Dedicated in Memory Of Bill
who made me promise never to give up.
And my sister Maria for all her help and encouragement.
Also my daughter Leah for her belief in me.

Prayer

Saint Michael the Archangel,
Defend us in battle
Be our protection against the
Wickedness and snares of the devil;
May God rebuke him, we humbly pray;
And do thou, O Prince of the heavenly host,
By the power of God, thrust into hell
Satan and all evil spirits
Who wander through the world
For the ruin of souls

Amen.

Chapter 1
Belfast 1973

Agnes Kenny reached across the worktop and switched off the radio. She stood at the kitchen window, gazing out at the flowers in the garden. However, her thoughts were not there in Belfast but in the border town of Crossmaglen where, it had just been reported, another British soldier had been shot in the head by a sniper. He was only nineteen years old.

"What for?" she asked herself, silently. "What's it all for?"

The Kenny's were a decent, law-abiding, Catholic family who prided themselves in having friends from both sides of the community and all walks of life. But like so many others in Northern Ireland in the early seventies, they found themselves plunged into a war-like situation that was not of their making and over which they had no control. She shook her head sadly. All of those being murdered were sons, husbands or fathers. Her country was fast becoming one of widows and orphans. Grief was still grief. Tears were still tears, no matter where they were being shed or by whom.

Agnes put it out of her mind and continued making the lunch when her husband, Robert, came down the hallway and into the kitchen. He pulled out a chair and sat down at the table. He was a fine man for his years, of stocky build with sandy coloured hair and piercing blue eyes. He was dressed in his working overalls with the Council logo stitched on them.

"Is it that time already?" asked Agnes, looking at the clock on the wall. "The girls will be in soon."

Robert put his newspaper down and taking his glasses out from the inside pocket of his dungarees, he placed them down beside it.

"I'm a bit early," he said. "I want a word with you before they get here."

Agnes turned down the heat on the cooker and joined him.

"What's wrong Robert?"

He looked quite serious.

"To tell the truth, Agnes, I'm a bit worried about Sheila. She's only seventeen. She should be out enjoying herself with her pals instead of doing a steady line with Raymond Burns."

"Oh for God's sake, Robert, nearly all the young girls around here are going steady."

"Well, I'm not worried about the rest of them. I'm worried about mine. He hasn't even got a job."

"Jobs are hard to find these days. I'm sure, like a lot more, he doesn't really want to draw the dole."

"Agnes, Raymond would rather draw the dole than draw breath!"

She smiled, a nicely featured woman with short, brown hair, and a kind, friendly face.

"Now, Angela's different," he continued. "She's all set for going back to College and boys don't seem to be her main interest. She wants to do something with her life and she might as well, she's got the brains."

"God knows, it's costing enough."

"Well, won't it be worth it, if she gets a good job and maybe meets someone who will be able to keep her and give her a good life?"

"That's if she ever leaves her books long enough to find him."

"Agnes, our Angela would have made a great nun."

She looked at him and laughed.

"Robert Kenny, there was never a nun on your side of the family or mine!"

"There's always a first time, you know," he said smiling. "By the way, I got that overtime I asked for a couple of weeks ago. I start today. I have to help clear away some barricades that were put up the other night during the riots. So if I'm late, don't be worrying."

"Be careful, Robert, they might start throwing bricks at you."

"Well the roads have to be cleared to let the traffic through and it's the council's job to do it. I'll be alright."

Agnes nodded.

"I suppose you're right, love, somebody has to do it. And the extra money will be a great help."

"Some of it can go towards buying Angela's books. I just hope the rest isn't needed by Sheila for a shot-gun wedding!"

"Robert Kenny, that's an awful thing to say!"

"Well, don't tell me you haven't noticed the way Raymond keeps following her around. He is older than her, Agnes. I hope she's looking after herself, if you know what I mean. I have nothing against the lad. I like him. But it's not right to see him propped up against the factory gate waiting for Sheila to come out – especially on Friday's! By God, times have changed. It's the women who keep the men now, and she's daft about him!"

He stared thoughtfully into space. "You know, I always thought Raymond fancied Angela."

"For Heaven's sake, if he's going steady with Sheila, how could he fancy Angela? Would you have wit!"

"Oh, I have wit alright, Agnes, I've seen the way he looks at her but I suppose she wasn't biting. Sheila was, though, like a trout with a fly!"

"Don't you worry about your daughters, Robert," said Agnes, patting his hand with her own. "They'll sort themselves out."

Just at that, voices could be heard coming through the front door. Agnes got up and pointed a finger at Robert.

"Not a word," she warned, "Do you hear me?"

Robert nodded, put on his glasses and lifted the paper.

"Hello Mr Kenny," said Raymond as he arrived in the kitchen with Sheila.

"How are you son?" asked Robert, not really expecting a reply.

Agnes was standing at the cooker now.

"Raymond, would you like some lunch?"

"I wouldn't mind, Mrs Kenny. Thanks very much." He sat down, while Sheila went upstairs. "Did you hear about Pete Flanagan?"

"No, what," asked Robert.

"He got a big win on the horses yesterday and went out last night for a drink. On the way home he got beaten up and all his money stolen. He was brought to the hospital and got ten stitches in his head."

"My God, that's terrible!" exclaimed Agnes. "Does he know who did it?"

"No, but I wish I did. I'd give them the same."

Robert gave a deep sigh.

"This country's getting worse," he said. "You can't walk the streets any more. You know, Agnes, if I had thought things were going to get this bad, I'd have gone to America that time your Aunt Bridget wanted to bring us out."

The kitchen door opened and Angela appeared. Raymond looked up and smiled at her.

"Is that a new outfit, Angela? You're looking well. But you'd look good in a bin-bag!"

"You never say things like that to me!" came Sheila's voice behind her.

Robert looked over the paper and nodded slightly at Agnes, as much as to say, "I told you so!"

Everyone gathered round the table while Agnes filled the plates. Raymond began tapping his fingers on the edge of the wood. A habit he had always had and one which annoyed Robert greatly. Finally, he asked, "Can I use your bathroom, Mrs Kenny?"

"Of course you can. You don't have to ask," she replied, putting the plates down on the table.

"Thanks."

Raymond disappeared upstairs.

Robert looked across at Sheila.

"Every time he comes in here, he always has to use the toilet. Don't they have one in his house?

A few moments later, Raymond began to sing.

"There he goes again – the shithouse crooner!" said Robert, folding the paper and taking off his glasses.

Angela started to laugh.

"It's not funny! said Sheila, looking annoyed. "Everyone says Raymond has a really good voice."

"Is that a fact?" he replied. "Well, why doesn't he take a stroll down to the dole office and use it to get himself a job?"

"He wants to sing with a group daddy. There's good money in it, especially when you play the pubs and clubs."

"Well that's a relief, because he won't make any by sitting in other people's toilets!"

"Alright, that's enough," said Agnes, as she heard Raymond coming.

As everyone began to eat, Robert looked around. Sheila very much resembled her mother, the same face and the same colour of hair. Angela, on the other hand, favoured him in looks. With her long red hair and blue eyes, she was a Kenny alright. For brains? Well, he didn't rightly know. After all, he was only a council worker. He glanced at Raymond, who was leaning protectively over his plate as if he feared someone would snatch it from him at any minute! He wasn't a bad looking lad, except for the shoulder length curly hair. Maybe the hair had something to do with the group he wanted to sing with, who knows? He wasn't big in build but he was big in ideas! Perhaps that's what Sheila liked about him.

"Oh well," he thought, "what can you do?"

As he watched, Sheila gazed over at Raymond as if he were a film star. Robert wondered which one it could possibly be. One thing was for sure, Raymond was no Robert Redford!

When lunch was over, Agnes began clearing the table. Raymond, trying to be the perfect gentleman, stood up and handed his plate to her. Robert watched with interest.

"I enjoyed that, Mrs Kenny," Raymond smiled, "you're a great cook."

"And you're a great eater!" muttered Robert, under his breath.

Sheila got up.

"I'd better be getting back to work."

"I'll walk you to the factory gate," insisted Raymond.

Robert and Agnes looked at each other. Sheila leaned over and put her arm around her father's shoulder.

"See you later, daddy."

"Right love. Have a good day now," he replied, touching her hand.

As she and Raymond were about to leave the kitchen, Raymond turned back.

"Hi Mr Kenny, did you hear the one about the Irish Cowboy?"

"No."

"He sat backwards on his horse all day – waiting for the cows to come home!"

"Oh, very good," replied Robert, nodding his head.

He listened as Raymond's laughter faded into the distance.

Angela smiled at Robert.

"I think you'll see a marriage there, daddy."

"Well if there is, he won't be bringing her home much money but he'll be able to bring her home plenty of jokes. At least she'll have a permanent smile on her face!" He winked, jokingly.

"Sheila won't want," smiled Agnes

"No, she won't," he agreed, "not while I'm around. None of my girls will. I'll work all the hours God sends to make sure of that." As he got up from the table he continued, "You know, Agnes, I can see a day coming when we won't have to use the bin."

"Why's that?"

"With the way that lad eats, we'll be getting one on two legs for a son-in-law."

They laughed.

"You're in a good mood," she commented, opening the back door.

"Well it's pay day!"

Without warning, a small Jack Russell terrier came running in, barking loudly. He excitedly wagged his tail and jumped up on Robert, who in turn bent down and stroked the dog affectionately.

"Come on Prince," he said. "I know what you want." He put his hand in his pocket and took out a bar of chocolate.

"Honestly, Robert," remarked Agnes, "you spoil that dog like you would a child."

"Well Agnes," he smiled, "he's the son I never had!"

After feeding Prince the chocolate, he went back to the table and lifted his paper and glasses. Then he turned to Angela.

"Are you working tonight, Angela?"

"From five till midnight, daddy."

He shook his head.

"That's a lot of fish and chips love. Would you not try for some part-time work during the day?"

"Oh, I don't mind working nights. Mr Nolan's a nice man and good to work for. Besides, I need the money for next term. I've a lot of books to buy."

"Now, don't you worry about that," he assured her. "You'll get whatever you need. I'll see to it."

Angela got up and put her arms around her father. "I know you will, daddy. I just hope I don't let you down."

"When do you get your exam results?"

"It won't be long now."

"Don't you worry, you'll do well." He patted her back gently. "Who knows, maybe one day you'll be standing in front of important people giving a speech and I'll be there among them all applauding and feeling very proud. My Angela, mixing with the cream of society."

"Well it would be a big step from serving in a chip shop!"

"Maybe it's just as well!"

They hugged each other tightly.

"I love you daddy."

"And I love you."

Agnes interrupted.

"Robert would you do something with that dog! If he keeps on barking like that, old Mrs Murray will be out to see what's going on."

"He's just excited, Agnes. He thinks I'm taking him for a walk. "Down Prince. That's a good boy. Daddy has to go to work but I'll see you when I get back. Come on wee son."

Robert took the dog by the collar and led him through the back door into the garden. Agnes looked across at Angela and turned her eyes up towards the ceiling.

"No wonder our Prince doesn't bother with other dogs – the poor thing thinks he's human!" laughed Angela.

"Well so would you, if your 'Daddy' had two legs instead of four!"

"He loves the dog though."

"Oh I know. I'm surprised he hasn't got it a job on the council."

"I heard that!" said Robert, putting his head round the door, "and believe me – if I could, I would! He could do a better job than some men I could mention."

The two women started to laugh. Robert came back into the kitchen and closed the door.

"Well, I better be going," he said, making his way to the kitchen window. "Bye Bye Prince," he waved. "Be a good boy till daddy comes home."

He kissed Agnes on the cheek.

"See you later darlin'," he smiled.

She nodded, not needing to say anything.

Angela came over and put her arm through his.

"Come on daddy. I'll leave you to the door."

Agnes watched as father and daughter left together.

"He's a good man," she thought. "One of the best. He just lives for his family and his dog. I love that man so much!" She returned to her dishes.

As they stepped out into the path Angela turned to Robert.

"Daddy, when I see you tonight, can we talk?"

"What about? Is anything wrong?"

"Oh no, nothing like that. I've just got something to ask you, that's all."

"Alright love. I'll see you then."

Angela stood and watched him walking up the street. When he reached the corner he turned and waved. She smiled and waved back.

"You watch yourself coming home from work," he shouted.

"I will," she nodded, stepping back into the house and closing the door.

He always worried about her and Sheila when they were out. That's the kind of man he was and that's what made him the loving father she adored.

Nolan's chip shop was full that night, when the door opened and Sheila came in. She pushed her way to the counter. Angela looked at her and smiled. "Just because I work here doesn't mean you don't have to wait your turn!"

"Angela, I have to talk to you."

"What's wrong?"

"I'll tell you outside," Shelia replied, nodding towards the door.

Gerry Nolan looked at Angela. She came from behind the counter and followed her sister outside. Sheila turned around with tears in her eyes.

"Daddy didn't come home from work. He was working overtime tonight but he should have been home hours ago. Mum's in a dreadful state."

"Is she on her own?"

"No, Raymond's with her. I phoned him and he came straight over."

Angela looked through the window at the large clock on the wall. It was just after eleven. She felt a surge of fear and panic sweep over her.

"I think you'd better come home," sobbed Sheila.

"You wait here. I'll be back in a minute," Angela promised.

She rushed back into the shop, pulling off the apron and then taking Gerry to one side, she whispered to him. He nodded.

"Go on home Angela, I can manage."

"Thank you Mr Nolan."

She then went through to the back of the shop and grabbing her coat and handbag, she hurried out. When the two girls arrived home, Agnes was pacing up and down the kitchen in tears. Raymond was sitting on a chair pulling hard on a cigarette. He looked worried.

Angela went over and put her arm around her mother.

"Mum, did you phone Eddie Spence?"

"He was the first one I did phone. He said your father was working in Wellard Street until eight o'clock. The job was finished so he said goodnight to the other men and left to come home. But he isn't here, Angela! If he's stopped off somewhere he'd have phoned. This has never happened before. He always comes straight home on pay-day. You know that."

Angela tried to comfort Agnes while Raymond put his arm around Sheila's waist and held her close.

"What are we going to do?" pleaded Agnes.

"I know what I'm going to do," said Angela. "I'm phoning the police!"

Raymond stamped out his cigarette on the ashtray.

"That might not be a bad idea. It mightn't make us very popular, but who cares."

Angela went out into the hall and dialled the number. After she'd explained everything, a short conversation followed. Then she returned to the kitchen.

"What did they say?" asked Agnes.

"Not a lot!" replied Angela, in an angry voice. "They said he's probably in someone's house or maybe a pub. But if he isn't back by morning I've to phone again."

"Right, that's it!" yelled Raymond, jumping up from the chair. He stormed down the hall and opened the front door. Shelia ran after him.

"Where are you going?" she cried.

"To get Jamie Doyle and a few boys. If the fuckin' police aren't going to look for your father, I will!"

He walked quickly down the path.

"Raymond, it's too late to be roaming the streets. You'll be lifted."

He spun round.

"Good! It'll give those bastards something to do besides drinking tea and coffee all night in the barracks! I'll do every street if I have to, from here to where he was last seen. And if anyone stops me to ask why – I'll kick their fuckin' face in!"

He put his hands in his pockets and hurried along the street. All the commotion brought Mrs Murray out onto her doorstep.

"Daughter dear, what's wrong? She asked Sheila.

"You better come in Mrs Murray. My mum needs you."

Old Mrs Murray was wearing her dressing gown and slippers as Shelia ushered her into the kitchen.

"Agnes, what's wrong? She asked, her arms outstretched. Agnes threw herself into them.

"It's Robert. He never came home form work. Something's happened to him, Mrs Murray. I just know it has." She began to sob uncontrollably.

""Oh, Agnes don't say that. What could possible happen to him? He's a quiet, inoffensive man and he doesn't bother with anything that's going on. Angela, make your mummy a wee cup of tea and we'll try and get her settled."

Angela turned on the cooker and reached for the cups. Suddenly, she was aware of a noise coming from underneath the kitchen table. The room fell silent as everyone listened. Prince lay forlornly, staring straight ahead. His whimpering became louder and louder as the atmosphere chilled.

Angela's eyes darted towards Mrs Murray, who was clutching the top of her gown. Their eyes met and the old woman shook her head. Angels knew then that everyone there was thinking the same thing, only no-one wanted to say it.

The lights burned in the Kenny household all night as the women inside waited for some kind of news with feelings of hope and dread. Raymond returned at about 4.30. Jamie Doyle and a group of men left him to the gate. He entered the house sad and depressed. All eyes looked at him, but he shook his head in despair.

"I'm sorry, Mrs Kenny, we had no luck. There's not a trace of him. Jesus, I don't understand it." He looked at Angela. "Did you phone the hospitals? He might have met with an accident."

"I phoned the police again. They're checking the hospitals for us. They said they'd ring back."

Agnes grabbed Raymond's hand.

"Do you think my Robert might be in a hospital?"

"There's every chance, Mrs Kenny. Maybe he's had a fall or been knocked down with a car. These things happen, you know." He hugged her protectively. "If he was admitted to any of the hospitals unconscious, it would take them a while to notify relatives. That's probably what's happened. I bet the police will phone you any minute now and tell you where Mr Kenny is. You wait and see."

Time went on. It was now 6.30. Angela was just about to pick up the phone again, when she heard the roar of armoured cars coming along the street. They came to a halt outside. As she opened the front door she saw both police and military taking up positions. An elderly man in plain clothes was making his way up the path, flanked by two constables and accompanied by a young woman. He looked at Angela.

"I'm Detective David Morris. May I come in?"

She nodded and led the way into the living-room. Everyone came through from the kitchen.

"Mrs Kenny?" he asked, looking a bit confused.

"I'm Mrs Kenny," said Agnes, stepping forward.

"Mrs Kenny, my name is Detective David Morris. I'd like a word with you, if I may."

"Please sit down."

He did so, and motioned her to do the same.

"Have you found Robert?" she asked in an anxious voice.

He hesitated.

"Mrs Kenny, we've found someone but we don't know who it is."

"What do you mean?"

He sat silent for a few moments, then continued, "Just before six o'clock this morning we received an anonymous phone-call, telling us to go to Melmont Street. We checked it out and found the body of a man lying in a derelict house."

A loud scream could be heard echoing in the silence of the early morning. Agnes Kenny sat shaking her head from side to side in disbelief.

"No, not Robert," she kept saying over and over again. Mrs Murray collapsed onto a chair. Raymond put his arms around Sheila. Angela stood rooted to the spot. The detective spoke again in a quiet, gentle voice. "It might not be your husband, it could be anyone. But we need to know for sure. Could someone come with me to Melmont Street."

"I'll go," volunteered Raymond.

Agnes looked at the detective, tears streaming down her face.

"How was he murdered? What did they do to him?"

"The man we found had been viciously beaten and shot in the head. Maybe it's best if this man here does come with me." He glanced at Raymond.

"No," cried Angela, "He's my father. I'll go."

"I'm going too," insisted Agnes. "If it's my husband I want to see him." She looked up at her two daughters.

"We'll all go!"

Detective Morris took her hand.

"I warn you, Mrs Kenny, it's not something you will want to see."

He stood up as Sheila and Raymond went to fetch the coats. Looking at Agnes and then at Angela he shook his head.

"I'm so sorry," he said in a sad and sincere voice. "It's at times like this when I really hate my job."

Melmont Street had been cordoned off with white tape. Detective Morris's car came to a halt as it was waved down by an army patrol sergeant. He and the young policewoman got out and all three talked for a few moments. Then he opened the door for Agnes and Angela. Shelia and Raymond got out of a second car and came to join them. Angela, pale and silent, gazed around. The street was crawling with land rovers, soldiers and police. The detective led the way as they followed, stopping at the door of an empty house guarded by two soldiers and a policeman. He turned and looked at Agnes.

"Are you ready to go in now and get this over with, Mrs Kenny?"

Agnes nodded her head and went inside with him. Angela took a step forward but the policeman put his hand out and stopped her, staring into her face.

"You don't want to go in there, dear," he said, shaking his head.

At that moment there came a heart rendering cry. The policeman quickly grabbed Angela as the impact of what she's just heard became a reality. She struggled, freeing herself from his arms.

"That's my father in there!" She screamed, running in. Raymond held Sheila tightly.

"You're not going!" he commanded, almost on the verge of tears himself. "I don't want you to see your father like that."

Angela followed her mother's cries until she arrived in a dusty, dirty, litter ridden room. Detective Morris was standing with a look of helplessness on his face. She looked down at the floor. The body of a man lay there. Agnes was kneeling beside it rocking backwards and forwards crying uncontrollably. Angela ran over and knelt down, too.

There were large black bruises on Robert Kenny's face and forehead where he had been badly beaten. His piercing blue eyes that had always been so full of life and laughter, were now glazed and stared, it seemed, into eternity. His head lay in a pool of blood.

"Daddy, oh Daddy!" she sobbed stroking his blood soaked hair.

"Please don't touch the body, miss. You're not allowed," said Detective Morris.

Angela looked up at him, tears streaming down her face. "This is my father lying here," she shouted. "My father!"

She bent over him once again, putting her hands under his head as if to make him more comfortable. The fact that he was dead did not deter her. When she took her hands away, they were covered in blood and tissue. She wiped them on her skirt and then put her arms around her mother. They clung to each other. Agnes was unable to speak.

The detective turned away. He understood how Angela felt. He had children of his own. The fear of being taken from them was there every day. After he'd composed himself, he beckoned the policeman and a colleague to come in.

"Sergeant, take this young lady outside. She's seen enough."

Agnes got up but stood motionless, as if in a trance.

As the sergeant reached out, Angela leaned over her father once more. She stroked the side of his face with her fingers, a habitual show of affection she's had since childhood. She bent down to kiss him when she noticed something that sent a freezing chill down her spine. For there on his cheek, the track of a single tear could be seen. Whatever had taken place in that dark and sinister room had frightened Robert Kenny. Frightened him so much, he cried.

Angela could feel her body shaking, in all her life she'd never seen her father cry. But whoever murdered him had filled him with such terror, they'd broken a once strong, brave and dignified man. Maybe he'd been begging for his life. Maybe he'd been pleading with them to let him go. As her thoughts ran out of control she threw herself over his body. "Daddy! Daddy! Who did this to you? Who could do this to you?"

As the police picked her up and led her away she stopped at the door and looked back. What she had just seen would stay with her for the rest of her life. As each day would dawn she would remember her father's face and that solitary tear. She would carry the memory of it to the grave.

"Daddy," she kept crying, over and over again. "Daddy."

Only Agnes and Detective Morris remained in the room now. She stared down at her dead husband, oblivious to the world around her.

Finally, the detective took her arm and guided her out of the house.

"Have you got children, Mr Morris?" she asked him in a faint voice.

"Yes, I have Mrs Kenny."

"I'll pray for them, I'll pray they never have to see what my child has. Never." She turned and looked back. "He was a good man, my Robert. A good husband and a good father. Our lives will never be the same again."

Over a period of time, many men who'd belonged to certain organisations were either ambushed and shot by the security forces or arrested and imprisoned by the courts. Someone was feeding information to British Intelligence and whoever it was had become known in the streets of Belfast as "The Nightingale". Just where this name had originated no one knew for sure but one thing was certain, "The Nightingale" was someone the people would never suspect.

The rumours began almost immediately and what began as hearsay to some people became a fact to a lot more as the day wore on. Word had spread like wildfire that Robert Kenny had been this informer. His murder bore all the hallmarks of an execution. The police issued a statement saying they did not know this man, he had nothing to do with them. But leading organisations were not as forthcoming, neither confirming nor denying the claim. This only added to the speculation.

By whoever or wherever the rumours started was a mystery but they were in full circulation. So much so that the dead man and his family were the topic of conversation in every street corner, book makers office and public house in Belfast. This had a devastating effect on Agnes Kenny and her daughters as they mourned the husband and father they loved so much.

Although Robert Kenny had always been a quiet, respectable and well liked man, not many people came to offer their sympathy or condolences and this did not go unnoticed by Angela. A large wreath was delivered to the house with a card which read: 'From Eddie Spence and The Boys.'

They were his Protestant workmates who would not come to the house in case it started trouble for the family. The Kenny's understood this and were grateful for the kindness they'd shown in their grief.

On the morning of the funeral, having no relatives to speak of, Robert Kenny's coffin was carried from his home by Raymond, Jamie Doyle and a few others. Agnes, Angela and Sheila walked behind them, accompanied by Mrs Murray and a handful of neighbours. As her father left his small terraced house in Glensdale Park for the last time, Angela's eyes looked around. The absence of many of their friends was obvious. Fear of intimidation had kept many of them away. Even those who believed in their hearts Robert Kenny was innocent, were too frightened to walk behind his funeral for fear of reprisals on them or their families. They, after all, had to go on living there and the last thing they wanted was for someone to point the finger at them, singling them out for being at the funeral of a notorious informer. That Northern Ireland had come to this, was a sad day indeed for its people.

After the funeral Mass, the small crowd of mourners made their way to the cemetery. When the priest ended his short service, Robert Kenny's coffin was lowered into the ground. His wife and daughters went to the edge of the grave and, one at a time, they dropped a red rose on top of it. As Angela stared down at the crucifix on the lid she whispered, "Good-bye daddy. I love you. Rest in peace."

The three women then embraced each other and loud sobbing erupted. Mrs Murray tried to console them but eventually joined in their tears. Raymond looked at Jamie and the other mourners and nodded to them appreciatively. Then he went over and put his arms protectively around Agnes and the girls.

The priest took Agnes's hand. She looked at him. "Why, Father? She asked. "Why my Robert?"

"I don't know Agnes. All I can say is these are hard times for everyone. He's not the first and he won't be the last."

Angela clenched her fists.

"I hope one day whoever did this, will get the same" she seethed.

"Now Angela," he replied, "don't be bitter."

"Don't be bitter?! My father was shot like a dog and left lying in an empty house for the rats to gnaw at. How can I not be bitter?"

She remembered only too well the state her father's body had been left in and she could only guess what he must have come through before they finally pulled the trigger, enough to make him cry. Once again the priest tried to reason with her. "Angela, my dear, don't have hatred for these men. Pray for them. They have strayed from the Commandments of God. 'Thou shalt not kill'. Always remember that."

She gripped his hand tightly and stared into his face.

"Oh I'll remember it alright," she assured him, "the same way they did, when they were murdering my father!"

The Kenny's soon realised that life would never be normal for them again. People they had known all their lives changed from friends to hostile enemies. Some did remain loyal but they were few in number. On more then several occasions Sheila came home from work crying, where abuse and insults concerning her father had been hurled at her. The taunts did not stop there. When Agnes and Angela went into the corner shop the conversation among the customers would stop immediately and those concerned would stand glaring at them in silence. Then on their way out, the whispering would start. Some local shopkeepers served them reluctantly, hardly uttering a word. Young men would stand on the street making remarks as they passed by, calling them names and in some cases forcing them off the pavement. All things considered, their lives were being made a misery.

Angela had been to the police station every week to ask if anything was being done about her father's murder. But she was either sent home with excuses or treated with indifference. She was becoming increasingly hurt and angry by the whole situation, not eating or sleeping properly since her father's death and suffering greatly from headaches and nervous tension.

It was after one such visit to the police station that she came home crying. As she let herself in, Agnes and Raymond were in the living room. Agnes looked at her and signed,

"I take it by the look on your face they didn't say very much."

"They never do," replied Angela, "I don't know why I bother to go. They make me feel like a nuisance."

Raymond looked at her.

"If it was one of them they'd handle it a whole lot differently." He stood up and took her by the arm,

"Come On!" he insisted

"Where are we going?"

"Back to the police station. If they're going to treat you like a nuisance you may as well act like one!"

Raymond flung open the door of the police station and walked up to the desk with Angela still in tow.

"I want to speak to someone in charge," he demanded.

The duty sergeant looked him up and down.

"And who might you be?"

"Father Christmas! Who are you?"

"Listen here, do you know where you are?"

"Well, let me guess," said Raymond cheekily, as he leaned his elbow on the desk. "Isn't this the place where men in dark green uniforms sit around all day developing piles, when they're supposed to be our helping the public?"

"Just what do you mean by that?"

"What I mean is, this girl's father was murdered nearly two months ago. She's been in here every week to ask what's being done and she's getting no information at all... but then why should we expect anything different – he was only a Catholic." Raymond raised his voice deliberately. "Last week a policeman was shot outside his house. He didn't die, he was only wounded. But within twenty four hours the man who shot him had been arrested and locked up."

"Now you listen to me," said the sergeant, pointing a warning finger at him. "You watch your mouth or I'll have you locked up. I don't like your attitude!"

"Well I'm not crazy about yours. And I'll tell you something else. If you're not going to help people, what the fuck are you doing standing there?"

"Right that's it," said the sergeant, angrily. "I've had enough of your cheek!" He slammed his pen down onto the desk and beckoned a constable with his finger.

"And up yours too!" smirked Raymond sarcastically, as the constable took him by the arm and forcibly led him away.

Angela was in a state of panic as the sergeant looked at her sternly.

"Is he your boyfriend?" he asked

Before she had time to speak, Raymond looked around.

"No. We're the travelling Punch and Judy Show!"

"Get him out of here!" yelled the sergeant, as the constable hurried Raymond to the door. On opening it he pushed him outside and stood guard to make sure he wouldn't attempt to come back in.

Just then an office door opened and a head appeared.

"What the hell's going on here?"

Angela recognised him at once. It was Detective Morris. He saw her and came over to the desk.

"Miss Kenny, what's the matter?"

"I come here every week to find out if there's any information about my father's murder and I'm being sent from one policeman to another and none of them can tell me anything. It's not right, the way I'm being treated."

He nodded his head

"Come through to my office."

The sergeant looked at him, Detective Morris stared back.

"Do you have a problem with that, Sergeant?"

"No sir. My problem is standing outside the door waiting for this young lady."

"Well if he's outside then that's alright. Get on with your work."

Angela walked into the office followed by the detective, who closed the door behind him.

"Angela. My name is Angela."

They sat down together, one at either side of the desk.

"Well Angela, I know you think nothing is being done but that's not so. I have tried, believe me, but I've come up with nothing. We know your father and the other Council workers cleared the debris from the barricades in Wellard Street that evening. The job took longer than anyone thought it would so we believe when your father left to go home he took a short cut round by the old factory and down Melmont Street. He could have been followed or attacked where he was found. I just don't know. And the truth is, if an organisation is responsible for killing him they aren't going to tell us. We can't get any information anywhere."

"Detective Morris, will you be honest with me?" she asked.

"Of course."

"Do you believe my father was an informer?"

He looked at her sympathetically and shook his head.

"Well if he was he certainly didn't give us any information. But unfortunately we can't prove anything."

Angela leaned forward and rested her hands on the edge of the desk,

"If my father was being paid to inform, where's the money? What did he do with it? He never had any money to spare and we certainly didn't have it. Whoever murdered him stole his wages and the little loose change he had. Doesn't that seem odd to you?" She was close to tears now.

"Yes it does," he replied, "But I know only too well that when you're dealing with an organisation, they are a law onto themselves."

"What you're really saying is, you don't think the people who murdered him will ever be caught and the truth of my father's innocence will never be made known."

"I'm sorry Angela. I wish there was more I could do. We'll go on with our investigations. Who knows, maybe we'll get lucky. For what it's worth, I think your father was an innocent man in the wrong place at the wrong time. I just wish I could prove it really I do."

"So do I," Angela whispered, as she got up. "Well, after today, I won't annoy anyone here again. I know now there is no point in coming back."

She turned to leave but Detective Morris stopped her.

"Just a minute Angela. Did you get your father's things back after we'd sent them off to be examined?"

"Yes, they brought us his clothes, his watch and some tickets he's bought earlier in the week from one of his workmates." She smiled sadly. "They were for funds for a children's flute band. Daddy was like that, you know. When it came to children, he'd have given his last penny."

He paused for a moment, then opened his desk drawer. "These were found in his overalls. There was a mix up and they were sent here instead of being included with his other belongings. I intended to call to your home with them but seeing as you're here...."

He put his hand inside and took out a small plastic bag. Inside was a pair of glasses. Part of the frame had been broken and one of the lenses shattered.

"I don't know if you want them," he said, "but they are your property."

Angela took the bag from him and held it tightly to her breast.

"Yes I want them," she sobbed.

Detective Morris got up and came from behind the desk. He put his arm around her and said softly, "I won't give up on this one Angela, I promise."

"Thank you," she whispered, opening the door. He watched her leave the police station still clutching the plastic bag. He shook his head in despair and looked over at the sergeant.

"I don't think we'll be seeing her again and quite frankly I don't blame her!"

"Cheer up Sir. After all, we can't catch everyone who commits murder. It's getting tougher all the time."

"I know. But this is one time when I'd really like to nail the bastard who did this one."

He walked back into the office and closed the door.

Outside, Raymond was waiting patiently for Angela to appear. When she finally came through the door he stamped out his cigarette.

"I'm sorry, Angela. I lost the head in there."

"It's alright, Raymond," she replied, wiping the tears from her eyes. "You were just trying to help."

"What have you got there?" he asked.

Angela held out the plastic bag.

"Jesus Angela, are they your father's?"

"Yes, Detective Morris had them."

"Had they any news?"

"No, it looks like they're never going to find out who killed my daddy."

Raymond put his arms around her and hugged her.

"Don't think like that, Angela," he pleaded. "Some day something will turn up, just when you least expect it. You'll see."

He fixed the collar of her coat and led her away.

Angela passed her exams but hadn't the heart to go back to the college. So when Gerry Nolan phoned her and asked her to go back to work at the chip shop, she agreed for two reasons. Firstly, she thought it would help her to come to terms with everything that had happened. Secondly, they needed the money. With her father gone, money was tight and the strain was beginning to show on Agnes.

Friday night had been busy, especially around teatime, but by 10 o'clock the shop was quiet. The next big rush would be when the crowds left the pubs and clubs. Gerry and Angela were standing talking when suddenly a huge brick smashed through the large window, shattering the glass. He grabbed her and they both crouched down onto the floor behind the counter. Voices began to chant outside, "Touts Out! Touts Out!"

"Jesus Christ, what's wrong with these people? said Gerry, looking into Angela's pale and frightened face. She tried to answer but couldn't, her body shaking.

"Listen Angela, there's no way you can leave here on your own tonight. I'm going to phone the police."

He began to crawl through the broken glass to reach the back of the shop. Angela followed him and gripped his arm tightly.

"Please don't get the police, Mr Nolan," she pleaded, finding her voice at last. "It will only make things worse for me."

She covered her face with her hands and started to cry. He nodded his head.

"Alright Angela. But if they come in, what are we gong to do?"

Angela sensed panic in his voice.

"I don't know," she cried. "Oh God, this is a nightmare!"

They both knelt there, surrounded by broken glass and listening to the threatening voices.

"It's always when you bloody need help there isn't any!" Said Gerry, as another missile was hurled through the window, just missing his head.

"Mr Nolan, I'm so sorry about all this. Look at the glass." She nodded to the floor.

"Don't worry about that, Angela. I'm insured."

"It's all my fault."

"It's their fault. For God's sake, you'd think someone would hear all that racket and come and see what's wrong."

Within a few moments they heard the sound of feet running round the side of the shop. Angela put her trembling hands on Gerry's shoulders.

"Oh God, they're coming to get me."

Then she heard familiar voices shouting.

"It's Raymond and Sheila," she cried with relief.

"Thank God it's somebody," sighed Gerry, wiping the sweat from his brow.

Raymond ran to the front window.

"What the fuck's going on?" he yelled, lifting a brick and firing it into the crowd of young teenagers.

"We don't want touts," they jeered.

"I know what you want. And if I come over you'll get my foot up your asses. Now clear off!"

He lifted another brick and charged at them. "Did you hear me? Fuck off!"

One young man moved forward.

"You think you're a big man, Burns," he shouted.

Raymond swiftly lunged at him, grabbed him by the neck and shook him violently.

"I'm big enough for you, you wee bastard!"

"I'll tell my Da!"

"Don't fuckin' bother. I'll tell him myself in the bookies tomorrow – while I'm banging his head off the fuckin' wall! Anybody else got anything to say?" he threw his prey back into the crowd, looked at all their faces, then picked up the stones lying at his feet. He began attacking them with their own ammunition, watching them scatter and run in all directions.

Sheila ran into the shop just as Gerry and Angela came out from behind the counter. She put her arms around her sister.

"Are you alright?" she asked.

Angela nodded, still shaking from her ordeal.

Raymond came in.

"That's some carry on. Are you hurt?"

"I don't know how we're not," said Gerry. "But I'll tell you something, you were the answer to a prayer."

Raymond looked around.

"Jesus, your shop's in some state! You won't be selling many fish and chips tonight, boy."

"Believe me, Raymond, that's the last thing on my mind."

Angela went and got her coat. She took Gerry's hand.

"Good-bye Mr Nolan, I won't be back. I've caused you enough trouble."

"Angela, I'm sorry this happened. You're a nice girl and a good worker." He looked at Sheila. "How did you know what was going on?"

"We heard it when we were coming down the street to get chips for the supper."

"Well, I think our Raymond here deserves a free fish supper for what he did tonight. We all do."

"Hold on Gerry. Are you sure the food's alright?" asked Raymond, trying to make light of the whole situation. "I mean I don't want to be on the toilet all day tomorrow, trying to pass fragments of glass!"

"Never fear, Raymond, I always keep the pans closed when the shop's quiet. The food will be o.k."

"Well in that case – plenty of salt and vinegar please!"

Gerry Nolan went behind the counter, made up the suppers and handed them out. As they walked towards the door together, Raymond took a chip from his bag and held it to his mouth.

"You know, Gerry, I'd stay and help you lock up but it's hardly worth the bother!"

He pointed the chip towards the large window with no glass. "But never mind, he continued, "you can put in for a big claim."

"To tell you the truth, after what happened here tonight I wouldn't care if I never opened again. If I was a wise man I'd pack up and get out while the going's good."

"Why don't you go to Italy and open an Irish Chip shop?" joked Raymond. "After all, they come over here and open Italian ones!"

"Now that's not a bad idea. Only they've got the mafia."

"Christ, Gerry, so have we! Only ours is known by a different name."

Gerry nodded in agreement.

"Goodnight girls. Goodnight Raymond and thanks for everything."

"Don't mention it."

As Angela turned to walk away, Gerry reached over and put his hand on her arm, affectionately.

"Take care of yourself, Angela," he said, in a sad voice. Then moving his hand towards her coat he slipped some money inside.

"I will Mr Nolan," she replied, trying hard to smile. "Thank you."

Raymond squeezed in between her and Sheila. "Nothing's going to happen to the Kenny's – not while I'm around!" he promised.

Gerry Nolan stood and looked after them for a few seconds, stared at his shop and the empty street, and then returned his gaze to Raymond and the young girls. He watched as they turned the corner and disappeared from view.

He shook his head. Raymond Burns was one brave lad and Robert Kenny would have been proud of him tonight!

At 2 o'clock the following morning, the Kenny's were awakened from their sleep by the sound of crashing glass. They came down stairs to discover the living room window totally smashed and a large brick lying on the floor. Glass was scattered over the furniture and carpet. Agnes began to cry. After what had happened to Angela at work and now this, her nerves were so bad she was on the verge of a breakdown. Both mother and daughters sat huddled in the kitchen waiting for daylight to come, using only a small lamp in fear of whoever did it returning.

Angela suspected it was the same group of youths who had attached the chip shop and as they all sat crying, each one knew how they were being victimised by an element of people who wanted to drive them out of their home. And this made Angela angry. Later that morning she made a phone call and a couple of hours later the window was replaced with new glass. Sheila went to work as usual. It was more a show of protest by both young women. Agnes and Angela spent the day clearing up the glass and getting everything back the way it was. Just as Angela thought her mother had settled, Agnes would break down in tears again. This went on for most of the day. As Angela sat her down to a cup of tea, she lifted it with shaking hands.

"They want us out, Angela," she sobbed, "they want us out of this house. What are we going to do?"

"We're staying, mum. We haven't done anything wrong. This is our home."

"What if they won't stop? What if they come back? What happens then?"

"I don't know."

"I was thinking," said Agnes, in a half whisper," I was thinking of phoning Aunt Bridget and telling her about all this."

"Mum, Aunt Bridget lives in America! What can she do?"

"Maybe she could help." Agnes's voice was becoming desperate. "Aunt Bridget is there a long time. She might be able to sort something out for us. She wanted your father and me to go and live with her years ago."

Angela stared at her.

"Do you mean we should pack up and go to America? Mum listen to me. You're too old now to go so far away."

"Maybe. But you and Sheila are young enough to start a new life, away from all of this trouble."

Angela got up from her chair and knelt down beside Agnes.

"Mum, I've been thinking. Maybe last night was the end of our trouble. When they see we aren't going to run away, we might be left in peace."

She spoke in a soothing voice and stroked her mother's hand.

"Well, it was a thought," replied Agnes.

"I don't want you thinking like that anymore. You're not well enough to move to another town, never mind another country. Sheila wouldn't leave Raymond, you know that. And besides, they can't do any more to this family than they've already done."

Agnes nodded.

"Maybe you're right Angela. But don't tell Sheila about this conversation, I don't want to upset her."

"I won't, I promise. But don't phone Aunt Bridget."

Agnes looked at her with tears in her eyes.

"Angela you've lost your job and most of your friends but you're well educated and you're young. Sheila has Raymond. You have no one. Would you consider going?"

"Mum, what would take me to America? I don't know anyone there. Come to think of it, I don't even know Aunt Bridget," she smiled. "No. We belong here. I belong here."

She got up and put her arms around her mother. "Don't worry about me, some day I'll find someone or maybe they will find me."

Those were going to prove to be the truest words Angela Kenny had ever spoken. Fate was already at work, preparing a path for her by putting together all the dramatic events in her young life. It would only take one more link before the chain would be completed. Then Angela was ready to take that path, with destiny leading the way.

Agnes Kenny had changed from being a healthy, happy woman into a worrying, nervous, complaining one who seldom left the doctor's surgery. Angela was cut off from her friends at College and withdrew into her books for comfort and consolation. Hardly a day passed that she wasn't upstairs in her room reading, with Prince lying at the side of the bed. He had become her constant companion since her father died and she made a fuss of him the way Robert had done. Apart from her visits to the library and the cemetery, she didn't go out much except to take him for a walk.

Agnes worried about her. She knew it was no life for a girl her age and although a couple of weeks had passed without any incidents, it didn't make her feel any easier in her mind. She had phoned Aunt Bridget a few times when Angela was out, keeping her informed about everything and confiding her innermost thoughts. Bridget was getting on in years and her health wasn't good, but she was most sympathetic and genuinely concerned. She wanted to help Agnes and her family and couldn't understand how they could live in Belfast after what had happened to Robert and the comeback it had had on them. She wanted Agnes to go to America and look after her. The girls were welcome too, but Agnes kept this to herself as so far they were being left in peace and she was thankful for that.

The following Saturday night, Sheila and Raymond were going out. Angela walked with them to the top of the road, as Prince followed behind. They stood talking for a few minutes, then Angela left them and went into the corner shop. Once inside she bought sweets for her mother and a bar of chocolate for the dog. She walked him back down and fed it to him, one square after another.

Agnes smiled, "you're spoiling him the way your father did."

"Well that's what he would have wanted," Angela replied, opening the back door and watching him run into the garden. "When I look at him I feel as though part of my daddy is still here."

Agnes looked serious now.

"Why didn't you go out with Raymond and Sheila when they asked you?"

"I'm going to watch the late film. I'll take a bath now and then make the supper. Maybe we could watch it together?"

"Alright love," said Agnes, as Angela left the kitchen to go upstairs.

The film had just started, when a loud knock came to the front door. Angela, in her dressing-gown, crept down the hall and called out, "Who's there?"

There was no reply, so she cautiously opened the door and looked up and down the street.

"Who is it?" asked Agnes from the living room.

"I don't know. There's no one here."

Angela was just about to close the door when she noticed something lying beside the step. She opened the door wide and switched on the outside light. Prince was lying motionless.

"Prince, what are you doing there?" she smiled. "Come on, boy, come inside."

Still, he didn't move. She bent down to pick him up, when his head fell to the side. He had a large wound on his neck and his coat was covered in blood. Angela screamed his name and lifting him quickly, she went back inside. Agnes came out into the hall.

"What's wrong?" she shouted, becoming distressed. She stood and stared in horror as Angela cradled the dog in her arms.

"He's dead!" she sobbed. "He's dead!"

It was then Agnes noticed a piece of paper tucked under his collar. She took it out and opened it. The paper contained the usual words – 'Touts out' in large letters. She held it up to Angela.

"Oh God," cried Angela, "they killed Prince! They killed my father and now they've killed his dog!"

Agnes held out her arms, as she too let the tears flow.

"Give him to me, Angela."

"No! I want to hold him. How could anyone do this, mum? How could anyone kill him? He's only a dumb animal, he never hurt anyone."

"Your father never hurt anyone either, Angela. They have no regard for life – any kind of life."

Angela bent her head and kissed Prince, lovingly. Then she stared at Agnes in a way that was almost frightening.

"I hate them!" she screamed hysterically, shaking from head to foot. "I hate them for what they did to my father and I hate them for this! I'll never forgive them, I swear it! I'll remember what they did for the rest of my life!"

Agnes sobbed loudly. Her daughter was a pitiful sight standing there, the lifeless animal lying in her arms. She knew she'd meant every word she'd said. She'd never heard her speak like that before, with such hatred. But then, they had taken away the only link Angela had left, with her father. As Agnes watched her helplessly, she knew she could never blame her daughter for feeling the way she did. Because, in her own heart, Agnes Kenny hated them too, and would do until her dying day.

It was after midnight when Sheila and Raymond let themselves in. Raymond looked into the living room.

"Is everything alright, Mrs Kenny?"

She looked at him and shook her head.

"What's wrong? he asked.

Angela came out of the kitchen.

"I'll show you what's wrong."

They followed her through. She went over to the dog basket in the corner and pointed down to Prince.

"The dog's dead," she said, bursting into tears.

"What happened to him?" cried Sheila. "Was he knocked down by a car?"

"No. Someone killed him and left him at the door with a note."

She handed the piece of paper to Sheila, who held it in trembling hands and then gave it to Raymond. He read it, then turned to Agnes who was now standing behind them.

"Jesus Christ, Mrs Kenny, I'm sorry. This has really gone too far."

He put his arms around her and held her for a few moments. Then he knelt down and looked at the dog, examining its neck.

"For fuck's sake," he said in a disgusted voice, "What kind of people would do that? I can't believe this."

He covered the dog with its blanket. "What are you going to do with him?" He looked at Angela. "Will I get him taken away for you?"

"No," she sobbed, "I want to keep him here with us. I want him buried in the back garden where he always played. My father would have done that."

He nodded his head

"Have you got a spade?"

There's one in the garden shed," Agnes informed him.

"I'll need a lamp or some kind of light."

Angela went over to the cupboard and took out a large torch that belonged to her father. She and Raymond went outside to the shed. After he'd found the spade he asked,

"Where do you want me to put him, Angela?"

"Under the rose bush at the bottom of the garden."

She stood with the brightly lit torch as he started to dig. Agnes and Sheila watched with their arms around each other.

When Raymond had dug a grave large enough, he went inside and wrapped Prince carefully in his blanket. He carried him out and placed him gently into the dark earth. He stood for a few moments, as if to pay his respects. After all, Prince was one of the family and Robert Kenny had loved him.

At that moment a bedroom light was switched on in the house next door. The window opened and Mrs Murray poked her head out.

"Raymond Burns, what are you doing?"

"I'm digging for buried treasure!" he shouted. Then turning away he muttered, "Nosey old biddy!"

Mrs Murray ignored him.

"Agnes what's wrong," she called.

"We're burying Prince, Mrs Murray. Somebody killed him."

Two minutes later, Mrs Murray appeared in her own garden and leaned over the fence.

"Doesn't she ever sleep?" said Raymond, under his breath. "I bet she lies in a coffin instead of a bed!"

The old woman shook her head in disbelief.

"Dear, dear, poor Prince. Who would do such a thing? I'll tell you something, Angela, there's more to this than meets the eye. Your father was a good man. There was no rhyme or reason for his death, I've always said so. And now his poor, wee dog is gone too. Where will it end?"

"When you shut your big mouth and mind your own business!" muttered Raymond, as he filled in the grave. Mrs Murray watched until he was finished and then, with a look of sadness, went back inside.

Raymond took Angela in his arms to comfort her as she sobbed loudly.

"If I ever find out who did this, Angela, I'll break every bone in their body," he promised. "They won't be fit to kill another animal, believe me! And as for that note, if I get the bastard who wrote it, I'll kick the shit out of him!"

The anger he felt flashed in his eyes and showed itself in every feature in his face. When he put the spade back in the shed, they all went inside.

An hour later, Raymond left. Angela washed the dog's bowl. Robert had bought it for him and had his name, 'Prince' printed on the side in black, capital letters. She dried it carefully and took it upstairs to her room. Agnes and Sheila sat talking for a while, then Sheila went to bed.

Agnes walked around, her mind in a turmoil. She went upstairs and quietly opened Angela's bedroom door. She found her daughter kneeling at the side of the bed with her head buried in her hands, crying. Beside her sat the bowl. Agnes closed the door, silently.

The killing of her husband's dog had proved one thing to her. None of them could take any more. If one of her children got hurt, she'd never forgive herself. She wanted to avoid that at all costs. But it was the look on Angela's face that night that really made her mind up. America might be far away but she didn't care. If Bridget could sort things out for them, they would go. She'd had enough. She was at breaking point and so was her eldest daughter. Agnes was going to get out of Belfast while her children were still safe. There was nothing left for them there, except hatred and victimisation. The majority of decent people were being ruled by a minority whose hold over them was getting more powerful every day.

It was with a heavy heart that Agnes Kenny made her way to the front hall, picked up the receiver and dialled. She waiting in desperation as she heard another phone ringing....

When the Sunday lunch was over, Agnes called the girls into the living room.

"Sit down," she told them. "I want to talk to both of you." They did so and she continued, "I thought I could learn to accept what happened to your father, but I can't and I never will. We're not going to get any peace to live here. Last night was proof of that. If they would kill the dog, what would they not do? I'm worried about us. If they started a fire in the middle of the night we'd be burned alive and if not, we'd have no home. Sooner or later it will come to that. They'll burn this house down just to get us out. I'm not going to wait for that to happen. I phoned Aunt Bridget. She knows everything and she's willing to help. She wants us to go to America and we are, my mind's made up. The sooner we go, the better."

There was silence. Then Sheila spoke.

"I can't go, mum."

"Sheila, I know it will be hard for you to leave Raymond but we are a family, we have to stay together. It's for the best."

"You don't understand," replied Sheila in a low voice and looking at the floor. "I can't go to America – I'm pregnant."

This news sent Agnes reeling. She looked at Angela.

"Did you know about this?"

Angela, dumfounded, shook her head.

Agnes's gaze returned to Sheila.

"How long have you known?"

"A while."

"How far gone are you?"

"Just over three months."

"What?" said Agnes, in an angry voice. "And when were you going to tell me, or weren't you going to bother?"

"Raymond and I talked it over and we were going to tell you last night, but with the dog being killed on top of daddy's death and everything else I couldn't do it, mum. I just couldn't!" she broke down. "I'm sorry."

Agnes got up and stared at her.

"How could you keep this from me, your own mother?"

Then she left the room without another word, leaving one daughter to comfort the other. A little while later, Angela found her mother in the kitchen, standing looking out of the window, crying.

"Dear God," she sobbed, as Angela put her arms around her, "isn't anything going to go right for this family?"

"Mum, please listen. Raymond wants to marry her."

"She's only seventeen. What if something should happen to her?"

"No-one will touch her when she's married to Raymond, they wouldn't dare. If anyone can look after her, he can and you know that. It's what she wants, mum. Don't spoil her happiness, please. She feels bad enough as it is. You're all she's got and it was your feelings she was worried about all this time. Don't be angry with her. She needs you now.

Show her you care, show her you love her."

Agnes nodded and wiped the tears from her eyes. When she went back into the living room, Sheila was still crying. On seeing her again Agnes embraced her and stroked her, the way she did when Sheila was a little girl. Then she kissed her face, as Angela looked on.

"Raymond loves me, mum and we're getting married. But we'll do it quietly. We won't tell anyone."

Agnes stepped back.

"Now, you listen to me, Sheila. You are going to have a proper wedding, with a white dress and flowers and a wedding car. We're going to do this right. It's going to be your day and I want you to be happy. When you walk out of this house to be married you'll walk out like a Kenny and make your father proud!"

Sheila smiled, gratefully.

"Thanks mum."

"Now go and tell my future son-in-law everything's going to be alright."

Sheila left to find Raymond while Agnes went upstairs to her and Robert's bedroom. She closed the door, went over to a drawer and took out an old wallet. It contained the policy money that was left over from her husband's funeral. She sat down on the bed and started to count it. Half way through she stopped. Remembering the last conversation she had with him, she could hear his voice joking about his over-time money being needed for Sheila's wedding. She told him to have wit! Perhaps he had more wit that day than she gave him credit for. After all, he had more or less told her this would happen. His fears and worry for Sheila had not been unfounded. Maybe Robert had been aware of something that she had not. She looked at the money in her hand and started to cry. He had been wrong about one thing. It wasn't his overtime money Agnes would have to use, it was money she had received from his death insurance. Fate had been so cruel to her. She closed her eyes, still moist with tears, and said a silent prayer that it would be more kind to her daughters.

The next few weeks were hectic as preparations were made for the wedding. Agnes knew there would be a lot of talk about her daughter. She also knew that by giving her a proper white wedding some people would say that it was the money Robert Kenny had received for informing, that was paying for it all. But by now she didn't care. She knew the truth and that was all that really mattered.

With the excitement of the wedding plans, America had not been mentioned by Angela or Sheila. Agnes suspected that deep in their hearts they thought, and hoped, she had changed her mind. The wedding was a quiet affair under the circumstances, but dignified. Both her daughters looked beautiful as bride and bridesmaid and Agnes went out of her way to make sure it was a happy occasion. Sheila and Raymond went away for a few days and it was during that time Bridget contacted Agnes to tell her everything had been taken care of and she was sending the money for the airline tickets to America. After the telephone call she went upstairs and opened the bedroom door. Angela was lying on the bed, reading. She sat down beside her.

"That was Aunt Bridget on the phone just now. She's sending on the money for our tickets."

There was a long pause, then Angela sat upright.

"Mum, do you really want to go? Have you thought it all out?"

"I've thought about it every night."

"But you love this house. Think of what you're giving up."

"I have, Angela, and when all's said and done it's only four walls. It's not the same without your father and it never will be, you know that. People aren't the same either. So many of our friends have deserted us. Others will never let us forget why your father was murdered. They'll never believe he was innocent and I can't live with the worry of what's going to happen next. We have been through so much and the sad thing is, it won't end, we'll always be made to suffer."

Angela leaned over and put her arm around Agnes's shoulder.

"We'll be among strangers, mum. People we don't know."

"Angela, we're living with people like that now. There are people here I thought I knew all my life but they have become strangers. I know you have strong doubts about going but what life have you got here? You rarely go out and I'm frightened when you do. I certainly don't see how America could be worse than this, we're not living, Angela, we're only existing."

The sadness in her mother's voice made Angela realise just how unhappy she really was.

"Alright mum. If you feel so strongly about this then we will go. I just hope we're doing the right thing."

"We don't have much choice. Whoever murdered your father and spread those rumours about him have brought us to this. I hope God will forgive them because I never will."

She got up and went over to the door.

"Maybe it's for the best," she continued, lowering her head. "Maybe out of all the bad things that have happened to us, something good will come out of it. Who knows? We'll just have to wait and see."

After seeing the door close, Angela got off the bed and kneeling down she opened the bottom drawer of the dressing table. She took out her father's glasses, still in the small plastic bag and Prince's bowl. She held them to her breast and began to sob. Her mother was right. Life here would never be the same again and Angela would never forgive or forget.

When Raymond and Sheila returned from their honeymoon they moved in with

Agnes, who'd asked Angela not to mention anything about their intended trip until she got some things sorted out. One of these, was a visit to the local housing office. After stating her case she was successful in procuring the house for Sheila and she was contented to know that her daughter and son-in-law would be the next tenants. At least when she left, there would still be a Kenny living there, the house would not go to strangers. When she arrived home she called them both into the living room. She looked from one to the other as they sat down. Then she explained,

"I've been to the housing office today and they are putting this house in your name, Sheila. You and Raymond are not leaving here, not with a baby on the way."

"Oh mum, you're not still thinking of going to America?"

"Yes I am. Aunt Bridget is sending on the money. It should be here any day now. I'm leaving the house the way it is. Everything will be yours, you won't have anything to buy. It will be a good start for you both."

Raymond stared at the floor, then at Agnes.

"Mrs Kenny, I don't think you should leave. This is your home, yours and Angela's. We could get a flat. Why should you go all the way to America?"

"Because I want to, Raymond, and besides I have Angela to think about. She has no life here."

"She might not have one out there either. Have you thought of that?" asked Sheila.

"Listen mum, aunt Bridget is old now. You'll have to look after her and you're really not fit, not after all that's happened. If you should fall ill, then Angela would have to take your place – and nurse you as well! Do you honestly think that's fair?"

"Life's not fair, Sheila. But maybe she will go back to College and get a good job. She might even meet someone with the same interests and qualities as herself. I have to give her that chance."

"Angela married to a yank? I can't even picture it!"

"Why not?" asked Raymond, in a sharp voice. "I can't picture her married to a Belfast man and, believe me, she could have had her pick."

"I suppose that includes you!" she snapped.

Raymond stared at her.

"I suppose it does – if that's what you want to think!"

Sheila got up and left the room.

Agnes and Raymond looked at each other uncomfortably.

"Pay no attention to her, Mrs Kenny, she's depressed. It's just the way she is, with the baby and all."

She nodded.

"You like Angela, don't you Raymond?"

"I've always like Angela. She was different, you know? But Sheila's my wife and I'll take good care of her, I promise, so don't you worry. I know Mr Kenny had his doubts about me going with her. He probably thought I was too old for her, but we'll be alright, you'll see." He got up and hugged her, just like a son. "I want to thank you for this house. You've done a lot for me and I won't forget it."

"Just make her happy, Raymond."

"I will. I know we'll both be happy here."

Agnes went to find Sheila, leaving Raymond alone.

He looked around, knowing he was very lucky compared to most newly weds. Agnes Kenny had always prided herself on her home. It came second only to her family. Both she and Robert had worked hard over the years to build it up and it showed. The furniture and carpets were like new. The pictures and ornaments were tasteful and decorative. Everything blended in and complimented. Soon it would all be his and Sheila's. He could hardly believe their good fortune. The day was coming when he'd take over Robert Kenny's home but he knew he could never fill Robert Kenny's shoes! He lit a cigarette and stared out of the window. Remembering the time when that home was full of love and happiness. Maybe one day it would be again. At least he could try to make it so. He owed it to his dead father-in-law to carry on and bring up his grandchildren in the home he had loved so much.

Aunt Bridget's envelope arrived by registered mail and Angela booked the flights. When she returned, Agnes sent her for Mrs Murray.

"Agnes, is everything alright?" she asked, sitting down at the kitchen table.

"Mrs Murray, Angela and I are going to America."

"For a holiday?"

"No, to live."

"Oh Agnes, you're not leaving for good! What about the house?"

"Sheila and Raymond are staying on. I want you to keep an eye on them. You're the nearest person Sheila will have to a mother when I'm gone, and Raymond will need your help when she comes nearer her time."

Agnes began to cry and so did her elderly neighbour.

"Of course I'll see to her and help in any way I can, but I'll miss you Agnes and you too, Angela. My God this is awful, the way a family can be torn apart. I blame it all on whoever killed Robert."

Just then, Sheila and Raymond walked in.

"You've heard the news?" asked Sheila.

"I have," she nodded, "and I will miss them. America is so far away. I'm going to tell you something, though. Whoever has caused all this heartache will never have luck."

"Oh, I don't know about that," said Agnes, drying her tears. "I'm beginning to think the more evil you do, the more luck you have."

"It won't last, Agnes, believe me. There will come a day of reckoning. I'm just surprised no one had let something slip before now."

"What do you mean, Mrs Murray?" asked Angela.

"Well, you know what some of them are like when they get a few drinks, it tends to loosen their tongues." She looked at Raymond. "Did you never hear anything in the pubs and clubs?"

He pulled out a chair and sat down, folded his arms and stared at her.

"Do you know what happens to people who eavesdrop on other people's conversations? Because if you did, you wouldn't ask."

"Well, I just thought there might be a way, that's all."

"Oh, there's a way alright," said Raymond, in an annoyed voice. "I could just stand outside and wait on everyone coming out, tap them on the shoulder and say, "excuse me, did you shoot Robert Kenny?" but then I'd be shot! And as for sticking my head into people's conversations – I'd soon get it kicked in!!

After saying his piece, Raymond left the kitchen, followed by Sheila. Mrs Murray looked at Angela. "Leaving his head out of it, a good kick in the ass wouldn't go amiss," she whispered. Angela smiled. "You know," she continued, "I don't think he likes me."

"Now that's true!" muttered Raymond, as he stood in the hallway. He looked at Sheila. "I wonder if we bought another plane ticket would she go to America. With any luck she'd poke her nose into somebody else's business and end up getting it shot off!"

Sheila giggled.

"Oh Raymond you don't mean that, she's an old woman."

"She's an old busy-body! I'd give her half an hour in 'The Punters Bar' and she'd be found with her head down the toilet. Come to think of it, that wouldn't be a bad idea. After all, if your mouth's full of shit you can't talk it!"

The suitcases sat in the living room. As Agnes looked at them she felt sad and bitter. After all these years of hard work, she had ended up with very little to show for it. She and her eldest daughter were about to start a new life in a new country with nothing more than a few suitcases. It was enough to break anyone's heart. Mrs Murray stood in tears as the taxi came to a stop and sounded its horn. Raymond lifted the cases and carried them down the path as she stepped forward and put her arms around Agnes,

"I can't believe this is happening," she sobbed.

Agnes returned her embrace.

"I'll miss you. We've been neighbours a long time. Don't forget and be there for Sheila."

"Agnes I'll be here. Just the way you were always here for me. Don't worry about that. Take care of yourself." She turned and hugged Angela. "I'll pray for you and your mother every night."

"I know you will Mrs Murray."

"Listen to me Angela," she said, gripping her hand tightly. "If there's a God above, then someday he will put all these wrongs to right. Don't give up hope. If we all live long enough we might just see the day when your father will be proved innocent and the guilty brought to justice."

Angela's eyes filled with tears.

"I want to thank you for the way you stood by us, through his death and his funeral. I will never forget you for that."

"Angela, you've been running errands for me since you were a little girl. I love you like my own daughter and so did my Johnny, God rest him. Your father and mother helped me in my sorrow, the least I could do was to be there for all of you. I hope you'll meet someone who'll give you the happiness you deserve. You're a good girl and someone good is waiting for you. One day you'll remember what old Mrs Murray said."

"Right, that's everything," said Raymond, coming into the hallway. He looked at Agnes and Angela, "its time to go."

Sheila was standing at the front door, crying. Raymond put his arm around her and walked her down the path. Angela and Mrs Murray came outside.

"I'll send you a card now and then and Sheila can give you all the news," said Angela, trying hard to smile through the tears.

In the meantime, Agnes stood inside on her own. She looked around the living room and then went into the kitchen and did the same. On walking down the hallway and reaching the front door, she stopped and looked back. She was leaving her home but she was taking the memories with her. She came out and closed the door for the last time. Then she and Angela walked to the waiting taxi. Mrs Murray watched as they got in and waved to her as they drove away. She shook her head and sobbed loudly. She had lost a good friend. Robert Kenny had always done odd jobs for her around the house and garden. Agnes and Angela had been there to look after her when she was ill, forever making sure she had help when she needed it. They weren't going to be there anymore. Even little Prince was gone.

Walking down the path and closing the gate, she stopped and looked back at the house. She wondered what kind of country she was living in. It had become a place where good, innocent people were suffering for the guilty. "And out there in the streets of Belfast," she thought, "are a lot of guilty people."

Agnes and Angela were going to Heathrow, then getting another flight to America. Sheila and Raymond insisted on waiting with them until the announcement was made for all passengers to go on board. There were tears and they embraced as each bid farewell to the other.

"Say 'hello' to the 'Big Apple' for me, Angela," said Raymond in a choked voice. She nodded.

"Raymond, be good to Sheila. She needs you now more than ever."

"I will. Nothing's going to happen to her, after all, she's Mrs Burns now."

"And be nice to Mrs Murray. She's very fond of Sheila. I know she annoys you sometimes but she means well."

"Angela, listening to Mrs Murray's ranting and raving would annoy a Saint, and they're supposed to be the one's with patience! She's always predicting what's going to happen. I think I'll get her a job."

"Doing what?"

"Fore telling the future. If I tie a scarf around her head and put a curtain ring in her ear, we'll be in business. I'll put a sign up, '*Mrs Murray – come and hear your date with fate*'! Then he smiled and assured her. "I'll be nice to her, don't worry. Besides, she could make me a fortune!"

Angela smiled too,

"Mrs Murray – The Medium! Well she might just surprise us all one day, if her predictions come true."

After the final goodbyes, Agnes and Angela left to board the plane. They had only gone a short distance when Angela turned and beckoned Raymond. She put her hand on his arm and looked into his eyes, earnestly. "Promise me if you ever hear anything you'll tell me."

"Angela, I'll always be watching and listening. Sooner or later someone will talk. You know what these blokes are like when they argue amongst themselves or get too much to drink. They'll say something someday, and then we'll all know."

She nodded.

"You see, Mrs Murray's words are coming in already. Find them Raymond. Please, try and find who murdered my father."

"I'll try, Angela, I promise."

He kissed her cheek. She held his hand tightly for a moment, before walking away quickly.

Raymond and Sheila stood watching them board the plane.

"Do you think they will stay?" she sobbed.

He put his arm around her.

"I'll give your mother a couple of months and she'll be back. Agnes won't settle in America," he said, waving his hand in farewell, "but Angela? Well, to be honest with you, I'm not so sure about her."

As the plane moved along the runway and gathered speed. Agnes pressed Angela's hand. Both women were silent, each with their own thoughts. At that moment Angela wished she'd had a brother. Things might have been different. He could have looked after them and maybe he could have found his father's killers. One thought consoled her, Raymond was the brother she never had and she knew if anyone could find out anything, it would be him. She felt sure he would keep his promise and that one day she would know who killed the father she loved so much – and why.

As the plane left the ground and left Belfast behind, Angela Kenny wondered what the future would be like and what New York and its people would have to offer someone like her...

Chapter 2

The long, black limousine pulled up outside the very exclusive "Safe Haven" restaurant. Inside was Joe Morrelli with his girlfriend Antonia Flemming, his best friend and minder, Rooney and Mandy, a friend of Antonia's and Rooney's date for the evening. They laughed and chatted as they entered the building. It had been a while since Joe had been there. He'd been out of town on business combined with a well earned vacation, but because he owned the place he liked to call now and then just to keep an eye on things.

As they approached the large dining area, Joe was greeted by Freddie Barrett who managed the restaurant for him

"Mr Morrelli, what a pleasant surprise! It's so good to see you Sir."

"Thanks Freddie. How's business?" enquired Joe.

"Booming as usual Sir!"

"Good, good. That's what I like to hear."

Freddie walked in front of the party, leading the way to Joe's special table from where he could see everything and everyone. As Joe and Rooney pulled out the plush, red velvet seats for the ladies, a voice was heard.

"Joe! How are you?"

Joe looked around.

"Judge Thompson, nice to see you."

He went over to his old friend and shook his hand.

"How are they treating you, Judge?"

"Fine Joe. Just fine. Good food, good service" replied the Judge, smiling broadly.

"We aim to please! Freddie, a bottle of the best champagne for Judge Thompson – on the house," called Joe, patting the Judge on the back.

"Coming right up, Mr Morrelli," assured Freddie.

"That's very kind of you, Joe." Judge Thompson remarked.

"Not at all. Special customers deserve special treatment."

Joe returned to his table and as he sat down he observed the large crowd in the elegant dining room. Freddie handed out the menus.

"I'll have someone take your order right away, Mr Morrelli," he said, before rushing off.

Joe was studying the menu, when a quiet voice with a soft lilting accent asked.

"Excuse me, sir. Would you like to order now?"

Joe looked up. Standing beside him was a very young and extremely attractive girl. He shot a glance at Rooney, who was openly staring at her.

"Yeah," replied Joe, looking at the two women. "I think we are just about ready."

Antonia and Mandy nodded. Rooney remained silent, his eyes still fixed on the young waitress.

"What would you recommend?" Joe asked.

"Anything on the menu sir. All the dishes are excellent. We serve only the finest cuisine."

Joe nodded his head in approval.

"Good answer! He thought to himself.

"Well. I'll have a steak – medium rare," he said. "Ladies, what will it be? Rooney?"

They all decided on steak and the young waitress began to write the order down.

"O.k." Joe continued, "that's three steaks – medium rare and one well done." He pointed to Rooney.

"Will that be with all the trimmings, sir? she asked.

"Yeah, steak and everything that comes with it."

"Side Salads?"

"Only for the ladies. And a bottle of the best wine."

"Red or white, sir"

"Red."

Joe studied her casually. She wasn't wearing much make-up. Just enough to set off her large, deep blue eyes and classic cheekbones. Not only was she pretty but she had long, thick red hair that gave off a golden sheen under the lights. It was pulled back and gathered into a black velvet bow.

"Thank you sir," she said as she left the table.

She wore a white blouse and straight black skirt. Black nylon stockings and black high heel shoes. The outfit showed off her trim figure and slender legs. Joe reckoned she was about 5ft.4ins. – without the heels!

He glanced around the table. Rooney was staring after her. Joe snapped his fingers in Rooney's face.

"Hey, what's with you?"

"Nothing Joe. Except...."

Rooney looked at Antonia and Mandy, who were deep in conversation. He leaned over the table and in a low voice continued, "I think that waitress is Irish."

"Yeah," agreed Joe. "Now that you come to mention it, she does have an accent something like yours – only more refined! Why don't you ask her?"

"Maybe later," said Rooney.

The young waitress returned and proceeded to serve dinner.

"Looks good," commented Joe.

She was very careful to serve each guest individually and gave particular attention to the pouring of the wine. After she gave Joe a sample he told her,

"That's o.k... I'll take it from here."

"Thank you sir."

"Thank you."

Everyone seemed to be enjoying dinner when Joe noticed that Rooney's steak was untouched.

"What's the matter?" he asked. "Is the steak o.k.?"

"Sure, Joe. It's fine."

"Well, if it's so fine why aren't you eating it?"

"Oh, I guess I'm not very hungry after all."

But Joe knew if Rooney suddenly lost his appetite it had something to do with the young waitress. He couldn't blame him. He'd been impressed by her, too. But he decided he wasn't going to say anything. After they had finished dinner she came back to clear the table.

"Would you like something else sir? Dessert? Coffee?"

"Coffee will be fine. And Four large brandies."

After she disappeared from view, Judge Thompson came over to Joe's table.

"Antonia, you look radiant – as always!" he said.

Antonia laughed, "Thank you Judge."

He turned to Joe.

"Joe, I've got to hand it to you. You don't only serve the best food in town, you also have some of the best looking waitresses I've ever seen. So charming and polite. Take that young red-head for instance?"

"Yeah, what about her?"

"She'd make any man want to come here," he said and after glancing quickly to the two ladies he added, "and bring his wife or girlfriend! It's a pleasure to be served by someone like her. I don't know where you get them from."

"Perhaps it's just as well!" joked Joe.

Judge Thompson laughed and then bid everyone a very 'goodnight' especially Antonia!

After a few minutes, Joe rose to his feet.

"Excuse me, ladies. I won't be long."

He made his way to the end of the dining room where Freddie was supervising the staff.

"I want to talk to you for a few minutes, Freddie." He said motioning towards the office.

Once inside Freddie asked nervously.

"Is anything wrong, Mr Morrelli?"

"That young waitress. The one with the long, red hair."

"You have a complaint about her sir?"

"No, but I'd like some information."

"Information?"

"Yeah. Like who is she? How long has she been here? You know what I mean!"

Freddie stared at the ceiling as he tried to recall.

"Well, her name is Angela Kenny and she's been here about four months now."

"Go on," urged Joe.

"She came in one day and asked for a job. I'd put an ad in the paper. We were short staffed, you see."

"Yeah, yeah" Joe was becoming a little impatient.

"I really didn't think she'd suit. She'd never done waitressing before but she begged me to give her a trial. She said she really needed the job so I agreed. I must admit, she picked it up very quickly and has become extremely popular with a lot of our customers."

"Did she say why she needed the job?"

"Not really, just something about having to support her mother. They'd come here form Ireland and were going through a difficult time. I suppose I felt sorry for her. Anyway, I agreed to take her on for a while."

"Anything else?"

"No, I don't think so – except that she works double shifts a lot of the time. You know, weekends. I did hear one of the girls saying Angela went to College back home and wants to go to one here if she can fit the classes in between her different shifts."

"What does she study?"

"I don't know Mr Morrelli."

"Then find out! Find our where she lives. Where she goes? Who she goes with? Find our anything you can."

"But how sir?"

Joe stepped forward and tapped Freddie on the arm. "Let me give you a tip, Freddie. If you want to find out about a woman – ask another woman. They love to gossip especially about each other."

"Well I suppose I could ask Cindy. She doesn't like Angela very much though, because she's so popular."

"Even better!" Joe smiled. "Find out what you can and let me know."

"Certainly Mr Morrelli"

They left the office. Joe went back to his table and lit a cigar. Now he could enjoy his brandy.

When Antonia and Mandy went to the powder room, Joe turned to Rooney.

"Listen," he said, "Why don't you have a word with her on the way out?"

"Who?"

Joe turned his eyes up towards the ceiling.

"Come on Rooney. I'm not blind. I know you like her. I've never seen you look at anyone that way before." "Was it that obvious"

"Not to them." Joe nodded towards the powder room. "But it sure was to me!"

On the ladies return they all decided to leave. Rooney escorted Antonia and Mandy away from the table while Joe opened his wallet and counted out thirty dollars, one twenty and one ten. It was his tip for the young, Irish waitress. Then he followed the others until he reached the cashier's desk. Even if he did own the place, Joe always made a point of paying and as he was settling the bill he felt a gentle tap on his shoulder and heard the same lilting accent as before.

"Excuse me sir. You left this behind."

On turning round, he came face to face with her as she stood with his thirty dollars in her hand.

"That's yours!" he said, rather surprised. "That's your tip!"

"I'm sorry sir, I can't take it."

"Why not?"

"Because it's far too much."

Joe stared at her for a few moments.

"Keep it!" he insisted, waving his hand.

"I'm sorry. I really can't."

Joe smiled and looked amused. Then he glanced at Rooney, who was taking in every word.

"O.K. I'll tell you what," Joe said, taking the money from her. "Why don't you take what you think isn't too much."

She glanced shyly at Rooney and then looked at Joe, her face red with embarrassment. She picked out the ten dollar bill.

"That's more than enough. Thank you sir."

"Thank you," he replied, as he watched her walk away. He and Rooney were helping the ladies with their coats when Joe suddenly caught sight of her again as she headed for the kitchen. He kissed Antonia on the cheek and explained,

"Wait here for a minute. I have to see Freddie about something."

He went to the entrance of the kitchen and leaned against the wall out of sight. Then he heard a loud female voice.

"Are you mad? Turning down a thirty dollar tip! Don't you know who that guy is? He's Joe Morrelli – the owner!"

"What?"

"Yeah, he owns this joint. He can afford to give 30 dollar tips! Why the hell didn't you take it?"

"But it was far too much, Cindy. I didn't earn it. I only served them dinner and I already get paid for that. It's my job."

"Oh come on! I just wish I'd served him. Honestly, Angela you're such a damn fool!"

"Well Cindy, better a fool than a thief."

There was silence. Joe smiled and nodded his head as he turned. Now there was someone who could be trusted! He joined the rest of the party and they all went on to 'The Portland', Antonia's favourite club.

As the evening wore on, Rooney's thoughts were miles away. He sat at the table, glass in hand. He moved it from side to side and watched as the alcohol swirled around. Joe had never seen him like this. He was showing all the signs of someone in love. Joe was also in deep thought. He recalled Judge Thompson's comments. There was no doubt about it, she was an attractive girl in every way. And an honest one, when it came to the 30 dollars! If she weren't so young he'd be interested in her himself. She'd make someone a very happy man. Unknown to Rooney, Joe had a secret desire that the someone in question just might be him.

A few days later, the phone in the study rang. Joe answered it.

"Mr Morrelli, it's me Freddie. I've got the information you wanted. I'm at the restaurant."

"That's fine, Freddie. Are you alone?"

"Yes sir."

"Good. I'm on my way out. I have some business to take care of first so I'll see you in about an hour."

Joe left the house and got into the waiting car. Al was already in the driver's seat.

"Where to Boss?"

"Stacey's Gym first. Then 'The Safe Haven'."

After some discussions with some associates at the gym, concerning a big fight that was coming up and who should win, Joe left in a happy mood knowing his bet was a sure thing and he'd make a small fortune!

His next stop was to see Freddie.

When he reached 'The Safe Haven', it was closed. Freddie was waiting in the entrance hall and unlocked the door to let Joe inside.

"I thought it best to speak to you before the staff turn up for the next shift, Mr Morrelli."

Joe nodded as he walked into the dining area and sat down at one of the tables. Freddie joined him and took a folded sheet of paper from his pocket while Joe lit a cigar.

"I wrote it all down, just in case I'd forget something."

"Was Cindy any help?" enquired Joe.

"More than helpful. Especially after the incident concerning the tip!"

Joe smiled and said, "I figured you'd hear about that."

"Mr Morrelli, I hear everything. That's part of my job."

Freddie cleared his throat before continuing. "Now, as you know, she's Angela Kenny and she came to New York with her mother about six months ago. She's originally from Belfast and her father died there last year. When they arrived here, she and her mother lived with an old aunt who has since passed away. They still stay in the same apartment just a few blocks from here."

Freddie paused. "This might interest you sir. When she went to College in Ireland she studied English Literature, particularly the Classics. You know, Shakespeare, Dickens. She's also into poetry and the great poets. You know…"

"Yeah Freddie – I know. And I'm impressed!"

"I thought you might be. On her days off she likes to visit art galleries and museums, especially if there are exhibitions."

"What did you do, Freddie – hire a private detective?"

"I didn't have to, Mr Morrelli. You were right, women love to talk and I'm a very good listener!"

Joe shook his head and looked puzzled.

"I don't get it," he said "What's a girl like that doing in a restaurant waiting on tables?"

"To be perfectly honest with you, Mr Morrelli, I'm not sure myself. On the other hand, she starts her courses at Wendelle College next week. The money that she earns from her double shifts here may be going towards her tuition fees and books."

"If that's the case, I can understand why someone like Cindy wouldn't be all that keen on the girl! She obviously wants to make something of herself. I admire that."

"Exactly," said Freddie, politely.

Joe stared down at the stiff, white, linen table cloth. He tapped the ash of his cigar lightly into an ashtray.

"Any boyfriends?" he asked.

"Not that I know of. At least, no one ever comes around looking for her."

Joe raised his eyes and stared at Freddie.

"What's she like, Freddie? I mean as a person?"

"She's a nice girl, sir. She seems a little quiet and shy until you get to know her, then you see a warm, friendly side to her. I think that's what appeals to our customers. She's very approachable but yet, a little reserved. She doesn't talk about herself a lot. Likes to keep her personal life her own business. It's taken me until now to find out what I've told you."

"You've done very well, Freddie. I really appreciate it. But there's just one more thing. How old is she?"

"Eighteen – I think."

Joe rose from the table and patted Freddie on the shoulder.

"Good work," he said.

He walked towards the door and Freddie followed.

"I hope what I've told you has been of some help, Mr Morrelli."

"It's been a great help," replied Joe, shaking Freddie's hand. "Goodbye Freddie and remember, this conversation never took place."

"What conversation?" asked Freddie, tearing the sheet of paper into tiny pieces. He held the door open as Joe left.

"Where to now, Boss?" asked Al, as Joe got into the car.

"Home," came the curt reply.

As Al drove along he noticed that Joe was unusually quiet, so he kept checking in the mirror to see if his boss was alright. Joe sat in the back of the car looking very thoughtful.

"Everything o.k. Boss?"

"Yeah, fine," came the reply. But Al had his doubts. Joe had left Stacey's Gym all smiles. Al had wondered what had happened at 'The Safe Haven' to change all that. The Car stopped in front of the house and Joe got out.

"I won't need you for a few hours," he said. "Take the rest of the afternoon off."

"Sure boss. I'll pick you up later on, to go to Miss Flemming's."

Joe didn't answer but let himself into the house and closed the door. He went straight to the study, poured a large scotch and sat down behind his desk. He gazed into space while he sipped his drink.

Here he was, a successful business man. He had money and power. People admired and respected him. Some even feared him. Yet through it all he felt there was a void of some kind. As if something was missing. It wasn't until today that he discovered what exactly it was. He needed someone to share his life with. He knew Antonia would be more than willing, but deep down inside he knew he'd always wanted someone like this young girl. This Angela Kenny. If Freddie's information was anything to go by, she had all the qualities he'd ever admired in a woman, but had never come across – until now. He felt sad that a man of nearly forty should find his ideal woman in a slip of a girl young enough to be his daughter! There's no way she'd even be interested.

"No, you fool," he murmured. "You can't buy what you want this time."

Remembering the 30 dollars and his talk with Freddie, Joe Morrelli decided to put Angela Kenny out of his mind. She was far more suited to a younger man – like Rooney. His search for information had only led him to wishful thinking. He got up, poured another scotch and raising his glass said in a low voice, "Here's to what might have been, if I were ten years younger"!"

When Joe Morrelli first opened 'The Safe Haven', he made quite a few house rules but the most important one of all was that the staff must not date the customers. He had his reasons. In his time he'd seen a lot of pretty, young waitresses make plays for successful, mostly married men. Just the same way he'd seen successful, mostly married men make plays for pretty, young waitresses! Either way, a lot of women got hurt and a lot of children were torn between feuding parents. Joe was determined that no such events would ever be attributed to his establishment and that 'The Safe Haven' would live up to it's name. Rooney had always supported him in this, until they met Angela Kenny.

Rooney arrived into the study unannounced. Joe looked up from his business papers.

"What's the matter with you?" he asked. "You look like a pane where there isn't a window."

"Oh, very droll," replied Rooney, walking over to the fireplace and resting his elbow on the mantelpiece.

"Well, what is it?"

"I've just been to 'The Safe Haven' – again."

"Oh!" said Joe, deliberately burying his head in the pile of papers.

There was silence. Then Rooney finally spoke.

"Joe, these rules at 'The Safe Haven'...."

"What about them?"

"Well, don't you think some of them go a bit far?"

"You never thought that before Rooney. Would this have anything to do with Angela Kenny?" asked Joe, looking up again.

"Come on, Joe, you know how much I like her. We get on so well and enjoy seeing each other but she still won't come out with me. She says she likes 'The Safe Haven' and needs the money. She can't take the chance of having to leave."

"Yeah well, in my restaurant if you take the job you must abide by the rules. Angela knew that from the beginning, just like the others."

"But you're the owner. Couldn't you make just one exception?"

Joe leaned back in his chair and rubbed his brow with one hand, while he tapped his pen on the desk with the other.

"You know I can't do that Rooney."

"Can't or won't?" asked Rooney, in a stern voice.

Joe threw the pen down and leaned over the desk, looking directly at his friend.

"I can't! How would that look if I started showing favouritism? What would people say?"

"I don't care what people say."

"But I do! My restaurant has a fine reputation, Rooney. But if I start changing things around for one friend, I'll have to do it for another and another and pretty soon the name will be changed from 'The Safe Haven' to 'The free for All' I just can't do it, not even for you."

Rooney thought for a few moments, then nodded.

"You're right Joe. I'm sorry. I should never have asked you. It wasn't right of me."

Joe reached over and grabbed Rooney's arm. "You listen to me," he said. "I know it's getting to you but Angela won't be waiting on tables for much longer. She's too smart for that. She'll find herself something better, Rooney, you wait and see. And when she does, there'll be nothing to stop you two going together."

Rooney forced a smile as Joe continued, "Now why don't you go on into the lounge and relax for a while. Frankie and Al are already in there playing cards. Make sure Al doesn't cheat!"

As Rooney left the study, Joe couldn't help but feel guilty. Unknown to his best friend he had more personal reasons for not wanting Angela Kenny to date any customers. More selfish reasons!

A few weeks went by. Joe left Antonia's early. She had a script for a new Broadway play and was giving him a headache, going on and on about how great it was and how it would be a huge success. Joe decided he needed some peace and a quiet drink so he made his excuses to her about having an important business meeting the next morning, and phoned Al to come and get him.

It was about 11.30pm when Joe settled down into the back seat of the car and breathed a sigh of relief.

"You wanna go home, Boss?"

"No. Just drive."

They cruised along one street after another going nowhere in particular. Then Joe leaned over and said "Stop at 'The Safe Haven.'"

As Al made his way there, Joe sat quietly thinking to himself. Why should he stay away from his own restaurant? After all, he was the Boss! The car came to a halt and Joe sat looking towards the entrance. After a few moments he noticed a couple of girls coming out of the side door, used only by the staff. They talked for a while and then split up. One of them waved and called "goodnight", then turned and started to make her way along the sidewalk on her own. Joe recognised her at once. It was Angela Kenny. He got out of the car and turned to Al.

"Wait here for about five minutes, then come along behind me slowly. But try and keep out of sight."

Al nodded.

Joe pulled his collar up and putting his hands in his pockets, he walked quickly behind until he finally caught up with her.

"Hi, how are you?" he smiled.

Angela jumped nervously with a startled look on her face. Then putting her head down she walked quickly away from him.

"You don't remember me, do you?" Joe asked, catching up with her again.

"Should I?" she replied, trying not to look at him.

"I'm Joe Morrelli. You know – the big tipper!"

Angela stopped and stared at him. Then she looked relieved.

"Mr Morrelli? My Boss?"

"Yeah, that's me. I'm sorry if I scared you but you shouldn't be walking on your own. It's too dangerous. There are a lot of weirdos running around."

"I don't have far to go," she replied.

"You don't have to go far to meet them! You should be more careful. Do you mind if I walk with you? I'd feel better knowing you got home o.k."

"No, I don't mind at all. It's very kind of you to offer. But I wouldn't want to take up your time if you're going somewhere else."

"Oh, that's ok. Don't worry about it."

Angela smiled and held her hand out towards him.

"I'm Angela. Angela Kenny."

Joe took her hand in his.

"Well, you already know who I am!"

After the official introduction, they continued the walk to Angela's home.

"So, how do you like working at 'The Safe Haven'?" asked Joe, trying to make small talk.

"Oh, I like it fine. Mr Barrett is a nice man and a good man to work for. I like him a lot.

"Yeah, Freddie's a good guy," replied Joe.

For a moment there was silence, then Angela said, "Mr Morrelli, about that night in the restaurant when I gave you back the money, I apologise if I offended you. I had no idea you were the owner."

Joe stopped and looked at her.

"Would it have made any difference if you'd known?"

"No, not really. But I'm surprised you didn't fire me on the spot!"

"Why should I do that? After all, honesty is a good quality to have. It's one you don't come across too often these days. Anyway, I promise to leave a smaller tip next time!"

They both started to laugh and walked a few more yards.

"Well, this is it. I'm home," said Angela, looking up at an old, discoloured building.

Joe thought for a moment and then took his hands out of his pockets and started rubbing them together. "You know," he said looking up and down the street, "it's always when you'd really like a cup of coffee, there never seems to be any place that's open."

Angela looked uncomfortable, if not a little embarrassed.

"Goodnight Mr Morrelli. And thank you."

She turned to climb the steps.

"What's the matter, Angela?" asked Joe. "Don't you like where you live?"

"Yes I do. But somehow I don't think a small furnished apartment would be what you're used to, Mr Morrelli."

"Really? You should have seen some of the places I was used to. Furnished apartments - without the furniture! Goodnight."

Angela stood and watched as he began to walk away. Then, without even realising it, she called to him.

"Mr Morrelli...."

Joe turned around.

"....would you like to come in and meet my mother?"

Joe smiled, "Do I get a cup of coffee?"

She nodded. So Joe followed her up the steps and into the apartment building. Three flights up she stopped at a door with 30A printed on it. She took a key from her pocket and opened it.

"Mum, I'm home," she called, as they both stepped inside and Joe closed the door.

Angela led him through a narrow hallway and into a brightly lit room. A gas heater blocked up the centre of a large old fashioned fireplace. Beside it was an armchair and seated in it, with her back to them, was a woman. She was reading a book and wearing a dressing gown and slippers. As she turned around, she asked, "Is that you, Angela?" in a strong Irish accent.

Angela walked across the room.

"Mum, I'd like you to meet Mr Morrelli – my boss. He walked home with me to make sure I'd be alright."

She then looked over at Joe and said,

"Mr Morrelli, this is my mother, Agnes Kenny."

Joe walked over and shook Agnes's hand.

"Nice to meet you Mrs Kenny," he said.

"Oh, call me Agnes. And please sit down beside the fire. Mr Morrelli."

Agnes put her book down and nodded to the couch facing her. Joe held his hands out in front of the heater as he sat down. Agnes smiled at him.

"It was good of you to see my daughter home. Would you like a cup of tea or coffee? Angela get Mr Morrelli whatever he wants, love."

"Coffee would be fine," he said, as Angela went through to the kitchen.

Agnes waited until she and Joe were alone. Then she leaned towards him and in a low voice said, "You know, I worry about her when she's working these late shifts. I can't go to bed until she's home. I'm always keeping her going and telling her if she'd find herself a nice taxi driver she wouldn't have to walk. Do any nice taxi drivers go to your restaurant, Mr Morrelli?"

"Not unless they own the company!" joked Joe.

Agnes studied him for a moment.

"Are you a family man yourself, Mr Morrelli?"

"No I'm not married, and no kids either."

"I'm very surprised that a handsome man like you is still single!"

Joe gave an embarrassed smile.

"And such a nice smile too," Agnes added.

Joe was still smiling, "Well maybe I never met the right woman."

"You must be looking for someone very special, then. Do you have a girlfriend, Mr Morrelli?"

Angela cringed in the cramped kitchen as she listened to the conversation.

"Yeah, I do."

"What does she work at?"

"As a matter of fact, she's an actress."

"You mean in the movies?"

"No, on the stage. She acts on Broadway."

"How wonderful!" said Agnes, "You must be very proud of her?"

"Yeah, she has a lot of talent."

Angela peeped out from behind the kitchen door.

"Mum, she insisted, "will you stop asking Mr Morrelli such personal questions."

Anyone would think you were working for the F.B.I.!"

"Now Angela, I'm only making conversation," said Agnes with an innocent look on her face. Then she turned to Joe and winked. They both started to laugh. Joe liked Agnes right away. She was open and friendly. Angela came into the room with a tray and put it down on the coffee table. She handed Joe a cup of coffee and gave Agnes tea.

"Have you taken your medicine yet, mum?" she enquired in a serious voice.

"No, not yet love."

Angela turned and reached up to the mantelpiece. From it she took down two bottles of tablets and counted out two tablets from one bottle and one from the other. She gave them to her mother, as Joe watched with interest. He realised that besides working long hours, this young girl had a sick mother who was very much dependent on her. He wondered how she coped with it all on her own. After Agnes took her medication she returned to conversation with Joe.

"Does your girlfriend do Shakespeare, Mr Morrelli?"

"No," said Joe shaking his head. "Somehow I don't think Shakespeare's really her bag!"

"When Angela went to College back home, she studied all his plays. She used to stand in the living room and recite pages for her father and me. I don't know how she kept half of it in her head. Angela, recite something for Mr Morrelli."

"Mum, please!" said Angela feeling extremely uncomfortable. "Let Mr Morrelli drink his coffee."

"Her father used to buy her books on all that stuff," said Agnes, looking up at the mantelpiece. "He was so proud of her."

Joe followed her gaze and saw a large framed photograph. He stood up and lifted it.

"Is this your husband?" he asked.

Agnes nodded.

"And that's Angela, and Sheila, my other daughter. She's married now and still lives in Belfast."

"He's a fine man," commented Joe, quick to observe that Angela looked very much like her father. At least he knew now where she had gotten her red hair from!

The smile on Agnes's face had faded and in it's place was a look of deep sadness.

"He's dead now," she explained. "I miss him very much. We all do."

Angela got up and went into the kitchen.

"He had such high hopes for her," Agnes whispered to Joe. "No offence, Mr Morrelli, but she would never have been a waitress if my Robert had been spared. She's too independent though and wanted to pay her own way. So she took the waitressing job. But now that she's gone back to school who knows what might turn up in the future. She always studied so hard and got such good grades."

Joe listened intently. He noticed that Agnes certainly didn't look well and knew that doctors and medication had to be paid for. That was probably the main reason why Angela had ended up working for him.

He also observed the apartment. It was clean and tidy but small and cramped, even for just two people. The furniture was old and the pictures on the wall, faded. Life had not been kind to them, he thought. He felt almost compelled to find out more about them, to get to know them better. He decided he'd like to see the books Angela's father had bought her and see for himself what she studied. It might help him to become that little bit closer to her. Agnes had wet his appetite to discover more about her daughter and her background. Perhaps if he were to call on Agnes when she was alone. She was obviously a friendly woman who liked company and liked to talk.

"Well," said Joe, "I'd better be going."

Agnes went to get up but Joe put his hand on her shoulder.

"No. You stay where you are."

He took her hand and added in a soft voice, "Maybe I'll call and see you again."

"Oh yes, that would be nice," she replied. "We don't get many visitors and I really enjoyed your company. You will be welcome any time, Mr Morrelli."

Angela came back from the kitchen.

"I'll show you out."

She led the way and opened the front door for him.

"Your mother's a nice lady, Angela," he said.

"She has one fault. She asks too many questions! I hope she didn't embarrass you."

Joe looked at her and smiled, "I think she embarrassed you more than me!"

Angela started to blush. At that moment, Joe wanted to put his arms around her and tell her how much he admired her. But he wasn't her father or her boyfriend. He was only her boss.

"Thanks for the coffee," he smiled.

"Was it worth all the questions? She asked.

"Yeah, I think so." Then his face broke into a happy grin. "I'd have another cup anytime!"

Angela laughed, "Goodnight, Mr Morrelli."

Joe waved his hand as he made his way down the stairs.

"Goodnight."

Angela closed the door and went back to her mother.

"What a nice man that Mr Morrelli is," said Agnes. "How come you've never mentioned him before?"

"Because I didn't really know him until tonight, mum."

"You know Angela, I was so surprised when he said he wasn't married."

"Yes. I heard you!"

"Well, you'd wonder why someone like him isn't. After all, he's a very attractive man and he must be nearly forty. He's not getting any younger. You'd think some girl would have snapped him up by now, wouldn't you?"

"To be honest, mum I haven't really paid as much attention to him as you. I've only met him twice. Once when I served him and his friends dinner, and then tonight. The first time I was too busy to notice anything and everything happened so quickly tonight I just never thought of studying him the way you did!"

"That's your trouble, Angela. You pay more attention to books than you do to people!"

Angela was getting tired of this conversation.

"Mum, he's my boss. I hardly know the man. What does it matter to me if he's married or not married, or getting married? I only work for him. Now, can we go to bed and get some sleep?"

Joe tossed and turned in the kingsize bed. He lay awake in the darkness going over all the events of that evening. He remembered every word of his conversation with Angela as he walked her home and everything Agnes had said concerning her daughter. The more Joe saw and heard about Angela Kenny, the more he was drawn to her. It didn't seem right that a man of his age should be so physically attracted to someone so young but he couldn't help how he felt. He reminded himself that many mature men had fallen for younger women but it didn't make him feel any better. He wanted to do something to help make life a little easier for Angela and her mother but he knew he couldn't offer money. They weren't that sort of people to accept handouts. They might live in a crummy apartment but Angela Kenny had her pride. That was one of the things he liked about her. No, he'd have to find another way.

There was something else keeping him awake. If she got another job he'd most likely never see her again. He didn't want that to happen. Besides having good intentions for wanting to help her, he also had his own reasons for keeping her at 'The Safe Haven'. At least he could see her and talk to her whenever he wanted. He had to admit to being selfish and it did make him feel guilty, but he could see no other solution. Perhaps he should have a talk with Freddie and square something, that way he could help the Kenny's and himself.

And then there was Rooney! He'd have to tell him about tonight and what he intended to do. He surely wasn't looking forward to that. Rooney had always been like a brother to him and Joe knew how he felt about Angela, from the first time he ever saw her. He decided not to tell Rooney how he felt, not yet anyway. After all, Angela didn't seem interested in him and he could understand that. Agnes had been more interested. He couldn't help wishing it was the other way round. But then Angela was probably looking for someone young and intellectual, like herself. Unfortunately, he didn't fit the bill. When it came to school he didn't have much of an education. But when it came to 'Street College', Joe Morrelli graduated with honours!

With the brains and manner Angela Kenny had, she could go all the way if she had someone to point her in the right direction. And there was no one better to do that than him. Joe had always admired people with knowledge and intelligence and from what

Agnes had told him, her daughter had plenty of both. Maybe what happened tonight was fate. If Antonia hadn't gotten her script that day, he wouldn't have turned up at 'The Safe Haven' and none of this would have happened. This thought eased his conscience. He turned over and taking a pillow, he held it tightly in his arms.

"Angela Kenny," he whispered, "I could take you all the way to the top."

After an uneventful night's sleep, Joe summoned Rooney to his study. Sitting in the leather armchair behind the desk, he asked Rooney to sit down.

"I've got something to discuss with you Rooney," he said, putting his hands together and resting his chin on them. He proceeded to tell Rooney what had happened the previous night, from he left Antonia's apartment until he said "Goodnight" to Angela and her mother.

Rooney sat in silence throughout and waited until Joe was finished. Then he got up from the chair, leaned across the desk and stared at him.

"Before you say anything," advised Joe, "Just hear me out."

"I'm listening!" came the reply.

Joe got up and walked over to the window.

"They need help, Rooney," he explained, "Especially the mother. She's an ill woman and looks older than her years. Her daughter's paying for an apartment, doctor's bills, and medication. Not to mention food and clothes. As well as that she's trying to pay her way through college. The girls' going to spend the best years of her life worrying about which bill is going to arrive next! So here's what I think should be done. I see to it that Angela Kenny gets a better job at 'The Safe Haven', a more suitable job, with more pay. That should help solve some of her problems. The job would be less demanding so she'd be able to carry on with her studies. What do you think?"

"Does it really matter to you what I think?"

The two men looked at each other.

"If it didn't," replied Joe, "we wouldn't be having this conversation!"

"Alright then," said Rooney, but why the sudden interest in Angela and her mother?"

"Because I know what it's like to struggle, Rooney. I gave up my youth to do it and maybe that's why I'm alone today. I don't want to see someone else make the same mistake, especially someone who could do so much with their life. It's a waste Rooney. It's time taken out of your life you can never replace. Believe me, I know."

Rooney was thoughtful for a moment. Then said,

"O.k. Joe, I think you're doing the right thing. But there must be another reason why you're taking this all so seriously. You really like, Angela, don't you?"

"Admire is the word I would use," contradicted Joe. "I admire her guts and determination, and her love for her mother. She's loyal and there's a lot to be said for loyalty."

"Well," said Rooney, "if anyone can give her the break she needs, you can."

"I just want to help," insisted Joe, as he walked over to Rooney and put his hand on his shoulder. "Anyway, look on the bright side. Now that she's back at school, Angela might not be at 'The Safe Haven' for much longer. And if she leaves, then at least I'll have done my bit."

Rooney nodded and said, "Yes, you're right. But maybe I just feel this way because I've fallen in love with her Joe."

"A lot of men could fall in love with Angela Kenny. But there'll only ever be one winner Rooney."

"I'll leave that choice to Angela. I only want the best for her and I know she'll make the right decision."

"I hope so," said Joe. "She might never get a second chance."

Rooney opened the door and left the study without another word. As the door closed, Joe rubbed his face with his hands. He knew Rooney suspected how he felt about Angela and he'd neither confirmed nor denied it. He thought it best to leave things as they were for now. No point in jumping the gun. Rooney went out into the driveway and lit a cigarette. He stood deep in thought, upset by the whole situation. Joe was the only family he had. He loved and respected him. But this was too much! It was like two brothers falling for the same woman. Then he started to think about Angela and everything Joe had told him. He had to admit that she did need help, even if she didn't realise it herself and Joe was in a better position than him to do something about it. Joe Morrelli had contacts all over the city. Through him, she could meet all the right people. If she wanted a better job, a better life, then Joe could open doors for her that he couldn't.

Rooney remembered the way Joe had helped him and wondered where he'd be now if he'd never met him. Probably in a crummy apartment like Angela. Or maybe even worse – just another nameless face in the crowd. It was a jungle out there and Rooney knew from bitter experience, when you're a nobody – nobody gives a damn!!

Joe Morrelli had given him a chance. Now he was willing to give Angela one. She might take it but then again she might not. However, Rooney knew that if he really loved her he'd have to leave her to choose for herself. It was the only thing for him to do. He stamped out the cigarette and went back inside to join Joe in the study. For a few seconds there was silence between the two. Then Rooney spoke.

"O.k. Joe, they do need help. She's not street wise. Anything could happen to her and if something did, I'd never be able to live with myself. You do what you have to, Joe. I just want to see her safe and happy."

"Well, I guess now that we've agreed on it, we can get down to business," said Joe, relieved that Rooney had come round to his way of thinking.

He went over to the desk and lifted the telephone.

Rooney sat on the edge of the desk while Joe dialled and waited. After a few seconds, Joe greeted the person on the other end of the line.

"Hello Freddie, how are you? Yeah, it's me! Look, I was wondering if you could drop by and see me today. I've got a proposition I'd like to put to you. I'd value your opinion. Say in about an hour? Good! See you then, Freddie."

Joe replaced the receiver and looked at Rooney.

"Do you think he'll go for it? Asked Rooney, "He's a bit touchy about running the place on his own."

"Relax, I can handle Freddie," smiled Joe. "I pay his wages, don't I? By the time I'm through with him, he'll be begging me to make her a partner!"

Just over an hour later, Freddie arrived at Joe's house. Rooney had made himself scarce, so Frankie let him in and brought him to the study, knocked on the door and waited for a reply.

"Come in," Joe said in a loud voice.

Frankie opened the door and announced,

"Mr Barrett is here, Boss."

"Good! Send him in."

Freddie walked into the study, looking a little nervous.

Joe put out his hand.

"Nice to see you, Freddie. Take a seat."

Freddie waited until Joe had sat down behind the desk, before he made himself comfortable in the chair opposite. Joe studied his hands for a moment, then raised his eyes and looked at Freddie.

"How long have you worked for me now? he asked.

"About three - nearly four years, Mr Morrelli. Since you got rid of your first manager."

"Oh yeah," replied Joe, "I remember him. I seem to recall he was skimming off the top. Treating the place like his own property. Forgetting I was the boss. Sadly he's no longer with us." Joe crossed himself. Freddie gulped.

"Now you," he continued, "by all accounts you do a real good job, Freddie and that pleases me. It's good for business and anything that's good for business is good for Joe Morrelli. Tell me, Freddie, do you like your job?"

"Of course! It's what I do best. It's a pleasure to manage such an exclusive establishment."

"But hard work," Joe interrupted. "I can understand that. Therefore, I'd like to make one or two changes. You see, 'The Safe Haven' makes a lot of money – but it could make even more. I've been thinking, and what we need is a little touch of P.R."

"P.R."

"Yeah. Public Relations. Say, an attractive, well dressed young woman to go around tables, mix with the customers, make sure they're happy, well taken care of, you know? That way they will tell other people who'll come. More customers means more business. More business means more money. Everybody's happy. See what I mean?"

"This... er... woman, will she manage the place?"

"No, no," replied Joe. "I don't see why you shouldn't remain manager. Unless of course, the idea doesn't suit you."

"Oh no, Mr Morrelli! Actually, I think it's an excellent idea. Had you anyone in mind?"

"As a matter of fact, I was considering Angela Kenny for the job. I think she could carry it off and you said yourself she's very popular with the customers. If she proved suitable she'd be able to take some of the pressure off you. She could see to the customers while you have more time to see to the staff and keep everything running smoothly. What do you think Freddie?"

Freddie was relieved.

"I'm glad it's Angela. At least I know her and like her."

"Well, from what I hear she's a likable person. That's why between the two of you. 'The Safe Haven' could be the place in town for everybody who is somebody. And, of course, if the business does well, that means I do well. And if I do well, that means you do well – if you get my meaning."

Freddie's eyes lit up!

"You know Mr Morrelli, I think it will work. I think you've hit on a great idea."

"I take it then, you have no objection?"

"None whatsoever. As you've already said, it will be good for everybody."

"That's fine. But there's just one thing, Freddie."

"What's that?"

"I want you to offer Angela Kenny the job. Let her think it was your idea. After all, you are the manager." Joe knew Freddie lived for his job. Freddie smiled.

"That's very considerate of you, Mr Morrelli," he said, with a tone of importance in his voice.

"Not at all, Freddie. You've been loyal to me and Joe Morrelli never forgets loyalty. So who better? Besides, I'd prefer it if my name wasn't mentioned, just the same as I'd prefer it for this conversation to remain private – just between us."

"Anything you say, Mr Morrelli. You can trust me!"

"If she takes the job," said Joe, "give her the money for some outfits. Tell her its standard procedure. But I don't want any money deducted from her wages."

"Leave it to me. I'll take care of everything."

"Well, that's about it," Joe said, getting up and coming around the side of the desk. "Unless you have something to add?"

Freddie got up.

"Not a thing," he replied, "I won't take up any more of your time, Mr Morrelli. I know you're a busy man."

Shaking Freddie's hand, Joe said,

"Remember, this is just between you and me. Give me a call if she accepts your offer."

Freddie nodded as Joe showed him to the door, but before leaving the room he asked,

"Mr Morrelli, may I enquire as to why you chose Angela Kenny? I mean, she hasn't worked for you for very long and now she's gone back to school, she might not stay."

Joe put his hand on Freddie's shoulder.

"Let's just say, I have my reasons!"

Joe didn't have long to wait to find out if his plan had succeeded. Two days later, Freddie phoned to tell him that Angela Kenny had taken the job. This pleased him. He told Rooney, who seemed happy enough with the situation. His only worry now was whether or not Angela could actually cope with her new position. 'The Safe Haven' meant a lot to Joe. It was one of the few legitimate places he owned and he was very proud of it. But if it were to loose money instead of make it, then Freddie would be suspicious and Joe's accountant, Reuben, would be breathing down his neck. That could prove very embarrassing for him but he decided to give it a while and see. Time would tell.

After a few weeks had gone by, Joe had a word with Rooney, they were in the lounge watching a baseball game, when Joe got up and turned the sound down.

"Have you been to 'The Safe Haven' lately?" he asked Rooney as he poured himself a drink.

"No," replied Rooney, as he opened a can of beer. "I thought it best to stay away for a while. Why?"

"Well, I'm just wondering how things are. I haven't heard from Freddie. I hope we're not losing business. Why don't you go over there? Have a look around, see what's happening. Just find out if everything's o.k."

"In other words," said Rooney, "you want me to spy on Angela!"

"No, I don't want you to spy on her! Just see how she's doing, that's all. She might not be up to the job and if that's the case Freddie would be to scared to tell me seeing as it was all my idea. Drop in for a drink, a meal – whatever, and see what's going on. Then get back to me."

Rooney agreed. He knew by the tone of Joe's voice he was anxious for information. Anyway, it was the weekend and it would be good to see Angela again.

Rooney turned up at the restaurant and went inside. The dining room was full and the lounge was packed with people waiting on tables. Even though it was a Saturday night, he'd never seen the place so crowded. The staff were busy coming and going with trays of booze. It took Rooney ages to get a drink from the bar. After mingling through the crowd, he caught sight of Freddie, rushing around as usual. He moved quickly towards him and caught him by the arm.

"Hey, Freddie, what's going on? Is someone having a party?"

"Yes Rooney, we are! It's party night most nights of the week now. That idea of Mr Morrelli's is going to make him a fortune. Things have really taken off. Come with me and I'll show you."

Rooney walked with Freddie to the dining room. On arriving, Freddie pointed and

Rooney followed his direction. There was Angela. She moved from table to table smiling, shaking hands, chatting. The customers talked and joked with her.

"I can tell you this, Rooney," said Freddie in his polite voice, "a lot of these people are here because they're treated like Royalty – Angela sees to that! She makes them feel special and they love it. She caters to their every whim. She'd make a great business partner. She's shrewd and had more brains than any of us gave her credit for – except Mr Morrelli that is. Yes, I have to say, when it comes to people, Angela Kenny just can't go wrong!"

Freddie waved his hand and called out to her. She looked up and saw them. After excusing herself from one of the tables, she made her way through the dining room towards them. Rooney watched her. She wore a short styled evening dress in cream lace, with a round neck and three quarter length sleeves. Its straight cut showed off her slender figure and she wore cream high heels to match. Her hair was swept back at the sides and fastened up on the top of her head, adding to her height. Rooney thought she was the most beautiful girl he'd ever seen. She stopped in front of him and took his hand.

"Rooney," she said smiling, "it's lovely to see you. Where have you been?"

"Oh, around."

"Are you with someone?"

"No. I just came in for a drink." He looked at her. "Can I have a few minutes of your time?"

Angela turned to Freddie.

"Would that be alright with you, Mr Barrett?"

"Of course!" replied Freddie.

Rooney guided her towards the lounge.

"Come on, Angela. Have a drink with me."

"O.K. I'll have a beer."

"A Beer? Are you sure?"

Angela nodded, amused.

Rooney went to the bar and came back with a glass of beer.

"Hadn't we better go to the office, Rooney? We can't let the customers see us drinking beer while they're drinking champagne. It's bad for business!"

Freddie was right, Angela was shrewd. Joe would approve!

"Do you always drink beer?" Rooney asked, closing the office door behind them.

"Not always. But I'll let you in on a secret. I like it better then most drinks. It's all I ever drank at home – not that I'm much of a drinker anyway."

"Oh, congratulations on your new job," said Rooney. "I didn't know about it until Freddie told me tonight. How do you like it?" Angela sipped at her beer.

"Well, I was nervous at first but I'm fine now. I'm really getting the hang of it. Besides, its better money and that's a big help to me. When Mr Barrett offered me the job I really didn't know what to do. I was worried in case Mr Morrelli would be upset. But then Mr

Barrett told me that Mr Morrelli left all the decisions to him and told him to get whoever he wanted."

"Another lie!" thought Rooney.

Angela drank a little more and then said, "I'll have to go now, Rooney, we're very busy tonight. I'm glad you came by."

"Yes. Well maybe we can have another beer sometime," he said taking the glass from her hand. She smiled and joked, "You'd know we were Irish. No champagne for us. We stick out like sore thumbs!"

She waved goodbye to him as she walked out the door. He was glad she was doing so well, but in a way he felt sorry for her. All this had been planned and set up for her and she'd probably never know. But maybe one day Angela Kenny would look back on her job at 'The Safe Haven' with fond memories. He and Joe would just have to wait and see.

Rooney called at the house the next day with the information Joe wanted. He was more than happy with what he had to tell. Joe was sitting by the pool, he liked to relax on a Sunday. Rooney got a beer from the fridge and went out to join him. He sat down, grinning like a cat who'd just gotten all the cream because inwardly he felt very proud of Angela. He proceeded to tell Joe everything, but left out the bit about Angela ordering the beer! Joe didn't like beer so Rooney thought it best not to say that Angela did, especially as she was mixing with people who only drank the best wines and champagnes money could buy, Joe listened, taking in everything that Rooney had to say. A broad grin spread across his face as he heard just how good business was and how the restaurant was really making a name for itself with Angela Kenny's help.

"Tell me, how did she look?"

"She looked terrific, Joe. Honestly," replied Rooney, who then started to describe her in detail. "The place was full of beautiful women but she stood out on her own. She just has that certain something."

Rooney sighed as he gazed into the pool, then began thinking aloud.

"You know, I wouldn't be surprised if one night some young, handsome, rich guy sees her, falls in love and marries her. I sure wouldn't blame him. She could do really well for herself and she does deserve it. A lovely, young girl like her."

Joe stared at him. The expression on Rooney's face said it all. He really did mean what he'd just said. Joe felt a pang of guilt. Rooney was right and it was unselfish of him to think that way, especially about a woman he cared so much for. Joe got up.

"Yeah, well, I have to go. I've got things to do. I promised Antonia I'd bring her out tonight. I'll see you later Rooney."

Rooney also got up and asked,

"Are you going to 'The Safe Haven'?"

Joe shook his head.

"No, not tonight. I might drop by in a week or two, just to see how things are for myself."

Rooney nodded and left.

Joe stood in deep thought. The truth was, he was scared of seeing Angela Kenny again. He was frightened of his feelings for her and after Rooney's detailed description of her and what he had just said, Joe felt guilty about his emotions.

Rooney was right. She belonged with a younger man, not someone Joe's age. He's been living in a dream world and hoping for something that was way beyond his reach. It was time to face reality. After all, he had Antonia. The restaurant was up-market now, where he had always wanted it to be. Freddie and Angela were doing a good job. The time had come to take a back seat and let everyone get on with their lives. He decided he had no real reason to see Angela Kenny except where business was concerned. But unknown to Joe Morrelli, something was about to happen that would change all that.

Chapter 3

It was late when the phone rang in Antonia's apartment. After rubbing the sleep from his eyes, Joe reached over and picked up the receiver. Rooney's voice was on the other end.

"Joe, it's me. I've got some bad news for you. Angela was attacked tonight after leaving work."

Joe sat upright in bed.

"What happened?"

"Some guy jumped her. When he didn't get what he wanted, he hit her and stole her purse."

"Is she badly hurt?"

"I don't know. I haven't seen her. Freddie phoned the house to tell you."

"Jesus! I warned her about walking home on her own."

"And I told you she wasn't street wise!" insisted Rooney.

"O.K.," said Joe. "Where is she now?"

"Well when Freddie phoned she was at the restaurant. He wanted to get the police and a doctor but she wouldn't let him. She just wanted to go home to her mother, so Freddie was going to bring her there after he phoned."

"Listen to me, Rooney," said Joe as he quickly got out of bed, "I want you to call Doc Arden. He doesn't ask any questions, he can't afford to! Tell him what's happened so he'll know what to do. Say it's a favour for Joe Morrelli and give him the address."

"What is the address?" asked Rooney, impatiently.

"30A Westmere Avenue. I want you and Frankie to go over there now and send Al here for me. I'll be there as soon as I can. And Rooney – keep the police out of this!"

Joe put the phone down.

"Joe honey, what's wrong?" came Antonia's sleepy voice.

"Something's come up. I've got to go. You go back to sleep."

Joe dressed hastily and left the apartment. After travelling down in the lift he made his way through the lobby, still stunned by what he'd just heard.

"Jesus, I hope she's o.k.," he whispered, as he paced up and down on the sidewalk waiting for Al.

About ten minutes went by. It seemed to be the longest ten minutes of his life. Finally, Al drew up beside him, Joe got in and they drove off to Angela's apartment.

On arriving, Joe saw Frankie standing outside the building.

"Where's Rooney?" he asked, getting out of the car.

"Upstairs Boss, with the Doc."

When Joe came to the third floor he knocked on 30A. The door opened and Rooney came out accompanied by Doc Arden.

"How is she?"

"She took a bad blow to her face, Joe. I'm surprised her jaw isn't broken. And she's very badly shaken, but I've given her some tablets to calm her down and left some more for tomorrow. The mother's in a worse state, though. I had to use something a lot stronger on her. It should start working pretty soon now."

"Doc, I really appreciate what you've done. Thanks for coming." The two men shook hands.

"That's o.k. Joe just as long as it's between us. I can't afford to get involved with the authorities."

"I know," acknowledged Joe.

"If you need me, you know where I am."

As Doc Arden disappeared from view, Joe shook his head and turned to Rooney.

"He could have been one of the best," he explained, "but Vietnam ruined all that. You can't blame the guy for turning to drugs himself. He was giving them to most of his men. They sure needed something to keep them going,"

He went inside and Rooney followed.

Joe was deeply upset by what he saw. Agnes was walking around, wringing her hands and crying hysterically. Angela was sitting on the couch. Her eyes were red and the left side of her face was badly swollen and bruised. Agnes turned and on seeing Joe cried,

"That's it! There's no way she's going to work at night ever again! I don't care about the money, I care about my daughter!"

Joe went over and put his arm around her.

"Agnes, Agnes, Calm down," he said gently, nodding for Rooney to come over. "I'm here to help. Now, I need to talk to Angela for a few minutes. Rooney here will make you a cup of tea, or something."

Rooney took over and led her into the kitchen, closing the door. Joe sat down beside Angela.

"I want you to tell me what happened," he said in a low voice.

She shook her head.

"No, I don't want to talk about it."

She held her hand up to her face and stared directly in front of her, her whole body overcome with nerves.

"Please, Angela. I have to know"

There was silence. Then she spoke.

"I ordered a cab but it didn't come. So I decided to walk home the way I used to. This man just seemed to come out of nowhere. He asked me how much I wanted. I told him I didn't know what he as talking about and to leave me alone. He followed me and pushed me against a wall. He took a knife from his pocket and held it up to my throat. Then he started to smile as he described all the things he wanted to do to me."

The look on Joe's face was a mixture of anger and disgust. Angela got up and stood with her back to him.

"I can't repeat what he said, Mr Morrelli. I just can't, it was pure filth. Then he started touching me with his hand, still smiling. It was also awful and disgusting!"

She broke down and sobbed.

Joe clenched his teeth,

"Did he....?"

"No. He didn't rape me. But I knew he was going to. So I lifted my fist and swung my arm, knocking the knife out of his hand. I kicked him and started to run but he ran after me. He caught my coat and held on. I hit him on the face with my purse and then he grabbed it. Then he punched me in the face and I fell. He ran away, shouting he'd kill me the next time."

She covered her face with her hands as she began crying again. Joe got up and put his hands gently on her shoulders.

"Angela, listen to me," he said. "There won't ever be a next time. You must believe that."

He turned her around and took her hands down from her face. He put his right hand under her chin and lifted her head up. The tears were streaming down from her face and her cheek had a large black mark just below her eye. She was so innocent and had been so brave, his heart was aching. He touched the bruised cheek very gently with his finger and looked into her eyes.

"Can you describe him?" he asked.

She nodded.

"He had long fair hair combed straight back. He was young. Heavy set. Strong. His eyes were kind of crazy looking. And he had a tattoo."

"A tattoo?"

"Yes. A small tattoo of a bird on his neck. I saw it plainly under the street lamp. I'll never forget him. Never!"

Joe put his arms around her and held her tightly. She rested her head on his shoulder and clung to him. He could feel every movement of her body as it shook uncontrollably against his. He buried his face in her long, soft, golden hair.

"Oh, Mr Morrelli, he could have killed me."

"You'll never see him again," he whispered. "I promise and Joe Morrelli never breaks a promise!"

The kitchen door opened and Agnes returned still in tears, followed by Rooney who looked across at Joe and shook his head. Angela hurried to her mother and the two women stood hugging each other tightly.

"Mum, please don't cry anymore." pleaded Angela. "I'll be alright."

"Oh God," sobbed Agnes, "if anything had happened to you, what would I have done? What would I have done? I couldn't come through it all again." She looked at Joe and continued, "Mr Morrelli, I know none of this is your fault but I can't let her go back to that job."

Joe moved towards her.

"Agnes, she won't ever be on her own again. I'm gong to see to that. Please let me explain what I intend to do. Just listen……"

"No, you listen!" Agnes demanded. "My daughter could have been killed tonight. Found dead on the street or in some empty building. Murdered coming from her work. Just like her poor father was!"

When she realised what she's said. Agnes put a hand up to her mouth. She hadn't meant to expose the past. Silence filled the room as Joe and Rooney stared at each other.

Angela looked at them both and then, putting her hands over her ears, she cried out, "I don't want to hear anymore! I can't bear to go through all that again!"

She ran to her bedroom and locked the door. But Joe was curious. He wanted to hear more. Agnes sank into the chair.

"I didn't mean to hurt her. I never wanted to bring all that pain back to her. She's suffered enough."

"Would you like to talk about it, Agnes?" Urged Joe. "You might feel better if you did!"

He sat down facing her, the way he'd done the very first time they met. Rooney turned towards the door.

"No," said Agnes, "I'd like you to stay too, my Angela says you've both been very good to her. I think after what happened tonight, its best you both know the truth."

Rooney lifted a chair and placing it between Agnes and Joe, he sat down. Agnes seemed calmer now. The drugs she got from Doc Arden were starting to take effect. She began to relate everything that had happened in Belfast, leaving nothing out. She remembered every word and detail as though it were only yesterday.

"You see, Angela wasn't meant to see what they'd done to her father. A police man was holding her back but she struggled free and ran inside after me. I was kneeling beside my husband's body and Angela knelt down too. She kept calling to him, "Daddy, daddy." Stroking his face and hair. Her hands were covered in his blood, then two policemen came and even as they were carrying her away, she was still calling to him. She loved him and he loved her. But I'd have given anything for her not to have seen him that way. She's never forgotten it. She never will." Agnes went on to tell of the terrible accusations regarding Robert and all the many things that happened because of them. The way they were ignored by one-time friends and neighbours. How Angela had to leave her job because of the danger to her employer.

"He was such a nice man. And so good to Angela. He didn't want to loose her but one night a crowd of young boys and girls gathered outside his shop and smashed the windows. Angela left that very night. She didn't want to bring him any more trouble."

After a pause she continues her story.

Telling of 'Prince', Robert's dog, and how Angela had found him lying dead on the step one night after a knocking at the door.

"There was a note around his neck,' Touts out'. Angela cradled him in her arms. In a way he was all that was left of her father. My Robert loved him, he was more than just a pet. He was one of the family. The girls were in such a state but Raymond buried him in the garden. He said that way 'Prince' would always be there with us."

Joe could hardly believe what he was hearing. He stared in disbelief.

"They even killed the dog? My God! What kind of people are they? What kind of country is it?"

Joe Morrelli had known some tough – even ruthless people in his time, but to persecute women and children and even animals? You'd have to be an animal yourself! He glanced at Rooney, who was staring at the floor.

"I just couldn't take anymore," said Agnes. "I was frightened for my girls, especially Angela. She's not like her sister, she has a temper and she lost it more than once back there. She was determined to stand up for her father's good name no matter what was said about him. But I knew it was just a matter of time before something bad would happen again so that's why we came here to New York. And you know what, Mr Morrelli? Just a few weeks after we'd buried Robert. Angela got her exam results. She's passed with the highest grades. She brought them with her to the cemetery, to her father's grave and said "Look Daddy, I did it! I hope I've made you proud." But my Robert was always proud of his family, Mr Morrelli. He loved us."

Rooney couldn't take any more. He got up and walked over to the door, opening it quietly. Before leaving, he turned and looked at Joe with tears in his eyes. Joe was taken aback. He'd never seen Rooney so emotional before. Then without hardly a sound, Rooney was gone. Joe leaned over and took Agnes's hand.

"I'm glad you told me all this," he said in a choked voice, trying to conceal his own feelings of sorrow and anger.

"So am I. There has been so much heartache and painful memories. Angela doesn't talk about it much but I know she carries the burden around with her all the time. I thought by coming here she'd have the chance of a new life and some happiness. She deserves it. Loosing Robert was bad enough but if I'd lost her...."

"Now Agnes, don't" advised Joe.

"She told me she realised for the first time how frightened and alone her father must have felt that night. She can't get it out of her mind. I just hope and pray that one day someone will find out who murdered him. Maybe then Angela and I will know a little peace."

"Is it o.k. if I speak to Angela before I leave?" Asked Joe.

Agnes nodded, so he got up and went to the bedroom door. After knocking gently, he heard the key turn in the lock. Joe waited for a few minutes and then slowly opened the door. Angela was sitting on the bed. He went over and sat down beside her. She looked at him.

"She told you, didn't she?"

"Yeah, I know everything. I am really sorry Angela."

"My father was innocent, Mr Morrelli. You must believe that- please! He was in the wrong place at the wrong time. Just the way I was tonight."

"I know, I know," said Joe, nodding his head.

"What about my job?"

"What about it?"

"Do I still have one?"

"This doesn't change anything Angela. Not for me anyway. But your mother doesn't want you to come back."

"But we can't manage without it. What am I going to do?"

"I'll come back and talk to your mother in a day or two. Until then I'll take care of everything. You'll still get your wages, don't worry. Now, I want you to get some sleep. You've been through hell."

He got up from the bed, bent down and stroked her face.

"I'll see you soon," he promised.

At that moment she looked so confused and helpless. Joe wanted desperately to make all her pain go away and the feelings that were with it. He wanted to look after her, not just for now but for always. No one had ever made him feel like that and he was doubtful that any one else could. He left the room and closed the door.

He put his arms around Agnes and after reassuring her once more, saw himself out. The story of Angela Kenny's life had touched a place in Joe Morrelli's heart, and what could have happened to her tonight weighted heavily on his mind. As he made his way down the stairs he could not hide his rage. With clenched fists he swore that Joe Morrelli would have revenge.

Rooney, Frankie and Al were standing on the sidewalk when Joe came storming out. He walked straight over to the car and banged his hand hard on the bonnet. He turned and looked at them, his eyes flashing with anger. "I want that bastard! You hear me? I want him! Frankie, put the word out on the street. Pay a visit to every club, every brothel, every gambling joint in town. Somebody must know something."

After giving the description of Angela's attacker, Joe pointed to his own neck and added,

"He's got a tattoo here, some kind of bird. So keep your eyes open. Al, you go with Frankie."

"Sure Boss" replied Al. "But don't you think it's kinda late? Some of our contacts might be asleep."

Joe roared like a lion, "Then wake them! I don't care if you have to wake up half of fuckin' New York – just do it!"

"Anything you say Boss," Al replied, jumping at the sound of Joe's angry voice.

"Good! Now take a hike," ordered Joe.

The two men went to Frankie's car. Al got into the driver's seat but before his companion could join him, Joe caught up, took Frankie's arm and walked him around to the back of the car. He took out a notebook and pen and after scribbling down a number, he tore out the page and handed it to Frankie.

"Now listen," he said in a low voice. "I want you to stop off at a phone booth and call this number. No private phones. Ask to speak to Carlo Capaldi. When he answers, just say 'Joe Morrelli sends his regards'. Wait a few seconds and then put the phone down. He'll understand. When you've done that, burn the paper."

Frankie nodded his head.

"Sure thing, Boss. I'm on my way."

Then he got into the car and he and Al drove off. Joe went back to Rooney. They stood silently for a while as Joe looked around the deserted street. Then out of the silence he said,

"This city never sleeps. That scumbag's out there somewhere right now. I can feel it!"

As Rooney drove the car home both were quiet. Each had his own thoughts. Rooney knew Joe was in a foul mood after the way he's snapped at Al. It had been one hell of a night for everyone. Once there, Joe opened the door and hurried inside, making his way to the lounge and the drinks cabinet. Instead of pouring one, he lifted a bottle and a glass.

"You want a beer?" he asked Rooney.

"No, I need something stronger," he replied, helping himself. Joe poured himself an extra large scotch, sat down on the couch and put the bottle on a small table beside him. He took a long swallow from the glass and then held it between the palms of his hands. He looked at Rooney, who by now was sitting opposite, and said,

"I can't believe what I heard tonight! Jesus, what kind of a country is it that could do that to its own people?"

"Joe, there's a war going on over there. We only see the half of it on T.V."

"Well, I sure as hell wouldn't like to see the other half. Can you even begin to imagine what it was like for that family? What they went through? I often wondered why Agnes Kenny came here at her age. Now I know." He poured himself another drink.

"Listen Joe," said Rooney, "Over there they have their own ways of doing things."

"Who's side are you on?" demanded Joe, raising his voice.

"Oh, come on Joe. That's not fair!"

"No, wait a minute!" he insisted. "Over here the Italians have their own ways of doing things, too. But we leave women and children out of it!"

Rooney nodded.

"O.K. you're right. You win. But that's not all that's bothering you. Be honest here. You know that Angela could have been raped tonight – even murdered. If she hadn't fought back like she did, God only knows what that guy would have done to her. You feel bad about it. Well, so do I and Agnes didn't help matters by telling us what Angela had already been through. But at least now we know. She's had enough heartache to last a lifetime. The best thing we can do is to try and help her get over it and get this guy."

"Yeah, well, I'm working on that. I just feel so angry, Rooney. At everything. And I'm angry with myself. I feel partly to blame. From now on none of my staff will be allowed to walk on their own. If that had been the rule to start with, none of this would have happened."

Just at that the phone rang and Joe answered it.

"It's me," came the voice on the other end. "What's up?"

"I've got a problem," explained Joe. "Maybe you can help me solve it."

"I'll call this evening," came the reply. Then the phone went dead.

"Carlo?" enquired Rooney.

"Yeah. It's best not to name names or discuss business over the phone. Always remember that, Rooney. Even telephones aren't safe anymore."

Joe leaned back and stared into space. Then continued, "Whoever he is, that bastard made a big mistake tonight when he jumped Angela. Thank God he didn't get to do what he wanted. But he'll pay dearly for trying, Rooney. I can promise you that. He'll pay!"

Rooney reached over and gripped Joe's arm gently.

"We'll get him Joe. And when we do we'll both make him pay for hurting her. Now try and get some sleep."

Rooney went upstairs to bed, leaving Joe to come to terms with everything that had happened. He went over it all in his tired mind. When he closed his eyes he could still see Angela's bruised and tearful face. He remembered how good it felt, holding her in his arms. He longed to do it again but wondered if he'd ever get a second chance. Joe Morrelli fell asleep with that thought on his mind, and her name on his lips.

He was wakened by the heat of the sun and someone shaking him gently. He opened his eyes and Rooney was standing there.

"What time is it?" asked Joe.

"11.30. Frankie and Al are here. And you have to go and see how Angela and her mother are."

Joe got up and said,

"Tell the guys to come on in."

Rooney called them and they appeared looking tired and none too happy. He closed the door.

"The word's out Boss." said Frankie, "Just about everybody knows you're looking for this guy. But so far we've drawn a blank in getting any information."

"Well, its early days yet," replied Joe. "Did you go around everyone?"

"Boss, we've been everywhere and covered everyone's territory. It's like he doesn't exist."

"Oh, he exists alright," insisted Joe, "And somebody knows him. They're just not saying, what I'd like to know is why."

"If someone's hiding him, they must have a reason," said Rooney.

"Yeah, and I'm gonna find out what that reason is."

Joe then looked at Frankie and Al.

"O.k. that's it for now. Frankie, I want you to go home and get some sleep. Spend some time with your family. I won't need you until tomorrow. Al, I want you to drive me over to Angela's apartment after lunch. Then you can go home too."

Al looked at Joe and nodded.

"Sorry we didn't have more luck, Boss," relieved that Joe had calmed down since the last time they'd talked.

Joe looked back at him and said,

"I know, Al. But it's o.k." They were on good terms again.

As Frankie and Al were leaving the lounge Joe called to them.

"Hey, guys. You did the best you could."

They both nodded and left, closing the door behind them. Joe looked at Rooney.

"I sure hope Carlo can throw some light on all this. We're gonna need all the help we can get."

"Christ, Joe! When you're walking around New York with a bird tattoo on your neck, someone's bound to know you."

"Yeah, I'm thinking the same thing myself. Well, I better go and get ready. I'll have to go and see if Angela and Agnes are o.k."

Joe left the room and made his way upstairs.

After lunch, Al drove over to Westmere Avenue. On the way they stopped at a florist and Joe bought two large bouquets of flowers. When they arrived at their destination he got out of the car and instructed Al,

"Wait for me."

"O.K. Boss."

He went into the building and up to the third floor. A few seconds after he rang the doorbell, Agnes answered the door.

"Mr Morrelli, come in."

Joe followed her through and then presented her with the flowers.

"How are you now, Agnes?" he asked.

"Oh, a little calmer. But what beautiful flowers! You're such a kind man, indeed you are."

Joe was still holding the other bouquet.

"Where's Angela?"

"She's sleeping." Agnes voice turned to almost a whisper. "Her face was so painful she never slept all night. She cried and cried until finally she cried herself to sleep just a little while ago."

Joe nodded and quietly put the flowers down on the coffee table.

"Do you need anything?" he asked.

"No thank you, Mr Morrelli. But please sit down. Can I get you anything? Tea, Coffee?"

"No thanks, Agnes. I won't be staying long. I just want to say how sorry I am about last night and what you told me. If there's anything I can do for you or your daughter, you just have to say."

"I'm so worried about her," Agnes confided. "I don't know if I've done the right thing by bringing her here. She has no one but me."

"She has her job and her friends," replied Joe. "Don't take that away from her. When she's well, let her go back. She'll never be on her own again. None of my staff will. I'll make sure they all get taxis home. Who knows, she may even meet that nice taxi driver you keep ribbing her about! What do you say?"

Agnes watched as Joe smiled genuinely.

"You really want her back, Mr Morrelli?"

"We all do. Mr Barrett, Rooney, me. We'll take good care of her, I promise."

Agnes became inquisitive.

"Why do you like Angela so much? I know you must. Other bosses wouldn't go to all these lengths just to keep someone on their staff."

He looked at her straight in the eye, his smile fading.

"Your daughter is very special. I've never met anyone like her. To be honest with you, Agnes I was beginning to think women like her didn't exist."

"Is that why you never married?"

"Maybe. But I'm not fooling myself. I know I'm too old for her. That's not to say I can't be good friend. I can – the best she'll ever have if she'll let me. And if you don't object."

Agnes returned his gaze.

"You know, Mr Morrelli, sometimes what starts out as a friendship, ends up as love. I hope you know what you're doing?"

Joe nodded and assured her.

"I have my reasons."

In her trust of him she conceded.

"All right then, Angela can go back to work when she's feeling better. But only if she wants to and somehow I have the feeling she will want to. Even so, promise me she'll never walk home on her own ever again."

Agnes got up and walked with him to the door. Then she put her hand on his arm, knowingly.

"I won't say a word, Mr Morrelli. But who knows what the future holds. Maybe one day you might be able to tell her yourself."

Al dropped Joe back at the house. Rooney and Evie, the housekeeper, were in the kitchen. She was preparing dinner. Joe put his head around the door and nodded for Rooney to follow him to the study. Once inside, Joe unlocked the safe and took out a handful of used bills which he sealed in a large brown envelope.

"I want you to deliver this to Doc Arden," he instructed.

"That's a lot of money Joe."

"Yeah well, favours don't come cheap but sometimes they're worth it. Anyway the Doc prefers cash in hand. Tell him the girl he treated last night needs some pain killers for her face. He'll know what to give you, then drop by and give them to Angela. Tell her the doctor sent them and also recommended she use plenty of ice packs to put the swelling down. Then come back here. I'd like you around when Carlo comes."

Rooney went and opened the study door.

"Hey Rooney," added Joe, "don't stay too long at the apartment but pay attention when you're there. I want to know how she is."

"Didn't you see her?"

"No, she was sleeping. But according to Agnes she had a pretty bad night."

Rooney left and Joe went upstairs to shower and change before dinner. Just over an hour later, Rooney returned. He had hardly been in the house five minutes when a car pulled up outside and the doorbell rang. Rooney was opening the door as Joe was coming down the stairs. A smiling Carlo Capaldi was standing on the step.

"How are you, Rooney?" he asked as he came in.

"Fine, Carlo."

"Carlo!" called Joe, going over and shaking his friend's hand. "It's been a long time."

"I know Joe. Too long. But I'm here now."

The three men made their way into the study and Joe closed the door.

"Sit down Carlo. Would you like a drink?"

"Sure. Scotch would be fine."

Rooney went to the cabinet and after pouring out the drinks he handed one to Carlo and left one on the desk for Joe, who by now had settled into his leather chair. Carlo raised his glass and looked at Joe.

"Here's to old friends and old friendships."

Carlo Capaldi was a handsome Italian in his mid-thirties. He was highly respected by his colleagues in the police department and by his small circle of friends on the outside. After taking a drink from the glass he sat it down on the desk.

"Now Joe, what can I do for you?"

Joe put his hands together and looking at him, spoke in a serious voice.

"Carlo, one of my girls was attacked last night."

"Was she a hooker?"

"No, she works at my restaurant 'The Safe Haven'. She was on her way home when some guy appeared out of nowhere and propositioned her. When she told him to get lost he pulled a knife on her and started to describe what he'd like to do to her. The usual stuff. You know better then me what these weirdo's are like."

Carlo nodded his head. Joe continued.

"Anyway, he started coming on to her and kept the knife at her throat. She was very frightened but she managed to fight him off. He smacked her so hard he almost broke her jaw, and then he stole her purse. He warned her the next time he'd kill her. Carlo, I don't ever want there to be a next time. She's a quiet, decent girl and she's in bad shape. I honestly believe if she hadn't acted the way she did, that guy would have raped her. She might even have been murdered. I can't allow this slime to get away with that. If I do he'll come back. I've already put the word out on the street but that will take time. I can't afford to wait, Carlo. I need to stop him now."

"Could she give a description of him?"

"A very good one. He's young, probably in his twenties. Long fair hair combed straight back. Heavy set, strong. She said he had crazy looking eyes and a tattoo of a bird on his neck."

Carlo stared at Joe and asked,

""A tattoo of a bird?"

"Yeah, you know him?"

"I'm not sure, but it does ring a bell."

Carlo leaned over and took another drink from the glass. Joe kept looking at him.

"Carlo, someone must know who he is. What's puzzling me is why they're keeping quiet. That's why I need your help. I don't want him on my territory."

Carlo understood perfectly.

"I'll tell you what I'll do, Joe. When I get back to the precinct, I'll run that description through the computer. If he's done the same thing before there's a good chance he's been hauled in. If so, I'll pull his file and get you all the information you need."

"I'd be very grateful. Will it take long?"

"No, not really. If there's anyone of that description I should know in a couple of hours. I could bring you all the details tomorrow morning. Say about eleven, when I've finished my shift?"

"Fine. I wouldn't ask you to do this, but it's important to me."

"It's o.k., Joe. There's no need to explain," said Carlo as he got up from the chair.

"But that tattoo of a bird, I'm almost sure I've seen or heard something connected with it. Anyway, I'll do my best for you, Joe."

Rooney opened the door and let Joe walk Carlo across the entrance hall. He watched as Joe put his arm around Carlo affectionately.

"I'd appreciate any help you can give me on this one," he said. "I don't like the thoughts of any woman being treated that way by a crazy psycho."

"I don't blame you, Joe. I'm dealing with scum like that all the time and you're right, if they get away with it once they keep coming back. This guy will only get more confident. Next time, she wouldn't get the chance to fight him off."

"Thanks for coming, Carlo. By the way, how's your little girl?"

"Great Joe. But only for that specialist, she probably wouldn't have made it. You want to see her now. It's hard to believe she was so sick. Thanks Joe."

The two men parted after shaking hands.

"That's what friends are for," insisted Joe as Carlo made his way to the door. "I'll see you in the morning."

Joe stood on the step and watched as Carlo waved and drove off. He smiled as he turned to come back in. "It's good to have friends," he thought. "Real friends."

Evie had just served dinner so he joined Rooney in the dining room.

"Do you think Carlo will come up with anything, Joe?"

"Well, he's smart. If there's anything on this guy, he'll find out. That's the advantage of knowing a cop with a bit of authority. Mind you, he wouldn't do it for everybody. But Carlo and me, we go back a long way. We both got our education on the best 'Campus' money can buy – the streets! When I was young you didn't survive if you weren't street wise. You always had to be one step ahead. Carlo was like me – shrewd. That's why we're both still here."

"Why did he become a cop?" Rooney asked.

Joe looked sternly into space for a moment.

"I guess we all have our own way of dealing with injustice. Carlo decided to do it through the law and he's been very successful. Too many innocent lives are taken for no good reason."

He put his knife and fork down and turned his gaze to Rooney.

"But we both agree on one thing. The punishment should always fit the crime!"

Rooney watched in silence as Joe slipped into deep thought. Then, in order to make conversation, he said, "Oh by the way I nearly forgot, Doc Arden sends his regards and many thanks for the money." Whatever thoughts were going through Joe's mind he left them for another time.

"Did he give you the medication for Angela?"

Rooney nodded.

"Yes, he gave her strong painkillers. He said to tell you the swelling should go down in a couple of days but the pain won't go away for a while. If you want him to check her out again, he will."

"How is she? Did you see her?" there was obvious concern in Joe's voice.

"Yes. She was trying to drink a cup of coffee. She won't be going anywhere for a while. Not with a face like that, anyway."

"My God! Is it that bad?"

"Under her eye is turning black. That guy must have thrown some punch."

"Yeah, well if I have my way he'll never throw another!"

"I felt sorry for her," Rooney said sadly. "She can't eat. She hasn't had any food from way before it happened. She's living on coffee and pills. I hope it doesn't last. She can't afford to loose a lot of weight. She's slim enough just the way she is."

Joe lifted his wine glass and held it.

"You know," he said wistfully, "that's one of the first things I noticed about her. She's got a really nice shape, not too tall and slender. The kind of woman you feel you'd like to protect."

"You know what I think Joe?" If you put Angela Kenny in an expensive evening gown, with her looks and figure, any guy would be knocked out by her."

"Yeah, especially with that beautiful hair. Sometimes I can't believe it's natural. I've never seen a colour quite like it."

"Red hair's common enough among the Irish," Rooney informed him.

Joe pushed his plate away. He'd lost his appetite just by thinking about her.

"Yeah, but when you look at it under a bright light it has a golden sheen to it. I guess I'm attracted to that colour because all Italian women have dark hair."

"Antonia has blond hair!"

"Yeah, but it wasn't always that colour. Jesus! That reminds me, I'll have to call her. I left her last night in bed and she'll be wondering what the hell's going on."

He put the wine glass down and hastily made for the door.

"Women!" he muttered. "It's a full time job just to keep them happy!"

"Oh, I think you do alright in that department," smiled Rooney, broadly. "Especially with Antonia!"

Joe stopped and looked over his shoulder.

"I've had my moments," he grinned. "And I've never had any complaints. I always aim to please and, so far, Joe Morrelli's age has never interfered with Joe Morrelli's love life. But Rooney – don't be a smart ass!!"

The door closed and Rooney sat at the table, shaking his head and smiling to himself.

Carlo Capaldi was as good as his word. A little after 11.00am he was ringing Joe's doorbell again. Frankie answered this time and the two men beamed as the saw each other.

"Frankie Rossi, are you still around?" asked Carlo as he slapped Frankie on the back.

"It's good to see you, Carlo."

"Don't tell me Al Colleano's around here too?"

"How did you guess?"

"I'm psychic!"

They both laughed as they made their way to the study.

"I didn't know you were still with Joe," said Carlo.

"Yeah, from the old neighbourhood. Remember?"

"That's a long time. You've never thought of moving on?"

Frankie shook his head, "Joe's been a good friend and a good boss."

"Yeah," agreed Carlo. "He was always one of the best."

After knocking on the door, Frankie opened it and showed Carlo in. Joe stood up and greeted him. Rooney was standing by the window. Then all three sat down.

Carlo smiled.

"I have some good news for you, Joe. I've found out who you're looking for, we have a file on him at the precinct." Joe was relieved. He leaned back as Carlo checked his notes.

"That's good to hear Carlo." He said.

After glancing over what he'd written down Carlo began,

"Well, the guy's name is Lenny Shultz and you're right, he's a real psycho when it comes to women. He has previous convictions from indecent exposure to rape and assault with a deadly weapon. He's getting bolder though. Within the last couple of months he's attacked three women with a knife. Your girl was lucky, Joe, the others weren't. Two were beaten up and raped and the third had her face slashed open. He gets his kicks by pulling a knife and talking dirty to them. He really likes to elaborate! He's like a snake. He hypnotises them with fear first and then strikes. He's one sick son of a bitch!"

Joe was puzzled.

"So why the hell is he still walking the streets?" he asked. "He should be behind bars with a record like that., Carlo."

Carlo nodded in agreement.

"We hauled the bastard in after every attack but we had to let him go."

"Why, for Christ's sake?"

"None of the women would give evidence against him. They were too frightened. He swore he'd come back and kill them. But he was our man alright. All those women remembered the tattoo on his neck. I read their statements, Joe. What he said to them I couldn't even repeat to you, so I'll let you use your imagination. No wonder your girl is in a bad way. It's enough to put her off men for life!"

Carlo's last remark hit home and Joe could feel the anger swelling up inside him.

"Can't you bring him to court without the evidence?" Rooney asked.

"We tried that already, Rooney, but he always had an alibi."

Carlo paused for a moment and then looked at Joe.

"Do you know Benny Bangles, Joe?"

"I don't so much know him as know of him. He's a young smart ass who wants to make a name for himself. Why?"

"Well this Lenny Shultz hangs out at his club. From what I hear he drug deals for Benny, mostly to young kids. We arrested him twice for it but this big shot lawyer came and got him off on a technicality. It got to the point where it was a waste of time bringing this guy to court."

Joe stared at him and said,

"Well I can tell you now. What he did the other night is one court case he won't be going to!"

Carlo understood.

"It would be less paperwork for us if he weren't around. He's going to end up on a murder charge sooner or later but he'll probably walk away from that one too. The guy's a fuckin' headache, Joe, one we'd all love to be without."

"He's also a menace to every woman walking the street," added Joe. "It's time he was stopped. I have no feeling for dirty scum like that, except maybe disgust!" "You know what I don't understand? How someone like Lenny Shultz can afford those kind of lawyers."

"He can't – but Benny Bangles can!"

Tell me Carlo, how would you feel if you never heard the name of Lenny Shultz again?"

"Relieved!" sighed Carlo. "And so would those women he attacked."

"Yeah," agreed Joe. "So if he were to disappear it would be doing everyone a favour?"

Carlo didn't answer. He didn't have to. Instead he smiled, got up and shook Joe's hand.

"I'll leave it up to you, Joe. Whatever you think."

Joe got up, went over to him and put his arm around Carlo's shoulder.

"Good work Carlo. Thanks for all your help."

"Where this guy's concerned, I was glad to help. I saw photo's of that woman's face – the one he slashed. It wasn't a pretty sight. She's ruined for life, Joe. I'm just thankful it wasn't that young girl the other night."

"So am I," Joe assured him. "So am I."

Rooney opened the study door as Joe led Carlo out into the hall.

"Remember, Carlo," he said, "anytime I can ever do you a favour, don't hesitate to ask."

"Just like the old days, Joe!"

"Yeah. We all need a friend sometime, but the best friends are those we can trust. The old neighbourhood taught us that."

"That's right. We learned a lot on the street."

Joe patted Carlo's back.

"We sure did," he smiled, "but the most important thing we learned was loyalty!"

"Well, Joe. You know where I am if you need me."

"I sure do, Carlo. Goodbye and thanks for everything."

Joe stood and waited until Frankie had shown Carlo out then he turned to Rooney and said," There goes a man I have always respected and trusted. Carlo Capaldi has always claimed to be my friend but today he has really proved that friendship."

Then he called out,

"Frankie, could you come in here a minute? I want to speak to you."

"Sure thing, Boss," Frankie replied, as he followed him.

Once inside he closed the door. He knew Joe liked privacy.

"What's up?" he asked looking from Joe to Rooney and back again.

Joe rested on the edge of the desk and folded his arms. His voice matched his serious look.

"Frankie, I want you to think carefully about this. When you put the word out the other night, did you go to everyone?"

"Everyone. Just like you told me."

"Did you happen to see Benny Bangles or any of his boys?"

"As a matter of fact I did. Al and me called in at the club he owns, 'The Blue Paradise.' It stays open nearly all night. We had a drink."

"Was Benny there?"

"Yeah, it was Benny who bought us the drinks."

"Go on," urged Joe.

"Well, we were at the bar and Benny and his crowd were at one of the tables. He came over and started to talk to us. Asked if everything was o.k. I gave him a description of the guy we were looking for and asked if he's seen anyone like that hanging around."

"What did he say?"

"He said he didn't know anyone of that description. No one with the tattoo of a bird came to his club, or he'd remember."

"Did you tell him Joe Morrelli wanted to know?"

Frankie nodded.

"He said because it was you, he'd keep his eyes open, but he never heard of or seen anyone like that. In fact he swore on his mother's life he's never seen the guy. We finished our drinks and left."

"I see. O.K. Frankie, you can go."

After he'd gone, Joe unfolded his arms and grabbed the edge of the desk with his fingers.

"Can you imagine that bastard, swearing a lie on his mother's life. Pretending he doesn't know someone who works for him. If he knows Lenny Shultz then he knows what he's doing. That sick scumbag is walking the streets because of Benny Bangles and his lawyers. But not for much longer. When he said he's never seen the guy he lied, but one thing's for sure, in a little while he won't ever see him again. Nobody makes a fool out of Joe Morrelli. We're going to get this Lenny Shultz, Rooney. And I swear that – on my life."

Angela Kenny was also having visitors but of a different kind. Freddie called at the apartment with a bunch of flowers and Angela's wages. When she answered the door bell she was surprised to see him.

"Mr Barrett! How good of you to call."

She brought him in and introduced him to her mother. After Freddie had given Angela the flowers and her wages, he took an envelope from his inside pocket.

"This is for you Angela." He said. "Cindy sent it."

She opened it to discover it contained money in five, ten and twenty dollar bills.

"Cindy sent this?" she asked, more shocked than surprised.

"Yes, she had a collection for you at work. The staff were going to buy you something but Cindy thought the money might come in handy while you're not working. She was really quite upset when she heard what happened. She said it could have been her or any of the girls."

"Well, that was very kind of Cindy and very thoughtful of all the staff," said Angela, with tears in her eyes.

"It just goes to show that they all like you."

"I never thought Cindy did."

"Oh, maybe not at first," said Freddie. "But since you took the other job, you've brought a lot more custom to the restaurant and that means extra tips. And, of course, there's one more very important thing, you've always treated the staff with courtesy and consideration. You've never let the job go to your head. Actually, Cindy thinks you're o.k. Angela. We all hope you'll be back with us soon," he smiled warmly.

Angela was very touched by all this and it showed. Agnes knew then that Mr Morrelli was right. Her daughter had friends, good friends who cared about her. It was only fair that she should go back to them. If Angela was happy, that's all that mattered.

"I'll be back just as soon as the bruising goes away," she promised.

"Oh, there's no big hurry. I'll bring your wages over every week and if you need anything just let me know."

"I don't know what to say, Mr Barrett. Everyone's been so good to me."

For the first time, Angela felt wanted. She had found somewhere she felt she belonged. It was a nice feeling. After she saw Freddie out, Angela returned and took Agnes's hand.

"Mum, I'm going back to my job. I want to."

Agnes nodded in approval. She could think of one person in particular who would be very pleased at the news, Angela's boss – Mr Joe Morrelli.

Joe had a lot on his mind over the next few days. He hadn't seen Angela since that night she was attacked and although he'd phoned to ask how she was, he felt guilty at not visiting her. So he decided to pay her a call. Dressed casually in a blue open-necked shirt, grey trousers and a black jacket, he got Al to drive him over there, stopping off at the florist as usual. Joe was a great believer in treating women with respect and always liked to give them flowers or perfume to make them feel special. When they arrived, Al was the first one to speak.

"You want me to wait for you, Boss?"

"Yeah. But drive around for a while. Get a cup of coffee or something. No point in just sitting here."

As Joe went inside the building, Al drove away. At 30A Joe rang the doorbell. Angela answered.

"Hi. How are you?" he asked smiling.

"I'm fine," she replied, trying very hard to return his smile.

"Come in."

Joe followed her into the sitting room. She was wearing a white cotton short sleeved blouse, a knee length black flared skirt and flat black shoes. Her hair was tied back loosely. He couldn't help but notice how young she looked, as he handed her the flowers.

"Thank you, Mr Morrelli. They're beautiful. I'll put them in water right away."

She disappeared into the kitchen. There was a small table and a chair over by the open window. The table was littered with books. Joe walked over and went through them one by one. Some names he recognised – Shakespeare, Dickens. Others he didn't – Bronte, Milton, Wordsworth. As well as all these there was a note book and some pens. Angela came out of the kitchen with the flowers in a glass vase and sat them on the mantelpiece.

"I see you're back to your studies," commented Joe.

"Yes. My teacher called and left some work for me to do at home. That way I won't fall behind in class."

"It's pretty heavy stuff by the looks of it."

"Well, it is hard work. I just hope it's worth it."

Unless Joe was mistaken, her voice had a sort of down tone to it.

"Where's your mother? he asked.

"She's gone to the supermarket. I hope she's alright. She's not really fit to carry shopping now. I didn't want to go."

He noticed she was quite pale.

"Haven't you been out at all, Angela?"

"No. I don't want to go out," came the determined reply.

Joe went over to her.

"Hey, let's have a look at that face," he said, putting his hand gently under her chin. She nervously backed away.

"Please, don't touch me!"

"O.k. are you like this with everyone or just me?" although he was hurt he tried to make light of it by putting his hands up.

Her eyes became moist as she explained,

"Mr Morrelli, I don't know what's wrong with me. I'm frightened, I'm confused. I'm embarrassed…."

"You're depressed!" interrupted Joe. "And no wonder, if you're going to shut yourself up in this apartment. Angela, listen to me. What that guy did must have scared you to death, not to mention what he said. But it's wrong to think that every man is the same. If you close yourself away like this then he'll have won. That's exactly what he wants you to do."

"But I feel so awful about that night and all the trouble I caused everyone – especially you. And then on top of all that, my mother telling you about my father."

"Angela, I don't believe for one minute that your father was anything other than an innocent man."

He could see she was becoming upset.

"You see, I just keep going over everything in my mind, Mr Morrelli. I keep wondering if my father felt the same fear I did. I can't help it!"

"Hey, come on," said Joe, gently. "you've got to try to put it out of your mind. You want to know what I think? You need to get out."

"I'll be going back to work soon."

But Joe shook his head.

"No, I mean a proper night out. You know, somewhere nice where you'll meet people. Hear some music. Dance a little. Be able to relax. Would you like that?"

"I…. I don't know."

"Look. What if I were to call for you next week and bring you somewhere? After all, I am your boss. I owe you that much."

"You don't owe me anything, Mr Morrelli," she insisted. "And you don't have to go to all that trouble for me."

"But I want to. That is unless you don't want to be seen with your boss. Or maybe you think I'm too old to take you out."

"Oh no! It's not like that. I just don't think I'd fit in. I mean, I'm not glamorous like Miss Flemming and I don't know the kind of people you do."

"Well, maybe it's time you did. Come on, what do you say?"

Joe could be so persuasive when he wanted to be!

"Alright. But only if you really want to." She smiled broadly for the first time since he arrived.

"I wouldn't have asked if I didn't. Now, let me get a look at that cheek."

She came over and stood looking up into his face.

"Yeah, it should be back to normal next week, so you can't use that as an excuse for not going!"

He smiled and for a moment his eyes met hers and his heart skipped a beat.

"I'd better be going," he said. "I'll phone you during the week and tell you what time to be ready."

"Aren't you forgetting something?" she asked. "You haven't told me what night."

"Oh yeah. Would Friday night be o.k?"

"Friday night would be fine." She smiled at him again. Angela Kenny could have no idea of the effect she had on Joe when she looked and smiled at him like that. And he knew he couldn't tell her. She left him to the front door and thanked him for coming. Joe took a deep breath going down the stairs, then he smiled to himself. He had finally done it! He had a date with Angela Kenny and he felt good. No – he felt great!! He came out onto the sidewalk and stood in the sunshine. A few minutes later, Al stopped the car beside him. Joe opened the rear door and got in. "It's a beautiful day, Al, and life's good," he said, smiling broadly as they drove away.

"Sure Boss," Al checked Joe in the driving mirror. "You look real happy with yourself."

"I am," replied Joe, "You're looking at one very happy man."

When Agnes arrived back form the supermarket, Angela was bright and cheerful.

"Mum, Mr Morrelli called to see me and you know what? He wants to bring me out on Friday night!"

"That's very good of him," replied Agnes, slumping into the chair.

Angela became concerned.

"Are you alright, Mum?"

"It's those stairs. They're so steep they leave me out of breath."

Angela fetched her mother's tablets.

"I'm sorry. I should have done the shopping."

"Never mind that, I'll be fine. Now tell me all about it."

Agnes looked up at the flowers on the mantelpiece, as Angela related everything to her.

"It's not a date," she insisted. "He's just bringing me out as my boss. I'm sure he'd do the same for any of the other girls."

"Where is he taking you Angela?" Agnes was all ears.

Suddenly there was silence. Then Angela exclaimed, "Oh God! I never thought to ask. He'll probably want to go somewhere fancy and expensive. He's that sort of man. Well what I mean is, he's been used to places like that. I'm sorry now I said I'd go. I should have made some excuse."

"But why?"

"You don't understand mum. The women who go to those places wear the latest fashions. I've seen them in 'The Safe Haven.' Some of those dresses must cost a fortune. What am I going to do? I don't have anything like that to wear."

Agnes got up, went into the bedroom and opened the top drawer of the dressing table. After rummaging around for a few seconds, she came back clutching a small book.

"We still have some of Aunt Bridget's money left."

"No mum," said Angela. "We can't touch that money. It's for emergencies and we use it to help Sheila and Raymond too, now that they have the baby."

"Well now it's your turn."

"No," Angela maintained. "I'm not wasting any of that money on a dress. I'll get in touch with Mr Morrelli and tell him I can't go after all."

"You'll do no such thing!" her mother insisted. "Now, sit down and listen to me."

After they'd both sat down Agnes continued, "If your father had still been alive and we were back home, what do you think would have happened if you'd come home one day and said one of your teachers or lecturers wanted to bring you somewhere special? Somewhere classy and out of the ordinary? Do you think for one minute your father would have let you back out just because of the price of a dress? Your father would have worked round the clock to get it for you. He'd have been happy to see you go and see you go dressed in the best he could possibly afford."

"That's different."

"Well I don't see how. If Mr Morrelli is used to seeing women in nice dresses, then he's going to see you in one. Alright, it might not be the most expensive but it will be the best our money can buy. Your father would have wanted it that way and so do I."

Agnes forced the book into Angela's hand. Her daughter meant more to her than any amount of money.

"Thanks, Mum!"

They hugged each other and Agnes smiled both with gladness and relief. It was good to see Angela so happy. It had been the first time in quite a while. Someone had finally managed to do it.

"Now," she instructed Angela, "you take whatever money you need out of that account and go shopping for the nicest dress you can find. When you walk out of here on Friday night, you'll walk out like a Kenny and make your father proud!"

Rooney, Frankie and Al waited in the entrance hall with anticipation, as Joe made his way down the stairs. When he reached the bottom he stopped, looked at his friends, raised his hands and asked,

"Well, what do you think?"

There was no doubt about it, Joe cut a dashing figure in a navy, Italian pin-striped suit, white shirt, navy tie with gold tie-pin and cufflinks to match, and expensive black leather shoes.

"You look terrific Boss," said Frankie.

Al bent his head to straighten his jacket.

"He looks like Kojak with hair!" he whispered to Frankie.

"You said something," snapped Joe, pointing an accusing finger in Al's direction.

"What was it?"

"I said you'll make people stare, Boss. You look great."

"Yeah, I do, don't I? Not bad for a guy my age."

He smiled as he pulled in his stomach.

Rooney took his arm and led him away form the others.

"I want a word with you," he said. "Now, don't get carried away and don't try anything on. Angela's not that kind of girl."

"How do you know?"

"I just do, that's all. She's not the pushy type."

"Well, for someone who's never been out with her you sure seem to know an awful lot. Are you certain you haven't dated her?"

"You know damn well I haven't, but I know the kind of girl she is – so you behave yourself."

"Yes mother!" replied Joe, sarcastically. "Is it o.k. if I talk to her? I mean, I wouldn't want you worrying in case I said the wrong thing. Maybe I should call and cancel my date with her and take you out to dinner instead."

"Don't be so childish!" said Rooney angrily.

"O.k. Let me run something by you, then," Joe answered in a cocky voice. "What if she gives us all a surprise? What if she gets carried away? What if she tries something on? What if she really is the pushy type? What do you want me to do – fight her off with my fork?"

Joe walked over towards the front door but after catching sight of himself in the mirror once again, he stopped for one last look…

"I feel like it's my first date," he informed them. "I feel like…. You know…. Like…"

"Cinderella?" interrupted Rooney.

Joe shot a glance in his direction.

"Let's hope the limo doesn't turn into a pumpkin at midnight," joked AL as he opened the door for his boss.

Frankie stifled a laugh, but Joe had already heard the remark.

"One of these days," he thought to himself," "Al's going to be in for a big surprise. He may have a big mouth now, but leave it to me and it'll be even bigger!"

But for all this, Joe was determined that nothing and no-one was going to spoil this special night for him.

Rooney checked his watch for the right time.

"Get a move on, Joe. You're going to be late."

Joe turned around.

"Well, aren't you going to wish me luck?" he asked.

Rooney smiled, "I do Joe. Really I do."

The door closed, leaving Rooney and Frankie behind.

"I have to admit it Rooney, he looks really swell."

"Yes he does. I didn't want to say too much, his heads big enough as it is. If it had gotten any bigger, we'd never have managed to get him through the door! Well, Frankie, what do you say we open a bottle and play some cards? Maybe Evie has left some of her famous meatloaf out for us."

"Keep talking, Rooney, I sure like the sound of your voice!"

The two friends headed for the kitchen. "Are you going to stay over tonight?"

"You better believe it! I wouldn't miss the end of this for anything. Ten dollars says he's home by midnight."

"You're on! Hey, did you hear Al about the pumpkin?"

Rooney nodded and they both burst into laughter.

Joe was feeling quite confident that Friday evening, as he sat in the back of the limousine on his way to Angela's apartment. He'd made reservations at 'The Imperial Palace.' Everybody who was anybody liked to be seen there. If you wanted to impress a woman, it was the place in town to bring her to. The owner was also a good friend of his, Ralph Lennox, who was famous throughout the city for his high society parties which had made him a lot of money.

On arriving at Angela's, Agnes showed him in.

"She'll be with you in a minute, Mr Morrelli," she said, going over and knocking the bedroom door.

"Angela, Mr Morrelli's here. Are you ready?"

The door opened and Joe could hardly believe his eyes. A beautiful young woman appeared before him. She was wearing a black cocktail dress. The top ended just above her breasts, showing nothing but leaving a lot to the imagination. It had short sleeves gathered in at the arms giving them a soft puffed up look. It was straight and ended just above the knee, really showing off her figure. The outfit was completed by black high heeled shoes and a black purse. Her makeup was lightly applied but her eyes proved to be her most important feature. The long, black eyelashes were complimented with pale blue eye shadow and thin black eyeliner.

She gazed at Joe, almost looking for approval. When he smiled at her, she knew he'd given it and her pale pink lips broke into a relieved smile, too.

But Joe paid particular attention to her hair. It was pulled gently back from her face and done up in a mass of soft curls, each one perfectly placed. She was really something. She looked like a woman in her twenties – and a very elegant one at that.

Agnes couldn't help noticing the look on Joe's face as he helped Angela with her coat, and after saying their good-byes, they left. Agnes waited by the window and watched as Joe put Angela into the limousine. She smiled to herself. She'd never seen her daughter look lovelier and neither, she suspected, had Mr Morrelli!

When they arrived at 'The Imperial Palace' restaurant and casino, Joe led Angela inside and stopped to hand her coat to the cloakroom attendant. They then proceeded to the dining room. The maitre'd jumped to attention when he saw Joe approaching.

"Mr Morrelli, such a pleasure to see you. If you would care to follow me, Mr Lennox has a special table for you."

"Thank you, Pierre."

Joe put his arm around Angela lightly and guided her along as Pierre led the way. She was overcome by the size and splendour of the place and decided that the name given to it was very appropriate. In fact, she was so in awe of her surroundings, she was beginning to develop an attack of nerves in her stomach.

Everyone seemed to know Joe Morrelli. They spoke to him or called his name. He must have went to several tables to talk to people and shake hands, bringing Angela with him and introducing her. She couldn't help but notice he had this easy going quality. He seemed to fit in perfectly , as if he's been used to places like this all his life. As they walked along, a voice called out.

"Hey Joe! Long time – no see!"

Joe stopped and looking over at one of the tables he smiled broadly. He led Angela over.

"Gene! Good to see you," he said, shaking the man warmly by the hand. "Angela, I'd like you to meet Eugene O'Brien. That is – Congressman O'Brien!"

"Not yet, Joe" came the reply, "not till all the votes are in."

"Oh you'll walk it," said Joe dismissingly. "Every Italian in New York is going to vote for you – I've made sure of it!"

Gene O'Brien stood up.

"How do you do little lady?" he asked, extending his hand in greeting. He then introduced the rest of the company. "I'd like you to meet Alan Bailey, my personal assistant, Jeff Lang, District Attorney and Judge Thompson."

Angela smiled and shook hands with each one in their turn.

"I'm please to meet with you all," she said. "But Judge Thompson and I have already met."

The Judge nodded in agreement.

"Say now, that's not a New York accent," remarked Gene O'Brien.

Joe smiled.

"Gene, fellas, I'd like you to meet Angela Kenny. She's from Ireland."

Gene's eyes lit up!

"Well, you just sit yourself down here beside me," he said, pulling out a chair. "I'm Irish myself – well, third generation. But once an Irishman, always an Irishman. That's what I say!"

Gene O'Brien was a very pleasant, friendly man. He was a larger than life figure, well built with a warm smile. Although he wasn't old his hair was turning grey, making him look quite distinguished.

"We Irish all stick together, Angela. That's why I'm almost sure of the Irish/American votes in the election. Now tell me, what part of Ireland are you from?"

"I'm from Belfast, Mr O'Brien."

"No kidding? You'd know all about the trouble that's going on over there, then. I hear things are pretty bad."

Angela nodded as her smile noticeably faded. Gene continued, "That's some sweet accent you've got. But tell me, what are you doing with him?" he smiled over at Joe.

"She works for me!" Joe informed him. "She hasn't been in New York very long and she doesn't know many people."

"Well, if she hangs around with you, she'll end up knowing everybody!"

"What are you all doing here, anyway," Joe asked.

"Business," replied Gene. "and besides, it's better discussing it on a full stomach. Better to have too much, than too little, Joe."

"Yeah, yeah. We all know there was a famine in Ireland, Gene. God knows you've told us often enough!"

Everyone laughed.

"Well, we'd better go. Good to see you all. Have a nice evening."

Angela got up and after shaking Gene's hand again, left the table. He called out to her as she walked away, "Hey, Irish – you're o.k.!"

Angela smiled. As Joe turned to follow her, Gene pulled him gently by the arm.

"Tell me something, old buddy. Where the hell do you get staff like that? I wish I could find them for my office."

"It wouldn't do you much good, Gene. You're a married man – remember?"

"Don't you start! The wife reminds me about that every day." Gene stared at Angela as she stood waiting for Joe. "Man, she sure is good looking. And what a figure. Now, that's the kind of woman you dream about."

Joe patted his friend on the back.

"You dream about the election, Gene. We're all counting on you."

Gene laughed,

"Yeah, I guess she would be a bit much to handle on a full stomach! Enjoy yourself, old buddy. With someone like that it would be hard not to – know what I mean?"

Joe smiled as he left the table and made his way over to Angela. They proceeded through the dining hall and were shown to a quiet table in the corner. A bottle of champagne was waiting for them in a silver ice bucket.

"Compliments of the House," they were told. The waiter pulled the chair out for Angela, and she sank into it.

That walk through the dining hall had been the longest walk of her life. By now she felt as though her stomach was being tied up in knots. She opened the menu and stared in disbelief. The price of a meal here was more than she'd paid for her dress! She was out of her depth in 'The Imperial Palace' and inwardly she was starting to panic. She knew she wouldn't be able to eat a thing and she didn't know how to tell Joe Morrelli. Gazing around at all the tables, she hoped she would see someone like herself. But everyone seemed so at ease she felt close to tears. She didn't even notice that Joe was speaking to her. On getting no reply he'd looked up from the menu and sat staring at her. He watched as she looked around, both hands clasped tightly in front of her. For a moment she resembled a lost child. Joe leaned over and touched her hands lightly.

"Angela, are you alright?" he asked.

She looked at him and nodded.

"I'm fine," she replied in a low voice.

"No you're not. What's the matter? Don't you like it here?"

"It's beautiful, Mr Morrelli, but I'm not used to a place like this. The truth is, I've never been in one. I feel so nervous I don't think I could eat a bite, I'm so sorry."

She lowered her eyes, almost ashamed to hold his gaze any longer.

Well, this was something new for Joe Morrelli! Most women he knew would give anything to be seen in this place. They'd go to any lengths just to be in the company he and Angela were sitting among. They'd brag about it all week to their girlfriends. But as Joe studied her, he realised that Angela Kenny wasn't impressed and he liked that. At least she wasn't out with him just to be seen and for Joe, that was a nice change.

"O.k.," he said. "Come on, let's go."

She looked at him.

"Don't you mind?"

"Why should I mind? We'll find somewhere else."

He took her arm and they began the long walk through the dining hall again. Joe looked a commanding figure as he strode along gently leading Angela towards the door. Gene O'Brien caught sight of them as they were leaving. He turned to Alan Bailey,

"Jesus! I knew he wouldn't be able to wait!" he said, laughing loudly and shaking his head.

Al was leaning back in the driver's seat listening to the radio, when he saw Joe and Angela come out onto the sidewalk. He could hardly believe it was them. It hadn't been that long since they'd gone inside. Either something had happened or that was the quickest meal his boss had ever eaten. He jumped out of the car and opened the rear door for them. Angela climbed in first. Joe followed.

"Anything wrong, Boss?" Al asked.

"No. it was just a little crowded tonight, that's all."

Angela sat silently. She felt embarrassed, awkward, and so angry with herself she just couldn't speak. Joe sat for a few moments, deep in thought. Then he said, "Al drive to Mario's."

"Mario's?" asked Al , sounding surprised.

Joe leaned over towards him.

"Yeah, Mario's. And turn that music down. I think it's effecting your hearing."

"But Boss, Mario's is in the ..."

"I know where it is! Now just drive."

They left the splendour of 'The Imperial Palace behind and headed across the city. The limousine finally came to a halt outside a small building on the corner of a narrow street. Al held open the door of the car as Joe and Angela got out.

"Do you like Italian food?" Joe asked her, as he pushed open the small wooden door in front of them,

"Yes I do," she replied, still feeling guilty about the whole situation. She stepped inside and looked around. Angela found herself in a small, plain restaurant with round tables covered in red and white check tablecloths. A little lamp was in the centre of each table holding a red candle which burned discreetly. The place looked so warm and inviting she felt at ease for the first time that evening. A young man in his twenties came over to them.

"Joe? Joe Morrelli! Do you remember me? It's Gino!"

He shook hands with Joe excitedly.

"Sure I remember you. How are you Gino?"

"Never better," said Gino as he ran towards the kitchen and called out, "Papa, look who's here."

A small elderly man appeared with grey hair and a grey moustache. He wore a large white apron which was securely tied around him.

"Joe!" he yelled, with arms outstretched. "Joe Morrelli!" Both men embraced each other.

"How are you, Mario?" Joe asked.

"Fine, fine. What brings you here?"

Mario's broken English accent made him sound as though he's just arrived from Italy itself!

"Oh. I was in the neighbourhood and thought I'd call," said Joe.

Mario held onto Joe's hand and looked at Angela. "You see this man?" he asked. "He's a good man. When I open my business some men come. They want money from me. I tell Joe. I never see them again." He then looked at Joe. "We miss you, Joe. The old neighbourhood, it not the same anymore. And my Gino, he all grown up now. He's a good boy Joe."

Joe nodded and then took Angela's arm.

"Mario, I'd like you to meet Angela."

Mario took her hand as she smiled at him warmly.

"How do you do, Angela? Welcome to my restaurant. Please sit down. Hey Gino! Where your manners? Show the young lady to a table. You stay and eat Joe. Mario will cook for you – on the house!"

Angela liked this place and she certainly liked Mario and his son Gino, who by now was showing her to her seat, and helping her off with her coat. Joe was just about to follow her when Mario pulled at his arm.

"She your wife Joe?" he asked in a low voice.

"No. I'm not married yet."

"A fine man like you? Ah, I know, she your girlfriend. Look. Look at her. She so beautiful. That face, so innocent." He put his fingers to his lips and blew a kiss. "She has the face of an angel!"

Joe looked over his shoulder and stared at Angela. He nodded his head and started to smile. "Yeah, she has. Hasn't she?"

He went over to the table and sat down beside her. Gino came over.

"What would you like to drink?" he asked them.

Angela looked towards the small bar and then looked at Gino.

"Could I have a beer please?"

Joe could hardly believe his ears. Tonight had certainly been full of surprises!

"Better make that two," he informed Gino. "What's he cooking in there?"

"Anything you want Joe. You know papa."

"Well then, I'll have the house special. I don't suppose it has ever changed!"

He looked across the table and smiled at Angela. She returned his smile without hesitation.

"Do you have lasagne?" she asked. Gino nodded. "Then I'll have that please."

With the ordering done they both relaxed in their seats while Gino brought the beers and then retreated to the kitchen.

"It's not very grand," said Joe looking around.

"I really like it," Angela assured him, "And I like your friends. They're so warm and friendly towards me."

"We aim to please!" he grinned.

Still smiling, they lifted their glasses and began to drink their beers. It was then that Angela found herself actually studying Joe Morrelli for the first time. He was a handsome man in a rugged sort of way. With black hair and brown eyes he looked every inch an Italian. When he smiled his whole face seemed to light up. She paid particular attention to a mole he had on his right cheek.

"What's the big attraction?" he asked.

"Your mole," she said smiling and pointing to his face.

"Oh that!" this time it was Joe who felt uncomfortable and embarrassed.

"A mole is supposed to be a sign of beauty, they say."

"Yeah, well, maybe for a woman it is," he replied.

Angela put her glass down onto the table and looked into his eyes.

"Oh, I don't know," she said. "Beauty doesn't always have to be on the outside, Mr Morrelli. After all, its whats inside that really counts."

Joe felt quite complimented!

Gino appeared from the kitchen with a tray. Lasagne for Angela and a large plate of spaghetti and meat balls for Joe. He looked down at it.

"See?, he pointed. "I knew the house special had never changed!"

They both started to laugh. For the first time in years, Joe Morrelli could be himself.

Angela had never been much of a drinker, so after a couple of beers and a bottle of Mario's best table wine she became very relaxed and talkative. Joe did observe on how intelligent her conversation was. She seemed older then her years, so he decided to find out more about her.

"Do you have any boyfriends?" he asked.

She shook her head in silence.

"What about back home? Didn't you have any there?"

"Well, there was one boy I liked. He was a college student. We used to go about together quite a lot. I didn't talk about him much to my parents but I had planned to bring him home to meet them. I was going to ask my father if it would be o.k. but he was killed before I got the chance."

"What was his name?"

"Michael, Michael Conway."

Joe saw a look of sadness come into Angela's eyes as she lowered them.

"Anyway," she continued, "after my father was murdered I never saw him again."

"You mean he never came to see you or even pay his respects?" Joe was shocked.

Angela raised her eyes again and looked at him.

"You don't understand, Mr Morrelli, he was probably frightened. He could have been beaten up – or worse. I never blamed him. You'd have had to be there to know what it was like. I hope he does well. Really I do. He wanted to be an Art teacher. I hope he makes it."

"Didn't you ever feel bad about him at all? I mean, just disappearing like that?"

"None of us really know how we're going to react in a situation until we're in it! Besides, not long afterwards my mother decided to come here. We stayed with my mother's aunt Bridget. She wasn't in good health and died not long after we arrived. My sister, Sheila, was supposed to come with us but she was already pregnant and we didn't know. It was quite a shock to us, especially my mother. Sheila was so young. Anyway, she stayed behind and married her boyfriend, Raymond Burns. My mother gave them the house and all the furniture and half of our savings because of the baby. We came to New York and I got the job at 'The Safe Haven.' When Mr Barrett offered me the job I do now, I took it because of the extra money. It's a great help. Every few weeks we can send Sheila and Raymond something to help them out. She's having another baby and my mother worries in case she can't afford the things she needs."

"He didn't waste much time!"

"Raymond wants a boy this time. Their first was a little girl. Sheila called her Senga, after my mother."

"But your mother's called Agnes," said Joe puzzled. Angela laughed, "I know, but Senga spelt backwards is Agnes!"

Joe leaned on the table and thought for a moment. "Oh yeah," he agreed, "So it is." So tell me, this Raymond, doesn't he have a job?"

"No. Work is hard to come by over there."

"Well, couldn't he do something? Manual work? Bartender? I mean, it's bound to hurt his pride, taking handouts from a young girl who's working all the hours she can. Or maybe he's happy with the way things are."

Angela seemed hurt at Joe's comments.

"Raymond was good to us, Mr Morrelli, especially when my father was killed. He stood by us and did everything he could to help. He's like a son to my mother and a brother to me. I don't mind helping out my own family. They'd do it for us."

Joe looked at her thoughtfully. He admired her loyalty and realised he'd been hard on Raymond. It was obvious the Kenny's were a close, loving family and that was the one thing Joe had always missed in his life. Never the less, here was a young eighteen year old girl who was the breadwinner for everyone. She worked long hours for him and studied hard. He couldn't help but feel that in a way she was being taken for granted. Not by Agnes – she was an ill woman. But from what Angela had told him, Joe felt that she was the one doing the giving while everyone else did the taking. Although this annoyed him, his admiration for her was growing by the minute.

He changed the subject.

"What's that around your neck?" he enquired.

"Don't you know, Mr Morrelli? It's a Horn of Plenty. An Italian Charm."

"Yeah I know," he laughed. "I just wondered why someone from Ireland is wearing it?"

Angela explained, "My father bought it for me for my sixteenth birthday and I've worn it ever since. I'd seen it in a jeweller's shop and fell in love with it. It was so unusual. When I told him about it he didn't seem all that interested so I never mentioned it again. I had no idea that he was paying money off it every week out of his wages so I could have it for my birthday present."

Angela's eyes glazed and her voice became emotional as she continued, "But that's the kind of man my father was. He was just a road sweeper and never had much money to spare, but he'd have gotten us the moon if he could."

She put her hand up and touched the charm gently with her fingers.

"If I had all the money in the world I wouldn't exchange it for diamonds. It has too much sentimental value for me and memories that money can't buy."

She stood up and excused herself to go to the ladies room. Joe watched her. Angela Kenny didn't just have a beautiful figure and walk. She had a beautiful heart as well. He had learned a lot about her tonight. She was loyal and unselfish to those she loved, and to Joe that was a rare quality. She was also open and honest and he liked that especially as she seemed to be getting very little out of life. What she should be getting, he felt, was a lot of love and it would be very easy for any man to give her that. Easy even for a man like Joe Morrelli, who has never let his heart rule his head! Joe began to look around. He had been so interested in Angela, he hadn't noticed that the other customers had gone. Mario came out of the kitchen and walked up to the front door. He locked it and pulled down the shades on the windows. He went behind the bar and opened another bottle of wine which he then brought to Joe's table.

"You stay as long as you like, Joe. My restaurant is yours. In the early days, I not have my business but for you. Mario not forget! You not let anyone spoil things for me, so tonight, I not let anyone spoil things for you.

Joe smiled at him and took his hand.

"Thanks Mario," he said.

"Listen, Joe I'm an old man but I tell you something, that girl, she special to you I can see the way you look at her. Tonight I think you fall in love. I know these things. It is easy for a man to find a woman, Joe. Not so easy for a man to find an angel. Don't let her fly away!"

Mario dimmed the lights and went back into the kitchen, closing the door behind him Joe poured himself another glass of wine and started to drink it. Angela came towards him. He watched her again, his eyes slowly moving over every inch of her. Maybe Mario was right. Maybe he was falling in love.

Angela looked around her as she sat down.

"It must be time to go," she said, "there's no one else here."

"Oh, don't let that bother you," replied Joe, as he lifted the bottle of wine and poured some into her glass.

"Mr Morrelli, I really don't think I could drink anymore. I'm not much of a drinker at any time."

"It's only table wine. Go on, it's good for you."

She smiled and raised the glass to her lips.

"Tell me something," enquired Joe. "Why did you go to College? And why do you still go to classes here? Is there something you want to be, or do you just like books?"

"You ask a lot of questions, Mr Morrelli," Angela commented.

"Well I guess I'm just curious."

She put her glass down onto the table and met his gaze.

"I'd like to get a really good job one day. To do that, I need the proper qualifications. That's why I'm studying. If you've got degrees you stand a much better chance when you go for interviews. I love books and I'd like a job that would involve them. Maybe, if I'm lucky, I could get a job with a publishing firm. I think writers have a great talent and I'd like to be part of that. After all, where would we be today without the great authors and poets of past generations? We can learn so much from them."

"Yeah, well I guess it would be a lot better than working at 'The Safe Haven'."

"I like my job, Mr Morrelli, but I can't stay there forever. And besides, if I could do really well and save some money then Sheila and Raymond could come over for a holiday. I'd love to see their children."

"Would you like kids of your own one day?"

"Oh yes, I would. But for now I have my mother to care for. She's not well and she needs me. She's never been the same since my father was killed. I think part of her died with him. When she was looking after aunt Bridget she collapsed one day and I had to call the doctor in. She's had a heart attack and was in hospital for a while. They told me she could take another one at any time."

Joe sensed that Angela was becoming a little anxious.

"What about some music?" he asked, pointing to a juke box in the corner. He got up and took her hand.

"Come on, let's see what's there."

She went with him.

"It looks very old," she whispered.

"Yeah," agreed Joe, studying the titles of the songs. "It's nearly as old as Mario – and so is the music! Here goes."

He dropped the coins into the box and pressed the buttons. As the music started to play he looked at her.

"Would you like to dance Angela?"

"Well, seeing as there's no one else here you can ask…"

They both laughed quietly.

Joe put his arms around her, gently placing his hands on her back. Angela put her hands on his shoulders and they started to dance slowly to the music.

Mario and Gino came out from the kitchen and watched. Mario smiled and then pushed Gino back into the kitchen. Father followed son, and closed the door behind him. Joe had often wondered what it would be like to hold Angela in his arms like this and now he knew. It was the best feeling he'd ever had. Slowly, he moved closer to her, feeling her body swaying to the music. He could smell the sweet fragrance of her perfume. He bent his head, deliberately touching her cheek with his own. He closed his eyes and moved his hands gently over her back. She put her head on his shoulder and her arms moved up around his neck.

There, in the dimly lit restaurant, Joe and Angela clung to each other as though they were already lovers. Joe Morrelli was the happiest man alive. 'Ol Blue Eyes' was singing a romantic ballad from the juke box and Joe had his arms wrapped around the woman of his dreams. What more could any man ask for?

When the music finally ended, Angela looked up at him.

"Thanks you for the dance, Mr Morrelli."

"My pleasure, Angela."

He smiled, looking into her eyes and holding the gaze. Angela stepped back and lowered her eyes away for him.

"I think I'd better go now," she said.

They went back to the table and Joe helped her on with her coat. He called towards the kitchen, "Hey Mario,"

"You leaving now Joe?" Mario asked.

"Yeah, we'd better. It's getting late. What's the damage?"

"On the house, Joe! I'm just so happy you come back. It's been a long time."

Joe put his arms around the old man.

"I'll tell you what," he said. "I'll come back again, only next time you let me pay." "O.k.?"

"Anything you say, Joe. Hey Gino! Open the door for Mr Morrelli and his beautiful lady."

Gino hurried and unlocked the door. Angela went over to Mario and shook his hand.

"Thank you so much for a lovely evening."

Mario kissed her hand.

"You come back soon and bring Joe. Don't let him wait so long next time."

"I will, I promise. Goodnight."

As they were going through the door, Joe turned to Gino.

"Are you married yet, Gino?"

"Not yet."

"Got a girlfriend?"

"Yeah, she lives two blocks away. Her name's Theresa."

Joe pushed two twenty dollar bills into his hand.

"You buy her something nice," he said, winking at him. Joe and Angela stepped out onto the sidewalk. He looked at her and then around at the buildings.

"It's been a long time since I stood here. I don't suppose things have changed much."

"Well, why don't you take a walk and see? I'll walk with you."

Joe looked surprised.

"Would you mind?"

"Of course not. I'd like to see it for myself. I've never been in this part of the city."

He knocked on the car window and Al lowered it.

"Anything wrong Boss?"

"No. I'm just taking a walk."

"A walk?"

"Yeah, a walk! You follow me slowly."

Joe and Angela began their walk along the street, leaving Al with a look of bewilderment on his face.

As they made their way from one street to the next, Joe pointed to different buildings explaining to Angela that these were places where he'd played, worked and run errands. He could remember everybody's name, what they did and how things used to be. He was right, though. Nothing much had changed. Some of the signs had new names but they were still the same old buildings. Still the same old streets.

About four blocks down, he stopped in front of an apartment block and pointed upwards.

"I was raised there. We lived on the top floor. That's where my mother died."

"What happened to her?"

"She took cancer. She died when I was ten years old. She was only thirty two."

Angela could sense the deep sadness in Joe's voice even though he was trying desperately to hide it.

"My old man couldn't take it. He felt guilty about not being able to give her enough, especially when she got sick. I felt guilty because I was too young to help."

"What happened to him?"

"He took to drink and became so wrapped up in his grief he forgot he had a son. I got jobs running errands for the big guys on the block. They were good to me. At least I earned enough to keep food in my mouth and clothes on my back, and keep my old man in booze. I dropped out of school and did my learning on the streets. Later on, I went to work for those same guys. My old man drank himself to death. I swore I'd never end up like him. Don't get me wrong, he wasn't a bad man but he had no determination. I guess I had enough for both of us."

Angela soon realised that Joe Morrelli had fought hard to get where he was today, and she admired and respected him for it. She wanted to tell him so but just couldn't find the words. Instead, she moved closer and slipped her hand into his. Joe held it gently but firmly. What she's just done had pleased him. It felt sensual, yet innocent.

"What were their names? She asked softly.

"My mother was Sophia Morrelli. My father was Joseph."

"I'm sure they'd be very proud of you today. You've come a long way, Mr Morrelli."

"Yeah, well you can take the man out of the Bronx but you can't take the Bronx out of the man!"

Angela smiled.

"You know, my father would have liked you. He may have swept roads for a living but he always used to say, "If you forget where you've come from, you'll never know where you're going!"

"No kidding? Well, I think me and your father would have gotten along just fine!"

Angela looked up at the tall buildings.

"It must be nice to come home. Like you did tonight."

Joe gazed at her intently and tightened his grip on her hand.

"Will you ever go home?" he asked in a half whisper.

She shook her head.

"No. I won't ever go back."

They walked through the rest of the old neighbourhood hand in hand. Inwardly, Joe was feeling pretty good. He had finally met a woman who had understood the real Joe Morrelli and he felt relieved that she wasn't going to go home. After all, Belfast was a long way from New York.

Joe hadn't had an evening like this since he was a young man. He never thought at his age, he'd be back in the old neighbourhood, having a meal at Mario's and enjoy it so much. He didn't want it to end. He was happy and relaxed in Angela's company and it had been years since he'd held hands. He felt like twenty again – but it was getting late. He stood and waited for Al to come along.

"Better get you home Angela," he said looking at his watch. They got into the back of the car and Al headed back across the town.

When they stopped outside her apartment building, Joe walked Angela to the front entrance. She was the first to speak. "Mr Morrelli, I'm sorry about earlier in 'The Imperial Palace'. I know you must have gone to a lot of trouble to bring me there. I hope I didn't spoil your night."

"Don't worry about it," he replied. "I had a good time in Mario's . Did you?"

"Oh yes, I did. But there's something I have to tell you. I'm afraid I wasn't very truthful tonight."

"What about?"

]"Well, it was when you asked me if I liked Italian food and I said I did. To be honest, I'd never even been in an Italian restaurant before. You didn't get many Italian restaurants where I lived!"

"Then how did you know to order lasagne?"

"It's on the college menu."

Joe smiled.

"Yeah well, I wasn't so truthful myself," he admitted.

"Really? What about?"

"When I ordered those couple of beers we had and pretended to enjoy them, the truth is, I don't like beer!"

They both looked at each other and laughed.

"Come on," he said, "I'll walk you to your door."

They climbed the stairs together. Then Joe asked,

"Could you tell me something?"

"What is it?

"How do you spell your name? Is it A.N.G.E.L.A.?

"Why do you ask?"

"Maybe I want to put you on my Christmas card list!"

Joe smiled broadly as he waited for her reply.

"Yes, it is," she answered, puzzled at his question.

"Just like you'd spell angel?"

"Yes, I suppose."

"Then would you mind if I called you Angel from now on?"

"Why would you want to do that, Mr Morrelli?"

"Oh, just something an old man said to me," he replied shrugging his shoulders, "and besides – I have my reasons!"

"Well, if that's what you want, I don't mind."

Joe stood looking at the floor for a few moments. He felt like he was on his first date. For such a smart guy, he really didn't know what to do next!

"I better be going in now, Mr Morrelli. Thank you for a lovely time."

Angela leaned over and kissed his cheek, touching the mole lightly with her finger. She smiled and then turned to put the key in the lock. Joe's hand covered her's as he turned her around to him once more and leaned her back up against the door. He slipped his hands under her coat and held them around her waist.

"I forgot to tell you how beautiful you looked tonight," he whispered. He kissed her forehead and her cheek. Then he buried his face in her neck and shoulder, kissing them tenderly he lifted his head and looked into her face, his eyes gazing deeply into hers. She felt as though he was seeing right into her soul.

"Goodnight Angel," he said in a low voice.

His mouth was only inches away from her own. She lowered her eyes and looked at it. Then on impulse, she touched it gently with her lips.

"Goodnight Mr Morrelli."

Joe moved away and headed for the stairs. As he was about to descend, he stopped.

"How would you like to go back to Mario's sometime – only without the walk?"

She smiled and nodded.

"I'd really like that."

"What about next week? After all, the guy has to make a living. We may as well give him some business."

"Next week would be fine."

"Good. Well, goodnight again!"

Angela disappeared inside the apartment and Joe watched as the door closed slowly behind her.

After coming outside, he stood for a while deep in thought. It had only been a kiss on the cheek and a very slight touch of her lips on his, but if he took his time and played his cards right it could lead to a proper kiss. He had a strong feeling that Angela could be quite passionate with the right man. And Joe Morrelli wanted to be that man! For the first time in his life he knew what kind of woman he wanted. He made up his mind to go after what he really wanted in life and that was Angela Kenny. He was going to go all out to get her!

Rooney and Frankie drank and played cards until 12.30am. There was no sign of Joe.

"Well, I'd better be going," said Frankie , holding out his hand and smiling. Rooney nodded and gave him the $10. after Frankie had left, Rooney headed for the lounge and made himself comfortable. As time passed, he kept checking the clock. 1.00am, 1.30am. he was getting tired and wondering where the hell Joe had got to. The last time he looked at the clock it was quarter to two. After that he fell into a deep sleep that would last till morning. Just before 3 o'clock, the front door opened and Joe came in. he walked across the hallway, humming to himself. It was a tune by one of his all time favourite singers. He smiled as the words came to him and as he began to climb the stairs he started to sing them softly, "strangers in the night…"

When Rooney woke up, the first thing he did was look at his watch. It was 9.30. he could hear faint voices coming from the kitchen so he left the lounge and went through. Evie was cooking breakfast and Frankie was sitting at the table with a cup of coffee, the morning papers spread out in front of him. There was no sign of Joe or Al.

"Hi Rooney. What time did the Boss get in?" Frankie asked.

"Search me. I don't even know if he's here. I waited that long for him last night, I fell asleep. Do you know if he's home Evie?"

"No I don't! But then nobody bothered to tell me he was going out in the first place!"

She sat a cup of coffee down noisily in front of Rooney. About ten minutes later Al came through the back door. His eyes were red and swollen and he was yawning.

"How did the date go?" enquired Rooney, waiting for the details.

"You mean last night?" asked Al

Rooney nodded.

"The Boss didn't go on a date Rooney. He went on a tour!"

Al poured himself a cup of coffee and sat down at the table, leaning his head in his hands.

"What do you mean – a tour?"

Al looked at Rooney through two tired eyes.

"I mean, he walked all the way through the old neighbourhood holding hands with Angela."

"Mr Joe, holding hands? Now isn't that nice!" said Evie, putting the plates on the table.

Frankie leaned over towards Al.

"You mean to say the Boss was back in the old neighbourhood, after all this time?"

"Yeah, and he covered every inch of it on foot. I had to follow behind. I was driving so slowly, I bet people who saw me from their windows thought I was a funeral!"

Just at that, loud humming came from the entrance hall. They all recognised the tune – "Strangers in the night." There was a big scuffle! Joe appeared at the kitchen door looking bright and cheerful. Everyone around the table was silently holding a paper.

"What's the matter?" asked Joe, as Evie handed him a cup of coffee, smiling knowingly.

"Hey you three. You look as though you've just been to a funeral."

Al looked at Rooney and whispered," I thought I'd been to one last night!"

Joe slapped the back of Al's head with his hand.

"What did you just say?"

"I said I had a late night last night."

"What have you been telling these guys?"

"Nothing Boss. Honest."

"Well I sure hope it was nothing or New York will have one more driver standing in the unemployment line."

"I'm just tired!" said Al.

"How the hell are you so tired? I'm the one who did all the walking."

Everyone stared in Joe's direction.

"Oh, I see," he said. "You want to know all about what happened. Well, that's a pity because I'm not telling!"

He walked towards the kitchen door, adding,

"Rooney, I want to see you in my study."

He then made his exit.

The three men were left staring at each other. Frankie leaned over to Al and whispered,

"Were they really holding hands?"

Al nodded. Frankie and Rooney began to laugh.

"Can you see the boss actually walking through the Bronx, holding hands?" Frankie asked his friend.

"Yes!" said Evie, in an angry voice, lifting the plate from him before he had a chance to eat what was on it. "Just the way I can see you without a job – if you keep this up!"

Ever since the visit by Carlo Capaldi telling him about Lenny Shultz, Joe had heard nothing from the street and this bothered him. Things had been quiet. Too quiet. And he couldn't help but wonder why. He thought constantly about everything Carlo had told him and he didn't like what he's heard. Now that he'd gotten to know Angela Kenny it made him realise how women like her were such prey for a scumbag like Lenny. The very thought of what had been done to her and especially those other women, made Joe all the more determined to make sure it would never happen again. One thing Joe Morrelli had, was respect for women. And he couldn't understand any man who didn't. From that night he'd held Angela in his arms in Mario's, he'd thought about Lenny putting his slimy hands on her. That was bad enough, but what angered him more was what he'd threatened to do to her and the language he's used. Joe knew the kind of sordid slang these guys used on the street. No wonder Angela had been so frightened. It made him sick just thinking about it. Lenny Shultz would have to be taken care of.

As Joe sat in the study one evening, going over some business deals Reuben had left for him, Rooney open the study door.

"Joe, it looks like you've got visitors," he said pointing to the window.

Joe got up from the chair and looked out. A long, black limousine had pulled up in front of the house, followed by two other cars. When they'd all come to a halt, a man got out of the back of the limo and held open the door. Then a tall, handsome, Italian man in his late twenties emerged. The doors of the other two cars opened and six men joined him. They stood together talking for a few minutes, but then the young man made his way to the front door as the others remained behind at the cars they arrived in. Joe turned to Rooney.

"Get me my jacket. Then you, Frankie and Al wait in the hall."

"Who is it? Can you see?" asked Rooney.

Joe nodded as he put on the jacket and straightened his tie, "Unless my eyes deceive me, it's Nick Andretti's grandson, Anthony. I'm just wondering what he's doing here."

The doorbell rang and he motioned to Rooney, "O.k. let him in."

A few moments later, Rooney showed Anthony Andretti into the study and closed the door securely as he left.

Joe went over and both men embraced, greeting each other in Italian. Anthony smiled, "My grandfather sends his regards."

"And I send him my respects. Please sit down. How is your grandfather?"

"Well thank you."

"I'm glad to hear that, Anthony, Can I offer you anything?"

"No thanks, I may have some business to see to later tonight. My grandfather expects me to keep a clear head!"

Both men sat down.

"I'll come straight to the point, Mr Morrelli," said Anthony. "We heard you were looking for a man by the name of Lenny Shultz."

Joe nodded, "Yes, I am."

"We've been following him on my grandfather's instructions, ever since the word was out. You don't have to tell us why, this we already know from our own sources. My grandfather wishes to extend his regards further by letting you know where this man will be tonight."

"I accept your grandfather's most gracious gesture."

Anthony nodded, "Lenny Shultz will be in Benny Bangles brothel at 11.20 to do a drugs deal. The buyer is one of our men. The deal has been set up with the promise that if the stuff is of good quality, a very young woman will be brought along as an added bonus. That should take care of Mr Shultz for an hour or two! There's only one entrance into the brothel, and just down the street from it is a dark, secluded alley. The perfect place for an accident, if you know what I mean."

"What about the young woman? Will she be safe?"

"That's all been taken care of. She works for us and she'll be well watched. The place will be full of customers tonight, most of whom will be our men. After he leaves, he's all yours – if you want him."

Joe nodded,

"Oh , I want him alright!"

Anthony smiled.

"Well then, everything should go according to plan,"

He then became quite serious,

"I suppose you were wondering why you hadn't heard anything before now?"

"As a matter of fact, I was. I didn't expect it to take so long."

"Well, Mr Morrelli, my grandfather decided to deal with this himself. He doesn't like what Lenny Shultz has been doing to innocent women."

Anthony stared at Joe and added.

"He doesn't like Lenny Shultz!"

"I know the feeling!" replied Joe.

Anthony Andretti stood up.

"So, after tonight your problem should be well and truly taken care of."

Joe got up from the chair and shook his hand.

"I'm very grateful to you for your visit, Anthony. You remind me a lot of your father. It's a tragedy he was killed so young. He would have been proud of you today. Thank you for coming. Please tell your grandfather I appreciate, most sincerely, what he had done. He is a man of honour."

"He always liked you, Mr Morrelli. You never interfered with business but you were a loyal friend to my father. We never forget loyalty. Goodbye."

"Goodbye, Anthony," said Joe, opening the study door.

He watched from the window as Anthony Andretti and his men left. He stared at the floor for a few minutes and then yelled,

"Rooney!"

Rooney appeared.

"What's up Joe?"

"Get Frankie and Al in here. We've just been handed Lenny Shultz on a plate and we're going to take him!"

"When?"

"Tonight!"

Rooney smiled,

"That's the best news I've heard for a while, Joe. At least Angela will be safe now and so will a lot of other women."

"That's right," said Joe, in a determined voice. "Cause there'll be no more Lenny Shultz!"

That night, the four men got into Rooney's car and headed for Benny's brothel. It was a quarter to midnight. They didn't talk much. Joe had gone over every detail earlier and each man knew what he had to do. On arriving, Al stopped the car across the street from the alley and they all got out. Al and Frankie walked back towards the brothel, while Joe and Rooney stood on the sidewalk watching. Al went inside the building, Frankie stood across the street leaning against a lamp post, smoking. Once Al had had a quick look around, he ordered a drink and began to mingle with the clients, making sure to stay in full view of the front hall and the desk. He watched to see which one of the girls was getting the most business. After a while he went over to the desk clerk.

"That blonde," he said smiling, "the one in the tight red dress. Is she worth the money?"

"Hey man, you can see how busy she is. She's the best, but if you want her you'll have to wait. I can promise you she'll be worth it. You won't be disappointed."

Al shrugged his shoulders,

"I don't mind waiting. I'm not going anywhere."

The desk clerk nodded. As far as he was concerned, this guy was just another customer after a good time and that's exactly what Al wanted him to believe. He sat down to wait his turn, knowing it would take a while. He studied everyone coming and going. Just after 1am a guy came down the stairs. He fitted the description alright and as he threw a door key onto the desk, the clerk asked,

"Everything o.k. Lenny?"

"Couldn't be better!" he beamed broadly, lighting up a cigarette. "I'm going for a walk.

Who knows, I might even find another woman I don't have to pay for. I feel really lucky tonight!"

He left. Al followed.

Once outside, Al pointed his finger at Lenny from behind. Frankie nodded and began to walk down the other side of the street.

"Here he comes," said Joe. "O.k. Rooney, you know what to do."

Rooney started to walk slowly in Lenny's direction, fumbling with a packet of cigarettes. As they came face to face, Rooney blocked his way and held up one of the cigarettes.

"Hey buddy, got a light?"

Lenny took out a lighter to oblige and held it out to Rooney, who put his hand up to cover the flame. Then, in an instant, Rooney gripped Lenny's arm, twisted it up his back and ran him towards the alley. Frankie crossed the road and both men pushed Lenny further back into the darkness. The only light, came from a dimly lit street lamp on the sidewalk. Rooney drew his fist full force against Lenny's jaw. He's been waiting to do that for a long time. He then lifted his foot and kicked him between the legs, bringing him down in a heap, moaning. When Lenny finally looked up he saw three figures towering over him. His voice was high pitched with fear.

"Who the hell are you guys?"

Joe bent down and gripped him by the throat.

"I'm fuckin' Robin Hood and these are my merry men!"

"I don't know you guys," insisted Lenny. "I've never seen you before. What do you want with me?"

His eyes stared wildly in panic as Joe banged his head off the ground and yelled,

"I'll ask the questions!"

"O.K., O.k., what the fuck do want, man?"

"I want to show you what fear feels like, Lenny. I want you to know how those women felt."

Lenny struggled to get up but Joe pulled a knife and held it to his throat as he cried,

"Hey, come on man, don't do that. Jesus Christ, leave me alone."

"Is that what those young women said to you? 'Cause if it is, you didn't listen to them. Did you? So give me one good reason why I should listen to you?"

Joe pressed the blade against Lenny's cheek and then ran it back down to his throat.

"You like knives. Don't you?" he asked. "It makes you feel good. Gives you power."

Lenny began to squeal. Rooney booted him once more.

"One more sound out of you and your throat won't make another," he promised.

Frankie pinned Lenny's arms to the ground as Joe took the knife away and put it in his pocket. A look of relief spread over Lenny's face.

"Look man," he pleaded," I've got money. Take it. Just leave me alone. Please!"

Joe stood up.

"Sorry Lenny, I can't do that," he said, replacing the knife with a gun.

Lenny looked at Rooney.

"This guy's crazy, he's got a fuckin' gun!"

Rooney reached inside his jacket and took out his own.

"That makes two of us!" he said.

By now Lenny Shultz was trapped like a frightened animal.

"Look, guys, I don't know who you are – I don't want to know, but I swear I'll never touch another woman on the street. Come on, fellas, what do you say?"

Joe bent down and gripped his face hard with his hand.

"Not good enough," he said, shaking his head. "I want to know what you say to them and I want to know now so start talking. It's your only chance to get out of this."

"I just tell them things."

"What fuckin' things?" Rooney aimed his gun.

"O.k., O.k,......"

Lenny began to relate his sick and sordid fantasies in a trembling, frightened voice. All three men were silent, unable to believe the filth they were hearing. Joe Morrelli listened, his stomach churning but he had to bear with it. He had to know what Angela Kenny had been subjected to that night, because he knew she would never tell him. When Lenny finished, Joe shook his head. He looked at him in disgust. Rooney looked at him with contempt.

"Jesus Christ," said Frankie, "this guy's a fuckin' pervert!"

"Yeah," replied Joe, "and it doesn't stop there. He likes to beat them up too. O.K., Lenny, I have one big problem, I don't know whether to shoot you in the balls or the brains!"

"Why not both," advised Rooney. "If you shoot him in the balls he'll still be able to think about it. This guy's a psycho!"

Joe knew Rooney was right. Here before them was the lowest form of life. What they'd all just heard made them sick. It wasn't difficult to imagine how a woman would feel, listening to it and having it done to her afterwards. Joe nodded to Rooney.

Two shots rang out in the alley. The three men came back out onto the street, crossed the road and got into the waiting car. Al moved off quickly and headed away at full speed, leaving the body of Lenny Shultz in the dark alley. And what better place was there to leave garbage!

Chapter 4

Joe and Angela chatted happily as they sat at the dimly lit table in the small restaurant she'd come to know so well. However, inwardly Angela was anxious.

"Mr Morrelli, may I ask you something?" She enquired in an almost whisper.

"Joe. Call me Joe," came the reply.

"It's a bit difficult for me to call my boss by his first name," she explained.

"Well," said Joe, "when you're not working and you're in my company just try to forget that I am your boss. Anyway, what did you want to ask me?"

Angela moved her fork around the plate nervously.

"It's about Miss Flemming."

"Yeah, what about her?"

Angela put the fork down and looked directly at Joe.

"Does she know you've been taking me out? What I'm trying to say is, I don't think she'd like it."

"I can handle Antonia."

Angela still wasn't satisfied.

"I wouldn't like her to walk into a place like this and cause a scene."

"Why should she do that?" asked Joe. "We're only having a meal. It's not to say she's going to find us in bed together."

Angela could feel her face starting to burn. Joe noticed.

"Did I embarrass you?" he asked in a half amused voice, cutting through his steak. " I did, didn't I?"

"No...no..." she stammered trying to avoid his gaze.

Joe put the knife and fork down, leaned his elbows on the table, closed his hands and rested his chin on them.

"Let me explain something to you, about Antonia."

"You don't have to do that," said Angela.

"I think I do," replied Joe. He stared at Angela.

"Antonia and me go back a long way. She lived three blocks away from me when we were kids."

"You knew her when she was young?" Interrupted Angela.

"Yeah, I knew her," recalled Joe smiling. "She was a funny sort of kid though, not like the rest of us. We'd run errands , do odd jobs. Make a few dollars any way we could. But not Antonia. She was always going to the movies, sitting all starry eyed watching the screen. Then she'd come out and act all the parts. Some of the other kids used to make fun of her. Her mother used to do some cleaning work for a lady up-town and Antonia used to go along sometimes to help. This lady had a daughter called Antonia and our

Antonia fell in love with the name. maybe it was because this other girl came from such a privileged background. You know the type, well educated, elegant. She used to give our Antonia her old clothes and shoes. She'd dress up in them and parade up and down the block. Yeah, she was an actress even then! Her old man ran out and her mother took up with a guy called Stan Flemming. She liked that name too."

"Are you saying that Antonia Flemming isn't her real name?" asked Angela lifting her glass.

"That's right. But if you're going to be an actress on Broadway, you sure wouldn't want top billing as Mavis Finkle. Good old Mavis Finkle from the Bronx!!"

Angela made a choking noise and leaned over the table coughing, as the wine seemed to stick in her throat.

"Hey, are you alright?" Joe was concerned as he patted her on the back. Angela nodded but couldn't speak. She took a few deep breaths.

"I'm fine – really I am."

"Yeah and shocked too I suppose?"

She didn't answer, just nodded her head.

"Anyway," went on Joe, "I left the old neighbourhood and forgot all about her, until one night some years ago I went to a nightclub and there she was in the cabaret. Every now and then she'd try to edge her way forward to get a share of the spotlight! She hadn't changed – but her name had. Everyone called her Antonia Flemming and so have I from that night. Now she's on Broadway and famous. Just what she always wanted."

Angela was stunned.

"I can hardly believe it. She's so glamorous."

"Yeah well," said Joe, "it just goes to prove one thing – very few people are what they seem to be. Always remember that, Angel."

Joe took Angela out on a constant basis over the next two or three months, but only once a week or so as he didn't want to appear over anxious. She always treated him as her boss, calling him 'Mr Morrelli' until the night in Mario's when he's explained about Antonia and asked her to call him 'Joe'. He was really drawn to her and the more he got to know her, the more he realised he didn't want to be with anyone else.

Sometimes he would call in at 'The Safe Haven' just to see her. He found himself constantly wondering what she was doing and where she was on her days and nights off. He looked forward to spending time with her. She was a very intelligent young woman and could talk about anything. Joe enjoyed that. It was a rare thing for a woman to have beauty and brains, and this was part of the attraction for him. However, he'd hoped by now they'd be more intimate but Angela always managed to keep her guard up. He was still getting the friendly kiss goodnight treatment, which was leading him to believe he was nothing more to her than her boss. That part was becoming difficult for him. He wanted to show her how he felt. It wasn't easy caring for a woman the way he did, and not being able to touch her. The truth was, Joe had never met anyone quite like Angela before and he was scared of rejection. The last thing he wanted was for her to think she had to please him just because she was in his employ.

Their next date was set for the weekend and Joe decided on a change of scenery for them both. Angela had never been to a proper Nightclub before. He thought it was time she had. He also thought it was time for them to be seen out in public together. Joe chose 'The Little Venice Club' as he felt sure Angela would like it. It was popular with people from all backgrounds who just wanted an enjoyable night out. As they walked into the club that night, Joe Morrelli was a very proud man. A lot of men stared admiringly at Angela as he escorted her to a table near the front of the dance floor and not far from the bar. She looked just as she had done on their first night out together. Same dress, same hairstyle, same grace and charm. She reminded Joe of pictures he'd seen once of Roman and Greek goddesses. As she sat down, he couldn't help but notice again those lovely legs. Those high heels she always wore really did set them off! Joe and Angela were enjoying their meal and talking to each other, while the music played softly in the background. Everything was just as he'd wanted it, until he heard loud laughter at the bar. At first, Joe tried to ignore it. But it continued. He looked over and saw Benny Bangles leaning against the end of the bar, accompanied by his 'boys'. Benny was whispering and sniggering as he kept looking over towards Joe's table. He was holding a large martini and, as always, was the centre of attraction.

Benny got his name because of his love for flamboyant jewellery. He wore a rolex watch and gold bracelets, his wrists virtually covered in them. Gold chains, plain gold ingots, some with diamonds studded in them. A large, ornate gold ring adorned almost every finger and chains and medallions hung around his neck.

As Joe observed him, he thought Benny must be worth a fortune in jewellery alone. He thought, too, it must weigh an awful lot. What a pity no one had ever pushed him into the Hudson. With all that gold he'd have sunk without a trace. The guy was bad news! Joe continued with his meal but so did the loud laughter that he knew belonged to Benny. He glanced over just in time to see him make a gesture with his arm and fist in Joe's direction, to the roar of approval from his friends. Angela, unaware of what was going on, leaned over the table and placed her hand gently on top of his.

"What's the matter, Joe? Don't let them annoy you. They're probably drunk."

"Yeah, I guess you're right."

But it all became too much and after another five minutes, Joe excused himself from the table and walked along the bar heading for the men's room. As he passed, Benny turned and sneered,

"Hey Joe, I didn't know you liked them young. I could have been supplying you all along. Nice juicy ones, used or unused. Whatever turns you on, man!"

Joe smiled at him. Then suddenly, without any warning, his arm shot forward and his hand closed around Benny's throat. He pulled him from the bar and dragged him around the corner, out of sight. As he pushed him up against the wall his grip tightened until Benny could hardly breathe. Benny's 'boys' followed but on viewing the situation, stood back looking on helplessly.

"Didn't I tell you," one of then exclaimed, not to fuck with Joe Morrelli!"

"You should have listened to your girlfriend, Benny!" said Joe, as his fingers dug deeper into his neck. By now, Benny was gasping, a frightened look in his eyes. He struggled to speak.

"Come on Joe, it was just a joke."

Joe banged his head off the wall.

"Now, you listen to me you son of a bitch! If you ever try and fuck with me again, you'll wish you lived on another planet! I know all about you. Kids are your bag – not mine. You buy your fuckin' jewellery from the misery of young boys and girls on the street, selling themselves after you've had them first."

Benny stared at him and stammered, "I ....I'm sorry Joe, honest."

Joe stared back.

"Not as sorry as you're going to be, you bastard, if you ever pull a stunt like that again! Now, Read my lips, you fuckin' walking jewellery store – YOU KEEP OUT OF MY WAY! If you ever walk into a place and see me – walk out. Because if you don't it's going to be very bad for your health. Do you understand?"

Benny nodded. Joe took his hand from around Benny's throat and put it over his face instead as he banged his head against the wall once more.

"Don't you ever try and fuck with Joe Morrelli!"

Joe stepped back, straightened his clothes and returned to his seat. When Angela looked into his eyes, she knew something was wrong. Anger flashed in them. She grew concerned.

"Joe what is it? What happened?"

"Nothing Angel, Forget about it."

A few minutes later, a bottle of champagne was delivered to their table. As the waiter sat it down Joe said, "Just a minute. Where did that come from?"

"The gentleman at the end of the bar, Sir."

Joe got up and lifted the bottle. When Angela saw the look of rage on his face, she also got up and lifted her handbag. He walked straight over and slammed the bottle down onto the bar in front of Benny. He glared in his face, his eyes narrowing.

"You bastard! Do you think you can buy Joe Morrelli?"

Benny raised his hands in the air.

"Joe, come on. What can I do here? It was just a misunderstanding."

"A misunderstanding? Well, I didn't misunderstand the way you were laughing at me tonight. And I didn't misunderstand that dirty gesture you made. Why don't you do it again, only this time do it to my face."

Benny froze.

"No," said Joe, "I didn't think you would, I don't blame you, Benny. You know I've killed men for less!"

Then lifting the bottle of champagne, he turned it upside down and poured it over Benny's expensive, black patent shoes. He waited until the last drop had fallen, took out his wallet and pulled out a $100 bill. After folding it neatly, he tucked it into Benny's breast pocket with the words,

"I've just bought the champagne and you've just bought yourself an enemy – remember that!!"

Benny Bangles cowered as Joe pointed at him in anger and warning. Joe Morrelli was a man of his word. Everyone knew that.

As he turned he discovered Angela standing directly behind him. She took his arm.

"Come on Joe. Let's go home."

As they walked through the crowded Nightclub, Joe noticed how Angela kept hold of his arm and held her head up high as if to say, "This is Joe Morrelli. And I'm proud to be with him!"

As Al drove them to the apartment, both remained silent. Joe was annoyed at what had happened and felt bad that Angela had been there to witness any of it. She, on the other hand, had her own thoughts. Tonight, she'd seen a side to Joe Morrelli she didn't know existed. When the car stopped they got out and walked into the entrance hall. Joe stood still.

"I suppose you want to ask me what happened back there?"

Angela sat down on the stairs.

"No, I'm not going to ask. If you wanted me to know, you'd tell me. Besides, where I come from you learn not to ask questions."

Joe sat down beside her.

"What do you mean, Angel?"

"Well, I lived in a place where people got murdered every day. I hated it all so much. The violence, the bitterness. But I thought if I didn't get involved and didn't ask questions, it would never happen to me or any of my family. But it did. And even then, I still didn't ask questions. It was too dangerous to even try. But I've often asked myself one."

"What was that?" Joe asked, gazing at her as she stared straight ahead.

"If what they said about my father was true and he had been an informer, then he'd have been well paid by someone, somewhere. Money should never have been a problem. Yet, when they found his body, he didn't have a penny on him. Not even his wages, though he'd been paid that very day. Wouldn't you think that whoever killed him would have left some kind of evidence to prove he was what they said? Instead of doing that, they took everything he had, why would they do that?"

"It beats me, Angel."

She turned and looked into Joe's eyes.

"No one else seemed to think about that – or want to. People I'd known all my life, Joe, friends and neighbours, they changed. They turned against us. The whole family was branded, accused of being traitors and turn coats. It was a nightmare! The abuse, the threats. They stayed away from his wake and funeral and watched to see just who would come to pay their respects to the 'Kenny Touts'! Our lives were made pure hell and we never knew why. Never allowed to ask. I lost all respect and trust for people, Joe, except for Raymond and our neighbour, Mrs Murray. She always believed my father was innocent and there was more to his death than any of us realised. When she heard anyone accusing him she always said, "How can you tell what you don't even know?" She was good to my mother too. I send her cards now and again, just to let her know I haven't forgotten."

Joe smiled, confidingly as Angela continued thoughtfully, "What happened between you and that man tonight, Joe, there was probably more to that than I realised. But I think I know you well enough to know that he must have said or done something really bad, to make you act the way you did."

Joe just nodded.

"Then you don't have to explain."

They both stood up and started to climb the stairs. As they reached the apartment Joe touched her arm gently.

"Angel, can I ask you something?"

"Of course."

"Do you go out with me because you feel you have to? You know, because I'm your boss and you think you might loose your job if you don't?"

"No," she replied, almost puzzled.

"Do you think I'm too old for you, then? I wouldn't want you to be embarrassed at being seen with me, after all, I am twice your age."

"So that's what happened tonight! That man said something to you about me. Didn't he Joe?"

Joe looked at the floor.

"You know Angel, your job's safe. You can work for me for as long as you want to, without ever coming out with me again."

"But I like going out with you Joe, and I want to tell you something. I admired you for the way you stood up to that man tonight and I respect you for doing what you thought was right. But I also trust you, for the decent, caring man you are. Believe me Joe, it's been a long time since I had those feelings for anyone."

"Look at me," she said softly. He did. "You've shown me nothing but kindness since the first time I met you. After all, you were the very first customer who ever left a thirty dollar tip!"

Joe smiled broadly.

"Yeah, but you didn't take it!" he joked. Then he grew serious. "Listen Angel, I want to thank you for the way you walked out of that club with me tonight. Holding my arm in front of all those people. You've got guts. It made me feel good!"

"That's because you are good! You're a good man, Joe Morrelli."

She put her arms around his neck and moved her face towards his, her eyes had a look of tenderness he'd never seen before. She closed them slowly as she kissed him gently, yet passionately.

He wrapped her in his arms and pulled her body against him. She did not resist in any way, but moved willingly. He'd waited for this moment for so long, wondering just what it would be like. Now he knew. It was all he'd expected and more. Joe put his face on her shoulder and held her tightly.

"Oh, Angel," he said, "I hope you meant that."

"I think you know I did."

He kissed her cheek and then moved to her mouth once more. A long, lingering kiss as he fondled her gently. Then he held her tightly in his arms again, not wanting to let go. He knew now, more than ever before, what it was like to really need someone. As he reluctantly released her and said "Goodnight", Joe Morrelli knew he was falling in love with Angela Kenny.

Life was good over the next few weeks for Joe and he was happy. The more he thought about Angela, the more he knew in his heart she was the one for him. However, Joe was a passionate man who liked to show his feelings but Angela never got carried away and she never let him, although there were times when he wanted to! Angela's kisses were always warm and tender but he knew if she would just let her emotions go, he could teach her to be a little more uninhibited. But there was plenty of time for that. He was pleased that things were going well for him at the moment and it showed. Joe was always in high spirits!

Frankie and Al got some extra time off and he was letting Rooney handle some of his business deals. It was his way of showing his friend that he had confidence in his judgement, and Rooney liked that.

One afternoon, Joe had some time on his hands so he decided to go over to Westmere Avenue and pay Angela a visit. He dressed casually and as Al had gone to see his elderly parents, Joe took one of the smaller cars and drove over, himself. When he arrived, Agnes opened the door.

"Mr Morrelli! How nice to see you. Come on in."

He followed her through to the sitting room.

"How are you doing, Agnes? Is Angel around?"

"No, she's at college. Won't you sit down? Can I get you something? Coffee maybe?"

Agnes couldn't help but fuss when visitors called.

"No, really I'm fine. Thanks."

They both sat down and there was a momentary silence. Then Joe spoke.

"Actually, Agnes, maybe it's as well Angel isn't here. It gives me a chance to talk with you."

He looked quite serious as he joined his hands and leaned forward.

"Agnes, I like Angel a lot and I think she likes me. She's very young, I know that, but when I'm with her it's so easy for me to forget that I'm twice her age. But what I'd really like to know is what you think, about me I mean. After all, she is your daughter."

Agnes studied him for a few seconds.

"I never interfered with Sheila, Mr Morrelli, I'm not going to do it with Angela. If she likes you, then that's all that matters."

"But how do you feel about the age difference?"

"Well I must admit I always thought she'd end up dating a College student like herself, or perhaps a teacher of some sort. But it just goes to show, you never can tell. The age difference does bother you, though, doesn't it?"

Joe nodded.

"Yeah, I guess it does. You see, Agnes, I think I'm in love with Angel."

"Does she know?"

"No, I haven't told her because I don't really know how she feels about me. I don't know if she could ever love me the way I love her. I think that might be asking too much. But I want you to know how I feel. It's only right you should."

Agnes leaned forward and placed her hand on his.

"Well, you've asked me what I think and I'm going to tell you. I don't mind about your age. You've been good to Angela and if she were to fall in love with you the age difference would never occur to her anyway. But give her time, Mr Morrelli, she's not like most other girls. What I mean is, she never ran around. Her head was always buried in books. Oh, I'm not saying she didn't have boyfriends – of course she did! But what I am trying to say is that you're a man of the world, Mr Morrelli. Angela has never experienced life the way you have, especially with the opposite sex."

"That's what I like about her, Agnes, amongst other things. And I want you to know I do respect her for it."

"Well, then, I have no complaints. So if you're both happy to see each other, then I think you should just wait and see what happens. After all, you're an Italian, you should know Rome wasn't built in a day! Besides, you're good for her and you'd be good to her. Given time you just might get what you hope for. Who knows?"

Joe got up smiling. At least he had Agnes's approval. Now all he needed was Angela's love and life would be complete!

"What time do her classes end?"

"About four o'clock."

"You won't tell her I've been here?"

"Don't worry, Mr Morrelli, your secret's safe with me!"

Joe hesitated.

"Agnes, would you call me Joe? I'd like it better if you did."

She smiled and nodded.

"Well I suppose we've known each other long enough for that and it does sound more friendly."

"Good, I'll see myself out. Take care, Agnes."

She watched until he reached the front door, then called out after him, "Goodbye… Joe."

As he got into the car, he checked his watch. It was 3.40. he decided to drive to the college to meet Angela. Maybe they could go somewhere for a cup of coffee. He smiled to himself. She'll be surprised to see him in an ordinary car and even more surprised to see him driving it!

Joe stopped the car across the street from the College and waited. Shortly after four o'clock the students began to leave the building. Almost ten minutes had passed when he finally saw Angela but she wasn't alone. She was accompanied by a young man and they were talking and laughing. They came out through the main gate and stood together. Angela was wearing jeans and a sweater and carried her books in her arms. Her hair hung loosely around her back and shoulders and every now and then she'd sweep it back with her hand.

Joe noticed that the young man was in his late twenties, well built and very handsome. He was dressed smartly, yet casually and he seemed to be on really good terms with Angela. Joe felt a pang of jealousy. They looked like an ideal couple. The young man handed her a slip of paper and she started writing on it. After she's finished and handed it back to him, he smiled and gave her a quick hug. Joe thought she must have given him her address and telephone number. No wonder he looked happy!

It never dawned on him until now that Angela could met someone like that at school, but she had, someone like herself. Intelligent, studious, attractive – young! He knew just by looking at the two of them together, that this young man was far more suited to her than he could ever be. Joe Morrelli felt as though his whole world was falling apart. How could he have been so stupid to think that Angela Kenny would want a man his age, when she could have one her own. Eventually, they parted company and walked in different directions. Suddenly, the young man turned and called out,

"Angela, what time would suit?"

She looked around and answered,

"About eight thirty or nine,"

Then they both smiled and waved to each other. Joe sat and watched her walk away. He didn't move. He felt so bad. The only thing he was glad about, was that Al wasn't there with him to witness any of it. If he had, he'd have told Frankie and Rooney. Joe would never have lived it down – especially in front of Rooney! No wonder Angela never got passionate with him. She was keeping that for someone else! All this time she'd been leading him on. Letting him think she really liked him. It was plain she had a date with another man, he'd heard it with his own ears. Joe was very upset. This young girl had taken him for a fool and he didn't like that. The hurt soon turned to anger as he thought of someone else making love to her. Doing all the things he's longed to do. As soon as Angela was out of sight he started the car and drove off, determined to find out more about what was going on behind his back.

For the rest of the evening, Joe couldn't settle. In his mind, he kept going over everything he'd seen and heard. He wandered aimlessly around the house, ending up in the bedroom lying on top of the bed, in deep thought. Firstly, Angela had told him she'd had a boyfriend back home. A student, just like the young man he'd seen earlier that day. Secondly, Agnes had admitted that she always thought Angela would go for someone like herself. And thirdly, when it came to having something in common, Joe and Angela were worlds apart. Yes, the whole thing was starting to add up. They only thing that still remained a mystery was, why was she still going out with him? That was the big question, Joe wanted an answer to. Maybe she wanted to get on in life and decided to use him to further her career. There could be a dozen reasons. The more he thought about it, the more he realised the only way to get answers and find out the truth, was to ask Angela herself. Maybe there was a perfectly good explanation for what happened today. Joe made his mind up to go to 'The Safe Haven' that night and ask her.

Joe arrived at 'The Safe Haven' at round ten o'clock. He walked through the entrance hall and just as he reached the dining area, he caught sight of Angela. She was sitting at a table in the corner talking and laughing, and there next to her was the same young man he'd seen that day at the college.

Joe's heart sank as he stood hidden and unnoticed behind one of the wood and glass panels. They weren't on their own. There were others at the table but he never gave them a second glance. His eyes were fixed firmly on Angela and her companion. "It's definitely the same guy!" he thought. "Only this time he's wearing a suit."

Angela was wearing the cream lace dress she had on the night he sent Rooney to check up on her. No wonder Rooney had been impressed. Joe could see for himself how beautiful she looked. He could feel the disappointment and resentment starting to build up within him and it was as if he was seeing every movement in slow motion.

He watched as Angela rose from her chair, smiling. She began to leave the table but the young man also rose, grabbed her hand and pulled her gently back towards him. He smiled as he kissed her, to the laughter and applause of the others. That was it! Joe had seen enough and he didn't want to see any more. He stormed out of the 'The Safe Haven' angry. So angry he was ready to explode. He decided there and then that Angela's friend from college would probably get further in one night than he's done in months!

Maybe the same had applied to Michael Conway! But more than anything, Joe was deeply hurt. After all this time he finally discovered that Angela Kenny wasn't as innocent as she pretended to be. She had played him along and was like most other women – out for what she could get. Well, as he'd always maintained, nobody made a fool out of Joe Morrelli, and Angela would soon find that out!

He sent Al home and headed for the nearest bar. He was going to stay there until he got drunk enough to put what he'd just seen out of his mind and try to put Angela Kenny out of his heart. It was going to take more than alcohol to do that. The pain and jealousy he felt was so consuming, he knew he was hopelessly in love with this woman.

Angela hadn't seen Joe for a couple of days until he walked into 'The Safe Haven' that afternoon, un-announced. She and Freddie were doing a stock take of all the wines and spirits needed for that week. As Joe strode up to her, she smiled.

"Hi."

Instead of greeting her, he took her hand and gripping it tightly, pulled her away form the table.

"I want to talk to you!" he snapped, walking her halfway down the dining area. Freddie made a quick exit into the lounge bar. Finally, Joe stopped and let go of her hand. She could see he was angry.

"Joe, what is it? What's wrong?" she pleaded.

"Is there something you want to tell me?"

"No, I don't think so."

"Are you sure about that?"

"O.k." said Joe nodding his head, "let me help you out here. Are you seeing someone else?"

"What are you talking about?"

"I'll tell you what I'm talking about. I came in here the other night and I saw you at that table over there, with a young guy. He was holding your hand and he kissed you. And you were smiling at him – like you wanted more!"

"You were here?"

"Yeah, I was here. And I saw the whole thing."

"But Joe, I can explain…"

"Oh Really? Well let me explain something to you. I don't like anyone going out with me and having someone else on the side!"

"What!!" Angela's temper was starting to rise.

"You heard!"

"Oh, I see. It's alright for you to do it but it's not alright for anyone else!"

"What do you mean by that?" Joe's voice was full of anger.

"You have Antonia on the side, don't you?"

"That's different. A man has needs."

"And a woman doesn't, I suppose. We're not allowed to have needs. You think it's quite alright to go out with me one night and sleep with Antonia the next. You think by keeping us both happy, you're in the clear. Well let me tell you something, Joe Morrelli, I thought you were different!"

By this time Angela was yelling at him. "I even thought you were special! But you're just like every other man- you're all self. And worse than that, you're a user. You use me and you use Antonia. But that doesn't matter to you, does it? Just as long as you get what you want!"

Joe was ready to explode.

"How do you know about Antonia?" he demanded.

"Oh, come on," replied Angela, a little calmer than before. "I might be young, but I'm not stupid. If you'd stopped seeing Antonia Flemming because of me, she'd have paid me a visit long before now."

"O.k.," he admitted, waving his hands around, "I still sleep with her – but only because I'm not getting anywhere with you! Don't you think you're carrying this innocent act a bit far? I only went to Antonia out of respect for you!" now Joe was yelling at her. "I've always treated you with respect! But you know something maybe I was wrong. Maybe I'm the one being used. Maybe respect isn't what you really wanted from me and I was too blind to see it. I guess you thought if you played hard to get for long enough, I'd set you up in a nice little apartment, pay all the bills. That way you could be Joe Morrrelli's mistress – and still have you young boyfriends. Satisfaction all round!!"

Angela stared at him. That remark wounded her deeply. She could hardly believe what he'd said to her.

"My God!" she exclaimed, "is that what you really think of me?"

When Joe didn't answer she composed herself, saying, "I don't think we should see each other again. Go back to Antonia, Joe, you belong with her. I guess you always have."

"Yeah well, at least she's not frightened of her emotions. She shows she cares."

"Yes, she does," Angela nodded. "In the only way she knows how! I'm just sorry I wasted so much of your time without knowing what you really wanted from me."

He turned and walked away but she followed. Gripping his arm she stopped him and stared into his face, "No doubt this means I'll be fired for being 'over friendly' with the customers. After all, that is your house rule, isn't it Mr Morrelli?"

Joe stared at her for a few seconds. Then looking down at her hand, he pulled his arm away. "And why should I do that, Miss Kenny?" he asked sarcastically. "After all, it's your job to keep the customers happy. That's what you do best!"

As she watched him leave the restaurant, Angela broke down in tears. Freddie came through to console her. He's heard that last remark. Putting his arm around her shoulder he said, "Don't cry, Angela, he didn't mean it. He's upset."

She shook her head.

When Joe got outside he stood on the sidewalk for a few moments, pondering what to do next. He was angry and upset, not to mention hurt, at some of the things Angela had said to him. He got into the car and told Al to drive home. He sat deep in thought, not uttering another word. Al thought it best to keep quiet.

On arriving back at the house he opened the front door and called out,

"Evie!"

"Yes Mr Joe."

"If anyone wants me, tell them I'm not to be disturbed – and I mean anyone!"

"Yes Mr Joe."

Evie emerged from the kitchen, drying her hands on a towel. She was concerned. She sensed something serious had happened. She watched as Joe slammed the door of the study behind him and locked it from the inside.

He poured himself a large scotch and sat in the leather chair. Leaning his elbows on the desk he covered his face with his hands. After a few moments his anger subsided and guilt crept in. he uncovered his face, revealing two sad eyes with tears beginning to build. He blinked hard and brushed them away. He knew he'd gone too far with Angela Kenny and said a lot of hurtful things to her, especially the part about her wanting to be his mistress. He could have bitten his tongue out there and then. She had said some hurtful things to him but, the sad part was, the more Joe thought about them the more he knew they were true! He, on the other hand, had said things that weren't true. He wanted to hurt her just the way he'd been hurt the other night. He lifted the glass to his mouth and drank the scotch in one go. Joe knew that after today, he had lost the one thing that mattered most to him – the only woman he had ever really loved. And it had all happened though his own stupid jealousy!

A man only ever meets one Angela Kenny in a lifetime – and that's if he's lucky! Joe Morrelli had met her. What was tearing him apart now was the fact that he'd not held on to her. He'd ruined everything. He sat alone in the study, a sad figure, his hopes and dreams disappearing like the scotch in the bottom of his glass!

Nearly two weeks later the elections were held in New York and Eugene O'Brien won. He'd gotten so many Irish and Italian votes, he swept the board and was now officially known as Congressman O'Brien. Angela watched the result on T.V. and was delighted for him. She liked him. By all accounts he was a decent family man and a man for all people. The people, in return, had made him their choice.

On arriving for work, Freddie called her into the office. He was jumping around like a scalded cat.

"Angela, did Mr Morrelli call you?"

"No, I'm probably the last person he'd call. Why"

"He's throwing a party for Congressman O'Brien and he wants to have it here."

"When?"

"Tomorrow night."

"What? Mr Barrett, that's very short notice."

"I know. But I wasn't going to be the one to tell him! What are we going to do?"

Angela sat down and thought hard.

"Well, we'll have to close all day tomorrow to get ready."

Freddie nodded in agreement.

"Mr Barrett, it seems to me there's only one way round all this. May I make a suggestion?"

"Oh, please do Angela!"

"If we put some of the larger tables together along one side of the dining area we could lay out a hot and cold buffet. The chefs could carve while the guests help themselves. That way the rest of the staff can tend the tables and see to the drinks. And we can help out. What do you think?"

"I think it's a wonderful idea!" Freddie sighed with relief.

Angela got up and opened the door.

"We'll have to order some of the food and get the staff organised."

"Angela, there's something else."

"Oh?"

"Yes. Mr Morrelli wants to know if we can provide some music and maybe decorate the place a little. You know, with signs of congratulations …or…something…"

Freddie's voice faded as Angela gave an icy stare.

"And what does Mr Morrelli think we're going to use for all this – a magic wand?"

She stormed out slamming the door.

Freddie turned his eyes up towards the ceiling. He knew whatever Mr Morrelli had said to her that day, was still causing her to smart. He just hoped she'd hold her temper until the party was over.

The next day was a hectic one but by the time all the tasks were completed, 'The Safe Haven' looked really well. The last thing to be put in place was a huge banner. Two delivery men brought it and, under Angela's supervision, hung it across the dining area in full view from the entrance hall. It had 'Cead Mile Failte' written in green, edged with gold on a white background. Underneath it was translated, 'A Hundred Thousand Welcomes.' A large green shamrock at each side completed the spectacle. Anglea had hired the banner from a department store that catered for the St. Patrick's Day Parade. She had provided the music too. A group of musicians in their late twenties and thirties who played at the college dances. Her teacher had recommended them to her as she wanted music to suit the age group of Gene O'Brien and his many friends.

When all the preparations were finalised, everyone went home to get some rest before the party.

Freddie and Angela were the last to leave.

"You did a great job, Angela," praised Freddie. "I couldn't have managed it without you. Mr Morrelli will be pleased."

"I didn't do it to please Mr Morrelli!" she insisted. "I did it for Mr O'Brien. After all," she continued, pointing to the banner and smiling, "I'm Irish too!"

It was 9 O'clock. Freddie stood in his black suit, white shirt and black bow tie. Angela was at his side. She wore a long rich green velvet evening dress that clung to her body and was held up by two thin straps. One side of the dress has a slit that came up to the knee, helping to reveal a pair of rich green velvet shoes. She'd hired the outfit for that one night. She thought the colour appropriate....

The sides of her hair were lifted up high and fastened, allowing the rest of her curls to hang down her back, shining in the bright lights. Her makeup was done to perfection. Not too much. Just enough to give her a natural, radiant glow. She knew what kind of crowd to expect, so she'd gone to great lengths to make sure she'd blend in. the only thing she wasn't looking forward to was seeing Joe Morrelli.

Freddie and Angela looked at each other as the sound of cars stopping and approaching voices could be heard. The doors were opened and in they came. Freddie rushed to greet them and on giving Angela the signal, she waved to the band who started playing "For He's a Jolly Good Fellow". Gene O'Brien entered the dining area with his wife, Kate, on his arm, followed by Joe Morrelli and Antonia Flemming, Jeff Lang and his wife, Alan Bailey and his girlfriend, Reuben and Miriam Goldman and Judge Thompson. Others followed. On seeing the banner, Gene held his hand up and everyone stopped in their tracks. He studied it for a few seconds and then grinned broadly. Angela went over and took his hand.

"Cead Mile Failte, Congressman O'Brien and many, many congratulations!"

"I don't believe it," he replied, gazing at her. "Hey Joe, I've just walked into a restaurant owned by an Italian and what do I see?" he pointed to the banner. "Irish greeting, shamrock and this beautiful colleen speaking to me in my own native tongue. I think I've died and gone to heaven!"

The company roared with laughter while Joe assured his friend,

"We aim to please!"

"Thank you, little lady, for all this. You've made my night."

He then introduced her to his wife.

Angela greeted all the guests, shaking their hands and chatting to them. She never once looked at Joe Morrelli but she knew he was looking at her. She could feel his gaze as he stood a few feet away from her, talking to Judge Thompson.

Antonia came forward, looking as though she'd just stepped out of 'Vogue Magazine'.

Angela smiled,

"Miss Flemming, how nice to see you. What a beautiful dress."

"Yes, I think so too." She replied. "Joe bought it for me. Didn't you darling?" she called across to him. "He's so thoughtful!"

Joe and Angela's eyes met briefly as he walked by, Antonia taking his arm. He looked most uncomfortable as he made his way through the crowd, Antonia in tow.

Being the host, he sat with his guest of honour and both men chatted happily. But every now and then he'd glance towards Angela. She looked stunning. His eyes took in every inch of her, every movement. He couldn't help but notice how people responded to her. They genuinely liked this young Irish woman. She had a way about her. When the last of the guests had been settled the band started to play and the waitresses came along with trays of champagne for every table. It wasn't long before the party was in full swing. Everyone seemed to be enjoying themselves and many couples were heading for the temporary dance floor.

Angela made a tour of the tables making sure the guests were all well taken care of. She stopped off at Gene O'Brien's table.

"Is everything alright Mr O'Brien?" she asked.

"Just great! You could have a job with me anytime. That is ...." turning to Joe "... if my good friend here doesn't mind the opposition."

Angela kept her eyes fixed on him as she smiled, "I just might take you up on that sometime."

Gene O'Brien sensed something was wrong. Joe Morrelli couldn't take his eyes off this young woman, yet she was trying very hard to avoid looking at him. He leaned over and quietly said, "Hey Joe, isn't that the girl you introduced me to one night in Ralph's place?"

Joe nodded.

"Well, what's going on? Are you having an affair with her?"

Joe shook his head, "No. I took her out a few times that's all. But not anymore."

"What happened?" He put his arm round Joe's shoulder.

"She's too young for me, Gene. It wouldn't work out."

"Are you serious! Since when did anything like that stop you? Come on Joe, you must admit she's one of the best looking women in the place. And with a figure like that I bet she'd be one hell of a lay. Don't be a fool – go for it!"

Joe smiled, but inside he was hurting.

Angela was standing at the entrance of the dining area tapping her feet to the music when a hand touched her shoulder. She turned round.

"Rooney!! Am I glad to see you!"

"How's it going Angela?"

"Very well, considering we didn't get much notice."

Judge Thompson had taken Antonia onto the floor to dance, even though the music was quite fast.

"Can you jive, Rooney?"

"I can try."

"Come on." She took his hand, "Why should they have all the fun."

On their way to dance they passed Joe's table but Rooney was so busy looking at Angela, he didn't even notice Joe was there. They started to jive. Angela had always been a good dancer but Rooney gave her quite a surprise. He could move, too. They were so good together that many of the guests applauded. Angela felt really happy and it showed. She and Rooney smiled and laughed as they twisted and turned in time to the music.

Gene studied them both for a minute and then turned to Joe.

"You know what I see over there, Joe? Breeding material! He's Irish, she's Irish. Put those two together and you'll have strong sons and beautiful daughters for Ireland. That is, of course, unless you'd like strong sons and beautiful daughters for yourself! Who else are you going to leave all your money to?"

Joe stared at Angela as Gene continued.

"You won't do any better than her, Joe. Think about it. A man's got to settle down sometime."

Joe didn't answer but he knew Gene O'Brien was right. Angela Kenny was a beautiful woman and for Joe Morrelli, the only woman.

He had hoped that tonight they'd become friends again and more. He wanted desperately to talk to her. But he knew she would not forgive or forget so easily, all the hurtful things he'd said to her. As he sat watching her in Rooney's arms, he was beginning to think that this party hadn't been such a good idea after all!

Antonia and Judge Thompson returned to their seats. Antonia wasn't pleased.

"Joe, I thought you told me the Irish girl you hired was young?"

"She is."

"Well, the way you described her I though she had pigtails and freckles! I didn't expect that!"

She waved her hand towards Angela, who was just leaving the dance floor. Joe was getting a bit riled. "What's the matter, Antonia? Are you jealous of every one who's attractive or just her? Or is it because she works for me?"

"I hope that's all she does for you – darling! I've seen the way you've been looking at her all night."

Gene O'Brien held his glass up to his mouth and smiled into it as he listened intently.

"That's enough!" snapped Joe.

"Well, she's hardly your type. I mean, I bet she doesn't own that dress she's wearing. Anyway, why would you want someone like her when you can have me?" she smiled sweetly.

"Breeding!" replied Joe.

Antonia looked totally bewildered.

"Breeding? Oh , you mean race horses?"

"It's o.k. Antonia, you wouldn't understand."

Gene gave a loud laugh and shook his head.

"Jesus," he whispered to Joe, "how did she get on Broadway?"

"With a great deal of help!" came the reply.

"I can well believe it!"

Both men roared with laughter as Antonia glared at them.

"What's the big joke?" she asked. "Did I miss something?"

Neither man could answer!

A little while later, Rooney came over to the table and threw his arms around Gene.

"Congratulations, Congressman!"

Joe looked up at him.

"Are you enjoying yourself, Rooney?"

"I'm having a great time."

"Why don't you sit down and join the company?"

"No thanks, Joe. I think I'll go over and chat to Angela."

Joe threw him a sarcastic glance.

"Lucky you!"

Rooney moved over and bent down beside him.

"Are you two still not friends?"

"Friends? That would be aiming high, seeing as how she won't even look at me! You know something, Rooney, I don't know why Agnes was so worried about her back home. She could take on anybody and win."

"What do you mean?"

"I mean she doesn't need a gun. She can blow you away just by pretending you don't exist! I tell you, that is one stubborn woman."

Rooney stood up.

"Well, maybe that's what you like about her, Joe. She won't do the running."

"Yeah well, two can play at that game. If that's the way she wants it, that's o.k. by me."

Rooney knew by Joe's voice he really didn't mean it. But he decided to leave things as they were and went over to join Angela and Freddie.

Joe was called to make a speech.

He got up and proceeded to tell everyone about how well he knew Gene O'Brien, how good a man he was and how well Joe had supported him in the elections.

Angela looked at Rooney and Freddie.

"That's typical!" she said. "He starts out by praising Mr O'Brien and ends up praising himself."

Joe went on and on about how Gene was going to help toughen up the laws and clean up the streets, and how he was going to help him fight crime.

Of course, this was all for Angela's benefit. He was trying to remind her in his own subtle way, of the night she'd been attacked. Angela glanced at the banner.

"So much for the luck of the Irish."

"Why?" asked Rooney.

"Congress gets Gene O'Brien – we get Humphrey Bogart!"

She stared at Joe, as Rooney and Freddie laughed uncontrollably.

"Jesus, Angela," Rooney said, eventually, "Sometimes you remind me of Joe!"

"Well, I wish someone would remind Joe to sit down. My feet are killing me!"

A few minutes later Joe did sit down. Gene O'Brien took over. He thanked Joe for the party, the guests for coming and everyone who gave him their votes, time and effort. He finished off with the promises that he'd do a good job. As the band played, "When Irish Eyes are Smiling", he waved to the crowd and took a bow.

It came to the last dance of the evening. Rooney took on a serious tone.

"You know, Angela, Joe's very cut up that you didn't make friends with him tonight."

"Oh really? And does that look like a man who's very cut up?"

She nodded towards the dance floor. Rooney looked and saw Joe and Antonia with their arms wrapped around each other. He could have cheerfully gripped him by the neck but then no one knew Joe better than Rooney. When Joe enjoyed a good night out he always liked to round it off in the company of an attractive woman. Rooney asked Angela for the last dance, watched from a distance by Joe. After a few moments, Rooney felt a tap on his shoulder. It was Gene O'Brien.

"Mind if I cut in, Rooney?"

Rooney reluctantly stepped aside as Gene held his arms out to Angela.

"Hey, Irish," he grinned, "what about us two kindred spirits taking the floor?"

Angela smiled as he took her in his arms.

"It was a great night and I want to thank you."

"I'm glad you enjoyed it, Mr O'Brien."

"You know, Joe's a lucky guy to have you working for him. He thinks a lot of you."

"I don't know about that!"

"Well, I do. You're doing well here but you could do even better. Joe's a good guy, one of the best. Sure, he can be a bit hot tempered sometimes – even stubborn, but then so can we. The Irish are well known for it but it doesn't make us any less likeable. We all do things we regret, know what I mean?"

Angela nodded as Gene continued,

"I'd like to see Joe with someone like you. You'd be good for him. He deserves the best. You both do. After all, he isn't getting any younger."

He looked over his shoulder at Joe and winked. Joe nodded and smiled. Here were two people Gene liked a lot. He'd like to see them find happiness, especially with each other.

The music ended and the guests got ready to leave. Angela joined Freddie in the entrance hall to say goodnight and thank them for coming. Eventually, Gene and Kate and Joe and Antonia were ready to go too. Gene took Angela's hand and kissed it.

"Remember little lady, don't let these Italians get the upper hand. We Irish just let them think they're the boss, it keeps them happy. But they never had a famine in Italy. If we can come through that and make good, what can we not do?"

"Oh, Gene," laughed Kate, "not the famine again!"

Gene turned to his old friend.

"Joe I have to hand it to you, you couldn't have found a better woman for the job if you'd gone all the way to Ireland yourself. Look after her. She's worth her weight in gold."

He returned to Angela. "Goodnight, sweet lady, I had a ball. Anytime I can do anything for you just get in touch with Eugene Patrick O'Brien. We Irish have to stick together."

"Thank you, I'll remember that."

The foursome made their way out chatting loudly. The party was over and had been a great success. Angela felt very relieved but very tired. She looked at her watch. It had gone 2.30am. she had spent most of the day on her feet helping to get things ready and the last five and a half hours walking around tables fetching and carrying for the guests. What she really wanted to do was sleep but the staff had worked hard too and they were due a well deserved break. Angela watched them clearing the tables and thought for a while. Then she turned and went into the kitchen, reached for a large white apron and carefully put it on. She started to lay out the unused food as a buffet for the staff. When she's finished she took her purse and went in search of Freddie.

"Mr Barrett I'd like to buy a bottle of our best champagne.

"What for, Angela?"

"For the staff. They've earned it."

"I tell you what, there should be an unopened bottle in the dining room. Why don't you take it?"

"Thank you, but I'd rather pay for it myself."

"It's very expensive."

"That doesn't matter. Please take what it costs out of that."

Angela took all the money from her purse and gave it to Freddie. He did as she asked and Angela carried the large bottle back to the kitchen. Then she came into the dining area.

"Just leave everything and come into the kitchen," she called. "Now it's your turn to be served."

Everyone stopped what they were doing and followed her.

During this time Joe and Gene stood outside 'The Safe Haven' in deep conversation. Antonia and Kate were waiting in the limousine.

"Listen to me Joe," said Gene, "Don't be a fool. If you walk away from what you really want in this world you'll regret it for the rest of your life."

"You don't understand, Gene. It's not as simple as that."

"Do you want her?"

"Yes I do."

"Do you love her?"

"Yes I do."

"Then let her know – any way you have to! If she won't let you tell her, then show her. Take a tip from an old married man. Believe me, Joe, it works every time. What have you got to loose? Let her know, for Christ's sake, before it's too late!"

Joe opened the door of the limousine.

"Al, take Antonia home. I'll get a cab."

Antonia tried to clamber out. "Joe, I want you to come home with me!"

He grabbed her arm and put her back into the seat.

"I won't be long," he assured her. " I have to see Freddie about something."

Gene nodded and got in beside her. Their plan had been put into action!

"Al, you can drop Mr and Mrs O'Brien off on the way."

As the car pulled away, Gene gave Joe the thumbs up signal from the rear window. When they were out of sight, Joe took a deep breath and went back inside. The place was deserted.

Making his way past the empty office, he wondered where everyone had gone to but as he approached the kitchen there was the sound of voices and laughter. He paused and looking through the half opened door he saw Angela, wearing the white apron, serving food to the staff as they all sat around the table. When she'd finished, she pulled over a chair and joined them. She sat almost facing him and Joe could see her clearly.

"Aren't you having anything Angela? Asked Cindy.

"No. I'm too tired to eat."

"You looked really well out there tonight. That's a beautiful dress."

"Yes it is, but it has to go back to the store today."

"You mean it's not yours?" Lisa asked her, surprised. Angela shook her head.

"No, I only hired it. And that cost me a small fortune. There's no way I could afford to buy a dress like this!"

Just at that moment Freddie came along, humming to himself. Joe looked at him and put his finger up to his lips. Freddie nodded and tip-toed away.

"Did you see some of those dresses out there tonight?" Cindy asked, reaching for the salt. "They must have cost a half a years wages."

"Never mind that," said Jimmy the young kitchen boy, "did you see all that food? Hey Angela, can I have a doggy bag?"

Lisa shook her head.

"Here he goes again!"

Everyone laughed.

"Well, somebody might as well eat it," he protested. Angela reached over and patted him on the back.

"Don't worry, Jimmy, I'll make up a doggy bag for you before you go."

"Are you sure you've got a dog?" one of the other girls asked. "I think you're having us on."

Angela looked at him and winked.

"Of course he's got a dog. Isn't that right Jimmy?"

"Yeah, that's right, it's a guard dog."

"How come you need a guard dog in a tenement apartment?" Asked Lisa. "Loan sharks?"

The laughter continued, with both Jimmy and Angela joining in.

"Oh come on," giggled Angela, "leave the poor boy alone!"

On hearing this, Jimmy got up and went over to her. He knelt down on his knee.

"Angela, would you marry me – and be my mother?"

She raised her hand to her heart and in a dramatic voice resembling Antonia said,

"You mean, your not after my body?"

"No, just your doggy bags!" he grinned.

She gave him a gentle smack on the back of his head.

"Sit down and finish your meal!" she ordered.

Joe was enjoying all this so much, he was smiling.. Angela got up, took the bottle of champagne from the cooler and started to pour it out into glasses.

"Where did you get that?" asked Cindy, as she watched it bubble and sparkle. "Was it left behind?"

"No."

"I hope not. If Mr Barrett sees us drinking this, he'll go mad."

"No he won't," piped Jimmy, "not if we all drink it quickly. Then he won't know."

Angela smiled.

"He knows all about it. I bought it tonight."

"It must have cost you, Angela. Why did you do it?" Lisa was puzzled.

"Well, you deserve it. You all worked very hard and besides, today is my birthday."

She checked her watch. "That is, yesterday was my birthday!"

Joe's smile faded.

Jimmy jumped to his feet.

"Angela, why didn't you say something? The band could have played a request for you."

"No, Jimmy. It was Mr O'Brien's party. It was his night."

"But it's not fair! You should have been out celebrating, or something."

Everyone agreed with him.

She touched the charm around her neck gently and gazed at the floor.

"I guess some birthdays matter more than others...."

She poured some more champagne.

"Happy birthday, Angela!!" they all said together, raising their glasses in a toast.

Lisa put her glass down on the table.

"Come on, Angela, you'll have to do a party piece for us."

"I don't think so."

"Oh yes, you will. Do something from one of those books you're always studying."

"Well.... O.k. I'll recite something."

She started off with the words:

"Friends are always there for you, when you need a helping hand. To share the good times and the bad, to care and understand......."

As she continued on everyone was silent. Joe had never heard this poem in his life before but was amazed at it's content. Angela spoke with great emotion and never faltered. It was as if the words were engraved on her heart. He studied her, wondering how she could remember it all, but she did.

When she'd finished there was a round of applause.

She smiled in appreciation.

"Now, lets have some fun before we go home!" she said, getting out of the chair and grabbing Jimmy by the arm. "We're going to do Shakespeare."

"Shakespeare?" he asked. "It sounds like a medical condition!"

"We'll do Romeo and Juliet. Cindy, you're Juliet."

"Not me! You're the one with the fancy dress, Angela."

"Alright then, I'll be Juliet." She took off the apron.

"Jimmy, you're Romeo."

"Who the hell's Romeo? Never heard of the guy!"

"Well you have now."

Angela pulled Jimmy onto the floor and put him down on one knee.

"Now stay there," she warned him, "and I'll explain. You really love this girl and you're waiting in her garden just to see her. Try and look romantic! She comes out onto the balcony...."

"What's a balcony? We don't have any of them in my neighbourhood."

"Alright then, she comes out onto the fire escape. Does that suit you?"

Everyone laughed as Jimmy made faces.

Joe laughed quietly. He was seeing Angela as he'd never seen her before. Free and fun loving. The joker in the pack, making sure the people enjoyed themselves, even for a little while.

"Are you alright?" she asked, as Jimmy tried to keep his balance.

"No, I feel like an idiot!"

"You look like one!" laughed Cindy.

"Now be serious everyone. I'm about to make my entrance." Angela took a few steps, then stopped. She clasped her hands to her breast and sighed:

"Romeo, Romeo, where for art thou, Romeo?

Jimmy gazed at her romantically.

"Give me a few of those chicken legs and I'll be anywhere you want me to be!"

The whole kitchen erupted in squeals of laughter.

Jimmy rolled onto the floor, giggling. Angela knelt down beside him, slapping him playfully.

"Jimmy Peterson, you are going to be the death of me!"

Without realising it, she revealed a very tempting amount of cleavage which Joe was quick to notice.

Jimmy lay on his back.

"You know something? I'm glad I didn't have to climb that fire escape. I'm getting a better view from down here!"

Joe agreed with him.

Angela got to her feet quickly, smoothing the creases from the velvet.

"I'd better be careful with this dress," she muttered to herself. Then she continued, "O.K. , fun's over. I'm surprised Mr Barrett hasn't been in to see what all the noise is about."

"Oh, that old fart!" snapped Jimmy. "He probably thinks we're not good enough for him. Not like you, Angela."

"Now, Jimmy, watch what you say about Mr Barrett."

"Well, it's true. He's a real pain. I wouldn't get any left-overs from him."

Cindy turned to Jimmy.

"Whoever said the way to a man's heart was through his stomach, really had your number."

There was more laughter. That expensive champagne had certainly done it's job.

"Here," said Angela, "hurry up and drink the rest of this. Jimmy, you take mine."

"Don't you want it?"

"No, it gives me a headache. Just leave everything, it's too late. The other shift can clear up for us. I'll have to go and see Mr Barrett about ordering the taxis for us. I'm so tired, I just want to get home."

"Are you working tomorrow?" asked Lisa.

"No, it's my day off. It's going to take that long for me to recover. I'll be back in a minute."

As she walked towards the kitchen door, Joe quickly stepped out of sight. As her hand reached for the handle she turned and looked at her friends.

"After tonight, every time I see Eugene O'Brien on the T.V. I'll remember that he had his election party on my birthday."

She walked out of the kitchen, turned, and found herself face to face with Joe Morrelli. She was startled at first but managed to close the door so that none of the staff would see. Angela couldn't believe it was him. She thought he'd gone home with Antonia ages ago.

Neither of them spoke. Joe just stood staring at her with a serious expression on his face. Angela began to feel uncomfortable, even nervous but was trying very hard not to show it. She returned his stare with one of her own. Then she moved by him, sideways, and walked towards the lounge. He put his hand out and gripped her arm.

"I didn't know it was your birthday."

"Do you always listen to other people's conversations?"

"Only when it suits me."

Angela pulled her arm away and continued walking. Joe followed her, moving in front and blocking her way.

"Why didn't you tell me?"

Her blue eyes flashed at him.

"Why, what would you have done? Bought me a nice apartment?"

"I could have given you the night off."

"Oh no. That's one thing you couldn't have done. You needed me here tonight, to keep your guests happy. After all, that's my job. That's what I do best – remember?"

"I was wrong. What you do best is care, about people and things that really matter. Like in that poem you learned."

"Well, what I learn outside 'The Safe Haven' doesn't really concern you, Mr Morrelli."

"O.k." Joe nodded, "I can see there's no point in even trying to talk to you."

"Good!" came the reply. "Now, will you please get out of my way? I want to go home."

Angela tried to push past him but Joe grabbed her by the shoulders, tightening his grip with every second.

"You don't want to look at me. You don't want to talk to me. You don't want to be near me. O.K!! but there's something I want to do. Now you can fight me, Angel. You can scream the damn place down but I'm going to do it anyway!"

He pulled her towards him and covered her lips with his own. She struggled to break free but Joe wouldn't let her. By this time he had her pinned against the wall,, pressing the full weight of his body against hers. His strength frightened her. She was helpless as she felt his tongue search her mouth, hungrily. All his emotions were in that long, lingering kiss. Everything he felt for her. Love, passion, anger and need.

Angela could hardly breathe. She knew she couldn't fight him anymore. He was too strong. Too overpowering. As she fell into his arms, he grabbed her once more. But this time, gently and protectively. He eased his mouth away from hers and relaxed his body. Angela instinctively clung to him, breathing deeply. Joe could feel the firmness of her breasts as they heaved against him. He kissed her hair and her cheek. Then again he searched for her lips with even more passion than before. He wanted this woman and if Angela Kenny didn't know it by now, she never would. Finally, they separated and looked deep into each other's eyes. He released her and whispered,

"Happy Birthday, Angel."

Angela watched Joe walk through the entrance hall and out of the restaurant. He had never kissed her like that before. She never dreamed he could. She stood with tears in her eyes and trembling hands. She knew if she stayed at 'The Safe Haven' he would be back. Only the next time he might not stop where he did tonight – and she might not want him to! Angela was scared and confused. The feelings she had for this man went far beyond anything she'd every felt before. She gazed at the front door and decided there and then to look for another job. Angela Kenny knew in her heart the time had come to leave 'The Safe Haven and Joe Morrellli.

As he walked along the sidewalk, Joe's mind was in turmoil. After what had just happened he wanted to go home but he had told Antonia he wouldn't be long. She'd be expecting him and he knew if he didn't turn up she'd be hurt and angry. She might also suspect he was with Angela. The last thing he wanted was for Antonia to show up at 'The

Safe Haven' and cause a scene. There had been enough arguments between him and Angela without someone else causing more.

He surely hoped Gene O'Brien had given him the right advice. It was too late now if he hadn't. But Joe had to admit one thing, he had enjoyed every second of the time he'd spent with Angela tonight and he'd gladly do it all again. Everything about her turned him on. She was one very sexy young lady, even if she didn't know it. He could still feel the warmth of her mouth and body next to his. He hailed a taxi.

It was late and with any luck by now Antonia would be asleep. Joe opened the door of her apartment and quietly let himself in. The lights were on in the lounge and Antonia was pacing up and down wearing a black lace negligee and drinking a Martini.

"Where have you been?" she asked, raising her voice. "I was beginning to think you weren't coming."

"I told you, I had to see Freddie."

"What about?"

"Antonia, you know I never discuss my business. So just drop it. I'm here now, aren't I?"

She went over to the bar and poured him a large scotch. She took an extra large Martini for herself. "Was that girl there?" she asked, as she handed the glass to him. "The one everybody seems to like so much? Even Congressman O'Brien seemed quite taken with her. I suppose it's because she acts the little miss innocent. She probably tells every man she meets she's a virgin, just to get him interested. Well, she doesn't fool me! No girl keeps herself for Mr Right these days and I should know."

Joe tried to change the subject.

"Antonia, don't you think you've had enough to drink for one night?"

She sat her glass down and put her arms around him a little unsteadily. She smiled saying, "Honey, you know what drink does to me and you like it! A real man needs a real woman – not some young girl who's only out for what she can get. At least I know what to do to please you."

Antonia took Joe's hand and on leading him towards the bedroom, she giggled, "I hope you're not tired, honey!"

This was the last thing Joe wanted. He started to undress, slowly, as Antonia lay on the bed waiting for him. Before he joined her, he made an excuse to go to the bathroom and closed over the door behind him.

Joe stared at his face in the mirror. He didn't want to spend the rest of the night with Antonia but there was no way he could tell her. This was one situation he couldn't get out of. Then he heard her call,

"Joe, honey, I'm waiting......"

He stared at himself once again, then shrugged his shoulders. There was nothing else for it, he'd just have to carry it through. As he climbed onto the bed beside her he asked,

"It's been a long night, aren't you tired?"

Antonia leaned over and put her arms around his neck.

"Not yet!"

She started to kiss him, moving her body against him in all the right places. It wasn't long before he responded. Joe took her in his arms, closed his eyes and began to make love to Antonia.

However, as one embrace led to another his thoughts began to turn to Angela. It was her mouth he was kissing, her body he was caressing. He could even smell her perfume. He couldn't help himself. He was with Antonia but it was Angela's voice he heard whispering,

"I love you, Joe. I love you."

It was her sighs and cries that filled the room as he made long, passionate love. When it was over, he opened his eyes. But it wasn't Angela who lay in his arms, it was Antonia.

"Oh, Joe," she whispered, breathlessly, "you were wonderful! You were so loving and passionate – we should go to parties more often. You were always good in bed, but I can't remember a night like tonight."

Joe got up feeling very guilty. He put on his shorts and headed for the door.

"Where are you going, Joe?"

"I need a drink!"

When he arrived in the lounge he stood at the bar and leaned his elbows on it. He rubbed his face in his hands saying, "Jesus, what's happening to me?"

Was Joe Morrelli loosing his mind?

He was surprised and angry with himself because nothing like this had ever happened to him before. He poured himself a drink then sat on a chair and stared out of the window.

In the bedroom Antonia lay on the bed smiling to herself, happily. She knew tonight was different. She knew Joe was different. He had something special on his mind, she could tell. Maybe he was leading up to something – a marriage proposal, perhaps! Her face beamed with joy.

Back in the lounge, Joe was thinking long and hard. What had happened was something he had no control over. He couldn't stop it, or maybe he just didn't want to. But one thing was for sure, it wasn't fair on Angela and it certainly wasn't fair to Antonia. He did love Antonia in his own way but he knew it wasn't the right kind of love. He realised he couldn't share the rest of his life with her. He could never marry her. If he did, he'd only be playing a game of pretend and he would be miserable doing it.

No. He loved Angela Kenny. He knew it deep in his soul. She was the only woman he wanted. He would never have to pretend with her. Being with her for the rest of his life would make him the happiest man alive. To make love to her was the one thing he wanted more than anything else in the world. If he couldn't have her, he didn't want any other woman, even Antonia.

Joe wanted to marry Angela, to take care of her always. But would she let him? Would she love him enough to bear his name and his children? He didn't know but decided to find out.

Antonia's voice came from the bedroom, "Joe honey, come back to bed…"

He returned to her but instead of taking up where he left off, he started to get dressed.

"Where are you going now?" she demanded.

"Home! I'm tired and I've got a lot of things to take care of today."

He bent over and kissed her on the cheek saying, "You could do with some sleep yourself."

"When will I see you again?"

"I'll call you."

When he reached the bedroom door, he stopped and looked back. As he watched Antonia drift off to sleep he felt both sadness and regret. They had had a long affair but that's all it ever was and all it ever could be. Joe wanted more. He wanted marriage and a family with a woman who would want the same. That someone could never be Antonia. The theatre was her one, true love. As he left the apartment he knew there could only be one Mrs Morrelli and her name was Angela.

When she arrived home, Angela went straight to bed. She took care not to waken Agnes. All she wanted to do was sleep. But she couldn't. Lying in the darkness, she kept going over all the things that had happened at the party, especially afterwards with Joe Morrelli. He had been a totally different man to the one she had come to know. Angela realised for the first time that there was another side to Joe, one that left her feeling at odds with herself. If he had deliberately set out to make an impression, he had succeeded. Not only did she care for him emotionally, but physically, and this frightened her. For the first time she felt awkward and embarrassed by her own lack of experience. She tossed and turned, full of self doubt. How could someone like him want someone like her? How could she ever satisfy a man such as Joe Morrelli? How could she even begin to compete with the kind of women he was used to? The fact was, she couldn't, and she knew it. So she made up her mind she wasn't going to try. Angela would be doing Joe a favour if she left 'The Safe Haven'. After all, out of sight – out of mind! If he didn't see her he'd soon forget about her and they could both go their separate ways. It would be best for everyone.

As soon as it was light, Angela got up and ventured to the kitchen for some coffee. A while later, Agnes appeared and found Angela in her dressing gown, carefully folding the evening dress and putting it and the shoes back into the large box.

"Angela, what are you doing up so early?" She asked, surprised.

"I couldn't sleep," came the reply. "Besides, I have to leave this outfit back."

"You have all day to do that."

There was silence as Agnes studied her daughter.

"Angela, are you alright?"

"Yes mum, I'm fine."

"Well, you don't look fine! Did something happen last night at the party?"

Angela didn't answer, so Agnes moved closer and put her arm around her, lovingly.

"You looked so beautiful in that dress. I bet quite a few of the guests thought so, too."

Two large tears fell onto Angela's cheeks. Her mother embraced her tightly and grew concerned.

"Angela, what happened? Did someone say something to you?"

"No."

"Well then, did someone do something to you?"

Angela returned Agnes's embrace.

"Yes."

"Who was it?"

"It was Joe Morrelli. Oh Mum, I did try to stay away from him but he wouldn't let me."

"What did he do?"

"At first he tried to talk to me and when that didn't work, he grabbed me and started to kiss me. But it wasn't like the way he kissed me before. It was different. I can't explain it. I only know I've never felt this way before. Mum, I think I'm in love with him."

Agnes cradled her, relieved that the situation wasn't more serious.

"Angela, Angela, is that so terrible?"

"It is for me. I never expected all this to happen. He's my boss and my friend. He can have any woman he wants. Why me? What can I possibly give him? Oh mum, I feel such a fool, especially after all those things he said to me a couple of weeks ago. He hurt me so much."

"I know. But maybe he's had time to think about it. Maybe he realised just how wrong he was. In his own way he might be trying to say 'sorry'. Trying to put things right between you."

"Well, it doesn't really matter," replied Angela, drying her wet cheeks.

"What do you mean?

"I don't know what he wants or why he's acting this way. But I can tell you, it won't make any difference to our relationship now."

"Now Angela, don't be hasty. Did you never stop to think that he might be in love with you? He might have acted on impulse, afraid of loosing you."

Angela looked at Agnes.

"He's going to loose me anyway. I'm going to look for another job and when I get one, I'll be leaving 'The Safe Haven' for good. It's the best thing to do. Mum. The only thing."

"Do you honestly believe you can run away from your feelings?"

"Yes, I do. If I can get a job where I don't have to see him or talk to him, I'll be fine."

"And what about Joe Morrelli and his feelings?"

"He's not in love with me, not really. He won't give me a second thought when I'm gone. He's a man who has everything, mum. He doesn't need me – or my hired clothes!"

She closed the lid of the box.

Agnes sighed.

"I hope you're doing the right thing, Angela."

Angela squeezed her mother's hand gently.

"I am, I know I am. I've made up my mind and nothings going to change it."

A week passed and it was one of the longest in Joe's life. Although he hadn't seen Angela, he had hoped he'd hear from her. He didn't. His original high spirits soon reached an all time low. When he began to realise she wasn't going to be in touch, Joe became sullen and depressed around the house. He vented his moods on everyone around him, not wanting to admit his fear that the good times he and Angela had shared, had finally come to an end.

He had phoned a couple of times and always knew when it was Angela who answered the receiver was put down every time he started to speak. It was obvious she didn't want to have anything to do with him, so Joe decided to seek comfort with Antonia and go back to the 'high life'.

Antonia's new play opened on Broadway and Joe was there in the audience to lead the standing ovation. Afterwards he escorted her to a party for the cast, in the hope that he might enjoy himself. As they walked into 'The Portland Club', Joe recognised some of his old friends and associates but there were a lot of other people there he didn't know. As Antonia mingled with the guests, overjoyed by the reviews in the late editions, Joe got himself a drink and stood at the bar looking around. A little while later a very attractive young woman came up to him. She wore a very sexy evening dress that was so low at the front it left nothing to the imagination. She smiled at him, coyly.

"Hi, you're Joe Morrelli, Antonia's boyfriend."

Joe took in all the information he needed in one glance. This was one well built female!

"Do I know you?" he asked, as she sipped a glass of champagne.

"No, but you will. I'm an actress on stage. Just small parts at the moment, you understand. But I really want to be in the movies."

"Really? Well that's nice. I hope you make it."

"Well, if I had someone like you I would. You seem to know all the right people. If I could just get an introduction to a producer it would make things so much easier. After all, I hear that's how Antonia got started."

"Yeah well, it's just getting that lucky break, I suppose."

She smiled as she moved up against him, stroking the lapel of his suit with her fingers, seductively. "If someone would give me that lucky break I'd be grateful. Very grateful, if you know what I mean."

She stared into Joe's eyes and slowly ran her tongue across her lips.

"I'd do anything," she whispered.

"Anything?"

"Anything!"

She walked away looking back at him, invitingly. Judge Thompson appeared on the scene, staring after the young woman who by now had stopped a few yards away," "Hey Joe," he said in a low voice, "that's a nice piece of ass – not to mention the rest of her!"

"Yeah, she wants to be an actress."

"No kidding? Well, maybe I can help her."

"I don't think so Judge. She wants to be in the movies."

"Oh, I don't think that will be a problem."

Joe looked at him, puzzled.

"So what are you, a producer in your spare time?"

"Come on Joe," he laughed "you don't have to be a producer to know a producer. I deal with all kinds of cases. I've met a few in my time, believe me. Besides, if I give her a name it'll make her happy. Then she'll make me happy. Know what I mean?"

The Judge winked and Joe nodded his head.

"Yeah, Judge, I know exactly what you mean."

"Mind if I try?"

"Not at all, be my guest. What's a piece of ass amongst friends!"

Joe watched as Judge Thompson made his way over to her and introduced himself. They stood talking for a few minutes, then suddenly her face lit up.

"Really!" she shrieked in excitement. "You know him?"

"He must have dropped some big shots name!" Joe thought aloud.

The Judge nodded and went on talking. A few minutes later, as they left arm in arm, Judge Thompson stopped, turned around and smiled at Joe.

Joe shook his head.

"There she goes," he whispered into his glass. "Another beautiful young woman, who's just sold herself to the highest bidder for the ultimate prize – fame."

As he looked around the crowd he became lost in his own thoughts. It seemed everybody was a hustler. They all wanted something and they'd do anything to get it. They were using each other without any hesitation. Just as Joe was beginning to feel grateful for not being like them, Angela's words came back to haunt him.

"You a user. You use me and you use Antonia."

She was right! He wasn't any different to the people around him. He left the bar and made his way to the phone booth. After putting in some change, he dialled a number. Holding the receiver, he heard it ringing.

"Hello," came the voice at the other end.

Joe remained silent.

"Hello, can I help you? Who is this?"

He could hear Agnes's voice in the background.

"Angela, who is it love?"

"I don't know, there's no reply. It must be a wrong number."

Joe closed his eyes as he heard her replace the receiver. No, it wasn't a wrong number. He just wanted to hear her voice. The voice of the only woman who had never asked Joe Morrelli for anything. And he'd never given her anything except for a few bunches of flowers. One thing was for sure, he could never accuse Angela Kenny of being a user!

Although he continued with the constant round of social parties and get-togethers, Joe's heart was no longer in it. Even Antonia had noticed a change in him. He was more quiet and subdued and there were times when his thoughts seemed to be miles away. She put it down to business but there were two things that did bother her. Firstly, Joe never invited her back to his house to stay anymore. Secondly, he never went to dinner at 'The Safe Haven'. When Antonia tried to bring either subject up to him, Joe always had an excuse.

Antonia was becoming a success in her own right now. Thanks to good plays and fine casting, she was moving in different circles with people from the Arts and High Society. Joe was proud of her but he wasn't impressed by her new found friends. He found them false and boring. When it came right down to it, none of them were contented with who they were. They all wanted to be someone else. And for all their many talents, he hadn't heard an intelligent conversation take place between any of them. They were all too busy complimenting each other on how wonderful they were! He'd never heard one of these so-called actors or actresses recite anything from the Classics. They were all so wrapped up in themselves they forgot about everything else – and everybody else. Joe was becoming increasingly disenchanted with the whole charade. The 'Dah-ling' set were beginning to get to him.

He found himself thinking of Mario's and the conversations he's had there with Angela. At least they were honest and interesting. When he thought about the books she'd read and the subjects she was studying, it was obvious she had more brains than all of these other people put together. For someone who lived on Westmere Avenue, she could teach them a thing or two. He missed those conversations and he missed her company. The truth was, he missed her. But Joe Morrelli had gotten the message loud and clear. Angela didn't want him so he was determined to leave her alone.

That Saturday night there was a big fight coming off at Semples Stadium, so Joe and Rooney went along. Joe was greatly involved in the world of boxing and loved a fight-night. It didn't last long, but it wasn't supposed to. It was basically good entertainment with everyone getting a slice of the action and Joe was pleased with his share. When they came back outside, Joe decided to take a walk. It had been a long time since he'd walked through this part of the city. Rooney wanted to go with him, but he insisted he'd go on his own.

"I just need to think about some things, Rooney."

Rooney was worried. He'd never seen Joe behave like this over any woman. So, he sent

Al home and followed Joe at a safe distance.

Joe walked along, stopping to light a cigar and study the brightly coloured lights and the people they shone on. He was looking for a diner to get a cup of coffee, when a young girl's voice came from a doorway.

"Hey Mister, you looking for a good time?"

He watched as she approached him, smiling. No more than a child, she stood dressed in a short, tight skirt, skimpy top and back patent, high heeled boots.

"What age are you?" he asked

"Sixteen. Is that young enough for you?"

"Too young – and you're not sixteen!"

"What does that matter. I can still give you a good time. What do you say?"

"No thanks," he said, shaking his head and walking away.

She followed him and touched his arm.

"I'm good. You won't regret it."

Joe stopped and looked into her face. She was smiling, but her eyes were full of sadness.

"You shouldn't be on the street, kid. Jesus, you look like you should be in a kindergarten!"

She looked nervously over his shoulder as he spoke.

"Look mister, you seem a nice man, so do me a favour. Talk to me for a couple of minutes, like you're interested. There's a guy watching me."

Joe glanced across the street and saw the figure of a man hanging around the street corner.

"Him?"

"Yeah."

"Well, I'm sorry kid. I can't help you."

Just at that, the man came across the street and walked up to Joe. He was brash and dressed in bright colours that gave every clue to his profession.

"Well…you want to do business?" he asked.

"What's it to you?" retorted Joe.

"Hey man, you pay me and she's all yours."

"How much are we talking about?"

"Thirty Dollars – but she's worth it. She'll do anything you want and you can do anything you want."

He put his arm around the young girl, smiling at Joe and winking. Joe took an instant dislike to this guy and he could see how anxious his young victim was becoming, in his menacing grip.

"And how much does she get?"

"Enough! Well, are you interested?"

"Sorry. She's a bit young for me."

"Come on, man, she's young but she knows what to do. What's your fuckin problem?"

Joe lunged forward and grabbed him by the throat.

"You're my fuckin problem!" he yelled. "She can't be more than fourteen or fifteen. I could have you arrested, you bastard! Now get out of my way!"

Suddenly, a voice came from beside him.

"What's going on here?"

Joe looked and saw Rooney standing there.

"Nothing I can't handle," he replied, releasing his prey.

Rooney took over, grabbing the man and pushing him into the doorway. Joe turned to the girl who looked frightened and confused.

"How much does he actually give you?"

"Ten. Maybe fifteen, if I keep him happy."

Joe put his hand up to his forehead.

"Jesus Christ!" he said, more to himself than to her. Then, he took her arm and led her further along the sidewalk.

"Here," he whispered, putting his hand into his pocket and taking out fifty dollars.

"Take this but don't tell him you've got it. O.K.?"

He pointed a warning finger at her but could see by her expression she'd do exactly as he'd said.

She took the money and quickly stuffed it down her boot.

"Thanks mister. He can be really mean to me."

"In that case, shout at me."

"What?"

"Shout at me, like you're angry. That way he'll think you're on his side. And, kid, for Christ's sake go home. Nothing could be worse than this."

She didn't answer but touched Joe's hand in a grateful gesture. Then she started yelling and cursing at him for wasting her time, and for her companion's benefit!

By this time Rooney had freed him and both he and Joe started walking away. After a few yards they stopped and looked back.

The guy had gone over to her, gripped her by the arm and was shaking her.

"I'm warning you!" he screamed into her face. "If you don't make some money tonight, Benny's going to fix you good! Now start earning!"

He pushed her away roughly and went back across the street to hang around again.

Joe looked at Rooney.

"I might have known. Benny Bangles just can't get them young enough."

"Look at her, Joe. She's just a child," said Rooney, mournfully.

"Yeah, I know. But the sad part is, she's not innocent like one."

Joe looked around at all the seedy, sinister characters.

"Come to think of it," he continues, "it's hard to find a woman who won't fall into bed with you at the mention of money or the promise of a good time."

"You're right enough. But that Benny should be locked up. He's a slime. If he goes on like this, there won't be a decent girl left in the city. He'll have ruined them all."

"There aren't many decent ones anyway." Joe remarked, sadly, "and certainly not around here. Come on, Rooney, lets find a cab and go home."

As he stepped off the sidewalk to hail a taxi, Rooney looked at him. It was obvious Joe was thinking about Angela, and he was right. Good women were hard to come by

Joe went to bed but couldn't sleep. He lay thinking about that young girl and all the others like her, and how many men must have used them in their sad, young lives. Then he thought of Angela. What if she had another man in her life, past or present? Compared to what was going on around him, not just on the street but in Antonia's circles, it was no big deal and he was a sorry man he'd made so much out of it. She was entitled to go with whoever she wanted. He didn't own her and he knew he'd behaved very selfishly. The way he felt at that very moment, he wanted her so badly he didn't care who she'd been with. She couldn't have had a lot of experience – if any. Even Agnes had led him to believe so. Anyway, he didn't really care! He loved her and not being with her was eating him away. He wondered how she was and what she was doing. Above all, he wondered if the time would ever come when she'd forgive him for hurting her so much. He came to realise that although he missed her gentle embraces and kisses, he also missed her companionship and the contentment it brought him. There was so much more to love than he'd ever dreamed. If only she had felt the same way about him. He could have moulded her into the kind of lover he'd always wanted. Their last meeting in 'The Safe Haven' had given him hope, not only of reconciliation, but of a more intense love affair. But it looked like Angela had other ideas. Not surprisingly. After all, he was twice her age and certainly no match for her I.Q. But he was so desperate he felt he'd settle for any kind of love she could give him even if it wasn't what he'd hoped for.

As night turned into day, Joe finally drifted into sleep wishing for the one thing in his life that seemed beyond his reach.

Chapter 5

If Joe was feeling disillusioned about life and the people he was meeting, unknown to him, Angela wasn't having much fun either. The day after Gene O'Brien's party, she'd taken down the two birthday cards she'd received and put them away. One was from Agnes and the other from Sheila and Raymond. She returned the dress and shoes to the store and on her way home, bought some newspapers. She was determined to look for another job but soon found that it wasn't easy. She worked most nights and spent her mornings and afternoons going after every suitable job advertised. Her world was a million miles away from Joe Morrelli's. While he spent his evenings at shows and dinner parties, Angela spent her nights off at the movies and the bowling alley with her friends from work. The constant job hunting was beginning to show on her. She was always tired and had skipped so many meals she was beginning to loose weight. On top of this she'd had many sleepless nights, some of which were spent hoping and praying that she was doing the right thing, while others were spent thinking about Joe. Angela had tried to put him out of her mind but she couldn't. She missed his company and, although she didn't want to admit it, she missed him. Having to leave 'The Safe Haven' was breaking her heart but it was Joe's restaurant. He could walk in any time and she couldn't face that. In fact, she was surprised he'd stayed away so long. In the end, she'd come to the conclusion that what had happened at their last meeting, hadn't really meant anything to him. And why should it? He had Antonia. How could she forget? Hadn't he thrown that into her face, about a man's needs and Antonia's emotions? Every time she thought back to that argument she became more convinced that she had to get another job, somewhere, anywhere, far from him and 'The Safe Haven'.

Angela persevered and toured the streets with the wanted ads, ending up in a large book store across town. After waiting for over an hour to be interviewed, she was offered the job. The wages were less than those at 'The Safe Haven' but she didn't mind. She was just so relieved to have found something after so many disappointments, that she couldn't wait to get home and tell her mother.

Angela came into the apartment and threw herself down into the chair.

"Well, how did it go today, love?" Agnes asked, anxiously.

Angela smiled.

"I got a job, mum! It's in a book store. I'm only an assistant but I told the manager I've been studying at College and he seems to think that if I do well, there may be a chance of promotion to the invoicing and ordering department. There's just one thing."

"What's that?"

"I'll have to take a cut in wages. The pay's not as good as 'The Safe Haven'."

"Angela, that doesn't matter. As long as you've found something to suit you. Do you think you'll like it?"

"Yes, I do, everyone seems really nice. I don't have to start for a couple of weeks. The girl I'm replacing is leaving to have a baby. Anyway, it will give Mr Barrett time to get something sorted out at work. I'll miss him. He's been very good to me."

"What are you going to do about your classes, Angela? What about your exams? You've worked so hard."

"I've already thought about that. I'll finish my courses at night-class and the manager said I could always change my day off to take any exams."

Agnes smiled and nodded as Angela got up from the chair and sighed.

"I'll think I'll lie down for a while, mum. I need to get some rest before I go to the restaurant."

As she reached the bedroom door, she stopped and came back a few steps. Looking at Agnes she asked,

"Mum, will you be alright on your own all day?"

"Of course I will! I'll miss you not being here but I'll be fine."

Angela went to bed. Agnes sat with tears in her eyes. She didn't want to say anything but she had grown very dependant on Angela's hours at 'The Safe Haven' and she would miss her daughter's help and companionship through the day. The drop in wages would make a difference too. They wouldn't be able to help Sheila and Raymond as often now and Agnes felt guilty. Angela had taken over from her father in many ways but deep inside Agnes knew it wasn't fair to expect so much of her. She was entitled to her own life and her own happiness, even if it meant her leaving 'The Safe Haven'. Agnes wished she could phone Joe and confide in him but knew if she did and Angela ever found out, she'd be very upset. Anyway, Joe would hear about it soon enough. He was her boss. She wondered how he would take the news and just how he would feel when he realised he wasn't going to see her daughter again. Casting her mind back to the times when she and Joe would talk, when he'd ask her advice and when he'd tell her his secrets, she couldn't help but feel so much more could have come out of the friendship he and Angela shared.

Angela lay on the bed going over the day's events in her head. She felt lucky to have gotten such a job. She'd be right at home among all those books! But Agnes's health worried her and she hoped she'd be alright and able to cope without her. She knew the wage difference was going to make thinks a bit tougher for everyone, but Angela consoled herself with the thought that it might only be for a while. Who could tell where this job might lead? Maybe her decision to leave 'The Safe Haven' would be for the best. She might do really well and find happiness along the way. Angela closed her eyes and smiled. She had a good feeling about the future. Unknown to her, her luck was about to change in a way she'd never dreamed of.

Angela arrived for work as usual. The place was crowded, so she got on with her job and didn't say anything to anyone about leaving. When the last of the customers had gone and the staff had cleared everything away, she went to the office to see Freddie. She knocked and entered. He was sitting behind the desk, sorting out the night's takings.

"We did well tonight, Angela," he smiled. "Very well. Now, what can I do for you dear?"

"Mr Barrett, I'm giving you my notice. I'm leaving."

The smile quickly disappeared from Freddie's face and his mouth fell open.

"Leaving!"

"Yes, I'm afraid so. I've found another job."

"Now Angela, let's not be hasty! Can't we talk about this? I mean, if it's a matter of money I'm sure I could sort something out."

"No, it's nothing to do with money, really. I just feel it's time to move on."

"But I thought you were happy here, Angela. I know you worked long hours but I thought you liked it."

"I've loved it here Mr Barrett and you've been very good to me – like a father almost. But I can't stay here forever," she replied, her voice becoming emotional.

Freddie stood up and stared at her for a few seconds.

"Would this have anything to do with Mr Morrelli and what happened here a few weeks ago?"

Angela looked at the floor.

"Well, we both know what Mr Morrelli thinks of me, he made that quite clear. To be honest with you, Mr Barrett, he made me feel like a prostitute. I'm good for business. My job is to keep the customers happy, that's what I do best. You heard him. I guess in his eyes I'm not good for much else."

Freddie became very flustered.

"Angela, you should have let me explain things to him when I wanted to!"

"It doesn't matter. He'd already come to his own conclusions about me and I'm glad I found out what they were. Anyway, I won't be leaving just yet. I hope you can sort out a replacement."

"When do you start your new job?"

"Not for two weeks. But I had hoped for a few days to myself. I've been out almost every day looking for something else and to be honest with you, I'm exhausted."

"I can well understand that. It can't have been easy. I don't know how you've kept it up," he said, giving her a sympathetic look. "Where are you going when you leave here, if you don't mind my asking?"

"To the 'Carson/Mills Bookstore'. You might be hearing from them regarding a reference – if that's o.k."

"Of course, of course. They must pay very well, if I can't persuade you to stay."

"As a matter of fact, Mr Barrett, they pay less than I earn now but it does have prospects and you know me and books. It'll be home from home!"

She tried desperately to sound light-hearted.

Freddie nodded his head and smiled, forlornly.

"We did have some conversations, didn't we Angela?"

"Yes, we did."

"And thanks to you I can now hold my own when it comes to writers and poets! What was it you used to say? There's no point in reading what they wrote unless you know why they wrote it. I'll miss you, Angela, and so will the staff. I wish you well in whatever you do. I'm just so sorry to see you go, my dear. You did a great job here. Our loss is certainly their gain."

Freddie put out his hand and Angela took it. Then on impulse, she leaned across the desk and kissed his cheek.

"Thank you, Mr Barrett. You were always very kind and understanding. I won't ever forget you. Goodnight."

As Angela closed the door behind her, Freddie stood with a sad expression on his face and a lump in his throat. He looked at his watch. It was too late to phone Mr Morrelli now but he'd make sure to call him first thing in the morning and give him the news.

Yes, he'd make sure to!

Early the next morning the phone rang in Joe's study and he answered it.

"Hello."

"Mr Morrelli, it's me, Freddie."

"Hi Freddie. What can I do for you."

"I've got something to tell you. Something I think you should know."

Joe leaned forward in the chair.

"We weren't robbed, were we?" He asked anxiously.

"No. Worse!" snapped Freddie.

Joe glanced at the receiver. He didn't like Freddie's tone of voice.

"Well what could be worse than that?" he asked dryly.

Freddie opened up like a floodgate.

"It's Angela, she's leaving. She gave in her notice last night. She's got another job. I thought you'd like to know right away. Mr Morrelli, are you still there?"

First there was silence, then

"Yeah, I am. Where is she going to work?"

"In the 'Carson/Mills Bookstore' across town."

"When is she going?"

"In about a week or so. But that's not all, Mr Morrelli, there's something else I think you should know but I can't discuss it over the phone."

"Is it important?"

"I think so," he replied, in a sharp, agitated voice. "You may be very interested in what I have to tell you."

Joe knew Freddie was very fond of Angela, but he didn't much care for his 'It's all your fault' tone. It sounded almost as if he was responsible for her leaving. He thought for a moment.

"O.k.. is she working today?"

"Not until tonight. I'm here on my own."

"Good. I'll be over to see you in about half an hour."

"I'll see you then, Mr Morrelli. Goodbye."

Both men hung up at the same time. Joe stared at the phone. It wasn't like Freddie to talk like that but he could understand how upset he was at Angela leaving 'The Safe Haven'. That made two of them! This was one thing Joe hadn't seen coming. He never thought for a minute she'd actually get herself another job. He leaned back in the chair and put his hands together. He'd gotten through the last few weeks consoled in the knowledge that Angela was still at the restaurant and he could call in and see her anytime, if he wanted. But if she left, the chances were, he would never see her again. She may even move from Westmere Avenue and be out of his life completely. Joe suddenly realised he didn't want that to happen! Yes he was being selfish and he knew it but he wanted Angela were he could see her, even if it did mean keeping her at 'The Safe Haven' and Westmere Avenue. But he also knew how stubborn she could be, wanting to do things on her own, in her own way – just like him!

He would go and see Freddie but there was no way he'd make her stay if she didn't want to. He wouldn't and knew he couldn't. but the thought of never seeing her again was too much to even think about right now. one thing was for sure, the restaurant would never be the same without her. The day Angela Kenny would walk away would be the day Joe Morrelli would see 'The Safe Haven' for the last time. There would be too many memories there for him and although he'd always been a strong man, he knew he wasn't strong enough to handle the heartache those memories would bring.

Joe arrived at 'The Safe Haven', pushed open the front door and walked through the entrance hall. Freddie was waiting.

"I'll be with you in a moment, Mr Morrelli. I'm just going to lock up. One can't be too careful."

Joe nodded, went into the office and sat down behind the desk. A few moments later Freddie came in and took a seat facing him.

"Well Freddie, what is it you think I need to know?"

Freddie cleared his throat.

"Mr Morrelli, since the day you first hired me my policy has always been to do my job and mind my own business. But the last day you were here, I'm afraid there was a grave misunderstanding."

"Oh yeah?"

"Yes, when you left, Angela was extremely upset. She was in tears as she told me some of the conversation you'd both had."

Joe lowered his gaze as Freddie continued,

"The point is, Mr Morrelli, that young man you'd seen her with is her teacher, Dean Prescott."

"So, she's going out with her teacher. It happens."

Freddie shook his head.

"No, you don't understand. He's her teacher and her friend, and he'd just gotten engaged."

"Engaged?"

"Yes, to Helen, a secretary at the college. Angela was so delighted for them she offered to arrange a special dinner here for them and some friends. She knew Mr Prescott wouldn't be able to afford it on a teacher's salary, so she asked if they could have it on her staff discount. She paid for the wine and champagne herself. I deducted it from her wages, a few days later."

Joe's expression said it all. If he'd never been in the 'dog house' he was in it now!

"But... but I saw him kiss her," he stammered.

"Yes, and if you'd waited long enough you'd have seen Helen kiss her as well! He was just thanking her Mr Morrelli, that's all."

There was silence in the office as Freddie's revelation sank in. Joe hurriedly gathered his thoughts.

"Freddie, why didn't you tell me all this before?"

"I wanted to, believe me, but Angela made me promise not to and I agreed. Now I wish I hadn't. I feel so guilty."

"You feel guilty!"

"But after last night and what she said...."

"Yeah... what did she say?"

"You're not going to like it."

"Try me!"

Joe was starting to get agitated so Freddie decided to come clean.

"She said you'd made it obvious what you thought of her, so there was no point in even trying to explain..."

When Freddie got to the part about Joe making Angela feel like a prostitute, Joe hung his head shamefully. So that's what was wrong with her all this time! That's why she avoided him. At least now he knew. He'd never meant to hurt her like that. He'd never dreamed he'd made her feel so bad about herself and her job. He listened carefully until Freddie had finished.

"This job she's going to, is it better paid?"

"That's what I thought, but she'll be taking a cut in wages."

"So it's got nothing to do with money."

"No. I even offered her a raise if she'd stay but she's determined to leave. I'll miss her, Mr Morrelli. The staff will take it badly, especially young Jimmy."

"Yeah, I've been meaning to ask you about him. What does he do around here?"

"Anything Angela asks him to! He came to the staff entrance one day looking for work. I said "No," but Angela pleaded with me to give him a chance, the way I'd given her one. So I took him on as a kitchen boy. Angela mothers him! His own mother's ill most of the time and his father drinks a lot. I told her you might not approve but she said you'd understand."

Yes Joe understood.

Freddie continued,

"Anyway, he has younger brothers and sisters so Angela lets him take home any unwanted food. She's always maintained he'd make good and I must admit she's been right."

"What do you mean?"

"Well, he started off as a kitchen boy. Now he's assisting the chefs. She's a good judge of character, that's for sure."

"Yeah well, she cares about people."

"Indeed. Last night I wished her well and shook hands with her and you know what she did?"

"What?"

"She kissed me – on the cheek, and thanked me. She said I'd been almost a father to her. Can you imagine? That's the first time anyone's ever said that to me."

Joe could believe that!

Freddie's voice took on an apologetic tone.

"Mr Morrelli, I'm sorry if I sounded a little abrupt with you earlier but I feel so terrible about all this."

"Forget it, Freddie," said Joe, as he got up from the chair. "Tell me something, will she be working tomorrow?"

"For a few hours in the afternoon."

"Can you arrange for her to be here on her own, no staff?"

"If you'd prefer."

"Maybe you could make an excuse, too. I'd like it to be just her and me."

"Of course, Mr Morrelli. I understand perfectly. You have something in mind?"

"I'm not sure yet and even if I do come up with something there's no guarantee it'll work. But leave it with me."

Freddie nodded and followed Joe out of the office and to the front door. Unlocking it he said,

"I'm glad you came, Mr Morrelli. I feel so much better now that you know the right way of things."

"So do I, Freddie. Thanks for telling me. Goodbye"

"Goodbye, Mr Morrelli."

Freddie closed the door, leaned his back against it and breathed a huge sigh of relief!

Joe may have left 'The Safe Haven' a much wiser man but he was carrying a heavy burden of guilt. No wonder Freddie's voice had a tone of accusation. Everything that had lead to Angela's leaving was all his fault. Now he didn't know what to do. He needed time to think. He got into the limousine, quiet and subdued.

"Home," he said.

Al studied him in the mirror as he drove. His boss had changed, he wasn't the happy-go-lucky guy he used to be and whatever news he's just heard surely wasn't good judging by the expression on his face. When they arrived home, Joe got out of the car.

"Al, I won't be needing you. Take the rest of the day off. Tell Frankie to do the same." He wanted to be on his own. Rooney was taking care of some business for him and he'd be gone all day. Joe was glad. This was one time he didn't want company. He wanted the place to himself.

In the study he went over everything Freddie had told him. That night at the restaurant he hadn't seen the teacher's girlfriend. Come to think of it, he hadn't seen anyone except Dean Prescott and Angela. And even then he'd only seen what he wanted to see! He knew he had accused her of things she'd never done – nor would do, and he knew he could never take back the hurtful things he's said to her. He made her cry and that was unforgivable but was there more behind her leaving 'The Safe Haven'? Joe thought deeply. Angela always liked her job. The money was good and the hours suited her because of her mother. she was popular with the staff and customers alike, and ever since Gene O'Brien's party Joe had stayed out of her way. So why on earth was she willing to give it all up and go to a lesser job at the other side of town?

Could it be that Angela Kenny was running away from something – or someone? Maybe him, for instance and if so, why? If he was the reason, then she was going all out to get away from him. Did she really hate him that much> O.K., he'd handled things badly and he was sorry. But not sorry enough to stand back and let her go, just like that. He loved this woman and his happiness was at stake. Joe Morrelli never walked away from a fight, especially when it concerned the one person who mattered most in his life. He left the study with a determined look on his face. He would talk to her tomorrow. Meanwhile, there was something he had to do. After a shower and change of clothing Joe phoned a taxi.

"Where to mister?" asked the driver, as his passenger settled in the back seat.

"The city," replied Joe, "I'll tell you where to drop me off when we get there."

As they began the journey, Joe relaxed. His mind was made up and he was fully prepared for what he intended to do.

At 3 o'clock the next day, Joe stood across the street from 'The Safe Haven' and watched as Freddie Barrett came to the front door and nodded to him. As one made an entrance, the other made an exit but not before Joe patted him on the back in a gesture of appreciation.

Angela was in the dining area inspecting the tables and putting out the menus. Joe stood for a moment, watching her. She was wearing a white blouse and black skirt, just the way she'd done the first night he'd ever seen her. He couldn't help but notice she had lost weight since the last time he's been there and she looked pale.

Angela turned around and saw him walking towards her. She closed her eyes tightly and took a deep breath, bracing herself. Joe stopped at her side.

"Hi. How are you?" he asked

Angela opened her eyes but kept her gaze on the table as she moved the cutlery and smoothed the cloth.

"I'm fine, thank you."

There was a short silence.

"Look, Angel, I've come to see you. I blamed you for something you didn't do and I said some pretty hurtful things. I didn't know that guy was your teacher and I didn't know he had a girlfriend."

"You didn't want to know. I told you I could explain but you wouldn't let me. Anyway, it doesn't matter now."

"Yeah , I know. I've heard you're leaving, Angel. I'm just interested in why/"

"I once told you I wouldn't be here forever."

"That's right, you did. But you also told me you wanted degrees. You don't have then yet, so why the big rush just to be an assistant in a bookstore?"

"I feel it's time to move on, that's all."

Joe was becoming annoyed as Angela was paying more attention to the table than to him.

"Don't do that!" He snapped, as he gripped her hand. "And look at me when I'm talking to you! Now tell me the truth."

Angela met his glare and pulled her hand away.

"You really want to know?"

"I'm asking, aren't I?"

"Alright. Ever since I took this job, I've tried my best to please you in my work. I've tried to please Mr Barrett. I've tried to please my mother. I've tried to please the customers. I'm trying to please everyone but myself! It's alright for you. You can go where you want, when you want. I work long hours in here nearly every night and do you know where I go? To the movies or the bowling alley once a week. I watch people come in here and have such a good time. They enjoy life. I don't even have a life – not one of my own anyway!" her voice broke with tearful emotion.

"At least in my new job I'll be working from 9 – 5 and my nights will be my own."

Joe stared at her. It was taking every ounce of strength he had to keep from sweeping her up in his arms.

"I hope that's the real reason," he said. "You must want out of this place really bad if you're willing to give up your studies."

"I don't have to give them up, but even if I did it really wouldn't matter."

"It would matter to me!" He insisted, raising his voice. "I won't let you throw away everything you've worked so hard for, just to run around some store all day."

Angela's voice was more determined than angry.

"If you've come here for another argument, Mr Morrelli, then I'm sorry to disappoint you. I really can't and won't take any more of this. Besides, I already know what you think of me. I don't want to hear it all over again. Please, just leave me alone."

Joe shook his head.

"Sorry, Angel, I can't do that."

"What do you want from me?" She asked pleadingly.

"I want you to marry me."

A look of total disbelief spread over Angela's face.

"Marry me? Why on earth would you want me to marry you?"

"Because I love you. Don't ask me to explain it. I can't. It just happened. God knows I never meant it to, but it did." He began to mock himself. "Imagine me, Joe Morrelli, falling in love! And with a woman young enough to be my daughter! Doesn't that beat all?" He became serious again. "I know you could never love me in the same way, and I don't expect it. Angel, I never thought I'd ever hear myself say this, but right now I'd settle for any kind of love you could give me."

In her shock she tried to reason with him. "You can't be serious."

"I've never been more serious in my life. But I don't want an answer now, I want you to think about it. I want you to think about the real reason you're leaving here. I won't stop you from going if it's what you really want. Just be sure it's the job you're leaving and not your feelings, because you can't ever run away from them. Believe me, I've tried."

Now it was Angela's turn to hold back the embrace.

"But why me, Joe?" She whispered. "What can I possibly give you?"

"More than you know," came the reply.

Lowering his eyes, he put his hand in his pocket and took out a small, velvet box. Setting it down on the edge of the table he said,

"It's up to you now, Angel. Whenever you decide, you know where I am."

Joe turned and walked away. As she watched him leave, Angela sank into the nearest chair. Then with shaking hands, she opened the box. Inside was an engagement ring. Three large hearts were joined side by side. The centre heart was slightly larger than the other two and was a deep blue sapphire, whereas the others were sparkling diamonds. It was the most beautiful piece of jewellery she had ever seen. It was obvious that Joe Morrelli had given a lot of thought, time and money in choosing it for her and she was so overcome with emotion, she wept.

After leaving 'The Safe Haven', Joe made his way to Westmere Avenue on foot. Agnes was surprised to see him.

"Joe, it's you! I thought you'd stopped your visits for good."

"Agnes, I've got to talk to you. Can I come in?"

She sensed the anxiety in his voice.

"Of course you can. Is anything wrong, Joe?"

He followed her through and sat down.

"Has Angel phoned you?" he asked.

"No. Should she have?"

Joe thought for a moment.

"I've just left her, Agnes, and the truth is....well... I've asked her to marry me."

She wasn't prepared for such a statement, as Joe could clearly see.

"You look surprised, Agnes."

"I am. I can hardly believe it."

"Well, I don't think Angel can either!"

"What did she say?"

"Nothing. I told her I didn't want an answer just yet. I want her to think about it. To be honest, I'm not sure if I've done the right thing. All I know is that I love her and I'd do anything to keep her near me."

"I take it you know about the new job?"

Joe nodded.

"Yeah, I heard. It was then I realised I couldn't let her go without telling her how I felt. I know I've hurt her, Agnes, I didn't mean to. But I'd make it all up to her if only she'd let me. Maybe I've left it too late."

"Oh, Joe," said Agnes, reaching out and taking his hand, "I wanted to get in touch with you and tell you what was going on, but if Angela had found out she'd never have forgiven me. I'm sorry."

"That's o.k. I just hope I haven't made a fool of myself. I don't think she loves me. I don't expect her to, with the age difference and all. We're so opposite, yet so alike. It's difficult to explain. Agnes, maybe I should just have let her go."

He looked at her, pleading for her advice.

"Do you really think that would have been the best thing to do, Joe?"

"I don't know," he replied, shaking his head. "But one thing's for sure, if she says 'No' and walks out of my life I don't know what I'll do. I'm scared to even think about what it would be like, never to see her again."

"You talk as though Angela would find it impossible to love you."

"I can't help it, that's how I feel. I only wish she could love me, for her own sake as well as mine. I'd be good to her, Agnes. I know I could make her happy and give her all the love she'd ever need. My own mother never got the chance to have any of those things but I'd give them all to Angel, I swear."

Agnes's heart ached for him. She knew he loved her daughter and that he'd meant every word he'd said. She put her hand up to his face.

"Joe, look at me."

He did.

"Tell me something. Do you believe in the Virgin Mary?"

"Yes I do."

"And do you believe she gave birth to God's son?"

"You're talking to an Italian Catholic, Agnes. I never had any cause to doubt it."

She leaned over and smiled.

"Then it just goes to show you that nothing's impossible!"

"Yeah," said Joe forcing a smile, "but she had God on her side!"

"Maybe He's on your side too, and you just don't know it yet."

She gave him a knowing look and then relaxed in the chair. Joe got up and kissed her cheek.

"I hope so. But I'll just have to wait and see."

Agnes got up and followed him to the door.

"Will I tell her you called?" she asked.

Joe shrugged his shoulders.

"It doesn't really matter, Agnes, I've got nothing to hide anymore. Angel knows how I feel now."

When he told Angela he wanted her to think about his proposal, Joe never thought she would take so long. Three days had passed and he still hadn't heard from her. She was due to leave 'The Safe Haven' soon and this made him even more anxious. What if she didn't get in touch? What if she just walked away without a word to him? There was no one to confide in. no one knew what he'd done, except Agnes. He wasn't sure if Angela would tell Freddie but that didn't worry him. Freddie always knew when to keep his mouth shut!

Late the following evening, a phone-call came through for Joe. It was Angela, asking to meet with him at the restaurant the next afternoon at 3.00. He was happy and relieved to hear from her, but the tone of her voice gave no clue as to her decision. This played on his mind the next day but as he got ready for the meeting he consoled himself with the knowledge that in a short time all the waiting would be over and he'd know the outcome for sure.

Al drove him to 'The Safe Haven' but didn't wait.

As he entered the building, Joe took a deep breath. It was make or break time! Freddie met him.

"She's in the office, Mr Morrelli. You won't be disturbed in there."

Joe nodded.

Sure enough, there she was. She was silent as Joe closed the door and then pulled over two chairs. As they sat down she swept her red hair back over her shoulders so she could look straight into his face.

"Well, I've thought about it Joe," she said, softly. "I've been over it a thousand times in my mind and I'm sorry, the answer's 'No'. it just wouldn't work."

Joe was devastated.

"Why Angel? I mean, why do you think it wouldn't work? Is it because I'm too old for you or because you don't love me? What? I'd really like to know and I'd like the truth."

"Oh Joe, it's got nothing to do with your age or how I feel about you. Don't you understand?"

"No, no I don't understand."

"I'm not the right woman for you. I don't fit in. We're worlds apart, Joe. You must have seen that for yourself the first night you took me to 'The Imperial Palace', having to leave in front of all your friends because of me. Marrying me would be a big mistake and I care enough about you to stop you from making it, Joe."

Joe leaned back in the chair.

"Oh, I get it. You think I should marry someone like Antonia?"

"Yes, I do. She knows all the people who matter and goes to all the places that matter, not like me."

"Don't you ever put yourself down like that, Angel," he said sternly. "It's because you're the kind of person you are that I want to marry you. Sure, I've had women in my life but I never had the happiness with any of them that I found with you. I never had the feeling for any of them that I have for you. Why do you think I never married before now?"

Angela knew he was being honest but she wouldn't be swayed. She stood up.

"And what would people say if we got married? They'd say I married you because of who you are. A nobody married Joe Morrelli because of what he could give her. They'd never believe any different."

Joe jumped up and kicked his chair away from him.

"Yeah!" he yelled, "and they'd probably say I married you because I like young girls or because I get a cheap thrill from going to bed with a kid half my age! But do you want to know something? I don't give a damn what they say or what they think because none of it's true! Is it?"

"No," she replied, shaking her head and lowering her gaze.

"No," he agreed. "And if you're going to go through life worrying about those kinds of people, you won't get far. It they don't care about us or how we feel, why should we care about them?"

She looked up at him as he took her arm gently.

"Do you love me, Angel?" he asked. "Do you have any feelings for me at all? Because if you do then we should only care about each other and how we feel, not the rest of the world."

"But Joe, you frighten me sometimes," she finally admitted.

"How?" This was news to him.

"The people you mix with, the friends you have. Judges, Congressmen, businessmen. I don't see how I could ever be a part of that. And then there are all those society women…"

"I want a wife, not a socialite!" he snapped. Then taking her in his arms he whispered, "I want you." He held her close and for a few moments she returned his embrace. Then she broke away and taking the ring box from her pocket, handed it to him. Joe reluctantly conceded.

"Well, at least I gave it a try. You can't ever say I didn't," he said, with a half-hearted smile. He took the box from her and joked, "I wonder what I'm supposed to do with it now?"

"Actually, I think you're supposed to take the ring out and put it on my finger!"

Joe's expression changed in an instant.

"You mean… you mean…..," he stammered, "you will? You will marry me?"

"Yes, if you're still asking," she smiled.

He fumbled as he opened the box and took out the ring. Placing it on her finger he looked into her eyes and said,

"You won't regret it, Angel, I promise. Your life's only beginning."

"I'm going to hold you to that, Joe Morrelli."

He brushed his lips against hers.

"I think you can do better than that," she smiled. "In fact I seem to remember you doing rather well one night in this place after a party."

"Yeah, well – we aim to please!"

He wrapped her tightly in his arms and kissed her passionately. To his delight she responded in a way she'd never done before. Joe Morrelli was a very happy man. He knew that Angela Kenny loved him.

As he stood there with her in his arms, he couldn't believe how lucky he was. But there was something on his mind and although he didn't want to spoil this moment for anything, he knew he had to tell her.

"Angel," he said, in a low voice, "I have to talk to you about Antonia."

Angela stepped back and looked at him.

"What about her?"

"I'm going to go and see her this evening. I want her to be one of the first to know about us and I think it's only fair that I should be the one to tell her. I'm going to end our affair. It won't be easy, she was a part of my life for a long time. But I need you to know that I can't turn my back on her. I'd like to remain her friend if she'll let me and always be there for her if she ever needs my help.

"I understand, Joe, and I wouldn't have it any other way. But I want you to listen to me for a minute." She pulled away from him gently and stared into his face. "Don't you ever sleep with her again – or with any other woman! If you ever do I'll never forgive you, Joe. I'll leave and I won't ever come back. I won't just leave you, I'll leave the country. You'll never see me again and that's for sure?"

Joe smiled,

"Do you really like me that much to be so jealous?"

"No, but I love you that much to want you to be faithful to me."

That was the first time Joe had ever heard her say she loved him and he was overjoyed! He took her in his arms again and stroked her long hair.

"Angel, you've got nothing to worry about. There'll never be anyone else in my life but you. I almost lost you once, I'm not going through that again!"

There was no need for any more words. They held each other close and expressed their feelings and emotions in long, passionate kisses and tender, loving caresses. This new language proved an experience for both of them.

After a while, Angela found it necessary to pull away from Joe – but he understood.

"Hey," he said, in a bid to spare her blushes, "what do you say we go out tonight and celebrate? Where would you like to go?"

"I'd like to go back to Mario's, but I'm working."

"You're not working tonight! We have plans to make."

"Well, I hope one of then isn't to get me into bed, Mr Morrelli! Just because we're engaged doesn't mean I'm going to do that, you know."

"Now, did I say that? Did I even suggest it?"

"No, but I wouldn't be surprised if you were thinking it."

Joe smiled broadly.

"Well you can't condemn a guy for thinking. I mean, I can't be arrested for my thoughts. And even if I could I'd probably be up in front of Judge Thompson and have my case dismissed!"

"Oh, very funny!" said Angela, trying hard to keep a straight face. "But I'm serious, Joe. I'm not ready for that yet."

"Then I'll wait till you are ready."

"Do you mean that?"

"I've waited this long haven't I? But do me a favour, Angel. Don't ever feel frightened of me, please. It makes me feel bad because I'd never do anything to hurt you."

Angela nodded.

"I know," she whispered. "It's just that you seem to know so much about the world outside."

"Then who better to teach you? Besides, we can learn a lot from each other and we've the rest of our lives to do it in."

He stepped closer.

"Well, that may be!" said Angela, putting her hand on his chest. "But right now I think you'd better go. I have work to do."

"Are you still leaving? He asked.

"What do you think?" came the reply.

"I think, Angela Kenny, you've made me the happiest man in the world!"

"Well , don't get carried away. We're not married yet. After all, there's a lot you don't know about me."

"Maybe, but just think about all the fun I'm going to have finding out!"

Angela hurried to the door and opened it.

"Good-day Mr Morrelli!"

"Good-day Miss Kenny! I'll see Freddie on the way out and tell him you won't be working tonight. I'll call for you around 9."

He stopped and kissed her on the cheek, then turned and walked away. As Angela watched him go, she knew in her heart she's done the right thing. Looking down at the ring on her finger she couldn't remember a time when she felt such happiness. As Joe walked through the dining area, he thought of Gene O'Brien and smiled. If Gene gave as good advise in Congress as he'd given him then all Joe could say was "Look out Oval Office, here comes another Irish President!"

Walking out of 'The Safe Haven', Joe Morrelli couldn't have been a happier man. Only two things overshadowed this very special day in his life, Antonia and Rooney. One had been his long time lover, the other had been his long time friend. He knew he would have to see both of them and explain about his plans for the future. It wasn't gong to be easy and as he hailed a taxi he couldn't help but feel a certain amount of dread at the outcome. He loved them both but his love for Angela Kenny far out weighted anything he had ever known. If nothing else, this gave him the courage he would need to see it through.

Joe arrived home and followed the sound of voices coming from the kitchen. On looking in he found Rooney, Frankie an Al sitting at the kitchen table talking, while Evie prepared some vegetables. Al, on looking up, was the first one to see Joe.

"Boss, you're back. Why didn't you give me a call? I'd have picked you up."

"That's o.k., Al, I had some business to take care of. Rooney, could you come with me? I want to talk to you in private."

Rooney followed him to the study and closed the door. Joe stood with his back to him, looking out of the window.

"What's the matter, is something wrong?" asked Rooney.

The room fell silent for a few moments, then Joe turned around and looked at him

"I'm going to come straight to the point here, Rooney. I've asked Angel to marry me, and she's said 'Yes'."

Rooney was stunned. He went to speak but Joe put his hands up to halt him.

"I know what you're thinking but before you say anything, just listen to what I have to say. Just hear me out. I know how you feel about her. I know you fell in love with her the first time you ever saw her. Maybe I did, too, but I didn't know it. I never meant it to happen, you've got to believe that, Rooney. In fact, more than once I made my mind up to keep away from her but every time I tried, something always happened to lead me right back. It was like fate. Something I had no control over. The more I got to know her, the more I realised I was falling in love with her. When we stopped seeing each other I went back to my old ways. The parties, the night-clubs, the fancy restaurants. You know that,

Rooney." He pointed towards his friend, hoping it would jog his memory. "I tried to forget her but I couldn't. I love her. I just never thought she could love me, but she does and we're going to be married."

Rooney had listened to every word carefully and continued to stare at Joe in silence. Finally he said, "I've known for some time you really liked Angela, Joe. But I had no idea you loved her the way you do." His voice was tinged with sadness. "When I first asked her out and she refused because of her job, because of the house rules, I should have pushed it. I should have asked her to leave and helped her find somewhere else to work, but I didn't. Looking back on it now, I guess that's where I made my big mistake and I'll regret it for the rest of my life."

Rooney was the kid brother Joe had never had so he knew he had to come clean. "Angel found another job, Rooney, and gave in her notice. When I heard she was leaving I decided to tell her how I felt and ask her to marry me. I knew if she'd left I'd never see her again so I had to take the chance. But I want you to know something, Rooney. If she'd never loved me and never wanted me, you're the only other man I'd ever want to see her with – and I really mean that."

Rooney nodded.

"Well, when it came to Angela you certainly had more guts than me, Joe. You went after what you wanted, but then, you always did. 'No guts – no glory', isn't that what they say?"

"Yeah, and remember that for the next time. If you want something badly enough, then go for it!" his voice took on a more serious tone. "I'm sorry we both fell in love with the same woman, Rooney. But if it's any consolation, I'll be a good husband to her and do everything I can to make her happy. I know how you must be feeling. I'd be feeling exactly the same way if she'd agreed to marry you. Come to think of it, I still can't believe she's agreed to marry me!"

"Well, there's only ever one winner, Joe. You said that yourself right here in this room – remember? It looks like the best man won and I know you'll be good to her. But as much as I love you Joe, I'll be watching. No more Antonia!" Now it was Joe's turn to be on the receiving end of the pointed finger. "No more women! I mean it. And I want you to promise me you'll never tell Angela how I feel."

"I can live with that if you can," smiled Joe, putting out his hand. Rooney clasped it with his own. Then the two men embraced each other like the brothers they had become.

"Congratulations, Joe!" exclaimed Rooney, as he patted Joe on the back. Joe grabbed him tightly by the shoulders.

"I want you to be my best man! And if anything ever happens to me I want you to look after Angel. That's what family is all about."

His voice sounded choked. Rooney smiled at him.

"I'll always be here for you and Angela. You can count on it. Now, who else knows you're going to become an old married man?"

"No one, you're the first. And hey – less of the old!"

Joe was beaming now.

"Come on," said Rooney, ushering him to the door, "let's tell the others. Wait till you see Al's face!"

"Wait till you see Evie's!" replied Joe. "She hasn't even met her yet."

"She'll probably think you're bringing another Antonia into the house."

"Yeah well, don't tell her any different, not yet anyway. I want her to get a surprise."

"Oh, she will," insisted Rooney, nodding his head.

"Believe me, she will!"

Joe's limousine pulled up in front of the luxurious Marlton Apartments. The smartly uniformed doorman hurried over and opened the car door.

"Good evening, Mr Morrelli."

"Hello Jake," came the reply as Joe stepped out.

He looked over his shoulder at Al.

"Don't wait around for me. I'll call a cab."

As he walked he pulled a $20 bill out of his pocket and handed it to Jake who by now was holding open the large glass door.

"Here," he said smiling, "buy the wife some flowers."

"Thank you, Mr Morrelli," said Jake, tipping his hat.

Joe crossed the spacious lobby and made his way over to the private lift that went up to the penthouse. Once inside he shuffled about with an uneasy look on his face, while the lift took him to the top of the building. He stepped out into the hall, took out a key and opened the door of the expensive apartment.

"Joe, honey is that you?" came Antonia's voice as she ran towards him, flinging her arms around his neck. Her face was alight with joy as she took his hand and led him into the plush bedroom.

"Antonia we have to talk," faltered Joe.

"Darling, you don't have to say anything," insisted Antonia. "I always knew you'd come back to me. You're here where you belong. Nothing else matters."

By now Joe was feeling very uncomfortably.

"Antonia, I have something to tell you." He hesitated for a moment. "I've asked Angela to marry me, and she's accepted."

Antonia's smile faded, replaced by a look of rage.

"You bastard!" she screamed, lunging at him with clenched fists. "you dirty bastard!"

Within seconds she was raining blows on Joe's chest, hysterical from the news she had just heard.

"Antonia, please let me explain," pleaded Joe.

"Explain? Explain what? You used me, Joe Morrelli! You got what you wanted from me and now you're throwing me to one side like a piece of garbage, for a young girl you hardly even know! You used me!!"

Joe grabbed her arms and pinned them to her sides.

"I used you?" he shouted, anger flashing in his eyes. "No, no Antonia," he said shaking his head, " I took you from a chorus line in a sleazy club. I paid for acting lessons, elocution lessons – you name it, I footed the bill! I bribed producers to give you parts. I called in favours to get you your big break on Broadway. I even bought you this apartment. But I didn't do all that just because I was sleeping with you. I did it because I cared about you and I knew it was what you wanted. That was all o.k. then, but now I want something it's not. No, Antonia, I didn't use you – we used each other!"

On hearing this, Antonia burst into tears and shook uncontrollably. Joe took her in his arms and pressed her tightly against him.

"Now baby, come on," he said lowering his voice to a soft, gentle tone. "you'll always be special to me. You're not loosing me. I'll be here for you, just like always."

She leaned her head on his shoulder, sobbing loudly.

"Joe," she said pleadingly, "will you stay the night – just for old times sake?"

She looked up at him and stroked his face lovingly.

"Antonia," he replied in a choked voice, "of all the things you've ever asked of me, this is the one thing I can't do for you."

"You love her that much, Joe?"

Joe nodded, "Yeah, I love her that much."

He cradled Antonia in his arms, rocking her gently. He closed his eyes tightly for a few seconds, shaking his head in silence. This was the hardest thing he'd ever had to do.

Over the next few weeks, Joe and Angela became almost inseparable. For the first time they went out together during the days when she wasn't working. Joe found himself visiting places he'd never been to before, like museums, art galleries and even the public library where Angela got her books. She was a world of information to him. Not only could she pin-point paintings but she could tell about the artist who painted them, and even some of the things they said or did. The same went for writers, how they lived, what they wrote and why. Sometimes when reading a poem, she could sense if the poet was in a happy or sad mood. Joe watched her and listened with great admiration.

On some days they would end up in a diner for a cup of coffee or in a quiet bar for a drink. They even strolled through the public park arm in arm, chatting and laughing like any ordinary couple. Angela had opened up a whole new world for Joe and he was enjoying it. He was also getting to know every thing about her and one thing he soon discovered was that besides being intelligent Angela Kenny was a very kind hearted and witty young woman. She was fun to be with, yet caring. He liked that.

Joe found himself dressing in a more relaxed and casual style. It wasn't that he wanted to look younger than his years, it was more the fact that he felt younger and was happy. As he and Angela sat in the park one afternoon, he decided it was time to bring up the subject of the wedding.

"Angel, I'd like you to visit my home. After all, it's going to be your home, too, when we get married. I'd like you to get to know it."

A sad expression came over her face.

"Joe, I've been wanting to talk to you about that."

His heart sank.

"What's the matter?" he asked, in an anxious voice.

"Well, it's my mother, Joe. What's going to become of her when I marry? I'm so worried about leaving her."

"Who said anything about leaving her? She can move in with us. It's a big enough house."

Joe sounded so matter-of-fact about it, that Angela thought he might be joking.

"Joe, you don't really mean that," she tutted.

"Of course I do! You don't think I'd leave Agnes in that apartment all by her herself, do you?"

"To tell the truth, I thought you might suggest some kind of sheltered accommodation, you know, with someone to look after her."

"Agnes in sheltered accommodation? I wouldn't stand for it! Come to think of it, Agnes probably wouldn't stand for it either…"

Angela slapped him playfully.

"Joe Morrelli, I hope you're not going to be like Frankie and start telling crude mother-in-law jokes!"

"Certainly not! Besides, Frankie's mother–in–law's really Mussolinii in disguise!"

They rolled about the grass, laughing, until Angela sat up and tugged at Joe's sleeve.

"Seriously, Joe," she said. "What about my mother?"

"Angel, I've already told you, she can come and live with us. She can have her own rooms. We'll just need to make a few alterations, that's all."

"But won't you mind? Not every man would want his wife's mother in tow."

"Yeah well, not every wife would have a mother like Agnes. I like her. I like her a lot. We've become good friends and I don't see a problem. I know you both love each other. There's no way I'd want to separate you, ever."

Angela leaned over him.

"Thank you, Joe. I can't tell you how relieved I am."

"That makes two of us! You had me worried there for a minute. I thought you were going to tell me you'd changed your mind and the wedding was off."

"How could I change my mind when I love you so much?"

"Speaking of love…." Smiled Joe, broadly, "would you mind if we didn't have a long engagement? I mean, I don't want to be here like this in six month's time. I don't think I could hold out that long!"

Angela began to blush.

"What did you have in mind?" she asked.

"Well, we'll see what needs doing to the house first. Maybe you'd like to re-decorate or something. Say, a couple of months?"

"That's not much time, really."

Joe reached up and pulled her down towards him.

"O.k., three months – but that's the best I can do!"

He rolled on top of her, kissing her lovingly in the bright sunshine.

"I love you so much," he said. "I'll be counting the days."

Secretly, she felt the same. She drew him close. "Joe, I want a small wedding in my own Church. Sheila's having trouble with this pregnancy so she and Raymond can't come. There'll just be my mother."

"That's' o.k."

"And there's something else… I'm buying my own wedding dress and everything that goes with it."

"Damn it, Angel, you're the most independent woman I've ever met! O.k. I'll make a deal with you. You can have your way with the Church and the dress, but I'll handle the reception. We'll have to have one, for all my friends. They'll expect it of me once the word gets out that Joe Morrelli's finally getting married! By the way, where would you like to go on your honeymoon?"

"I don't know," she answered, thoughtfully. "But I do love the sea. I don't mind where we go as long as there's a beach and the sea."

Joe gazed at her and smiled.

"Well, I'll give you one thing, Angela Kenny, you're not hard to please!" then his face became more serious. "You won't change your mind, will you, Angel? You do still want to marry me don't you?"

"I won't change my mind, Joe. I'm going to marry you – in three months time!"

They kissed again, his hands fondling her body before coming to rest on her breasts.

"Joe, you're in a public park," she reminded him.

"Yeah, but nobody's looking. Besides, I need the practise for that beach you've been talking about.

After he's dropped Angela off, Joe headed home. He couldn't help but smile at what had happened in the park. He'd finally gotten one over on Angela. She never would have dreamed he'd touch her like that in public, but then she had a lot to learn about Joe Morrelli. He did it knowing full well she wouldn't want to create a scene, and of course he was right.

As he stopped the car in the driveway the smile had become a broad grin. His thoughts were still in the park as he arrived into the kitchen. Frankie and Al stood at the back door, smoking. Joe poured himself a cup of coffee as Al studied him from top to toe. He observed Joe's blue denim jeans and blue open necked shirt. Looking across at Frankie and pulling on the cigarette at the same time he nodded in Joe's direction and murmured,

"What's with the Boss? has some studio offered him a role in a western movie?"

Joe banged the coffee pot down and spun around.

"That's it!" he yelled. "What did you say just now?"

Al panicked.

"I was just saying, Boss, you look really... groovy!"

Joe walked over to him and pointed at the jeans.

"My intention is to look casual!" he said sarcastically.

"Well, you look that too, Boss!" came the reply.

Joe took him by the shoulders and pushed him out onto the back porch.

"Go and find something to do!" he ordered him.

Al stood looking at Frankie, as Joe disappeared inside. Then he whispered, "You know what Frankie, ever since the Boss decided to marry an Irish Woman with red hair, he's been acting like John Wayne!"

Joe appeared suddenly in the door way and made a swipe at him. Al's eyes widened as he ran out of Joe's reach. Frankie roared with laughter.

"One of these days, Al – I'm warning you!" shouted Joe, pointing his finger. "Now, go clean the cars or something."

"I've done all that, Boss."

"Then go to the movies. Better still, go and get laid. At least when you're concentrating on something else you won't be thinking of my wardrobe. Now, get out of here!"

Joe turned his attention to Frankie, who was still laughing.

"You're as bad as he is. I want the two of you out of my sight – now."

He went inside and slammed the door leaving the two friends together.

"You shouldn't have said anything!" snapped Frankie, as they walked away from the house. "Why can't you keep your big mouth shut?"

"I know, I know," agreed Al. "I don't mean anything by it, honest. But at least my big mouth's got us some time off with pay, so don't knock it."

They both laughed as they made their way to Frankie's car.

That Saturday there was a buzz of excitement throughout the house. Angela was coming early that evening. Joe was gong to show her around his home and she was staying for dinner. He was in high spirits. Evie, however, was in a state of nerves. She had been trying to find out about Joe's intended but nobody was saying anything – on Joe's orders.

Rooney and Frankie had the night off. Al was to call for Angela and bring her to the house. Then he, too, was free to go. Joe kept watch at the window as the time arrived for Angela's visit. A little after six, Al drove up to the front door and he and Angela got out. Joe greeted her with a broad smile and open arms.

"Hi, come on in," he said ushering her into the entrance hall. "Angel, this is Evie, my housekeeper."

Evie stood with her hands clasped in front of her, lowering her gaze and bowing her head as Angela looked in her direction. Angela reached out and took a shocked Evie's hand.

"It's so nice to meet you, Evie," she smiled warmly.

"It's so nice to meet you too Miss," replied Evie, clearly surprised by Angela's approach.

"Come on, Angel," said Joe, "Let's have a look at the house before we have dinner."

As they walked away, Evie hurried to the kitchen. Joe showed Angela the large dining-room and lounge. Both were expensively furnished. He may not have been the most educated of men but over the years Joe Morrelli had acquired a great deal of taste and it showed in his surroundings. On escorting her to the kitchen, Joe was puzzled as Angela stopped and knocked the open door.

"May I come in, Evie?" she asked.

"Why…yes, of course," replied Evie, surprised and flustered.

"Oh, what a lovely kitchen!" Angela deliberately sounded impressed. "You could fit our whole apartment in here with room to spare. And everything's so clean and fresh. You mush work awfully hard, Evie."

Evie didn't answer, as they turned to leave. She didn't know what to make of Angela Kenny but one thing was for sure, she certainly wasn't what Evie expected.

As they climbed the wide stairs, Angela pointed to the study door.

"What's in there, Joe?"

"That's my study, Angel. That's were I sort out my thoughts, my plans, my business; and there's something I'd like to say. When we get married I aim to share every inch of this house with you, but the study I claim as my own. Can you understand that?"

Angela looked at him for a few moments, then nodded.

"Yes, Joe, I understand. Everyone needs their own space, even when they're married. Heaven knows. I'll have plenty to choose from!"

With every passing day Joe was becoming more convinced that Angela was the right woman for him. Today was no exception.

On reaching the landing, he led her along a hallway and then opened a door.

"I was thinking of this room for your mother. it was always the guest room. I hope you like it."

Stepping inside Angela found a spacious bedroom and sitting room combined.

"Joe, it's beautiful!"

"It's ensuite too. Look, the bathroom's over there."

"She'll love it. It's just perfect."

Making their way back along the hallway, Joe pointed to the next door.

"That room belongs to Rooney," he informed her.

"I didn't know Rooney lived here, Joe."

"Well, he doesn't, he's got his own apartment. But this is like a second home to him and there are times when he needs to stay over. He keeps some of his stuff here, too,, but he'll be moving out permanently when we get married."

"Why?"

"Well, he doesn't think it would be right to stay on. He feels he'd be in the way. You know how it is. You might want the house to be more private."

"But I wouldn't want Rooney to move out, Joe. After all, he was here long before me. You didn't want to separate my mother from me. I don't want to separate Rooney from you. We're all going to be family. I'd like him to stay, Joe. The house is big enough for all of us. Will you tell him?"

"No problem!" said Joe, beaming. "He'll be delighted – not to mention relieved!"

They worked their way along the next two small bedrooms, vacant but beautifully furnished. Inside the bathroom, the walls were covered in glittering, white tiles. The shower screens were decorated with white swans. Placed on one towel rail was a set of pink towels and on a second was a set of blue. The floor was also covered in white tiles, but these had a faint speckle throughout.

Finally they came to the master bedroom at the top of the stairs. Joe grinned.

"And this is my room," he said, opening the door to reveal a large room with mirrored wall units along one side. A vase of fresh flowers sat in the window and a velvet armchair was placed so that a view of the garden could be easily obtained. Angela hovered in the doorway.

"Come on in, Angel," he coaxed. "In three months it's going to be your room, too."

She stepped in and sunk into the thick, rich carpet. It was a lovely room, true, but one thing that made an instant impression on Angela was the king size bed! She'd never seen anything like it. The cover and pillowcases matched the drapes on the window and at the foot of the bed stood a velvet chest, a perfect match for the bedroom chair. At each side of the bed was a small cabinet with matching lamp.

Joe could see Angela was lost for words. She noticed another door in the room and on following her gaze, he opened it.

"In here's the bathroom," he said. "It's not as big as the main one but it has everything you'd need."

Angela looked around her.

"It's lovely, Joe. It's all so lovely and so big – just like the bed!"

"Oh, you noticed?"

"I'd be blind not to. At least if I take a headache I'll be safe for at least an hour."

"What do you mean?"

"Well, it'll take you about that long to find me."

"Don't kid yourself, Angel. I've had my moments in that bed and the best has yet to come!"

He went over and sat down on it.

"Why don't you come and sit here beside me?" he smiled, patting his hand on a place next to him. She joined him. He leaned towards her.

"I don't suppose you'd care to try it out?"

"Not today, thank you!"

"Yeah well, you can't blame a guy for trying," he joked. He got up and took her hand, gently pulling her up towards him. Then he took her in his arms.

"So do you like the room?"

"Yes, I do. But I guess so did all the other women you brought here."

"Well, I never asked any of them. They were never here long enough." He stared into her face. "With you it's different. You'll be here with me for the rest of our lives and that's what I want more than anything. I love you, you know."

"I know. And I love you, too."

He covered her face in small kisses before their lips met and they exchanged warmth and desire. Eventually Angela pulled away gently and kissed the mole on his cheek.

"Come on, Joe Morrelli, let's get something to eat before you eat me!"

As she walked through the door she could feel her heart pounding. Joe's experience always came through and there were times when it left her feeling inadequate and a little frightened.

Joe watched as she left the room. She wore a simple outfit, just a cream blouse, brown skirt and high heels but she looked lovely. Casual but classy. He knew with care and grooming she could blossom into an elegant and sophisticated woman. It would just take a little time, that's all.

Evie served dinner. As she sat talking to Joe, Angela couldn't help but notice that every now and then Evie would glance at her nervously. She also noticed that Joe was going a little overboard with the table wine, with her more than himself. Every time she got halfway down her glass, he'd fill it up again. She was relieved when it came time for the coffee to be served.

As the evening had progressed, Angela was having a few quiet thoughts to herself about Evie. So when she returned with the coffee and a large brandy for Joe, Angela looked at her.

"Evie, could you bring another cup, please?"

Evie looked puzzled but disappeared and came back carrying another cup and saucer. Angela took them from her and sat them down on the table. Then she pulled out the empty chair beside her.

"That was a wonderful meal, Evie. Now, I think you deserve a rest. Please sit down and join us."

"Oh, I really don't think I should."

"Of course you should."

Angela lifted the coffee pot and poured a cup for Evie, who by now was settled in the chair looking a little embarrassed.

"Here you are, Evie."

"Thank you, Miss."

Then Angela poured some for Joe and herself. She then gave Evie her full attention.

"It must be hard work for you, looking after Joe and his friends."

"Oh, I don't mind."

Joe lit a cigar and sat in silence, listening to every word. He knew where Angela Kenny was coming from!

"Well, I've never had to do it," she continued, "and I'm not sure I could if I had to. That's why I was wondering if you'd stay on here with us when Joe and I get married? I'd be very grateful. That is, unless you've made other plans."

"Oh no!" said Evie, without hesitation. "I have no other plans, none at all."

"Well then, would you stay, for me?"

A look of relief came into Evie's moist eyes. "I didn't think you'd want me. I thought maybe you'd have someone else in mind."

She lifted her cup with a shaking hand.

"I can't think of anyone better. You see, Evie, just because I'm moving in doesn't mean to say things have to change. I'd rather everything went on like before. The only difference being that I'll be one of the family too."

Evie's face lit up as Angela went on, "Besides, I was a waitress and I know how demanding these men can be. They'd run you off your feet if you'd let them."

"Oh, Miss Angela, you don't know the half of it!"

"I can imagine. We girls will just have to stick together."

"Why, you took the words right out of my mouth!"

Evie started chatting quite happily to Angela about all the comings and going of the Morrelli household.

Joe lifted the brandy glass and looking across at the two women he smiled and shook his head. At last, Evie had been put out of her misery by the very woman she had dreaded and was now in deep conversation with. He had to admit it, Freddie Barrett was right about her. Angela Kenny was one shrewd lady when it came to people and Joe felt proud of her for the way she'd been so observant with Evie. She'd been quick on the uptake and wasted no time in putting Evie's mind at rest. She'd also treated her like an equal. Not many white women he knew would have done what she did. Joe was filled with admiration. One thing was for sure, there was no prejudice in her and if Evie's laughter was anything to go by, Angela had made a friend for life.

It was a more happy and relaxed Evie who cleared the dining table, as Joe took Angela into the lounge and closed the door.

"I've got to hand it to you, Angel, I'm impressed by the way you handled that situation back there."

He smiled as she looked at him.

"Well, I know what it's like to be nervous. I remember the first time I ever waited on tables in 'The Safe Haven'. I was so scared in case I'd do something wrong. In case people wouldn't like me."

Joe poured a small scotch for himself and a beer for Angela from some chilled bottles Evie had left.

"Tell me something," she said, taking the glass from his hand, "how did you meet her?"

She waited patiently as Joe cast his mind back several years to the day he and Evie first met.

Coming out of Isaac Goldman's office that day, Joe was in a great mood. Isaac had proved to be a good accountant and an even better friend. Thanks to his shrewd business plans and investments, Joe was fast becoming a wealthy man. He was on the ladder of success and climbing it daily. The icing on the cake had happened earlier that morning when Joe signed the final papers and bought his first home.

As he stood on the pavement, he smiled to himself. No more apartments for him, furnished or otherwise. Joe Morrelli was moving to Roseberry Avenue, a very classy neighbourhood. His home would have a driveway, garden – front and back, and even a small swimming pool. Some might have thought it modest by certain standards but to Joe it was 'The White House!'

He looked around for the car but it was nowhere to be seen. Then he remembered Al saying it was low on gas. That's probably where he'd gone, to get the tank filled up. Joe looked at his watch. He'd have time for a cup of coffee, so he crossed the street to the diner opposite.

On sitting down he was approached by the waitress.

"Can I get you something?" she asked in a low voice. Joe looked up. There stood a Negro woman in her thirties, plump, not pretty but quite shy in appearance. The badge on her uniform said just one word, 'Evie.'

"I'll have a cup of coffee and one of those doughnuts," he replied, pointing to the display cabinet on the counter.

"Surely," she said, turning to fetch his order.

As Joe relaxed and enjoyed his coffee and doughnut, the waitress tried to busy herself in the almost empty diner. She kept coming back to his table, re-filling his cup but never spoke to him, nor him to her except to say 'thanks.'

As Joe checked his watch again and looked out of the window in the hope of seeing Al. the door of the diner was thrown open and a group of construction workers piled in. they took their seats, talking loudly and laughing. After they'd settled, the waitress went over to them with her notepad and pencil.

"Would you like to order?" she asked.

They ignored her. She tried again. This time their conversation halted and they all looked at her. The ringleader, Larry spoke up.

"Well,. If it isn't Miss Black America!" he sneered.

It was the mid sixties and a time of racial tension, both north and south.

The rest of them roared with laughter and before long she was subjected to jokes and jibes about her colour, her looks and her sex. Larry especially made a meal of it,

"There's always one!" thought Joe, in disgust. "There's always one who's all mouth and no brains!"

The waitress persevered until she was able to provide the cook with the orders. Then she came back to Joe. He put his hand over the cup.

"I've had enough," he said, not really meaning the coffee.

He noticed the tears in her deep, brown eyes and for a few seconds he remembered his childhood and how the other kids made fun of him because of his background, his clothes and his lack of intelligence. Some even refused to sit beside him in school and that had hurt.

Joe sat on as she returned to serve Larry and his cronies.

"I didn't order that!" he snapped, as she put the plate down in front of him.

She checked her notepad and held it out to him.

"Yes, you did. You ordered double cheeseburger and French fries."

"Are you calling me a liar?"

She didn't reply but lifted the plate.

"I ordered chicken, French fries and a side salad. Now go and get it while I go and take a piss!"

The others sniggered as he left the table. After a few seconds, Joe followed.

The cubicles in the men's room were all empty except for the one occupied by Larry, so he was surprised to hear a gently tapping on his door.

"Who's there?" he called.

There was silence. Then the tapping began again.

"Who the hell's there?" he called again, as he unlocked and pulled open the door.

In a split second Joe grabbed him, pushed him back inside the cubicle, forced his head down the toilet and pulled the chain. Larry struggled but was no match for Joe Morrelli's temper. The water swirled around his head and muffled cries could be heard as he banged his fists off the sides of the cubicle. As the water subsided so did his strength and he fell limp, as Joe picked him up and sat him on the floor.

"The next time you order something I suggest you eat it – while you've still got a set of teeth!" advised Joe as he threw Larry down and walked over to the mirror. After brushing the drops of water from his clothing, he straightened his tie and casually walked out, leaving Larry still gasping for breath.

"Thanks for the service," he said handing the waitress the money to cover his bill and a generous tip. She smiled at him for the first time.

"Thank you," she said, "Thank you very much."

There was no love lost between the Italians and Negros, it was true. But at that moment in time they were neither, just two people who had both been on the receiving end of prejudice – and didn't like it.

Joe reached into his pocket and handed her a printed business card.

"Just in case you ever need a job," he said.

She took it from him and watched him leave.

A few days later, Joe was standing in the doorway of his new home talking to a delivery man, when a taxi pulled up. The rear door opened and out stepped the waitress, still clutching the business card he's given her. She stared at him, not really knowing if she'd be welcome. He returned her stare and then grinned.

"Come on in, Evie," he said. "I've been expecting you…"

When Joe had concluded his story, Angela put her glass down on the table beside his and said,

"You know what, Joe Morrelli? You collect people the way others collect antiques!"

"Shush! Don't let Evie hear you call her an antique, I get enough hassle from her as it is!"

"Well, you're certainly not as tough as you'd like people to believe."

"Yeah well, keep it to yourself Angel. I've got my reputation to think about!"

"Oh, and what reputation would that be?"

"I'll show you!"

He suddenly grabbed her and pushed her back onto the large couch. They wrestled playfully, laughing and giggling. As Joe weighed down on her, Angela began to move her body around in the hope of freeing herself.

"Oh come on, Joe, that's not fair!" she laughed in a deep throaty way. Not only did she look sexy, she sounded sexy. It was at this point when Joe's playfulness became something more serious. He buried his head in her neck as his hands explored her struggling body. She writhed beneath him but the movement of her body against his aroused him even more. He tried to kiss her as he fumbled with his zip, but she freed her hands and putting them on his shoulders, pushed him away – "no!!!" she said, defiantly staring into his face.

Joe paused. Then breathing deeply, he shook his head, "Jesus Angel, don't you ever get the urge?"

"No. I want it to be special for both of us."

"I'm sorry. I got carried away. It won't happen again, I promise."

He sat upright and straightened his clothing. He sounded both apologetic and guilty. Angela couldn't bring herself to be angry with him, so she reached out and took his hand.

"I'm sorry, Joe," she said softly, "I know it can't be easy for you. But this isn't the time or the place."

"I know," he replied, nodding his head as he stared at the coffee table. "I just love you so much, Angel, I couldn't help myself." He turned towards her. "Forgive me?"

"There's nothing to forgive." She took his face in her hands and kissed him.

Joe decided some music was called for and 'Ol Blue Eyes' was soon serenading them.

"Would you like to dance, Angel?"

Angela took his hand and they embraced as they swayed to the gentle rhythm. Neither spoke as they enjoyed the warmth and closeness of each other. Eventually, they returned to the couch. Joe put his arm around Angela's shoulder and she leaned her head against his chest. The silence continued as the words of the love songs filled the room. She held his hand gently but firmly, and every now and then they would instinctively kiss. Joe had never spent an evening like this with any other woman and he felt good about himself. Angela and the rest of the world.

When the taxi arrived to take her home, Joe walked Angela to the front door.

"I'll remember this night for a long time, Angel!"

"There'll be plenty of nights just like it, Joe."

The driver kept sounding the horn but every time Angela tried to leave, Joe kept pulling her back to kiss her. After several attempts Angela said,

"Will you let me go? The poor man will think he's come to the wrong address!"

"So let him think!"

"Joe, you've kept him waiting so long you'll probably have to pay him by cheque!"

"So, I'll pay him by cheque!" he laughed, as she finally made her way to the taxi.

Joe paid the driver and gave him a large tip to help calm his nerves.

After watching them leave, he returned to the lounge and poured himself a drink. He turned off the music and stood staring at the couch.

He was glad nothing happened tonight. Angela was right, it wasn't the time and it certainly wasn't the place. The more he thought about it, the more convinced he became. He smiled to himself. Joe Morrelli had met a woman with dignity and self respect. In fact, she was one in a million – and soon she was going to be his!

Breakfast time had come and gone before Joe got up the next morning. He took his seat at the kitchen table, facing Rooney. Evie was humming happily as she stood by the kitchen sink.

"Good morning Mr Joe, Would you like some breakfast?"

"No thanks Evie, Coffee will do just fine."

Rooney closed the file he had been looking through and studied Joe as Evie gave him his coffee and stood hovering over him.

"Perhaps I'd better bring Miss Angela her breakfast now," she said.

"That's fine by me. I'll have Al drive you over to Westmere Avenue with a tray!"

"You mean she didn't stay over?"

"That's right."

"Well, that's a first." Evie was surprised. "But then, I knew she was different," she went on as she turned back towards the sink. "She's so friendly and has such nice manners. Not at all like that Miss Flemming."

"What do you mean by that?" asked Joe.

"Well, she swept in and swept out, waving her hands in the air and giving orders to everybody."

"She's an actress," shrugged Joe.

"That's her problem. She doesn't know when to stop acting. Why, when I think of all the times she just came into this house and took over without so much as a 'by your leave', it makes my blood boil!"

"Do you mind!" snapped Joe. "You happen to be talking about my girlfriend."

"Ex-girlfriend!!" interrupted Rooney.

"Yeah well, that's what I mean," he insisted as they both looked at each other.

"Well, she's not the one for you, Mr Joe," Evie continued. "I've always known it. And believe me, I know what I know."

"That's the trouble with everyone who works for me, they're know-alls!" he shot Evie a sarcastic look before leaning his elbows on the table and turning his attention to Rooney.

"Take Al, for instance. I swear Rooney, one of these days I'm going to kick his ass!"

Rooney laughed.

"He really gets to you sometimes, doesn't he? Like the other day."

"Oh, so you heard about that?"

"Yes, Frankie told me."

"That's what I mean! Everybody's a know-all and they tell everybody else what they know. I wouldn't be surprised if I ended up having to send my wife coded messages by carrier pigeon!"

Rooney shook his head and laughed loudly. Joe went on, "And there's another thing…"

"Rooney, Miss Angela has asked me to stay!" Evie interrupted, over Joe's shoulder.

Joe stared in disbelief and then threw his hands up in the air.

"You see what I'm up against here?" He yelled. "I can't even get to finish a conversation in my own home without someone putting in their two cents worth!"

He glared directly at Evie, who totally ignored him.

"And are you staying, Evie?" smiled Rooney.

"Why of course I am! She needs my help, and she's so young. I just couldn't leave."

"Wouldn't is the word I would use." Muttered Joe as he turned his eyes up towards the ceiling.

Evie continued in a pleased voice, "Why I think Miss Angela and me will get on just fine. You know, Mr Joe, it was a lucky night for you when you met her. Someone must have been praying for you."

Joe looked across at Rooney and shrugged his shoulders.

"Yeah well, maybe it was you, Evie."

"Maybe it was, Mr Joe," she replied, nodding her head and smiling, knowingly. "Maybe it was…."

As Gene O'Brien walked into his office, the first thing he noticed was a large bottle of expensive champagne sitting on the desk.

"What's this?" he asked looking across at Alan Bailey.

"Have I won first prize in a raffle?"

"Beats me, Gene. It arrived a little while ago with a note."

He nodded towards an envelope, then leaned back in his chair and put his feet up on the desk. Gene opened the envelope and read the note. A broad grin appeared on his face as he shook his head.

"Well, what do you know, that horny Italian friend of mine has finally been brought to heel!"

"Who?"

"Joe Morrelli! He's getting married. Well, I'll be damned. I never thought I'd see the day. And do you want to know the best part? He's marrying that young Irish girl."

"The one who works for him?"

"The very same. He surely won't get it all his own way with her! Being Irish and a redhead she's bound to have a temper. What I wouldn't give to be a fly on the wall when they have an argument!"

He roared with laughter.

"Don't you think she's a little young for him, Gene?"

"I guess a lot of people would. Joe thought so too. But what the hell, if you're happy, age doesn't matter. Besides, Joe's played the field, he's no fool... she must be very special."

Gene stared into space, rubbing his chin with his hand.

"Just think, Alan," he said, "when Joe Morrelli was starting to make a name for himself and enjoying the pleasure of women's company, a baby girl was born in Ireland. That baby girl would grow up, leave her home and come thousands of miles and you know why?"

Alan shook his head, so Gene continued.

"Because fate decreed that they should be one. How's that for a story?"

"It beats the hell out of Hollywood, Gene!"

"You can say that again. I must admit I feel rather proud, I had quite a roll to play in all of this myself."

"Now you sound like an actor!"

Gene sat down on the edge of the desk.

"Well, it just goes to prove I'm in the right job, doesn't it? I've never met so many actors in my life!"

He paused thoughtfully.

"You know, Alan, there are times when I've thought of this great country of ours as a wagon train. Except, instead of keeping us out of danger, the wagon masters are leading us straight into the pass and right slap, bang into the Indians."

Gene had a serious tone in his voice, as he pointed his finger like a gun, and pulled the trigger.

"Oh, and I suppose you could do better?"

"Well, I sure as hell couldn't do any worse!" he said shrugging his shoulders and getting off the desk.

"When I walk down those corridors of power and past all those portraits of the Presidents, there's only one I stop to salute."

"And we all know who that is – J.F.K.!"

"Got it in one," smiled Gene. "Who knows, maybe some day the people will want another Irish man in the White House." He leaned his hands on the desk. "And when that day comes, Eugene O'Brien will be waiting in the wings. So stick with me, buddy.. we could be on our way."

Alan sat upright.

"You really believe that one day you could run for President?" he asked, surprised and excited.

"Well, you've got to aim high! After all Joe Morrelli did and its paid off for him. Times are changing, Alan, and if you get Italians marrying Irish then you get a lot of backing and a lot of votes. Especially if you know people like Joe Morrelli and Angela Kenny." Gene became thoughtful once again.

"You know, this young Irish girl will figure in my own fate. She's marrying a guy with all the right connections. We Irish are very superstitious, Alan, and I've got a hunch about her. Next to my wife, she's the only other woman I'd like in my camp. Sure, I'd run for president – when the times' right. God knows I'd be as good as some we've had, if not better than most! But don't worry, Alan, I won't expect you to call me Mr President, you can still call me Gene!"

He ducked just in time as Alan Bailey's paper weight zoomed over his head.

Chapter 6

As far as the wedding was concerned, everything was going according to plan. Agnes's health wasn't all it should have been but Angela put most of it down to excitement. Joe was anxious that nothing should interfere with the preparations, so he insisted that Agnes have regular home visits by the doctor. When he couldn't see Angela, he phoned. However, on this particular day he was having great difficulty in contacting her. Finally, Agnes answered the phone. She told him that Angela had hardly been at home all day and she sounded a little upset and tearful. After their short conversation, Joe decided to drive over to the apartment after dinner. Surely Angela would be home by then.

It was 8.30pm

"Hello, Joe," said Agnes, leading him into the sitting room.

"Hi Agnes. How are you?"

She didn't answer, but as she turned to face him under the light he could see how red and puffed her eyes were. She was so pale and drained. He put his hands on her shoulders.

"What's the matter, Agnes, don't you feel well? Maybe I should call the doctor. You shouldn't be here on your own. Where's Angel?"

"She's not here."

"You mean she's still out? What's going on, have you two had an argument?"

"I wish it was that simple, Joe."

"I think she's in Church. At least, that's where she said she was going."

"Church, at this time of night? I don't understand."

He paused for a moment then said anxiously, "She's not having second thoughts about the wedding, is she?"

"Oh no, nothing like that. Didn't she tell you, Joe? I thought she would."

"Tell me what?"

Tears came into her eyes.

"This is Robert's anniversary. He was murdered a year ago today."

Joe stared.

"Agnes, I'm sorry. Angel never mentioned it."

"Well, I suppose with the wedding and everything, she didn't want to say. She knows how happy you've been. She's been out walking around on her own. I'm worried about her, Joe. Angela's taking it so badly. I thought maybe the excitement of the wedding would have helped her a little but I dare say it has made her miss him even more. That's probably why she went back to Church again this evening." She broke down. "Oh Joe, I just wish she'd come on home! There's nothing any one can do. Her father's gone and nothing can bring him back."

"It's o.k. Agnes. I'll go straight to the Church now. if she's not there I'll go and look for her. I won't come back unless she's with me. Now, you sit down and stop worrying."

The Church of our Lady of Lourdes was dimly lit when Joe arrived. A few parishioners were still kneeling and as he looked around he caught sight of a lonely figure sitting before the marble alter. It was Angela. Joe respectfully bent one knee, crossed himself and slipped into a seat beside one of the large pillars. He watched as Angela gazed silently at the large, gold crucifix. Eventually, the others left. Just the two of them remained. Quietly, the vestry door opened and the elderly priest came out onto the alter. He glanced towards Angela, then made his way down to her. He bent over and placed a hand on her shoulder. They talked. Joe couldn't hear what was being said but when he saw Angela point towards the back of her head and the expression on the priest's face change, he knew she'd confided in him about the death of her father. She covered her face with her hands and sobbed, uncontrollably. The priest put his arm around her in a consoling way, shaking his head and looking at her, helplessly. Joe knew Angela Kenny would never forget what happened to her father or her family. It was a nightmare she'd always have to live with and he'd have to live with it too. In a few weeks they'd kneel before that alter and become man and wife. He knew he'd never be able to take away the pain of her father's murder, but maybe he could ease it a little by making her happy. By loving her.

As the priest ushered Angela onto the aisle, Joe hurried out of the church and stood in the darkness of a side entrance. A few minutes later they both appeared.

"Thank you for listening, Father Ryker. It's just that sometimes I get so confused."

"Sometimes I can't even pray." She looked down at the rosary beads in her hands.

"I know, my dear. But you must remember that God sees everything and forgets nothing. He's all powerful."

"Well, if that's true why doesn't he do something to stop the pain and suffering in the world? Why let old people get mugged? Or innocent children abused? Or decent men murdered?!"

Father Ryker was silent.

"Good question!" thought Joe. And she wasn't getting any answers!!

After a while, Father Ryker took Angela's hand and looked into her face.

"I know this is hard to understand, even harder to explain – believe me! But there is justice in Heaven, Angela."

"Shouldn't there be some on Earth too? Surely we deserve some kind of justice?"

"He said 'Vengeance is mine'."

"I'm sorry father, but I think vengeance belongs to everyone who suffers for no reason. In my heart I want vengeance for my father and I always will. I just hope that someday the person who murdered him will get what he deserves."

At this point Joe came forward, pretending he'd just arrived. Angela was surprised to see him.

"Joe!"

"Hi, Angel. Your mother said I'd find you here. Hi Father Ryker, how are you doing?"

"Hello, Joe. It's nice to see you again - even if it isn't at Mass!"

"Yeah well, I've been meaning to get around to it, Father, but something always crops up."

"I can imagine! Just as long as you're here on the day."

"Are you kidding, Father, miss my own wedding?"

Father Ryker smiled and nodded.

"Here, Joe, you take this young lady home. I'm sure Agnes is worried about her. Go on, Angela, and just keep thinking about how happy your father is for you. You're a good girl and you've found yourself a good man. God bless you both."

After saying goodnight to him, Joe and Angela got into the car.

"Angel, why didn't you tell me this was your father's anniversary?"

"I didn't want to, Joe. Everything's going so well, I didn't want to spoil it. I thought maybe if I had the day to myself I could get through it o.k. but I'm glad you're here."

She took his hand and held it against her cheek.

"We're getting married Angel and marriage isn't much good if you can't share the sad times as well as the happy ones."

"I know. But there are nights when I close my eyes and see it all again so clearly, Joe. His brains on the ground. His blood on my hands. I call to him. I scream at him to answer me but he can't. As long as I live I'll never hear his voice again."

She threw herself into Joe's arms and he hugged her tightly.

"Listen to me, Angel, we all loose people we love. Sometimes it's through death, sometimes it's through fate. Either way it's still damn hard to deal with. But as long as we remember them and keep them in our hearts, they're never really gone. Are they?"

Angela found that comforting.

"You're right, Joe. My father's always with me. I can sense it."

"You see."

She looked up at him.

"There are times when you're so like him."

"I'm honoured. But I don't want to be your father, I want to be your husband. There's a big difference, you know? I want to be sure of your love for me. No misunderstandings, Angel."

"I am sure of my love for you. I want to be your wife, not your daughter. No misunderstandings, Joe."

"That's good enough for me!" he hugged her again.

"You know what?" he asked.

"What?"

"I get the feeling that maybe we didn't meet by chance after all."

"Really."

"Yeah. In fact, I think your father guided you right to me and I can promise you this, Angel, I'm going to repay him – no matter how long it takes!"

Angela gave Joe the job of dealing with the invitations for the wedding reception. Fancy cards were printed with each individual's name and as he sat in his study going over each one he couldn't help but notice that his guest list varied quite a bit; from Nicholas Andretti in the city , to Gene O'Brien in Congress, to Mario and Gino in the Bronx. There was no getting away from the fact that Joe Morrelli was well known in New York and had a lot of friends. As he picked up the gilt edged card with Antonia's name on it, a sad expression came over his face. He hadn't seen her since the night he'd ended their affair and although he'd phoned her several times, she refused to speak to him. Joe knew she was angry and upset and that she'd probably never forgive him, but he had hoped that the ice between them might thaw a little and enable them to be friends.

Slipping the invitation into the envelope he felt it was all going to be a waste of time. She wouldn't come. That much he was sure of. However, with or without Antonia, Joe was determined to make it one of the best receptions anyone had ever had. So as all the invitations went into the post, he was happy enough to carry on with his plans for 'the big day'!

A few nights later, Angela was at work as usual when Freddie approached her with a worried look.

"Angela, you have a visitor." He nodded towards the office.

"Who is it?"

"Miss Flemming! Perhaps I should phone Mr Morrelli."

"No, its alright, Mr Barrett. I've been half expecting her. Excuse me."

When she reached the office, she closed the door gently behind her. Antonia stood in a smart black and white suit, black high heels and black purse. Her blond hair and make up were done to perfection. She was a very attractive woman who always maintained she wasn't a day over twenty eight. In face, she was thirty two her last birthday but only Joe and a very few others knew it. She certainly didn't look her age as she'd always been kind to herself. In her profession she had to be.

"What is this – some kind of joke?" she said, sarcastically, as she threw the wedding invitation onto the desk. "How dare you send me an invitation to my ex-lovers wedding!"

"I take it you're not coming, then."

"Why should I come to see Joe make a fool of himself? I've been on to you since the very beginning. Little Miss Nobody meets Mr Somebody. She knows she's onto a good thing so she pretends to fall in love with him. Plays hard to get until he falls in love with her, then she climbs into bed with him making him believe he's half his age because she's young enough to be his daughter! Shall I go on?"

Antonia was getting angry, Angela stared long and hard at her.

"I really don't care what you think, because none of it is true. You've had Joe for years.

You above all should know he's no fool. I don't love Joe Morrelli for what he is, I love him for who he is. I'm in love with the man – not the image, but I guess you'd find that hard to believe. If your little story were true then why am I still working here at the restaurant earning my own money? I'll tell you why, Antonia. Because since the day I first met him, I've never asked Joe Morrelli for anything!"

At that last remark, Antonia lowered her gaze to the floor, looking uncomfortable. She was silent for a moment but when she spoke her tone was more natural.

"Look, you're a very young girl. There are plenty of men you could have, why choose him? Don't you have any consideration for my feelings?"

They both stared at each other.

"I didn't choose him, he chose me. If things were the other way around and Joe had asked you to marry him, would you have considered my feelings>" asked Angela.

Antonia remained silent. Angela continued, "Joe loves you, Antonia, in a special way and he always will. You matter to him more than you know. I know he's been phoning you and he's been deeply hurt by your response. You've turned your back on him. That's something he's never done to you and never will. It was he who sent you the invitation, not me. Even after everything that's happened, he still wants you to be part of things. I know you think I don't love him but I do. In time you'll come to see that for yourself. But if you have any love for him, and I know you do, then at least phone him and wish him well. It would make him so happy. After all, he'd do it for you."

Angela politely opened the office door. Antonia straightened her shoulders and holding her head up high, she walked passed her, leaving the invitation lying on the desk. Angela picked it up and was holding it in her hand when Freddie appeared.

"Is everything alright, Angela?"

"Everything's fine, Mr Barrett, but I'd rather you didn't tell Mr Morrelli about this."

"Oh, Angela, is that wise? Remember what happened the last time we kept a secret!"

"This is different. It was just between Miss Flemming and myself."

Freddie nodded.

"Alright, but I must say, by the look on her face she didn't seem pleased."

"Well, sometimes the truth hurts, Mr Barrett. And besides, you can't please everyone."

Rooney was puzzled. He's been keeping a careful eye on the calendar and Joe's birthday was in a week's time. Any other year it would have been the topic of conversation but so far Joe hadn't even mentioned it. As they sat in the study that evening, Rooney decided to bring it up.

"What are you doing for your birthday this year,, Joe, or is it a secret?"

"Oh, nothing much. I think I'll just have a quiet night at home."

"What, no party? Why?"

"I have my reasons."

"What reasons?"

Joe paused.

"Well , to be honest with you, Rooney, I've been so busy with the wedding arrangements I haven't given anything else much thought."

"Come on, Joe, you've always thought about your birthday from ever since I've known you."

"Yeah well, this year it's different."

"Why, because you're forty?"

"It's not because I'm forty!" mimicked Joe, slapping his gold pen down on the desk. "It's just that,…. well… people might think it's silly."

"People never bothered you before," said Rooney, with a raised eyebrow.

Joe looked at him, then threw his hands up in the air.

"Oh, alright, then! Angel might think it's silly!"

"I see," smiled Rooney. "Doesn't she know?"

"No, she doesn't. and don't you go telling her. She'd only buy me a present and I don't want her spending her money on me. She's saving for the wedding."

"She might be hurt if you don't tell her and she finds out."

"Well, if she finds out I'll find some excuse for not telling her. O.k.? Now, can we drop the subject and just forget about my birthday. I'd like to get back to business here."

He picked up the pen.

"Sure thing, Joe, said Rooney. "I've forgotten about it already."

"That was quick!"" muttered Joe.

That same night, Rooney paid a visit to 'The Safe Haven' to see Angela.

"Is anything wrong?" she asked, closing the office door and then sitting down facing him.

"No, nothing's wrong, Angela, but I think you should know that it's Joe's birthday next week and he doesn't want anyone to tell you."

"Why?"

"Well he says he has his reasons."

Angela went quiet. With her father's anniversary just passed and Agnes's health so bad, she felt sure that these were probably the reasons Joe had in mind.

"I think I know what those reasons are," she said, in a soft voice.

Rooney faltered.

"Yes…well… I think there's something else you should know. Joe has a party every year."

"Really, who gives it for him?"

"Himself."

Angela was astonished.

"Joe gives himself a birthday party!"

"Well, it's sort of a tradition with Joe," shrugged Rooney. "He's never had any family to speak of so if he doesn't remember it, who will? Besides, he reckons that the ones who are invited and don't show, are the ones he should keep an eye on!"

They looked at each other and laughed.

"Anyway," he continues, "there'll be no party this year. He's decided to spend his birthday at home – no fuss."

"That's what he thinks!" said Angela, determinedly. "I'm glad you told me, Rooney. We'll have a small surprise party for him right here. What do you say?"

"Great! But how are we going to get him here on the night?"

"Leave that to me. The big problem is what to buy him. What do you get the man who has everything?" She bit her lip while trying to think.

"Maybe the party would be enough," said Rooney.

"Not if it's going to be a small one. We'd need something extra. Something special. What are you going to get him?"

"No idea."

"Then how would you feel if we bought him a present between us. Something really different. Maybe something Irish," she smiled.

"That's a great idea. What had you in mind?"

Angela became secretive.

"Can you meet me tomorrow?"

"Sure I can. Where are we going?"

"Shopping. Meet me at Davis Street at noon."

"What if Joe finds out?"

"He won't. I'll phone him and tell him I have an appointment with the dressmaker."

They both got up.

"O.k." said Rooney, "I'll see you at high noon. We'll be just like Grace Kelly and Gary Cooper."

"Only you'll be driving a car instead of a buggy."

"Yes, Angela," he thought, as he watched her leave the office. "And I won't get the girl at the end!"

Rooney had asked Joe for the following Thursday off. Joe agreed but was a little disappointed as Thursday happened to be his birthday and he thought Rooney might have spent it with him even if it did mean staying at the house. He was beginning to wish he's asked Angela out to dinner but as she had spent her birthday organising Gene O'Brien's party, he felt guilty at wanting to celebrate his own.

He decided that Thursday would be a day for business. First he'd go to Stacey's Gym, then visit the Escort Agency to make sure everything was o.k. with the girls. He'd make a few calls on his business associates who owned a couple of nightclubs of which he had shares and finally pay a visit to Reuben and find out just how much money all of this was making him. It would be the first time in years he wouldn't be out enjoying himself.

That Wednesday night Joe sat watching a ball game on T.V., consoling himself with a large scotch. It looked like his fortieth birthday was going un-noticed by everyone, including him. Just then the phone rang. It was Angela.

"Hello, Joe."

"Hi, honey. It's good to hear your voice. Is everything o.k.?"

"Everything's fine but I need to ask a favour."

"Sure, what is it?"

"Could you meet me at 'The Safe Haven' tomorrow night? There are a few things I need to talk over with you, about the wedding."

"Will I call after you've finished work?"

"No need. Mr Barrett said I could take a couple of hours off during the evening. I thought maybe we could have a drink while we sorted things out."

"A couple of hours? That was big of him! Why don't you ask for the night off? Listen, Angel, I don't know why you're putting in all those hours when you have so much to take care of at home. You know how I feel about all this. I have the money to pay for everything you need and….."

"Oh, Joe, let's not get into all that again. Please."

"O.k. o.k! Forget I said anything. What time would suit you?"

"About 8.30?"

"No problem, honey, I'll be there."

"Thanks Joe, Goodnight."

"Goodnight Angel. And hey – I love you."

"I love you, too."

Joe put the receiver down and smiled broadly. That unexpected call had made his night. He'd be spending his birthday with Angela after all, even if she didn't know it. Two hours was better than nothing and gave him something to look forward to. He was in a good mood for the rest of the evening.

Al accompanied Joe on his business calls the next day. The last stop was at Reuben's office, where Joe was surprised to find that Reuben had already left for home., it wasn't like him, he always kept his appointments, especially with friends. Maybe something was wrong. Al drove Joe to Reuben's house. The maid answered the door.

"Mr Goldman isn't here, Mr Morrelli. Can I take a message?"

"Yeah, Louisa. Would you tell him to give me a call? I'd like to have a word with him."

"Of course."

On driving home Al complained of not feeling well, so Joe gave him the rest of the day off. "I won't be going out until later and I can always call a cab." He told him.

"Thanks Boss."

The house was silent as Joe entered and made his way to the kitchen. There was a note on the table from Evie, telling him she's gone to a meeting at her church and that she'd left him some chicken in the refrigerator. He hadn't seen Rooney all day and even Frankie was nowhere to be found. He opened the refrigerator door, took out the plate and stood staring at it.

"Cold chicken," he muttered, "and an empty house. What a birthday this is turning out to be!"

His sudden loss of appetite made him put the plate back and he went upstairs to shower and change. When he'd told Rooney he'd decided to have a quiet night in, he surely didn't think it was going to be this quiet. Even Reuben hadn't been home.

"Thank God Angel phoned," he thought. "This is one night when I'll be really glad to see 'The Safe Haven.'

After paying the taxi driver, Joe glanced at his watch. It was almost 8.30 and as he entered the restaurant, Freddie Barrett was there to greet him.

"Good evening, Mr Morrelli."

Hello, Freddie. Is Angel around?"

"She's waiting for you at your private table. Allow me to lead the way."

As they walked through the dining area, the lights suddenly went very dim.

"Have we got a power cut? Asked Joe from behind.

"No, Mr Morrelli," replied Freddie, "But we've got a party!" he moved away just as the lights went back on.

"Happy Birthday Joe!" came a chorus of voices. Angela stood holding a large birthday cake, accompanied by Rooney, Agnes, Evie, Frankie, Al and Reuben. Joe had never been more surprised in his life. His face beamed as he looked at them all.

"Happy Birthday, Joe," repeated Rooney, as he stepped forward and grabbed his shoulders.

"Why you.... So this is why you wanted the day off!"

"You didn't honestly think I'd desert you on your birthday, did you?"

"Well, I was beginning to wonder about that!"

Reuben came over and shook Joe's hand."

"I'm sorry about the run-around, Joe."

"You had me worried, Reuben."

"Why?"

"Well, you weren't at your office and you weren't at home. I was beginning to think you were having an affair!"

Reuben laughed loudly.

"No kidding? Just wait till I tell Miriam!"

"Don't even think about it!"

"Happy Birthday, Joe," said Agnes, giving him an affectionate hug.

He turned and looked at Evie.

"What's the matter?" he asked, holding out his hands. "Don't I get one from you too?"

"Oh, Mr Joe," said Evie, shyly. "Of course you do!"

Frankie and Al were all smiles.

"Happy Birthday, Boss," said Frankie.

"Same here, Boss," said Al.

"Thanks guys!" he looked at Al, "I thought you were sick?"

"Well, you know how it is, Boss," he replied, shrugging his shoulders. "I couldn't think of anything else to say."

"I find that hard to believe!"

Everyone laughed.

Finally, Joe looked towards Angela.

"Happy Birthday, Joe," she smiled.

He went over and put his arm around her.

"Thank you," he whispered.

"Don't mention it. I'm getting used to organising parties at short notice. What do you think of your cake? Jimmy made it."

Joe had to admit it looked pretty good. It was round and the white icing was set off by a thick, blue ribbon tied in a bow. On the top was written "Happy Birthday Joe" in blue icing.

"How many candles are you putting on it?" he asked

"Why, forty of course," she replied.

"Oh come on Angel," I'll never blow all those out."

"Yes you will, Joe Morrelli."

"Well," he whispered in her ear, "I suppose I could pretend we're making love and there's only a few seconds left. That ought to do it!"

"Honestly, Joe! Can't you think of anything else?"

"Not when I'm with you!"

It was an embarrassed Angela who put the cake down in the centre of the table. Joe took her hand and in an amused voice said,

"Sit down Angel. You look kind of flushed. It must be the excitement!"

He kissed her cheek and as he pulled out the chair he whispered.

"Or maybe it's the thought of our honeymoon!"

Rooney uncorked the champagne and filled the glasses. Joe sat down between him and Angela. "Hey what's this," he asked looking at the table, "presents too?"

He started to open them. There was a large box of his favourite cigars from Evie, Frankie and Al. a brown, leather wallet with his initials stamped on it from Agnes and a book from Reuben about all the great 'Boxing Legends'.

Rooney and Angela looked at each other as Joe opened the last gift. It was a small box and in it was a gold tie-pin.

"That's from Rooney and me," said Angela, touching his hand. "Do you know what it is?"

"Sure, it's a tie-pin," he grinned.

"It's not just a tie-pin, Joe. Here, let me explain."

Joe looked more closely, as she took the box. A heart was held between two hands and above it sat a crown. Joe had never seen anything like it before. Angela went on,

"It's an ancient Irish symbol called 'The Claddagh'. The hands signify friendship, the heart, love and the crown. Loyalty. It's very special to us as a people. Joe, and we only give it to those we love and trust."

Everyone was silent.

"It's beautiful," said Joe, unable to take his gaze away from it. "And what it means is even more beautiful. Where on earth did you get it?"

"Don't ask!" said Rooney. "We did every jewellery store in the city and ended up finding it in a little 'Irish Heritage' place."

"It was waiting there just for me, Rooney!" laughed Joe.

"Well, it was Angela's idea. She thought with both of us being Irish, it was the one thing we could give you to prove how we feel about you."

"Well, love and friendship are the two greatest things you could ever have in life. And when you've got them, you've got loyalty. Thanks, Rooney."

He put his arm around his friends shoulder and then turned to Angela.

"I'm going to treasure this for the rest of my life. Would you put it on?"

Angela took it out of the box and clipped it onto his tie. Everyone applauded.

Joe looked down at it, proudly. It had been given to him by the two people he cared for most in the world. It was part of their history, part of their culture, part of them.

"This is a very special birthday," said Joe, gazing around the table, "and I'm celebrating it with very special people."

Angela got up, looking lovely in a short, sleeveless floral dress and lit the candles on the cake.

"O.k. stand up and make a wish."

Joe stood and closed his eyes. After a few seconds he opened them again and smiled broadly.

"Ready?" she asked.

"Yeah, but you'll have to help me."

"Oh, alright, then. On the count of three."

Everyone counted – ONE, TWO THREE…

Joe and Angela blew out the candles together. Everyone applauded again.

"It looks like you'll get your wish," she smiled. He took her in his arms. "I already have!"

Not to be outdone, Freddie came along with his own present. A silver tankard. As some of the staff laid a buffet on the table, Joe insisted that Freddie join him in a glass of champagne.

"I hope everything is satisfactory, Sir," he said. Feeling very important to be sitting next to his boss.

"Couldn't be better, Freddie. Thank you."

Joe looked around the table. Frankie and Al were swapping jokes, Rooney and Reuben were in deep discussion and Agnes and Evie were chatting away like they'd known each other all their lives. Evie had never been a guest at any of Joe's parties. As they'd always been held in different nightclubs. He was happy she was here tonight and by the look on her face, so was she! Agnes was in a jolly mood and greatly interested in everything Evie was saying. That's what Joe admired most about the Kennys. It didn't matter who you were or what you were, and he liked that.

Freddie raised his glass and in a polite voice said "Happy Birthday Mr Morrelli. I hope I can make everything as satisfactory for you and Angela on your wedding day. I'll certainly do my best."

Joe looked at him.

"Freddie, I'm closing the restaurant. Didn't Angel tell you?"

Freddie gulped down his mouthful of champagne and a look of shock and panic spread over his face.

"Closing the … But, Mr Morrelli, I don't understand. Why close down a perfectly good business? The place is doing so well. Oh dear, this is a bad blow to me. I've enjoyed working here so much. Why, I don't know what I'll do now."

His voice was full of disappointment. Joe looked at Angela.

"Will you tell him or will I?" he asked.

"It's your restaurant."

"Yeah, but it's your idea."

Freddie looked from one to the other in total confusion before blurting,

"I know what you're going to say, Mr Morrelli. You're going to tell me that my services are no longer required."

"No, I'm going to tell you I'm closing 'The Safe Haven' for two days. The day I get married and the day after. You see, there'll be no-one here anyway. Angela has invited all the staff to the reception."

"Reception?"

"Yeah. It's being held in 'The Imperial Palace'. Ralph Lennox is a good friend of mine. He's taking care of everything."

"Oh, I see," said Freddie, wiping his forehead with his handkerchief. "So you're not closing for good?"

"No way! I know a good thing when I see it. It's o.k. Freddie, your job 's safe."

"I can't tell you how glad I am to hear that, Mr Morrelli." Now he was wiping his hands.

"That's o.k. – your face is doing that for you!"

"Excuse me, Sir, but did you say all the staff were invited?"

"Every last one."

"Well no one asked me"," he said in a hurt voice.

"Well. Maybe that's because you're getting an invitation to the Church as well. Go on, Angel, you tell him the rest." Joe looked amused. Angela took over.

"Mr Barrett, I'd always believed that when my wedding day came, my father would be there at my side. But as this can't be, I'd like you to take his place and give me away. It would mean a lot to me if I could walk up the aisle on your arm."

For a few seconds, Freddie was dumbfounded.

"Oh, Angela! I would be delighted, it would be an honour and a privilege. I can't believe it!"

"Thank you, Mr Barrett. I know my father would approve and apart from him there's no one else I'd rather have. It's only a small, church wedding you understand."

"Angela, big or small, I'm very flattered you should ask me."

"Good. There is one thing you could do for me, Mr Barrett."

"Anything Angela."

"Could you give Jimmy some time off and the use of the kitchen? He wants to make my wedding cake."

"Consider it done, my dear." Freddie got up from the table, all smiles. "Just imagine it. Me giving the bride away. I'm so excited! I must go and tell the staff. Oh…. And see to the other customers of course!"

Joe nodded his head and watched as Freddie strode down the dining area. He turned to Angela.

"Well, you've made somebody very happy. Just do me one favour, Angel. When you get to the altar make sure you're the one who stands next to me. I'd hate to end up marrying Freddie, and I sure as hell wouldn't want to go on honeymoon with him!"

They both burst out laughing.

"Speaking of honeymoons," said Angela. "Where are we going?"

"Oh, all that's been taken care of. I've rented a beach house in Miami for a month – six weeks if you want to stay that long."

"A beach house, Joe?"

"Well, you wanted sea and sand so I got us a house right beside it."

"Joe, I can't believe it! You mean we'll have the beach and an ocean at our door? Oh, that's wonderful!"

Angela sounded like an excited child. Joe smiled at her, "We aim to please!"

She tried to calm herself.

"Are you sure a month won't be too long for you, Joe?"

He grinned broadly.

"Not for what I've got in mind, Angel, I'm looking forward to it."

"That's what's bothering me! I might not get to see the beach or the ocean."

"Now, would I do that to you?"

"I don't know," she replied, in a serious voice,

179

"Would you Joe?"

His smile faded, as he put his arm around her and kissed her cheek.

"Everything's going to be o.k., honey. When two people love each other, everything else comes naturally. I promise, you'll see as much as you want of that sea and sand, Angel. We'll see it together. We'll be so happy. You'll see. I love you."

"And I love you too," she smiled.

"Well then, all that's left for us to do is show each other in the way we were meant to.."

"I know. But, it's just that…"

Joe placed a forefinger on her lips. She went silent.

"Trust me," he said.

And she did.

Everyone was relaxed and in a happy mood. Joe in particular was delighted with the way his birthday had turned out, and every once in a while he would look down at the tie-pin. As the night wore on the subject of the wedding inevitability cropped up.

"So, it's going to be a small Church wedding but a big reception," said Reuben.

"That's right," replied Joe. "With Angela not having any one here except Agnes, it seemed more appropriate to have just immediate family. So there'll be Angela and her mother, me and Rooney, Evie and the guys."

This surprised Evie.

"You mean I'm going to the Church, Mr Joe?"

"Sure you are. You live in my house, don't you?"

"Have you got a room there, Evie?" Asked Agnes.

"Well , there used to be a games room right across from the kitchen, but Mr Joe had it made into a bed/sitting room just for me so I can keep an eye on everything."

"Especially the refrigerator!" muttered Al.

"Am I going to the Church, Boss? smiled Frankie.

"Yeah, and don't forget to bring your wife and kids to the reception."

Al looked at Joe in anticipation.

"What about me, Boss?"

"What about you?"

"Well, am I going to be at the Church?"

"Why wouldn't you be?"

"But I'm not family."

"Oh yeah? Well, the way you've been eating me out of house and home all these years, I thought you were my twin!"

"That's right, Mr Joe," chirped Evie. "Why he just can't keep his hands to himself. He won't leave my meatloaf alone!"

Al stared at Frankie and raided his eyebrows.

"She should be so lucky!"

"Rooney here is my best man," continued Joe.

"Who's bridesmaid?" asked Rooney, casually.

"Cindy," replied Angela.

"Oh come on Angela, give me a break!"

"What's the matter?" Asked Joe.

"She's a know all!"

Joe stared at him with a straight face.

"Congratulations! I hope you'll both be very happy! Anyway, Reuben, Freddie Barrett will be giving the bride away."

Rooney sullenly poured another glass of champagne.

"Well. It's the only thing he'll have given away from ever I knew him!"

Joe turned his head and laughed.

"I'm sorry it wasn't a big party," said Angela, changing the subject, "but with the wedding and everything, Joe, I just didn't have the time."

"That's o.k. honey. At least this year my party was a surprise and I'm really enjoying it."

Angela looked around the table, smiling.

"I think everyone is."

"I notice you're not drinking beer tonight," he commented.

"Well, it's such a special occasion, I decided to have the champagne instead. But I must admit, I think it's going to my head."

"I must remember that!" he muttered to himself.

It was now 12.30 and Freddie Barrett had ordered taxies for everyone. Angela and Agnes were taking the first one, and after saying their goodbyes to the others Joe put his arms around them both.

"Thanks for coming, Agnes."

"I had a great time, Joe. I haven't enjoyed myself so much since before…. I'll leave you to say goodnight to Angela."

She walked on and Joe took Angela in his arms

"Thanks for my birthday, Angel, and my present."

"I'm glad you liked it," she said, putting her arms around his waist.

He noticed the champagne had put her in a romantic mood, so he kissed her.

"I wish you were coming home with me," he whispered. "That big bed can be pretty lonely."

"Well, look on the bright side. At least you've got plenty of room. My bed's only a single one there's only enough space for me."

"I wouldn't bet on it. I've had my moments in beds like that."

"Is there anywhere you haven't had your moments, Joe Morrelli?"

He smiled broadly.

"No, I guess not. It must be the Italian in me."

"Or the alcohol," she laughed.

"Well, Angel, in a few weeks we'll be going home together. That's the one thing I'm really looking forward to. And I want you to know something. I'm in love with all of you. You're a very intelligent young woman. Your mind turns me on as much as the rest of you!"

"Do you really mean that, Joe?"

"Yes=, I do. And I've never said that to any other woman."

"Thank you. That's quite a compliment."

She kissed him, passionately. "Goodnight, Joe"

"Goodnight, honey. Take care,"

He stared after her as she followed Agnes. Then Rooney came up and put his arm around him.

"Well,. Joe, how was your birthday?"

"Just great, Rooney."

They walked towards the door together. Then Joe stopped and looked at Rooney.

"I learned something tonight."

"You did?"

"Yeah. I learned about friendship and love from the two people who matter most in my life. And to Joe Morrelli, friendship and love means loyalty too."

He smiled as he pointed to the tie-pin!

The time passed quickly for Joe and Angela and as the wedding day drew near, all the preparations had been taken care of except for the wedding rings. They had decided to leave those until the last.

As Al sat waiting, Joe emerged from the house looking very happy. Al got out and opened the rear door for him.

"Where to Boss?"

"Westmere Avenue to pick up Angel, then head up town," he smiled.

When they got there, Joe went inside and a few minutes later he and Angela came out and got into the car.

Al drove along following Joe's directions, and finally pulled up outside an exclusive looking jewellery store.

"Is this the right place?" asked Angela, as Joe opened the large glass door. "It seems so expensive. I'm surprised they don't charge people for just looking in the window!"

"Yeah, it is a bit up-market but what they sell has that little bit of class. This is where I bought your engagement ring."

She feared to think what it must have cost! When Joe explained to the assistant why they were there, they were immediately shown the wedding rings on display in the glass covered counter. They began to try them on. Every ring was beautiful but very pricy.

Eventually they settled for 'His and Hers' plain, thick, gold bands. As the assistant wrapped them up, Joe took out his wallet. At the same time, Angela took out her purse.

"Excuse me," she said, leaning slightly towards the assistant. "Could you give us two separate receipts, please?"

The assistant looked surprised.

Joe looked shocked.

"Angel, what are you doing? He whispered. "Put that purse away!"

"No," she whispered back, "I'm buying your wedding ring."

"Would you please put it away," he insisted. "This is getting embarrassing!"

He then looked at the assistant and smiled.

"Excuse us for a moment," he said, taking Angela's arm and leading her over to a corner.

"What's the matter with you, Angel? I'm buying the rings!"

"You're buying mine, but I'm not letting you buy your own."

"What's the difference? It's no big deal."

"it is to me Joe, and it should be to you if you're going to take this marriage seriously."

Joe shrugged his shoulders and was becoming annoyed.

"I don't understand," he said.

"Then let me explain it to you. When I look at my ring, I'll always know that you bought it for me. I want you to be able to do the same. I want you to look at your wedding ring and know that I bought it for you. What's the point in wearing a wedding ring you bought yourself?"

He put his hands on her shoulders.

"Look honey, it's too expensive."

"It's my money, Joe, I've earned it. I want to buy you your wedding ring. It's my gift to you. Is that so awful?"

"No, it's not that," he said in a low voice.

"Then maybe you're ashamed."

"Of what?"

"Of standing here in a fancy jewellers with a woman who wants to use her own money to buy you something you really want. And I know you want that ring, Joe." She was almost in tears.

He was silent for a moment as he stood looking at the floor. He shook his head.

"I'm not ashamed, Angel, but I'm deeply touched. You see, no other woman has ever done this. Antonia used her credit card, the rest of them used mine. None of them ever used their own money. They didn't need to when they were with me." He raised his eyes and looked at her. "I forgot you were different."

She bent her head.

"I've embarrassed you, haven't I?"

He put his hand under her chin and lifted her head up.

"No, just surprised me. But then, nothing you do should really surprise me, Angela Kenny. Come on."

He took her arm gently and walked her back to the counter. The assistant was waiting.

"The lady would like a receipt for my ring," he told her. "She's paying for it."

Angela opened her purse and started to count out the money. Joe leaned his elbows on the counter and watched closely. He always carried large bills but Angela's were a lot smaller. Tens and twenties – even a few fives! When she'd finished, she looked at him and smiled. In his heart, Joe Morrelli knew she wasn't marrying him for his money and what she'd said and done had proved that beyond the shadow of a doubt. He turned to the assistant.

"I wonder if you could unwrap those rings for me?"

"Certainly sir, Is anything wrong?"

"No, but I'd like you to do something for me."

She undid the wrapping paper and handed Joe the two boxes. He opened them and looked carefully at the rings.

"I'd like an inscription inside. Is that possible?"

"Yes sir, we can do it for you now, what would you like?"

"I'd like the words 'I love you' inside each one."

She pressed a buzzer and an elderly man appeared.

"This gentleman would like these two rings to be inscribed with the words 'I love you'," she explained, pointing to the inside of each one.

"I'll do it right away," he smiled. "It will only take a few minutes."

He took the rings away and ten minutes later, reappeared.

"Here we are. What do you think, Sir?"

He handed them to Joe for a closer look.

"That's fine" Joe smiled, nodding in approval. "Thank you."

He then gave them to Angela. After reading each one she smiled with tears in her eyes and carefully placed them in the boxes.

"Now you can wrap them up," he told the assistant, who by now was almost in tears herself. She did so and placed the fancy package on the counter in front of Joe. He paid for Angela's ring and received his receipt. Then Angela paid for his and folded her receipt neatly before putting it into her purse.

Joe put his arm protectively around Angela and smiled broadly at the assistant.

"She's Irish – and a very independent lady! I love her for it. That's why I'm marrying her."

She nodded and smiled.

"May I wish you both every happiness!"

"You may. I have a feeling I'm going to be a very happy man. I know I'm going to be the luckiest!"

He and Angela walked towards the door and as he held it open for her, they both paused and smiled back at the assistant.

"What a lovely couple," she thought. "They were meant for each other."

Chapter 7

Joe and Angela's wedding day had finally arrived and even though the marriage wasn't taking place until noon, Joe had been awake for hours. He had watched the dawn break from the large bedroom window and could hardly believe that by the end of the day he'd be "an old married man"! He smiled at the thought and wondered if Angela was still asleep. He'd spent a couple of hours with her the day before but hadn't seen her since. As it happened, Angela had hardly slept a wink herself. She had watched every hour pass on the clock and as she did so, became more nervous. So unknown to each other, they had both had a sleepless night. The morning was passing quickly, bringing great excitement and activity at Westmere Avenue and at Joe's house especially. At 10o'clock, Frankie and Al arrived looking very smart in new suits. As they made some coffee in the kitchen, Al turned to Frankie.

"Did the boss mention to you who was driving us to the Church? More to the point, who's driving him?"

"No, he didn't say. I guess he must have hired someone. You know, I still can't believe he's getting married."

"I don't think he can believe it either! And where's Evie?"

"Oh, you know what women are like when they're going somewhere," shrugged Frankie.

"She's a bit carried away at the thought of the wedding and really excited about going to the Church."

"Yeah, well let's hope she doesn't get too carried away and wears a long, white dress; or too excited and ends up marrying Rooney!"

"Or you!!" laughed Frankie, as he left the kitchen.

"Hey, that's not funny!" snapped Al, as he followed.

Both men had just made it to the entrance hall when a familiar figure appeared and walked straight past them with her head held high. It was Evie, dressed in a red and white suit, carrying a large white handbag and wearing white shoes. She never spoke a word but made her way across to the lounge, to wait for the car. Neither of them noticed just how well she looked as their eyes were glued to Evie's head. For there sat a wide brimmed straw hat, decorated with artificial fruit of every kind and description!

"Well there goes Carmen Miranda!" said Al, in a low voice as he watched her disappear.

"I don't know what we're getting for lunch, but I sure know what's for dessert!"

It was just approaching 10:30 when Joe and Rooney came down the stairs. Rooney looked handsome in a light blue suit, white shirt, grey and light blue tie and black shoes. But Joe was a sight to behold! Dressed in an expensive royal blue suit, white shirt and royal blue tie, he looked every inch the successful, self-made man he was. He wore gold cuff-links, black Italian leather shoes, and on his silk tie was the gold, Claddagh tie-pin Angela and Rooney had bought him.

"Oh, Mr Joe, you look wonderful!" smiled Evie.

The guys had to admit it too.

"She's right, Boss. You look terrific!" said Frankie.

"You and Rooney look like big time actors!" Al commented, hoping his compliment would be appreciated. But Joe hadn't forgotten the "John Wayne" episode in the kitchen.

"So help me, Al, I'm warning you!" he glared, holding up his forefinger. "If you make one smart-ass remark today, your feet won't touch the ground!"

Just then a black, stretch limousine pulled up outside the house and a uniformed chauffeur got out. By this time, everyone had made it to the front door.

"Mr. Morrelli," he smiled, touching his peaked cap. "I'll take the guests first and then come back for you. The other chauffeur will collect the bride".

"That's fine," replied Joe. "These are guests". He pointed to Evie, Al and Frankie who were standing aghast at the car and it's driver. "There's one more at Westmere Avenue. It's the bride's mother."

"Of course, Anything you say, Sir."

"Jesus, Boss," whispered Frankie, "this must have cost you a fortune".

Joe shook his head.

"Courtesy of Nicholas Andretti and his grandson".

Evie and Al climbed in but before Frankie could follow Al stuck his head back out. "Hey, Frankie!" he yelled, "it's got a bar in-case we get thirsty. And if we get hungry – there's always Evie's hat!"

Frankie pushed him back in and climbed in himself, hastily shutting the door. As the limousine pulled away Al's voice could be heard all over the driveway,

"See you at the Oscars, Boss!!!"

Joe stared after it.

"One of these days, Al" he muttered. "One of these days....!"

Joe looked at his watch again. It was now 12:10 and still no sign of Angela. He was getting anxious. The Church was silent except for the odd, low whisper that came from the two front seats. Frankie and Al were on the groom's side, Agnes and Evie on the bride's. Agnes, in a floral dress, plain jacket and matching accessories, looked happy and well as she waited patiently for her daughter. Father Ryker was checking his sermon but after a quick glance towards the entrance, he moved onto the front of the alter and beckoned Joe and Rooney to come forward. When they did so, he coughed loudly and nodded towards a small gallery where an organ began to play. Joe felt a wave of relief sweep over him. Angela had arrived. As the music played, Joe kept his eyes fixed firmly in front of him as he and Rooney stood together. But the suspense proved too much for

Rooney, so he turned and looked over his shoulder. When he saw Angela he smiled, leaned towards his friend and whispered, "Jesus, Joe, wait till you see her. You'll wish it was bed time!"

He turned his head back to find Father Ryker peering into his face with a disapproving look. "Young man, may I remind you, you are in the house of God!"

"Sorry, Father", said Rooney, looking at him sheepishly.

Angela came up the aisle on Freddie Barretts' arm. He walked slowing, feeling and looking very proud. He cut a fine figure in grey trousers, light grey shirt, maroon and gold tie and a very attractive maroon blazer with an elaborate gold crest embroidered on the breast pocket. Soft grey shoes completed his outfit.

Angela was a vision! Her white, satin dress had a round scooped neckline trimmed with small rose-buds set with tiny pearls. The snugly fitted bodice and old fashioned leg of mutton sleeves gave it an added touch of elegance and made her look taller, almost regal. The skirt of the dress reached down to her white high heels and sat out around her. Her red hair was gathered up in soft curls and the same small rosebuds were placed carefully around them. She wore no jewellery except for her gold charm and her bouquet was a mixture of pale pink and white roses finished with green fern.

Cindy followed in a deep lemon satin dress with a plain, round scooped neck line and short puffed sleeves. A headdress of small lemon rosebuds adorned her lovely dark hair and her bouquet was of lemon and white roses finished with the same green fern. Her shoes were dyed the same colour as her dress and as a bridesmaid she looked stunning. As Freddie and Angela reached the alter, Joe turned to greet his bride. She looked at him as if for a sign of approval. He studied her for a few seconds, then smiled broadly as he gazed into her eyes and held out his hand. Relieved, she smiled back. Close to tears, Freddie placed her hand in Joe's and stood back, watching them press each other's fingers gently and lovingly. They let go as Father Ryker began the Mass.

After Freddie officially gave Angela away, he joined Agnes and Evie. Freddie Barrett may have been a proud man that day but there was no prouder man alive than Joe Morrelli. He listened intently to everything the priest was saying. This was the most important day of his life and he wanted to remember every detail.

Now and then, he and Angela would glance at each other instinctively and smile. Everything was going perfectly. That was, until Father Ryker reached the part of the ceremony where he asked the congregation if anyone knew of "just cause" why they shouldn't be joined together as man and wife. For it was at that exact time when the Church door was heard to open and close, and the sound of high heels echoed throughout the building. Joe knew who those footsteps belonged to. Antonia!! As they got nearer, they got louder. Al was the first to look around. When he saw who it was, he turned to Frankie, "Looks like we got dressed up for nothing!" Father Ryker was now silent as all heads turned. All that is, except Angela and Joe. She looked at him nervously but his attention was elsewhere. As he gazed pleadingly at the large, gold crucifix on the alter he thought, "Oh God, please don't do this to me! Not Now! Not after all I've been through to get here! Please!"

Joe's prayers for divine intervention were answered, as the Church fell silent once more. Antonia had taken a seat without uttering a sound.

Father Ryker continued with the marriage service. Everyone breathed a sigh of relief. Joe looked now towards the chalice. No disrespect to the priest, but this was one time when he really could do with a drink! Antonia's arrival was one surprise he could have done without but luckily there were more pleasant ones in store. When it came to the taking of the vows Joe realised that his new wife had two names, Angela Christine. She'd never mentioned that to him – but then, there was something he'd never mentioned to her about his earlier years. Rooney had placed the two wedding rings on the red velvet cushion. Joe and Angela exchanged them in an atmosphere of peace and happiness and were just about to turn their attention back to the ceremony, when an angelic voice could be heard coming from the gallery. It was a young boy, singing in Latin. The Church of Our Lady of Lourdes was filled with the sweetness and glory of the "Ave Maria." As he listened, Joe Morrelli found himself going back in time.

The streets of New York were never busier than at Christmas time. The hustle, bustle and excitement began in November and carried right through. The young Joseph Morrelli liked this time of year. Christmas meant business and business meant money. Like so may streetwise kids, he was always finding things that had fallen off the backs of lorries – usually things that would be in great demand! Every day was a "wheeling-dealing" day, except for Christmas Eve.

Joe would make an excuse to the other guys and go off on his own. He'd walk along the streets, looking at the festive decorations and window displays. And then there were the people. Yes, the people. Parents and children, whole families even, on shopping expeditions.

Eventually he would make his way to the local Church, not to hear Mass but to listen to the choir singing all the hymns and carols associated with the Saviour's birth. His favourite hymn of all was "Ave Maria". Each time he heard it, he thought of his own mother and how different his life would have been if she'd lived. He remembered how beautiful she was and how much she loved him. Even though times were hard, he never went without – she made sure of that.

He couldn't recall when she first became ill but he did notice how thin and weak she became and how much time she spent in bed with the shades down. Doctors came and went but she didn't get better. Sometimes he'd feel angry. His father would walk around like a lost soul. Joe felt he should be willing his wife to get well again for all their sakes. He was too young to understand that all the will in the world would not make cancer disappear.

On the day she died, Joe felt as though part of him had died too but he could not have known the devastating effect her passing would have on his young life.

Tears stung Joe's eyes as he turned and gazed at the young woman by his side. How right he was to call her "Angel", for that's just how she looked. As the past was replaced by the present he realised with a great sense of satisfaction, Joe Morrelli had come a long way over the years and, at last, had found true happiness.

As the hymn ended, he looked down at the ring of his finger. Angela had been right all along. Living with the knowledge that she'd bought it for him would keep him both comforted and contented. He looked across at her hand. She was admiring her own wedding ring and as she looked up at him, he couldn't help but whisper,

"I love you."

She didn't need to answer. The tears in her eyes said it all. Here were two people who's love for each other had come through test and trial but remained strong and steadfast. They would remember this day for the rest of their lives.

As Father Ryker drew the Mass to a close he smiled at them both, "I now pronounce you man and wife. You may kiss the bride."

Joe held Angela in his arms and kissed her tenderly. Muffled sobs could be heard coming from the direction of Agnes and Evie. Freddie took a sudden attack of the sniffles and Al blew his nose loudly with his handkerchief! All in all, there wasn't a dry eye in the place, for whatever the reason. But one thing was certain, Angela Kenny was now Mrs Joe Morrelli and her husband was a proud and happy man.

Joe, Angela, Rooney and Cindy went into the vestry to sign the register. Father Ryker invited Agnes too. As she watched her daughter pose for photographs and sign her maiden name for the last time, Agnes couldn't help but feel sadness as well as joy. Robert Kenny had loved his two children so much, yet he hadn't lived to see them on the happiest day of their lives, their wedding days. She shed a quiet tear when no one was looking. Then she embraced her daughter and kissed her saying,

"God bless you, Angela, you and Joe. I know you're going to be happy."

Hugging Joe she smiled,

"Well, you did it!"

He nodded.

"Now don't you worry Agnes. I'm going to take good care of her and that's a promise!"

"I know you will," came the reply.

When all congratulations had been said, Rooney approached Angela and put his hands on her shoulders.

"I hope you will be very happy, Angela, really I do. You look beautiful."

"Thank you, Rooney. Aren't you going to kiss the bride?"

He smiled, as he bent his head and looked into her face. She reached up and kissed him on the lips. For those few moments, Rooney forgot about everything that was going on around him. The only thing that mattered was that he was kissing the woman he loved, even if she didn't know it.

"I'll always be around if you need me", he assured her.

"I know. Now, be nice to Cindy, won't you? Please."

She smiled and squeezed his arm gently. How could he refuse her?

Joe escorted Angela out of the vestry and onto the alter. Everyone followed and so did more congratulations! Rooney watched Angela closely, then turned towards Cindy. In a way, she was really quite attractive with her dark hair and her big brown eyes. Not a bad figure, either. Still, she could never come up to Angela Kenny but then again, no one ever would. That was going to be something he'd have to live with.

As Angela walked down the aisle on Joe's arm, Antonia, stepped out in front of them. Her dazzling cerise pink dress was off the shoulder and it's straight cut showed her voluptuous figure. Her broad brimmed hat was of the same colour but had a black bow attached to it to set off her black accessories.

"Joe, darling!! she beamed, holding our her arms to him." "I just had to come". She kissed his cheek.

"We're happy to see you Antonia."

"Congratulations, darling! you look wonderful."

"So do you."

She turned and pecked Angela's cheek lightly whispering, "I knew when I didn't hear from him, you hadn't mentioned our little chat…."

Rooney heard. And noticed that Antonia hadn't congratulated Angela or commented on how lovely she looked. He had a gut feeling that Antonia had something up her sleeve so he decided to keep an eye on her. After all, there was no reason for her to be at the Church. She should be at the reception like everyone else.

More photographs were being taken outside the Church but Joe managed to take Father Ryker to one side.

"I want to thank you Father, for everything."

"I was happy to do what I could, Joe."

Joe took a thick, sealed envelope from his inside pocket and gave it to the priest.

"I want you to take this, Father. Churches are always needing their roofs fixed!"

Father Ryker was startled but accepted the envelope gratefully.

"This is a very poor neighbourhood, Joe. I think people matter more than roofs. Don't you?"

"Whatever you say, Father, That's yours, to do whatever you want. And if you ever need anything, just let me know."

"Thank you, Joe, Thank you. I know a lot of people will be grateful to you, believe me."

"Before I forget, will you do something for me, Father?"

191

"Of course."

"Will you give this to the kid who sang the 'Ave Maria'?"

He handed Father Ryker a twenty-dollar Bill.

"I'll see he gets it. God Bless you, Joe."

"Well, He has today!" he smiled.

When the final photograph had been taken, Antonia asked if she could pose for one with Joe – "for old time's sake." Angela stood back as Antonia grabbed Joe's arm, snuggled in to him and beamed in to the camera. Rooney was getting angry. He went over and stood by Angela's side.

"I heard what she said earlier. I take it she paid you a visit?"

"Yes, I asked her to consider Joe's feelings but I never asked her to the service. I almost died when I heard her footsteps".

"Didn't we all!"

Joe managed to break free from Antonia and came over looking rather embarrassed.

"I want a word with you, Joe" said Rooney, leading him away. But before he could continue, the two stretch limousines appeared and Antonia came after Joe.

"Joe, how am I going to get to the reception?" she asked innocently.

"How did you get here?" Rooney asked, sarcastically.

"In a taxi!" she snapped.

Joe looked at her and then at the cars.

"Well, one is for the four of us and the other is for the guests. There'll be plenty of room for one more".

"Really, Joe! Do you expect me to arrive at 'The Imperial Palace' with the hired help?"

She sounded almost insulted as she threw a side glance at the others.

"I don't see what else I can do, Antonia."

"But I have my reputation to think about, Joe! I wouldn't mind in the least going with you. We could walk in together."

Angela stood quietly, looking from one to the other. Joe didn't like where things were leading. Rooney, however, walked off towards the vestry and Father Ryker.

"Excuse me, Father, do you have a phone I could use?"

A few minutes later, Rooney returned.

"Well, that's all sorted out," he smiled at Antonia.

"What?"

"A taxi's coming to pick you up and take you to the reception."

"What?!"

He ignored her and checked his watch.

"We better go," he advised Joe and Angela. "People are waiting for you."

He took Angela's arm and lead her away. Joe remained. He stared at Antonia, angrily.

"Don't ever do that again!" he warned. "Don't ever try and bring my wife down. Not now, not ever!"

"But Joe, I only wanted…."

"I know what you wanted, Antonia, because I know you! It's finished – over. And if you don't behave yourself our friendship is, too. This is my day and my wife's day and no one is going to spoil it. Do you understand? When I walk into "The Imperial Palace" today, I walk in with my wife – no one else!"

Antonia never spoke but lowered her gaze. Rooney and Angela looked at each other. Then Joe came over and took Angela's hand in his. He held it firmly.

"Come on, Angel let's go." He turned to Rooney. "You know, for an actress her timing's lousy. I hope this taxi driver's not going to be the same."

"Don't worry," smiled Rooney. "I told him he wasn't needed for fifteen minutes."

"Good thinking! That gives us plenty of time to get something sorted out and it gives her plenty of time to think about what I've said."

Joe helped his wife into the car and Rooney helped Cindy. As they drove away the second car followed leaving Antonia alone on the steps of the Church. Joe was still holding Angela's hand. "I'm sorry about that honey," he whispered, "but it won't ever happen again. Not with her, not with anyone."

She looked at him and nodded.

Rooney was watching. He knew Joe was telling the truth, because he knew he loved her. As Rooney and Cindy entered into conversation Joe kissed Angela and said,

"You look beautiful."

"You look very handsome yourself."

"You think so?"

"I do."

"Well, we aim to please!"

They both laughed but then Angela squeezed his hand, anxiously.

"I'm nervous, Joe."

"Well, don't be. It's only a restaurant and you're with your husband. When you walk into "The Imperial Palace" this time you'll be walking in on my arm as Mrs Joe Morrelli. From now on you're going to have the respect you deserve and I'll make sure you get it!"

Both limousines arrived at their destination together. Joe turned to Rooney.

"Go and tell Frankie I want a word with him."

Rooney got out and came back with him.

"What's up, Boss?"

"I want you to go inside and tell Judge Thompson I'd like a word with him. When you've done that, bring the others into the entrance hall. We'll join you in a few minutes."

"Sure, Boss." Said Frankie, closing the door.

A few moments later, Frankie and the Judge appeared at the main entrance. Joe opened the car door and got out.

"This won't take long." he said, looking at Angela.

He beckoned to Rooney and both men went over to speak to Judge Thompson, as Frankie ushered everyone else inside 'The Imperial Palace'.

"What can I do for you, Joe?" the judge asked.

"I've got a small problem I'd like you to take care of for me."

"Don't tell me you got a parking ticket on your wedding day!"

"I should be so lucky!"

"Well, what is it?"

"Who is it, would be more to the point", said Rooney. "The problem has a name."

"Yeah," said Joe, "and one you know well. It's name is Antonia."

"Really? How can I help?"

"Well, you see Judge, she's arriving in a taxi and she doesn't have anyone to escort her into the reception."

"Say no more," he smiled. "I'd be delighted to do the honors. We can't have a Broadway actress walking in on her own, now can we? Why don't you go in, Joe, and I'll wait here.

"Thanks, Judge, I owe you one."

Joe and Rooney came back to the car. The chauffeur reached in and helped Angela and Cindy step out. Their respective partners lead them towards the huge glass doors of the 'The Imperial Palace." Judge Thompson smiled.

"Angela, you look breathtaking, my dear."

"Thank you, Judge Thompson, I'm so glad you could come."

As the four made their way into the entrance hall, they found Agnes and Evie admiring the surroundings. Evie couldn't take her eyes of the tiled floor.

If she didn't know better she'd swear it was real marble! Even Freddie Barrett was impressed. Joe gathered them all together.

"Freddie, you escort Agnes. Al, you escort Evie. Frankie, you go on ahead."

"How come he gets to go in on his own, Boss?" asked Al, nodding towards Frankie.

"He could walk with me."

"Not on your life," said Frankie, "my wife's in there. If I walk in with you I'll never live it down. Come to think of it – I'll never live!" he smiled as he walked away.

Freddie and Agnes lead the way. Evie was still staring at the floor.

"Are you ready" asked Al, impatiently. "All you have to do is put one foot in front of the other and follow the yellow-brick road!"

Evie looked at him coldly and cast her eyes. Joe shook his head.

He waited until the others had disappeared from view, then turned to Angela, "O.K, this is it," he smiled.

Cindy flitted about, fixing the long, full skirt of Angela's dress. Angela took Joe's arm and holding her bouquet with her other hand, she took a deep breath and nodded.

"You'll be fine," he whispered, as they walked towards the reception room. "Don't let it throw you. The last time I brought you here, I wanted to make an impression. This time, you'll be making the impression. I want everyone here to see what a lucky man I am. I love you."

The doors opened and the happy couple appeared before their guests, followed by Rooney and Cindy. Cheers of approval and a rapturous applause could be heard, as Mr and Mrs Joe Morrelli took their place among the many people who were waiting to express their congratulation and very best wishes.

Within seconds they were surrounded and on the receiving end of embraces and handshakes. Some of the people Angela knew but most of them she didn't. However, they were all relaxed and friendly, and very loving in their attitude. One face she did recognise as it came towards her smiling. It was Eugene O'Brien. He stood with his arms outstretched,

"Hey, little lady, you look beautiful."

"Thank you, Mr O'Brien."

"Oh no, it's not Mr O'Brien any more. Now that you're married to my buddy here, it's Gene." He put his arm around her. "I'm very happy for you, Irish," he whispered," and I'm delighted for Joe. By the expression on his face, he's delighted for himself!"

Angela looked around. Kate O Brien laughed and joked with Alan Bailey, while Jeff Lang fetched drinks for the rest of the company. Mario, Gino and Theresa smiled and waved to her. She was becoming more at ease with every minute, especially when Reuben and his wife, Miriam, approached. Miriam reassured her.

"Angela, make sure and take in every moment. This will be a day to remember for all of us but especially for you and Joe. This is just the beginning of years of happiness."

Frankie took pride in introducing his wife, Elena, an attractive and pleasant woman, who was obviously very much in love with her husband.

Joe took Angela by the arm and steered her towards two very distinguished looking men.

"Angela, I'd like you to meet Nicholas Andretti and his grandson, Anthony. They're both very dear friends of mine. Also Anthony's wife, Maria and his sister, Victoria."

After many more introductions, she met Carlo Capaldi and his wife, Sandra. In the meantime, Antonia's taxi pulled up outside. Judge Thompson hastened over and opened the door.

"Antonia, you look radiant, as always."

He smiled broadly as she got out.

"Thanks Judge."

"Joe told me you were coming."

"That was nice of him," she replied, forcing a smile.

"I'll escort you in. Don't you think it's quite a coincidence that we should both be here on our own?" he beamed.

"Well, I suppose we could stay together – for the reception, I mean."

"I'd like nothing better," he said in that suave voice everyone knew so well.

As they entered the dining room, a large crowd was gathered around Joe and Angela. This was one grand entrance Antonia had made unnoticed. For once in her life, she was not the centre of attention. No one batted and eyelid except for Judge Thompson who took her arm and led her to a table, telling her once again how attractive she looked. After all the formalities were done with and Angela had been congratulated by Jimmy and the rest of the staff from "The Safe Haven", everyone dispersed to their tables. She and Joe and Rooney and Cindy, went to theirs. Champagne was brought to every table and lunch was to follow. Joe finally sat down and viewed his guests. Everyone was in a great mood. He turned and motioned Frankie to join the others. Not needing to be told twice, Frankie made a beeline for Elena – Al made a beeline for Frankie!!

Lunch was a sumptuous affair. With Ralph Lennox being such a good friend of Joe's, he made sure that only the best and most expensive food and drink was served. Angela glanced around, then turning to Joe she smiled.

"It's nice to see so many children here."

"Yeah well, I've never seen an Italian wedding without any," he smiled back. After a few glasses of table wine and champagne, Cindy was in a talkative mood and determined to get Rooney's attention. She leaned across the table.

"I was just saying to Angela the other day, Mr. Morrelli, that Miami can be very warm. I was there on vacation once and do you know something? The heat was so bad I couldn't even wear a nightdress in bed. Of course, I told Angela weeks ago not to buy anything heavy. Isn't that right Angela? I told her it would probably have the same effect on her that it had on me."

Joe lifted his glass and looked in to it.

"Yeah, I guess Miami can be pretty hot," he whispered.

Cindy, unaware of the last comment, continued.

"Of course, I was with my boyfriend at the time. I suppose that makes a big difference."

Rooney's face lit up.

"I didn't know you had a boyfriend," he said.

"Oh, I don't," she smiled, "At least not anymore. To tell the truth, I don't really understand what happened between us. We seemed to be having such a good time and I was so considerate. I always told him the best times to sit in the sun, the best skin lotion to put on, the right food to eat. I told him, light healthy food was the best, especially at night. After all, who wants to go to bed on a full stomach? You'd be too tired to do anything but sleep!" she looked coyly at Rooney, who quickly glanced away.

"Anyway," she went on, "When we got home, he broke off our relationship. He said I was wasting my time with someone like him as I knew far too much about everything, and I never saw him again."

Rooney looked at Joe,

"Well, that says it all!"

Over at another table, Al was sticking like glue to Frankie – which was beginning to annoy Elena. This was one day she wanted Frankie to spend with just her and the kids, but Al was talking and joking so much, she could hardly get a word in edgeways. Every now and again she would give Frankie one of her looks. Eventually, he got the message.

"Al, would you take my kid to the toilet?"

"But Dad, I don't need the toilet." the little boy insisted.

"Sure you do, son. Now run along."

Frankie lifted him off the chair.

"Better do as your Father says. Now you come with your Uncle Al."

Al took the child's hand and as they made their way from the table, Frankie looked at Elena.

"What's the matter, honey?"

"You really want to know? How come the only day you're not working, you still end up in his company? You know, Frankie, I often wonder why you didn't marry him instead of me!"

"Oh come on, honey, what could I do? He followed me."

"Why doesn't he follow something in a skirt!"

"But he's my friend. I work with the guy."

"Exactly! Well, Frankie Rossi, if you think you're going to spend the day with 'my pal Al', forget it. There's bound to be somebody like himself."

"There is," he replied, in a sarcastic tone, "your cousin, Rita. Maybe I should give her a call."

"Just what do you mean by that?" she snapped.

"What I mean is, she can't get anybody either."

"I'll have you know Rita can have her pick of men."

"So that's why she spends every weekend at home, watching old movies and stuffing her face with pizza."

"Don't you get smart with me!"

Elena's eyes flashed a warning sign that Frankie knew only too well.

"O.k., honey, I'm sorry. I'll tell you what, after the meal and the music starts, I'll find him someone and you and me will spend the rest of the day together, I promise."

"You promise?"

"Sure. There's bound to be someone here I can pair him off with. You leave it to me."

He kissed her lovingly. Elena looked across the dining room.

"Here he comes she said, "The Lone Ranger looking for Tonto!"

Frankie laughed, "That's like something he would say."

"I know" she sighed, "but when you listen to Al long enough you begin to sound like him. I should know – I'm living with you!"

When lunch was over, Jimmy carried in the wedding cake, putting it down in front of Joe and Angela, he smiled.

"Mr Morrelli, Angela, this is my wedding present to both of you. I hope you like it."

"Oh Jimmy, it's beautiful."

"It sure is," agreed Joe.

As they looked more closely they could see it was three tiered and each tier was in the shape of a heart, ornately decorated with silver horseshoes, cherubs and tiny posies. The icing was whipped and swirled around to make it even more elaborate. On the top tier stood the statue of the bride and groom. The three hearts were certainly appropriate.

"I got the idea from your engagement ring, Angela."

He drew their attention to the top tier where the initials A and J were entwined.

"Good thinking Jimmy. It's terrific!" said Joe.

Angela put her arms around him.

"Thank you, Jimmy, it's a wonderful present."

"Well, I couldn't have done it if you hadn't given me the chance to learn. Thanks for everything," he smiled.

Joe felt pleased at Jimmy's little speech, which reminded him – Rooney had one to make before the dancing and socialising could begin. Rooney dutifully got up and after making a few jokes about Joe and his new status, he gave a short but touching speech wishing Joe and Angela every happiness. Everyone stood up and raised their glasses for the toast. When they'd all sat down, it was Joe's turn. On behalf of himself and his new wife he proceeded to thank everyone for coming, Rooney and Cindy, Ralph Lennox and his staff and especially Father Ryker who had managed to join them and sat at the top table between Agnes and Evie. When he finally came to the end, he announced free drinks for everyone, which brought loud applause from all – especially Gene O'Brien!! The orchestra began to play and the reception was well and truly underway. Joe proudly led Angela onto the dance floor. As he took her in his arms, he could hardly believe the day had come when she had accepted him as her husband. He gazed into her eyes, almost loosing himself in their blueness.

"I love you, Mrs Morrelli," he whispered.

"And I love you," came the reply.

Rooney and Cindy joined them on the dance floor, followed by the other guests. Eventually, the two men swapped partners.

"Well, how's it going?" he smiled.

"Fine. There are so many people, Rooney."

"I know. Joe has a lot of friends and associates."

"I just hope I can fit in. I can't help but feel he should have married someone as well known as himself."

"Like Antonia, you mean? Listen to me, Angela, Joe couldn't have done any better than you – and he knows it. You've made him a very happy man. I've never known Joe to love any woman the way he loves you."

She bit her lip.

"I hope you're right, Rooney. I know Joe's had a lot of experience with women, I just hope I don't disappoint him."

It was then that Rooney realised that Joe and Angela had never slept together. He couldn't help but feel envious of his closest friend, but was determined not to let it show.

"Don't worry, Angela. There's a big difference between sex and love. No one knows that better than Joe."

When the dance had ended, she hugged him tightly.

"Thanks, Rooney, I feel more contented now."

As he watched her join her husband, he wondered how different things might have been if Angela had fallen in love with him instead of Joe. Maybe today he would have been the one saying, "I DO."

Judge Thompson left Antonia just long enough to dance with Angela and tell her how delighted he was for her and Joe. A well built, attractive man, he knew how to treat a woman and make her feel extra-special. His dark hair and blue eyes, combined with his charm and wit, made him quite successful with the opposite sex. Being divorced, he's made sure to enjoy the freedom it provided, by wining and dining some of the prettiest women in New York. However, he had a soft spot for Antonia and was looking forward to the rest of the day, hoping that by the end of it, she might have a soft spot for him!

"Would you like a drink from the bar, honey?" asked Joe. "You're not drinking much champagne."

"I'll have something later," replied Angela. "But right now a glass of iced water would be nice."

"What – no beer?"

"Not in this place. Why don't you go and talk to some of your friends. I'm going to sit with my mother for a little while."

"O.k. Are you sure you don't want to come, too?"

"I'm fine, Joe, really."

Joe fetched her the iced water and then went off to mingle with his many friends.

"I'll be back in a little while," he assured her. "We have to cut the cake!"

She watched him disappear through the crowd, then looked around at all the children. They were getting a little bored. She went over to Jimmy and whispered in his ear. He got up, collected the children and led them onto the dance floor. Angela and Agnes followed, accompanied by some of the staff from "The Safe Haven.". They all made a large circle in the middle of the floor, joined hands and began to dance.

Frankie spotted Lisa, standing in the middle of the circle and immediately grabbed Al's arm. He walked him down and put him into the circle beside her. Lisa smiled happily as she took Al's hand. Frankie returned to Elena and put his arm around her.

"I think we can say goodbye to Al for the rest of the day," he chuckled, "and the kids are having a great time!"

The first people Joe made his way to were the Andretti's. He embraced old Nicholas first, then Anthony. Maria and Victoria went to watch over the children, leaving the men to sit down and talk.

"I'm honored you could come," he said to Nick.

"I'm happy to be here, Joe, it's like old times. Besides, how could I miss Joe Morrelli's wedding? My Dominic would never have forgiven me! I was beginning to think it might never happen. She's very beautiful, Joe," he nodded towards Angela.

Joe followed his gaze.

"Yeah well, I think so."

"She respects her mother, that's good. I see she likes children, that's good too. I like that, it makes the foundation for a happy marriage."

Joe watched as Angela danced with the children.

"I'm a lucky man."

"And a happy one," smiled Nick.

Joe turned back.

"I want to thank you for the limousines."

"My pleasure. There will be one waiting at the airport in Miami, for you and your wife. Everything has been taken care of. The beach house is ready for you, food, alcohol, flowers, cigars. My driver in Miami has been told to take good care of you. Anything you want, anywhere you want to go, just call his number."

He motioned to Anthony, who took a piece of paper from his pocket and gave it to Joe. Nick continued,

"My men know you're coming."

"How did you know which beach house I'd be renting?" asked Joe, surprised.

"It's my business to know these things." He grinned. "The man you rented it from works for me. I own a lot of property in Miami, Joe."

Once again he motioned to Anthony, who this time gave Joe a large sealed envelope.

"This is your deposit, Mr Morrelli." said Anthony. "The house is yours for as long as you want it – compliments of the Andretti family."

He smiled as Joe took the envelope from him. Joe shook his head.

"How can I ever thank you for your kindness?"

"What are friends for?" asked Nick. "Besides, you were a good friend to my son. One of the few he ever trusted. I'm just repaying a debt with gratitude."

Joe took the old man's hand.

"Believe me, I miss Dominic. I miss his friendship and his loyalty. I think of him often."

Nicholas Andretti was deeply moved and hugged Joe tightly. Then Anthony embraced him.

"He should have stayed with friends like you," said the old man.

As Joe leaned back, he looked at them both.

"I won't forget this. If ever I can do something for you, just let me know."

Nick nodded his head and said,

"You're a good man and a shrewd one. What is it they say about you? If Joe Morrelli does something, he has his reasons!"

Joe smiled,

"Yeah well, it makes a lot of people think twice before they do anything!"

The three men laughed, then Joe rose.

"Excuse me, please. There's someone else here I'd like to thank."

He made his way towards Gene O'Brien.

"How are you, Congressman?"

Gene looked around, surprised.

"Well, if it isn't the happy groom!" he beamed.

"I see the gang's all here," smiled Joe, looking around at the rest of the company.

"All but the Judge, Joe. He seems to be holding his own private court over there and by the look of things, he might well win his case!"

"Yeah well, you win some, you lose some and that applies to Judges as well."

"Come on," said Gene, getting up and putting his hand on Joe's shoulder, "let's go and get a drink."

Gene led the way past the waiters who were holding trays of champagne, and arrived at the bar. He ordered two large whiskeys (one Irish, one Scotch) and handed a glass to Joe,

"Congratulations, old buddy!" he said, raising his own.

"Thank's Gene. And thanks for the advice."

Both men emptied their glasses and leaned on the bar.

"I didn't know you knew the Andretti's, Joe. I didn't think you moved in those kind of circles."

"Well, Nick gave me my first real job years ago in the Bronx. Me and his son, Dominic, were friends.

"Wasn't he killed?"

"Yeah, he was shot. Some kind of feud or something. I wasn't involved so I don't know an awful lot about it. It looked like he'd been set up by a couple of his so-called friends. His father never really got over it, but at least Dominic's kids were here for the old man. That helped. Dominic and me had some good times together but as the years went on he got in with the wrong kind of people."

"Did they ever get who did it?"

"Who knows?" shrugged Joe. "The Andretti's play their cards very close to their chest. One thing I do know, they voted for you and made sure all their people did, too."

"You're kidding!"

"No I'm not. I told you I'd get you in," grinned Joe.

"I sure didn't think guys like that would back me." Said Gene, almost in disbelief.

"Gene, guys like that carry a lot of weight in a lot of places. Besides, you're a good man. They know that. You like the Italians and you're Irish descent, just how many of our people are there in this country? Make no mistake guys like that could help put you in the White House. After all, it wouldn't be the first time the Irish and Italian votes made a President, now would it? Remember that, Gene."

"I will, Joe," he nodded. "Believe me, I will."

Joe ordered two more drinks.

"Now that we're here, I'd like a quiet word," he said, in a low voice.

"Sure," replied Gene, looking a little concerned. "What about?"

"Well, it's about Angela. I think she might be a bit nervous, about me I mean."

Gene stared at him. "I don't understand!"

"You know," said Joe, looking embarrassed, "the honeymoon."

"You mean you haven't slept with her yet?"

Joe shook his head. Gene started to laugh.

"Jesus, Joe, I never would have believed it."

"I can hardly believe it myself! I think she's nervous because I've been around."

"Oh, you've been that alright! When the rest of the guys were playing baseball, you were playing with some young woman's body. Boy, did we envy you. We had to sit around waiting while you were making out. Cars, alleys, roof-tops – you weren't choosey!"

Joe smiled into his glass.

"Yeah, that was the one thing I really liked about the old neighbourhood – variety. And there was always some girl willing to explore with you and oblige. But I fell in love with someone who wasn't!" His voice became serious. "I don't think she's been with a man, Gene. In fact, I'm almost certain. There was someone back in Ireland. She must have liked him, she was bringing him home to meet the family."

"What happened?"

"Oh it just didn't work out. I don't think they ever 'got it together', if you know what I mean. One thing's for sure, I'm still waiting."

Gene put his hand on Joe's shoulder, knowingly. "Join the club!"

Joe stared in surprise.

"You mean, you?"

Gene nodded.

"Well, I wouldn't tell it to many but when I was dating Kate, nothing happened either. She went to a strict convent school. Most of the teachers were nuns – and I don't have to tell you what they're like! And besides, her old man would have killed me. Anyway, I didn't make love to her until our wedding night. Believe me, Joe, if something's worth having then it's worth waiting for. You'll find that out for yourself. Maybe that's why Kate and me are still together after all these years. Let me give you a bit of advice.

Angela's very young but she probably suspects you've had other women besides Antonia. She may be scared she won't live up to your expectations. Don't rush her, Joe, let her take her time and you do the same. She's not like the rest but then I don't have to tell you that. She's a lady. Treat her like one and everything else will follow. I know."

"I love her, Gene."

"Sure you do and we're old enough now to know that love just isn't sex, it's a lot of things. If you're the first then you're a lucky man. I'm happy for you."

Joe was relieved.

"Thanks, Gene, for everything. I'd better be getting back."

Gene nodded.

"Anytime Joe. Just remember our little chat."

"I will."

Joe smiled to himself as he left the bar and made his way back to Angela. She was at the other side of the room, talking and laughing with the guests. He watched how easily she mingled with everyone. The way she looked at them that smile, those eyes. She looked beautiful in her wedding dress. Gene O'Brien was right. She was every inch a lady and he was a very lucky man.

"Joe!" came a voice from the crowd. He turned and found Mario standing beside him.

"Joe, I never see such a place. And the food, the food I never taste before. What they serve here, Joe? That man who owns all this, must be big-shot!"

Joe put his arm around his old friend.

"Yeah, he is. But between you and me, Mario, his spaghetti and meatballs sucks!!"

Mario's face lit up.

"So that's why you come to Mario's, Joe Mario's is better."

"That's right but don't say anything. I don't want to hurt the guy's feelings!"

Mario tapped his nose with his finger and smiled, "Not a word, Joe, not a word. And for that I won't change the house special."

"After all these years, Mario – I didn't think you would!"

He walked over to Carlo Capaldi, who shook his hand.

"Hey, Joe, so you finally decided to be like the rest of us – married!" he laughed.

"Well, you know how it is. I'm getting a bit old now to run around."

"Maybe, but not too old to land a catch like that,"

Carlo nodded towards Angela.

"I got lucky, Carlo."

"Joe, as far as women went, you were always lucky. Remember the old neighbourhood? The way we'd all cruise around looking for the local talent. You and Dominic got the pick of the bunch while we had to settle for what was left."

"Yeah, I guess we did make it tough for you guys," smiled Joe broadly.

"You know what I could never understand? How come we got chased by the girls' fathers but you and Dominic were always invited in."

Joe laughed and decided it was time to come clean.

"Well, you see we knew this old Jewish guy who sold imitation jewellery. It looked just like the real thing. We'd give it to the women, you know, fancy engagement rings, lockets and chains. They thought we were going to marry them. Their fathers thought we were making plenty of money. By the time the black circles appeared on their fingers and necks we were long gone. I bet every good looking woman in the Bronx had a piece of jewellery from that old Jew, and we'd have a piece of her."

"So that was the secret," smiled Carlo.

"Yeah, that was it. We had some good times, thanks to him. He was very fond of us, especially Dominic."

"Why Dominic?"

"He bought it in bulk."

Carlo laughed and shook his head.

"No wonder you went about with a permanent smile on your face! And speaking of smiles, you're looking very happy today. Would that by any chance be the girl that worked for you?"

Joe nodded, "Yeah, that's her, Carlo."

"She's very beautiful, Joe. I'm glad nothing bad happened to her. Well, apart from what she had to listen to. Did she ever tell you?"

"No, she never did. But it isn't hard to imagine. Anyway, she won't ever have to listen to some creep like that ever again. Thanks for everything, Carlo, and thanks for coming."

"Be happy, Joe, you deserve it and so does she."

As Joe walked away his face became serious for a moment as he remembered Lenny Shultz and what he had heard that night. He looked over at Angela, who was sitting talking to her mother. He knew she'd never tell him what had been said by Lenny but it didn't matter, he already knew. Maybe she was a bit frightened of all men because of it. It was up to him to lay those fears to rest. He hoped tonight he could.

After a quick chat with the guys from Stacey's Gym and his associates from the various night clubs, he returned to Angela.

"I'm sorry, honey, things took a bit longer than I thought," he said, kissing her lightly and sitting down beside her.

"Oh, that's alright, Joe. I've been kept busy myself, there are so many people to get around."

He called a waiter and lifted three glasses of champagne off the tray. He gave one to Agnes and handing one to Angela, he raised his own.

"To us," he said.

They took a few sips, then Joe put his glass down and took Angela's from her hand.

"Come on," he smiled, "let's dance."

Angela held his hand tightly.

"Joe, I think you should dance with Antonia."

"No Angel, I want to dance with you."

"You can't ignore her like this, Joe. Not in front of all your friends and hers, it's not right. What she did this morning was wrong but what you're doing now is wrong too. Don't let her down. Not here."

Joe stared at the table for a moment.

"O.k.," he nodded, getting up. "Just so long as I know I'm coming back to you."

He went over to where Antonia and Judge Thompson sat in deep conversation. She looked up at him in surprise.

"Judge," he said, "I'm sure you won't mind if Antonia has this dance with me."

Her face lit up as Joe took her arm and led her onto the dance floor.

"I see you and the Judge have hit if off," he said. "He often asked about you and wanted to know how you were."

"Hasn't he ever heard of a telephone?"

"I guess he didn't have you number. You know, he's a nice man and he likes you."

"Joe, just because you got married today, doesn't mean that I have to. I have my career to think of."

"Yeah, and your friends," added Joe. "You know something, Antonia? You've changed. You're surrounded by people who think they can say what they like and get away with it. They treat other people like dirt because they think they're better and you're doing the same. But just remember, if your plays start to get bad reviews they won't be around because they won't want to know you. There'll come a day when you won't be top billing anymore, Antonia. Someone younger will come along, they always do. We'll see how many of your so-called friends will be around then. But people like the Judge – well, they stay around no matter what."

"And you, Joe," she said in a low voice, "are you going to be there for me?"

"I'll always be around if you want me, Antonia. I think you know that. But you'll have to drop your fancy act with me. I like the old Antonia better."

She lowered her gaze.

"I'm sorry about today, Joe I never thought you'd go through with it, and I didn't want you to. I hope you're not making a mistake by marrying her."

"I'd have made a bigger mistake if I hadn't. I love her very much but that doesn't mean I don't care about what happens to you. I'll always be your friend. I'll help you in whatever way I can. I just want you to know that."

"I'm sorry for the way I behaved, Joe."

"It's not me you should be apologising to, it's Angel. You tried to ruin her day."

"Well, she ruined my life!" she replied sharply. "She took the one thing I loved most."

"Come on now," said Joe, looking her in the eyes, "let's be honest with each other. You love the theatre more than anything or anyone. It always came first, I came second. We just drifted along and had each other when we wanted sex or a good time. We were never really committed to each other. I had my home, you had your apartment. I had my business, you had your parties. We had everything we wanted except for the kind of love people really need. Would you have given up being an actress on Broadway for me?"

She looked away from him and remained silent.

"Now do you understand, Antonia? Angel can be a wife in every sense of the word. She can give me the special love I need. We all need it, Antonia. I've found mine, I hope someday you'll find yours."

She looked at him and smiled sadly,

"We had some good times, Joe. Didn't we?"

"The very best," he smiled back.

After the music ended he escorted her back to her seat. She glanced around, haughtily, to see who had been watching Joe Morrelli leave the dance floor with Antonia Flemming.

On his way back to Angela, Joe stopped to chat with Reuben and Miriam.

"I wish my father could have seen this day, Joe!" joked Reuben, peering through gold-rimmed spectacles.

"Yeah well, if he'd never had a heart attack, he sure would have had one now!"

"What's it like being an old married man?"

"Ask me tomorrow!"

Reuben Goldman had been Joe's accountant and financial adviser since the sudden death of his father, Isaac, a few years before. Joe only trusted a handful of men – Reuben was one of them. When it came to money and business he had a gift, almost sixth sense, for knowing what deals and investments would profit and what ones wouldn't. As a child and young boy, he remembered his father's friendship with Joe and how Joe often compared the loss of his own parents with the loss of Isaac's in the 'camps' during the war. They had both been so young when left to fend for themselves. Joe, Reuben and Miriam recalled old times and laughed and joked while the children played around them.

When Joe finally got up to leave, Reuben rose too.

"I'm so happy for you, Joe. Every man should have a family. My father always said a man lives through his family – even when he dies!"

"Your father was one of the finest men I ever knew."

Reuben hesitated, then said,

"Joe, I just want to thank you."

"What for?"

"For letting me carry on where my father left off. Not many men would have trusted me with their business affairs. After all, I was barely out of College and still wet behind the ears."

Joe looked serious for a moment and then put his hands on Reuben's shoulders.

"You were Isaac Goldman's son – and that was good enough for me!"

When Reuben asked Angela up to dance, Joe decided he'd go and have another look at the cake before he and Angela cut it. He was standing admiring the three hearts when one of Frankie's kids came up and stood beside him. The little boy poked his finger into the side of the bottom layer, scooped up some icing, put it into his mouth and sucked his finger hungrily.

Joe watched as the child put his finger back to the cake for more.

"Hey, Junior, don't do that!" said Joe, in a warning manner.

"Why?"

"Because it's not nice."

The boy looked up at him innocently, a ring of white icing surrounding his little mouth.

"But I want some," he explained.

"You'll get some," mimicked Joe, impatiently.

"When?"

"When I cut it."

"But I want some now."

"Well, you can't have some now! Your mom can give you a big piece on a plate if you take your finger away."

"When?"

Joe turned his eyes up towards the ceiling.

"When I cut it!"

"You promise?"

"Yes, I promise. Now be a good little boy."

Just then Frankie came over and lifted the child in his arms.

"Sorry about that, Boss."

"Oh, that's o.k.," smiled Joe. "What age is he now?"

"Frankie Junior's three years old and he's full of fun." Said his proud father, walking away.

"Really?" muttered Joe, to himself. "He'll be full of lead if he comes back near this cake!!"

Angela came over to him and putting her arm through his she said, "Come on, there's someone I'd like you to meet."

She led him over to a table. Joe recognised the young man sitting there, but Angela continued,

"Joe, I'd like you to meet my teacher, Dean Prescott and his fiancée, Helen."

Helen smiled and nodded as Dean got up and shook Joe's hand.

"Congratulations, Mr Morrelli. It's nice to meet you at last."

Although a little embarrassed, Joe managed a smile.

"Hi there. Nice to meet you, too. Angel has told me a lot about you."

"I hope it was all good!" he laughed.

At that moment, Jimmy called Angela for a private word.

"Excuse me," she said leaving the table. "I won't be long."

Joe sat down and entered into conversation with Dean.

"So, how's she doing in her studies?" he asked, leaning his elbows on the table.

Dean smiled,

"She's one of the best pupils I have, but then she was clever before I got her. She just has a natural gift for understanding whatever's put in front of her. She also has a thirst for knowledge and an ability that can be quite rare these days. I hope she doesn't waste them."

"What do you mean?"

"Do you want the truth?"

"I'd appreciate it."

"Well, Mr Morrelli, if Angela passes her exams and stays on at College for another couple of years she could really excel. But in order to do that she'd have to keep her mind on what she'd be doing, with very few distractions. That might prove to be very difficult, now that she's chosen to be a wife and possibly a mother."

Joe was thoughtful for a moment.

"Have you spoken to her about this?"

Dean nodded,

"I explained it to her. She's still young. She has her whole life ahead of her, and it could be a very successful life."

"Do you think she'll pass these exams?"

"Yes, I do. I've been putting her over all the things she's learned and I can't see her having any problems. She can recite Shakespeare like he taught her himself! And when it comes to writing, the words just flow from her. She should be a teacher herself."

Joe felt proud.

"Well, one thing I can promise you," he said, "I won't ever stand in her way, whatever she decides. Not if you think she's that good."

"I'm glad. I'd hate to see talent like that go to waste."

Joe got up.

"I'm grateful you told me all this. Angel doesn't go into detail about her studies. But at least now I know. Thanks."

They shook hands once more as Angela returned to the table.

"Joe, we'll have to cut the cake soon, so I can go and get changed."

"Don't stay away from classes too long." Smiled Dean. "Your exams are coming up soon."

"Don't remind me!" she laughed as she and Joe walked away.

"He's a nice guy," said Joe.

Angela looked at him.

"You've changed your tune! I remember a time when you didn't think so."

"Well that was different," he shrugged. "That was before I knew you loved me – not him."

"I don't recall telling you I loved you at that particular time."

He stopped and took her arm.

"Angel, you loved me alright. You just didn't want to admit it. Come to think of it, I did a lot of worrying for nothing. I mean, how could you resist my charm? No one else did!"

He smiled broadly.

"Joe Morrelli, you're a big head!" she retorted.

He leaned over and whispered,

"If I were you, Mrs Morrelli, I wouldn't make any comments like that just yet. After all, you haven't seen the rest of me!"

Her eyes widened and her mouth fell open. Joe burst out laughing.

"I'm only kidding! Come on, let's go and see the wedding presents."

As they walked towards the back of the dining room, Angela quickly lifted a glass of champagne from a tray being carried by a passing waiter, and started to drink it. Joe smiled to himself. That was the first time, all day, he'd seen her actually wanting a drink!

A number of tables had been joined, covered by expensive, embroidered tablecloths. They were piled high with boxes of every shape and size, wrapped up in pretty paper and coloured ribbons. Others were stacked neatly on the floor and there were quite a few envelopes containing money.

"Joe where are we going to put all this stuff?"

"Oh, we'll find somewhere. Maybe we can move Evie into a tent and use her room for storage!"

"Have you been to the bar? You've suddenly become very witty."

"I'm just happy. The truth is, I haven't had much to drink. I guess I'm in a good mood because it wont' be long until we can be on our own, just the two of us. I'll be glad to leave everyone behind and get on that plane."

Angela felt a twinge of nerves in her stomach.

"What's the matter, Angel?" he asked. "You're very quiet."

"Oh, nothing," she smiled. "It's been a long day and I didn't sleep last night."

"I couldn't sleep either. I was excited about getting married."

"I was nervous."

He took her hand and looked into her eyes.

"Nervous about getting married – or me?"

"A little of both," she whispered.

He brought her hand up to his lips and kissed it gently.

"Everything's going to be o.k." he assured her. "You'll see."

Rooney called on everyone for their attention as Joe and Angela held the knife and cut their wedding cake, to the flashing of cameras. Lifting out the first piece, they divided it into two and fed it to one another as more photographs were taken and the room erupted in applause.

Afterwards, the photographer assured Joe that he'd gotten all the important shots and more besides, especially those of Joe and Angela in each others arms. He was rewarded with a hefty tip!

Jimmy then took over, cutting the cake into portions and distributing it amongst the guests and staff. As the dancing continued, Angela left to get changed accompanied by Agnes and Cindy. Joe went over to Reuben.

"I want you to settle all bills while I'm away, Reuben."

"Don't worry about it, Joe, I know what to do."

"Just tell Rooney if you need anything. Speaking of Rooney, where the hell is he? I've hardly seen him all day."

Reuben laughed,

"Try the bar. You'll most likely find him in the middle of a crowd – hiding from Cindy!"

Joe was taking Reuben's advice when Judge Thompson came over and took him by the arm.

"Joe, could I have a word?" He glanced around, cautiously.

"What's the matter, Judge," did you lose something?"

"No, I'm just watching for Antonia. She's gone to the powder-room. Actually, it's her I'd like a word about."

"Go on, I'm listening."

"Well, I don't know what you two talked about on the dance floor but she's been very nice to me ever since. I was thinking of asking her out. You know, to dinner. But I wouldn't want you to think I was trying to take over – from you."

"Listen Judge, I got married today. Remember? Antonia's free to go out with anyone she pleases."

Judge Thompson smiled with relief.

"You mean, you're not going to be seeing her again? You won't be...."

"Sleeping with her? No, that's all over. We're just good friends now."

"I thought, maybe, you'd still see her from time to time."

"Not a chance. I'd have too much to lose."

"It's really over between you two, then?"

Joe nodded,

"Yeah, it's really over."

"Well, I suppose this is as good a time as any to tell you, Joe. I really like Antonia, I always have."

"I know. I'm not blind. I've known it all along. You've seen her on stage more often than I have and you probably know her lines better than she does!"

"Weren't you ever jealous, Joe?"

"Why? After all, I was the one she was with."

The Judge smiled and shook Joe's hand.

"You know, I'm glad you asked me to escort her, Joe. This could well turn out to be my lucky day!"

"You'll never know unless you try," said Joe, encouragingly.

"Thanks Joe."

"Glad to be of help," he winked. "I have to go now. I've got a plane to catch."

"Enjoy yourself."

"I'm sure going to try!"

Joe pushed his way through to the bar and found Rooney propping it up.

"How are you doing?" asked Joe.

"I'm having a quiet drink and, believe me, I've earned it. I've listened to Cindy's voice for so long I'll probably waken up in the middle of the night with a nightmare!"

"Oh now, Rooney, it can't be that bad."

"It's worse! Everywhere I go, she's there. Trying to make an impression by knowing something about everything. Gazing at me like I'm about to keel over!"

"Well, maybe she's got the hots for you," explained Joe. "It's not unusual for the bridesmaid to fall for the groomsman. I know people who met like that and ended up getting married."

"It won't happen here – I can promise you that!" Rooney said, determinedly. "No wonder her boyfriend dumped her after their vacation. He must have had the patience of a saint to wait that long. I'd have tied her to a motor boat and paid some guy to take her out to sea and dump her!"

Joe couldn't help but laugh.

"It hasn't been your day."

"You can say that again. I wouldn't relive this day for anyone – not even you!" he said, draining his glass.

"Well, it was Angel who asked you to be nice to her."

"I know. That's where I made my big mistake. How was I to know you can't be nice to Cindy for one day? She thinks you should be nice to her for a lifetime."

"Come on, Rooney," Joe put his arm around his friend's shoulder. "Angel has gone to change and I have to freshen up. After that I have to see Ralph. Come with me. Cindy can't get to you if you're in Ralph Lennox's private room."

"Lead the way, Joe. I'm right behind you!"

Rooney sat and listened as Joe went over all the things he had to do while he'd be away. "And don't forget to have Agnes settled in before we get back. I don't want Angel to have anything to worry about while we're in Miami. If she knows her mother's o.k. she'll be more relaxed and…"

"Joe, everything will be fine. I'll see to it."

Joe came out of the bathroom, buttoning up a new white shirt."

"What's wrong with you?" he asked.

"Nothing."

"Nothing?"

"Well, alright. I had a talk with Angela earlier and she seemed a little nervous."

"About what?"

"About tonight."

"Oh, I see," said Joe, as if the penny had just dropped.

"And you want to tell me to be a good boy and not jump on her as soon as we get on the plane! Well, just so it'll put your mind at rest, I've packed 'House and Garden' instead of the 'Karmasutra'!"

He put his tie on and clipped on his tie-pin. Reaching for his jacket, he looked back at Rooney.

"I love her, Rooney, and she loves me. I'm not going to do anything to ruin that."

Rooney got up and straightened the tie-pin.

"That's all I wanted to know," he smiled.

Joe buttoned his jacket and checked himself in the mirror.

"Come on," he said, "let's go and see Ralph."

Ralph Lennox greeted them warmly in his personal office-cum-sitting room. As they sat down in the comfortable chairs, he fetched them drinks from his own bar.

"Well, was everything o.k. for you, Joe?" he asked.

"More than o.k., Ralph. It was terrific. Reuben and Rooney here, will settle up with you tomorrow."

"There's no hurry, Joe. It can wait."

"No, I insist. No one could have done it better, Ralph. I'm really grateful."

"And I'm really happy to oblige a friend," he said, joining them.

The Lennox family were to New York what the Kennedy's were to Boston. Ralph could trace his wealthy family back for generations. A tall, distinguished, handsome man, he was in his mid-forties with greying hair, a thin moustache, a winning smile and impeccable dress sense. He knew what high society wanted and gave it to them in 'The Imperial Palace'. It had been a gamble to begin with, bought by money left to him in his grandmother's will. But it had paid off and made him, not only wealthy in his own right, but the toast of all those he'd set out to impress. Ralph Lennox was an important man and a valuable friend.

After they'd chatted for a while, Ralph, got up and went to the safe.

"This is your money and credit cards," he said, bringing them to Joe. "And these, my friend, are your tickets to Miami – or should I say 'Heaven', judging by the company you're going with! I've got to hand it to you, Joe, she's delightful."

"Yeah, I guess I did o.k., Ralph. Thanks for everything."

They shook hands.

"My pleasure, Joe. And my wedding present will be deducted from the bill!"

As Joe turned to go, Ralph stopped him.

"Joe, how's Claudia?"

"Now Ralph, I thought you'd know better than me," he said, holding his hands in an upright gesture.

"I haven't seen her for a couple of weeks. I've been away on business and then I had your wedding to take care of. I have sent her some flowers, though, to the Agency. Just to let her know I'm thinking of her."

"I'm sure she knows, Ralph, and it was a nice thing to do. The girls appreciate it, when they're appreciated."

"Maybe I could give her a call later this week?"

"You do that. She'll be glad to hear from you. But be careful. The next wedding you take care of, might be your own!"

Ralph laughed,

"I'm sure stranger things have happened, Joe. And besides, it wouldn't be the first time a Lennox female had a bit of a 'reputation'!!"

Rooney and Joe left the office and returned to the dining hall to wait for Angela. Cindy came in, followed by Agnes.

"She won't be long, Joe. She's almost ready," Agnes told him.

"How is she?" he asked.

"A bit sad that none of the rest of the family could be with her today. Sheila and Raymond would have loved it, and I just wish her father could have seen her. He'd have been so proud. I never thought my little girl could look so beautiful."

"She's that alright. I still can't believe I'm married to her."

Agnes put her hand on his arm.

"Well, I did tell you miracles can happen, didn't I?"

"You sure did Agnes, and let me tell you something. I love your daughter. She's everything in this world to me. I'm going to take good care of her."

"I know," she smiled.

At that moment, Angela appeared. Rooney gazed at her, admiringly. Her hair and make-up were redone and she wore a light peach, two-piece cotton suit. The short, straight skirt was covered by a three-quarter length jacket which was unbuttoned, showing a plain, cream top. Cream high heels and shoulder bag completed the outfit. Joe's eyes made their way from her face down to her ankles and back up again.

Gene O'Brien's voice muttered from beside him,

"Jesus Joe, she's beautiful."

"I know," whispered Joe.

"Then let her know – tonight! A special lady deserves special treatment."

"You can count on it," he replied, going over and taking Angela's arm, proudly.

"You look beautiful, Angel."

"I'm glad you think so," she smiled.

After saying goodbye to their guests, Joe escorted Angela to the entrance, followed by Rooney, Cindy, Agnes, Freddie and Evie. Frankie and Al were already outside, making sure that all the luggage was safely in the limousine.

As the car door closed and they began their journey to the airport, Joe and Angela looked back and waved. Joe saw Gene O'Brien standing on the sidewalk with the others. His old friend smiled and gave him the 'thumbs-up', just as he had done that night outside 'The Safe Haven'.

Joe took Angela's hand and held it gently but firmly. Then leaned over and kissed her, as they finally left 'The Imperial Palace' behind.

Chapter 8

By the time the plane touched down in Miami and they were driven to their destination, it was just after ten o'clock. On arriving at the secluded beach house, they were greeted by a man called Charlie, who shook hands with them and told them he was the caretaker. He opened the door and led them inside. The chauffeur followed with the luggage.

"Where would you like these, Mr Morrelli?" he asked.

"The bedroom would be fine," replied Joe, looking around. Charlie pointed to a door.

"That's the bedroom over there."

When the luggage was brought through, Charlie showed them around. It was a spacious house with polished wooden floors and expensive rugs. The walls were white and had prints of famous artists hanging on them. The furniture was upholstered in rich, pastel fabrics with large, soft cushions and footstools to match. There were several lamps situated around the room and tall, green plants stood in the corners. The fitted kitchen was compact by design but had the latest electrical appliances and was large enough to hold a pine table and six chairs. The master bedroom was luxuriously furnished and en-suite. The two smaller bedrooms were tastefully decorated and the bathroom just across the hall from them had everything guests could require.

Charlie smiled.

"As you can see, Mr Morrelli, everything is designed for comfort, because it's all on one floor." He pointed to an alcove off the lounge. "A table has been set for supper. It's a cold buffet but you should find the food to your liking." He handed Joe the keys. "I live just up the beach. If there's anything you want, just call my number – it's by the telephone. Good night Mr Morrelli, Mrs Morrelli." He smiled at Angela. She smiled and nodded in appreciation.

"Good night," said Joe "and thanks for everything."

"My pleasure," he replied, closing the door behind him.

Joe looked at Angela.

"Well, what do you think?"

"I can't believe it! It's so beautiful! And have you seen the flowers?"

She pointed around to various locations were expensive flower arrangements adorned the room.

"Yeah well, we might as well live in style," he smiled. "O.k., honey, do you want to unpack first or would you rather eat?"

"I think we'll eat. I'm not unpacking everything tonight."

They went into the alcove where a long, glass topped table was attractively laid with food. A large bottle of champagne stood in a silver ice-bucket. They took off their jackets. As Angela filled the plates, Joe uncorked and poured the champagne.

"To us," he smiled. "I know it's not your favourite drink, so if there's something else you'd like…."

"No, this will be fine, Joe."

"I've heard you say it gives you a headache!"

"It's o.k. I'm a little more used to it now. Besides, it's a shame to waste it."

They enjoyed their meal, happy and relaxed.

"Sheila and Raymond phoned last night to wish us luck."

"I bet you missed them not being here, Angel."

"I did," she replied, sadly. "It would have meant a lot to me to have them at my wedding, especially as I'd been their bridesmaid. Sheila should really have been mine."

"I think Rooney would have preferred it that way!" he joked.

"Why? Didn't he hit it off with Cindy?"

"I'd say it was the dead opposite. By now I reckon he's probably gone into hiding. We'll be lucky if we ever see him again! To make things worse I told him that sometimes the groomsman ends up marrying the bridesmaid. I think that just about did it!"

Angela laughed. Then Joe thought for a moment and said, "But that's not strictly true, is it? After all, you didn't marry Sheila and Raymond's groomsman. Who was he, anyway?"

"Raymond's best friend, Jamie Doyle. He married someone else, thank goodness!"

"Why? Didn't you like him?"

"Yes, I liked him, but there's no way I'd have married him. My father used to say if Jamie had brains he'd be dangerous!"

"He sounds a bit like Cindy!" laughed Joe, as he poured some more champagne.

After they'd finished their meal, Angela became very still.

"Joe," she whispered, "can you hear something?"

Joe was silent for a moment, then got up and went to the window, pulling back the drapes. He returned and lifted his glass.

"Come on," he said smiling. "And bring your drink with you."

She followed him and watched as he pulled back a large, sliding glass door and stepped out onto a veranda. Again she followed him. He held his hand towards the distance and smiled.

"Well, there you are, Angel. Just what you wanted."

At the bottom of a white path was the beach and the sea.

"It's so near!" she exclaimed. "And it's so beautiful! Oh, Joe!"

He put his arm around her shoulder, as they both stood quietly, listening to the sound of the waves lapping onto the sand, and sipping the champagne. For the first time they were completely alone. After a while Joe said,

"Can I ask you something? Why do you like the sea so much?"

"I think it's because of the feeling it gives me. When you're brought up in a city everyone's always rushing around trying to deal with problems, worries and stress. But the sea gives such a feeling of contentment. Calm. It's in no hurry. It's not going anywhere. People don't really appreciate it. It's the only thing I can look at and enjoy. It makes me glad to be alive. It's beautiful."

"I sure never thought of it like that."

She looked at him and smiled.

"Not enough people do. But like the saying goes, 'Beauty is in the eye of the beholder.' I'd better go and unpack a few things."

"Yeah, it's been a long day," he sighed.

He watched her walk through the lounge, then looked back at the ocean.

"Beauty is in the eye of the beholder," he murmured. "I must remember that."

Then stepping back inside, he closed the door and followed Angela to the bedroom. She was unpacking some of her night things when he went in. As Joe did the same, he noticed Angela looking a little uneasy. So he said,

"You use the shower in there, Angel. I'll use the one in the other bathroom."

"Are you sure?"

"Sure, I'm sure!" he smiled, picking up his things and leaving the room.

He made sure to take his time in the hope that Angela would be ready for bed by his return. After all the advice that had been given to him that day, he decided to take things slowly. Angela came out of the bathroom wearing an ankle length white satin nightdress that clung to her body. It had a low neckline and was held up by two thin straps. She brushed her long, loose curls down over her shoulder and looked at herself in the mirror. Cindy had been right, Miami was warm. She lifted her matching robe and went over to the bed. Pulling down the top cover she folded it neatly along the bottom, leaving just the sheet, then laid her robe on top of it. Going across to the window, Angela opened the drapes and discovered another sliding door that led out onto a small, white concrete path that seemed to go all the way around the house and join with the one leading to the beach. She opened the window slightly, closed the drapes again and climbed into bed. She lay on her side, watching the drapes blowing gently in the night breeze. Angela was nervous. Joe was so much older than her and she had no idea what he would be really like now that they were finally married. She didn't know just what he would expect from her.

When Joe walked in, her stomach did a summersault. There was no going back now! Normally, he only ever wore boxer shorts to bed but as this was the first night of his honeymoon, he wore pyjama bottoms. As he pulled the sheet down and got into the bed, Angela couldn't help but notice how well built and supple his body was.

Joe sat up and looking down at her, he smiled.

"I see you're feeling the heat. I suppose that's why you chose the side of the bed nearest the window."

"Yes, it is very warm. I opened the window a little. I hope you don't mind."

"Not me," he replied, looking around the room.

Angela edged away from him, then did the same thing again as Joe watched her out of the corner of his eye.

"Hey," he joked, "I know I'm not twenty one anymore and I know I've gained a few pounds, but I didn't think I needed all this space!"

She kept moving slowly until she reached the edge of the bed, then clung onto the mattress as if for protection. Finally, Joe said, "Angel, if you move anymore you'll be sleeping on the beach!"

"I just want you to be comfortable," came the reply.

Joe knew that wasn't true and his face became serious as he looked at the large gap between them. He moved across the bed and leaned over her.

"Why don't you get some sleep," he advised, kissing her cheek. "You must be worn out."

He got out of bed and made his way to the lounge, where he switched on a small table lamp and sat down in one of the chairs with his back to the bedroom door.

"Boy, am I glad the guys aren't here to see this!" thought Joe. "There's no way Rooney would believe it, Joe Morrelli sitting alone on his wedding night. And as for Al....!"

He was just glad they were both in New York.

The sound of the bedroom door opening broke his train of thought. Angela came to the back of the chair and put her arms around his neck.

"Joe, I'm sorry," she said in a low voice.

He stared straight ahead but put his hand up and stroked her arm.

"It's o.k. honey."

"No, it's not o.k."

She took her arms away and slipped onto the arm of the chair. He put his hand on her waist and pulled her gently onto his lap.

"What's wrong, Angel? Is it me?"

"No. It's just that I'm scared you might wake up tomorrow morning and realise you've made a mistake by marrying me."

"That will never happen."

She put her head on his shoulder and moved her hand along his chest. He kissed her hair and stroked her shoulder lightly with his fingers, pulling down the thin strap of her nightdress. She raised her head and began to kiss his cheek, slowly moving towards his mouth. Their lips met and what started as a soft, sensual kiss became a hot, passionate one. Joe embraced her, feeling her now willing body against his own. His hand moved to slip inside her nightdress and cover her breast. She pressed her finger tips into his strong shoulders, as she felt the gentle movement of his hand.

Taking her lips from his, she whispered,

"I want to go to bed now."

Joe held her tightly, burying his face in her neck and smelling the fragrance of the perfume that seemed to linger on every part of her bare skin. Then, without another word he rose, lifting her in his arms like a baby. She held onto him as he carried her to the bedroom and on going inside he put his heel to the door, closing it securely. The small lamp glowed in the darkness of the lounge and as the waves rolled onto the shore, Joe and Angela Morrelli became castaways on their own sea of passion.

Joe wakened with his arm around Angela and strong sunlight through the light drapes. He rolled onto his back and after rubbing his eyes, he lay looking at the ceiling with a smile of satisfaction on his face. His watch on the bedside table said eight thirty, so he quietly edged over and sat on the side of the bed. Lifting his pyjama bottoms off the floor, he put them on and went over to the window where he opened the drapes a little and looked out. He gazed at the ocean, feeling the warm fresh air on his face. Then he turned and looked at Angela. She was sleeping soundly, one arm lying loosely over her waist the other reaching under her pillow. The sheet covered the lower part of her body and Joe watched as her breasts moved up and down to the rhythm of her breathing. He knew she'd felt some discomfort during their lovemaking. There had been times when he'd felt her body stiffen and heard her gasp, and he was experienced enough to know that passion was not responsible.

Any doubts he'd ever had about Angela and Michael Conway had disappeared completely. He knew now for certain he was the first man who'd ever had her, and he was glad. A younger man might not have been as caring or understanding as he had tried to be. He couldn't bear the thought of someone being rough or demanding with a woman like that. It had been a very special night for him. Not only had Angela given him all her love and affection, she'd given him the one thing no other woman ever did – her virginity. He felt a proud and happy man as he closed the drapes, went over to the bed and kissed her shoulder lightly. She didn't stir, so he left her and went through to the lounge. After switching off the lamp and opening the drapes, he made his way to the kitchen to cook breakfast.

Angela woke just after nine. She looked around for her nightdress but couldn't find it, so she reached for her robe and put it on, then went in search of Joe. He was standing in the kitchen, humming happily and watching the coffee pot boil.

"Hi," he smiled. "Would you like some coffee?"

She nodded, so he poured a cup and handed it to her. Then he leaned over and kissed her.

"Are you o.k." he asked.

"I guess so. No pain, no gain," she replied as she slid stiffly onto the chair.

Joe watched her, then sat down.

"You'll be fine," he said, nodding downwards. "It doesn't last long."

"And you would know all about that, I suppose."

"Well, you know how it is, Angel... you hear about these things. It's not only women who talk, men talk too. You know what I think?"

"No, but I've a feeling you're going to tell me."

"I think making love for the first time is like doing anything for the first time – you always remember it. It's like your first ride on a roller coaster, the subway, a greyhound bus..."

"Joe! Can we please change the subject" asked Angela, glaring at him over her coffee cup.

"Yeah, sure. But I'm only trying to explain. It's like going somewhere really special."

"But we didn't go anywhere."

"Speak for yourself!" he grinned.

Angela put the cup down and pointed her finger at him.

"You're enjoying this, aren't you?"

He grinned even more.

"It's alright for you," she continued, "But I'm the one who's having difficulty sitting down."

"Well honey, I did try to warn you at the reception!"

"Well, you didn't try hard enough!"

She got up and walked past him. He put his hand out and caught hers.

"Oh, come on, Angel. I'm only having some fun."

"I've noticed," she replied, looking down at him. "You're just full of it this morning."

He pulled her gently onto his knee.

"The truth is," he said, putting his arms around her, "I'm just very happy and very proud."

He moved his hand inside her robe and stroked her thigh. "I love you," he whispered.

"Well, you'll have to put it on hold," she whispered back.

"O.k.," he agreed. "Now, what do you want to do today, besides riding roller-coasters or buses?"

She got up off his knee and slapped it playfully. He, in turn, slapped her bottom.

"Seriously though, what are you going to do?" he asked again.

"I'm going to unpack and have a shower."

"I think I'll come with you and do the same," he replied getting up.

"Oh no you don't!" she insisted, pushing him back down.

"You stay here and calm yourself. Now, drink your coffee and eat some breakfast. You have to keep your strength up!"

Joe's eyes gleamed as Angela left the kitchen.

"Yeah, I'd better," he thought. "Now, where are those eggs?!"

Miami had been a good idea and the beach house was the ideal place for Joe and Angela to really get to know each other as husband and wife. They sunbathed, went swimming and took long walks along the beach talking about everything and anything. Joe especially liked the evenings, when they would stroll hand in hand beside the ocean and then sit on the veranda just enjoying each other's company. He would take her on his lap and hold her protectively. He'd never been more relaxed or contended in his life. Sometimes, they went out to dinner but Angela liked to cook for him so most evenings they dined alone. Joe couldn't help but notice that a lot of young men came to the beach during the day and when Angela walked by in a bikini, she turned quite a few heads. He could understand why. One afternoon as they lay on the beach, she left him to go for a swim. A little while later he sat up to see where she was and caught sight of her further along the beach, talking to a young muscular male. As she left him and made her way back, he quickly lay down again pretending he hadn't seen her. He thought she would mention it but as time wore on and they got up to leave, she still hadn't. This gave Joe and uneasy feeling as they walked back to the beach house.

"Joe, how would you like a nice steak for dinner?" she asked him, as she went to change.

"Sounds fine by me."

"I'm going to the supermarket to get some groceries."

"Do you want me to come with you?"

"No, it's not far. I won't be long," she assured him.

"Well, if you're sure honey."

"Yes, I'm sure. Besides, it's only a ten minute walk away."

Angela made out her grocery list.

"You'll need money," he said. "It's in the drawer of the bedside cabinet."

"It's o.k., I have money here." She held up her purse. "We don't need that much, anyway."

She kissed his cheek and left.

Joe was in deep thought. He wondered if the trip to the supermarket had anything to do with the young man on the beach. After he got changed he sat on the veranda with a large scotch. He kept looking at his watch. He realised he was keeping time on her but he couldn't help it. The truth was, he was feeling jealous. Not only had that young man been talking to his wife, but she'd failed to mention it to him even in passing. Joe was worried that something might go wrong to spoil his happiness.

Angela came back with the groceries and left them in the kitchen. Then she poured herself a beer and joined Joe on the veranda.

"That supermarket was busy. I could hardly find what I wanted," she said casually. Joe couldn't contain himself any longer. He looked at her.

"That guy on the beach earlier, what did he want?"

Angela turned to him, surprised.

"He wanted to know if I was with someone. I told him I was with my husband. He said that didn't matter these days but I told him it mattered to me."

"He looked a handsome guy," said Joe. "You know, well built."

"Haven't you noticed? They all look like that. They strut up and down the beach like they're God's gift to women, thinking no woman can refuse them. If you want my opinion they're all brawn and no brains, that's why I married you," she smiled. "Although to be honest I never though I would."

"What do you mean?" asked Joe, putting his glass down.

"Well, I knew Rooney a lot better than I knew you. He kept coming to 'The Safe Haven' and asking me out, but I couldn't go. I wasn't allowed to date the customers. Remember?"

"Would you have gone out with him if you had been allowed?"

"Yes, I probably would. I always liked Rooney. I often thought he'd ask me to leave my job because of the house rules, but he never did. I guess he wasn't as interested in me as I thought."

Joe realised just how close he'd come to not getting Angela.

"Anyway," she smiled, "you came along and now I'm married to you."

"Have you any regrets?"

"Not one. I'm in love with my husband and all the beach boys in Miami can't change that!" She got up.

"I got you something at the store." She disappeared and came back with a carrier bag. "Here."

"You got something for me?" he smiled. "What is it?"

He opened it and took out a black baseball cap. On the front of it written in white was, "I'M AN O.K. GUY – THE WIFE SAYS SO!"

Joe smiled broadly.

"Now, that's one thing I don't have. But you shouldn't be spending your money on me."

"It only cost a few dollars, Joe. And besides," she said putting it on his head, "I don't want you to get sunstroke!" She smiled and kissed him. "Now I'm going to see to dinner."

When she'd gone Joe took it off and held it, reading the words. It might have only cost a few dollars but to him it was the one present he'd always hold dear because he knew Angela had chosen the words. It was like a seal of approval. Her way of telling him he was her kind of man. He had never loved her more than at that moment. He put it back on again with pride, knowing he was a lucky man to have her.

On following her to the kitchen he watched her unpack the groceries, then went over and put his arm around her waist.

"Would you do this 'o.k. guy' a favour?" he whispered in her ear. "Would you wait until later to cook dinner?"

She turned and looked at him.

"Aren't you hungry?"

"Not for food."

He took her hand and guided her out of the kitchen, through the lounge towards the bedroom.

"Joe," she smiled, "why are you wearing that cap indoors? There's no sun."

"Maybe not," he grinned, opening the bedroom door, "but I have a feeling it might get pretty hot where we're going!"

Angela liked to go down to the beach in the morning when there was no one around. She'd go for a swim or just walk along enjoying the solitude. Joe let her do her own thing. He would read the newspaper and make a few calls back home, or just laze about. One morning, as she walked along the quiet stretch of beach, she heard a voice call to her, "Good morning Mrs Morrelli."

Angela put her hand up and shielding her eyes, looked around. Charlie was standing outside his small beach house.

"Good morning," she called back, waving. Then she made her way towards him.

"I see you like the ocean," he commented.

"I love it!"

"Then that makes two of us. There's nowhere else I'd rather be."

"You're very lucky to be living beside it."

"I know. I've just made some coffee. Would you like a cup?"

"Yes, I would. Thank you," smiled Angela, as she followed him inside.

Charlie's beach house was very compact but well furnished. He led the way through to the kitchen and poured the coffee. They sat at opposite ends of the table and helped themselves to milk and sugar. Angela found herself studying him. He was about fifty years old, maybe a little more. His dark hair was turning grey, making him look more mature than elderly. His tanned skin and brown eyes gave him a Latin look and this combined with his warm smile gave him an earthy charm. She couldn't help but think he must have been very handsome in his younger years, as he was quite an attractive man. Casually dressed in light grey trousers and white T-shirt, he offered Angela some cookies from a jar.

"I see you on the beach every morning, but you're always alone," he said.

She leaned her elbow on the table, placing her hand on the side of her face. "Well my husband isn't as excited by all this sea and sand as I am," she smiled. "I've never been here before, so I guess I'm over-awed by it. I like the mornings and the evenings best, when there's hardly anyone around."

"Yes, that's the best time alright."

Angela looked at him.

"You were surprised the night you met us, weren't you? I could tell by your face."

223

"Well, to tell the truth I wasn't expecting Mr Morrelli's wife to be so young." he smiled.

"I suppose you think I married him for all the wrong reasons?"

Charlie looked uncomfortable.

"That's alright. I guess a lot of people will think that of me, but its not true. Joe is a lot older than me but I love him. I know some people might not understand that or believe it. I don't think you do."

"Maybe not at first," he admitted, "but I've seen you both in the evenings, walking hand in hand and I've never seen two people look more happy and relaxed in each other's company."

"Are you married, Mr -?"

"Gordino, but call me Charlie. I was once. She left me a few years ago. She got bored and wanted to move to the city. I guess she wanted some excitement out of life. Anyway, I wouldn't go. I couldn't live in a place that was always so busy all the time. No I like it just fine where I am."

He stirred his coffee and continued, "You see, I was brought up in an apartment in the slums. My father was Italian, my mother was Anglo. It was a poor neighbourhood and a tough one. When I got older I moved around from place to place but I couldn't settle. I never seemed to fit it."

"I know the feeling," nodded Angela.

"Anyway, when I finally came here and got a job, I knew this was where I wanted to be. My wife didn't like it, though. Come to think of it, I don't think she liked me much, either." He shrugged his shoulders.

"When I was young I used to dream of going to sea. The ocean always fascinated me. I guess that's because I only ever saw it in books and magazines, until now. I used to read books about great voyages and travellers on the high seas. I loved anything like that."

He leaned back in his chair, clasping his hands behind his neck. "I remember once reading a poem about the sea and ships but I can't remember who wrote it." He stared into space, as if lost in his own thoughts. Then he jolted. "I'm sorry, I bet I'm boring you to death. Maybe now you'll understand why my wife isn't around!"

Angela looked at him and smiled,

"No, I'm not bored at all. I read quite a lot myself. Can you remember how the poem started?"

Charlie paused for a moment and then said,

'I must go down to the sea again.

To the lonely sea and the sky…'

"John Masefield," said Angela.

"Who?"

"John Masefield. That's who wrote the poem."

"Yeah!" Said Charlie, in a surprised voice, "that's the guy!"

They both began to recite the pieces of the poem they knew. Charlie was delighted with Angela's company.

"How on earth did you know about that?" he asked.

"I study English Literature at College. I know a little poetry." She smiled. They talked on and on.

"Well, I can't tell you what it means to me to be able to hold an intelligent conversation with someone like yourself, Mrs Morrelli. If you'll pardon me for saying, most of the young women who frequent this beach are high on beauty but low on brains! Mr Morrelli's a very fortunate man, he's married a woman with both! That's a rare thing these days."

She started to laugh and putting out her hand, she shook his in a warm, friendly manner.

"You must call me Angela," she insisted.

"O.k. then, Angela, would you do me a big favour?"

"Sure, if I can."

"Would you write out those words for me before the end of your honeymoon?"

"You really like that poem, don't you?" she smiled. "I can understand why. The sea works its own kind of magic."

Charlie leaned across the table.

"How would you and your husband like to go on a boat trip with me?" he asked. "I rent them at the marina. I also rent cars, water-skies, anything like that."

"I'd love to go! And I'm sure Joe would as well. I'll ask him just as soon as I get back. Come to think of it, I better be going. He'll be wondering what's happened to me."

Charlie left her to the door.

"I'm really glad I asked you in. I don't get much company living here. It's good to talk to someone on your own wavelength. It doesn't happen often."

Angela looked at him.

"Well, would you like me to call again?"

"Sure! Feel free. I'll look forward to it and if you want anything just let me know. Don't forget about the boat trip, now. I think you'll enjoy it."

"I won't forget about it. And I won't forget about your poem either! Goodbye Charlie."

"Goodbye Angela."

She walked a short distance, then turned and waved to him. As he watched her go down the beach, he shook his head and smiled. In the time he'd lived there he'd seen young women come and go. Beach parties, drugs, sex. It was a way of life to most of them. But this one was different. She didn't need or want the high life. Other things were more important to her. People were more important to her. It was refreshing for him to meet someone like her. In a crazy mixed up society it gave him hope for the future. He could understand why Joe Morrelli had married her. She had warmth, personality – and class.

"Joe Morrelli might come from New York," he thought, "but he's found the pearl in the oyster that only comes from the sea!"

Angela returned to the beach house to find Joe pacing up and down.

"Where have you been?" he asked, in an anxious voice. "I've been up and down the beach looking for you. I thought something had happened to you. I was just about to call the cops."

"I met Charlie."

"Who?"

"Charlie. You know, the caretaker. I was in his beach house talking to him."

"Well, doesn't Charlie have a phone? You could have let me know where you were. What did you find to talk about all this time?"

"Oh, this and that. He's really a very interesting man. A bit lonely, though. I think he needs a friend."

"Really!"

"Anyway, he's invited us on a boat trip. I said we would go."

"Oh great!" replied Joe, casting his eyes towards the ceiling. "My friends will range from Congressmen to caretakers. That's all I need!"

Angela stared at him as her eyes narrowed.

"What's the matter, Joe, isn't a caretaker good enough for you?"

"Well, considering the kind of people I know he rates pretty low on my scale," he retorted sarcastically.

"And that bothers you, I suppose? Well you went from a Broadway actress to a waitress. You can't go much lower than that."

Now Angela was hurt as well as angry.

Joe tried to explain.

"You can't just go talking to strangers and walking into their homes, for Christ's sake! There's a lot of crime here. There's a lot of crime everywhere. Don't ever do it again. Anything could happen to you. And another thing, if Charlie wants a friend let him go and get someone else. I don't want you going back there, Angel. Do you understand?"

Joe's voice was raised in anger. But Angela gave as good as she got.

"I understand one thing. If it were Gene O'Brien or some big shot it wouldn't bother you so much. But let me tell you this, if I want to go back and see Charlie then I will and you won't stop me! You're not going to choose my friends for me either. I'm quite capable of doing that for myself. They may not be your choice but they're mine!"

On opening the door, she stopped and looked back.

"You know," she sneered, "for someone who made his first dollar running errands in the Bronx, you think you're very high and mighty."

"Yeah well, I've earned that right!" he roared.

"Maybe the caretaker would have earned it too, if things had gone well for him!" she replied, slamming the door and walking down the path.

Joe opened it again and stepped out.

"Well, the honeymoon sure didn't last long!" he yelled after her.

"And who's fault's that?" she replied, without looking back.

"I suppose you're going back to Charlie's?!"

Angela stopped in her tracks and turned around. Even from a distance Joe could see her seething.

"No," she snapped, "but I think you should go back to Antonia. It sounds like you're missing her already!"

Now it was Joe's turn to slam the door. He went into the lounge, poured himself a drink and took it out onto the veranda. He watched as she walked along the beach. "If Gene O'Brien was here he'd love this," thought Joe.

He'd often heard his friend talk about the Irish temper and if he'd seen and heard Angela today, he'd be laughing from now till Christmas!

Lunch time came and went but there was still no sign of Angela. Joe's temper had subsided and he was feeling both sorry and guilty about his outburst. He knew he hadn't given her much of a chance to explain about Charlie. She looked so happy when she first came in but he'd ruined all that. To make matters worse he'd given the wrong impression as to why he'd acted the way he did. He really had been worried about her but it came across that he felt superior to everyone, including Angela. He'd acted just like Antonia would have and he didn't like himself for that.

Joe made something to eat and afterwards he walked around the path outside, but there was no sign of her.

The beach was starting to crowd with people and he was getting anxious. Angela had been gone for hours and had no money with her to buy anything, so he decided to go and look for her. He went down the path and headed in the direction he'd last seen her. He'd walked nearly the full stretch of the beach when he finally caught sight of her. She looked a sad and lonely figure as she sat gazing at the ocean. It reminded him of the night he'd seen her in the Church.

Joe went over and sat down beside her in silence. Then after a few moments, he turned to her.

"I'm sorry I shouted at you," he said, in a low voice. She didn't answer so he continued.

"I thought something bad had happened to you. I was worried and upset, that's all."

When Angela met his gaze he could see she'd been crying.

"No, that's not all," she replied in a voice close to a whisper. "When you make love to me, you treat me like a woman. When you're angry, you treat me like a child. You told me I couldn't see a friend, the same way you'd tell a child they couldn't play with someone. You once said you didn't want to be my father but you surely acted like one today!"

Joe tried to make amends.

"Look Angel, I'll tell you what. We'll go on the boat trip with Charlie and we'll invite him over for dinner. What do you say?"

"Don't do me any favours, Joe," she replied, looking away.

"Angel, listen to me. I want you to have your own friends, really I do. But when we go back to New York I'd like you to get to know my friends. You're always so nervous around them, yet you meet this guy, Charlie, and you can talk to him like you've known him all your life. I'd just like you to be able to do the same back home."

Angela kept looking straight ahead.

"Joe, your friends don't understand me and I can't talk to them about the things I like. Charlie understands. He never fitted in anywhere, especially the city, that's why he's here." Then she turned and looked at him. "What if I'm like Charlie, Joe? What if I don't fit in? That thought frightens me. I didn't fit in back home in Belfast and New York is still new to me. Sometimes I feel I don't belong anywhere. I was beginning to think I belonged here but you've spoiled that for me now. You're lucky, Joe, you belong in New York and you love it there."

"And you will, too, honey. Just give it time."

Angela got up and walked away from him. He followed, looking at the sand.

He didn't know she felt like this. He's been so wrapped up in the kind of life he wanted for both of them, he'd never thought to ask her what she wanted. His heart sank as he remembered his heavy handedness with her that morning and he knew she was right when she said he behaved more like a father than a husband. He swore to himself it would never happen again.

Eventually, he caught up with her and put his arm around her shoulder.

"Let's go back to the beach house, Angel. You must be tired and hungry."

They walked back in silence, Angela keeping her eyes fixed on the sand. Not once did she look at the ocean or the waves that crept up towards her. Joe knew she was hurting. All he wanted to do was to make everything the way it was before today but it wasn't going to be easy. He knew she was thinking he'd be better off with Antonia and that he'd made a mistake by marrying her. Nothing could be further from the truth. He'd just have to prove it to her in whatever way he could. And after what she'd said on the beach, he was more than willing to try.

When they got back, Angela poured herself some coffee and sat in the kitchen. Joe sat down beside her.

"You really should eat something, Angel. You haven't had anything all day."

"Maybe later," she replied, staring at the cup.

"I know, why don't we go out to dinner? That way you won't have to cook. You can relax and enjoy yourself."

"Not tonight. I'm going to take a shower and change." She got up and left. Joe sat on, staring at the table. He knew she was feeling pretty down but hoped things would get better as the day past. However, Angela remained quiet and subdued. As they sat through dinner there were no smiles, no laughter and very little conversation on her part. Joe did most of the talking trying to make everything as normal as possible.

"By the way I forgot to ask you, who got that kid to sing the 'Ave Maria' at our wedding? He had a great voice."

"I did," she replied. "Rooney told me it was your favourite." She kept playing with the food on her plate.

"And how come you never told me you had two names?" he smiled.

"It never came up."

Joe studied her and then asked.

"Aren't you going to eat that?"

"I'm not very hungry."

After an uncomfortable silence, she got up and started to clear the table, her glass of wine still untouched.

"Why don't you leave that, honey, and take your drink out onto the veranda?"

She shook her head, "I'm not in the mood. I'm tired I think I'll go to bed."

"Yeah," said Joe, agreeably, "that's a good idea why don't you get an early night. Then tomorrow you could go shopping, buy yourself anything you want."

"Like a thousand dollar dress?" she asked walking by him. Is that how you made up with Antonia? Why don't you just bring me to the store and buy me candy, like a child. It would save you a fortune!"

Joe got up quickly, took her arm and turned her around.

"O.k., that's enough!" he warned. "That's twice you've mentioned her name to me today and I don't like it."

"Well, excuse me!" snapped Angela, glaring at him. "But I got the impression this morning that you'd be more at home with a high class wife like her. Not to mention her high society friends. Yes, I think that arrangement would suit you just fine!"

"Will you stop it? O.k., I said things this morning I didn't mean and I'm sorry. But I married you, Angel, not her."

"Well, maybe that's been your big mistake, Joe. A wife who mixes with lower classes might be a novelty at first, but she can soon become an embarrassment. I'm not really what you need, am I? You deserve someone better."

She pulled away from him. "Like I've already said, Joe, I don't belong!"

He stared after her as she walked to the bedroom, closing the door loudly. A serious expression spread over his face. Things were going too far. He went out onto the veranda and sat down, gazing at the ocean and wondering what to do. Now he realised what it was like to feel sad and alone.

"Damn it!" he thought. "There must be some way of putting this right!"

Then he had an idea.

Joe opened the bedroom door and switched on the lights. He walked across the room, pulled over the drapes and opened the sliding door. Then he came to the bed and pulled back the covers. Angela, startled at his behaviour, sat up.

"What are you doing?" she asked.

"You'll see," came the reply.

Lifting her in his arms he carried her through the sliding door and out onto the concrete path, making his way to the beach.

"Are you drunk?" she demanded.

"No," he replied, as he kept on walking.

"Joe Morrelli, are you out of your mind? Put me down," she ordered.

"All in good time."

He walked onto the sand and gently laid her down on a large rug which already awaited them.

Angela was totally confused.

"What is the matter with you?"

"I'll tell you what the matter is. I want my wife to know how much I love her so I'm going to show her here and now!"

Now she was shocked. He joined her on the rug and started to remove his clothing.

"Joe Morrelli, you can't – not here," she protested, looking nervously around.

"Oh no? Well, you just watch me," he insisted.

"This is ridiculous!" she muttered, struggling to get up. "I'm going back inside."

He grabbed her and pulled her back down, rolling on top of her.

"You're not going anywhere. Not until we get things sorted out, Angel. I love you and only you. You've got to believe that."

Angela opened her mouth to speak but Joe kissed her hungrily. She struggled under his weight, remembering a similar night in 'The Safe Haven'. Then he whispered,

"Don't fight me on this, Angel. We've done enough of that."

His kisses were passionate, full of want and desire. As she felt the warmth of his hands burning into her skin, she put her arms around him surrendering to his need.

"You belong, Angel" he assured her. "You belong with me."

Slowly he pulled down the top of her nightdress, kissing her flesh and caressing it with his tongue. She stroked his back and shoulders in response. Finally, when he had freed her body from the delicate white lace, Joe made love to Angela and she made love to him.

The sound of their passion was carried on the gentle night breeze, only to be drowned by the waves that rolled loudly as if in an effort to give them anonymity and keep them safe. Afterwards, they lay wrapped in each other's arms, happy, contented, fulfilled. This was a special night for both of them and one they would always remember.

Two days later, Charlie drove up in his jeep to take Joe and Angela for their boat trip. On arriving at the marina, Charlie led them to his boat – "The Noble Neptune". Angela stopped to take photographs. Then on going on board, Charlie started the engine and they headed out towards the open sea. As the boat cut through the water and the marina was left behind, he pointed out the scenery and the various landmarks along the coast. Eventually, they reached an inviting stretch of water and Charlie stopped the boat. He handed out some beer and then relaxed in a deckchair provided by Joe, who had already stretched out and fixed his baseball cap to sunbathe.

"This is the life," said Charlie, looking around him and smiling.

"You rally like the sea, don't you?" asked Joe.

"I sure do. It's my refuge."

"You mean, like a safe haven?"

"That's right, Mr Morrelli. It's somewhere I can go for peace and quiet and just relax."

"That's funny," smiled Joe. "I own a restaurant called 'The Safe Haven' and that's exactly why people come to it!"

"Now that's a good name. It would be even better for a boat or a beach house."

Joe nodded.

"Yeah, it would. I never thought of that."

Charlie looked towards Angela.

"Your wife loves the sea. She's happy just to be near it. I guess she's a bit like me."

"I can understand her for that, Mr Morrelli. She feels she belongs and that's important. We all need to belong somewhere and know there's a place we can go to. Somewhere special, where you can just be yourself. You know?"

"Angel likes you a lot, Charlie. I guess you both have a lot in common."

"Well, I read a lot but I rarely get to talk about it. That's why meeting your wife has meant so much to me. She's a very understanding and sincere person, and they're hard to come by these days. You're a lucky man. Most of the women who hire my boats spend their time talking about the beauty parlour, the latest scandal or who they've slept with. They just don't seem to be interested in anything else. But your wife is different."

"Yeah," nodded Joe, "I guess I am lucky."

Angela joined them with a picnic basket and they had lunch.

The conversation went from one subject to another and Joe soon realised why Angela found Charlie so interesting. He was a world of information. Ranging from culture to current affairs to politics, he talked on and then listened intently as Angela and Joe put their own views across. Joe was beginning to like him just as much as Angela did. Charlie was a very nice, down to earth man. One who enjoyed good company and good friends.

As they had another beer, Charlie smiled at Angela.

"Now that we're out here in the middle of the ocean, why don't you recite that poem for me again? Before we head back"

"What? Here?" she smiled.

"Why not? It's the perfect place."

She looked around and agreed.

"Yes, it is!"

As both men listened she recited the poem. Charlie gazed out to sea. Joe gazed at Angela. When she'd finished, silence fell. Then Charlie spoke.

"Did you live near the ocean back home, Angela?"

"No, but we used to go to it for day trips and holidays. When the troubles began, my father used to say that if his pools coupon ever came up he'd buy a house by the sea, away from it all. Somewhere peaceful and quiet. But it just never happened."

"What's a pools coupon?" asked Joe. This was new to him!

Angela smiled and explained.

"How much money do you get?" he enquired.

"It all depends. But it would have been enough to make his dream come true. He never missed a week in the hope it would happen."

"Well, maybe someday it will happen for him," smiled Charlie.

Angela, got up and started packing the picnic basket.

"No, Charlie, it never will. My father's dead."

"That's a shame," he said, shaking his head and watching her walk away. "If I had a daughter like that I'd sure want to live and see her achieve something in life."

"Oh, she will," assured Joe.

"I guess it's all up to you now, Mr Morrelli. I hope she does well."

"You can count on it!"

"You love her very much."

"Is it that obvious?" laughed Joe.

"To anyone with eyes! But then, you've got someone very special there so don't' ever let go."

"I don't intend to Charlie, Believe me."

"I do, Mr Morrelli. I really do. Well," he said, getting up, "it's time we headed back." Charlie started the engine once again and headed back to the marina. Joe and Angela stood with their arms around each other. Charlie smiled. She may have lost a good father but she had found a good husband – of that he was sure.

As Charlie dropped them off at the beach house, Angela put her arms around him

"Thank you for a wonderful day."

"My pleasure."

Joe shook his hand.

"I really enjoyed today, Charlie. Why don't you come to dinner tomorrow night?"

"I'd really like that, Mr Morrelli."

"Good. Say about 8 o'clock?"

"I'll look forward to it," replied Charlie, getting into the jeep. He waved to them as he drove off. Joe and Angela went inside.

"Well, what do you think of him now?" she asked.

"He's a bit like me," he smiled, pulling down the brim of his baseball cap. "He's an o.k. guy!"

Angela smiled.

"I knew you'd like him when you got to know him, Joe. It was nice of you to invite him to dinner. Thank you. And speaking of dinner, why don't we go out this evening? It would be a lovely ending to a perfect day."

"Yeah," he agreed. "We could go somewhere for a meal and maybe catch a show."

"Anything you say," she whispered, kissing his cheek and smiling. "Now I'm going to call my mother and find out if she's alright and tell her all about today."

As she headed for the bedroom, Joe sat down feeling happy and relaxed. Angela was in a good mood and Charlie was right, she was different. What so many women would take for granted had made her happy. They had only gone on a boat trip but it had meant a lot to her.

There had been no all night clubs or expensive shopping malls for Angela. She was contended with the simple things in life and enjoyed them, not like most of the other women he'd known. But that was one of the reasons why he'd fallen in love with her. He knew that when the time came to leave, she'd be sad. So would he. This beach house would always hold a lot of memories for them both. However, they had a week and a couple of days left and he wanted her to enjoy herself. She deserved some happiness and if he had his way, he would give her that. Not just for now but for the rest of his life.

Joe was all dressed up and looking forward to his night out. After all, he was a New Yorker and knew how to paint the town!

He waited patiently in the lounge for Angela. Finally, the bedroom door opened and out she came.

"Well, what do you think?" she asked, turning so he could get a better look. The short low-cut, burgundy dress was in rich, crushed velvet. Too hot to wear stockings she let black high heels compliment her legs. Her red hair was gathered up and held in place by burgundy combs. She clutched her black purse in her right hand.

Joe stared.

"You look terrific! We're going to have a great time tonight, Angel. I can't wait to get you onto the dance floor," he smiled, winking.

Taking her arm, he escorted her to the front door.

"Joe, you're so obvious when it comes to women." she smiled.

"Correction, Angel," he replied, pointing his finger at her playfully. "A woman!" He smiled as he opened the door for her. "We're going to dance the night away," he promised.

"Well, that's a welcome change," she replied in an amused voice. "I was beginning to think you'd retired!"

"Yeah, maybe. But even God rested on the seventh day, you know."

He grinned broadly, then viewing Angela from head to toe he turned his eyes up and shook his head.

"But then, God wasn't married to a woman like this!" he muttered to himself, as he followed her to the limousine.

At 8pm, Charlie arrived carrying two bottles of wine.

"I didn't know what was for dinner, so I bought red and white," he explained, holding them up as he followed Joe through to the lounge.

Angela appeared.

"I hope you like roast chicken," she smiled. "I haven't learned how to cook Italian food yet."

"Don't worry about it. My wife couldn't cook it when she met me and she still couldn't cook it when she left!"

"How long have you been on your own?" asked Joe, pouring him a drink and sitting down with one for himself.

"About four years," came the reply.

"Don't' you miss her?"

"Not really, at least not any more. We never did have much in common. They say opposites attract but I guess we were just too opposite. I'd miss my boats more!" he smiled, roguishly.

"Well, at least you're honest about it," said Joe.

"What happened? Did she just up and leave you?"

"You could say that," Charlie nodded. "I came home early one day and found her in bed with my best friend. They left the same day. I haven't seen them since. At least I'd found out he had been communicating with her a lot better than I ever did," he sighed.

Angela got up from the chair.

"Joe, could you come through and open the wine? Dinner must be ready"

Joe followed her to the kitchen.

"What are you doing?" she whispered. "The man came here to dinner. Not to tell you his life story!"

"Well I was only making conversation," he shrugged.

"Well, make it about something else!" she snapped.

"O.k., o.k. I was just interested, that's all."

She pointed towards the kitchen door.

"May I suggest you go out there and get interested in something else – like changing the subject."

"It was just getting to the good part," he sulked, uncorking the wine.

"Joe!"

"Alright, I'm going!" he hurried to the kitchen door, put his hand on the handle and then turned, thoughtfully. "I wonder what his wife's doing now?" he whispered.

"Minding her own business, I should think. Unlike some people I could mention," she glared. He threw a sarcastic look and left.

Angela served dinner.

"Do you work for yourself, Charlie?" she asked.

"No. I have a boss who owns a lot of property here in Miami. I handle the beach houses, the cars and the marina for him. It's a good business. There's a lot of money in it and he's a good man to work for."

Charlie never once mentioned his boss by name but Joe knew it was Nicholas Andretti...he continued, "I own two boats myself, the one you were on yesterday and another that's getting repainted. I might even give it a new name."

Angela smiled.

"Why don't you call it after that poet you like so much?"

"Hey, that's not a bad idea!"

They all clinked their glasses. Then Charlie's mood became more sombre.

"I guess you'll be sorry when your trip's over."

"Yes I will. I love it here."

"We were going to stay longer," said Joe, "but Angela's got exams in a few weeks and I'd like to see her do well"

"And do you think she will?" smiled Charlie.

"I sure hope so. I have every confidence in her," replied Joe, reaching over and patting her hand.

"I have so much studying to do when I get back, I just hope I can remember it all when the time comes," sighed Angela.

"You will," he assured her. "What would you like to do with everything you've learned?" "Share it," she replied, in a serious voice. "Knowledge isn't much good if you keep it all to yourself. If the great authors hadn't written down their stories, if poets hadn't written down their thoughts and feelings and if artists had locked their paintings and sculptures away, we couldn't share in the pleasure and joy that has existed for centuries. By sharing what they did, they have educated the world. Passed on a great wealth that has made the world a better place. They'll live forever in the hearts and minds of people, all because they shared."

Joe and Charlie were silent as Angela rose and cleared away the dishes.

"I don't know about you, Mr Morrelli, but I've never heard a woman talk like that. Come to think of it, I've never heard a man talk like that either. Never mind being the First Lady, she could be the First Lady President! You must be the envy of New York or will be in time. One day she's going to make you very proud."

"Yeah, Charlie, I'm a lucky man. And when I listen to her, like just now, I can't believe just how lucky I am."

When Angela came back, they all moved to the lounge.

"That was a wonderful meal, Angela. Thank you," smiled Charlie.

She nodded gratefully, then went over and opened the sliding door. Charlie stood beside her.

"Isn't it beautiful?" he said.

"Yes it is, Charlie. I'll always remember it and I'll always remember you," she smiled, touching his arm affectionately.

He nodded towards the sea.

"Maybe that's why I never married again."

Angela followed his gaze saying softly, "I understand. The ocean is your wife and you love her. Your boats are the children you never had. They'll give you pleasure now and in your old age."

He turned his gaze towards her.

"Angela, you're the only person I've ever met who knows exactly how I feel. I'll never forget you."

Joe watched and listened. Once again his wife had proved Freddie Barrett right. She had a way with people.

The three spent the rest of the evening enjoying drinks and the various topics of conversation. Joe even insisted that Charlie share his Havana cigars! He liked him a great deal. Charlie had a knack of making a short story in to an epic. He could be serious and witty, packing one liners like punches. Joe appreciated the humour. After all, what New Yorker doesn't?! but for all that, he knew Charlie to be a sincere man, caring and genuine. A lot like Angela. Perhaps that's why they got on so well.

It was 1:30 when Charlie was leaving and he was in a happy frame of mind. He shook hands with them both, smiling broadly.

"Thank you for a wonderful evening. I've enjoyed the hospitality and the company."

Angela opened the front door.

"Good night, Charlie and thank you for coming."

Joe walked him down the path. As they reached the end, Charlie stopped.

"Mr Morrelli, would you do something for me?"

"What is it Charlie?"

"Don't ever let anyone try to change Angela."

"I don't think anyone ever could. She's one stubborn lady."

"She's also a very beautiful lady in more ways than one. And you know what?"

"What?"

"She really loves you. My wife lusted after every man but me. That's why I'm going home to any empty house and, believe me, I don't recommend it. You've got everything you could ever want in one woman and I'm not talking about sex. I mean love, friendship and understanding. The things that will withstand whatever life brings your way."

"I know, Charlie. I always hoped I'd meet someone like her but never thought I would."

The two men parted as good friends.

"Goodnight Mr Morrelli."

"Goodnight Charlie."

Joe closed the front door.

"Well, I think he enjoyed himself," said Angela. "He must get lonely sometimes."

"Yeah, I guess he does."

Joe walked over and putting his arms around her, held her close.

"What's brought this on?" she smiled.

"I'm just so glad to have you," he replied in a low voice. "I was surrounded by people at parties and clubs but I was lonely, too. But I never wanted to admit it, not even to myself. You know, you don't always have to be alone to be lonely."

"And how do you feel now?" she whispered.

"Thankful that I met you, happy that you love me and proud that you're my wife."

His arms tightened around her as he kissed her passionately.

"You're everything I ever hoped for but never thought I'd find. And believe me, Angel, I've been looking for a very long time."

The honeymoon was coming to an end. They had less than a week left in Miami. As they sat at breakfast, Angela brought the subject up.

"Joe, we've only a few days left here and I think we should do some shopping. We need to buy presents to bring home, if that's alright with you?"

"Sure. We could go today if you like. Only this time we use my money for a change. O.k." he smiled.

"O.k." she agreed. "We'll go this afternoon."

They made their way from one store to another. Angela was excited and stopped to look at and admire everything she saw. They decided on initialled gold cigarette lighters for Rooney, Frankie and Al, and initialled gold cuff-links for Freddie. Angela pointed out that he could wear them to work and add a touch of class to his position as manager. Joe smiled and nodded. He was sure Freddie would appreciate anything that would make him look more important and authoritive!

Angela chose a gold bracelet for her bridesmaid, Cindy and with great care and pleasure she wandered about choosing a present for Evie. She finally decided on a beautiful silk patterned scarf that she could wear around her neck to church and a broach to go with it.

"Joe," she said, puzzled, "I don't know what to get for my mother."

"Well, what do you think she'd like?"

"I don't really know. She doesn't go out much and doesn't wear jewellery." Angela stood and thought for a moment. "The only thing I can think of is maybe a watch. The one she's wearing now is old and belonged to Aunt Bridget."

"Well, there you are," smiled Joe. "Get her one of her own and make it a really nice one."

"O.k. but you help me choose it. She'd like that."

"Sure," he nodded, going back to the jewellery department, followed by Angela. "Now let's see…."

They studied the display cabinet closely.

"What about that one?" said Joe, pointing to a very expensive ladies watch.

"It's beautiful, Joe – but very pricey."

"Nothing's too good for my mother in law! Besides, I want to stay in her good books! We'll take that one, please," he grinned at the assistant. "Agnes is going to have the best or my name isn't Joe Morrelli!"

After their final purchase they came outside.

"Where to now, honey?" he asked.

"Why don't we go and get some coffee?"

"Good idea."

They found a quiet diner and ordered their coffee. Angela talked about all the presents and how she hoped everyone would like them.

"Thank you for the watch, Joe. My mother will be so pleased with it."

She leaned over and kissed his cheek.

"Well, is that everyone taken care of?" he asked.

"Yes, that's everyone."

"What about you?"

"Me?!"

"Yeah, you! You've bought something for everyone but yourself. Why don't you spend some money on you for a change? Have a look around. There must be something you want."

She put the cup down and gazed into his eyes.

"You've already given me everything I could possibly want. You've given me four weeks in a beautiful beach house with sea, sand and sunshine. But more important of all, you've given me your love. What more could I want when I have you, Joe?"

It took every ounce of willpower he had to stop himself from taking her in his arms and kissing her there and then. He struggled with his emotions, wanting her so badly it hurt. He wished they were back at the beach house. Pictures of their lovemaking flashed through his mind so clearly.

"What's the matter?" she whispered.

"Nothing," he replied, covering her hand with his own and forcing a smile. There was no way he could tell her of his thoughts and feelings at that moment. It would only embarrass her. "Why don't we go for a walk? Get some fresh air."

"I'd like that," she smiled, gathering up the shopping bags. Joe watched her. No other woman had ever paid him such a compliment or shown him such appreciation and no other woman ever would – because there'd never be another woman in his life. Joe Morrelli was hopelessly in love with his wife and always would be. Of that he was certain!

Early next morning, the doorbell rang. Joe answered, to find a delivery boy standing with a package.

"For Mrs Morrelli, Sir."

Joe signed for it and gave the boy a tip. He walked into the kitchen and put it down on the table beside Angela's coffee cup.

"That's just arrived for you. Did you order something?" he asked, sitting down to finish his breakfast.

"Oh, good! I thought it wasn't going to get here in time," she replied, picking it up and looking at the postmark.

"Well," he asked, "aren't you going to open it?"

"Joe, I know what it is."

"But I don't. You never told me you'd bought something."

"It's not for me. It's for Charlie."

She opened the package and took out a book.

"For Charlie?" asked Joe, surprised. "Well, what is it?"

Angela smiled.

"Remember that poem he liked so much?"

He nodded.

"Well," she continued, "he asked me to write it out for him before I left but I had a better idea. I bought him a whole book of poems written by the same poet. Look," she smiled, holding it up. "The Poems of John Masefield'. Do you think he'll like it?"

"I'd stake my life on it! "Where did you get it?"

"New York."

"New York?! How did you manage that?"

"Well, the day Charlie took us on the boat trip, I phoned my mother to tell her all about it."

"Yeah, I remember. But I don't see the connection."

"I told my mother to ask Rooney if he'd go to the Carson/Mills Bookstore and get this book for me. He did and here it is."

"I don't believe I'm hearing this," said Joe, in disbelief. "You ordered a book in New York and got it sent to Miami – for Charlie?"

Angela gazed innocently.

"But he's been good to me, Joe and I wanted to buy him a present. Something special he could always keep. He's my friend and besides, I might not ever see him again."

Her voice became sad.

"You'll really miss him, won't you?" Joe asked, looking at her, admiringly.

She nodded and lowered her gaze.

"I'll miss everything about this place," she sighed.

Then she looked up. "Would you mind if I went and gave this to him, Joe?"

"Of course not, honey."

She got up and lifted the book.

"If I go now, I'll catch him before he goes to the marina. I won't be long."

"Take your time, Angel. Stay and have a chat with him. I'll be busy for a while anyway. I have a few business calls to make."

"I hope he likes it, Joe. I can't wait to see his face!" she said excitedly, as she left the kitchen.

Joe leaned back and shook his head. Only Angela would have thought of something like that! She loved to give but never asked for anything for herself. They'd been in Miami almost a month and she hadn't asked him for anything. Come to think of it, she hadn't asked him for anything in New York either! Angela could be a stubborn woman but she was also the most unselfish one it had been his good fortune to meet.

When Angela got dressed she came back to the kitchen, carrying a small shopping bag with the book in it. She put her arm around his shoulder and kissed his cheek.

"I'll see you later," she smiled, going out the back door and down the path. Joe got up and went through the lounge and onto the veranda. He watched as she walked up the beach. When she was out of sight, lifting his notebook he flicked through it. Sitting on the side of the bed, he dialled a number and waited as he heard it ringing.

"Hello," came the voice at the other end.

"Hi, Nick. It's Joe Morrelli."

"Joe! How's Miami?"

"Well, that's what I want to talk to you about."

"Nothing's wrong, I hope?"

"No, everything's fine, Nick. But something's come up in the line of business. I'd like to discuss with you. That's why I've used your private number."

"You know me, Joe. I'm always interested in business. It must be pretty important for you to call so early – and on your honeymoon too!"

"Well, it is to me Nick. I have a proposition to put to you."

"I'm listening, Joe," came the reply....

Angela arrived back at noon and looked very happy.

"Well, did he like it?" asked Joe, getting up and switching off the t.v. set.

"He loved it," she smiled. "The poems about the sea and the ships are just what he really feels at heart. As a matter of fact, he's reading the book now."

"Really?" he said, glancing at his watch. "I was beginning to think he was writing one!"

"I'm sorry Joe. I've been a lot longer than I thought I would but it wasn't Charlie's fault, it was mine. I have something to tell you and I hope you won't be angry with me."

She looked guilty for some reason.

"What is it?" he asked, sitting down. "Let me guess. You've invited him to New York!"

"No, that's not it. Charlie doesn't like cities much, anyway."

"Angel, honey, if you've got something to say, spit it out. And sit down, you're making me nervous."

She did as he said and then continued, "I asked him to drive me into town to get something."

"Well, what was it you were in such a hurry for, that couldn't wait?"

Joe held out his hands waiting for an explanation. Angela looked at him and faltered a little.

"I know we decided to get Rooney a lighter from both of us, Joe, but he's been very good to me and I like him. With him being Irish, too, we seem, to get on so well. I can talk to him. In some ways he's the brother I never had. I know he'll always be there for me – he told me so, just the way he's always there for you. So, I bought him a present from me, out of my own money. I wanted to get him something personal and a little bit special."

Joe stared at her silently for a moment. Then said, "Well, if you've used your own money, it will be personal." His voice was dry. "Am I going to get the privilege of seeing this special gift?"

Angela leaned over and lifted a small package out of her shopping bag. If was wrapped in fancy paper with a ribbon. She thought maybe Joe would tell her not to spoil it by undoing it all, but he didn't. She unwrapped it carefully as he watched. Then opening the box, she handed it to him. As he took it he saw a dark blue velvet background and resting on it was a gold St. Christopher medallion and chain. He lifted it up and on closer examination discovered an inscription on the back of the medallion.

"To Rooney, From Angela."

"What do you think?" she asked, eagerly.

"I think he'll be very pleased with it," replied Joe, feeling a little put out. "Anyone would. But why did you find it necessary to go off with Charlie and buy it? Why didn't you buy it when you were with me?" He sounded disappointed.

"Joe, I couldn't?"

"I didn't want you to see what I was buying."

"For Heavens sake, why not? I'm seeing it now, aren't I? And I would certainly have seen it round his neck!"

Angela couldn't understand why Joe's attitude was changing. He was becoming sarcastic. What was wrong with him? She ventured on.

"Well, if you'd seen me buying that present, then you'd have seen me buying this one."

Once again she reached into the shopping bag and produced another package, handing it to him.

"Who else have you bought for?" he asked.

"Why don't you open it and find out," she said, taking the St. Christopher from him and making her way to the bedroom.

When he heard her close the door, he undid the wrapping to find a similar box. Inside, too, was the same velvet background but this time a thicker chain with a larger medallion was in place. On the medallion was the Virgin Mary and around her head were the words 'Ave Maria'. When he turned it over an inscription read, "To My Husband Joe, Love From Angela."

Joe could hardly believe his eyes. He felt so bad about his behaviour, he could have punched himself!

He opened the bedroom door and entered, his head slightly bowed. In his hand he clutched the gift box. He went over and sat down on the bed next to Angela.

"Angel, it's beautiful. I don't know what else to say."

"You don't have to say anything. I bought it as a kind of 'thank you' present. You've made me so very happy, Joe. And I know that she'll always take care of you for me! I'm just sorry it isn't something more expensive."

"I don't want anything more expensive. This means a lot to me and it always will. Will you put it on?"

Angela took it out of the box and fastened it around his neck, as he stared into her face. Then he put his hands on her shoulders.

"I'm sorry about what happened back there. I made too much out of nothing. I'm just scared that one day you might meet someone else and not want to be with me anymore. I don't think I could handle that, Angel."

"But Rooney's not 'someone', Joe. He's your best friend, almost your brother."

"Yeah, I know. I was stupid about that. Do you forgive me? He's going to like his present almost as much as I like mine!"

"I hope so. Who knows, he might travel somewhere one day and meet the right woman."

Joe took her in his arms and leaning his head over her shoulder, he looked at the St. Christopher on the bedside table. How could he ever begin to tell her that Rooney had already met the right woman and was very much in love with her. But she was another man's wife and that man had her in his arms at that very moment. There was so much she didn't know. So much he dared not tell her. Angela's gift of friendship to Rooney could so easily be taken to mean something else. But she wasn't to know that. Joe had always trusted Rooney in everything but where Angela was concerned, he was finding it hard to trust any man. He loved her too much and had everything to loose if some morning she woke up and decided she wanted someone else. The thought of another man having her was unbearable. He wanted her for himself – always. When it came to Angela, Joe Morrelli was a very possessive man, and he knew it.

"Joe, can I ask you something?" she said, softly.

"Sure."

"Do you trust me?"

"Of course I do! What makes you ask that?"

"Well, sometimes I get the feeling you think what we have right now, won't last." She pulled away from him gently and gazed into his eyes. "It will last, Joe, a whole lifetime if we let it. But that means trusting each other. If we don't have that, we don't have anything. Sometimes I blame myself."

"Why?" he asked, surprised.

"Well, I seem to know enough about certain things but maybe I don't know enough about things that really matter, like pleasing my husband for instance."

"Oh, come on, honey. Don't ever say that. You're giving me the kind of love I've always wanted. O.k., so you don't know everything, but I'm glad. At least that proves to me you haven't been around. A man isn't always turned on by how much a woman knows sometimes he's turned on by how much she doesn't know!"

With her spirits brightened, she hugged him tightly.

"I love you, Joe."

"Likewise, I'm sure!" he joked.

"Then you don't mind me buying Rooney the present?"

"No, of course I don't! What's a present between friends?"

They both began to laugh at they lay back on the bed. Then, after a few moments, Joe unbuttoned her blouse and reaching around her back, he undid the white brassier that cupped her full breasts....

The day before they were due to leave Miami, Charlie pulled up in the jeep and sounded the horn loudly. Angela opened the door and went outside, followed by Joe.

"Have you got an hour to spare?" smiled Charlie. "I've got something I'd like to show you, Angela."

"What is it?"

"Why don't you come and see for yourself – and bring your camera."

She turned and looked at Joe.

"Go on," he encouraged.

"I'd like you to come as well, Mr Morrelli," called Charlie.

"O.k.," agreed Joe with a smile. "We'll be with you in a minute."

They went back inside. Angela got her camera while Joe fetched his baseball cap and put it on.

"He seems very pleased with himself," she commented.

"Yeah, he sure does."

They closed the door and climbed into the jeep. Charlie drove off in the direction of the Marina. When they arrived, he parked the jeep and led them down the pier. Stopping near the end he raised his arm and waved towards a newly painted boat. "Well, what do you think?" he smiled broadly.

They looked, and there painted in large letters on the side was it's name "The Masefield."

"Charlie, you did it!" she beamed.

"Yes, I did. Thanks to you and that book you bought me. Do you approve?"

"Of course I do. It's beautiful. Congratulations! Now stand there till I take a picture."

"You must be very proud of it," nodded Joe.

"Yes I am Mr Morrelli, but there's something else I'd like you both to see." He walked the rest of the way to the end of the pier then stopped, folding his arms. "O.k. guys," he yelled. "you can take the canvas off now."

Some men rolled back covers to reveal an expensive white cruiser.

"My boss thought this beauty would be ideal for the tourists. I took delivery of her the other day."

"You never mentioned it Charlie," said Joe.

"That's because I wanted to name her first."

And sure enough, there was her name. "Lady Angela".

He continued, "It's by way of a wedding present to you both. This will mean that even when you're in New York, part of you will always be here."

Tears filled Angela's eyes.

"Oh, Charlie, never in my wildest dreams did I think I'd have a boat named after me."

She put her arms around him.

"Well," smiled Joe, "I remember a certain someone telling me nothing's impossible – and they were right!" He looked at the name proudly.

"Come on," said Charlie, "we'll go aboard and have a drink. We've got to christen her properly!"

Once on board he produced a bottle of champagne and filled some glasses. They raised them in a toast. Charlie did the honours.

"To 'Lady Angela' and all those who will sail in her."

"I'll drink to that!" said Joe.

After a few celebratory drinks, Angela went to look around. Joe put an arm around Charlie's shoulder.

"I want to thank you, Charlie. It was a really nice thing to do. You've made her very happy."

"Not as happy as she's made me. It was the least I could do. When she called at my home with that book I just couldn't believe anyone could be so thoughtful. She'd even signed it for me,

To My Dear Friend, Charlie

From Angela.

You know something Mr Morrelli? I'm really going to miss her. She makes you feel special, know what I mean?"

Joe smiled and nodded.

"Yeah, I know exactly what you mean; That's why she's my wife!"

After their outing to the Marina, Charlie dropped them off at the beach house.

"I'll see you tomorrow. I'll be at the airport to say goodbye," he smiled, driving off as they waved. When they went inside, Angela walked into the bedroom with the camera and Joe followed.

"I'll never forget our stay here or Charlie," she sighed.

"Angel, how could you forget?" he smiled. "You've taken enough pictures of everybody and everything to make a movie! But it sure has been something to remember, I will say that." He took off his cap.

"Anyway, we'll have to do some packing later on."

Angela smiled at him, as she laid a change of clothes across the bottom of the bed.

"You'll be glad to see New York again, won't you, Joe?"

"Well, I must admit I've enjoyed it here but I'm looking forward to going home. I'm really starting to miss it."

"You know, in a way I'm surprised you've stayed the pace."

"With Miami or you?" he asked, smiling. "Because I'll have you know, Mrs Morrelli, that your husband might be forty years old but he could teach guys half his age!"

"Now I can believe that, Joe," she smiled, leaning over the bed and pointing between his legs. "But with all the territory you've covered, I'm surprised there's any left for those young guys!" She laughed, as Joe's mouth fell open.

"Oh, very witty. What brought this on?" he grinned, pulling her onto the bed.

"Well, I remember you making fun of me one morning at breakfast."

"I wasn't making fun of you. I was just trying to prepare you for what was coming."

"Joe, nothing could have prepared me for what was coming!" she laughed.

Joe became flustered.

"Well, I think it must be the ocean or the heat or something, because I'm not like this in New York."

"I hope not because if you are, you're going to have a wife with a very peculiar walk!"

Joe raised himself up on his elbow, laughing.

"Why, Angel, I'm surprised at you talking like that!"

"Oh, maybe I'm just tired," she sighed. "Why don't we take a nap?"

"A nap? Honey, you know I never sleep during the day."

"Come to think of it, Joe, you don't sleep much at night either! But look on the bright side."

"What's that?"

"Well, if you ever go bankrupt Gene O'Brien can give you a job guarding the White House. After all, your friend down there loves to stand to attention!"

Joe was almost shocked.

"Oh, very funny! I never thought I'd hear that from you. You're just full of wit."

They both laughed loudly as they wrestled playfully for a few moments. Then he said, "Do you remember the last time we did this? You told me it wasn't the time or the place."

"Well, it is now," she assured him.

He put his hand gently on her stomach.

"Are you sure it's o.k.? I mean, its been a few days now and I didn't want to pry."

"I'm fine now, Joe, really," she whispered.

He turned his eyes up.

"You don't' know how glad I am to hear that," he said in a happy voice, kissing her.

"Why, was your vision becoming blurred?" she teased.

Joe stopped and lifted his head.

"What's the matter?" she asked.

"I've just thought of something. Al's really going to love you!"

Joe carried the luggage out and left it by the door.

"Well, that's it," he said. "There's only some hand stuff left and we can take that on the plane with us."

"I'll get it," Angela replied and made her way to the bedroom.

She'd been gone quite a while. When Joe put his head around the door he found her standing out on the path, gazing at the ocean. He joined her and put his arms around her.

"I know it's hard to say goodbye," he whispered, in an understanding voice.

"Oh, Joe," she sighed, "I won't ever forget it."

She put her arms around his waist as they stood admiring the view.

"You won't have to, Angel. We'll be back and that's a promise. We've had happy times here and I'd like to think there's a lot more to come."

"Do you mean that, Joe? Can we really come back?"

"Sure. And just to prove it, I bought you something."

He reached into his pocket, took out a key and placed it in her hand. Angela looked at it, puzzled.

"It's my wedding gift to you," he explained.

"But what is it?"

"This house."

She looked at him in disbelief.

"This house? You bought this house?"

"That's right," he smiled.

"For me?"

"Right again."

"Joe, I don't believe it!"

"Well, you better believe it, cause it's ours. And from today it's going to be known as 'The Safe Haven', too."

"Why?"

"Because I first met you at the restaurant and I first made love to you here. Can you think of a better name?"

Angela started to cry.

"No, I can't" she sobbed, "but this place must have cost you a fortune, Joe."

"So what? You're my wife and I love you. Hey, come on now, I thought you'd be happy!"

She held the key in her clenched fist.

"I am happy, Joe. I never expected anything like this."

He stepped back and looked into her face.

"Now you belong," he said tenderly, taking out a handkerchief and wiping the tears from her eyes. "Come on now, why don't' you give me one of those smiles I love so much?"

She obliged. "That's better," he grinned. "You can come here anytime you want to."

"I won't come without you, Joe. This is our special place."

"I'm glad to hear it!"

Angela's face brightened and she put her arms around his neck, drawing him close. Just then, the door bell rang.

"That'll be the chauffeur," said Joe. "I guess it's time to go."

"Not yet," she pleaded. I'm sure he can wait a few more minutes."

She kissed him lovingly and passionately as his arms tightened around her and their kiss lingered to the sound of the waves. Eventually, Joe reluctantly broke free.

"We'd better go, honey. But keep the rest on hold for tonight!"

He walked towards the door.

"That's if you can find me." She teased.

He turned and grinned.

"Angel, if I could find you in a city like New York, I can find you in a king size bed – you can bet on it!!"

As Joe and Angela waited in the busy airport for their flight to be called, she kept looking around.

"I thought Charlie would be here," she remarked sadly.

"Well, maybe he couldn't make it, honey."

When the flight was finally called, they got up and made their way to the departure area with the rest of the passengers. Just then, she heard a voice calling her name and on looking around, saw Charlie hurrying through the crowd, waving. Angela dropped the hand luggage and put her arms out to him.

"Oh Charlie, I thought you weren't coming."

She embraced him.

"Now, would I do that to you?" he smiled. "I'm sorry I'm late, I got stuck in traffic."

"Charlie," she said excitedly, "I've got something to tell you. Joe has bought the beach house!"

"I know," he nodded "my boss told me. So now we will be neighbours. Angela, I'm so pleased."

"I can't believe it. I thought I'd never see you or that beautiful place again."

"Oh, you'll see me alright and I'll be thinking of you every time I bring my boats out – or read my book!"

"Angel, we'd better go," interrupted Joe.

Angela turned and looked at him, then flung her arms around his neck.

"Isn't it wonderful, Charlie?" she said, in a raised voice, kissing Joe's face. "I love this man!"

"Alright!" yelled a man's voice. Followed by, "Right on!" from another.

Joe looked around and discovered they were surrounded by a crowd of onlookers. He took Angela's arms away, nodding at his audience with a red face and embarrassed smile.

"My wife," he explained. "we're only married a few weeks. Angel," he whispered, "come on, lets go. Everyone's looking."

She flung her arms around him once again.

"I don't care! I love you Joe Morrelli and I want the world to know it!"

She smiled and kissed him to the sound of loud applause and whistles. Joe put his arms around her. Although clearly surprised by Angela's behaviour, he was secretly enjoying the whole episode. Charlie was amused as he watched, then he embraced Angela once again and shook Joe's hand.

"Have a good trip," he smiled.

"Thank's Charlie," replied Joe. "Anytime you're in New York you're welcome to stay with us."

"Thank you, Mr Morrelli, I'll remember that."

He stood and waited until they went out to board the plane. They looked back and waved. He put his hand up in acknowledgement. He was sorry to see them go and he'd miss Angela.

As the plane taxied down the run way and took off, Joe settled back holding Angela's hand. He was going home to New York and Roseberry Avenue, just like he'd done many times before. This time, however, would be different. This time, his wife would be at his side. After being on his own for so long, he now had someone to share it all with. He was glad he had waited all those years. As he looked at Angela beside him, he knew she was the right woman. Joe had always set his heart on having the best and he couldn't do any better than her. He pressed her hand gently but confidently. In return she looked at him and smiled, convincing him even more that he'd found what he had always searched for. As she put her head on his shoulder, in his heart he felt a love he had never known before. Yes, this time Joe Morrelli was going home one very happy man!

Chapter 9

Rooney and Al were waiting in the arrival area, watching as the plane landed. They saw Joe and Angela disembark. Al was the first to comment. "The Boss looks really well."

He looked at Rooney, surprised. And he's lost weight, too. He looks thinner."

"Yes, he does. Maybe he's been doing a lot of sports."

"What kind of sports?" Al enquired.

"Well, I don't know! Probably swimming and jogging."

"Jogging? In Miami? In that heat? I don't think so!

Come on, Rooney. You know he was never a big fan of out-door activities. I think…"

"I don't want to know what you think!" replied Rooney, pointing a warning finger.

"Well, I was only going to say the Boss always did go in for more in-door stuff."

"Maybe he went to a gym and did some press-ups."

Rooney's voice held a sarcastic tone.

"Oh, I bet he did a lot of those!" smirked Al nudging Rooney's arm. "The Boss always did like to get on top of things!"

"Al," warned Rooney again, "If you still want to be around for the next pay cheque, keep you big mouth shut! Here they come."

"Well," shrugged Al, "if that's what a honeymoon in Miami can do for you, I wish I could go."

"So do I," muttered Rooney, casting his eyes. "So do I."

Rooney hugged Angela.

"How was Miami?" he asked.

"Hot!" she smiled.

He put his hand on Joe's shoulder and looked him up and down.

"I don't have to ask you about it – you look great!"

"Yeah Boss, you look terrific!" agreed Al, as he went off to collect the luggage.

Joe put his arm around Rooney and leaned closer.

"Cindy sure was right about one thing," he whispered. "You don't have a lot of use for nightdresses. Know what I mean?"

Rooney shook his head and smiled. Nothing had changed. He was still the same Joe.

They walked out to the limousine and Angela got into the back. As Joe went to follow her, Rooney caught his arm and pulled him back.

"I can tell by your face the honeymoon was a success."

"Rooney, it was an experience I'll never forget," he winked.

"Angela looks very happy."

"Yeah well, she has her reasons!"

As Joe joined Angela, Rooney climbed into the front with Al.

"Where's Frankie?" asked Joe.

"He's at the house, Joe. A lot of people telephoned today. They knew you were due back. Frankie's there to take any important messages."

Al looked in the mirror.

"You both sure have a nice tan. And you've lost a few pounds, Boss."

"Yeah, I guess it was all those out-door sports. Isn't that right, honey?" Joe smiled at Angela.

"Not to mention the in-door ones!" muttered Al, under his breath.

Rooney kicked Al's foot with his own. Al, coughed, checked the traffic, started the engine and then turned around in his seat.

"Home, Boss?" he beamed.

"Yeah", nodded Joe, leaning back and putting his arm around Angela, "Let's go home."

When they arrived at the house and got out of the car, the front door was immediately opened and there stood Agnes, Evie and Frankie.

"Well, if it isn't the Welcoming Committee!" smiled Joe, as he and Angela made their way towards them. Suddenly, he stopped and took Angela's arm.

"I'm only ever going to do this once, so I may as well do it right," he smiled. "I believe it's customary for the groom to carry the bride over the threshold, so here goes."

He lifted her in his arms.

"Joe," she whispered, "you're starting to make a habit of this."

"Well, maybe I like it. And besides, women like their men to act the tough guy sometimes. You didn't seem to mind in Miami," he reminded her, in a low voice.

"To be honest I quite enjoyed it but I wasn't going to tell you that!"

"Oh, so I did make an impression after all," he grinned.

"More than you know," she smiled, kissing his cheek.

The door-way cleared as Joe carried her through, putting her down in the entrance hall.

"Welcome home, Angela Christine Morrelli" he said, putting his arms around her.

Agnes watched. They both looked so happy as they stood smiling at each other. She knew the honeymoon had gone well. They looked more in love now than they had ever done. The tears came to her eyes as she went over and embraced them both.

"Did you have a good time?"

"Agnes, we had a great time," replied Joe. "Isn't that right, Angel?"

"Yes, we did." She held her mother tightly. "Mum, I have so much to tell you."

"Oh, Mr. Joe, Miss Angela, you both look wonderful!" chimed in an excited Evie. "And Mr. Joe, you look so trim."

"Well, Evie, it just goes to show what a month away from your meat-loaf can do!"

Evie's face took on a look of displeasure.

"I'm only kidding," he added quickly, putting his hands up.

"I should hope so, too!"

"By the way, what's for dinner?"

"Meat-loaf!" she replied, in an arrogant tone.

Joe looked at Rooney and turned his eyes up.

"Now what made me ask?" he sighed.

Frankie came over and put his hand on Joe's shoulder.

"You're looking swell, Boss. It's good to have you home. We all missed you."

"Even Al?" smiled Joe.

Frankie laughed.

"I think he missed you most. All I got every day was, 'I wonder what the Boss is doing now'."

"Well, if he ever gets married I'll send him to Miami on his honeymoon and then he'll know!"

Frankie kissed Angela on the cheek.

"Welcome home."

"Thank you, Frankie," she smiled. "It's nice to be here."

Al carried in the last of the luggage.

"Where do you want this Boss?"

"Upstairs in the bedroom," replied Joe. "Frankie, give him a hand. Then come down for a drink."

Frankie and Al took the luggage and made their way upstairs. Frankie opened the bedroom door and went in followed by Al, who promptly dropped the cases when he saw the king size bed.

"Look at the size of that!" he exclaimed, wide eyed. "You could have a party in there!"

"Well, you know the Boss," replied Frankie.

"Correction – I thought I did. What is he? A gymnast?"

"He just likes comfort and a lot of room."

"Why? Does he like to turn summersaults before making love? I'll tell you one thing, Frankie, if his wife gets into that she'll never find her way out."

"Maybe that's the idea," smiled Frankie.

Al shook his head.

"No wonder any woman he ever brought home never got up before noon. You'd need a map to find your way. You know, there's more to the Boss than meets the eye," he nodded.

"What are you talking about?"

"Well, that's one sure way of getting them to stay the night. Who wants to struggle out of that after a few drinks? Maybe I could buy one."

"You haven't got a wife. Come to think of it, you haven't got a girlfriend either."

"Maybe not," smiled Al, "but if I did get someone, at least I could go to bed contended, knowing she'd still be there in the morning."

"Aren't you forgetting something? The bed's not much good unless you can perform in it!"

Al looked at him.

"Well, I guess that's probably why Antonia ended up on Broadway. I'd say the Boss could give award winning performances! Know what I mean, Frankie?" he grinned.

"Yeah, I know what you mean. I never heard a woman complain about him in all the years I've known him. Anyway, we'd better go downstairs. If we stay up here much longer, the Boss is going to think I've got the hots for you. And to be honest with you, Al, you're not my type!" laughed Frankie, as they closed the bedroom door and came down to join the others.

When they walked in, Joe handed each of them a glass of champagne. A toast followed, then he looked around and smiled.

"Now that everyone's here, I think we'll give out the presents." He opened the small hand luggage bags that sat on the floor. "I'll let my wife do the honours!"

He motioned Angela to come over. As Joe took out the presents one by one, she distributed them by reading the gift tags.

"Why, it's just like Christmas!" remarked Evie, as they all opened their gifts together.

The guys were really pleased with the lighters.

"Hey Boss, Angela, this is really something," smiled Frankie.

"It's too much," said Rooney, a delighted look on his face. "They're real gold."

"Real gold!" echoed Al, taking a closer look.

"Only the best will do for my friends," smiled Joe.

Al held his in front of Frankie's face, flicking it like a big shot!

"What do you think? Will I make an impression?" he grinned. "All I need now is a woman – and a big bed!"

"Did you say something, Al?" enquired Joe.

"I was just saying, Boss, I'll knock the women dead!"

"Yeah," said Joe, giving him a sarcastic look, "I knew you said something to that effect."

Frankie and Rooney looked at each other and smiled. Evie stood with the scarf around her neck and the brooch fastened to it.

"Oh, Mr Joe, Miss Angela, you shouldn't have!"

"Now, that's what I said," replied Joe.

She cast a stern glance in his direction.

"They must have cost a lot of money," she added.

"Well, don't worry about it, Evie. I'll deduct if out of your next pay cheque." he grinned.

Angela put her arm around Evie and hugged her. "He's only teasing you, Evie," she smiled. "Don't pay any attention to him."

"I rarely do!"

"Now, that's very true," he agreed.

Evie put her arms around Angela, saying "Thank you so much – both of you. They're beautiful."

Joe nodded.

"Everyone's going to know you work for Joe Morrelli. You'll be the best turned out woman in that Church of yours!"

Agnes stared lovingly at the watch.

"Oh, Angela, it's just beautiful. And so expensive looking."

"Do you like it mum? Joe chose it for you."

Agnes went over and embraced him.

"It's far too much, Joe. It must have cost a fortune."

"Only the best for you, Agnes. After all, I got the best when I married your daughter."

He then turned his attention to the others. "Frankie, you can take the rest of the evening off. Al, you can do the same. Rooney, I'd like you to stay for dinner. We can have a talk about business."

Joe filled up the glasses again and Evie took her's to the kitchen, still wearing the scarf and brooch.

As the four sat at dinner, Angela told Rooney and Agnes all about the beach house and the view, about Charlie and the boats, and about Joe buying the beach house as a surprise gift for her.

Agnes was dumfounded.

"You bought the house?" she asked in disbelief.

Joe nodded.

"Yeah, I did. It's a good investment. And anyway, I couldn't think of anything Angel would have liked better. You know, she never bought herself anything the whole month she was there. I don't think she even brought back a souvenir."

"Yes, I did," she smiled, getting up and going out of the dining room. She returned with a white napkin.

Now Agnes smiled.

"I think I know what it is," she said, as Angela put it down carefully on the table and opened it.

The napkin contained sea shells, mostly large white ones. Rooney and Joe stared at first at them, then at each other.

"Is that all you wanted?" asked Joe, in a surprised voice.

"I collected them in the mornings," she explained. "If you hadn't bought the beach house, they would have always reminded me of it and the ocean."

"Her father did the same, Joe," said Agnes, with a sad smile. "Every time we went to the sea side, he took the girls to gather shells. He used to keep them in his garden shed so they would remember."

Joe looked at them both. He couldn't help but think just what simple people they were at heart and as he looked at Angela's collection from the beach, he realised they meant more to her than gold bracelets or diamond necklaces ever could. And he admired that greatly.

After dinner, Agnes went to her room and Evie came in to clear the table, still wearing her presents. As she went out, Joe lifted his brandy and cigar and led the way to the lounge.

"You know," he said. "I think Evie's going to sleep with that scarf on. If she's not around in the morning, we'll have to call the paramedics."

"Why? Enquired Angela.

"Because she'll have strangled herself, Angel. That's why!"

When they had settled in the lounge, Joe looked at Rooney with a sly smile.

"How's Cindy?" he asked, in an amused voice.

"Don't ask!"

"Why, what happened?"

Rooney took a deep breath.

"Well, I gave her the slip at the reception and went home. She told Al we had a date but she couldn't remember my address. Of course, 'rent-a-mouth' told her. The next thing I knew someone was banging on my door and when I opened it, there she was, smiling at me. She came half way across town in a taxi, still wearing her bridesmaid's dress and clutching a bottle of champagne."

"Did you ask her in?"

"What else could I do, Joe?"

"Did she stay the night?" Curiosity was getting the better of Joe.

"No, she did not stay the night!" snapped Rooney, giving Angela an embarrassed look. "We had a drink and I took her home and I've got news for you. 'The Safe Haven' isn't safe anymore! Well, not for me, anyway."

Joe laughed loudly.

"It's not funny, Joe," whined Rooney. "Every time she sees me there, she's over faster than the speed of light."

"Well, maybe she likes you. Maybe she finds you attractive, Rooney. I know I did."

Joe's smile faded as Angela got up.

"Really?" asked Rooney, pleasantly surprised.

She nodded.

"Why not? You're a very kind man. Well, I'll leave you two to talk. I'm going to unpack, then I'll look in on my mother. Oh, before I forget, I have something for you, Rooney."

She went to her bag, took out the small package and handed it to him.

"I'm sorry it's not wrapped up as fancy as the other one, but it's just a little something from me to you."

Joe sat silently, watching and listening.

Rooney undid the package and opened the box. His face said it all when he saw the medal. Angela leaned over the back of his chair.

"There's an inscription."

He turned it over and read it. Then he looked up at her.

"Angela…"

"Do you like it, then?"

"Like it? I love it!"

She bent down and kissed his cheek. He took her hand.

"I'll wear it for the rest of my life," he promised.

"Well," she smiled, "at least until you find a steady girl and fall in love!"

He looked embarrassed by this last remark. But when he composed himself, he got up, embraced her and kissed her cheek. As they stood smiling at each other, Joe continued to watch with an uneasy feeling and more than a hint of jealousy in his heart.

Angela said 'goodnight' and left the lounge. Joe and Rooney discussed some business matters but not for long. Joe wasn't really in the mood after what he'd seen and heard. Rooney got ready to leave.

"I'll see you tomorrow, Joe. We can go over everything then."

"Yeah, sure," replied Joe, getting up from the chair. He watched his friend go over to the door, open it, then stop and turn around.

"I'm glad you bought her the beach house, Joe," he said. "She's a woman in a million. She'd have settled for shells from the ocean just as long as they reminded her of your time together. You're a lucky man. Don't ever forget it," he smiled.

"I won't Rooney. Goodnight."

As the door closed, Joe stared at it thoughtfully. Rooney was right. He may have received a personal present from Angela, but Joe was the one who had her. And right now she was in his bedroom. The same room where he had lay so many nights thinking about her. Hoping and dreaming that this moment would happen for him. He made his way upstairs, opening the bedroom door. Angela was still unpacking. "You weren't long," she smiled looking at him over her shoulder.

Joe opened his suitcase and took out his baseball cap, putting it down on the bed. "Joe Morrelli, did you bring that all the way from Miami?" she asked, surprised.

"I sure did. Just like you with those shells, I want my memories too."

He walked over and put his arms around her waist. Angela stopped what she was doing and cuddled into him.

"You wouldn't happen to have that white lace nightdress handy, would you?" he asked.

"Why?"

"Well, I'd like you to wear it."

She turned and smiled at him.

"If I remember rightly, I didn't get to wear it for long the last time."

"Maybe that's the reason I want you to wear it now!"

She put her arms around his neck and drew him closer.

"In a bed this size, if I take it off I might never find it again!" she joked.

He closed his eyes and hugged her tightly, almost lifting her off the floor. Rooney was right, he was a lucky man.

As Joe settled down to married life, he got back to what he knew best – taking care of business. Angela, however, was finding things a little more difficult. She was attending her classes again, her exams being just a few weeks away. But with taking care of her mother and trying to spend as much time as she could with Joe, her studies were taking second place. She was anxious about this but didn't want to say anything to Joe. So at night while he was asleep, she'd slip out of bed and go down to the dining room to study. She would lay all her books on the table and go through them one by one, memorising and making notes. However, it was all starting to prove too much for her and she became increasingly tired and depressed.

Things eventually came to a head one night, when Joe awakened and discovered Angela wasn't there. He put on his dressing gown and went in search of her. He noticed the light coming from the dining room and pushed open the door, gently. Angela was pacing up and down, talking to herself quietly, or so he thought at first. Then after a little while he realised she was quoting from the books that lay open on the table. Every now and then she would refer back to them, resting a hand on her weary brow, deep in thought. As Joe walked in she looked up, startled.

"Angel, do you know what time it is?" His voice was full of concern. "It's 3:30 in the morning, for God's sake!"

"It's alright Joe, I'm not tired."

"Well, you could have fooled me. You look worn out and you sound exhausted." He studied the dining table. "How long has this been going on? You haven't written all these notes in one night."

"Nearly two weeks," she replied in a low voice.

"Are you telling me you've been going without sleep all that time? Why?"

"Well, it's the only real time I get to myself. I go to College, then at home I spend half my time with you, the other half with my mother, I just never seem to get any time to myself. I can't study in the bedroom, the lights would only keep you awake. At least if I'm down here, I'm not annoying anyone."

"You're annoying me by not telling me about all this!" he said, in a raised voice.

"Joe, keep your voice down. You'll wake Evie."

"I'm not concerned about waking Evie. But I am concerned about you. Just how long do you think you can keep this up? You're going to make yourself ill. What I don't understand is why you didn't explain all this to me!"

He was angry now. Angela's eyes filled with tears.

"Because I didn't want you to think I was making excuses for not being with you. I thought I was doing the right thing but maybe I can't do anything right."

She covered her face with her hands, sobbing loudly. Joe stared at her, then took her in his arms.

"It's o.k., honey," he whispered. "Everything's going to be alright."

"Is it?" she asked, pulling away from him. "You want me, my mother needs me. Nothing's changed, Joe, including your temper and I don't like it!" she yelled.

"Well, I'd say you've got quite a temper yourself," he said, looking at her in amazement.

"Maybe," she agreed, "but I'm not as quick to use it. I'm the one who's going without sleep, not you. So why don't you go back to bed!"

"Now listen, Angel, I'm not going anywhere until we get something sorted out here and you calm down!" he yelled back.

"Until I calm down? That's rich, coming from you! I'm not the one with a heavy handed attitude!"

She glared at him, her dark blue eyes flashing.

"O.k., Angel, o.k.," he apologised. "Now, can we talk about this – please?"

Angela stood in stoney silence.

"Believe it or not, I understand how you feel." Said Joe. "You're tired, overtired even. You need your sleep. I'm worried about you, Angel. Starting from today, I want you to use one of the spare bedrooms for studying. You can spend as much time there as you like. No one will bother you. I'll ask Evie to see to your mother. You know how well those two hit it off! Besides, it's only for a couple of weeks. What do you think?"

"That would be a great help, Joe, as long as you don't mind."

Joe was relieved to hear her soft voice again.

"Why should I mind? I know how hard you've worked, Angel, and I want to see you do well. I just wish you'd come and told me about this sooner."

"I'm scared, Joe," she admitted. "I think I'm going to fail. There's so much to remember I don't think I can do it."

He took her in his arms.

"You'll do it," he assured her. "You're a Kenny and a Morrelli. What more does it take!"

When she laughed quietly, Joe knew she was feeling better.

"Thank's Joe," she whispered.

"Come on." He escorted her towards the door. "I want you to come back to bed and get some sleep."

As soon as Angela's head touched the pillow, she fell fast asleep. Joe lay with his arm around her protectively, making sure she was comfortable and warm. He'd tell Al to help her move all her school things to one of the spare rooms, first thing. He couldn't help but smile.

"It's the closest he'll ever get to Shakespeare!" he thought.

It was time for Angela to take her exams and Joe insisted on leaving her to the College. He walked her to the front door and kissing her cheek, wished her luck. It was going to take some hours.

"Now you can call me, honey, when it's all over and Al will come and collect you," he said. After watching her go inside, he got back into the car.

"You know something, Al, I really hope she does well, she's put a lot of hard work into it. I'd like to see her get straight A's," he smiled.

"Just like you, Boss!" replied Al, driving off.

"What do you mean?" asked Joe, suspecting Al of being flippant.

"Well, just think about it. You've got three women in your life and all their names start with and A. There's Angela, Agnes and Antonia – straight A's! You sure didn't settle for anything less. Haven't you ever thought about that?"

"No, I never did and come to think of it, you're right."

"I don't think anyone else has cottoned onto it except me!" smiled Al proudly.

"O.k., so there's a brain in there after all," said Joe. "That doesn't mean you have to get carried away."

"It's funny when you think about it, though, Boss. Three women, all A's."

"Yeah, and three's enough, believe me. I sure hope it stops there. I've had enough headaches."

"Maybe you'll get another one and make it four. Now wouldn't that be something?" He looked in the mirror to see Joe's reaction.

"Are you trying to be funny?" snapped Joe.

"Well, you never know, Boss. Maybe some day you'll have a daughter and call her Annabell or something."

"What are you, my fortune teller all of a sudden?" He knew Al was enjoying this.

"Come to think of it, I just might call her Alberta and teach her how to be a chauffeur!" he said, leaning over and giving him an icy stare.

Al pulled up outside the house.

"All the same, Boss, it just goes to show that although you're not the one who's studying, you've done o.k. for A's! It sure makes you wonder," he said with a smug look on his face.

Joe got out of the car, then leaning his head back inside he said, "Well, I've got something else for you to wonder about."

"What's that Boss?"

"Why don't you start and wonder if you're going to get a pay cheque at the end of the month!" He slammed the door and walked away.

Al chuckled to himself. It wasn't often he got one over on the Boss. Just wait till he told Frankie!

Angela's exams were over and the pressure was off. She was getting used to the house and being married to Joe, and she was happy. It didn't go unnoticed. She would sing and play music, which delighted Evie and she would sit at the kitchen table and laugh and joke, which was right up Al's street! They all liked her because she was friendly and caring and would join in all their conversations. Joe was pleased. It was important to him that Angela should 'belong' just like in Miami.

As she and Joe sat at dinner one night, Evie came into the dining room.

"Miss Angela, there's a phone call for you."

Angela went out to the hall and took it. She was gone for a while, making Joe wonder what was going on. When she returned she looked both happy and relieved.

"Is everything o.k.?" he asked.

"Oh Joe, that was Raymond. Sheila's had a baby girl."

"Well, how about that! Another little girl. Is he disappointed? He wanted a boy, didn't he?"

"Well, now that it's all over, he really doesn't mind. He says as long as the baby's alright, that's the main thing."

"I admire him for that. I'd think the same way myself. That makes you an Aunt for the second time."

"And you and uncle."

"Yeah, that's right," agreed Joe. "I'm an uncle to two kids I've never even seen. We'll have to do something about that, Angel. Maybe later on we could bring them all over on vacation."

"Oh Joe, that would be wonderful," she said, excitedly.

"I'd love to see them and I know my mother misses not seeing her grandchildren. She'd be so happy."

"Well, that settles it! We'll bring them out and have a family re-union. How's that?"

Angela beamed.

"You look pretty happy," he remarked.

"I'm just so pleased everything's alright and relieved that Sheila and the baby are fine. I'm going to phone the hospital now and have a talk with her. Raymond gave me the number. Then I'll go up and tell my mother the news."

She hurriedly finished her meal while Joe watched, amused. Then she went back to the phone, while he went into the lounge.

When she finally appeared, Joe was reading the newspaper. He looked up.

"Well, did you get to speak to her?" he asked.

"Yes, I did. Then I went up and told my mother. She's delighted but a little sad. She feels she should have been there for her. But she knows Raymond can cope."

"How is Sheila?"

"She sounds a bit depressed, Joe. I tried to cheer her up but it was no good. Maybe when she gets a few days over her, she'll be o.k. I hope so."

"What is she going to call it?"

"Well, she likes the name Deborah."

Joe nodded.

"That's a nice name. You know, Angel, I've been thinking. Girls must run in your family."

"How can you read one thing and think something else at the same time?" she smiled.

"Because I'm a man of many talents," he replied, shrugging his shoulders. "You should know that!" He grinned as Angela went over and stood behind him, putting her arms over his shoulders the very same way she had done on the first night of their honeymoon. Joe folded the paper and put it down.

"Is there something you want to tell me? Is anything the matter?"

"No," she replied, cautiously. "But I would like to talk to you."

"O.k. Why don't you sit down?"

Angela sat down on the couch and looked at him, wondering just how to begin.

"Joe," she said, in a soft voice, "my exams are over now. My mother's health is picking up and Evie takes care of a lot of things here. I think, maybe, it's time I went to work."

Joe stared.

"Angel, you're not going back."

"What do you mean?" Angela was surprised. "I thought I still had my job in 'The Safe Haven'?"

"Well, you thought wrong!"

"But I don't understand."

"Do you think I want my wife out of the house until all hours, keeping other people happy? No that's all finished."

"Well, what about the day time? I could work then. I could help Mr Barrett."

"Joe Morrelli's wife doesn't work – ever!"

"But Joe…"

"Angel, I don't want to argue with you about this. I have other plans for you. No more working at 'The Safe Haven' or anywhere else and that's final. The subject is now closed."

Angela knew by the serious tone in his voice and the stern look on his face, he meant it. "Can I ask you something?" he continued. "Why do you want to work? Or better still, why, for God's sake, do you feel you need to? We have a lovely home, not to mention what's in it. You know you won't ever want for anything. Is it money? Do you need money to buy something? Because if you do you've only got to say." He looked and sounded annoyed.

She lowered her gaze, bowing her head a little. "It's not for me Joe, it's for Sheila. Mum and I always sent her what we could but with the wedding and all, we don't have anything left. I was counting on working again so I could help her out when she needed it, especially now with a new baby. It's hard for them over there, Joe, with no jobs, no prospects, no money."

"Hey, I don't mind helping them out," he replied. "I don't mind sending them some money."

"Well, I do mind! When I married you I didn't expect you to take on the upkeep of my whole family. You brought my mother to live here and you're wonderful to her, that's enough. My sister is my responsibility."

"Wrong!" he said, pointing a finger. "We're all one family now and if she needs help from time to time, it's our responsibility because what's mine is yours and what's yours is mine."

"But it's not right, Joe, I don't want to live off you."

"Well, I don't see how there's much you can do about it, Angel. After all, you're my wife and it's my duty as a husband to keep you."

Angela got up.

"What's wrong?" he asked.

"I don't like what I'm hearing."

"Sit down, Angel, I'm not finished yet."

She obeyed.

"Now, listen to me," he demanded. "I know you don't want to ask me for money – you're too stubborn and independent for that!"

Angela shot him a sarcastic look.

"But that's a good quality," he added, hurriedly. "And I don't want you to have to ask me every time you need something. It's degrading for any wife to have to do that. You're not a kid on an allowance and I'm not going to treat you like one. So here's what we're going to do. I'm going to get you a cheque book and credit cards in your own name. you can use them whenever and for whatever you want. And if it's cash you need, there'll always be some in your bed-side drawer. Take what you need. I'll replace it from time to time. That way you won't be asking me for anything." He went over and sat down beside her. "Angel," he said, putting his arms around her, "I have enough money to go around. I promised you a good life and I'm going to keep that promise. I want you to be your own person and be independent but I can't let you work. No wife of Joe Morrelli needs to."

"Joe, you're such a good man," she whispered, putting her arms around him and burying her face in his neck. "You're kind and thoughtful and I love you."

"I love you too. More than you'll ever know. All the money in the world couldn't make me happy if I didn't have you."

As he felt her warm breath on his skin he bowed his head, enabling her to kiss his cheek, then his lips. She did so freely and sensuously, then Joe decided that the night had finally come upon them and it was time for bed.

It was a few weeks later when Joe took Rooney into the study and closed the door. "Sit down, I want to talk to you," he said.

Rooney sat down on the chair while Joe leaned against the desk, folding his arms.

"I'm going to Chicago on business," he explained. "I'll be gone about a week."

"Chicago?" This was news to Rooney.

"Yeah. Some big names are putting together a business deal. Anthony Andretti has invited me along."

"What kind of business?" asked Rooney.

"Oh, respectable gambling casinos. High prices, high stakes and rich clientele."

"Are you going in on it, Joe?"

"I don't know yet," he replied shaking his head. "At the moment I'm just an interested party. I want to sit in and listen. If I think it's a good deal and the profit far exceeds the stake money, then I might. What I really need to do is get all the facts and figures. If I like what I hear then I'll have Reuben go over it all when I get back. If everything's legit I'll take it from there."

"Well, if the Andrettis are in on it, I'd say these men can be trusted."

Joe looked at him.

"Nobody's perfect, Rooney and there are very few you can trust when it comes to money. A lot of good intentions are forgotten when a man gets greedy. I've seen it happen before, that's why I'll leave the final decision to Rueben. I'd trust that man with my life. If there's something not right, he'll find it. That's why he works for me!"

Rooney nodded thoughtfully.

"Well, when do we go?" he asked.

"You're not making the trip this time. If I'm going to go as just an interested party I have to go alone. Anyway, if Nick is sending Anthony that's a clear message to these guys to be on their best behaviour. Besides, I need you here. I want you to look after things for me. And I want you to look after Angel."

"Oh, she'll be alright, Joe. She's got her mother and Evie."

"That's not what I had in mind, Rooney. I want you to spend some time with her. You know, bring her out to dinner. Get her out of the house. Let her enjoy herself."

"Maybe she won't come."

"Sure she will, she likes you!" smiled Joe.

"Well, if that's what you want, consider it done," said Rooney standing up.

"That's what I want. You'd be doing me a big favour and remember – I'm counting on you."

"When do you go, then?"

"The day after tomorrow."

Rooney went over and opened the door.

"Don't worry about a thing, Joe, you can depend on me," he smiled, broadly.

As Joe watched the door close, his eyes narrowed and a serious expression came over his face.

"I hope so, Rooney," he murmured. "I really hope so."

Joe watched Rooney drive away. He stood looking out of the window for a few minutes, then he opened the study door and yelled, "Frankie!"

"Coming Boss," came the reply and within a few seconds Frankie stood before him. "What is it, Boss?"

"Come in and close the door. I want to talk to you while Al isn't around."

"Where is he anyway?" asked Frankie, getting settled.

"He took Angel into town, so before they get back I'm going to come straight to the point. I'm going away for a week on business and there's something I want you to do for me while I'm gone."

"Sure Boss, just name it."

"I want you to keep any eye on Rooney and my wife."

Frankie stared at him, shocked.

"You mean – watch them?"

"Yeah, that's what I mean."

"Rooney and Angela? What reason would I have?"

"Hopefully, none," he replied. "Listen Frankie, they both like each other, you know that, but I have to know that's all it is. I don't like doing it. Rooney's family, the brother I never had and I love him. He's also my best friend." He was silent for a moment, lost in his own thoughts. Then, "Angel's only nineteen, I love her too. But I must be certain of their love and loyalty to me. I have to know if they'd be attracted to each other, or if they are. Do you understand?"

"Sure Boss," said Frankie, sympathetically. "What do you want me to do?"

Joe explained,

"Well, I've asked Rooney to spend some time with her. Bring her out when I'm not here."

"Don't you think that's sort of asking for trouble? You know, pushing them together like that."

"I've thought about that," nodded Joe, "but with me out of the picture they have the perfect opportunity and the perfect excuse. And I'll have given it to them. What I want you to do is watch and listen. He might invite her to his apartment. He might stay over in this house when I'm gone. He might take her for an intimate dinner somewhere where they're not known. He might do a lot of things. Then again who knows, she may well be the one who'll encourage him." He gave a deep sigh and put his hands together. "I don't like doing this, Frankie. I feel bad about it. But I really love her. That's why I have to know that she loves me. I must be sure I can trust her. I must be 100% sure I can trust them both. Now do you understand, really?"

Frankie nodded and tried to reassure Joe.

"You leave it to me, Boss. If anything happens you'll know about it, where and when."

"Thanks, Frankie," said Joe, putting a grateful hand on his shoulder. "And remember, this is strictly between us."

"You bet!" came the reply.

Frankie got up to leave.

"There's one more thing," said Joe. "When I'm coming home I'll call you. I want you to pick me up at the airport. If there's any bad news I'd rather hear it before I get back to the house. You can make some excuse to Al."

Frankie nodded but loitered in the doorway. Finally, he met Joe's gaze.

"Are you sure you want to do this, Boss?"

"I don't want to do it but I have to. I have my reasons!"

Joe forced a weak smile as Frankie left, closing the door behind him. Joe was left alone in the study in deep thought, remembering the night in Miami when Charlie told him about his wife and best friend.

Joe went to Chicago and true to his word, Rooney invited Angela out for dinner. An invitation she readily accepted. As they sat at a quiet table in 'The Safe Haven' she studied him closely, just the way she had done with Joe the first night he took her to Mario's.

He was taller than Joe, well built with fair hair and blue eyes. Although not exactly handsome, he was attractive in his own way with a very winning smile. He had a Northern Ireland accent but it wasn't strong. She got the impression that the time he'd spent in New York had crept into his voice.

"Tell me something," she said, lifting her glass. "Why does everyone call you Rooney? Don't you have a first name?"

"Unfortunately, yes," came the reply.

"What is it?"

"Don't ask – please!" He shook his head.

"Go on, tell me. It can't be that bad," said Angela, trying to coax him.

"Would you like to bet on that?"

"Oh, come on, Rooney."

"Alright," he sighed, giving in. "I was christened Ignatius Pius Rooney. How's that for a mouthful?"

Angela bust out laughing.

"You're having me on!"

"I wish I was," he said, lowering his head and looking embarrassed.

"Your mother must have been very religious."

"She must have been a bloody fanatic! I took some stick from the rest of the boys." He smiled and shook his head again as he recalled, "You should have seen Joe's face the first time he ever heard it, not to mention his mouth trying to pronounce it. The more he tried the worse it sounded. Finally he gave up and said, 'Kid, I've heard some very peculiar names in my time but that beats them all! From here on in you'll be known as Rooney!'"

Now he joined Angela's laughter. Then they continued their conversation.

"How did you meet Joe?" she asked.

"Well, it was really by chance – or by fate, I don't know." He looked at her and smiled, "Maybe we have something in common there. Anyway, my parents parted when I was very young and my mother put me in a home. It was run by priests who wanted as many of us as possible to follow in their footsteps. I guess with a name like mine they thought I was halfway there! But I wasn't having any of it, so I left at sixteen and fell in with a bad crowd. Living rough and acting tough, you might say. Then one night one of the priests from the home, Fr. Taylor, was sent for to come to the police station. I'd been arrested for taking part in a gang fight. He got me out and brought me back to the home, but I had turned seventeen and he knew he couldn't keep me there, so the next thing I knew my fare to America was paid and I was given $50 and an address that turned out to be a seedy room in a run down parish." Rooney's voice was serious as he related his story. "I arrived in New York with just one change of clothes in a canvas bag and no prospects at all."

He stopped to take a drink and then continued, "I looked older than my age so I never had a problem getting into bars. One night I was in a bar called 'The Cellar', when Joe came in. he was smiling and saying hello, making his way to a back room. Then all of a sudden, this guy next to me at the bar pulled out a knife and as Joe walked passed, he lunged at him. Before I realised what I was doing, I'd grabbed the guy from behind and wrestled him to the floor. I think I acted on instinct. There was no time for questions. He put up a fight but I got the better of him. Then a couple of other guys came over and carried the guy out. He was in bad shape, but Joe would have been in worse shape if things had gone to plan!"

"What did Joe do?" asked Angela, enthralled.

"Well, after the initial shock wore off, he thanked me up and down and invited me to have a drink with him. I told him it was o.k. and to forget about it, but that only made him more insistent so I agreed. We got talking and he said, 'Kid, I like your style. How would you like to work for me?'"

"And…"

"I jumped at the chance! He gave me a job, bought me clothes and rented me a nice room. We became close. I went from being his minder to his friend and confidant. Now I have an apartment and my own room at his home. I guess you could say we're like brothers now. He's the only family I have ever really had. In a way Fr. Taylor did me a good turn. Anyway, that's how I met Joe."

Angela gazed at him, admiringly.

"How long have you known him then?" she asked.

"Well, I'm twenty six now, so about nine years."

"Funny, I always thought you were older."

"You know what they say, Angela, every picture tells a story. Mine would be an epic!"

he smiled.

There was a short silence, then Angela said,

"Can I ask you something, Rooney?"

"Sure."

"You must know Joe better than most people. What kind of man is he really?"

He leaned back in his chair and smiled broadly.

"Joe thinks he's New York's answer to Robin Hood!" His smile faded as he remembered Lenny Shultz and believe it or not, Angela, sometimes he is."

"You saved his life, Rooney," she said gratefully.

"Yes, I guess I did. But in a way, he saved mine. He made me what I am today. Joe's loyal. He never forgot what I did but I'll never forget that night either. He changed my whole life and I'll always be grateful to him."

Rooney looked as his watch as Angela pondered on what she'd just heard.

"Well, now that you know my life history," he joked "I think It's time I was getting you home. It's late."

Angela nodded and got up.

"I really enjoyed hearing all that," she smiled. "Have you ever been back home for a holiday since you came here?"

"No, I've never been back. Just like you, Angela, I have nothing to go back for."

They said goodnight to the staff and Freddie and walked out of 'The Safe Haven', happy in each others company. Rooney hailed a taxi and they got in. But as the cab drove away, Frankie started his car and followed at a safe distance!

As Rooney continued to keep Angela company, things were going well for Joe. The more he heard about the business deal and its profits, the more he liked it. But being the shrewd man he was he didn't commit to anything. He had phoned home a couple of times to speak to Angela but he didn't ask any questions. He'd been in Chicago now for four days and decided to go out on the town. He visited a couple of clubs but left, unable to settle. As he walked along the streets watching all the activity, he couldn't help but think it was a lot like New York. Every city seemed to come alive at night, with a hooker on every corner plying her trade. He felt alone and he missed Angela. Without really thinking, he wandered into a bar and ordered a drink. Music was playing loudly and he looked in it's direction. There on small platforms, were topless dancers moving their bodies seductively to the rhythm of the music. They were surrounded by men, some encouraging, others abusive. Joe stood and watched. They were attractive young women not much older than Angela. In fact, one of them had a body just like hers. As she swayed around, Joe couldn't help but take in every movement. His eyes moved slowly from her breasts down to her feet. At that moment he wanted his wife, and only his wife. Any man could see this young girl's body just by walking in off the street. Angela was different. No one had seen hers except him. And even then she was still shy and embarrassed sometimes, when he looked at her. He smiled as he thought of how easily she'd blush when he'd tell her how beautiful he thought her body was, when they'd make love.

"Why don't you go down to the front?" said the bartender, breaking in on Joe's thoughts.

"You get a better view. When they're finished they come down and mingle. Know what I mean?"

"Yeah, I know what you mean," replied Joe, putting his glass down and shaking his head.

"Not tonight." He turned and walked towards the door.

"Maybe some other night," the bartender called out.

"I don't think so," he said.

Joe walked back to his hotel room and lay on top of the bed. He wondered what Angela was doing and if she would be home. His watch said 11:30 but he longed to hear her voice. He got up, sat on the edge of the bed and called home. The phone rang for a few moments then he heard a voice on the other end say, "Hello."

"Hi honey it's me."

"Joe! Is anything wrong?"

"No, why should anything be wrong?"

"Well, it's late."

"Yeah, I know. I'm sorry about that. I just wondered how you were"

"I'm fine."

"I didn't know if you'd be in. I thought maybe Rooney had brought you out to dinner or somewhere."

"He brought me out to dinner the evening you went away and I was out to dinner with him again last night."

"Anywhere I know?" enquired Joe.

"'The Safe Haven'."

"Well, that should be good for business," he joked. "My wife eating out in her husband's restaurant. I thought you might have gone to Mario's, it's small and quiet, you know – cosy." He had a serious look on his face now. There was a pause.

"Joe," said Angela, in a low voice, "Mario's is special to me. It's our place. I wouldn't go there with anyone but you."

Joe closed his eyes for a few seconds.

"I didn't know you felt like that Angel."

"You never asked. Anyway, we might be going to the movies tomorrow night, but he's promised to take me somewhere special the night after. He's being very secretive about it. He says I'll never guess where we're going and he won't give me any clues," she laughed.

"Well, that's great honey. It sounds like you're having a good time."

"How's Chicago?"

"Oh, it's ok."

"Are you enjoying your stay?"

"Well, you know, it's mostly business."

"When are you coming home?"

"I'm not sure. It might be another three days before I get everything sorted out, but I'll let you know." His voice became emotional. "I really miss you, Angel. It's so good to hear your voice."

"I miss you too."

"You do, even with Rooney keeping you so busy?"

He forced a laugh.

"I'm just wondering if someone's keeping you busy," Angela joked.

"Oh, come on, honey. Would I do that to you?"

When she didn't answer he continued, "I don't want anyone else, Angel, I love you."

"I love you, Joe." She assured him.

At that moment, he really hoped she did.

"Well," he said, "I'd better hang up now. Goodnight, honey."

"Goodnight, Joe....Joe?"

"Yeah?"

"It's nothing."

He listened as she put down the receiver. He lay down on the bed again, with his hands under his head, staring at the ceiling. Where was Rooney taking her that was so special? What had she wanted to say – but didn't? Well, he would know soon enough. Joe had told a lie. It wouldn't take three more days to finish his business. Two at the most should be enough. He didn't want Angela or Rooney to know exactly when he was coming home. He wanted to surprise them.

He closed his eyes, remembering the young dancer he had seen earlier and wishing he was home in bed with Angela. She had no idea just how much he missed her!

After long meetings and a lot of talking, the business transaction had come to an end. Everyone really seemed satisfied with the deal but a few like Joe and Anthony Andretti, wanted time to go over the finer details and this was agreed. It was also decided that because of the importance and secrecy of the deal they shouldn't all be seen out together, so Joe and Anthony were to meet up later that night for dinner to discuss business. Joe had been right, two days was enough to bring the deal to a close.

Back in the hotel room he showered and changed and was putting his files away, when a knock came to the door. On opening it he came face to face with a very attractive woman, her hair and make up done to perfection. She was in her late twenties and wore a straight, beige raincoat with a tie-belt.

"Room service," she smiled.

"Well, whatever it is, I didn't order any," replied Joe.

"Maybe some kind person ordered it for you." She suggested, pushing past him and walking into the room. She turned and looked at him. "My name is Mercy."

"Would that be your real name?"

"Does it matter? By the time I'm through with my men it's what they're begging for!"

"Really, you're that good, huh?"

"Aren't you going to close the door?" she asked.

"I don't think you'll be here long enough," he said, determinedly.

"Oh I think you'll change your mind when you see what's on offer."

She untied the belt and let the raincoat drop to the floor. Standing naked in front of him, she smiled,

"Well, what do you think?"

Joe stared at her, unflinching.

"I think you'd better leave," he advised.

She climbed onto the bed and Joe hurriedly closed the door.

"I thought you'd change your mind!" she laughed.

He stood looking down at her as she moved her hands all over her body. Then she rolled over, positioning herself on her hands and knees and looking at him seductively.

"Whatever you want, whatever turns you on, is alright by me," she purred.

He didn't doubt that for a minute!

"Whatever I want? You're sure about that?"

She smiled and nodded.

Joe grabbed her arm and quickly pulled her off the bed.

"O.k. then I want you out of here – now!"

He lifted the raincoat off the floor and pushed it into her hands.

"What the fuck's wrong with you? Are you gay?"

"No – I'm married."

"So what's the big deal? Most men are."

"Well, I'm not most men and the big deal is, I happen to be in love with my wife."

Mercy was getting angry.

"I'll bet she doesn't know half the ways there are to please a man. I do!"

"Well, good for you," he nodded, making sure she put the raincoat back on. He went over and opened the door.

"Your wife could never do for you what I could. You don't know what you're missing," she said, in a bitchy voice, walking past him.

"Well, I'll just have to live with that. Won't I?" replied Joe, sarcastically.

She stopped in the corridor and glared at him.

"What's the matter?" he asked. "Is your pride hurt because you've finally met one man who didn't' beg for mercy? Or maybe you're upset because you didn't earn your commission, plus a nice fat tip from me."

"You're a bastard!" she yelled.

"And you're a hooker," he reminded her, shrugging his shoulders and staring at her coldly. "But who gives a damn? Good bye Mercy, it was nice not knowing you!"

As Joe watched she stormed along the corridor, almost running into Anthony Andretti, who had just turned the corner at the same time. He stopped and looked after her, then walked towards Joe. He smiled.

"What was that, room service?"

"How did you know?" asked Joe, in a surprised voice.

"I got it too. But like yourself, Mr Morrelli, I refused it. I think we're the only two who did."

"Could I ask you why?"

"Maria's not just my wife, she's the mother of my children," replied Anthony. "What about you?"

"Step into my office," nodded Joe.

Anthony followed him into the room and closed the door.

"I have two reasons," explained Joe. "Apart from my wife who is reason number one, there's also another very important one. Sit down, Anthony."

Anthony made himself comfortable and listened intently to Joe, who began, "Let me tell you something. The last day of any business trip out of town, is for fun. Believe me, I know. I've been to quite a few. But no matter how nice or how respectable your associates seem to be, never take any chances. I want to give you a word of advice. Don't ever give them anything to hold over your head. Drugs, women, anything. That's the ace they'll keep up their sleeve. If a deal turns sour and they have something on you, then you can't ask questions. If you do, those things have a habit of coming to light. I've seen it happen. I've known men who had calls from these women. Pictures of them in compromising positions were sent to their homes to threaten their marriages. They had to go along with a deal, especially a bad one and some of them ended up being fleeced. Or worse, they were blackmailed and for what? For doing the same thing some of our friends are doing right now! You always have to be one step ahead to survive. Take that from me."

Anthony smiled.

"Thank you, Mr Morrelli, my grandfather has already told me all that."

"Yeah, well, that's why he's still around and respected."

"The same can be said for you. My grandfather always told me you were like him, a shrewd man."

"Well, it can't hurt. Not in business anyway."

Anthony looked at him, admiringly, and for a split second Joe could see his old friend Dominic. He put his hand on the young man's shoulder, affectionately.

"Anthony, wherever you go and whatever you do, there's something I want you to remember."

"What is it?"

"A reputation takes a lifetime to build – but just a moment to destroy!"

Joe knew by the expression on Anthony's face that he understood perfectly and would be determined to protect not just his own reputation, but that of the entire Andretti 'family'. "You're a bit early for dinner," said Joe, on a lighter note. "I wasn't expecting to see you so soon."

"I came to tell you I called the airport. We can get a flight out tonight. What do you think?"

Joe smiled broadly.

"I think we'll be on it. Come on, lets go to dinner now, then we can pack."

As Joe sat on board the plane, he was deep in thought. Before leaving the hotel he'd called Frankie, who was now on his way to meet him. This had been Rooney and Angela's special night out. He reckoned Frankie would be able to tell him where they'd been. He was glad he was going home, yet he harboured a certain amount of dread. Joe looked down at the wedding ring on his finger. At least he had kept his end of the bargain, he had remained faithful to Angela. He wondered if she had remained faithful to him. A week of Rooney's undivided attention might have been a big temptation for her. Anyway, he would know in a little while. He had no doubts that Frankie would be able to give him all the news. He just hoped in his heart he could live with it.

As Joe and Anthony came out of the airport, a large limousine was waiting. "Can I offer you a lift?" asked Anthony.

"No thanks. One of my men is here to collect me."

The two men shook hands but Joe was curious.

"Can I ask you something?"

"Of course."

"When you came to my room, how did you know I wouldn't be...well, you know....otherwise engaged?"

"I didn't, but my grandfather did. That's why he told me to invite you. He said you would know the score. That's why he wants you in on this deal. You play by the rules and you never commit yourself to anyone. Why are you so careful?"

"I have my reasons!" replied Joe, smiling.

"Well, goodbye, Mr Morrelli. When our accountants have done their job I'll be in touch."

"Goodbye, Anthony. Please give my deepest respects and thanks to your grandfather."

Joe spotted Frankie's car and made his way to it. After putting his suitcase on the back seat, he climbed into the front. Frankie looked at him but never spoke.

"O.k., Frankie," said Joe, taking a deep breath, "it's truth time. What have you got to tell me?"

"Not a lot, Boss. Rooney and your wife went out to dinner, twice. Both times at 'The Safe Haven'. They got a taxi home, I followed."

"And…"

"He left her to the door but didn't go in."

"Well, did anything happen? I mean, did he kiss her?"

"Boss, he didn't even kiss her hand."

Joe was silent for a moment.

"But how can you be sure he didn't go back after you'd gone?"

"Aren't you forgetting something, Boss?" Frankie said. "He didn't know I was following him. And besides, once he went home to his own apartment he stayed there."

"Are you sure?"

"Oh, I'm sure alright. I stayed awake watching. Look," "he pointed to his face, "I even have the dark circles under my eyes to prove it. And that's not all. I was almost arrested by the cops for kerb-crawling! I haven't slept in five nights. I feel like one of those private detectives."

"And nothing happened? He didn't stay over and she didn't visit his place?" Joe still needed re-assurance.

Frankie nodded,

"That's right, nothing happened. But I think something's about to…"

"What do you mean?" asked Joe, in an anxious voice.

"I think I'm having a fuckin' breakdown!"

"Well, don't worry about it. I'll pay your medical bills."

"You might have to pay more than that, Boss."

"What are you talking about?" asked Joe, becoming more confused as the conversation went on.

"I'm talking about my Elena, she thinks I'm seeing another woman. You know something? I think she'd be relieved if she was to find out it was my eyes that were working overtime – and not my dick!"

Joe threw his a sarcastic look.

"Can we please get back to the subject and discuss my wife," he snapped.

Frankie rubbed his hand over his drawn face and continued in a tired voice, "They went to the movies last night. When they arrived back at the house, she went upstairs to her mother, Rooney spent an hour or so in the study. Then he left. Any time they were together in the house someone else was always there. Mostly they were in the kitchen talking with the rest of us."

"What about tonight? He was bringing her somewhere special."

"They went to a theatre in the city. I lost them on the way back, I got stuck in traffic. But I tell you, Boss," said Frankie, sounding very sincere. "Rooney can be trusted. So can your wife. Believe me, I ought to know."

Joe breathed a deep sigh of relief and put his hand on Frankie's shoulder.

"I'm glad to hear that," he said. "Of course, I never doubted it for a minute."

"Sure you didn't!" replied Frankie, this time sounding very unconvinced.

"I just had to be sure, that's all," Joe smiled, happily. "And now that I am, you can have a few days off. I'll send a note to your wife, Frankie, saying you were doing a job for me and I'll enclose some money. Buy her something nice and take her out to dinner. That should end any problems you're having."

Frankie's face brightened up.

"Thank's Boss!" Joe nodded. "Does this mean I can finally get some sleep?"

"Do you want to go home now, Boss?"

"I sure do, Frankie. I have a big bed waiting and a wife who doesn't know I'm coming. She's in for one hell of a surprise!"

Frankie started the car and they began the journey back to Roseberry Avenue.

Joe let himself in quietly and made his way upstairs. It was 2:30 in the morning but instead of feeling tired, he felt happy. Nothing had happened between Angela and Rooney. His fears had been unfounded. He could trust his wife and his best friend, of that he was sure. He was excited at the thought of seeing Angela and never realised he could miss her so much. Those few days had proved one very important thing: Joe was deeply in love with her and no other woman could ever take her place.

Gently, he opened the bedroom door, switched on the lights and stood beaming – but not for long. His smile quickly faded as he saw the bed neatly made up and the room empty. Angela wasn't there! Dropping the suitcase and staring at the bed, he clenched his fists and a look of anger distorted his face. He walked out and along the landing to Rooney's room. He turned the handle sharply and flung open the door but after switching on the lights, discovered that Rooney's bed hadn't been slept in, either. There was no Rooney and no Angela in the house and it was the middle of the night. Joe nodded to himself.

"That can only mean one thing," he thought. "They must be at his apartment!"

After all, where else would his wife be at this time? Didn't Frankie tell him he'd lost them in traffic, when he tried to follow then home? But it was all becoming clear to him now. They didn't come home. They'd never intended to. Joe was becoming more angry by the minute but worse than that, he felt betrayed and he felt a fool. He closed the door and stormed downstairs to the kitchen.

After putting the coffee pot on the stove he lifted a cup, but unable to control himself he threw it onto the floor, smashing it into tiny pieces. The thought of Angela doing this to him hurt and humiliated him, but the thought of her and Rooney in bed together was just too much to bear. He banged the table with his fists. "Damn it!" he muttered, angrily. "Nobody makes a fool out of Joe Morrelli! If they're sleeping together I swear they'll answer to me!"

He lifted another cup and smashed it off the wall. At that moment, Evie appeared out of nowhere. Dressed in her nightgown, she was moving slowly and cautiously, brandishing a large umbrella.

"Mr Joe, it's you!" she said, both surprised and relieved. "Why, you scared me half to death. I thought you were a burglar."

"When an intruder comes into a house to steal things he does it quietly, Evie," he explained. "He doesn't announce he's here by turning on the lights, breaking crockery or making coffee!"

There was a sarcastic tone in Joe's raised voice.

"What's the matter, Mr Joe, didn't the trip go well for you?" She looked down at the broken cups on the floor and pointed. "How did that get there? And how on earth did you get here at this time of the morning?"

He turned his eyes up.

"I flew, all the way from Chicago and would you believe it, my arms are tired!"

"I can see Chicago hasn't improved your wit – or lack of it"!" she replied, giving him one of her looks.

Joe became impatient.

"Would you mind putting that umbrella down and stop waving it in my face!"

Evie placed it on the table.

"Why didn't you let someone know you were coming? Does Miss Angela know you're here?"

He stared at her, suspectingly.

"Speaking of Miss Angela, Evie, where is she? And I don't want any excuses," he warned, pointing a finger directly at her. "I want the truth!"

"Why I don't know what you mean, Mr Joe," she replied, puzzled.

"Oh, I think you do! I've already been upstairs and she's not in our bedroom. Rooney's not in his room, either. And before you start making excuses for her, I already know they went out together again tonight, only this time it was to 'somewhere special'. And I think I know where that 'somewhere special' is. So you better tell me!"

Joe's voice was stern and demanding. Evie glared at him with a face like thunder, while pulling the tie belt on her gown more securely. The penny had dropped!

"Mr Joe, how could you?"

"How could I what?"

"How could you think what I know you're thinking – and about Miss Angela too," she said, shaking her head, disapprovingly.

"O.k., Evie, why don't you tell me where she went tonight? And more to the point, where she is now."

He leaned his hands on the table, looked up into her face and waited for an answer. Evie pulled out a chair and sat down.

"Alright then, I will," she nodded. "Rooney brought Miss Angela to the theatre tonight. They went to see a play by that nice Mr Shakespeare. She wasn't going to go at first, on account of her mother being sick. But I forced her to go and told her not to worry, I'd see to everything for her. Then when they came back, Rooney took some coffee and left and

Miss Angela sat right here at this table and told me all about the play. She was so excited, seeing it all live on stage like that. Why, it even got a standing ovation!" Evie's eyes narrowed as she glared at Joe. "I also happen to know where she is right now. She's sleeping on the couch in her mother's room in case she needs her during the night."

There was an uncomfortable silence before Evie spoke again. "I'm disappointed in you, Mr Joe, I really am. Miss Angela would never do anything to hurt you. She loves you too much and she missed you so. Why, that last night you phoned, she was almost in tears. And as for Rooney, he's been a real gentleman! How could you think anything was going on behind your back?"

A guilty look came over Joe's face as Evie shook her head and got up. He sighed, rubbing his face with his hands.

"I'm just tired, Evie," he explained.

"That doesn't give you the right to go around accusing people of things they didn't do!"

"I know, I know," he nodded, looking at her shamefully. "I'm ashamed."

"So you should be. And just look at my floor!" she said in an angry voice.

Joe took her arm pleadingly.

"I love her Evie, I really do. If I lost her I'd be so unhappy and alone."

"If you don't' learn to cool your temper, Mr Joe, you could very well end up that way. And you'd only have yourself to blame!"

"You're right, but it's just that she's so much younger than me. I'm scared she'll meet someone else."

Evie could see the anxiety in his face, so she put a caring hand on his arm.

"She doesn't want anyone else, Mr Joe. She's in love with you, and I know what I know! But you'll have to trust her. Now, I won't say anything about tonight. I wouldn't hurt Miss Angela for the world – but I'm still disappointed in you, Mr Joe!"

Joe nodded as she reached over and lifted the umbrella off the table.

"Were you really going to confront an intruder with that thing?" he asked.

"Yes I was!" she replied in a confident voice, walking towards the door.

"And what were you planning to do with it?"

"I was planning on giving him a good smack." She turned and looked back at him. "And I'm sorely tempted to do the same to you, Mr Joe. Sorely tempted!"

As Evie disappeared, Joe shook his head and smiled, then poured himself a cup of coffee.

When he'd finished he made sure to clear away the broken crockery before he left the kitchen. He was in Evie's bad books enough as it was and he didn't want Angela finding out about tonight's little episode. After turning out the lights he went upstairs and along the landing to Agnes's room. He opened the door slightly and looked in. Angela was lying on the couch fast asleep with one hand almost touching the floor. Beside her lay a book. A lamp still shone on a small table next to her. Joe went over and picked up the book, placing it beside the lamp. He noticed it was a book of poetry which he'd bought for her some weeks before. He gazed at her for a few moments, then bent down and kissed her cheek. She opened her eyes slowly. "Joe!" she whispered, surprised.

He smiled, saying in a low voice, "No, don't get up. It's o.k."

He placed his hands gently on her shoulders.

"What time is it?" she asked.

"It's the middle of the night. I got home earlier than expected. You go back to sleep, honey. I'll see you at breakfast."

Angela put her hand on his arm and smiled.

"Joe, I'm so glad you're home. I missed you."

Her voice was sleepy and he knew she needed rest, so he kissed her forehead and stroked her hair.

"I missed you, too," he nodded, turning off the lamp. "You stay here. I'll see you in a few hours."

She drowsily moved her hand down his arm until he was able to take it in his own and their fingers gently entwined. Then she closed her eyes and drifted off to sleep. After waiting a few moments, Joe covered her with the white blanket that hung over the bottom of the couch, and left the room as silently as he had entered it.

Going into their own room, he undressed, got into bed and lay staring into the darkness. Joe was tired – but couldn't sleep! He felt so guilty about everything. Rooney, Angela and the way he'd jumped to conclusions about them. They had both proved themselves in more ways than one. His wife had spent part of the evening at a theatre, but the rest was spent with her sick mother. And what did she have for company? Just a book of poems given to her by a husband, who right now was feeling very ashamed of himself! At that moment he couldn't help but think how innocent and naïve she was to what was going on around her, especially out on the streets. But then, that's what had attracted him to her in the beginning. She hadn't been around. There was such a difference between her and most of the women he'd known – and had. He was glad and proud he'd married her. To the "Mercy's" of this world, sex was just getting laid. But with his wife, sex was making and sharing love and Joe knew only too well what the difference was. He reached out and pulled Angela's pillow towards him, embracing it as if it was her. The scent of her perfume contented him and dispelled all other thoughts but one: after all these years it was a great feeling to be genuinely loved by someone like her and an even greater feeling to love that woman as much as he did, in return.

Angela felt happy as she got dressed that morning. Her husband was home and she'd been so glad to see him. She left her mother's room and went along the landing to their bedroom, opening the door to look in on him. But Joe was already up and getting dressed.

"Good morning," he smiled.

Angela looked surprised.

"I thought you would still be asleep after arriving home so late."

"It's nine thirty," he replied. "I've had plenty of sleep. Here, I bought you something."

He handed her a neatly wrapped package. Angela sat on the bed and opened it.

"Joe, that is really expensive," she said, holding up the large bottle of perfume.

"Only the best for my wife," he smiled, sitting down beside her. "Angel, can I ask you something? The last night I phoned, I got the impression there was something you wanted to say."

"There was," she nodded, "but I didn't want to spoil your trip."

"Well, what was it?"

"I wanted to tell you I missed you so much I wanted you to come home." She looked at him with tears in her eyes. "But I knew you'd think I was being silly."

Joe put his arm around her.

"No honey, I wouldn't have thought that. I didn't think you'd miss me that much, with all the time you were spending with Rooney."

"I had a lot of fun with Rooney but he's not my husband. He's not you, Joe."

Angela couldn't have paid him a greater compliment. He just hoped she'd never find out what he'd done or the lengths he'd gone to for proof that he could trust her. If she did, he knew it would almost certainly ruin his marriage. Joe's heart was heavy with guilt but he wasn't going to let it show.

"Come on," he said, "let's go down to breakfast."

She got up and took his hand, smiling.

As they made their way downstairs, Angela chatted happily. But she never once asked him about Chicago, what he had done in his spare time or how he's spent his nights. It was obvious to Joe that Angela placed a lot more trust in him, than he had done in her. As they sat down at the kitchen table, Joe tried to avoid Evie's gaze. Angela was all smiles.

"Look, Evie, Joe's home."

"So I see," replied Evie, in a moody voice.

She came over to the table with two plates, putting one down in front of Angela and banging the other one down in front of Joe. Then she went to pour the coffee.

"What's the matter with Evie?" whispered Angela.

"Oh, I woke her up last night when I came home. I came in here for a cup of coffee and let something slip."

"You sure did!" said Evie in a sarcastic tone, putting the coffee down on the table.

"What was it?" asked Angela.

"A cup," he replied, looking uncomfortable. "Anyway, she thought I was a burglar. She came in waving this big umbrella like Errol Flynn with his sword."

Angela put her hand to her mouth, trying to hide a smile.

"You must have been very frightened, Evie. I bet you were relieved to find it was Joe."

"You could say that, Miss Angela," she replied, giving Joe a long look. "What I don't understand is why Mr Joe can't be like everybody else and travel in the day time instead of landing home in the middle of the night – causing a disturbance!"

"I happened to get an earlier flight than expected," said Joe, turning round and looking at her. "Do you have a problem with that?"

"Not me! The only problem I have is getting no sleep and being scared half to death. But then, the good Lord knows there are worse problems than that." She gave him a knowing look.

"Well, I think you were very brave, Evie," praised Angela "but didn't you stop to think for one moment that by coming in here you might have been raped?"

Evie clasped the sink with both hands.

"You know, Miss Angela, that thought did cross my mind."

"Well, it sure never crossed mine!" muttered Joe.

Angela started to tell him all about the play she had seen, her voice full of excitement as she went over everything.

"I didn't know you'd been to the theatre," lied Joe, convincingly. "I'm glad you enjoyed it," he smiled.

Evie stood with a smug 'I told you so' look on her face.

"Rooney sure looked after you," he continued.

"Yes, he was great company, Joe and he's a great friend," she smiled, getting up to prepare a breakfast tray for her mother.

"Well, maybe tonight you and me could go to Mario's."

"I'd like that."

She kissed his cheek and left the kitchen with the tray. Joe waited a few seconds, then got up and went to the kitchen door. He paused a moment, then turned.

"Thanks for not saying anything about last night, Evie."

Evie looked at him, forgivingly.

"I care about you, Mr Joe and I care about Miss Angela. It would break her heart to know you thought what you did. As for last night, well, it didn't happen."

Joe nodded in appreciation.

"I can promise you one thing, it won't ever happen again."

He left the kitchen and walked down the entrance hall to his study. There was a stack of mail on his desk, so he sat down in the leather chair and reached for the letter opener.

One envelope contained a gilt edged card, inviting him and his wife to a party at Gene O'Brien's home. Joe leaned back in his chair, tapping the card lightly on his lips.

"This is it," he thought.

Now was the time to introduce Angela into his circle of friends in high places. She had the brains, they had the position and power to help her climb the ladder of success. By knowing the right people, she could achieve a social standing in life. Joe knew the time was right to put his plans for Angela into action.

Rooney called after lunch and was surprised to find Joe sitting in the lounge, reading the newspaper.

"Well, the wanderer returns!" he smiled. "When did you get back?"

Joe put the paper down.

"In the middle of the night," he replied.

"How was Chicago?"

"Good. But you know me, Rooney, I never rush into anything. It sounds like a good deal but let Reuben be the judge of that. Anyway, how are things at this end?"

"Couldn't be better. Everything's running smoothly and you're still making money."

"I'm glad to hear it!"

"I thought you would be," smiled Rooney, sitting down.

Joe looked at him.

"Rooney, I want to thank you for taking care of business and Angel."

"My pleasure, Joe. I told you, you could depend on me."

Just then, Angela appeared and went over and put her arm around Rooney.

"How's my favourite escort?" she smiled.

"Fine, at least now I know about Hamlet!" he laughed, turning to Joe. "You should go and see it," he encouraged. "That is, if you don't mind sitting with a woman who recites the lines along with the actors!" He winked at Joe. Angela pushed him, playfully.

"I think Joe is more of a Broadway fan," she smiled.

"Oh, I wouldn't say that," said Joe, looking at Angela's arm around Rooney's shoulder. "I think I will go and see it. You know, find out about the guy, Hamlet. He must have something going for him if you like him so much."

"I'd like you to go," she smiled. "It's a wonderful play with some beautiful lines. And you're never too old or too young to learn."

"Now, that's just what I was thinking," he replied, feeling his emotions building up as he thought how sexy she looked with those dark blue eyes and beautiful smile.

"Where's Evie?" she asked. "She's not in the kitchen."

Joe shrugged.

"She's probably in her room. Why?"

"I wanted to tell her I'm going upstairs for a long, hot shower and a rest. Sleeping on a couch isn't very comfortable."

Joe watched as she ran her hands down the sides of her body.

"I'll see you later, Rooney," she said.

"O.k., Angela"

Both men watched as she left the room. Even when tired, hot and strained, Angela could still be attractive in her tight fitting jeans and t-shirt. When she'd disappeared from view, Joe leaned over.

"You know, Rooney, I've heard a lot of guys say that the secret to a good lay is a firm bottom. I believe every word!!"

"Well, what are we doing today?" asked Rooney, getting back to the subject of business. "Oh, I don't think there's much to be done. You seem to have everything pretty much under control and besides, I'm feeling a bit tired. I think I'll go upstairs and lie down for a while." Joe put his hand up to his mouth and yawned, deliberately.

"Joe, you never lie down during the day."

"Well, today's different."

"Oh, I get it," nodded Rooney. "You might be going upstairs but I'd lay odds you're not tired!"

Joe stood up and put his hands out.

"Well, you have to seize the moment, you know. Make the most of every opportunity."

Rooney looked at him.

"Joe, I don't know where people go when they die but if there's such a thing as reincarnation I wouldn't be one bit surprised if you came back as a rabbit!"

"Come to think of it, that might not be so bad. Rabbits have a lot of fun," smiled Joe.

"So remember," he warned, pointing a finger, "if anything happens to me always be nice to them. You never know, one of them could be your boss!"

"Don't worry," Rooney assured him, "when everyone else is putting flowers on your grave, I'll be putting on a bunch of carrots – just in case!"

Joe laughed and put his arm around him.

"I'll see you tomorrow," he said. "I have a feeling I'll be otherwise engaged for the rest of the day."

He turned and walked out of the lounge.

Rooney shook his head as he got up. In all the years he'd known Joe, he'd never known him to miss an opportunity. And by the look on his face as he left the room, this was one he was really going to make the most of. And who could blame him? As Rooney looked up at the ceiling he knew that if Angela was his wife, he'd do exactly the same.

Joe paid Agnes a short visit, then left to find Angela. When he walked into the bedroom, Joe could hear the water running and Angela singing in the bathroom as she often did. He closed the door quietly and going over to the bed, he took his shoes off and lay down on top of it. When he heard the shower being turned off, he half closed his eyes and lay very still. In a little while Angela came out in a knee-length, white bathrobe, brushing her hair. She looked over and saw him.

"Joe, what's the mater, don't you feel well?"

There was no answer. She looked more closely.

"Joe are you alright?"

He didn't reply and wasn't moving. Angela started to panic. She threw herself onto the bed and crawled over it, still holding the hairbrush. Gripping him by the shoulder, she shook him.

"Joe, speak to me!" she pleaded.

"Hi!" he smiled.

Angela hit him on the arm with the back of the hairbrush.

"Joe Morrelli, you frightened the life out of me. I thought you were dead."

"Come on, Angel, would I do that to you?"

"Why are you up here, anyway?" she asked.

"I thought I'd take a nap."

"Joe, you never sleep in the afternoon."

"Now, why does everybody keep telling me that? Besides, if I can't sleep I'll just have to find something else to do!" he grinned.

"Oh, I see. You're not tired – just horny," she replied.

Joe leaned on his side and looked at her surprised.

"Where do you hear words like that?" he asked, in an amused voice.

"I don't just read books, you know. I read magazines as well."

"Now that explains it. And do these magazines inform you of anything else?"

"What do you mean?"

"I mean variety!"

Angela stared at him.

"I hope you're not trying to tell me you're kinky!"

Joe hung over the edge of the bed, looking underneath it.

"What are you doing?" she asked.

"I'm looking for those magazines. With words like 'horny' and 'kinky', I wouldn't mind reading them myself," he joked.

She shook her head in despair.

"I don't know what I'm going to do with you!"

"I do."

He rolled back towards her but noticed a serious expression on her face as she spoke.

"Joe are you on some kind of tablet I should know about?"

"Me?" What would I take tablets for?" he asked, surprised.

"Energy," came the reply. "Because I just don't know where you get it from."

"Oh, I've always had plenty of that."

"Now, he tells me," she muttered, turning her eyes up to the ceiling.

Angela tried to clamber off the bed but Joe pulled her back.

"Where are you going?"

"To get dressed. Why?"

"Well, you know, Angel, I've been thinking. I'm not doing anything and we've got the house pretty much to ourselves, why not make the most of it. What do you say?"

"I hope that's all you've been thinking because if it isn't – forget it."

Joe knelt up on the bed and took her face in his hands.

"Angel, I'm not kinky, I swear it…. I'm just your average red-blooded male who happens to love his wife. Besides, I've missed you."

"Well, I've missed you too."

When Joe heard that, he quickly lay back down on the bed again, smiling.

Angela tried to keep a straight face.

"You've got half an hour," she said.

"What? Oh, come on, Angel, it takes me that long to enjoy a cup of coffee!"

"Well, how long will it take?"

"What day is it?!"

They both burst into loud laughter.

Joe pulled her towards him, undoing her loosely tied robe. He slipped his hands inside and gently manoeuvred her body until it lay on top of him. Angela slowly undid the buttons of his shirt, kissing his flesh as she moved lower and lower. After she unbuckled his belt, he drew her up in his arms, kissing her lovingly and passionately. As he opened her robe fully and slipped it from her body, he was reminded yet again of how soft and sensuous her perfumed skin was. And she was reminded of the strong, virile and considerate man she had married.

Joe and Angela remained upstairs for the rest of the afternoon, locked away from the whole world. What Angela had never known about love-making, Joe Morrelli taught her that day. Through his gentle persuasion she had become a willing student. No doubt in the future there would be even more to discover for both of them. But for now, nothing could be more perfect.

The next few weeks went well for Joe, both in his home life and on the social scene. There were the nights when Angela would curl up beside him on the couch with a beer and they'd watch t.v. or listen to music or just relax in each others company. Then there were the social events. Gene O'Brien's party had proved to be the perfect place for Angela to meet the right kind of people, and she had handled herself exactly the way he knew she could. When she walked in on his arm that night she was one of the best dressed women there. Joe had made sure of that. Her friendliness, good manners and intelligence had resulted in other invitations. As a couple they were becoming well known where it mattered and that pleased him.

When they were out together at parties, functions and clubs, she looked and sounded every inch the lady. He would watch and listen proudly, and as he did so he never failed to notice the attention she was getting. Being married to someone like her had given him a deep feeling of satisfaction and achievement. Everything, including his plans for Angela, was going well. He was happy and contended with life.

Joe had always lived by one golden rule and that was, 'always be one step ahead'. But he forgot one very important thing – fate was always one step ahead of everybody. And fate was waiting.

It wouldn't be long before Joe would take his final step and catch up with it. His life was about to change in ways he'd never dreamed of. Joe Morrelli could not foresee that his destiny and that of those he loved most and was closest to, would soon be in the lap of the Gods.

Chapter 10

Angela had not been well. She was suffering from severe headaches, which in turn brought on nausea. She had told Dr Chapman about her symptoms when he visited Agnes and he told her he thought she had developed migraine, brought on by the worry of her mother, who's health was slowly deteriorating. The weather at that time was quite hot and humid and he felt this was also having an effect. Angela didn't mention anything to Agnes. She thought it best not to worry her. She did tell Joe about the headaches but not how bad they really were. When he wasn't at home during the day she'd lie down and rest until they'd ease off, and when he was home she'd just take an aspirin and try and make light of them. Joe had no idea just how much pain Angela was suffering. He, like the doctor, thought she was worrying too much about Agnes. In fact, there were times when he even thought she was using them as excuses to avoid certain things. He had dropped a couple of gentle hints which Angela couldn't help but lift, so after that she decided to keep things to herself if at all possible.

On that particular morning she was awakened from her sleep by the pounding in her head and the straining behind her eyes. She didn't say anything to anyone because Agnes had decided to come downstairs for lunch, and Angela was so pleased that her mother seemed to be on the mend.

Joe, Rooney, Agnes and Angela sat in the dining room chatting and joking, while Evie served lunch. Suddenly, Angela could hear their voices fading into the distance as a dark shadow crept over her eyes. Rooney was sitting opposite her and was the first to notice that something was wrong. He jumped up from the table as he saw her eyes close. But he was too late, she fell off the chair onto the floor in a faint. Agnes screamed. Joe made a dash and knelt down on the floor beside her. Rooney poured some water into a glass and handed it to him.

"Jesus Christ," cried Joe, "she's out for the count!"

The tears streamed down Agnes' face when she saw how very pale and lifeless her daughter had become. Joe gently sprinkled some water on Angela's face and dabbed some on her lips with his fingers.

"My God, what's wrong with her?" sobbed Agnes.

"I don't know," he replied in a worried voice, "but I'm going to find out."

He lifted Angela in his arms and carried her out of the dining room. Evie was standing at the door, crying.

As Joe carried Angela upstairs to the bedroom he called back,

"Rooney, call Dr Chapman. Tell him to get over here right away."

Rooney rushed to the study, while Evie put her arm around Agnes and led her on through the lounge.

As Joe put Angela down onto the bed, she started to come round.

"What happened?" she asked, dazed.

"It's o.k., honey," he replied, sitting on the side of the bed holding her hand. "You fainted. The doctor's on his way."

"It's those headaches, Joe. They're getting worse."

"Don't you worry, Angel. We'll find out what's wrong and get it treated," he said in a soft voice. "Everything's going to be fine."

He lifted her hand to his lips and kissed it. Then he stroked her forehead, soothing her and comforting her until Dr Chapman arrived.

Evie showed him up to the bedroom and while he examined Angela, Joe waited outside pacing up and down the landing. It seemed a long time before the door opened and Dr Chapman finally appeared.

"What is it, Doc, what's the matter with her?" he asked in a concerned voice.

"I'm not sure yet, Joe, but I think she might be anaemic. I'd really need to do some blood tests, so I'm going to take her over to the City General Hospital. With any luck we may even find out today, what the problem is."

Angela came out and Dr Chapman took her arm.

"I'm coming too," insisted Joe. "I'm worried about her."

"No, Joe. I'll be alright. I want you to stay with my mother, she's had a dreadful fright."

"Angel, we've all had a scare but you're my wife. I want to go with you."

"Please," pleaded Angela. "There's no need. Stay here and look after her for me and explain what's happening."

"O.k.," sighed Joe, "if that's what you really want."

She kissed him, then followed Dr Chapman downstairs and out to his car.

Joe stood at the top of the stairs, gazing down. He was so worried, almost frightened.

He knew now those headaches had been for real and he bitterly regretted not taking them more seriously. He felt ashamed at the subtle hints he'd given Angela and the times he'd turned a deaf ear when she'd complained.

When he went into the lounge, he found Rooney sitting with Agnes, who was in tears.

"What's wrong with my daughter?" she cried.

Joe explained everything.

"She had headaches once before," she said, "after her father was killed. But she wasn't eating or sleeping then and that's what the trouble was. But she's not like that now, Joe, unless she's worrying about something."

As Agnes dried her tears, Joe hadn't the heart to tell her that she was the worry.

"Come on, Agnes," he said, "lets get you to your room. You've had quite a shock."

He put his arm around her protectively and brought her upstairs. He gave her the medication Angela had left out and sat down.

"Don't cry anymore, Agnes," he said. "She'll be o.k. I'll get her the best doctors money can buy. You just leave everything to me."

Agnes nodded.

"You love her very much, Joe. Don't you?"

"Yeah, I do. She's my life."

"She loves you too."

"How do you know that?" he smiled.

"She told me so – a long time ago. She wants to make you happy."

"Well, she's doing a good job. I've never been more happy in my life."

He got up and opened a window to keep her cool and comfortable. Then he put his arm around her once again.

"Don't worry, Agnes. I'll be back later to make sure you're alright and Angel won't be gone that long. You'll see her real soon."

He left and came back downstairs only to find Rooney and Evie in the kitchen, sitting in silence. Joe turned and went into the study, closing the door behind him. As he stood gazing out of the window, he prayed fervently that when Angela did come back she wouldn't have bad news.

Joe couldn't settle anywhere. He roamed around the house killing time. Everywhere he went seemed so empty. He missed not seeing Angela or hearing her voice. Without even realising it he ended up in the bedroom sitting on the side of the bed, his hands joined. It was the loneliest place of all. He had been so happy in that room. It was full of memories, ones he would never forget. Hours passed until finally he heard a car stop in front of the house. He leapt off the bed and looked out of the window. Angela was getting out of a taxi cab. Joe ran downstairs and had just made it to the front door when Angela walked in. She gave him a sad look. He took her and led her into the lounge, closing the door behind them.

"Well, did they do the tests?" he asked, anxiously.

"Yes, they did."

"Do they know what's wrong with you?"

She looked at him and nodded.

"Joe, I have to go into hospital."

"Oh, God!" cried Joe, putting a shaking hand to his forehead. "When?"

"In about seven months."

"But why?"

"Because I'm going to have a baby!"

Her face lit up as she smiled at him.

For a few moments Joe stared at her, then stammered,

"You mean…. You and me….we're…."

"Yes!" she said, still smiling. "We're going to have a baby."

He lifted her in his arms, overcome with joy.

"I can't believe it! I'm going to be a father! It's terrific! But Angel, honey, didn't you have any idea?”

"Well, I did suspect but I wasn't sure. I didn't want to say anything in case it was a false alarm. When Dr Chapman examined me he thought I might be pregnant but I asked him not to mention it until we were sure. We'll have to be careful for a while, though. Until I get over the third month.”

"Don't you worry about that, honey. I'll sleep in the study if I have to!"

"I don't think it will come to that," she laughed, as he held her close.

They stood for a little while, contended to be in each other's arms. Then Joe broke the silence. "You know," he said, thoughtfully, "wouldn't it be something if we knew, when it actually happened?"

"What do you mean?" Angela asked, looking up at him.

"Well, if we could figure out what day or night it happened, it would always be something special to remember.”

"If you want my opinion," she volunteered, "I think it was after your Chicago business trip when you followed me upstairs.”

"Oh, yeah," he said, smiling broadly. "Now that I do remember. I sure must have hit the target that day!"

"I'm not surprised," she answered. "You fired enough shots!"

"I feel really proud, Angel – I never thought I'd be a father at my age. It'll be great to have a kid in the house!"

"This is only the beginning, Joe," she assured him. "We'll have more. We'll make the name 'Morrelli' famous in New York.”

"Yeah," he grinned, "I can just see it now and it's all thanks to you. Breeding, that's what it's all about! The 'Morrelli' name is really going to mean something in this city. That's my dream, Angel – for all of us." He kissed her tenderly. "Of course, it'll mean a lot of overtime," he said, sounding amused.

"Oh, I'm sure you can handle it, Joe.”

"Angel, that's the one job I don't mind working extra hours at. Who knows, the Morrellis might go all the way to City Hall. And with your brains and my know-how, maybe even the White House!"

Angela went upstairs to tell Agnes the good news, while Joe went into the kitchen.

"Well, is Angela alright?" Rooney asked, anxiously.

"That depends," replied Joe.

"What's the matter with her? She scared me half to death. I thought she was a gonner.”

"She'll be o.k., in time, Rooney.”

"Well, what the hell's that supposed to mean?"

Joe raised his hands.

"Calm down," he said. Then throwing them in the air, "Angel's having a baby!"

He smiled broadly as Rooney's mouth dropped open. Evie's eyes widened in disbelief.

Rooney finally found his voice.

"You mean, that's what's wrong with her?"

"Yeah, I'm going to be a father. Can you believe it?"

"Joe, that's terrific!" smiled Rooney.

Evie leaned her back against the sink and folded her arms.

"Terrific for Mr Joe maybe, but what about poor Miss Angela?"

"And what's that supposed to mean?" asked Joe, looking at her with a puzzled look on his face.

"Well, I don't hear you complaining about headaches or see you fainting over." Then she turned and muttered into the sink, "But then women always did pay for a man's pleasure!"

Joe glanced at Rooney, then walked over to her.

"You know something, Evie? For someone who never married, you seem to know an awful lot about it."

Evie's head turned slowly and she looked Joe straight in the eye.

"I know, what I know!" she said.

There was no answer to that. Rooney got up from the table, smiling.

"She's just worried about Angela, Joe."

"That's right," replied Evie. "She's so young. Maybe you should have waited."

"Oh yeah, how long? Until I was shuffling around on my Zimmer frame?"

Evie put a defiant hand on her hip.

"Now don't you get shirty with me, Mr Joe! After all, we are going to have a baby in this house. The Lord be praised."

Joe leaned over to Rooney and pointed his finger at Evie's back.

"We," he whispered, "did she say – we?"

Rooney laughed loudly and put his arm around Joe's shoulder.

"Come on, Joe," he said, "let's have a drink. This is really something to celebrate!"

Later that evening, Angela was lying down so Joe went along to Agnes' room. As he opened the door she turned and smiled at him.

"Congratulations, Joe!"

"Yeah, it's great news," he said cheerfully, going over and sitting down in the chair opposite her. She was holding her rosary beads. "Am I disturbing you?"

"No, I'm always glad of your company, you know that."

Joe was silent for a moment, looking at the floor.

"Is something bothering you?" she enquired.

He raised his eyes.

"These headaches and things that Angel has, they'll go away. Won't they Agnes?"

"Of course they will. In another few weeks she'll be fine, once she gets some iron and vitamins. No woman feels well the first two or three months."

Joe shook his head.

"You know, I feel really guilty. She did tell me she wasn't well but I thought she was making excuses. I thought maybe she didn't want me anymore, maybe she'd realised I was too old for her, that she's made a mistake. I guess I'm just frightened of ever loosing her."

"Well, I wish she'd told me she wasn't feeling well," said Agnes. "I had no idea. I have to say one thing, my daughters didn't take after me. They've both become young mothers."

"That's another thing," commented Joe, "maybe she should have waited a year or two. To be honest, I thought she would. Sometimes I feel I've taken her youth away from her, that she should be out somewhere enjoying herself. After all, I had a good run," he said, lowering his voice and his eyes.

Agnes reached out and took his hand.

"Joe, listen to me. Angela loves you very much. She couldn't enjoy life if you weren't part of it. You are her life. She doesn't see you as being older, she never did. You were meant for each other. Angela always thought she wasn't good enough for you but she gets that from her father. Robert courted me for so long I thought he'd never marry me, so one night I asked him out right and do you know what he said? 'Agnes I wouldn't marry anyone else but I don't think I could make you happy. I'm not good enough for you. You deserve better.' No wonder it was such a long courtship. I didn't have Angela until I was in my thirties. Now, Sheila is different. She wanted Raymond since she was fourteen and she got him. Although, Robert had his doubts."

"What do you mean?" asked Joe.

"Well, Robert always thought Raymond really wanted Angela. He always wondered if Sheila had just been second choice. Anyway Joe, I'm going to pray that God will give you sons as well as daughters. I love both my girls but I can't help thinking if I'd had a son, he'd have done something to find out who murdered his father and dealt with the ones responsible."

"Would you have wanted that?"

"Yes. I know it might not seem right to you, but whoever killed Robert, killed me inside and tore my family apart. They are still walking around somewhere and enjoying life. Why, I could even have passed them on the street back home and not realised it. That's a hard thing to have to live with, Joe. They left my husband lying like a dead dog. I'll never forget it and neither will my Angela. She'll carry the memory to her grave, just like her mother will."

Joe looked at Agnes's face and was so sad at what he saw. A woman, old before her time. Sick and weak, when she should have been in her prime. Surrounded by people who cared, but lonely for the man she'd loved and lost. Existing from day to day, when she should have been planning for the future. Lost in the past. She caught him studying her. "I know," she said, nodding "I'm a sick, bitter woman. I wish I wasn't. But I can't help it, Joe. Someone, somewhere destroyed our lives and I wish I could live to see them brought to justice, but I know I never will." She smiled at him, warmly and affectionately. "Robert would have liked you, Joe. You've given Angela the strength to go on. You've given her a good life and you love her. Don't ever doubt her love for you. Promise me that. She's delighted she's having a baby – your baby. You have nothing to feel guilty about."

Joe got up and kissed her cheek.

"Angel has given me the two things I wanted most in this world. The two things all my money couldn't buy me. Her love and a child of my own. How could I ever doubt her? I'm the happiest man alive. Goodnight, Agnes. I'm glad we had this talk."

"So am I, Joe. Goodnight."

He closed the door of their bedroom quietly behind him and walked over to the bed. He sat down on the side of it and gazed at Angela, who was lying there with her eyes closed, wearing only a bathrobe. He bowed his head and kissed her cheek. She opened her eyes. "Hi, how are you feeling?" he asked, in a soft voice.

"I'm alright Joe. Just a little tired," she smiled.

"Can I get you anything?"

"No, I'm fine. I'm not hungry."

"Angel, you haven't eaten since lunch. Are you sure you don't want anything? Evie could make you a sandwich or something."

"No, really, Joe. I've had a shower and all I want to do is rest."

"O.k. honey. But I'm going to phone Dr Chapman first thing in the morning and get you the best gynaecologist in New York!"

"There's no need," she said, taking his hand. "He's already taken care of that. I have an appointment with a Dr Weissman, the day after tomorrow."

"I hope he's good," he replied, in a concerned voice.

"Well, Dr Chapman says he's the best."

"I'm glad to hear it. Only the best is good enough for my wife – and this time I'm going with you!"

Joe looked away and was silent for a few moments. Angela moved her hand until it rested on his arm. She squeezed gently.

"Joe, what's the matter?"

There was no answer, so her hand reached up to his face and she made him look at her. "I guess I'm feeling guilty," he replied. "I don't like to see you ill."

"Joe, I'm not ill, I'm having a baby! In a few week's I'll be fine."

"Angel, I honestly thought you were taking precautions. You know what I mean. With going to College and everything, I didn't think you'd want kids for a couple of years. I thought you would take Dean Prescott's advice and graduate first."

"Joe," she said, stroking his face, "I'm nineteen years old. I can go back to College after the baby's born. I don't have to miss out on anything. But you're forty. I wanted to give you a child of your own, so you could enjoy watching it grow and achieve things. I want to give you something. Is that so wrong?"

Her voice was filled with emotion.

"No, it's not wrong, Angel," he replied, gazing into her dark, blue eyes. "It's just that you're so young. I never expected it, that's all."

"I've spoiled things for you, haven't I?"

"What do you mean?"

"You were enjoying being back on the social scene, weren't you? All the dinner parties and functions with all the right people."

Joe leaned over her with a serious look on his face.

"Now you listen to me, Angel," he said. "Joe Morrelli doesn't put anything or anyone before his wife or his kid! I don't care about the rest of the world, only you. When you came home today and told me we were having a baby, I felt ten feet tall. No one ever made me feel like that." He looked down and placed his hand gently on her stomach. "I love you. And knowing there's part of me growing in there, makes me love you even more. I haven't given you anything compared to what you're giving me." He kissed her. "You've given up so much for me. That's why I sometimes wish I was a much younger man."

She put her arms around him and pulled him closer.

"I don't!" she insisted. "I like you just the way you are."

"You do?" he grinned.

"Yes I do. I like older men."

"No kidding?"

"Now, could I kid Joe Morrelli?" she beamed.

"I guess not," he nodded, "but you've made him one very happy man!"

Joe lay down beside Angela and slipped his arm around her waist.

"You know," he said, in a serious voice, Dean Prescott isn't exactly going to be overjoyed when he hears the news. He'll probably blow a fuse."

"You let me handle Dean Prescott. After all, it's not his baby I'm having, it's yours."

"Yeah, and you don't know how glad I am about that," smiled Joe, thinking back to the time when he thought Dean and Angela had gotten together. And how happy he was to be proved wrong. "And how glad I am that you married me," he added.

"You made it difficult to refuse," she smiled.

"Yeah well, I had my reasons! And I'll never regret them. Jesus, Angel, you smell so good," he whispered, kissing her long and passionately. Then he raised his head and looked at her with a mischievous glint in his eye. "About the headache. I don't suppose .."

"Don't you dare!" she warned him. "You know what Dr Chapman said."

"I was only kidding!" he laughed. "But I'll be honest with you, Angel, it's at times like this when I'm glad it's such a big bed."

"I hope you can last the pace!"

"Oh, I'll last he pace alright. I'll just find another way around it, that's all. You leave it to me," he grinned.

"Maybe you'll find yourself another woman," she said, trying to smile but with a serious hint in her voice.

Joe's grin faded as he studied her face.

"The only woman I want is right here," he assured her. "You're all I'll ever need. I love you Angel."

"I love you too, Joe Morrelli. And you're going to make a wonderful father!"

Angela came down to breakfast late that morning. As she entered the kitchen, Joe was sitting at the table talking to Evie and sorting out his mail. She joined him.

"How are you feeling this morning Miss Angela?" enquired Evie, full of concern.

"I'm fine, Evie."

"What would you like for breakfast?"

"Just some coffee and toast, please."

"Well, I'll give you some fruit juice as well. It's full of vitamins."

Joe looked up, beginning to feel like 'The Invisible Man' as Evie continued.

"You'll have to eat more, Miss Angela, especially now you're having a baby."

"But I never could eat much in the mornings, Evie."

"I know," she nodded, putting the fruit juice on the table, "but I'm going to make sure you have a proper lunch. We want that baby to be strong and healthy. Isn't that right, Mr Joe?"

"That's right, Evie," he agreed, happy to be brought into the conversation at last. "And with the meals you've been cooking lately, it'll probably weigh a ton! I know I'm starting to put on weight."

Evie looked at him sarcastically.

"Well, nobody told you to eat so much. It's Miss Angela who's pregnant!"

"Yeah, but maybe I'm the one with the symptoms," he smiled, rubbing his stomach.

"The one with the big head about it, most likely," she muttered, pouring the coffee for Angela.

Joe turned to her.

"Well, I'm very proud of being a father. After all, at forty it's quite an achievement."

"And I suppose you're going to take all the credit. Why, anyone would think to hear you talking, you got this baby all on your own, Mr Joe."

He smiled at Angela and winked.

"No, Evie, I had a lot of help which I enjoyed enormously!"

"Mr Joe, I'm surprised at you!" she replied, flustered and embarrassed. "I don't want to hear anymore about it."

"Don't worry, Evie, you're not going to. I'll leave it to your imagination."

"I don't use my imagination for things like that!"

"What, never?" asked Joe, sounding amused.

Evie didn't know where to look.

"My thoughts are with the Lord," she insisted, looking up towards the ceiling.

"Then that explains why you're working for me," muttered Joe, as Angela tried desperately to hide a broad smile. "Oh, I nearly forgot, honey, there's a letter for you," he said."

"It will probably be from Sheila."

"I don't think so," he replied, handing her a large envelope.

Angela looked at it, then sat it down on the table

"Aren't you going to open it?" he asked.

"Later Joe."

The longer it lay on the table, the more curious he became. He lifted it and examined it, back and front.

"Who's it from?" he asked. "Do you know?"

"I think it's my exam results."

Joe put it down and pushed it in front of her.

"Why don't you find out," he said, telling rather than asking.

"I don't really want to know what it says," she replied nervously.

"Well, I do. Come on, Angel. Please."

"Honestly, Joe, you're like a school boy!"

"But you have to open it sooner or later. You can't just leave it there."

"Alright," she said, lifting the envelope. "Here goes."

Evie came over to the table and stood in anticipation. All eyes were on the envelope as she opened it and took out a folded sheet of paper. Angela's face showed no emotion as she read it.

"What does it say?" asked Joe, in an anxious voice, almost dreading the answer.

"It says I've passed with top grades and I'm getting a Certificate of Excellence for the English Literature."

She smiled as she handed him the paper.

Joe took it and read the contents. He nodded with pleasure and pride.

"Oh, Miss Angela!" cried Evie, clasping her hands. "Why, it's just wonderful!"

"Thank you, Evie," she smiled, putting a grateful hand on her arm.

Joe held the paper up and pointed to it.

"Does this mean you've got A's?"

Angela nodded.

"I didn't think I'd do so well with the others. I put all the effort into the Literature course."

"Well, they must have seen that. A Certificate of Excellence! Honey, what can I say? It's just terrific." He got up and put his arm around her. "I'm so proud of you."

"I know," she nodded.

He held her hands and kissed her. Evie watched, overcome with emotion. She made no attempt to stifle her sobs.

"Your father would have been a proud man today, Angel," whispered Joe. "I know I am. One day you'll go back and graduate. He would have wanted that and so do I. You've got what it takes and I'm going to make sure nothing stands in your way." He looked at Evie and smiled.

"I might have waited a long time but I couldn't have done any better in my choice of a wife. What do you say, Evie?"

"Oh, Mr Joe," said Evie, drying her face with her handkerchief, "you couldn't have done any better than Miss Angela and that's for sure! I told you once, it was a lucky night you met her." He smiled down at Angela and nodded.

"Yeah, you did," he agreed. "And I'll never forget just how lucky I was."

At that moment, the back door opened and Rooney appeared. He looked around at all the smiling faces - particularly Joe's!

"What's going on?" he asked.

Joe beamed,

"My wife got her exam results from the College this morning."

"Well?"

"She got top grades, Rooney. What do you think of that?"

When Rooney saw Joe filled with such pride he couldn't help but feel happy for him. He smiled broadly and said, "That's great news!" he went over and hugged Angela.

"Congratulations, Angela! All that hard work paid off after all."

"And," emphasised Joe, strutting up and down, "not only did she get top grades, Rooney, but she's only getting a Certificate of Excellence! Can you beat that?"

Rooney smiled at her.

"I'm really pleased for you, Angela. I always knew you had brains, from the first time I met you."

"So did I!" chimed Joe. Angela and Rooney stared at him. "Well, maybe not the first time," he shrugged.

"Or the second, or the third," Rooney whispered into her ear.

"But I knew," Joe continued, "as time went by."

Rooney nudged Angela.

"I suppose you're going to frame this certificate, Joe."

"Now, that's a good idea." He looked thoughtful for a moment. "Yeah, I'm going to get it framed and hang it where everyone can see it."

"Honestly, Joe, anyone would think I'd won the Nobel Prize," laughed Angela. "Sit down!"

"Well, just think about it," he replied, obeying. "When you join all those ladies committees, they'll have to make you chairwoman because you'll be able to talk them all under the table."

"Just like you're doing now," she muttered.

"Believe me, honey," Joe went on, "they will all want your advice and ideas. You just wait and see. These women only think they know it all but wait till they meet Mrs Joe Morrelli."

Angela lifted her coffee cup.

"I think one know-all in the family's enough," she whispered. "Unless we dress Joe in ladies clothes and send him."

Rooney burst out laughing.

"I can just see it!"

"See what?" enquired Joe.

Rooney coughed,

"A Morrelli on the ladies committee," he explained.

"Yeah, it's really going to be something," smiled Joe, proudly.

"It sure is - if it's you, Joe," Rooney muttered, looking at Angela.

They both started to smile as Evie poured fresh coffee.

Joe looked at Angela as she and Rooney talked about exams. She had many gifts. He was proud she was his wife but couldn't help but feel a little sad. She has passed tough exams and he knew how hard she'd worked but instead of going back to College for a career, she was now three months pregnant and only nineteen years old. Angela had given up a lot to have his baby and she had done it for him. She has also given up the best years of her life to become his wife. Thinking back to the day he proposed to her he now knew he hadn't realised just what he was asking of her. He couldn't change that, but as he gazed at her he made himself a silent promise that he would, when the time was right. He would make it up to her. Later on, she would enjoy her life and Joe would do everything he could to get her the place in society she deserved and the happiness he wanted her to have.

When her conversation with Rooney had ended, Angela got up from the table and lifting a breakfast tray, she started to lay it.

"Miss Angela, I don't want you running up and down stairs carrying things in your condition. I'll bring that up to your mother," said Evie, coming across the kitchen.

"It's alright Evie, I'll do it. You have enough to do down here," Angela replied, lifting the tray and walking out of the kitchen.

Evie watched her leave.

"You know, Mr Joe, if there were more people like Miss Angela this world would be a better place. There she goes, just the way she does every morning. Why, you wouldn't think she'd passed such important exams." She shook her head. "Miss Angela will never rise above herself, Mr Joe. She has her feet too firmly on the ground. She's a lady in every sense of the word."

"Yeah, she is," agreed Joe, following her gaze. "And in time I'm going to make sure everybody knows it." He looked at Rooney. "And that's a promise."

"One I know you'll keep, Joe, nodded Rooney. "I've known you too long to think otherwise. She's one in a million."

"Yeah, she sure is and Joe Morrelli found her against all those odds!" he replied in a low, emotional voice.

Joe and Rooney were just about to enter the study when Joe stopped and looked towards the stairs.

"You go on in, Rooney. I won't be long."

Rooney nodded.

"O.k. Joe. I'll get the files out and make a start."

He closed the door while Joe crossed the entrance hall and went upstairs. There was no sign of Angela, so he stood outside their bedroom door and waited. A short time later, she came out of her mother's room and along the landing.

"What are you doing, Joe?" she asked surprised "Is something wrong?"

"No, nothings wrong," he smiled. "I was just wondering if you'd like to go out somewhere tonight? You know to celebrate. We could go to Mario's. But only if you're feeling up to it."

Angela smiled back.

"I've got a better idea," she replied, putting her arms around his waist. "Why don't we have a nice dinner for two right here, listen to some music and have an early night?"

He put his arms around her shoulders and hugged her close.

"I think that's a great idea but maybe we should wait another week or two, just to make sure everything's o.k. for the baby. After all, you're just the three months, Angel."

"Wrong," she said, looking at him. "I'm past the three months now."

Joe took a step back.

"Do you mean you've been holding out on me?" he joked.

"I didn't know myself until Dr Weissman counted up the dates for me."

"Well, good for Dr Weissman!" he smiled, broadly. "Now that's one guy I don't mind paying."

"I thought you'd be pleased."

"Angel, I'm always pleased to hear good news."

"He said I was fine and the baby is safe, so everything is alright. I asked him."

Joe drew her close to him once more.

"I don't suppose you thought to ask him if you could have some champagne."

She pinched him playfully.

"I don't need champagne for you, Joe!"

"Yeah, I know - but it helps!"

She looked at him, knowingly.

"What you really mean, Joe Morrelli, is that you think it goes to my head."

"Amongst other places!" he grinned.

"Oh, I see," she nodded.. "Well, in that case I don't suppose one or two glasses will endanger my health."

"Even if they're very large glasses?" he teased.

"I think I could manage that."

"Well, it is a special occasion, Angel."

"For who, you or me?"

"For both of us, thanks to Dr Weissman!"

"Honestly Joe!" laughed Angela, shaking her head.

At that moment, he put his finger to her lips so she could not continue.

"I'm being serious now, Angel," he said, looking into her face. "I might have gone on a bit downstairs, about the exams and everything, But I just want to tell you in private how proud I am of you, honey, and I always will be." He held her tightly and kissed her gently. "Now, I'd better get back to business."

As they parted he turned to walk away, then stopped and looked over his shoulder.

"Are you sure that doctor's right about the weeks? I only make it four."

Angela put her hands on her hips.

"Joe Morrelli, have you been keeping count?"

"Every day, Angel. I have the calendar in my study to prove it."

She turned her eyes up towards the ceiling.

"I don't believe you sometimes. And here I was, thinking you didn't know how long to wait."

"Angel, I'm only human. My body kept reminding me of that from time to time," he said in an amused voice as he walked to the top of the stairs.

"Well, so much for your calendar," she replied. "You were wrong anyway."

"Maybe, but the doctor has put it right and he should know."

"That was an underhanded thing to do, Joe Morrelli."

He looked at her and held out his hands.

"I'll be even more underhanded tonight - when we're under the covers! Oh, and by the way, Angel, remind me to say a thanks - giving prayer for Dr Weissman at dinner."

"Why?"

"Because I'll be too busy later on to remember!"

Joe sang happily as he went downstairs, leaving Angela to watch and shake her head. Then she smiled to herself. She had to admit that he had been very caring and patient over the last few weeks, and had showed his love by the way he'd treated her. He was a good husband who'd given her a lot of attention and showed her a lot of respect. She loved him. But then, it would be hard not to love a man like Joe Morrelli. And with his wit and charm, life was never dull!

When Angela was five months pregnant, she and Joe decided to make one of the unused bedrooms into a nursery. The decorators were called in and Joe left all the details, such as wallpaper and colour schemes to Angela who knew exactly what she wanted. As he sat in his study, he could hear the sound of the workers coming and going and couldn't help but notice that Evie was doing the same. She was never around as often as she used to be but he didn't pay much attention. She was probably helping upstairs.

Unknown to Joe, Evie was taking a great interest in the nursery. She has always been very house proud and liked everything to be just right, so when the two workmen came she decided to keep a check on what they were doing.

They had started to put the wallpaper on that day, so she went upstairs to have a look. As she entered the nursery, she surveyed everything with the eyes of an eagle.

"Excuse me," she said, making both men turn around. "Are you sure that paper's straight?"

"Where?" asked the first one, who happened to be the senior employee.

"Over there," she replied, pointing to one of the walls.

"The paper's straight alright. It's the shape of the wall, it slants a little," he said.

"Well, I hope you're right, we don't want any mistakes. My employer would like a perfect job done on this room. That would be his wish."

He turned his face to the wall and muttered, "I wish you'd disappear!"

"I heard that! Let me remind you you're being paid good money for this work."

He turned back to her and bowed.

"Yes, your majesty," he said.

Meanwhile downstairs, Joe had gone to the kitchen for some coffee. He lifted the percolator. It was empty.

"Where is that woman?" he said out loud. "She's never around when you need her."

He slammed the coffee pot down and walked out of the kitchen. He spied the workman coming down the stairs, followed by Evie.

"I'm going to lunch, Mr Morrelli and with any luck I'll meet with an accident!" he said, looking back at her.

"What's going on?" enquired Joe, as the workman left.

"Oh, don't mind him, Mr Joe, he's the cheeky one," she replied, walking towards the kitchen.

Joe went upstairs and looked into the nursery. He was surprised to see the second decorator, a black man around fifty, still working on.

"Hi there, how are you doing?" smiled Joe, gazing around him. "Aren't you going to lunch too?"

"No Sir. The boss wants me to work through," came the reply.

Joe nodded but thought to himself, "Maybe this is the reason why Evie's upstairs most of the time!"

The kitchen door opened and Joe came in with the decorator.

"Evie," he said, "I'd like you to meet Mr…"

"Smith," came the reply.

"Smith? Now there's an unusual name," smiled Joe.

"Yes Sir, Isaiah Smith."

Joe pulled out a chair and motioned Mr Smith to sit down.

"Well, tell me, Mr Smith are you married?"

"No, Sir. I never felt the need. I'm pretty much a church going man."

"Now there's a coincidence," smiled Joe, putting his hands in his pockets while Evie stared at him. "My housekeeper never married and she's a real pillar of the church. So much so, I'll be very surprised if they don't name a pillar after her one of these days!"

Evie cast her eyes and looked away. Undeterred, Joe continued.

"Evie, I'd like you to give Mr Smith here some lunch. She's a terrific cook, you know." he added, into Mr Smith's ear.

"Oh, Mr Joe!" smiled Evie, embarrassed but grateful. He looked at his watch.

"Well. I'll have to go now. Nice meeting you, Mr Smith."

"Nice to meet you, Sir. Thank you, Sir," replied Mr Smith getting up from the chair.

Joe put a hand on his shoulder, making him sit down again saying,

"Enjoy your lunch, you're in good hands!"

He smiled at Evie as he left the kitchen, closing the door behind him.

He was just about to go into the study, when Angela came down the stairs.

"Joe, have you seen Evie?" she asked.

He rested his hand on the handle of the door.

"Yeah, she's in the kitchen - entertaining."

"You mean, the decorator?" she smiled broadly, as Joe nodded. "How did he get there?"

"I brought him down for lunch. At least now she'll have to stay in there and with any luck we'll all get something to eat!" he grinned.

Angela came over and put her arms around him.

"Are you sure that's the only reason?" she quizzed.

"If you start playing cupid we might loose a good housekeeper."

"I don't think so," he replied, shaking his head. "And besides, if a white guy can take his lunch break, so can Mr Smith! This is my house and I'm paying their wages."

Angela reached up and kissed his cheek.

"You're a kind man, Joe Morrelli."

He shrugged his shoulders and opened the study door.

"I like to think of it as just being fair, Angel."

She nodded in agreement as he kissed her forehead and went inside.

Angela's pregnancy and the thought of a nursery breathed new life into Agnes. She started coming downstairs more often and wanted to be a part of everything that was happening. She and Joe were sitting in the lounge when Angela came in and announced, "That's the nursery completed."

She smiled as she held up the key.

"Don't tell me I'm finally going to get to see it!" said Joe, winking at Agnes.

"You're both going to see it. Come on," insisted Angela leading the way.

Agnes took Joe's arm and they followed her upstairs. They stopped outside the door and watched as she turned the key and opened it.

"Well what do you think?" she asked, as all three stepped inside.

Joe could hardly believe his eyes, the room had been totally transformed. He was looking at bright, patterned wallpaper; expensive drapes; deep rich carpet and new furniture. In the middle of the room stood a baby's crib of white satin and lace with matching cover. Hanging from the ceiling above it were little birds and animals that chimed soft music as they moved around in a circle. A selection of soft, cuddly toys sat along the window seat.

Agnes put her hands up and clasped them.

"Oh, Angela, it's beautiful!"

"It sure is," agreed Joe.

"Do you really like it?" she smiled.

"Honey, its terrific. Just terrific," he replied, in a choked voice.

"You turn the chimes on from here," explained Angela, going over to a switch beside the door and pressing it to stop the music.

Agnes touched Joe's arm affectionately.

"Joe have you ever seen anything like it? I bet you can't wait to see your baby in here."

"I'm counting the days!"

"Joe's very good at that mum," said Angela, gazing at him.

They both smiled.

Joe looked around, for fear of having missed anything.

"You've done a great job, Angel," he praised.

"Well only the best is good enough for Joe Morrelli's baby!"

"Now that's very true," he grinned, nodding his head. "Why don't we all go downstairs and have a drink to celebrate?"

"That's a good idea," smiled Agnes.

She and Joe went out onto the landing, then looked back.

"Aren't you coming, Angela?"

"I'll be along in a few minutes, mum. You go on with Joe."

They left her gazing longingly at the crib, smoothing the cover gently with her hand and running her fingers along the ruffles of lace.

"She's so happy Joe," said Agnes, as he helped her down the stairs.

"We both are, Agnes."

"I know," she nodded. "Can I tell you something?"

"Sure."

"I liked you from the first time I ever met you."

"Yeah, no kidding?"

"I knew you were a good man."

"And what about later, when you realised I was falling in love with your daughter?"

She stopped and looked at him.

"I prayed it would happen."

"Even though I was twice her age?"

"What has age got to do with anything when you're in love? In fact, I think Angela was in love with you long before she would admit it, even to herself."

Joe smiled and joked,

"Well, I'll say one thing for you Kenny's - you sure can keep a secret !"

Agnes smiled as they continued on.

"I suppose you had a few anxious moments, Joe."

"A few? Agnes, that's the understatement of the year."

"I used to have my doubts about bringing Angela to America but now I'm glad I did."

"So am I. You'll never know how much."

"Oh, I think I do," she insisted. "After all, I am your mother-in-law. And speaking as such, have you noticed that Angela isn't putting on a lot of weight Joe?"

"Yeah, I did notice it and I had a word with Dr Weissman. He says it's early days yet. She'll probably gain it all in the last eight or nine weeks. Don't worry about it according to him, I'll probably have to buy a crane to get her up and down the stairs!" he grinned .

Agnes laughed as he continued, "One thing's for sure, she's gaining weight up top. We're going to have the best fed baby in New York! But I'm not complaining Agnes, I quite like it. That's going to be one lucky baby!"

"Oh Joe, trust you to think of that!" she smiled, slapping his arm, playfully. "I'm so excited. I never got to hold my first two grandchildren but I'm going to hold this one and I can't wait."

Suddenly, she stopped and gripped him tightly. She was starting to loose her breath. "Agnes, are you alright?" he asked, anxiously. She breathed deeply for a few moments, then nodded. When she'd recovered she leaned towards him.

"The old ticker hasn't been the same since Robert died, "she whispered. "You might not think it to look at me now, but I was a strong, healthy woman until that day."

Joe put his arms around her, thinking, "There are other ways to kill people, without ever pulling a trigger."

"Come on," she said, patting his back, "let's go and get that drink."

They made their way slowly to the bottom of the stairs.

"Joe, can I baby-sit for you and Angela?" she asked, sounding cheerful "I'd love to sit in that nursery with my grandchild."

"Of course you can! But I've got to tell you, Evie has her name down too."

"Oh, I don't mind that, Evie and me get on well. We can sit in the nursery together."

He leaned towards her.

"Just as long as there's no fighting on the premises."

"What do you mean?" she asked, surprised.

"Well, if you and Evie want a punch up over who will hold it, I'll arrange it at Stacey's Gym. But you'll have to go by the rules - no pulling each others hair!" he grinned.

"Oh honestly Joe," she laughed, "for a minute I thought you were serious!"

As they were walking into the lounge, the telephone rang.

"I'll get it honey," called Joe, as Angela came down the stairs.

He lifted the receiver and spoke pleasantly to the person on the other end for a few moments. Then he put it down gently by the side of the phone and walked towards the kitchen.

"Evie," he shouted, "it's Mr Smith."

Evie came out of the kitchen so fast she almost collided with him.

"Where?" she whispered in a panic, looking around.

"On the phone," he pointed.

She went over and lifted the receiver, staring at Joe who guided Angela into the lounge half closing the door behind them. He stood behind it in anticipation. Evie's voice was polite and nervous throughout the short conversation. When she had finished, Joe put his head round the door.

"What did he want?" he enquired.

She straightened her apron, looking embarrassed. "Oh, Mr Joe, he wants to escort me to the Church Social on Sunday afternoon."

"What did you say?"

"Why, I was so surprised I said 'yes'. But what will the congregation say? What will my minister think?"

Joe turned to look at Angela and Agnes.

"He'll think he's witnessing a miracle!" he muttered, then turning back to Evie, "You go and enjoy yourself with Mr Smith, "he said in a patronising voice. "What harm can it do?"

"Oh I don't know, Mr Joe. I don't want anyone to think I'm a loose woman!" she replied, walking towards the kitchen in a daze.

Joe shook his head and smiled, "I sure hope Mr Smith wears something with pockets."

"Why?" asked Angela.

"Because it's the only place he'll get to put his hands!"

Evie's voice was heard singing loudly from the kitchen, "Swing low sweet chariot, coming for to carry me home…."

He looked at the two women and grinned.

"If he tries anything someone will have to carry her home, only it won't be in a chariot - it'll be on a stretcher!"

Joe told Rooney about Evie and Mr Smith, he in turn told Frankie and Al. On the morning of the Church Social, she was up earlier than usual and standing baking when the back door opened and Frankie and Al came in. Al walked up behind her and put his head over her shoulder.

"I hear you've got a hot date," he smiled.

"And I hear you've got an appointment at the hospital," she replied, giving him one of her looks.

"Me? What for?"

"For the large lump I'm going to inflict on your head!" she warned, waving a wooden rolling pin. Frankie burst out laughing as Al hurried over to him, out of harm's way.

"Oh, come on, Eive" he said, once out of reach, "aren't you just a little excited?"

She carried on with her work.

"Why should I be excited? It's a Church Social with lots of people."

He turned to Frankie.

"At least she's safe enough," he whispered. "There's not a lot he can do in a place like that."

"Besides," Evie continued, stopping for a moment and looking thoughtful, "I'm not the excitable type. After all, we'll be in the Lord's house."

"I could think of a better house to be in!" he muttered.

She spun round and stared at him.

"Well, it wouldn't do you any harm to go now and again instead of the house you do visit."

"Oh yeah? Well, maybe I'm not like you," he shrugged. "Maybe I am the excitable type!"

"If you are it surely doesn't last long or you wouldn't be poking your nose into other peoples business."

"She's right Al," said Frankie, grinning broadly. "You should get yourself a steady girlfriend."

"I'm working on it!" snapped Al, looking very annoyed.

"You've been working on it for years."

"That's right," said Evie, "and so far I haven't heard of any women being trampled in the rush."

She smiled smugly.

Al looked at Frankie.

"Who's side are you on, anyway?" he sulked.

After lunch, Evie went to her room to get ready. Joe and Rooney came out of the study to find Frankie and Al standing in the entrance hall.

"What are you two hanging around here for?" asked Joe.

"I'm waiting for Rooney, Boss," said Frankie quickly.

"And who are you waiting for?" he asked, turning to Al and staring at him.

Al bowed his head and started to shuffle his feet. Frankie nudged him.

"Go on, tell him," he smiled.

"Evie," came the reply, in a low voice.

"What was that? I didn't hear you," Joe pretended.

Al looked up at him sheepishly.

"I'm waiting for Evie, Boss."

"Why?"

"I just want to see if she's wearing 'that hat'!"

"Well, would you both mind waiting over there?"

Joe pointed to a corner, then looked at Rooney and shook his head.

"What do you do with these guys?" he asked, as Rooney laughed.

Angela came out of the lounge and on seeing the four men standing around asked, "Have I missed Evie?"

"No honey, you're just in time," said Joe, as he watched Evie's door open.

Out she came, walking up the entrance hall dressed in a floral dress and a large hat.

"Well, would you look at that," said Rooney, in a low voice. "Evie's just full of surprises."

"You can say that again," replied Frankie. "She's switched from fruit to feathers!"

All eyes and attention went to the hat which was richly decorated with large, brightly coloured feathers.

"Hey Evie, you look great. Doesn't she?"

Joe shot a warning look at the others who, having been rendered speechless, nodded their heads in agreement.

Evie smiled, appreciatively.

"Oh, thank you, Miss Angela. Thank you Mr Joe."

Just then the door bell rang.

"That'll be Mr Smith," said Joe, glancing at his watch. "And he's right on time. Leave this to me." He went over and opened the front door.

"Mr Smith. Come in," he smiled.

"Thank you, Sir."

Isaiah Smith stepped inside and acknowledged the gathering.

Evie stepped closer to Angela.

"Oh, Miss Angela," she whispered, anxiously, "do I really look alright? I mean, I'm not overdressed or anything?"

"You're fine, Evie. Now don't be nervous. Come on, Mr Smith's waiting."

Evie went towards the door and everyone followed. Mr Smith watched as she drew closer.

"Why Miss Evie, you look mighty fine," he smiled.

"Thank you," she nodded.

Joe held the door open for them.

"Have a nice time."

"Yes Sir, we will," assured Mr Smith. Then looking directly at Joe he said, "Thank you, Sir."

"Hey, Evie, don't eat too much!" joked Al.

She threw him one of her looks.

"Why everyone knows I eat like a bird," she replied smiling up at Mr Smith, shyly.

After Angela waved them 'goodbye', Joe closed the door and everyone huddled around the hall window to watch them drive off.

As Mr Smith's old car pulled out of the driveway, all was silent until Al spoke, "Why everyone knows I eat like a bird," he said, mimicking Evie's voice. Then he turned to the others. "I don't know about eating like one, but I think she's got one on her head!" he grinned.

"You know, if she's not back by eight o'clock, I'm going to be very worried," said Joe.

"Why, Boss?" asked Al, his grin fading.

"Because she'll have probably flown south for the winter!" he shrugged and walked away smiling.

Al slapped Frankie's shoulder.

"Hey, that's a good one, Boss."

"Yeah?" asked Joe, turning round. "Well, I've got an even better one. If you don't get back to work you'll be seeing even more feathers."

"How come?"

"You'll be in Central Park and unemployed - just like the pigeons!"

Angela cleared away the dishes from the kitchen table as Joe studied his boxing manual. The back door opened and Evie walked in. Glancing at his watch, Joe saw it had just gone seven.

"Well, Evie, how did it go?" asked Angela. "Did you have a good time?"

"It was fine, Miss Angela. Just fine," she replied, smiling.

"Then come and tell me all about it."

Angela sat down at the table, pulling out a chair for her.

"Well, there's not a lot to tell."

"How did you get on with Mr Smith?"

"Oh, he's a gentleman, Miss Angela."

"What did the minister think of him?" enquired Joe, looking over the manual.

"Why, he was quite taken with him, Mr Joe," she smiled. "Especially during the prayer meeting. I've never known a man who could praise the Lord as loudly as he can. There he was, waving his hands in the air."

"Well, at least he got to use them!" muttered Joe, returning to his manual.

Evie continued, oblivious.

"Afterwards at the social, I introduced him to everyone and they liked him."

"And what about you, Evie?" smiled Angela. "Do you like him?"

"Yes I do, Miss Angela. Isaiah Smith is going to be a very good friend."

Joe put his manual down.

"I take it we're not going to hear the sound of wedding bells?"

She looked at him, somewhat surprised.

"Mr Joe, how could you even think that? I couldn't up and leave you after all this time. And there's Miss Angela having a baby. No! I'm going to be here just like always."

Joe and Angela looked at each other and smiled.

"You know something, Evie?" he said. "I'm really glad to hear it. This house wouldn't be the same without you."

"Really?"

"Really," he nodded.

She sat beaming, happy in her own thoughts.

Angela put her arm around her.

"It's good to have a friend like Mr Smith, Evie."

"Yes it is, Miss Angela. I just hope Mr Joe remembers that the next time he goes spreading rumours!"

"I won't say a word," Joe promised, putting his hands up.

"Oh, yes you will," Evie demanded, staring at him. "You're going to put everyone straight about my friendship with Mr Smith - especially that driver of yours!"

"O.k. O.k.!!"

She got up from the table.

"Well, I'll just go and change and then I'll start dinner."

"There's no need, Evie," said Angela, "We've already eaten. Joe's going to a boxing match."

Joe smiled and held up the manual.

"Yeah, I'd better go and get ready," he said, getting up.

On the way to her room, Evie stopped at the kitchen door and looked back at them.

"You know," she said, thoughtfully, "I really like this house and I'm going to like it even more when there's a baby in it. I just can't see myself living anywhere else."

"Neither can I," whispered Joe.

"Evie, don't you ever get fed up looking after all the men in this house?" asked Angela.

"Men? Why Miss Angela, in some ways they are all still babies. They grow up in some ways but not in others. And believe me, I should know!"

She looked at Joe, before turning and closing the door after her.

Angela got up and put her arms around his waist.

"She likes you so much, Joe. That's one housekeeper who'll never leave."

"I've had that feeling from the first day she arrived here!" he joked, putting his arm around her shoulder. "You know, Angel," he continued, as they walked towards the door, "you, me, your mom, Evie and the guys, we're all one big, happy family and I don't ever want that to change. I like everything just the way it is!"

Chapter 11

Evie said "goodbye" as she left for the market. Angela came along the landing that morning with a breakfast tray, the way she always did. She opened the door to Agnes's room and after setting the tray down on the bedside table, she turned to the large armchair at the window.

"Good morning mum," she said. "I didn't think you'd be up this early. I've brought you your breakfast. Let me make you more comfortable and I'll tell you all about my plans for today."

Angela leaned her mother forward and proceeded to prop up the cushions while telling her what a lovely morning it was. Suddenly Agnes slumped forward. Angela bent down and asked anxiously,

"Mum, what's wrong?"

Agnes made no reply but fell heavily to the floor, landing on her side. Angela quickly got down on her knees pleading loudly,

"Mum! Mum!"

Agnes's face was badly twisted and her eyes were glazed. Angela panicked.

"Mum - talk to me, please! Please mum!"

She put her arms around her mother and tried to lift her. She was struggling with the weight when suddenly a sharp pain cut right through her stomach. Almost loosing her breath, she tried to get up but the pain was so severe she couldn't move.

"Joe!" she screamed towards the open door "Joe! Rooney! Somebody come!"

Agnes's feeble hand gripped Angela's. Her mouth moved but no words would come. Heavy footsteps could be heard racing up the stairs. Rooney and Frankie burst into the room.

"Jesus Christ!" yelled Rooney, as he hurried over to Angela and tried to lift her. "Don't!" she screamed, holding her stomach. "I can't move. See to my mother." Rooney turned to Frankie,

"Get Joe - he's in the study, and call an ambulance. Hurry!"

Rooney then knelt down beside Agnes, he felt her neck and checked her pulse. Angela cried,

"Is she alright, Rooney? Is she alive?"

Just at that Joe rushed in and taking in the scene at one glance, ran over to Angela and kneeling down took her in his arms.

"Angel, honey!"

Angela was sobbing.

"Oh Joe! The baby. I'm going to loose it."

Joe stroked her hair and cradled her gently. She was trembling.

"What about my mum?" she asked, almost knowing the answer already.

Joe looked at Rooney, who shook his head. Angela saw. "My God!" she screamed as she tightened her grip on her husband's arm. "They've killed my father. They've killed my mother and now they're trying to kill my baby! What more can they do to me, dear God! What more?"

Within minutes two paramedics arrived and after quickly checking Agnes they turned their attentions to Angela.

"How far on is she?" one of them asked as they unfolded a stretcher.

"Seven and a half months," replied Joe in a distressed voice.

They lifted Angela gently and placed her on the stretcher. She was moaning loudly now, the pain increasing with every movement that passed.

"We'll send someone back to check out the death of the old lady," the paramedic informed Joe. "But better see to your wife first."

They carried Angela out of the room and down the stairs to the waiting ambulance. Joe followed, ashen faced. He climbed into the back of the ambulance, took his wife's hand and held it up to his lips.

Rooney watched from the hall window as the speeding ambulance made it's way out of the drive and onto the main road.

When it reached the hospital, Angela was rushed to the emergency room. Joe was by her side, still holding her hand.

A doctor arrived almost immediately and introduced himself as Dr Phillip Henley. Joe explained what had happened. The doctor then asked him to wait outside while he conducted his examination. A young nurse showed Joe into a waiting room. Minutes later the doctor arrived with a worried look on his face.

"Mr Morrelli, your wife is in deep shock and I'm afraid she had injured herself internally - quite badly. We'll have to operate at once to try and save the baby. Will you sign this consent form?"

Joe took the form from the doctor's hand and somehow managed to scribble his signature on it. The doctor turned to go but Joe grabbed him by the arm saying, "Doctor, whatever it takes, whatever you have to do, just do it. No matter what it costs."

The doctor nodded and then hurried out of the room. Joe followed, and stood in the corridor watching, as a team of doctors and nurses wheeled Angela to the operating theatre. He knew by the expressions on their faces - it was panic stations. He felt sick with panic himself as he returned to the waiting room and sat down, resting his head in his hands. Rooney appeared at the door, clearly out of breath.

"Joe, what's happening?" he gasped.

Joe looked up and joined his hands as if in prayer.

"I don't know, Rooney," he replied "I just don't know."

The two men sat in silence. Joe kept looking at his watch. He felt like he'd been in that room for an eternity. Finally, he got up, walked over to the window and stared out onto the busy streets in silent anger. Then he turned to Rooney,

"I'll tell you something now. If anything happens to my wife and child, someone, somewhere will pay. By God Joe Morrelli will make them pay!"

He yelled in an enraged yet tearful voice as he wiped the sweat from his brow with a shaking hand. Rooney, for the first time in his life, had seen Joe Morrelli in a way he never thought he'd see him - as a broken man. But he understood how Joe felt. Joe loved Angela - but then so did he! He got up from the chair, stubbing out his cigarette on a glass ashtray.

"I think I'll get some coffee. Do you want some?"

"Yeah," came the reply

The coffee was really just an excuse. Rooney thought it best if they both had a little time on their own.

After Rooney left, tears filled Joe Morrelli's eyes. He put his fist up to his mouth and bit on it so as to stifle any sound. Then he turned and pressed the same fist against the cold, concrete wall.

"Oh God," he pleaded. "I'm not a religious man, but please don't take away the two things I've wanted most in my life. Please!"

A while later, Rooney returned with the coffee.

More time went by.

Then the door opened and Doctor Henley appeared in a gown and cap, removing a surgical mask from his mouth.

"Mr Morrelli."

Joe and Rooney sprang to their feet together. Joe took a few steps forward.

"Mr Morrelli, congratulations - you have a son!"

For a few seconds Joe found himself unable to speak.

Then the words came,

"Is he o.k.?"

"Well, he's in intensive care. You must remember that he is six weeks premature. Besides that , he does have some breathing problems. However, he does seem to be a strong little fella and that's certainly in his favour. I'd say he'll be o.k. Mr Morrelli."

"Thank God! But what about my wife, doctor? Is she o.k.?"

"She will be, given time and plenty of rest. But I would like a few words with you - alone."

Rooney immediately left the room and waited in the corridor.

"Mr Morrelli," the doctor continued, "your wife had serious complications. In fact she's lucky to be alive. But I'm afraid she will never be able to have any more children. I'm sorry, truly I am."

Joe was clearly shaken by the news.

"I understand. Can I see her, doctor?"

"Well, she's heavily sedated but you can go in for a few minutes. After that, I'm sure you'd like to see your son."

"You better believe it!" came the reply. Joe shook Doctor Henley's hand and said "I want to thank you, Doctor, for everything. I owe you and I won't forget it."

Both men stepped out into the corridor. The doctor called to one of the nurses,

"Show Mr Morrelli to room 354, please."

Joe turned to Rooney

"Wait for me, will you Rooney?"

"Sure Joe."

Joe entered room 354 and closed the door quietly behind him. He approached the bed. Angela lay pale and drawn, with tubes and wires attached to her arms and body. Joe stood over her and fighting back the tears he lifted her hand and gently caressed her fingers. He leaned forward and kissed her forehead. "I love you, Angel," he said softly. "I always have and I always will."

Then putting her hand back down onto the bedcovers he turned and left the room.

He hurried back to the waiting room.

"Come on," he motioned to Rooney. "We're going to see my son!"

Joe and Rooney peered through the large glass window. The nurse did her best to turn the crib at an angle so the newly born baby could be seen. There he lay, tiny and helpless - with a head of black hair! Wires and patches led from his chest to a number of machines.

"Hey!" said Joe, smiling proudly and nudging Rooney with his elbow.

"That's my son. That's part of me lying there and believe me, Rooney, he's going to have all the things I never had!"

After they came away, Joe turned to Rooney,

"I want you to go back to the house and take care of things. Make a note of any important calls and put everything else on hold. Make arrangements for Agnes's body to be kept in the morgue until I can talk to Angel."

"No sweat, Joe. I'll see to everything."

"There's one more thing. Call Reuben, Gene O'Brien and the others. Let them know what's happened. I'll call Antonia and tell her myself."

The two men parted company in the lobby and Joe made his way to the phone booth.

Rooney hesitated and then followed him.

"Joe, will you let me know about Angela? When she comes around, I mean, and if she's o.k.?"

Joe put his hand on Rooney's shoulder and squeezed it knowingly.

You'll be the first to know. I promise."

Rooney smiled rather sadly and nodded his head.

"Thanks Joe."

Joe dialled Antonia's number and dropped the coins into the box. He told her everything that had happened. Of course, she wanted to come to the hospital straight away but Joe persuaded her not to. He wanted to be on his own. He needed time to think. So much had happened in such a short time. It was only beginning to sink in. He went back to room 354, lifted a chair, placed it beside Angela's bed and sat down to keep a vigil. As he sat looking at her, all sorts of things were going through his mind. Bits of his life flashed before him as though he were a drowning man.

The first time he ever saw Angela Kenny. The first time he walked her home. The first time he kissed her. Their wedding. The honeymoon. When she told him she was pregnant. How happy she'd made him. Thank God she was still alive and there with him. He couldn't picture his life without her.

And Agnes. Poor Agnes. So honest and loyal. All the little things she used to tell him about her husband and family. The secrets she shared with him – and the jokes. That Irish sense of humour! Now she was gone. His wife and baby had nearly gone too. A look of intense anger crept over his face as his thoughts turned to those responsible. Those men who murdered Robert Kenny had also murdered Agnes, just as sure if they'd shot her, too. And what of the other children he and Angela would have had? Murdered! Just like their grandparents.

He was consumed with hatred for the faceless men who had inflicted so much pain and grief.

"Scum," he murmured. "Murdering Scum."

He could never forgive them. They had taken away his wife's right to give life and robbed them both of their dream to have more children. They were the ones who didn't deserve to live. His greatest regret was not knowing who they were. His thoughts were interrupted by the nurse coming in and out to check on Angela's condition.

"It's been a long day and night for you Mr Morrelli," she commented. "Why don't you try and get some sleep?"

"I'm o.k. nurse," Joe replied. "How long do you think it'll be before she comes round?"

"I'd say another couple of hours."

Joe got up and stretched his tired body.

"I'll just go and see how my son's doing. But I'll be back. I want to be here when my wife wakes up."

Joe made his way back to intensive care and after putting on a gown and observing all the rules he was taken in to be with his son. He stroked the infant's arms and legs and stood studying his tiny form. He felt an overpowering love for his helpless baby he'd almost lost. There lay his dream and Joe Morrelli would make sure nothing and no one would ever harm his son again.

Later back in Angela's room, Joe sat beside her bed once again. Taking her hand in his, he wanted to tell her that the baby was alright. He knew she'd be happy. But he also knew she'd have to face Agnes's death all over again. Half of him was longing for Angela to come round, half of him was dreading it. There was so much she'd have to know.

Hours had passed when Angela's eyelids began to flutter and her fingers started to move. Slowly, she opened her eyes and gazed at the ceiling. Then she stared silently around the unfamiliar room. She became aware of a figure sitting beside the bed.

"Joe?" Her voice was weak.

"Angel, honey!"

"Joe, the baby? What's happened to the baby?"

"The baby's fine, Angel. It's a boy and he's just fine. I've seen him."

Angela began to cry.

"Oh, thank God! Where is he?"

"He's in intensive care but it's just so they can keep an eye on him. Now, don't you worry."

Joe leaned over and kissed her wet cheek. Then taking a handkerchief from his pocket, he dried her tears.

"Angel," he whispered, "you've given me the one thing I never thought I'd have. Now, my whole life has been worthwhile. I have a son! Tell me, is there anything you want? Is there anything I can do for you? Angel, just say the word."

Angela's mood changed.

"My mum's really dead?"

"Yeah, honey. She is." Angela gripped Joe's hand.

"Then I want you to send her home, Joe. She was parted from my father in life, I don't want her to be parted from him in death. Promise me you'll do it, Joe."

"I promise. Your mother and father will rest together, Angel. You just leave everything to me."

"Thank you, Joe." Joe nodded as Angela continued, "Now, what about the baby?"

"What about him?"

"Well, if he's in intensive care shouldn't we give him a name?"

"I never really thought about that."

"I think we should call him after you,"

Joe pondered for a few moments.

"Well, honey, I don't know. You see, I'm Joe and he'd be Joe. Two Joes in one house…" he screwed up his face, "…might be sort of confusing. I'd like him to have a name with a nice ring to it. What about Robert? Yeah, Robert Morrelli! I like the sound of that."

"You mean we can call him after my father?"

"Why not?"

"Oh Joe!" Angela cried, "Thank you. Thank you."

Joe kissed her hand and then her lips. As he soothed her brow, Angela's eyes began to close once more and her voice became more feeble.

"Maybe we can call the next one Joe. What do you think?"

There was no reply, but Joe Morrelli's heart was aching. How could he tell her that there'd never be another child?

Then came a faint whisper.

"I love you, Joe Morrelli."

"I love you too," came the reply as he wiped away the tears from his dark brown eyes.

Joe was awakened from his sleep by someone shaking him gently and a low voice calling his name. He looked up.

"Doctor Weissman! Where have you been?"

Joe rose from the chair.

"I was on vacation," explained the doctor. "Angela wasn't due for another six weeks and everything was fine. I knew I'd be back in time to take care of her. Doctor Henley called me and explained everything. I told him to go ahead with the operation and I'd catch the first flight back. I'm sorry, Joe. It's been a really tough time."

"Yeah well," replied Joe, "Doctor Henley did a really good job."

"I knew he would. He's one of the best."

The two men walked over to the door and continued their conversation in whispers.

"I suppose you know she can't have any more children?"

Doctor Weissman nodded.

"It's going to break her heart," said Joe. "She always wanted three of four. I can't bring myself to tell her. What am I to do Doctor Weissman?"

"Don't you worry about it, Joe. I'll break the news to her myself."

"Would you?"

"Of course."

"Thanks Doctor. By the way, this Doctor Henley – you don't happen to know if he's had his vacation yet, do you?"

"I don't think so. Why?"

"Because I aim to see he gets a damn good one!"

Doctor Weissman smiled and said.

"You're generous to a fault, Joe."

"No, he deserves it. After all, he's the one who's been generous. He saved my wife and child."

The Doctor nodded, opened the door and then hesitated.

"There's something I have to tell you, Joe. There must be no sexual relations between you and Angela for five or six weeks. She'll need plenty of time to heal."

"That's no problem."

"Good. I knew you'd understand. I'll be back tomorrow to check on her and perhaps have a little talk – break the news gently."

Doctor Weissman left the room and as Joe closed the door behind him, he breathed a sigh of relief that the task he most dreaded would be taken on by someone else.

Angela felt a little better the next day and was both relieved and delighted to see Doctor Weissman. He sat on the edge of the bed making small talk but there was no easy way around it, so he broke the news to her. She sobbed uncontrollably, feeling as though her whole world had fallen apart. The Doctor put his arm around her.

"Does Joe know?" she asked.

"Yes, he knows and he's accepted it, Angela. You'll have to do the same. You have a beautiful baby boy and you are both lucky to be here. Look at it this way, all the love you would have given to the rest of your children, you can give to him."

Angela nodded,

"I will. I promise I will."

Then with the aid of a nurse, Doctor Weissman put her in a chair and wheeled her up to intensive care to see her baby. When Angela saw little Robert her face lit up with joy and the love she felt for him went far beyond anything she'd ever known. After that, she seemed contented.

She was kept in the hospital for another week. Flowers arrived on a daily basis filling the room with a multitude of fragrances. Joe's friends and associates had sent them, with cards and telegrams of congratulations. Robert was growing stronger so Doctor Weissman had him brought to Angela's room towards the end of her stay. Joe was there constantly and Rooney kept popping in to admire the baby and see Angela. Antonia paid a surprise visit one afternoon, making a grand entrance with a basket of flowers that was so huge the young delivery boy almost had a coronary!

"Joe darling – you look wonderful!" she gushed, rushing over to him.

Rooney and Angela looked at each other. Anyone would have thought it was Joe who'd had the baby!

"And dear Angela," she continued, kissing her lightly on the cheek. She ignored Rooney who was studying her intently. "Congratulations all round. Now, I must see the baby!"

She went over to the crib and on seeing Robert for the first time, raised her hands to her face dramatically. "Oh my God! He looks just like you, Joe. And he's adorable!"

Rooney and Angela exchanged another quick glance. Joe smiled proudly.

"Yeah, he does look like me!"

"Thank you for coming, Antonia," said Angela.

"Oh, I just had to see the baby. I couldn't stay away a moment longer," Antonia replied, gazing lovingly at Robert.

"Would you like to hold him?" asked Angela.

"Oh, could I? Just for a few seconds."

Angela lifted Robert out of the crib and placed him in Antonia's arms. Joe was delighted as he watched Antonia cradle the baby.

"Joe, he's a darling. He's a darling, Joe," she kept saying over and over again.

Joe looked at Angela, smiled and nodded his head in appreciation.

Angela then took Robert and handed him to Rooney.

"Go on," she insisted, "you may as well start now!"

Rooney took the baby from her and rocked him gently in his strong, protective arms. "Now, isn't that a pretty sight!" exclaimed Joe, putting his arm around Angela's shoulder. "Our son, with his Uncle Rooney and Aunt Antonia."

There was no answer to that!

When Angela was discharged from the hospital, Robert was kept behind. Doctor Weissman told her it would only be for a few weeks, until the baby was really well. She and Joe arrived home. Once inside, Angela turned to him,

"What about the arrangements for my mother? What's going to happen now?"

Joe took her into the lounge and they both sat down. Taking her hand in his he said, "Well, you know I phoned Sheila the morning after Robert was born and explained everything."

Angela nodded and asked,

"How has she taken it all?"

"Not good, Angel. I've been talking to her a couple of times since and she breaks down every time. Raymond has taken it pretty badly too. Understandable I guess. He's known your mother for years. A lot longer than me. I told them we were sending your mother's body home to be buried with your father. They think it's the best thing, too. They know you can't travel, so they are going to meet the plane when it arrives and see to the funeral. I've already sent them on a cheque to cover expenses."

"It's all so tragic, Joe," said Angela. "One daughter and son-in-law will arrange her departure, while another daughter and son-in-law will arrange her arrival. And she won't know a thing about it. Not a thing."

"She'll know, Angel. There wasn't much went on around here that Agnes didn't know about!"

Angela smiled sadly,

"When is she going?"

"Tomorrow morning. It's all been taken care of."

"I have to see her, Joe."

"I know. And I'll take you to her. Just say the word."

"Now"

"Now it is."

They left the lounge and began the short journey to the funeral parlour.

Joe, Angela and Rooney stood in the cold morning air, watching Agnes's coffin being taken on board the large air craft. After the door of the cargo area was closed the giant propellers started to turn. A strong wind blew across the tarmac and around the three grieving figures standing motionless. The plane turned and gathered speed as it moved down the runway Joe held one of Angela's hands tightly and Rooney held the other one. They watched as the plane took off into a dull grey sky.

"Now you can go home, mum," whispered Angela. "Now you can go home."

Four weeks had passed when Joe and Angela went to the hospital to collect the baby and bring him home. Angela was so relived when the Nursing Sister handed him to her. He'd put on weight and looked so healthy no one would have guessed he'd been premature. She cradled him lovingly and kissed his tiny face and hands. Joe was over the moon and kept insisting to anyone who'd listen, that his son could recognise him instantly just by the sound of his voice!

The Morrelli household was on it's ear. Robert only had to whimper and everyone rushed to be of assistance. Joe complained that it was like being in a stampede. Evie, however, reminded him that the more love and attention a baby received the better person they'd grow up to be. Joe wondered how Evie was such an expert on the subject, seeing as how she'd never had any kids of her own. But when he saw the way she, Rooney and the guys fussed over Robert, he decided that she was most probably right. The day after the homecoming, Joe invited his many friends to the house for a celebratory drink. People kept coming and going and gifts for the baby were piled high in the entrance hall. Joe mingled among the crowd but every now and again he'd glance towards Angela. He couldn't put his finger on it but something just wasn't right. She was smiling and being very charming to everyone but she'd been acting strangely every since she got home from the hospital. In fact, she'd been almost distant towards him except during their visits to Robert. Only then did she seem like her old self. He hadn't mentioned anything to her because he knew she'd been through a lot. But the feeling he had just wouldn't go away. Now and then he'd catch her looking at him but she always managed to look away again even before he could smile at her. There was something else that bothered him. Although Doctor Weissman had advised him to leave Angela alone for a few weeks, it had gotten to the point where she didn't even want him to kiss her. Every night she'd lie in bed with her back to him hardly saying a word.

"Oh well," he thought, "I'll give it another week or so."

But even with time things didn't change. Except now that the baby was home he rarely saw her. She was always in the nursery.

One night as they lay in bed Joe leaned over to kiss her.

"Don't Joe," she said, "I'm not in the mood."

"O.k." he sighed but as he lay in the darkness he knew things had really changed between them.

The following day when Joe and Rooney arrived back to the house after making a few business calls, they were met by two delivery men coming down the stairs. Joe stared at them until they'd gone through the door and then made his way up the stairs nodding for Rooney to follow.

The were walking along the landing when they heard Angela's voice coming from the nursery. Joe and Rooney stopped at the door and on looking in, Joe saw a new single bed alongside the baby's crib. Angela was standing beside it with Robert in her arms, talking to Evie who was holding a pile of fresh bed linen. Joe stared at the bed and then to

Angela. Rooney stared at the floor! When Angela saw Joe she said,

"I'm going to move in here for a while, to be near the baby."

Joe turned and walked away without saying a word. Rooney followed. He too, was silent.

Time passed and Angela slept in the nursery every night. Joe tried to ignore it at first but eventually it became too much. One evening he went to the nursery and found Angela sitting in a chair with Robert asleep in her arms.

"Don't you think this has gone on long enough?" he asked her.

"I don't know what you mean."

"Damn it Angel! You know exactly what I mean - sleeping here every night."

"I'm worried in case something happens to Robert."

"What can happen to him? He's a strong healthy baby. Anyway, it's not just Robert. There's something else and I want to know what it is. I have a right to know. I'm your husband for God's sake.!"

Joe was almost yelling by this time and when he slammed his fist down onto the arm of the chair, Angela burst into tears.

"Alright! Alright, I'll tell you," she cried "I'm not the same woman you married. I've ruined everything for you. All the promises to you about a family - I can't keep them anymore, Joe. Why sleep with a woman who can't really give you what you want?. How can you be expected to make love to me when I'm only half a woman? I'm useless and I can't bear the disappointment I know I've brought to you."

Joe stared at her and then spoke in a low voice.

"My God … is that what this is all about? Do you honestly believe for one minute that I could think like that? Because if you do, you don't know Joe Morrelli. You don't know Joe Morrelli at all. You're the one who's thinking like that, not me. Your tearing yourself apart with guilt over something that wasn't your fault. I can't believe you'd think me capable of anything you've just said."

He shook his head, turned and walked to the door. On reaching it, he spun round.

"There's one more thing," he said, pointing an accusing finger at her. "You are going to make a nancy boy out of my son!"

"How do you make that one out?" she asked, stunned.

"I'll tell you how. Your face is the only one he sees these days. You won't let anyone else near him - including me! Your smothering him. You and this damn nursery are all he ever sees!"

Joe stormed out, slammed the door and thumped his way down the stairs. Rooney was standing at the bottom, having heard all the commotion.

"Al! Al, bring the car round!" roared Joe as he reached the hallway.

"Where are you going, Joe?" asked Rooney.

"Out!!"

"I'll come with you …"

"Hold it!" yelled Joe. "I've got a wife upstairs who's avoiding me, while your all over me like a nasty rash. Don't you think it ought to be the other way around?"

"But where are you going?" asked Rooney again.

"Oh, I get I!" said Joe, the penny having finally dropped. "You think I'm going to Antonia's."

"Well, are you?"

"No! I'm not!" yelled Joe into Rooney's face.

"O.k.!" Rooney yelled back. "That's it. I'm going home!"

"Good!" replied Joe.

Rooney's face was white with temper as he almost took the front door off it's hinges.

"Al!" Joe roared again. "Will you bring the damn car!"

Al pulled up outside Doctor Weissman's home. Joe got out and rang the doorbell. The maid answered but before a word could be spoken Doctor Weissman's voice was heard, "Joe!"

The maid was dismissed and the Doctor ushered Joe into the study. They sat down. "This is quite a surprise, Joe."

"Yeah, I guess it is. I sure hope I'm not interrupting anything, Doctor Weissman, but I really had to call and see you."

"What is it Joe? You seem very down."

"It's Angel."

Doctor Weissman listened as Joe explained everything to him. "I don't know what to do," said Joe, shaking his head.

"You've already done the right thing." replied the doctor.

"Do you think she needs professional help?"

"Well, I think she needs someone to talk to her about it. I'll call and see her later on this evening. You know, pretend I'm just passing on my way home."

"Thank's Doctor Weissman. I really appreciate it."

"Try not to worry, Joe. She's been through a pretty traumatic time and she's young. She probably feels she's let you down and that would be hard for her to deal with."

Doctor Weissman escorted Joe to the door and tried to reassure him once again. Joe left and headed for "The Safe Haven." After a few drinks he toyed with the idea of paying Antonia a visit but he knew if he did he'd end staying the night. No - this was one problem he'd have to sort out on his own. Meanwhile at Joe's house, Doctor Weissman had called and Angela had brought him up to the nursery to see Robert. After entering the room, Doctor Weissman nodded towards the bed.

"How long has this been going on?" he asked.

"A while," said Angela. "I'm scared to leave him on his own."

"What about Joe? Do you think it's right to leave him on his own? After all, Angela, Robert is almost three months old. If you think about it, that's a long time for your husband."

"I know …" she sighed "but the baby needs me."

"Joe needs you too. He loves you, Angela. Very much. Don't throw it all back at him or one day you may regret it and end up a very lonely woman. We're always there for our children, but they're not always there for us. Think about it. Please. Joe needs his family. Don't shut him out."

Doctor Weissman left Angela with a lot of food for thought.

Joe arrived home well after midnight. He went into the lounge and poured himself a large scotch. When he finished it he decided to go upstairs and look in on Robert. But then he thought about Angela.

"Better leave it," he said to himself. "No point in disturbing her. Besides, it might cause another scene!"

He poured himself another drink and carried it upstairs to the bedroom. He breathed a heavy sigh as he set it down on the bedside table. Suddenly he saw a shape in the bed and by the light from the landing he could see the glint of long, red hair on the pillow.

Angela!

He got undressed, went into the bathroom and splashed some water on his face. Then he came out, closed the bedroom door and quickly got into bed. He turned on his lamp.

"Where were you?" asked Angela.

"Oh, just out," Joe replied leaning his elbow on the pillow.

"I know that! But out where?"

"I called on a few friends. We talked."

"You talked all this time? I was worried sick about you. Why didn't you get in touch with someone?"

"Oh well," came the reply, "the next time I'm late I'll send you a telegram!"

"It's not funny, Joe. Rooney was worried about you too."

"Oh you know Rooney. Sometimes that guy acts like he's my mother!"

"You should be very glad he does. And by the way, don't you think you owe him an apology? I heard what you said to him."

"Yeah, yeah, I'll see him tomorrow."

After a few minutes of silence Angela asked,

"Were you with Antonia Flemming?"

"No I was not with Antonia Flemming. And Angel, do you think you could turn around?

It's not easy trying to have a conversation with the back of someone's head!"

Angela turned over and stared at him.

"Are you finished with the questions now?" he asked.

She nodded.

"Good! Can I ask you one?"

"Go ahead."

"Why are you back in our bed?"

After another few moments of silence Angela spoke.

"Well, I've been thinking about what you said. I've been very unfair to you, Joe. I'm sorry."

Joe switched off the light and lay down. Neither wanted to be the one to make the first move.

"You'd better get some sleep, Angel. It's late."

"I'm not tired," came the reply.

"Now isn't that a coincidence - neither am I! So what will we do to pass the time?"

"Well, I can think of one thing I could do. I could make you a very happy man!"

Angela put her arms around him and started to kiss his face and neck.

"I don't think that would take very long!" he joked.

"Oh come on, Joe Morrelli! I bet you can hold your own with the best of them."

Joe took Angela in his arms, rolled on top of her and kissed her passionately.

"I'm sure gonna try!" he whispered

Frankie and Al turned up for work as usual but there was no sign of Rooney and, more to the point, no sign of Joe. He had always been an early riser but not this morning. The guys headed for the kitchen in the hope that Evie might have some coffee on the boil. Joe lay in bed with his hands behind his head, staring at the ceiling. There was a broad grin on his face. Things were back to normal. No - better than normal! He could hear Angela singing in the nursery while she bathed Robert. Just as he was about to relive the previous night he suddenly caught sight of the clock.

"Is that the time? It can't be!" he thought aloud as he jumped out of bed. Once dressed he made his way downstairs to be greeted by Frankie and Al.

When Al saw Joe all smiles he nudged Frankie.

"It must have been some night!" he murmured.

"Did you say something?" enquired Joe

"It's the big fight tonight, Boss"

"Oh yeah, so it is. I almost forgot. I'll have to drop in at Stacey's Gym later. Where's Rooney?"

"He's not here, Boss" said Frankie.

"Oh," said Joe, not really surprised. "I guess I better call him. I'll be in the study."

After Joe walked away Frankie turned to Al.

"One of these days, Al, he's gonna catch you out and you'll be missing an arm and a leg - and I don't mean money wise!"

"I can't help it," replied Al. "It just comes out"

"I know. And if the boss's face is anything to go by you're probably right!"

They burst out laughing and started to slap and punch each other playfully.

Joe dialled Rooney's number.

"Rooney? Joe here! Listen. I've got to go to the Gym later on. Why don't you come over and have lunch with Angel and me? She was kinda worried about you yesterday. No, I'm not doing anything special today. I'm just going to spend some time with my family - that's why I was hoping you'd be here. What do you say? Good! See you later."

Joe smiled as he put the receiver down. It made him feel good to know that they were all friends again - especially where Angela was concerned. He'd really missed her. Rooney turned up for lunch and judging by the way Joe kept gazing at Angela, he came to the conclusion that the single bed in the nursery would no longer be required!

As they all sat round the dining table Joe looked at Rooney.

"About yesterday ..."

"Forget it, Joe I have."

Joe smiled. Apologies never did come easily to him!

"By the way, Rooney, Billy Wilson will win tonight. I'd say round about the sixth or seventh round."

Joe gave Rooney a knowing wink.

"How can you be so sure?" asked Angela

"Just a hunch"

"Just a bet more like!"

"Well, Angel, you have to bet on somebody. So me and Rooney are going for Wilson. Right Rooney?"

Rooney agreed.

"Oh well," said Angela, "I don't like boxing. You two go on ahead tonight. I have some things to do."

"Are you sure you don't mind. Honey?"

"Why should I mind, Joe? You go and enjoy yourself."

"Only if your sure Angel. I'd be just as happy to stay here at home with you and the baby."

Rooney stared at Joe and thought,

"Well that's a bloody lie for a start!"

After lunch Joe and Rooney headed out to the car that was waiting to take them to Stacey's Gym.

"What's with all this happy to stay at home talk?" asked Rooney mimicking Joe.

Joe put a brotherly arm around Rooney's shoulder.

"Have you ever known me to miss a fight, Rooney? Especially where there's money involved?"

"Never."

Joe smiled.

"You know, Rooney, women are funny creatures. If they think you really want to go somewhere - they won't let you go. But if they think you don't want to go - they'll force you to. See what I mean?"

Rooney stared at him and then said almost admiringly.

"By God, Joe Morrelli, you could give acting lessons!"

Angela heard the car stop and the sound of voices.

A few moments later the front door opened and Joe called,

"Angel honey, I'm home."

Angela appeared at the door of the lounge,

"Don't you honey me, Joe Morrelli. I want to talk to you!"

She turned and went back into the lounge. Joe followed her, closing the door behind him.

"What's wrong?" he asked in a low, concerned voice.

"I'll tell you what's wrong," she replied with a stoney look on her face. "I've just had Antonia Flemming on the phone telling me how delighted she is that we have asked her to be Robert's godmother!"

For a moment, Joe was lost for words.

"….Oh, yeah…." he stammered. "I was meaning to talk to you about that."

"Really? When? The morning of the christening?"

"Oh, come on Angel, let me explain…"

"Forget it Joe! This has gone far enough. Listen to me, I have a sister in Ireland and…."

"No - you listen to me!!" Joe raised his voice to her in a way he'd never done before.

"I've known Antonia for years. She looked up to me and respected me long before the big shots in this city ever did. She loved me! Now, I couldn't return that love the way she wanted me to. I couldn't marry her and give her my name. she always thought that one day she'd be Mrs Joe Morrelli, but I married you, Angel. You have my love, my name, my son. You have all the things she ever wanted. Your sister doesn't even live here. Robert would never see her. Antonia will always be here for him. O.k., I admit I should have talked it over with you first. I'm sorry. But I'm not going to change my mind! Believe me, I have my reasons."

He moved closer to Angela and put his hands up to her face. "Angel," he continued, calmer than before, "I don't want to hurt her any more than I have already. Let her be your friend. Please honey, do this one thing for me."

Angela sat down as Joe went across to the window and gazed out into the garden beyond. She had been surprised by his outburst but she understood how he felt. Eventually she broke the silence.

"You're right, Joe, I'm the lucky one. I've got you and your baby - and you've been good to me."

"Angel, it's you I love. But Antonia was always there when I needed her. She could do the same for you. Just think about it. Please."

"I already have," replied Angela. "Antonia would be a good godmother to Robert - but you should have told me all this before you spoke to her. That's what really hurts."

Joe watched as she got up, crossed the room and opened the lounge door. She beckoned to Frankie who was waiting outside the study, whispered to him and then came back in to join her husband.

Within a few minutes, Rooney appeared. Angela nodded for him to close the door.

"Anything wrong?" he asked.

"You'd better ask the boss!" she answered.

Joe turned to Rooney with a guilty look on his face.

"Antonia is going to be godmother to Robert," he said, trying to smile as he broke the news.

Rooney dropped his gaze as if to study the pattern on the carpet.

Angela took over.

"Antonia is like family to Joe and family is important to both of us Rooney. That's why we'd like you to be Robert's godfather. You are the nearest thing to family that I have in this country and we know you'd love him and take care of him like your own flesh and blood."

Rooney's mouth broke into a broad, happy smile.

"I'd love to be a godfather - especially to Robert." He laughed and shook his head. "I can hardly believe it!"

"Well, everything's settled then," said Angela. "I'm sure Joe's just as pleased as I am. Right Joe?"

Joe walked over from the window and put his hands on Rooney's shoulders.

"One big happy family!" he grinned. "And it's all down to my darling wife."

He slipped his arm round Angela who pulled away, making the excuse she had to check on Robert in the nursery. She left the room and climbed the stairs. She knew she'd done the right thing, but she was still angry with Joe for not confiding in her until now.

Rooney's patience was wearing thin.

"You'd think she'd make the effort and be on time for her own godson's christening!"

Angela, with the baby in her arms, nodded in agreement.

Joe tried to smooth things over.

"Now Rooney," he said, "you know what these actresses are like. They always have to make an entrance. It makes them feel important."

"Well, if she doesn't get a move on," replied Rooney, "he'll be getting married instead of christened!"

Joe said a silent prayer to himself which was answered immediately as Antonia's limousine drove up to the church and pulled up at the steps.

"At long last," sighed Rooney, as he stamped on his cigarette. Al opened the rear door.

The first things to emerge were two long, slender legs in four inch stilettos. Then Antonia struggled out of the car wearing the biggest white, satin hat anyone had ever seen! She pushed past Rooney and Angela as if they were non existent.

"Joe!!" she shrieked, holding out her arms to him.

Joe rushed towards her.

"Antonia! You look terrific!"

"She looks like a flying saucer!" commented Rooney.

"Never mind," quipped Angela, "at least she's landed!"

Rooney was on his way to the kitchen, when he noticed the study door ajar. On going over to close it he heard Joe's voice, conducting what seemed to be a one-sided conversation.

"Who are you talking to?" he asked, peering round the door.

"I wasn't talking," insisted Joe, startled.

"Yes you were. I heard you."

"Oh, so you're listening at keyholes now!"

"I wasn't listening at any keyhole. I was on my way to the kitchen and I thought somebody was in here with you."

Joe tutted.

"Well, if you must know, I was talking to Robert."

Robert was now nine months old, sitting in a baby chair beside Joe's desk.

"Really," smirked Rooney, coming in, "and what was he saying?"

"Don't get smart!" warned Joe.

"Me? Get smart with you, Joe? I wouldn't dare!"

"Well, for your information, I read an article in one of those magazines that said whatever a kid learns in the first four years of his life, paves the way for his whole future."

"I see," nodded Rooney. "So you were just filling him in on a few things."

"Yeah."

"Showing him the ropes."

"Yeah."

Rooney could hardly keep a straight face.

"So we've got a little Orson Welles in the family."

"Now listen Rooney!" Joe yelled so unexpectedly that little Robert burst into tears. Joe panicked. "Are you happy now?" he asked Rooney. "Now look at what you've done!"

"What have I done?"

"You've upset him! All that talk about…. About Orson Welles and stuff!"

"Oh come on!!" cried Rooney, disgusted that Joe could clutch at such flimsy straws!

"He's probably just hungry."

"You think so? Well, I'll tell you what, Rooney. Seeing as how you're so much smarter than anyone else in this house, you can take him to the kitchen and get him something to eat."

Joe thrust a sobbing Robert into Rooney's waiting arms.

"There, there son," he soothed. "Bad Uncle Rooney!"

Rather than say another word, Rooney left the study with Robert and closed the door. Once outside into the hallway, he almost doubled up with laughter. Ever since this baby first hit Roseberry Avenue, Joe Morrelli was in a constant tizwaz!

A half an hour later, Joe came into the kitchen ready for lunch. He looked around. "Where's Robert?"

"He's not here," said Rooney.

"Well, I can see he's not here! If he was here would I be asking you where he is?"

Joe shook his head in despair. "What a house!"

"He's in the garden with Al, Mr Joe," Evie informed him, as she took a casserole out of the oven.

Joe went over to the door and gazed out. Sure enough, Al was taking a leisurely walk around the garden with a smiling Robert in his arms, stopping to point at the different plants and shrubs.

"What the hell…" said Joe, as he went out to investigate.

"What are you doing?" he asked.

"Oh hi, Boss. I'm just telling Robert here all about the trees and the flowers."

"Well now, isn't that nice. And I suppose any minute now, Julie Andrews is going to come skipping up the driveway, singing!"

Al was cut to the quick.

"As a matter of fact," he said, "I read an article in one of those magazines that said whatever a kid learns in the first four years of his life…"

"Did you read that too?" asked Joe, quite surprised.

"Yeah."

"What did you think of it?"

"I thought it was pretty good, Boss."

"Me too. Rooney thinks it's a joke."

"Oh, you know Rooney. He always has to make light of everything. Besides, those guys are experts. They know what they're talking about."

"Exactly!" exclaimed Joe, relived that someone was finally on his side. "It also said that if your child is naturally inquisitive, you're halfway there. And you must admit, he is a nosey little fella" chuckled Joe, as Robert grabbed hold of his finger.

"Yeah," agreed Al, "he's a real Morrelli! Oh look, Robert – rhododendrons…!!"

Angela went back to College after a great deal of persuasion from Joe and graduated with honours, much to his delight. He was proud of her and what they had. A good marriage, a loving relationship and a son they both loved and cherished, who was growing into a healthy, intelligent child now three years old.

There was one thing, however, that overshadowed them. In every respect Robert was a Normal happy little boy but from the age of two he was prone to nightmares.

Nightmares which were becoming more constant.

Joe and Angela spent many nights with him in the nursery. His loud cries and sobs could be comforted by his loving parents who would take turns in soothing him. Joe would walk up and down carrying him in his arms or Angela would nurse him, rocking him gently on her knee, talking and singing to him until sleep would be the victor. In some instances they had to bring him to their bedroom to dispel his fears. It was always the same dream. He would cling to them sobbing, telling about a bad man who was running after him.

"Mommy, daddy, don't let him get me!" he would beg.

Angela fretted. Joe tried to make light of it, saying it was just a phase he was going through but inwardly he was deeply troubled. It was after one such event that Angela came back from the nursery, sat on the side of the bed and started to cry.

"I blame myself for this, Joe!"

"What do you mean?" he asked, surprised. "How can you hold yourself responsible for his bad dreams?"

"I should never have called him after my father."

"What has that got to do with it?"

She looked at him, tears streaming down her face.

"Think about it, Joe. My father met with a terrible death and it was a bad, wicked man who pulled the trigger."

"Now, that's just superstitious nonsense!" Joe insisted.

"Maybe you think so but we Irish are a superstitious people. He was taken from this world too quickly, Joe. There were no goodbyes to his family. He probably never even got the chance to utter a prayer or bless himself. He must have been so full of fear, knowing what was going to happen to him."

Joe leaned over and put his arms around her.

"Honey, I don't want you thinking like that. There could be a hundred reasons why Robert has bad dreams. I'm going to take him to the best doctors and child therapists money can buy, until we find for sure what's causing this. Once we know, then he can be cured."

"Do you think so?"

"Yes, I do and that's a promise."

She put her arms around him.

"Oh Joe, I really hope so. He's all we have and it's breaking my heart to see him like this. It's not so bad for Sheila. She has three children now, even if they are all girls."

She looked at him and burst into fresh tears.

"I'm so sorry Joe!" she sobbed.

"Hey, come on now, Angel," he said kissing her forehead. "It's not your fault. If I could turn the clock back, I'd still marry you." He put his hand up to her face and wiped away her tears with his finger. "Some people can have a lot of kids but not much love. You and me have just one kid but a lot of love. So don't you ever feel bad or sell yourself short because I'm going to tell you something. I'll love you, Angela Morrelli, until I take my last breath."

He held her tightly as she put her arms around his neck and laid her head on his shoulder. He stroked her hair and stared straight ahead as he spoke in a low voice, "I don't want you ever to blame yourself because we can't have any more kids. What happened wasn't your fault." His eyes narrowed and a serious, almost cruel, expression crept over his face. "If it's anyone's fault, it's those bastards back in Belfast who murdered your father!"

Joe was determined to find out the cause of his son's problem. He contacted the best paediatricians and child psychologists in New York. Angela was a bit hesitant about bringing her son to a therapist but as Joe in his logic pointed out, they were all specialists in their own field. As Robert was taken from one to another they all agreed that he was a happy, healthy child living in a secure and loving environment. However, regarding his nightmares their opinions differed – Childish fantasy. Fetal distress. A fear of the night or darkened places. But whatever they thought the cause, Robert's nightmares didn't go away. After three months of therapists and treatment they were still occurring. Angela was extremely worried and felt completely helpless. One afternoon, when Joe and Rooney had gone out, she phoned a taxi and went to see Fr. Ryker. As they sat in the vestry she told him everything, including why she blamed herself.

Fr. Ryker sat and listened, then leaned forward.

"And what does Joe think about that?" he asked.

"He doesn't believe it, Father. You know Joe, he says it's superstition."

He nodded his head.

"I'm inclined to agree with him. Angela, listen to me." He took her hand. "Your father, by all accounts, was a good man. A kind man. Whatever is troubling your son has nothing to do with being named after him. Your father, may his soul rest in peace, wouldn't let anything bad happen to his only grandson. You must believe that."

She nodded and looked at him with tears in her eyes.

"But what am I going to do, Father?" she asked, in a low voice.

Father Ryker stood up and still holding her hand, he pulled Angela gently to her feet.

"We're going to pray," he replied, opening the vestry door.

He put his arm around her shoulder as they walked into the Church.

"You know, Angela," he said in a soft voice, "God really does work in mysterious ways. After all, he guided you to New York and you met Joe. Give him time and He'll guide you towards a cure for Robert. Who knows, maybe your father played a part in your coming here, too. It's not impossible, and if it's true he'll play a part in looking after your son. I've been in this neighbourhood for many years and I've learned one thing about dealing with people. Sometimes, what seems like a big problem, only needs a small solution."

They both knelt down in front of the alter and prayed silently. After a little while, he turned and looked at her.

"I remember the day I married you here. Any regrets?"

She shook her head.

"No, not one," she whispered.

"I didn't think so."

"I love him, Father. I always will."

"I think I can safely say that makes two of you!" he smiled. "I never saw a happier man than Joe Morrelli when he looked at you that day. I want you to go home and stop worrying Angela. Everything will be alright. I want you to pray for guidance and I will pray you get it."

They both rose and Angela shook his hand gently.

"Thank you for everything, Father. I feel so much better now, and so relieved," she sighed.

"We all need someone, Angela. To love, to talk to and to watch over us. We're only human. It makes us feel good and it can make us feel safe!"

A few weeks later, Angela went shopping in the city. She and Joe had received an invitation to a charity function, courtesy of Gene O'Brien. Joe was impressed because a lot of very important people would be there, and he insisted that Angela bought a new dress for the occasion. He wanted her to stand out in a crowd, not just because she had become a very attractive woman, but because she was also Mrs Morrelli! As Angela left the large department store with an expensive dress and matching accessories, she made her way along the busy street to a diner on the corner, where Al would be waiting. While walking along clutching the bags, she turned her head almost instinctively to look into a shop window. She stopped in her tracks and stood staring, as her eyes came to rest on something quite extraordinary. There, in front of the window, was the white statue of an angel. She stepped forward to examine it more closely. He stood with his sword drawn, pointing it downwards and one foot was poised on the head of a bad angel. The bad angel looked defeated as the large, white one was about to thrust him into the depths of Hell. In every way it was a symbol of good triumphing over evil and Angela felt drawn towards it.

She went inside and asked to have a closer look at it. As the elderly lady went and lifted it out of the window, Angela looked around. It was a small store, full of religious items and books. The lady smiled as she put the angel down onto a shiny wooden counter. "It really is a very unusual statue," she said. "In fact, it's all the one we have."

"I've never seen one like it," replied Angela, captivated.

"You might not see one like it again. We never had one before and we may never get another. It was made in Italy."

Angela smiled as the lady continued.

"I must admit I think it's rather beautiful. There's something about it that holds your attention. He looks like a real protector, but then, he is Michael the Archangel conquering the Devil." The lady gazed at it admiringly as Angela nodded.

"I'll take it, please," she said, determinedly.

"I thought you would," came the reply.

After placing the statute in its box and wrapping it up, the elderly lady took the money. However, Angela couldn't help but notice how she stared at her throughout.

"Is anything the matter?" she asked.

The lady shook her head.

"No, but just look out there." She pointed at the window. "Hundreds of people pass this store every day and that statue has been in the window for quite some time. Yet, you have been the only person who has ever stopped. Call me old fashioned but I'm a great believer in unusual things. I guess what I mean is, I don't think it was a coincidence that brought you here today." She smiled as she handed Angela the box. "I think that angel was waiting for you."

When Angela arrived home, she went straight upstairs and put the box into her wardrobe. She never mentioned what she had bought to anyone. After she bathed Robert that night, he sat in the lounge with Joe watching cartoons on the television. She slipped upstairs and taking the angel out of the box, she brought it to the nursery and placed it on the bedside table in front of the night lamp she always kept burning. The light shone on the white statue, causing a powerful, bright glow around it. Angela stood and looked at it for a long time. Then, she left the room, closing the door behind her. As she entered the lounge, Joe was switching off the television.

"Come on, son, it's time for bed." He said, taking Robert's hand.

Angela took the other one and they walked upstairs together. When they came to the nursery door, Robert opened it and stood wide eyed.

"What's the matter son?" asked Joe in an anxious voice, following him inside.

Robert pointed to the statue, then slowly moved towards it. Joe stared at it in surprise then looked at Angela.

"What is that?" he whispered.

Before she could answer, the child turned around and in an innocent voice asked, "Mommy, who is that man?"

She went over and sitting down on the side of the bed, took him on her knee.

"He's not a man, Robert," she explained, "He's an angel. A very good and powerful one. He chases away bad men so that they can never hurt or frighten anyone. Look, he's standing on the bad man so he can never run after you again. He's here to watch over you and keep you safe."

He gazed at the statue with large, dark eyes and then looked at his mother.

"Would he kill the bad man, mommy?"

Angela nodded and in a gentle voice said, "Yes, he would. That's why he has a sword.

A good angel will kill a bad man if he has to because bad men must be punished for the wicked things they do."

"Will the angel stay with me?"

"Every day and every night," she answered, kissing his forehead. "He has come to stay with you and be your friend."

Joe stood with his arms folded, listening. Angela put Robert into bed and tucked him in. As she leaned over to kiss him, he put his little arms around her neck.

"Will the bad man go away now?" he whispered.

She nodded.

"The good angel will make him go away – forever!"

Joe bent down and kissed him.

"Goodnight son."

"Night daddy," he replied, staring at the statue.

As they left the room and closed over the door, Joe stopped and looked at Angela.

"Do you think it will work?" he asked.

She shook her head and sighed,

"I don't know, Joe. But I'm so desperate I'll try anything."

Robert lay staring at the glowing statue until he finally drifted off to sleep and from that night on his nightmares ceased.

The Angel Had Come.

Chapter 12

Angela was in the lounge arranging flowers in a vase, when the front door opened unexpectedly and Joe's voice could be heard.

"Angel, honey, I'm home. Robert, daddy's home."

An anxious look appeared on Angela's face. He was supposed to be away all day on business, not due home until later that evening.

Joe walked into the lounge.

"Hi honey. Where's Robert?" he asked, looking around.

"He's with Antonia."

"Oh, that's nice. Did she bring him to her apartment?"

"No," replied Angela, still fixing the flowers.

"I know, she brought him to the park."

"No."

"The zoo?"

Joe's suspicions were becoming aroused.

"Actually, Joe, she brought him to the theatre," replied Angela, turning around.

"The theatre? What for?"

"Well, she had rehearsals and thought it would be fun for him to see the costumes and sets and see what she did for a living."

"And you let him go? For Christ's sake, Angel, he's only four years old. I thought you had more sense!" He sounded really annoyed.

"She came over and asked him if he'd like to go with her. He got so excited, Joe. He wanted to go and I hadn't the heart to say, 'No'. Besides, he's never been in a theatre before."

"Well, I'd never been in one either at that age. You should have said, 'No'."

"For God's sake Joe, it's only a theatre!" exclaimed Angela." What harm can it do? I just don't see why you should be so upset."

"Oh, you don't? Well, I'll tell you. I just hope she doesn't have my son prancing around a stage in make-up and tights!"

"Oh, so that's what's up your nose – apart from the usual!" she snapped, in a polite but angry voice. I'll have you know, some of the greatest actors in history pranced around in make-up and tights."

"Yeah? Well, they weren't called Morrelli!"

Angela folded her arms.

"Now why doesn't that surprise me?" she said, sarcastically.

Joe paced up and down.

"You don't know Antonia. If he can't act, she'll have him in the chorus line or the orchestra. She'll find somewhere to put him, believe me. You don't know her like I do."

He sat down on the couch and lifted the newspaper, turning the pages noisily. "I'm surprised at you!" he said, staring over at Angela. "If she had her way, he'd be an actor or end up marrying one. Well, that's not going to happen I've got plans for him." Joe tried to concentrate on his paper, while Angela tidied away the flower remnants.

A few minutes later, Antonia's car pulled up outside the house and she and Robert got out. Angela watched from the window, then turned to Joe.

"Here they come," she informed him. "Now don't say anything to Robert. Not a word." She warned pointing her finger.

Evie answered the door and Antonia swept in without even glancing at her. She held Robert firmly by the hand.

"Hi, Evie," he called back, as Antonia led him towards the lounge.

"Hi honey," she replied.

"I had a great time with Aunt Antonia."

"That's real nice," said Evie, glaring at Antonia's back. She watched as they both disappeared.

"Well, here he is," smiled Antonia, as she walked in. "All safe and sound. We had a wonderful time. Didn't we darling?"

Robert smiled and nodded his head. She bent down and took his face in her hands, kissing him.

"Why, he even got to conduct the orchestra. Didn't you, Robbikins'?"

Joe slammed the paper down.

"That's it! That's it! 'Robbikins'!", he muttered. Then, standing up he put his hands out and looked up to the ceiling.

"Now, why couldn't I have done what my friends all did? Why didn't I marry an Italian woman? It would have been so simple. But not me, oh no, not Joe Morrelli. I always had to make things difficult for myself."

"Oh, come on, Joe," said Antonia, "you never went with Italian women. You always said they were too jealous and they talked too much, they gave you a headache."

Joe walked over and stared into her face.

"Well, I take it all back. Because, do you want to know something, Antonia? You have given me some of the biggest headaches of my life!" He turned and took Robert's hand.

"Come on, son," he said, "let's see if there's a ball game on the T.V. upstairs."

He guided Robert to the door of the lounge. Then the child stopped and looked up at him, pleadingly.

"Dad, can I go with Aunt Antonia again? I really liked it."

"See!" he said, pointing to the boy. "See what you've started!"

He stared at the women, then cast his eyes and slammed the door as he left with his son. Angela and Antonia looked at each other, then started to laugh. It was the first time real friendship have ever showed between them.

"It's at times like this I'd rather you were married to him, than me," said Antonia.

"Oh, he'll be alright. Moods never last long with Joe," Angela replied.

Antonia stared at her.

"You really did love him, didn't you?"

"Yes, I did and I still do. I'll always love him. You just have to know how to handle him."

"Well, if anyone can do that, you can," smiled Antonia. "I'd better be going."

As she walked across the entrance hall, Joe was coming downstairs. She stopped and looked at him.

"You know something, Joe? Robert's a very bright kid. He'd make a great actor. I can just see it now," she said, putting her hands up high

"Appearing tonight for the first time on Broadway, Robert J.Morrelli, in big, bright lights."

"Oh yeah?" he replied. "Well, you're the only one who's going to see it!"

The front door closed and she was gone.

Joe and Rooney had been out most of the day. As they walked through the entrance hall talking, Angela came from the dining room.

"Joe, a lady phoned and left a message for you"

"Did she give her name?" he asked.

"Yes, she said her name was Lillian. One of the girls at the Agency has had an accident and won't be able to work for a couple of weeks."

Joe threw a quick glance at Rooney.

"Did she know who you were – when she left the message, I mean?"

"Well, I answered the phone but didn't say I was your wife. She probably thought I was the maid or housekeeper," replied Angela.

Joe nodded.

"Yeah, she probably did. I have to go out again, honey."

She smiled, "You never told me you had a Model Agency, Joe."

"Well, it's not exactly a Model Agency," he said, shrugging his shoulders and looking uncomfortable. Angela's smile faded.

"What kind of agency is it?"

Rooney looked at Joe, then looked at the floor. Joe went over, took her arm and led her towards the lounge. He opened the door saying, "I won't be long, Rooney."

Angela glared over her shoulder.

"I wouldn't bet on it!" she said, giving Rooney a cold look.

Joe closed the door behind them and was silent for a moment. Then he looked into her enquiring face.

"It's an Escort Agency."

She stared at him.

"And who's Lillian?"

"She works for me, you know…" he gestured with his hands, "she's sort of like a manager."

"A manager – or a madam? Joe Morrelli, I'm shocked at you!"

"Oh yeah? Well, you'd be even more shocked if you saw what goes on, on the streets! The girls who work for my Agency are very high class, let me tell you. And they go with very important men. I'm talking business executives, lawyers, men in government positions. They go to the top restaurants, nightclubs, shows – you name it. They dress in expensive clothes and if they have any kids, they go to the best schools and have all their medical bills taken care of."

Angela's eyes widened in disbelief.

"You actually make money from those girls?"

"Listen Angel. I take a percentage from the clients who hire them as an escort for the evening. Whatever they choose to do in their own time is their business. That's where Lillian comes in. She deals with that. Most of the clients are regulars anyway."

She put her hand to her forehead.

"I can't believe you could do that."

Joe stared at her and shook his head.

"You don't understand, do you? If it wasn't me it would be someone else. Only they might not care how those girls are treated. If that's the type of work they want to do, they'll do it regardless of anybody. The big difference is that with me they are safe." He pointed his finger. "If it wasn't for me they'd be working the streets with some pimp slapping them around and pushing them into drugs. I treat them all with respect and I don't take a cent from them that isn't mine. To me they're just doing a job and getting paid for it like anyone else!"

There was silence. Then Angela nodded slowly.

"When you put it like that….well, I understand. But have you ever…," she hesitated, looking at him.

"Have I ever slept with any of them?"

"No, Angel, and that's the truth. Joe Morrelli never mixes business with pleasure."

"What about Rooney?"

"What about him?" he asked, surprised.

"Is that the reason why he isn't married or hasn't a steady girlfriend?"

Joe smiled,

"No, that's not the reason. Rooney hasn't been with any of them either." He took her in his arms. "Now, don't you go worrying about Rooney. He'll find someone special, just the way I did. He's no fool. He's probably hanging out for someone like you and I don't blame him. You're a very special woman, Angel."

Angela put her arms around his neck and kissed him long and passionately.

"I'll see you at dinner," she whispered.

Joe smiled as he reached the door.

"I doubt if anyone at the Agency could top that!" he winked, as he left.

When he and Rooney got outside the front door, Rooney stopped.

"Well, how did it go?" he enquired.

"Better than I thought it would but then, I think I handled it pretty well. I got out of the situation, that's the main thing. But I'm not sure about you."

"Me?" asked Rooney, surprised.

Joe looked at him.

"Yeah. Angel wanted to know if the girls from the Escort Agency were the reason you're not married. I guess she figured with you not having a steady girlfriend, you were using their services. After all, the rules at 'The Safe Haven' don't apply to the Agency."

"Well, I hope you put her straight!"

Joe smiled.

"Now that's difficult. You see, I'm the married one and Angel knows I wouldn't play around." He stared straight ahead for a moment, enjoying the conversation. "I reckon I just had a better excuse. I guess I'm lucky. Like I've said already, I got out of it."

Rooney glared at him.

"That's the one thing about you, Joe, you can get out of anything. Are you sure your middle name isn't Houdini?"

"Well, it's your own fault!" replied Joe. "You should get yourself a woman. Or better still, let me get you one."

"No thanks!" snapped Rooney. "I still remember the last one."

"Oh, yeah," said Joe, scratching his forehead. "What was her name again?"

"Mandy."

"Yeah, that's right, Mandy. I thought the two of you were getting on great. You were real quiet that night."

"I didn't have any choice. She talked all night about the love of her life, which just happened to be a Persian cat called 'Fifi'."

"So she's an animal lover. What's wrong with that?"

Rooney was getting annoyed.

"Nothing, if you want to spend the rest of your life married to someone with photographs of a cat all over the house. I even heard the gory details of what 'Fifi' looked like, after it had been run over by her father's limo."

Joe pointed a finger at him.

"I was doing you a big favour setting you up with her. Her old man's loaded and Mandy had plenty of cash herself."

"Well, it's a pity she didn't have plenty of brains to match!" Rooney replied sarcastically, as he walked towards the car.

Joe was finding it hard to keep a straight face. He put his hand up and rubbed his chin, thoughtfully.

"You don't seem to have much luck with women. Do you Rooney?"

"Not the ones you pick, anyway."

"Well, I didn't pick Cindy."

"Oh come on, Joe, give me a break!" he replied in a loud voice, flinging open the car door.

"Yeah, the women in your life always seem to talk a lot."

"Just like my boss!" muttered Rooney. He turned to Joe, "I want you to put things straight with Angela because for your information I have plenty of women!"

"And where do you bring these women?" asked Joe, innocently.

"Around," came the reply. "I mean, I go around to their apartment or they come around to mine. Anyway, will you just drop it, Joe?"

"O.k., o.k., but if you ever need my help……"

Rooney interrupted.

"I've had your help on more than one occasion so would you do me a big favour Joe?"

"Sure, anything. Just name it."

"Don't do me any more favours!!"

Joe received an unexpected call from Gene O'Brien, asking him to lunch at "The Imperial Palace".

After being shown to a private table, where Gene was waiting, he sat down. A waiter appeared almost immediately.

"A large scotch for Mr Morrelli and a large Irish one for me," came the order.

"Right away, Mr O'Brien," the waiter replied, hurrying to the bar.

Joe smiled.

"You're really moving up the in world, Gene. Congressman, charity functions and your own table in 'The Imperial Palace'. Yeah, you sure have come a long way."

Gene was silent as the waiter put the drinks and the menus on the table, then left. He looked across at Joe.

"That's what I want to talk to you about," he said in a serious voice, "I'm thinking of going even further."

"What's the matter, have you got itchy feet?"

He nodded as he lifted his glass.

"You could say that. It's time to move on, Joe. The truth is, I'm thinking of running for the Senate. Oh, not right away," he shrugged, "but there will be an opening in the not so distant future and I intend to be ready. What do you think?"

Joe grinned, "Why not? I think it's terrific! You're a good man. Respectable. Decent. A family man with kids to be proud of. No-one can dish any dirt at you. Why, you'd be perfect. I say go for it!"

"Oh believe me, I will," smiled Gene. "But I don't intend to go on my own. I want to bring you and Angela with me."

Joe looked surprised as he continued.

"Politics can be a dirty business. I'll need friends I can trust and rely on. People like you in my corner, who are loyal, who can get me the votes that matter."

"Well, I did help to get you into Congress!" smiled Joe.

"I know, and between you and Angela I could get the Irish and Italian votes I need for the Senate." He leaned over the table. "Joe, I'd like Angela to be a big part of this but I didn't want to ask her until I'd spoken to you. Do you know Senator Dan Casey?"

"No, not personally. But I've seen him on T.V. a lot and read about him in the newspapers."

Gene smiled and nodded,

"Well, he and I have become very good friends. He has a lot of power and clout where it matters. He's sixty-three years old and has health problems. He won't be running for re-election but he's teaching me the tricks of the trade. He wants me to run in the next election and take his place in the Senate. After all, who better to take over from a staunch, Irish American, Democrat than another staunch, Irish American Democrat! Dan Casey's a good man, Joe A man of the people." He stopped to take a drink. "Anyway, his nephew, Kevin Mitchell, is throwing a surprise 40th wedding anniversary for Dan and his wife. It needs a lot of planning so I'm setting up a committee with Kate. Angela should be perfect for it, if she'd join. She has all the qualities. She's young, attractive and she knows how to treat people and talk to them. I'll never forget the way she handled everything in 'The Safe Haven' the night of my party."

"Yeah," smiled Joe, "I must admit she did a great job."

"Exactly!" replied Gene tapping his finger on the table. "And she has the one thing Senator Casey admires most – intelligence. If she would join this committee, she'd be there for me. And believe me, Joe, I'd really like her in my camp."

Joe shrugged his shoulders.

"Well, I'll have a word with her, Gene. Personally, I think she's just what you need and I know she'd really want to help you and Kate. I'll speak to her tonight, but why don't you phone her tomorrow. I don't think there'll be any problem."

"That's all I wanted to hear," smiled Gene, as he raised his glass. "Here's to the Senate!" Joe laughed as he raised his own.

"And the White House!" he added, waiting to see Gene's expression, which was one of great surprise. "Oh, come on," smiled Joe, slyly, "Don't tell me it hadn't crossed your mind that another Irish man might sit in the Oval office one day?"

"If dreams come true, Joe, it might happen!"

They clinked their glasses.

"Yeah, you've go to aim high," advised Joe.

"It sure didn't do you any harm, old buddy," came the reply.

Joe smiled happily as he drank his scotch.

Inwardly, he was feeling very pleased that the woman he loved and married had made such an impact. He always knew that if she met the right people she could go a long way, but in his wildest dreams he never thought it would be with Senators in the corridors of power. Angela Morrelli was about to come into her own and it was her brains as much as her beauty that was in demand. Joe knew it was only a matter of time before she would become a major part of Gene O'Brien's campaign and an important woman on the social scene. He would be with her every step of the way. She would bring respectability to the name Morrelli in ways he had never imagined possible!

After his conversation with Joe, Gene felt relieved… he knew Joe Morrelli was a man of his word, was grateful to have him as a friend and pitied those who had him as an enemy. He lifted the menus and handed one to his guest.

"Let's eat, I'm starved," he said.

"Well, that hasn't changed." Smiled Joe. "You were always hungry, even as a kid. Remember when I used to go over to your house? Your mother would have a pot of Irish stew on the boil. I swear, Gene, there were times I used to think she had everything in it but the kitchen sink!"

Gene smiled broadly,

"She probably did – and you always got second helpings!"

Joe winced.

"Yeah, she was always saying I was too skinny. Even yet, I don't know how I managed to eat it all."

"But you did. And I never heard you complain."

"I didn't dare! But I'll be honest with you, I spent a fortune in the drug store on medicine for indigestion."

Gene started to laugh.

"Well, at least your stomach was full for the rest of the day."

"Yeah, she was a nice lady, your mother, and she was good to me. So was you old man. Now there was someone who could eat!" Joe nodded. "He'd come home from work and tuck into that stew, mopping up the gravy with a slice of bread as thick as a door step!" His face became serious. "I remember the day word came he'd been killed in that accident at the factory. It was a tragic time for you and your mother, loosing him like that."

A sad expression came over Gene's face, as he nodded in agreement.

"Those were tough times, alright. You know, I always regretted he didn't live to see me win my scholarship."

"Yeah well, that's life, Gene. But I'll tell you something, your old man would have been proud of you. It takes guts and a lot of determination to go from delivery boy, to lawyer, to Congressman and probably to Senator."

Gene looked across at Joe and although he tried to smile, his voice was sad. "I guess we both did o.k. Joe. It just goes to prove that if you want something badly enough, you can make it happen," he said.

Joe decided to change the subject.

"Jesus, would you look at the fancy names Ralph has for food!" he said in a low voice. "What ever happened to plain spaghetti? After you went to College, I used to get all the guys over to my apartment and cook it. Dominic, Carlo, Frankie and Al. There wasn't room to move."

Gene smiled and asked,

"What about that little guy who always followed you around, what about him? I haven't seen him in years."

Joe thought for a moment, then shook his head and smiled.

"Little Louie! Now, there's a blast from the past. Louie Cumani, he was a real character. But it's a bit of a long story."

"I'm not going anywhere I'd like to hear it," replied Gene, as the waiter came to take their order.

"Well, Louie had this dream of becoming a big shot, even though he was only 4 foot 11. Mind you, being so small did have it's advantages. When I was cooking for the guys, I'd write out the list of ingredients and give it to him. Then, I'd go into the store for the spaghetti and keep the old lady behind the counter talking. Louie would sneak in and go from shelf to shelf stealing everything else. He was never caught because he was never seen." Joe paused and smiled broadly. "The guys used to call him 'The Jockey'. Jesus, he hated that!" He screwed up his face as he remembered. "Anyway, he fell in love with a blonde bimbo called Shelly, who happened to be 5 foot 8! I used to watch the two of them dancing and try to visualise what they were like, you know, making love but I never could." Joe looked puzzled, then continued, "Eventually they got married."

"She married him?" asked Gene, surprised.

"Sure, why not? Louie could steal anything that wasn't nailed down. Shelly didn't want for anything. Clothes, jewellery, perfume. I guess she figured it was worth her while keeping him around." Joe put his knife and fork down and smiled across at Gene. "I remember the day they got married. They had no money to go anywhere so they went back to the apartment. We decided to give Louie a present. Actually, it was Dominic and Carlo's idea. They left it outside his door, rang the bell and ran down to the next floor. Louie came out buttoning his trousers and started to unwrap it. He took off the coloured ribbons and the fancy paper and underneath there was this big wooden crate with a note saying, 'If you want to do it standing up you'll need this!'"

Gene O'Brien threw his head back and laughed loudly, as Joe shook his head and said, "He went fuckin' bananas! Dominic and Carlo flew. A few minutes later, Louie came out of the tenement cursing and swearing. He started running up and down the sidewalk, bare chest, bare feet, yelling and waving his gun around. Shelly was hanging out of the window screaming – and that's not all that was hanging out! 'You bastards' he kept yelling, 'I know you're around here some where.' We were all hiding in the five and dime store across the street, watching," grinned Joe. "Dominic and Carlo were crouched down on the floor under the window, laughing so much they had tears in their eyes. Louie was still running up and down going berserk. Then he started firing the gun in the air. You never saw a street clear so fast. Everyone ran for cover but somebody must have run for help. A few minutes later, this big car drove up and Nick Andretti got out. Very cool and very calm, Nick ordered him to shut up and go inside or he'd blow his balls off!"

"What happened?" asked Gene, still laughing.

"What do you think?" Joe replied, raising his eyebrow. "It was bad enough for Louie being 4 foot 11. Can you imagine what it would have been like for him being 4 foot 11 with no balls? He went inside immediately and stayed there for the rest of the day."

Gene wiped the tears from his eyes.

"I always thought he was a bit weird," he said.

Joe leaned forward.

"Weird? The guy was a nut!"

"But he always looked up to you, Joe."

"Yeah, well, he didn't have much choice – if you know what I mean."

"Go on," urged Gene, "this is the best story I've heard in years."

Joe shrugged,

"Well, the next thing I knew, we were all summoned to Nick's office. He lined us up and demanded to know what happened. We had to tell him the truth."

"What did he say?"

"Nothing," said Joe, smiling "I never heard Nick Andretti laugh so hard."

"Did Louie move out of the neighbourhood?"

"Eventually, he recruited a couple of nutcases like himself and went onto higher things. Don't get me wrong, he didn't grow any bigger. He just got bigger in ideas. He went from robbing stores around the neighbourhood, to jewellery stores in the city. He was caught leaving one with a dozen gold watches. When they took him down town to make a statement, he said he'd only gone in to find out the time! Can you believe the nerve of that guy? That was his big mistake – mentioning the word time," nodded Joe. "He ended up doing it! He got a fifteen year stretch for armed robbery. While he was inside, Shelly sent him a 'Dear John' letter saying she'd left him for a taller man. He couldn't handle it, so he committed suicide."

"Suicide? But how?" asked Gene, shocked.

"He hanged himself in his cell," Joe explained. "But nobody could figure out how. Let's face it, he could never had made it to the ceiling. Well, not without a great deal of help! Dominic said he knew how."

Gene leaned over.

"Really?" he whispered. "How?"

Joe leaned towards him and looked around cautiously before whispering back, "Dominic said he tied a sheet to the top bunk and jumped off!"

Both men burst out laughing.

"After all," added Joe, "his feet would never have reached the ground."

Gene O'Brien shook his head. This was one lunch he had really enjoyed, and this was one side of Joe Morrelli very few people ever got to see except those closest to him. Beneath the tough exterior of this hard, shrewd businessman, was a guy who could be humorous and witty, sometimes without even knowing it.

"Jesus, Joe, you never forgot the old neighbourhood, even after all these years," said Gene, admiringly.

Joe smiled broadly.

"Well, I guess we all try when we make the big time. But as my late father-in-law used to say, 'if you forget where you've come from, you'll never know where you're going'."

Gene nodded his head in agreement.

"You know, Joe, I've never heard truer words. Could I borrow them for my campaign? Would Angela mind?"

Joe looked over Gene's shoulder and stared down the dining room to the table he and Angela sat at, the first time he had ever brought her out. Then he looked at Gene and smiled,

"Mind? No! I think Angel would be proud. After all, when Robert Kenny was sweeping the streets in Belfast who'd have thought that one day he'd help elect a man to the United States Senate!"

Angela joined the committee, much to Joe's delight, and threw herself into it wholeheartedly. She was kept busy with meetings and lunches but she was happy and enjoyed what she was doing and the people she met. Angela had the chance now to show her worth and she was doing just that. She was also proving to be a great asset to Gene O'Brien, especially in ideas, and he was always keen to listen. As the night of the anniversary party drew near, everyone involved was anxious and excited. None more so than Kevin Mitchell, who was on the phone constantly.

Rooney opened the kitchen door that morning around eleven and was surprised to see Angela sitting at the table with a cup of coffee. Normally, she would be seeing to Robert or getting ready to go out somewhere.

"How's the committee?" he smiled.

"Fine," she nodded.

"Don't tell me they've given you the day off?"

"Everything I can think of has been taken care of. Evie has brought Robert to the market so I'm going to relax today."

"I think it's been a lot tougher than you've let on," he said, sitting down beside her.

"Yes it has," she admitted, looking a little wistful, "but don't say anything to Joe."

Rooney stared at her, then asked.

"What's the matter, Angela?"

"Oh, nothing, I guess all this is still new to me. I never dreamed when I was waitressing in 'The Safe Haven' that I'd end up rubbing shoulders with Senators and planning parties for them." She looked across at him. "You know, Rooney, when I married Joe I wanted nothing more than to give him children. I was only nineteen and it all seemed possible. After Robert was born and the doctor told me I couldn't have any more, my whole world fell apart. I guess Joe's did as well. We don't talk about it but there are times when I feel I've let him down. When I look at Robert I blame myself because he hasn't got any brothers or sisters. I know deep in my heart he would have liked that, so would Joe." She shook her head. "Apart from Robert, I couldn't give Joe Morrelli the one thing his money had never bought him - a family."

Rooney placed a comforting hand on her shoulder.

"You're wrong, Angela, Joe could never have bought the happiness and love he found with you."

She gave him a faint smile.

"Well," she said, "if I can't give him what I really wanted to, then the only other thing I want is to make him proud of me. I'm doing this for Joe."

At that moment the phone in the entrance hall rang and Joe answered it. As he made his way to the kitchen, Angela looked at Rooney and put her finger on his lips. Joe came in. "Honey, Kevin Mitchell's on the phone. He wants to speak to you, something about meeting him for lunch."

Angela got up with a sigh and hurried out. A few minutes later she returned.

"Joe, I have to go. There are a few last minute details to be taken care of. Is that alright?"

"Sure, you go and get ready, I'll see to Robert. And if I have to go out, Evie can look after him."

Angela shrugged her shoulders at Rooney, before going upstairs to get ready.

"So much for her relaxing day!" he thought.

Joe sat down at the table while Rooney got up and poured some coffee for them both.

"Angela's been working very hard on that committee," he continued, sitting down again.

"Yeah, she really has been in demand, especially with that guy Mitchell. But then, Dan Casey is his uncle. I guess he wants everything to be perfect, and Angel must be doing o.k. in that respect because he always seems to want her advice."

"This is turning out to be the biggest event of the year," said Rooney.

"And my wife is a part of it," smiled Joe. "Now that's really something!"

"You're moving in pretty high circles, Joe. Congressman, now Senators and God knows who else will be there."

"Well, it's by invitation only so you can be sure of one thing, is will be the very elite."

The door opened and Angela appeared wearing a straight black skirt, black top and a three-quarter length electric blue jacket, set off by black high-heels and shoulder bag.

"You look terrific, Angela," complimented Rooney.

Joe looked her up and down.

"Yeah, you sure do," he agreed.

She smiled,

"Oh, before I forget, Rooney, this is for you."

She reached over and put a large, white envelope down on the table in front of him.

"What is it?" he asked.

"It's your invitation to the party."

"Who invited me?"

"I did, on behalf of Senator Dan Casey."

"Oh come on, Angela, I can't go to that!" he replied, surprised.

Angela stared at him.

"Why ever not?"

Rooney shrugged.

"Well, I wouldn't fit it."

She pointed her finger at him.

"Now, you listen to me," she demanded. "You are every bit as good as anyone else who'll be there."

"But Angela, they're Senators, for God's sake!"

"I know. And just how do you think they got there? I'll tell you how, Rooney. You and me and everyone else." She put her hand on the door and held it open. "If it wasn't for the ordinary man and woman on the street giving them their support and their votes, they wouldn't be in the Senate. They need us even more than we need them, and they should never be allowed to forget that, Rooney."

Joe looked at Rooney and nodded.

"She's got a point. You know something, Angel? You'd have made a great First Lady!" he beamed.

She went over and put her arm around him.

"As long as I'm your First Lady, Joe, that will do for me." Kissing his cheek, she then turned to leave the kitchen.

"Now, don't you do all the hard work and let them take all the credit!" he called after her.

"I won't," came the reply. "You'd never forgive me and besides, I'm a little smarter than that, Mr Morrelli!"

"You sure are," he nodded, as the front door closed. Then he looked at Rooney and smiled, pointing to the envelope. "Well, it looks like you're going to be moving in high circles as well!"

Joe, Angela and Rooney stepped inside the very upmarket 'Royston Club', after handing in their invitations at the door. There was a large, polished dance floor with tables and chairs on both sides, a band stand complete with some of the finest musicians New York had to offer and a gold railed balcony that went the whole way round the room. The place was pretty crowded as they made their way past the long, mirrored bar to the table reserved for them.

"Not bad," smiled Joe looking around, as a waiter came over with a large bottle of champagne in an ice bucket, and put it down on the table. Joe lifted the bottle and looked at the label before pouring it into the long stemmed glasses. "Classy stuff. The champagne alone must be costing a fortune."

"Everything is costing a fortune," replied Angela, taking a sip. "Some of the food for the buffet was flown in especially. But Kevin wanted the best. Besides, he can afford it."

A little while later Dan Casey, his wife and their party (which included Gene and Kate O'Brien) entered the hall to loud applause. Dan Casey was visibly surprised as he stood for a few moments smiling, before being led to his table. Angela then excused herself and went out to the foyer. The band stopped playing and the sound of pipes could be heard. Then, to everyone's amazement, a pipe band marched down the centre of the floor playing Irish tunes, accompanied by a troop of Irish dancers in national costume, who followed behind. The pipers stood and played, then splitting into two sections they made their way up the steps to the balcony. The dancers took over, putting on a display of jigs and reels that was almost breathtaking. When they had finished, they held hands and bowed low, as everyone rose to applaud. They turned and marched out slowly, as the pipers descended from the balcony and followed.

Dan Casey stood, wiping the tears from his eyes. He was clearly showing great emotion at this unexpected and most appreciated show and display. After that, the party was in full swing. Joe and Angela were dancing when Gene O'Brien put his arms around them. "Come with me," he nodded, leading the way to his table. Once there he smiled, "Dan, I'd like you to meet two of my dearest friends, Joe Morrelli and his wife, Angela." Joe put out his hand.

"Nice to meet you senator." Dan Casey clasped it.

"It's nice to meet you too, Joe. Gene has told me a lot about you."

Joe smiled, "I hope it was all good!"

"Oh don't worry about that. He speaks very highly of you."

He turned and shook Angela's hand.

"And I'm told you're the one I have to thank for the floor show. My nephew tells me it was your idea," he smiled.

"I'm so glad you liked it."

"Liked it? I loved it! For a while I thought I was back in my grandfather's whitewashed cottage in Kildare. You've made me very happy."

"It was an honour Senator," smiled Angela. Then she turned her attention to Alma

Casey and Kate O'Brien, chatting happily to them.

Dan looked at Joe. "Your wife's a real lady," he nodded. "Gene thinks a lot of her and after tonight so will I. She's doing a great job and I know you both will, when Gene runs for election."

"Well, we aim to please," smiled Joe. Gene poured three glasses of champagne, handed on to the senator, one to Joe and lifted the third.

"Here's to the senate," he toasted, in a low voice, "and the Irish and Italian votes that are going to put me there." The three men looked knowingly at each other and nodded, then stood in deep conversation. As people came up to the table to congratulate Dan and Alma Casey on their anniversary, Joe decided it was time to go. He looked around.

"Where's Angela?" he asked.

"She's up dancing," replied Kate.

Joe shook hands with the Senator and his wife and made his way through the thronged dance floor, to his own table. Rooney had disappeared as well. Joe ordered a double scotch from a passing waiter and sat drinking it slowly, watching the dancers and looking around for his wife. When the music stopped and every-one was leaving the floor, Angela came through the crowd holding some-one's hand. He expected it to be Rooney but when they both came in full view it wasn't.

Smiling, she came up to the table with a young man. He was well built and extremely handsome, with a deep tan, blonde hair and green eyes.

"Joe, I'd like you to meet Kevin Mitchell. Kevin, this is my husband, Joe Morrelli."

She stood aside as Kevin stepped forward and smiled broadly, showing a perfect set of white teeth.

"I'm pleased to meet you, Mr Morrelli," he said, as they both shook hands.

However, a look of surprise crept over Kevin's face as he studied Joe more closely. A look he couldn't hide and Joe was quick to notice. He knew Kevin Mitchell had been expecting a much younger man, the look on his face said it all. For the first time since Joe had married Angela, he felt his age. He was forty-four and right now he felt every day of it. He didn't need a crystal ball to know what Kevin Mitchell was thinking. He knew he was wondering why a man of his age was married to a woman of barely twenty-four. As he looked at the two of them standing together, Joe felt uncomfortable and embarrassed. Although he didn't show any signs, inwardly that old green-eyed monster called "Jealousy" was awakening after a long sleep! They complimented each other so well Kevin, handsome and confident. Angela, beautiful and elegant in a white and silver evening-dress that sparkled under the lights. As Joe surveyed them both standing in front of him he had to admit to himself, they looked the perfect couple!

"Could I borrow your wife for a little while, Mr Morrelli?" smiled Kevin. "It's time for the cake to be brought it."

"Sure, be my guest," replied Joe, forcing a smile in return.

"I won't be long, Joe," she beamed happily. "And when I come back there are some people I'd like to introduce you to."

As they left the table, he couldn't help but notice the way Kevin looked admiringly into her face. Rooney appeared, pulling his seat out and sitting down.

"Who's that?" he said, nodding after them.

"Kevin Mitchell," came the reply.

"Oh, so that's him? Well, I must admit he's very good looking and a lot younger than I imagined."

"Yeah well, that makes two of us," said Joe, gazing after them.

In a little while the lights were dimmed, as Kevin and Angela wheeled in a large cake lit up with coloured sparklers. Afterwards, Senator Casey gave a speech thanking everyone for coming and a special 'thank-you' to all those who had organised the party. Angela had just rejoined Joe and Rooney at the table when another large, very expensive bottle of champagne was delivered and a beautiful bouquet of flowers, courtesy of Kevin Mitchell. Angela and Joe got up to dance.

"Are you enjoying yourself?" she asked.

"Yeah, it sure is some party."

"I'm glad it went so well, Joe."

"Why wouldn't it? The best thing that they ever did was ask you to help organise it," he smiled.

At that point in time , all he wanted to do was to hold his wife in his arms and move slowly to the music. But every few seconds someone was tapping her shoulder and chatting. In turn, Angela was introducing him. He'd never realised she'd come to know so many people. Some of them were going out of there way just to talk to her because of Senator Casey. Joe was feeling a little peeved. It was the first party he'd been to where he wasn't the one who knew most of the guests and wasn't doing the introducing. As they came back to the table and sat down, Rooney noticed a moody expression on Joe's face. As Angela poured herself some champagne. Joe looked at the glass. "Don't you think you're drinking a little too much of that, Angel?" he nodded.

She laughed, "I'm enjoying myself Joe. And besides, I've earned it!"

Rooney glared at him "Come on, Angela, lets dance," he said.

Then casting his eyes at Joe he led her on to the floor. When the music ended, Rooney made for the bar and Angela went to the powder room. Joe felt a hand on his shoulder and, looking up, saw Gene O'Brien leaning over him.

"Well, how's it going, old buddy?" he smiled, sitting down,

"Couldn't be better."

Gene looked at him and nodded, "You could have fooled me. I've seen you look happier."

"Well, maybe that was when my wife was in my company," he shrugged, glancing towards the crowd and seeing Angela and Kevin talking and laughing.

As the band started to play, they began to dance. Gene followed his gaze.

"I see you've met Kevin Mitchell. He's an interesting guy."

"Yeah, and he really seems to be interested in my wife," replied Joe, still watching them.

Gene smiled and decided to have a little harmless fun.

"He seems quite taken with that dress she's wearing."

"If you ask me he's more taken with what's inside it. What does he do for a living, anyway?"

"Oh, he's one of these high flying executives. You know, stays in the best hotels, owns apartments and villa's half way round the world."

Joe turned and stared at Gene.

"The guy must be loaded," he said.

"He is. You want to know something, Joe?. He's thirty years old and he's got more money than you and me put together. And that's not counting Dan Casey's money. Kevin is sole heir to everything he has."

"You'd think he'd be married."

"Well, he doesn't want for women, that's for sure. But it would take a special kind of woman to land that fish. He's very attracted to a good figure and good looks but he also admires personality and brains. Yeah, Kevin wants it all- a bit like you, Joe!" he said, hiding a smile. "He's on the lookout."

"Oh yeah? Well, he can look somewhere else!"

Gene shook his head.

"I don't want to worry you, Joe, but he's the new generation. You know, the new breed. He's the dinner in Paris type."

"What do you mean?" enquired Joe.

Gene smiled, "When he asks a woman out to dinner, he thinks nothing of flying her to Paris for it."

Joe leaned across the table.

"Well, I can promise you one thing. He won't be having dinner in Paris with my wife, not if I can help it! Who does he think he is, anyway? Walking around with that Florida tan and Hollywood smile," he snarled.

Gene got up from the table and patted his friend's shoulder.

"Every woman's dream, Joe," he smiled. "Every woman's dream!"

As Gene O'Brien made his way back to Senator Casey's table, he was still smiling. He hadn't lied about Kevin Mitchell's status or lifestyle, but he knew by the look on Joe's face he had taken an instant dislike to the guy. And after what he'd told him, he knew Joe would lose a lot of sleep if ever the phone rang and it was Kevin inviting Angela to dinner. He chuckled to himself. If he knew Joe (and he did) he would probably end up sitting in the airport watching every flight going to Paris!

Rooney came back to the table.

"Where's Angela?" he asked, sitting down.

Joe nodded towards the crowded floor.

"She's dancing with Kevin Mitchell – and he's loving every minute of it!"

Rooney looked at him.

"You don't like him much, do you?"

Joe lifted his glass and replied,

"He's paying too much attention to my wife."

"Really? Why? Is he watching every glass of champagne she's drinking as well?"

Joe threw him a look.

"Angel can't handle a lot of that stuff," he explained. "It makes her... you know," he shrugged.

"No, I don't know."

"Romantic!"

"Well, lucky you," said Rooney. "I'm surprised you're not filling her glass every five minutes! Listen Joe, she did a great job with the party. Why don't you just let her enjoy herself?"

Joe thought for a moment.

"Yeah, you're right," he nodded. "But I don't see why she has to pay so much attention to everyone. She's spent half the night talking to the guests, making sure they're happy."

"Well, if I remember correctly, she did the same thing when she worked for you and I never heard you complain."

Joe lowered his eyes and looked at the table.

Rooney nudged him saying,

"Here she comes. Forget about Kevin Mitchell, Joe. After all, he's only a guest like the rest of them."

Angela smiled.

"Have you got yourself a girl yet, Rooney?"

He looked around.

"I'm spoilt for choice! I must admit, there are some very attractive ones here but they're a bit too classy for me. I'm glad I came, though. It's nice to see how the other half lives. To be honest with you Angela, I've really enjoyed myself. It's been a great night."

"And it isn't over yet," she smiled, looking at Joe.

Joe met her gaze as she continued. "I've got a surprise for you. I've asked the band to play a special request. Here it is now."

As the band played the opening bars of "Strangers in the Night" she took Joe's hand and led him onto the dance floor. He smiled proudly as they put their arms around each other.

"I never thought you'd remember that, Angel," he said in a low voice.

She looked up at him.

"How could I forget? It was the first record we ever danced to in Mario's."

"Yeah, that was the night I knew I'd end up falling in love with you – and I did," he whispered.

As they danced closely, oblivious to all others, Rooney looked across the room and caught sight of Kevin Mitchell. He was leaning his elbows on the table, his chin resting on his joined hands. He was watching Joe and Angela with a bemused smile on his face.

A smile that puzzled Rooney.

Gene O'Brien got up and nodded towards the two,

"There goes a happy couple," he commented, taking Kate's arm in a bid to join them.

Kevin looked at him.

"Oh, I don't know, Gene. A lot of young wives have to keep their husbands sweet, but they like their action elsewhere."

Gene shook his head and leaned over the table.

"Not this one!" he assured.

Kevin made no reply but smiled broadly as he returned his gaze to the dance floor.

Joe came out of the men's room and was making his way across the floor when, on the stroke of midnight, a mass of coloured balloons with white satin string attached to them came floating down from the ceiling. As everyone cheered and tried to snatch them, Joe reached up and caught one. He held it tightly as he began battling through the excited crowd, towards his table. He wanted to give it to Angela and was smiling as he caught sight of her. However, his smiles soon faded. For just at the moment, Kevin Mitchell appeared at Angela's side. He, too, was holding a balloon and handed it to her. She accepted, laughingly. He put his hands on the table and leaned over smiling admiringly, as he gazed into her face. He then moved his head and started to speak softly into her ear, almost touching her cheek as she nodded and smiled.

As Joe watched Angela holding the balloon Kevin had given her, he could feel his temper rising. He opened his hand and let go of the one he had. It drifted away. Although people jostled by him, he stayed rooted to the spot until Kevin Mitchell finally left the table. Then Joe made his way over.

"Where have you been?" asked Angela.

"Oh, I was talking to someone. Anyway, I think it's time we were going. Are you ready?"

Angela got up as Joe stood looking around.

"Where's Rooney?" he asked.

"He's over there," she replied, pointing to the dance floor.

He went over and tapped Rooney on the shoulder.

"We're ready to leave. Are you coming?"

"I'm ready if you are but I didn't think you'd be leaving so soon."

Joe looked at him.

"Yeah well, as far as I'm concerned the party's over! Lets go."

When they arrived back at the table, Angela was waiting.

"What shall I do with this?" she asked holding the balloon.

"Whatever you want!" came Joe's curt reply.

She tied it to the back of the chair, then picked up her purse and the bouquet of flowers. The three then went over to Dan Casey's table. Joe was very gracious as he shook hands with both him and his wife.

"We have to go now, Senator," he explained. "Thanks for a wonderful night."

"I'm glad you enjoyed it, Joe, and I'm happy to have met you. I'm sure we'll meet again."

He took Angela's hand. "It was a marvellous party, thanks to you," he smiled "Kate tells me you really put a lot of effort into it. And my nephew is really singing your praises! He told me he couldn't have managed without you. You're a very special lady, Mrs Morrelli, and your husband is a very lucky man."

"I was glad to help in any way," she smiled, "but before we go, I'd like to introduce you to a member of our family. Senator, this is Rooney."

Dan Casey laughed as he shook Rooney's hand, "Don't tell me, let me guess. With a name like that you must be Irish! Are you two related?"

"Not quite, but you could say we're neighbours. We come from the same place."

"And where's that?"

"Belfast."

The Senator became more serious and shook his head.

"Belfast," he echoed. "I follow what's going on there very closely. In fact, I like to think I'm kept well informed about all of Northern Ireland. It's a bad state of affairs but we all have to do what we can, both now and in the future. Anyway, I'm glad you're both here in New York. If you want my opinion, things are going to get a lot worse over there before they ever get any better. But then, I guess I don't have to tell you that. After all, you've lived there." He looked at Joe. "You take good care of this wife of yours, Joe. Coming from the place of bombs and bullets, she deserves it!"

Joe nodded, then they said their 'goodbyes' to Gene and Kate. As they turned to leave, Kevin came walking towards them. He stopped and smiled

"Goodnight, Mr Morrelli. I'm sorry you both couldn't stay longer," he said, shaking Joe's hand but looking at Angela. "The place won't be the same without the prettiest woman in it! Thanks for everything Angela."

As she smiled at him, he gazed deeply into her eyes for a moment.

Joe stared at him, then put his hand on Angela's back to gently guide her away.

"I'll be in touch, Angela," he added. "Perhaps I could give you a call?"

Joe turned his head and leaned towards him.

"I wouldn't bet on getting a reply!" he said, in a sharp tone.

Angela and Rooney looked at each other but never spoke.

The three of them walked towards the foyer to the front door. As Joe stepped out onto the side-walk and into the waiting limousine, the expression on his face had changed to one of hurt and rage. Gone was the "Mr Nice Guy" Senator Casey had met. Joe Morrelli was consumed with anger and jealousy and ready to explode!

As the car pulled away from the kerb, there was silence. Then it was broken by Joe's voice.

"Well, he might fool you but he sure doesn't fool me."

"Who?" asked Angela.

"Mr 'Charm and Smarm Mitchell."

When she made no reply, he turned on her.

"I blame you!" he accused.

"Me?" she asked, in a surprised voice.

"Yeah, you! He was really getting your full attention tonight. Did you have to act so familiar with him? The guy was making a play for you and you were leading him on."

Angela gave a deep sigh.

"For God's sake, Joe, would you just drop it?" said and angry Rooney.

Joe looked at him.

"Maybe I should drop you – at the nearest corner."

"That suits me fine! Al, pull over."

As Rooney pushed himself off the seat, Angela grabbed his arm.

"No, Rooney, you're staying right here." Then she turned to Joe. "That's enough!" she warned.

They continued the journey in silence as Al watched them all in the mirror. He couldn't believe his ears or his eyes, as Joe simmered behind him.

Finally the silence proved too much and Joe broke it once again.

"I saw the way he looked at you. With that 'nobody can resist me smile' and those 'come to bed' eyes. But I didn't see you do anything to stop it. Oh no! Quite the opposite, in fact. You fell for it."

His sarcastic tone was wounding Angela. She stared at him. "I treated Kevin Mitchell the same way I treated everyone else tonight."

"Well, you could have fooled me. But as I've already said – he doesn't! I know what Kevin Mitchell wanted. What I'd really like to know is, would he have gotten it if I hadn't have been there?" he asked, raising his voice.

Angela stared straight ahead, tears brimming in her eyes.

"You have no right to speak to me like that."

"I have every right," he insisted. "I'm your husband. Or has Kevin Mitchell made you forget that?" he yelled.

Rooney dug his fist into the car seat as Al shook his head in disbelief. When they pulled up in front of the house, Rooney opened the door and got out. Then he leaned back in, took Angela's hand and waited until she'd stepped out beside him.

Joe got out through the other door, slamming it loudly.

"I'll have a word with him, Angela," whispered Rooney, as she turned and walked quickly towards the front door.

Joe walked around the back of the car, undoing his jacket. Rooney put his hand on his arm.

"You're making something out of nothing. Let it go or you might regret it."

Joe looked at him.

"She's my wife!" came the nasty reply.

"Then stop treating her like a whore!" snapped Rooney, as Joe pulled his arm away and followed her.

Al opened the driver's door.

"Jesus, Rooney, what's wrong with the boss? I've never seen him like that with a woman."

"Jealousy!"

"Well, whatever it is I feel sorry for her."

"So do I because it's all in his mind. And believe me I should know, I was there. Listen, Al, can you hang around for a little while? I've got a feeling I won't be staying the night after all."

"Yeah sure, Rooney. I'll be in the garage."

"Thanks, Al," he replied, then hurried to the front door, closing it behind him. As Al walked away, Joe's accusing voice could still be heard but this time he was really spoiling for a fight!

All the commotion brought Evie to the door of Robert's room, from where she watched the scene.

Angela walked towards the stairs followed by Joe, who was still ranting on about Kevin Mitchell. She stopped and turned to face him.

"Joe, will you please stop repeating that name over and over. You sound like one of those talking parrots and you're giving me a headache." She put her hand up to her forehead. "Why don't you do what Rooney said and just drop it."

"As long as that's all that's being dropped around here!" he sneered.

She gave him a long look.

"What do you mean?"

Joe pointed his finger at her.

"You know what I mean."

She shook her head.

"I'm not going to argue with you, Joe. I'm going to bed."

As she turned and stepped onto the bottom stair, he grabbed her arm.

"I haven't finished yet. Don't you ever turn your back on me when I'm talking to you. And stop clutching those stupid flowers!" he shouted, snatching the bouquet from her arm and throwing it to the floor.

"That's not fair," she protested. "I got those for helping on the committee."

"Yeah," agreed Joe, "and we all know who gave them to you – 'The Slick Prick'!"

"I wasn't the only one he gave flowers to. Kate got them as well."

"But Kate O'Brien wasn't running around all night after Kevin Mitchell like a bitch on heat," he said sarcastically.

Angela stared at him.

"How dare you say that to me."

Joe pulled his jacket open, put his hands on his hips and walked up and down in front of her. There was silence as he studied the floor. Then he spoke.

"Tell me something," he said. "All those lunches you two had together. Were they just cosy lunches or sex sessions in fancy hotel rooms with expensive champagne? I'd like to know."

Rooney looked and saw Evie cover her face with her hands. Then he turned and saw the look of shock sweep Angela's face.

"That's enough, Joe!" he warned. "You're going too far!"

Joe ignored him, as Angela made no reply. He stopped and put his hand up to his ear. "What was that? I didn't hear it. O.k.," he nodded, pacing up and down again, "I'll repeat the question."

Rooney had seen Joe do this before, but only with men. He'd seen him intimidate them by his attitude and tone of voice, to the point of fear. Now, he was watching helplessly as he did it to his own wife.

Joe never lifted his eyes from the floor as he continued.

"Did you sleep with Kevin Mitchell?" he demanded, stopping and looking at her. Then he lunged forward. "Did you spread your legs for that son-of-a-bitch?" he roared into her face, his own filled with uncomfortable rage. Angela gave a startled jump, visibly shaken by his outburst. She grabbed the stair-rail to steady herself. Her eyes were filled with tears and fear as she looked at him. She swallowed hard and took a deep breath. "I'm not going to answer that, Joe Morrelli, because deep in your heart you already know the answer."

Joe lowered his eyes, then looked away.

"Are you finished now?!" she asked. "You must be, because there's really nothing left for you to say. You certainly can't bring me down any lower than you already have. But there's something I want to say. I've had enough of your insults and accusations and I'm not going to listen to any more."

She walked across the entrance hall.

"Where are you going?" he shouted.

She turned and glared at him. Now her eyes were filled with anger. "To find Kevin!" she yelled, defiantly. "After all, if I'm going to be accused of it, I might as well do it!"

As she opened the front door, Joe caught up with her and grabbed her wrist tightly. "You're not leaving this house!" he ordered.

She pulled herself free.

"Oh no? Well you just watch me!" she replied, slamming the door in his face.

Rooney walked towards him.

"Well, you've really done it this time!" he said.

Joe nodded to the door,

"Follow her."

Rooney stopped in his tracks.

"No way, Joe. This is your mess, you clean it up!"

Joe stared at him coldly and shouted,

"What the fuck's the matter with you? I gave her everything and it was me," pointing to himself, "Joe Morrelli, who put her where she is."

Rooney stood in front of him, his face white with anger.

"Oh, come on, Joe, it's me you're talking to. Sure, you wanted her in with the right crowd but you wanted it as much for yourself as Angela. Why don't you just admit it? Yes, you wanted the big time for her and you got it. But now that you see how successful she's become and the attention she's getting, you can't handle it, and that's the sad part."

Joe shook his head.

"Don't say anymore, Rooney. I'm warning you."

"Why? I'm only telling the truth. But then sometimes the truth hurts, doesn't it?"

Rooney squared up to him like never before. "Did you ever wonder why she joined that committee?"

"Because she knew she could do it. She had the brains."

"Wrong!" yelled Rooney. "She did it because she feels she owes you. Because she can't give you any more kids. Because, more than anything else in the world, she wants to make you proud of her. She told me so herself the other day, when we were sitting in the kitchen. Any man would have been proud of her tonight, but not you. Oh no, you ruined her night and everything she worked so hard for. This was her one big chance to achieve all her goals and you destroyed it." He looked Joe up and down saying, "You know, for such a smart man you fucked up, Joe. And you did it in a big way."

Joe's eyes flashed with anger as he pointed to Rooney.

"Don't interfere in my life," he warned.

"If you carry on like this, pretty soon you won't have a life because you might not have a wife to share it with. But just stop for a minute and think about Angela's life. Her father was murdered, her mother died right next to her, she almost lost Robert and she can't have the children she longed for. Don't you think she's had enough hurt without you treating her like some two-bit whore?"

"Now you listen to me," demanded Joe.

"No, you listen for a change!" It was Rooney's turn to point "You know damn well there's nothing between her and Kevin Mitchell, but I'll tell you something. If I knew where he lived I'd take her there myself because you deserve everything you get!"

Joe looked at him in surprise. Rooney had never spoken to him like this before.

"Are you finished?" he roared.

"Not quite!" shouted Rooney. "Angela never gave you any reason to doubt her. She always loved you."

"Maybe that's what's bothering you," Joe sneered, "there's only ever one winner."

Rooney eased back, stared at him and nodded.

"O.k. Joe," he said, "you gave Angela a lot of things I never could, but you forgot one very important thing."

"And what's that?"

"Your trust!" Rooney replied, as he turned and opened the front door, feeling both hurt and angry.

Al was standing there with a glum look on his face. Joe looked at him.

"Did you see Angel outside?" he asked.

"Yeah, but she's gone now, Boss. I was coming to tell you."

"What do you mean, gone? Gone where?" yelled Joe.

"Well, I saw her walking down the driveway so I caught up with her and asked if she wanted me to drive her somewhere. She said 'No', it was better if I didn't get involved. If I didn't take sides you couldn't say anything to me. I guess she didn't want any more trouble," he shrugged.

"Where did she go?"

"I don't know, Boss. I walked her to the end of the drive and she hailed a taxi. Before she got in, she apologised for what happened tonight. You know.... On the way home."

"She apologised?" said Rooney, looking at Al. "She didn't do anything. He's the one who kept running off at the mouth!" he pointed to Joe, accusingly. Then turned and stared him straight in the eye. "You know something, Joe? I feel sorry for you because some day you might end up a lonely, bitter old man. With no wife and no friends, and you'll only have yourself to blame. Sometimes the winner ends up the loser – just like the fights you fix!!" He turned around. "Come on, Al, lets go I've heard things here tonight I wouldn't have heard in a 'dive'."

Rooney walked out, slamming the door so loudly it echoed through the house.

Evie crept down the stairs as Joe stood alone, gazing at the door and listening as the car drove off. Whatever thoughts were going through his mind were quickly interrupted by the sound of Robert crying. He turned and hastily made his way towards the stair-case Evie, dressed in her night-robe, was close by picking up the flowers. As he came nearer, she straightened herself slowly and looked at him with tears in her eyes.

"You said some bad things tonight, Mr Joe, some bad things. How could you treat Miss Angela like that and accuse her of doing things you know deep inside she would never do?"

Joe gave her a sorrowful look.

"He's everything I'm not, Evie. He's young, he's handsome, he's educated – and he wants her!"

"Maybe, but she wants you. She always did. It's not her fault if other men find her attractive. Didn't you? If they were in your shoes they would be proud. After all, wanting her is one thing but having her as your wife is something else. And you had her, Mr Joe. But after tonight, well, I'm not so sure."

"What do you mean?" he asked.

She nodded towards the top of the stairs.

"From the day that child came into this house, this is the first night Miss Angela hasn't looked in on him. She would never go to bed unless she made sure he was alright. She must be hurting real bad to leave her home and her son." She turned and walked away from him, shaking her head. "Yes Sir, she must be hurting real bad," she repeated, in a sad voice.

Joe hurried up the stairs and opened the door of Robert's room, which had once been the nursery. The little boy was sitting up in bed, bewildered and crying loudly. Joe lifted him in his arms.

"It's alright son," he said in a low, soothing voice. "Don't be frightened, Daddy's here."

Robert clung to him tightly, as Joe sat down on the bedside chair with the small boy on his lap. Rubbing his sleepy eyes with clenched fists Robert sobbed,

"I want my mommy."

Joe held him protectively, kissing his forehead. "Go to sleep, Robert. Everything is alright now," he murmured.

The child put his head on his father's shoulder and wrapped his little arms around Joe's neck. Tears still streamed down his face but gradually his eyes closed.

"I want my mommy," he sobbed again, drifting slowly off to sleep.

Joe patted his back gently as he stared at the angel. Tears filled his own eyes and he gave a deep sigh.

"So do I son," he whispered. "So do I!"

Joe sat for a long time holding Robert. His temper was replaced by a deep sadness and a strong feeling of guilt. Angela hadn't wanted an argument but he had provoked one that had driven her to walk out. He gave another deep sigh as he rubbed his face with his hand. This time he really had gone too far. He had treated her worse than some slut on a street corner and what was unforgivable, was that he had done it in front of other people. People she had to face every day because they were like family. He had shown no decency towards his wife and he was full of remorse. This was one side of Joe Morrelli's character he never wanted Angela to see. But she had. And he couldn't help but feel anxious at the effect it would have on her. He rose from the chair and gently put Robert into bed. After tucking him in, he leaned over and looked into his little tear-stained face. "Son, I know you love your mom," he whispered. "I love her too and I always will."

He kissed Robert's cheek, then left the room closing the door quietly behind him.

Joe came downstairs and went straight to the study. Once inside, he took off his jacket and tie and after unbuttoning his collar, he stood looking out of the window into the darkness. He glanced at his watch. It had gone 3:30. He was deeply worried about Angela. He had no idea where she was. She had no family to go to and he was certain she wouldn't trouble any of their friends. At that moment all he did know was that she was out there somewhere feeling unwanted and unloved, and it was all his fault. He could only hope and pray she was safe and that she's come home soon. The thought that she might not return weighted heavily on Joe's mind, but that wasn't all. What about Agnes? She had made him promise never to doubt Angela's love for him, but he had. For the first time in his life, Joe Morrelli had broken a promise. But what hurt most was that he had broken it to a woman he had loved and respected. Agnes had given him her trust and he had betrayed it by what he'd done to Angela.

He sat on the leather chair, leaning his elbows on the desk and clenching his hands tightly together, he closed his eyes.

"I'm sorry, Agnes," he whispered, from the heart. "Please, wherever she is, send her back to me."

Tears welled up in his eyes and he put his face down onto his hands. "I love you Angel Morrelli," he sobbed. "And I don't want to live the rest of my life without you!"

Joe sat for the rest of the night keeping a lonely vigil, watching the darkness slowly turn into light. Shortly after 6am he heard a car pull into the driveway and stop. He jumped up and looking out of the window, he was surprised to see Freddie Barrett getting out. Joe wondered what he was doing at his home so early.

Freddie walked around the car and opened the passenger door. As Angela stepped out, Joe's heart leapt for joy. He rubbed his face with his hands, his eyes red and swollen from tears and lack of sleep. Unshaven and dishevelled, he hurried to the study door. Opening it just enough to peer out, he heard the sound of footsteps and low voices. As he watched, Angela crossed the entrance hall and went upstairs. When she had disappeared from view, Joe opened the door and came out. Freddie was standing with his hands clasped in front of him. The two men looked at each other.

"Thanks for bringing her home, Freddie," said Joe. "Where did you find her?"

"I didn't Mr Morrelli. She found me. She came to 'The Safe Haven'. We were closed but I was still in the office when I heard the bell. I opened the door and she was standing there, distraught.... I took her inside and then brought her to my apartment. She hasn't had any sleep. She spent the night talking, crying and drinking coffee."

Joe nodded and put a hand on his shoulder.

"I'm glad she's safe. I've been out of my mind with worry. I really appreciate all you've done."

Freddie didn't reply but forced an uncomfortable smile as he shuffled from one foot to the other.

Joe watched him, puzzled

"Is something bothering you, Freddie?"

"Mr Morrelli, Angela has asked me to wait."

"What's going on?" asked Joe, staring at him.

"It's not my place to say, Sir," Freddie replied, looking embarrassed. "I think you should ask Angela."

He lowered his gaze as Joe raised his towards the top of the stairs.

"Oh, I will, believe me," nodded Joe as he hurriedly climbed them two at a time, leaving Freddie to stare after him.

As Joe entered the bedroom, he could not believe what he was seeing. There on the bed was a large suitcase and Angela was packing it. A look of shock and surprise swept over his face, as he walked over to the bed.

"What are you doing?" he asked, anxiously.

"You've always prided yourself on being a smart man – you figure it out!" she replied, keeping her eyes on the garment she was folding.

"Angel, listen, we have to talk."

She stopped and looked at him coldly.

"You did all your talking last night. Remember?"

Joe's expression changed to one of guilt, as Angela continued to pack. "You know, I've had a lot of time to think, Joe," she continued, "and looking back, I've been very naïve. You never trusted me, did you? Not with Michael Conway, a boy you didn't even know: not with Dean Prescott: not with those beach-boys in Miami. I don't think you even trusted me with Charlie, when I first made friends with him." She shook her head sadly then turned and stared into his face. "My God, I'm surprised you ever trusted me with Rooney! But then, I suppose you wouldn't have if he wasn't like a brother to you."

The last remark pricked Joe's conscience more than Angela would ever know.

"Now, that's not true!" he insisted. "I love you."

"I'm not talking about love, I'm talking about trust, Joe. Something you never had. But I always trusted you, especially with Antonia."

"And what's that supposed to mean?"

"Oh, Come on, Joe, I'm not stupid. I know you still see her from time to time."

"And just how do you know that?"

"I've heard you on the telephone."

He lowered his gaze for a moment, then looked at her and nodded.

"O.k., I do see Antonia now and again. But it's only to make sure she's alright. There's never been anything but friendship between us since the day I married you – and that's the truth!"

"I've never doubted that, or you. It's a pity you couldn't do the same with me."

She moved closer to him, her eyes fixed on his. As Joe gazed at her, he could clearly see the anguish he had caused.

"Do you want to know what hurts the most, Joe? The fact that you didn't think I had the brains to see right through Kevin Mitchell," she said in a disappointed voice.

Joe knew in his heart she was right and he had made a big mistake. He shook his head and held out his hands.

"Angel, you don't understand. I was scared of losing you to a guy like that. He could give you the kind of life I don't. He likes to travel, he could show you the world."

He watched as tears filled her eyes and she pulled back.

"Do you honestly think that's the kind of life I want? Jetting around the world, living out of suitcases in different hotel rooms, partying every night? And what about you Joe? She clutched the evening dress she was still wearing. "Do you think I married you for expensive clothes and all the things your money can buy? To be looked up to because I'm your wife – Mrs Joe Morrelli?! You've really disappointed me. I thought you were a much smarter man. You see, Joe, I'd have married you if you'd been a garbage collector."

She turned away with a disgusted look on her face and continued her packing. Joe stood ridden with guilt and remorse.

"Look, Angel, we can work this out."

"It's too late, Joe, I'm leaving you."

"For Christ's sake, Angel, we've had one argument," he said in a raised voice. "That's no reason to end a perfectly good marriage."

She quickly faced him.

"I told you once in Miami if we didn't have trust we had nothing. But you didn't listen. That's why I'm ending it. This marriage is over!!" Her voice was filled with anger.

Joe sat down on the bed. He knew she meant every word and was determined to leave. Inwardly, he was in a state of blind panic. He was prepared to do anything to keep her. He had only one trump card left to play. He didn't want to use it but he was a desperate man, and desperate times called for desperate measures.

Joe watched as Angela closed the suitcase.

"Where will you go?" he asked.

She kept her eyes lowered as she lifted the case onto the floor.

"I'm going to Miami and I'm taking Robert with me, Joe."

He'd been expecting this. He rose off the bed.

"You're not taking my son anywhere," he warned.

There was silence for a moment as Angela stared at him. Then she spoke.

"Oh, that's right, I almost forgot Everything's yours, Joe, isn't it? Your business, your friends, your house, your son. Well he's my son too and he belongs with his mother!" She walked defiantly towards the door but Joe got there before her. He held her arm gently but firmly.

"Now, you listen to me," he said in a serious voice. "My son stays here. If you leave this house you go on your own and you leave your son behind. Think about it!"

Angela remained silent as he let go of her arm. She walked along the landing, opened the door of her son's room and went inside. On reaching his bed she sat down, smoothed his hair gently with her hand and touched his cheek lightly with her finger.

Robert opened his sleepy eyes and put his arms around her neck.

"Mommy, I was crying and you didn't come" he murmured in a sleepy voice.

She put her arms around his back and lifting him up gently, she held him close. "I will always be there for you, Robert," she whispered. "I won't ever leave you, I promise."

Joe who had been watching from the door way, turned and motioned for Freddie to leave. As the front door closed quietly, he turned back to find Angela cradling her son in her arms, sobbing softly.

"Mommy loves you," she said in a broken voice, kissing him lovingly.

"I love you too," he replied dreamily.

She held him in her arms until he fell into a contented sleep. Then she laid his head on the pillows and draped the quilt over him. She left the room, passing Joe as if he wasn't even there. Going back to her own room she sat on the bed, her hands clenched tightly in front of her. Joe followed, closing the door, going over to the side of the bed and crouching down in front of her. He gazed up into her face.

"He loves us both, Angel," he whispered. "This is his home. It would break his heart to be separated from either of us. He's happy."

Angela looked at him and nodded.

"You win, Joe. But then, you always do. I'll be your wife everywhere but here." She pointed to the bed.

"I take it that means you'll be moving to another room?"

"No. if I did that, Robert would start asking questions. And besides I think everyone around here has enough to talk about," she replied calmly.

"Angel, honey, everything is going to be o.k."

As he leaned forward to put his hands on her shoulders she shrunk away from him and burst into tears."

"Don't!" she sobbed, hitting out blindly and helplessly at the space between them. "Don't you touch me! I'm staying because of my son."

She looked like a caged animal and it was only now he realised the full impact of what he had said and done. Angela lay down on the bed and curled up like a lost child. Even though she buried her face into the pillow, her cries still echoed around the bedroom. Knowing he could do nothing to comfort her, Joe got up and walked over to the window. He stood with his back to her, gazing down at the garden below but not seeing anything. He wasn't proud of himself or what he had done. The unhappiness he had caused his wife now made him unhappy too. He gave a deep sigh as he listened to her. There had been no screaming or tantrums from Angela. The truth was, he'd have felt better if there had been. She had every right to slap his face and give him abuse, but that wasn't her way. Angela carried her hurt inside but this time she had been hurt too much and for no good reason, except jealousy and mistrust.

Joe knew his marriage was on very shaky ground and he would have to tread very carefully in order to save it, and win back the respect of the woman he loved so much. As the room fell silent he turned and went over to the bed. Angela had finally cried herself to sleep. He lifted the neatly folded cover from the bottom of the bed and gently placed it over her. As he stood and stared into her face he saw how pale she was, exhausted from all the trauma. Her eyes had dark circles underneath them and her cheeks were still moist from the tears she had shed. At that moment, Joe Morrelli silently swore on his mother's grave that he would never hurt Angela again. He would do everything possible to put his marriage back together, the way it used to be. And he would never do anything to put their love or relationship at risk again. He swore vervently because he knew that for him, life without Angela just wasn't worth living.

As he left the bedroom, closing the door quietly behind him, he saw Robert coming along the landing. The child was oblivious to what was going on around him.

"Where's Mommy?" he asked, looking up innocently at Joe, who knelt down and put his arms around him.

"Mommy's got a headache, son. She's sleeping."

"Can I see her later?"

"Sure you can. Now, why don't we go downstairs and see what Evie has for breakfast. What do you say?" smiled Joe.

Robert nodded and Joe got up and took his son's little hand.

"Maybe you and me could go to 'Stacey's Gym' today," he suggested. "Would you like that?"

Robert grinned, broadly.

"Gee dad, that would be great!"

As they reached the top of the stairs, the boy stopped and looked back. He thought for a moment and then said,

"I love mommy and I love you too, dad."

Joe looked away and wiped two tears from his eyes. Then gazed down at him.

"I know you do son. And we love you," he nodded. "I guess we're very lucky people. It's a nice feeling, to love someone. But when they love you back, it's the best feeling in the world. I want you to remember that, Robert."

The telephone in Rooney's apartment rang every hour on the hour. He knew full well it was Joe but was determined not to answer it.

"Let him stew," he thought. "It'll do him good!"

But the truth was, it wasn't doing Joe any good at all! In fact as the day wore on, Joe became anxious, then worried, then dismayed. Every time he thought of the previous night and what had been said, he could have slid down a drain! And to make matters worse, Robert would constantly want to know,

"Dad, where's Uncle Rooney?"

Finally, it all became too much for Joe to bear.

Rooney had decided to go out to dinner and had just showered and changed, when the door bell rang. On answering it he discovered a familiar face. A face that looked guilty, sorrowful and forlorn. It was Joe.

The two men stared at each other.

"She's giving me another chance," Joe explained. "How about you?"

There was a deadening silence as Rooney glared at him with piercing eyes and tight lips. Then suddenly, he poked a warning finger right up to the tip of Joe's nose and said,

"If you ever fuck up like this again, Joe, you won't just lose Angela – you'll lose everybody!"

Joe never flinched but looked at Rooney, then at the finger, then back at Rooney.

"Is that a 'yes' or a 'no'?" he asked.

Rooney took a step back and lowered his hand. He thought for a moment, then gave a loud tut.

"I'll get my jacket!" he said, reluctantly.

When he disappeared from view, Joe breathed a deep and heavy sigh. Not only did he feel very relieved, he also felt very sick. Understandable. After all, he'd never ate so much 'humble pie'!"

Angela kept her word. As the weeks passed, their marriage looked normal to all those who knew them but in the bedroom it was strictly 'hands off'. Joe consoled himself with the thought that it wouldn't last and was trying hard in his own way to make amends. He had given Evie the night off on a few occasions and taken over the kitchen. Joe had always been a good cook and was very handy with a few pans. Having Evie around had made him lazy but he had cooked some really special meals and served them up amid flowers and candles, thinking the intimate dinners and suppers would set the mood. But it hadn't worked. Away from everyone, Angela was still distant towards him and it was getting to the point where he looked forward to receiving an invitation because being in a crowd was the only time he could get really close to her. Only then could Joe take her in his arms and dance with her or slip his arms around her waist as they stood talking to friends.

She devoted herself to Robert, bringing him to the movies or taking him on outings. In the evenings she would read with him. He was ready to start school and she had him well prepared. She often visited 'The Safe Haven' and resumed her nights out with the staff to the bowling alley. Joe didn't mind. He always knew Angela had never ended her friendship with them. What he did mind, was the way things were when they were alone. They didn't watch television together any more and although they were on speaking terms, things had changed. The conversations between them were strained and gone was the laughter they had shared. Joe wondered what on earth he could do to make up with her. Then he had an idea.

A couple of days later he arrived home and standing in the entrance hall, called to her. When Angela came out of the kitchen he walked towards her grinning, took her hand and said,

"Come with me. I've got a surprise for you!"

He led her out of the front door and pointed.

"Well, what do you think?" he asked.

Parked outside was a sporty, top of the range, red car. Angela looked at it, surprised.

"Who owns that?"

"You do! Ever since we got married I always said you should learn to drive."

"But Al's here," she reminded him, "and if he isn't I get a taxi."

"Not any more," he replied.

She looked at him, puzzled.

"Why did you buy me that? You know I'm nervous at the very thought of driving in traffic."

"Oh everyone's like that at the start," Joe insisted, "and besides if Al isn't here you won't have to take a taxi anymore. It's all yours, Angel," he smiled. "From now on you'll have your own car, you'll be able to go where you want and do your own thing."

Angela just stared at him.

"Somehow, Joe, I don't think that would suit you!" she said, turning and walking back inside.

Joe went over and leaned on the roof of the car looking at Rooney, who had gone with him to buy it.

"That is one stubborn woman," he said, throwing his hands up in despair. "I've tried everything!"

"Have you tried saying 'I'm sorry'?" asked Rooney, sarcastically.

Joe put his hand on his forehead as Rooney studied him for a moment and then continued, "Look, Joe, maybe you're trying too hard. Why don't you just give her time? She'll come around when she's good and ready."

Joe nodded,

"Yeah, maybe you're right."

"I know I'm right. I haven't worked with you all these years without knowing that Joe Morrelli can buy a lot of people. But you never could buy Angela, and you never will!"

Joe nodded again,

"Come on, let's go," he said, opening the car door.

"Where to?" asked Rooney.

"Back to the Sales room."

As they climbed in, Rooney smiled.

"It's not the car she wants Joe – its you!"

"I should be so lucky!" replied Joe, resting both hands on the steering wheel and turning his eyes up towards heaven.

"Well, why don't you turn on that old Morrelli charm? It always worked before."

"Yeah, well the women it worked on weren't called Angel!"

As they sat in the car, Rooney leaned towards him.

"It worked once before didn't it? "Why don't you give it another shot?"

Joe smiled at his friend.

"If the second time is as good as the first it will be worth waiting for. Believe me!"

Angela watched from the window of the lounge as Joe and Rooney drove away. She knew Joe was finding the condition of their marriage very difficult but she wasn't ready to forgive him. He needed to be taught a lesson and the best way to do that was to refuse him the one thing he wanted most – herself.

Angela wasn't a spiteful woman but she had decided to take a leaf out of Joe's book, and was being a little underhanded. She had gone and bought some very expensive and sexy lingerie, for night time. She was making things tough for Joe but after the way he had behaved, she felt it was no more than he deserved!

Joe decided to take Rooney's advice. After all, he had nothing to lose. So a couple of nights later, as he and Angela lay in bed, he moved over and slipped his arm around her waist. Then he began to kiss her shoulder.

"Joe, would you please get back to your own side of the bed!" came the response.

"Don't you think it's more cosy like this?" he whispered, leaning his head over and kissing her neck. She dug her elbow into his chest.

"I'm warning you," she protested. "If you don't move away, I'm going to another room."

Joe moved over and turning on the bedside lamp, he sat up.

"What are you made of, cast iron? Be honest, haven't you wanted sex just once after all this time?" he asked, in an annoyed voice as he looked at her back. Without turning around she replied,

"I was nineteen years old before I had sex. It wouldn't bother me if it were another nineteen years."

"Well it would bother me! I've known people who spent less time in prison for committing serious crimes!" His voice had a note of sarcasm.

"Oh I'm sure you could find someone else to oblige you."

"But I don't want anyone else. I want you and you know it Angel." He moved over and looked down at her. "Don't think I haven't noticed those sexy nightdresses and expensive perfume you wear to bed. You're doing this on purpose, aren't you?"

"I don't know what you're talking about," she replied casually.

"I don't believe that for a minute," he muttered, getting out of bed.

"Where are you going?" she asked.

"To take a shower. I've never had so many cold showers in my life!"

Joe went into the bathroom and started banging things around noisily.

"This is ridiculous!" he kept muttering.

He turned on the shower then leaning over the wash basin, he looked in the mirror…

"Nineteen years," he whispered. "That's a life sentence." He shook his head. "I'd rather be dead!"

After that night, Joe made no more advances towards Angela. She did notice, however, that he wasn't coming to bed as early as he used to. Some nights he sat up late watching the sports channel on T.V. but mostly he was shut away in the study where the lights burned until the early hours of the morning. He poured over files and studied business deals, much of which Reuben had already done for him, but he needed something to pass the time.

Sometimes he just sat and had a quiet drink, alone with his thoughts. Sharing a bed with Angela and not being able to kiss her good night or even touch her, was proving too much for him. During the day things were fine but in the bedroom they had become like strangers. Joe was not a happy man and he knew that the longer it continued, the chances of their marriage getting back to normal were slim. They would grow apart and that was the last thing he wanted. He was staying up late on purpose. Not because he wanted Angela to think he didn't care, but because he just couldn't handle her rejection. It was tearing him apart.

He wanted back the love and the closeness they had always had. But more than anything, he wanted to show her how much he still loved her, even though she was making that very difficult for him. As Joe sat in the study that night, he knew something had to be done. He thought long and hard. Then, finally Joe Morrelli came to a decision.

The very next night at around 10.30, Angela came into the bedroom. She closed the door and put the book she was carrying down on the dressing-table. As she took of her robe and laid it at the bottom of the bed, she noticed the lights were on in the bathroom and went over to switch them off. Suddenly, Joe appeared in the doorway. She was clearly surprised to see him and moved aside to let him past. He stared at her for a moment. Then after hitting the light switch with his hand, he walked by brushing her arm deliberately with his own. He stopped and turned around, put his hands on her shoulders and pushed her gently against the wall. Leaning his body firmly against hers, he pushed his thighs hard against her own.

"You want it just as much as I do," he said in a low voice, kissing her. "Why don't you just admit it?"

She struggled and putting her hands on his chest, pushed him away.

"Don't flatter yourself, Joe. Just because you think you're God's gift to women, doesn't mean we all have to!" He walked away saying,

"Well, I never heard any complaints from you."

"Maybe that's because I never knew any better. I never had anyone else to compare you with!"

He came back and stared into her face.

"You know something, Angel?" he said, "you have a tongue like a two edge sword. I'd rather you'd have slapped me as say what you just did."

Angela knew she had hurt him and she was sorry. She was just about to say when he continued,

"And what about you? Oh, you were very convincing."

"What do you mean?"

"I mean the 'wine me, dine me but don't touch me routine you pulled and I'm the mug who fell for it!" He pointed to himself, accusingly. "You'd have made a great actress!"

She pushed her hands against his chest, angrily.

"That was no act Joe Morrelli, and you know it!"

He glanced down, casually and sarcastically,

"Well at least we're making bodily contact."

She lowered her eyes and took her hands away, stepping back. Joe grabbed her arms firmly.

"I have been a very patient man. I could have had you anytime I wanted. I could have taken you fighting or lying like a statue. But I didn't and do you want to know why? Because that kind of sex doesn't turn me on." He let go of her and walked over to the bed.

"If the other party isn't willing then I don't want it. That's the kind of guy I am. So you can come to bed now Angel and feel safe. One sided love making doesn't appeal to me. I'm not interested in having sex with any woman who doesn't want it - or me." Joe pulled the sheet back and got into bed. He lay on his side with his back towards her and turned off the lamp on the bedside cabinet.

Angela decided to do the same and they both lay in the darkness without a word.. Finally, she turned towards him and in a low voice said,

"Why didn't you trust me? When I took my marriage vows I promised to love you and be faithful".

Joe rolled over on his back and stared at the ceiling.

"Yeah, I know. But I remember when I was a kid, my mother made me a promise. She'd been ill for a long time and I'd stopped going to school because I wanted to be with her. One day she forced me to go. I didn't want to leave her but she told me she was feeling better. She even said she'd cook something special for me when I got home. I asked her if she was sure she'd be alright. She put her arms around me, kissed me and said' I promise, Joseph, I'll be here for you!' She waved to me from the window as I walked along the street. I felt really happy that day. When school was over I ran all the way home, but she wasn't there. They'd already taken her to the funeral parlour." Joe's voice was full of emotion as Angela listened intently.

"I ran from one room to the other looking for her and crying. That apartment was so cold and empty. I just couldn't understand how she could do that to me."

Angela's eyes filled with tears.

"She didn't want you to see her dying, Joe. She felt she was doing the right thing by sparing you that."

"I know you're right. But she should never have made me a promise she knew she wasn't going to keep. I guess that's why I'm so determined to keep mine."

Angela realised that although Joe was a tough man in many ways, deep down inside he was insecure when it came to promises, especially those made by women. He had carried the memory of his mother's broken promise since he was a young boy. It had left him with a mistrust as an adult, he found hard to overcome.

"Joe, would you make me a promise?" she asked, softly.

"Sure, What is it?"

"Would you promise me you'll never doubt my love for you ever again?"

"I promise, Angel and Joe Morrelli has never broken a promise - bar one. One I bitterly regret because it was to you mother. The fact that she is dead should never have made a difference. When Agnes told me how much you loved me I should have eccepted it and been grateful to her. Instead, I let her down. I only hope she can forgive me." He gazed across the darkened room towards the window. "You know, Angel, if my biggest sin is loving you to much, then I'm willing to do my penance for as long as it takes."

Angela lay for a few moments, silently thinking every-thing over. Then she moved closer to him and raised herself up on her elbow.

"I think you've done enough penance", she said.

He turned and looked at her.

"Do you really mean that?"

She nodded. Joe put his arm around her and gently pulled her down beside him. Placing one hand on her face he gazed at her lovingly.

"I don't deserve you, Angel. I never wanted to hurt you but I did. Can you forgive me?"

"Just this once", came the reply.

"Once is all its ever going to take."

He kissed her, very slowly and very tenderly. Although it had been sometime since he'd made love to Angela, Joe was in no hurry. This was his chance to show her how much he loved her and just how much she meant to him. She put her arms around his neck, running her fingers through his hair and responding to each sensual kiss and caress. He became more passionate, pulling up her flimsy nightdress a little at a time until he had removed it. While kissing her neck and shoulders, his hands moved gently over every part of her body. He buried his face between her breasts, licking her smooth skin with his tongue. As their passion became more intense she explored his body, determined to give him as much pleasure and satisfaction as she could. She succeeded.

"I love you Angel, and I want you so much", he whispered. Angela closed her eyes as she felt the rhythm of his muscular body against hers. Clinging to him and pressing her fingers deeply into his back, she wondered who could possibly compare with this man. He knew all the right moves at exactly the right time, making sure that she got as much from their love-making as he did. As their passion reached it's height she kissed him hungrily, almost gasping for breath.

Later, as he lay in her arms she realised just how much she'd missed him.
"I love you, Joe," she whispered.
He didn't answer because he didn't need to. His powerful embrace said it all.

The next afternoon while Angela and Robert were at the movies, Joe decided to pay a visit to the travel agency. After the previous night he knew he could still save his marriage and he was going all out to do just that. He wanted desperately to put his marriage back on track and keep it there, so he had decided to bring Angela away for a break-just the two of them. He had nowhere specific in mind so the lady had given him a lot of brochures. Joe let himself into the house, humming happily, and after looking around to make sure he was alone, he went into the study and locked the door. After laying the brochures on his desk, he fixed himself a drink and sat down in the comfortable, leather armchair. He spread out the literature he had been given and studied the front covers carefully. Mexico, Hawaii, Acapulco, Barbados. They all looked great. Then one caught his eye - Paris! He was curious as he opened the brochure and began looking through the pages, reading about all the famous City had to offer. It had been home to a lot of famous artists. Monet, Renoir, Cezanne. The same men Angela had been able to tell him so much about on their trips to the art galleries in New York, before they were married. She had often spoken of how wonderful it must be to see the Louvre gallery. Well, here it was right in front of him. The great Victor Hugo and Emilie Zola had also lived there. Joe knew Angela would be really interested in a place like that. It had everything from fashion shows to "The Moulin Rouge", to roadside cafes. Notre Dame Cathedral would be just one of the sights.

Joe wanted to bring Angela somewhere special. He owed her that after everything that had happened and this struck him as being that somewhere. The more he read, the more interested he became and the more convinced he was she would love it. He had a feeling it would be a trip they would both remember for a very long time and he felt it would be the right place for them to enjoy together. He wanted to be completely alone with her and hopefully have the romance, conservation and laughter they'd had on their honeymoon. On coming to the last page, he stared long and hard at a picture of a couple having an intimate, candlelit dinner.

"That's it," he murmured, nodding his head. "I'll bring my wife to Paris for a second honeymoon." His face took on a serious expression as he tapped the picture with his finger. "I am going to have dinner in Paris. If it's good enough for Kevin Mitchell - it's good enough for me!!

After talking things over with Rooney and making a few plans concerning Robert, Joe went ahead and booked the trip. A couple of nights later, he watched in anticipation as Angela came out of the bathroom and got ready for bed. She pulled the sheet down and only then, she noticed a large envelope lying on her pillow. A single red rose was placed on top of it.

"What's this?" she asked, looking over at him.

"Oh just a little something for my wife," he smiled. He watched as she lifted the rose, then the envelope and opened it. When she saw the tickets a look of surprise and disbelief swept over her face.

"Paris! These are for Paris!"

"That's right," he nodded. "You and me are going on a trip."

"But, Joe, what about Robert?"

"That's all been taken care of," he assured her, "Rooney is coming over to stay, Evie's here, and Frankie Junior is coming to keep him company at night. You know how much Robert thinks of him he's like a big brother. He can have his other friends over in the day time. Our son will enjoy himself that much, he'll hardly notice we've gone. Besides, it will help to make him a little more independent for when he starts school. He needs that, so don't you worry about him, he'll be fine".

"You've thought of everything."

"You bet," he nodded "and no excuses!" Angela smiled and shaking her head, put her hand up to her face. She looked at the tickets once more, then at Joe.

"I can't believe it - we're really going to Paris!"

"Yes we are, Angel. It's first class all the way and I've booked us into the best hotel I could find."

She scrambled across the bed and threw her arms around him

"I'm so excited Joe! I'll be able to see so many things."

"I know. We'll be able to see them together. We're going to have dinner in Paris by candlelight."

"Joe that sounds so romantic," she whispered.

"That's the idea!" came the reply.

She kissed his cheek and put her head on his shoulder.

"I never would have expected you to think of something like that."

"Well, when you love someone as much as I do, why not show it?" He put his arms around her. "You know, Angel, I've been thinking. We should travel more. Spend some time on our own. Next time, we'll go to Italy. Yeah, I'd like to bring you there. At least I can speak the language!"

She looked up at him and smiled.

"You didn't have to do this," she said.

His expression became serious.

"Yes I did. I never appreciated what I had until I nearly lost it, but it taught me a lesson for the rest of my life. Without you and my son, I have nothing that matters. I pushed you to get an education but somewhere along the way I got my priorities all wrong. Well, not anymore! You know so much about so many places but I forgot just how important it was for you to see them. I was so wrapped up with seeing you do well here in New York. I should have realised that you had dreams too. I have the money to make them come true and I'm going to - that's a promise. I've been selfish in a lot of ways but I'm going to make it up to you. This is just the start."

Angela put her hands to his face and gazed into his eyes.

"Paris is a wonderful start, Joe. I couldn't have asked for anywhere better." she said in a low voice, kissing him. "You've made me very happy."

She put her arms around his waist and laid her head on his chest. Joe's arms tightened around her and he kissed her hair.

"I'm taking you on a second honeymoon Angel, and if it's anything like our first, I'll be one very happy man, because believe me, the time I spent with you in Miami is so precious to me I'll carry it to my grave. That was when I found out what real love was and I'll always be grateful that in this big wide world, Joe Morrelli found what he'd always been searching for but never thought he'd find. I'm a very lucky guy and I never intend to forget it!"

Rooney sat at the kitchen table with a newspaper spread out in front of him, talking to Frankie who was standing with his back to the window. The door opened and Al appeared, walking over to the percolator and pouring himself a cup of coffee.

"How was your day off?" asked Frankie.

"Fine," Al nodded.

Frankie put out his cigarette.

"I guess with you not being here yesterday, you haven't heard the news."

Al looked at him, puzzled

"News? What news?"

"About the boss."

"The boss?"

"Yeah, he's going to Paris."

"Paris?"

Rooney looked around the kitchen

"Is there a fuckin' echo in here? He asked.

Al lifted the cup and going over to the table, he pulled out a chair and sat down. A sullen look was on his face.

"What's he going to Paris for anyway?" he asked, looking at Rooney.

"A second honeymoon."

Al shook his head.

"Some people have all the luck. The boss is going on his second honeymoon and I haven't been on my first one yet."

Rooney flicked through the paper.

"Well, if it's any consolation, neither have I."

"That's different."

"How do you make that out?" enquired Rooney.

"Well, you're a lot younger than me. You've still got plenty of time."

Rooney leaned his arms on the table and looked at him.

"What is this, 'Feel Sorry for Al' day?"

"Oh, you wouldn't understand," Al muttered into his coffee cup.

"Well it's your own fault." said Frankie, folding his arms in a patronising way. "You're looking in all the wrong places. Why don't you join a club?"

"What kind of club?"

"I don't know. Maybe you should go to one of those singles bars? You might meet some nice, refined woman your own age."

Al stared straight ahead.

"Yeah, I'm starting to get a vision of her right now. Knowing my luck she'll have her hair in a bun, wear thick spectacles and have prominent teeth. No thanks!" He gave Frankie a sarcastic look as he got up from the table "I think I'll pass!" he closed the kitchen door loudly as he left.

"What's the matter with him?" asked Rooney.

"Oh he's just in a mood because he's the last one to know about Paris. Al always likes to be first with news - especially if it's about the boss."

Rooney pushed the paper aside and leaned back in the chair.

"I'm curious about him. Tell me something, Frankie. Did he ever have any girlfriends? You know proper ones?"

Frankie smiled,

"You might not believe it, Rooney, but Al had his fair share with women. The only trouble was, he always seemed to be more interested in the ones the boss was dating."

"What do you mean?"

"Well, the boss had a way with women. He could walk into a nightclub and meet someone sophisticated, or into a bar and meet a good time girl. Either way, he made them feel special. Like they were the only woman there. Al stuck to him like glue, watching his technique, listening to his chat-up lines. Then he would try it. The only thing was, it never seemed to work the same for Al!"

Rooney smiled.

"Maybe that's because he forgot, there's only one Joe Morrelli."

"Yeah," nodded Frankie, "the boss was really something in action. But he did Al a few good turns."

"How do you mean?"

"You see, Al's old lady and old man were very religious. They didn't approve of sex before marriage which meant he could never bring any one back to stay the night. So, Al figured if he went to a brothel the room would be included with the woman and he'd actually save money!"

"So there is a brain in there! But where does Joe come in to all this?"

Frankie grinned,

"The boss used to feel sorry for him, so sometimes he'd let Al have the keys to his apartment, when he wasn't using it. That really used to impress Al's lady friends! I'll always remember the first time he went there. That's the night Al Colleano discovered satin sheets! He raved about them for days. He reckoned no woman could resist them, so he ended up buying satin sheets for himself."

"But what was the point, if he couldn't bring anyone home to sleep with him?"

Frankie looked at him and nodded.

"I remember saying the same thing at the time"

"And ..." prodded Rooney.

"He said it didn't matter because, even without a woman, sleeping in them made him feel like a somebody. At least there was one consolation for him."

"What was that?"

"Well, if he couldn't get the same woman as the boss, at least he could get the same sheets!"

Rooney smiled and shook his head.

"I wonder if he's still got them?"

"Who knows," Frankie shrugged, "it was a long time ago. One things for sure - he's still got the same type of women! And the same admiration for the boss!"

Frankie turned and stared out of the window for a moment, as if recalling old times.

Then he looked at Rooney and continued,

"Things were tough in the old neighbourhood. Some guys tried to buy respect but not Joe Morrelli. No, believe me, he earned it. That's why he has so many friends and that's why Al and me are still with him."

Rooney got up from the table and put his hand on Frankie's shoulder.

"That's why we're all with him. Joe has qualities money can't buy. But as we say in Ireland, that's what separates the men from the boys."

"Yeah he's been good to us. The boss makes a good friend but a bitter enemy. Nobody ever crossed him and lived 'happy ever after', if you know what I mean."

Rooney nodded,

"I know exactly what you mean but none of us would have it any other way. That's why we work for him. And speaking of work, I'd better go." He glanced at his watch. "Joe might be going to Paris but his business isn't."

Frankie smiled,

"I guess Al will be driving them to the airport."

Rooney turned around as he opened the door. "If he keeps that long face, he's going to drive us all up the walls!!"

Chapter 13

When Joe and Angela returned from Paris, Robert started school. Although Joe Morrelli was a wealthy man, he and Angela had decided on a good local school for Robert where he would be with kids from all different backgrounds and cultures. This, they hoped, would help the boy to grow up accepting people for who they were – not what they were! Angela believed he would be taught just as well in such a school, insisting that if he didn't have the brains to start with, Joe's money couldn't buy them for him. Joe had agreed, remembering just how well Gene O'Brien and so many others had done in local schools. And besides, Robert was still very young and the main thing was he was happy and had made many friends.

Angela went back to her committee work. Gene was moving onwards and upwards with the help of Dan Casey and his closest friends, one of them being Angela Morrelli. She knew now he wanted to be the next Senator and couldn't think of anyone better for the job. She had his confidence and trust in all matters, and he had her originality and driving force. With the White House beckoning and as loyal supporters of the common people, they made a terrific team!

The trip to Paris had been a success in many ways. Joe and Angela had talked openly and frankly to each other. He had been able to lay his fears to rest concerning younger men like Kevin Mitchell. She had opened her heart about her inner most thoughts and feelings. She longed to see Sheila and her family and Joe's hunch about her wanting to see other places had not been wrong. She had, but kept it to herself. Angela had been reluctant to bring it up for fear of offending him, deciding to go along with his plans for her instead.

They had returned with a much greater understanding, trust and respect for each other. Because of their openness and straight talking they had achieved something they would both treasure – a stronger love.

Joe had saved his marriage and won back the one thing he wanted so badly, his wife. The days and nights they had spent together in Paris had been everything he hoped for. He was a contented man because he knew he still had Angela's love. He needed that to survive. Things between them were even better than they had been before all the unhappiness he'd caused, if that was possible. Yes, the Morrellis were a happy family again and he and Angela were still very much in love. Joe was going to make sure that's the way it was going to stay! He was a much wiser man and felt safe and secure in the knowledge that he'd handled everything the right way. His wife and son were first in his life, because Angela and Robert were his life.

Time passed quickly and before Angela realised it, Robert's first term at school was coming to an end. It was only weeks before his summer break. Every other year, Joe had talked about Miami for weeks before they were due to go. But this year he hadn't mentioned it and that puzzled Angela, so she decided to bring the subject up herself. A couple of nights later, after she had looked in on Robert, she came downstairs and into the lounge. She sat down on the couch quietly, as Joe sat on the edge of his seat watching a boxing match on T.V. going through all the motions with his fists. After a few moments of silence, she spoke.

"Joe, could I talk to you?"

"Sure honey," he replied, without taking his eyes from the screen.

Angela folded her arms and sighed, waiting patiently for some kind of response. Joe's eyes were glued to the television. She waited and waited. Then,

"How much longer is this fight going to last? Why doesn't one of them just knock the other one out?"

At that moment a roar went up. Joe turned with a surprised look on his face.

"One of them just did. That's it, it's all over. I'd almost swear that guy heard you," he said, pointing at the winner. "I feel sorry for the poor guy on the canvas. You know something, Angel, I sure would hate to step into a ring if you were in the opponent's corner."

"I'm sorry Joe."

"It's o.k., "he shrugged, switching off the T.V.

Angela bit her lip.

I'll bet you're going to be in a bad mood now."

He turned and smiled.

"Why should I be in a bad mood? I had my bet on the winner! Now, what do you want to talk to me about?"

She unfolded her arms and relaxed.

"It's near the end of Robert's school term so I've been thinking about our vacation."

Joe put his hand up and scratched his forehead.

"Oh yeah, I've been meaning to talk to you about that."

"When are we going to Miami?" she smiled.

"I'm sorry honey," came the reply, "we won't be able to make the trip this year."

Her smile faded.

"But Joe, we go every year. You know how much I look forward to it and Robert loves it there."

"Yeah, I know. But something's come up."

"Well, if it's business, maybe Robert and I could go on our own."

"That won't be possible, Angel. You see, we're having visitors"

Angela stood up, shocked.

"Visitors? When did this happen and why didn't you tell me?"

"Now, calm down. I was going to tell you."

"Really – when? when they rang the doorbell?"

"Now, honey, listen to me for a minute…"

"No! You listen, Joe. If you have invited people to our home, don't you think I have the right to know?"

"But I wanted it to be a surprise."

"Well, it certainly is! Now, would it be asking too much for you to tell me who it is? Or are you going to keep that a secret too?"

"Not any more," he said, shaking his head.

"Alright Joe….I'm waiting."

He looked at her.

"Sheila and Raymond!"

Angela's eyes widened and for a moment she was stunned.

"I don't believe it," she said in a half whisper.

"Yeah well, it's true," he smiled. "They're coming out for a vacation with the kids. That's why we can't go to Miami."

She began to cry.

"But I don't understand Joe. Sheila never mentioned it when I spoke to her on the phone."

"That's because she wanted to surprise you. Everything's been arranged and they are coming to stay for four weeks."

Angela threw herself into his arms.

"Oh Joe, you don't know how much this means to me!"

He put his arms around her.

"I think I do, Angel. Now don't cry. I want you to be happy."

"I am. Thank you, Joe, for making all this possible."

"Hey, I have my reasons! I want to see them, too. After all, they're my family as well."

She looked up at Joe, smiling through her tears.

"I can't believe it. Sheila, Raymond and the children all here in this house. It's going to be great. Robert will see his Aunt and Uncle for the first time, and get to meet his cousins."

"Yeah, and I will finally get to meet all those voices I keep talking to on the phone!" he joked.

Angela stepped back and put her hands on her face.

"Will we have enough room for everyone? Where will they sleep?"

"Oh, honey, don't worry about that. We have plenty of space. Sheila and Raymond can have your mother's room, the two eldest girls can have Rooney's and the youngest can go in with Robert. We can put up a spare bed. Besides, from the conversations I've had with Sheila, Raymond's so excited he'd probably settle for the bath tub!" he grinned.

Angela laughed.

"I just can't get it to sink in that they're really coming."

"Well you'd better because all the tickets are bought and paid for and they'll be on their way pretty soon. And believe me, they want to come so much, nothing short of a full scale war is going to stop them!"

She put her arms around his neck.

"Seven years is a long time. I can hardly wait."

"I know Angel. It's been too long."

Angela raised her head and looked into his eyes.

"You really are a good man, Joe Morrelli. And I really do love you."

They kissed.

"Why don't we have an early night?" he said, in a low voice. "We might not get any, once the in-laws arrive!"

"Anything you say, Mr Morrelli."

"Anything?" he grinned. "This is going to be my lucky night."

"Well, anything within reason," she smiled, guiding him to the door,

Joe stopped for a moment.

"What's the matter?" she asked.

"Oh, I was just saying goodbye to my fantasies!"

Angela opened the door saying, "I wouldn't be too hasty if I were you. It's a long time until morning!"

"Do I detect a promise of great things to come?"

She looked at him knowingly and smiled.

"Maybe, Joe, maybe…."

He put his arm around her and switched off the light.

Over the next couple of weeks, the Morrelli household buzzed with excitement. Angela and Evie talked about the visitors and they had both gone through the house getting everything just perfect for their arrival. Rooney helped as well, by cleaning out his room. As he carried his belongings downstairs in a suitcase, Joe was passing on his way to the study. He stopped and looked at Rooney, then at the suitcase.

"So that's were you've been," he said. "I've looked everywhere for you."

Rooney stared.

"I'm sorry Joe, it's just not working out so I'm leaving you. This is goodbye!"

"Oh very funny," he nodded, throwing him a sarcastic look as Rooney started to laugh.

"Tell me something, what are those two women finding to do up there?"

"Just about everything, Joe."

Joe shook his head.

"I tell you, Rooney, if I had known there was going to be all this commotion over my in-laws, I'd have booked them into the Hilton!"

Rooney came down to the entrance hall.

"Joe, if you've got a minute I'd like to talk to you."

"Sure, come on," he replied.

Rooney put the suitcase down and followed him into the study. Once inside, Joe turned to him.

"Well, what is it?"

"I've been thinking and it's like this, Joe. When your relatives come it's going to be a time for family. You know? You'll have to spend a lot of time with them and show them around. The truth is, I'd feel out of it so I was wondering if maybe I could take my vacation then."

"Sure you can. In fact, I think that's a good idea." He sat on the edge of the desk. "You see, Rooney, these people know I own a restaurant but that's all they know. And I'd like to keep it that way. Everything else is my own private business." He thought for a few moments. "You know, maybe I should give Frankie some time off as well. That way no-one will wonder what you guys do for me. If they don't see you around, they won't ask any questions. And they won't know I have other interests."

"Will you manage everything o.k.?" Rooney asked. "After all, there's the Agency, the numbers, the gym. Not to mention the nightclubs and the out of town business."

"That won't be a problem," shrugged Joe. "Lillian can deal with the agency. Reuben and I can square everything else with a few phone calls. It'll only be for a few of weeks. As for the out of town business, Reuben and me can handle that between us. Most of it's done on the phone anyway."

"What about Angela, have you spoken to her about things?"

Joe nodded,

"Yeah, I've had a word with her. She knows I like to keep my business interests private and she agrees they don't have to know anything other than Joe Morrelli owns 'The Safe Haven'. I'm just an ordinary businessman, nothing more. The only one who works for me is my chauffeur," he winked. "You and Frankie can go on vacation a few days before they arrive. I'll let you both know when they've gone."

"O.k., that's settled," said Rooney, making his way back out to the entrance hall and lifting the suitcase.

Joe followed him.

"Hey, Rooney!" he called

Rooney turned around.

"What?"

"When this visit is over, I want to see you bring that suitcase back. This will always be your home. I mean that!"

"I didn't think you cared," Rooney joked.

Joe looked at him.

"I might not always show it but I care, believe me, I care," he nodded.

"I know," smiled Rooney. "Hey, Joe, do you remember? You were the first one ever to buy me a suitcase."

"Yeah well, when you work for Joe Morrelli you don't go around carrying a canvas bag – it's bad for business!"

"Not to mention your image."

Joe smiled and waved his hand.

"Go on, get out of here!"

It was late that evening when Joe got back from Reuben's office. It had been a long day for him. He had paid visits to his business associates and had put all his affairs in order for the next few weeks. He'd had to skip dinner, calling home to say he'd be held up and he felt tired but relieved as he let himself in. Angela appeared from the kitchen and met him in the entrance hall.

"Have you already eaten?" she asked.

"I had a snack earlier on." he replied.

She put her hand on the side of his face.

"You look so tired. I asked Evie to wait dinner for you. Why don't you fix yourself a drink while I bring it through to the dining room?"

"You should have started without me, honey."

She shook her head.

"I wanted to wait for you. I know you've had a busy day. Evie gave Robert his dinner earlier in the kitchen. He's in bed now, fast asleep."

Joe nodded, went into the lounge and poured himself a scotch. He took a few sips, then sat down and joined Angela. She had set two places for dinner, complete with candles and a small vase of flowers. As she put the plates on the table and sat down beside him, he smiled.

"This is nice," he said, pouring the wine.

"I thought you'd like it," she smiled back.

Joe started to relax in the atmosphere of the dim lights and brightly burning candles. Soft music played in the background. It was cosy and he was pleased that Angela had thought of it – and him. As they came to the end of their meal she poured some more wine and looked at him.

"You know, it's only been a couple of days but I miss not seeing Frankie or Rooney around.

Rooney didn't say where he was going, did he tell you?"

"Yeah, he's going to Vegas."

"On his own?"

"No, he's going with friends. Two guys from the gym. They got together and planned a fun-filled, action-packed trip. The action being mostly with the ladies!" he grinned. "You should have seen Al's face when he heard about it. His eyes lit up like one of those slot machines they have out there!" He leaned his elbows on the table and rested his chin on his hands. "I think Rooney's hankering after one of those showgirls."

"Are they pretty?"

"You bet! they're young, nearly all six feet tall with long legs and big breasts."

"How do you know?" she smiled, lifting her glass.

"Oh, I've had a few trips to Vegas myself. As a matter of fact, the first night I ever saw you in 'The Safe Haven' I'd just come back from there."

Angela looked at Joe and shook her head.

"That's one thing I don't think I'll ever understand. How could you go out with such beautiful women and ever notice someone like me?"

He held his hands out and attempted to explain.

"It's more simple that you think, Angel. Most of those women have only two things going for them, their faces and their figures. So they have to make the most of them while they can. Who can blame them? After all, they won't have them forever. When they start getting older, they get replaced by younger girls. So they grab as many good times as they can. A lot of them end up marrying old men for money and security, love doesn't really come into it. When you bring women like that out, you know sex is going to be on offer by the end of the night. Everyone ends up getting what they want and a good time is had by all!"

"You seem to know a lot about it. You must have had some good times."

"I sure did," he nodded. "I was your regular 'Mr Party All Night'."

"Don't you ever miss that, Joe?"

He shook his head.

"Angel, I've seen the other side to the glamour. When some of them get a few drinks too many at a party, they get loud, sometimes embarrassing. They start flaunting themselves. Showing you what they're really like by the way they behave. You know, forward. If they want sex they let you know it. But believe me, when the false eyelashes and hair pieces come off and the make-up isn't there, they're not so startling. Take away all that, plus the fancy feathered costumes and dresses and I can tell you now, they look like difference people." He drank some wine, then put his glass down and looked at her.

"Let me try and explain something to you. Most men, if they were honest with themselves, tend to want the woman they can't have or the one that's hard to get. At the end of the day we don't really care about what we can get handed to us on a plate. We like to do the running and make the first move. When we do that, we have respect for that woman and we secretly admire her. She's the one we really want to make love to." He leaned towards her and put his hand gently under her face. "That's what happened with you. When a man gets on in years, sometimes it makes him feel good to have young, attractive women on his arm. But what he really wants and needs is to be able to relax in a woman's company and have an intelligent conversation. Looks and figure are fine but they don't compensate for a caring nature and shared interests – someone who's on your own wave length. It's not everything having a woman by your side who's all beauty and no brains. No matter what age a woman is, Angel, if you feel good with her, that's everything. You have to love the mind as well as the body. That's where a lot of men make their big mistake. You taught me that the night I brought you to Mario's. When you told me it was what was inside that really counts. As I'm getting older I realise that's very true. Personality counts for such a lot, that's why I chose you."

Angela smiled,

"What if I'd been an older woman?"

He shook his head.

"It wouldn't have made a difference, not to me anyway. You're everything I ever wanted. The fact that you were young was just an added bonus."

She gazed into his face.

"Will you still love me when I get older and have a few wrinkles?" she asked, in a soft voice.

"You bet!" he smiled, winking. "Besides, those other women wouldn't have gone to the brother of planning a cosy night like this. They would most likely be out on the town. Joe Morrelli's no fool! He always knew what he wanted." He poured some more wine and raised his glass. "I found the right woman!" he smiled.

Angela lifted her glass to join him.

"And I found the right man!"

As they finished their wine, she glanced at her watch.

"In a few hours time, Joe, I'll be seeing my family – our family."

"Yeah," he smiled, "Well I think we could both use some sleep. It's going to be an exciting day for us all!"

Joe and Angela stood with Robert by the hand in the busy airport and watched as the plane came to a standstill. As the passengers began to make their way through the arrival area, Angela pointed excitedly, "There they are!"

Raymond was the first one to see her. He hurried over then lifting Angela off her feet, he held her tightly and swung her around. As Sheila and the children rushed over to join them, Robert pulled away from Joe and ran towards the cousins he had never met....

Angela and Sheila hugged each other, crying and laughing at the same time and everyone began talking at once. Joe stood surveying the scene feeling more than a little emotional, when a small face peeped out at him from behind Sheila. It disappeared and a few seconds later a tiny child emerged and stood gazing at him. He smiled and winked at her. She hesitated. Then, oblivious to everything that was going on around her, she walked towards him holding out her arms. As Joe watched her getting closer, his heart melted. She had the same red hair and dark blue eyes as Angela and he couldn't help but think that if they have been blessed with a daughter, she would have looked just like this little girl. He bent down and lifted her into his arms.

"You must be Aisling," (Ashleen) he said softly. She nodded and smiled as she put her tiny arms around his neck and held onto him tightly. That smile was all Joe needed to convince him that he was looking at Angela when she was that age. From the family photographs that Agnes used to show him of when Angela was a little girl, he could hardly believe how alike they were. The resemblance was almost uncanny and from that moment, Aisling touched a place in Joe's heart.

Angela's voice brought Joe face to face with the family he had never seen.

"Joe, this is Sheila."

They embraced and kissed each other on the cheek.

"And this is Raymond," she added.

The two men greeted each other and shook hands firmly.

"Nice to meet you," smiled Joe.

"And I'm happy to meet you, Joe. Really happy! This is Senga and Deborah, and I see you've already met Aisling," grinned Raymond.

Joe kissed both girls.

"Yeah," he said, "And I've a feeling that Aisling and her Uncle Joe are going to get along just fine. Isn't that right?" he smiled, looking at her. "Well, let's go," he continued. "Al's gone to get the luggage and the car's waiting outside."

As he lead them all out of the airport, still holding Aisling in his arms, he was flanked at either side by Senga and Deborah. Angela and Sheila chatted excitedly, while Raymond took Robert's hand and looked down at him admiringly.

On stepping out into the bright sunshine. Raymond stopped and looked all around.

"I can't believe it," he grinned. "I'm in the Big Apple!"

"Welcome to New York," smiled Angela.

Hearing this, Raymond held out his hands and burst into song,

"I want to be a part of it – New York New York!!' You know Angela, when you think of New York you think of Frank Sinatra. They just go together. Like Americans and hamburgers!"

Al passed Joe with a suitcase.

"And you think I'm bad!" he muttered.

When the last of the luggage was packed away. Al came around and opened the door. Raymond stared at the limousine and in a stunned voice said,

"Jesus, Angela, is this yours? I've got to hand it to you. You've come a long way from sitting on the Saintfield bus back home." He leaned forward and looked inside." Would you look at this," he said to Sheila, "I've been in smaller flats in Belfast!"

Sheila laughed and turned to Joe.

"Don't pay any attention to him, Joe. He's just excited."

Joe smiled and nodded, then looked at Al.

"Well, I sure hope it doesn't last!" he murmured.

Everyone climbed into the limousine. Finally, it was Joe's turn. Al smiled,

"And who is this little lady?"

"This is Aisling," replied Joe, proudly.

"I might have known it," said Al, nodding his head, "That's another 'A' for you Boss!"

Joe opened his mouth but before he could say anything, Al hurriedly closed the door and got into the driver's seat. After checking the mirror he started the car and drove off, leaving the airport behind.

As the limousine made its way to Roseberry Avenue, the occupants talked, joked and laughed.

"I suppose you'll want to see all the sights," said Angela to her sister.

"Raymond has made out a list," Sheila smiled. "We'd like to see Broadway."

"Well, you're in luck. Joe used to go there quite a lot. Didn't you, Joe?" teased Angela.

"That's great!" beamed Raymond. "Maybe you could bring us, Joe?"

"Sure, no problem," came the reply. "Broadway it is."

Gazing through the window, Raymond started tapping his fingers and humming. Then he proceeded to sing the first verse of "Give My Regards to Broadway." Joe sat throughout all this with an outward smile but inward he couldn't help but wonder if this was the same Raymond Angela had told him so much about! Perhaps the trouble in Belfast had gotten so bad it had had a dramatic effect on this poor guy, leaving him five cents short of a dollar – upstairs!

Anyway, Joe had a feeling that four weeks of Raymond's company was something he was never going to forget. As the tune ended, he told himself that maybe Raymond just liked to sing. Or maybe he had a brother-in-law who was going to be the next Al Jolson! As the journey continued, he noticed that Al kept studying Raymond in the mirror. He knew that Al really didn't know what to make of this visitor from Ireland. Joe was going to keep it to himself but the truth was, neither did he!

On their arrival at Roseberry Avenue, Angela introduced Evie to her family. Then she and Joe showed them around. Sheila and Raymond were impressed by the house and it's contents, but Raymond was even more impressed when he saw the pool. He sat down on a sun lounger and leaning back he put his hand into the inside pocket of his jacket and producing a pair of dark sunglasses, he put them on.

"Hi Angela, what do you think?" he grinned.

"I think you look like Roy Orbison!" came the reply.

Joe put his arm around Angela and whispered

"If he was wearing a trenchcoat he'd look like one of those guys who guard the President."

Angela laughed,

"Maybe we could get him a job with Gene O'Brien."

"Well, considering he's Irish, it's not impossible," smiled Joe.

Evie appeared with a tray of soft drinks and cookies for the children. Joe went inside and came out with a bottle of champagne and four glasses. He put them down on the poolside table and uncorked the bottle.

"O.k., celebrate time!" he smiled as he poured it, handing the glasses around.

As they relaxed around the pool and the children played, Raymond held his champagne up and looked at it.

"If Jamie Doyle could see me now," he grinned, shaking his head. "He'll never believe it when I tell him. Hi, Sheila, where's the camera? We'll have to take a photograph of this!"

"How is Jamie? enquired Angela.

"Well, his circumstances might have changed but he hasn't."

"What do you mean, Raymond?"

"Him and the wife have split up. She's living with someone else. This other fella owns a contracting business and that's right up her street. With all the explosions he's making a fortune selling wood and boarding places up. Eileen knew a good thing when she saw it. She always did want to be better then everybody else. Yes, Eileen always was the fur coat and no knickers type!"

Joe coughed, choking slightly on his drink.

"Are you alright Joe?" Asked Angela, patting his back.

He nodded but couldn't speak. She looked at him and explained,

"What Raymond means is, she wanted people to think she was better than she really was."

At last Joe found his voice.

"I just never heard it expressed like that before!"

Sheila laughed, "You'll probably hear a lot of expressions you've never heard before."

Angela looked at her. "Will the house be safe while you're away?" she asked. "You never know what might happen."

"Oh, it will be alright," Sheila assured her. "Jamie is staying in it until we get back."

Angela then turned her attention to Raymond.

"How did you manage to get the Social Security to let you come here for a month?"

He smiled triumphantly.

"It was a piece of cake, Angela. There's so much unemployment back home that if you walked into the Dole office and told them you were going on a trip up the Amazon to look for work, they'd be delighted! I just told them I was coming out here to look for suitable employment. It's easy when you know how."

Joe's eyes looked across the pool and watched the kids playing. Sheila followed his gaze.

"She's very like Angela," she smiled, pointing to Aisling.

"Yeah, she is," he nodded.

"I think she resembles my father," said Angela, fondly.

"Same difference," replied Raymond. "You and your father were always very alike."

Joe turned to Sheila.

"You're like your mother."

"Everyone says that," she nodded.

There was silence for a few moments as both sisters wiped the tears from their eyes. Joe didn't want them to get melancholy about the past on their first day together, after so many years. So he got up and poured out more champagne, filling everyone's glass.

"To us!" he smiled. "Together at last!"

Raymond sat up and took the sunglasses off. "I'd like to propose a toast," he said, raising his glass. "To both of you, Joe and Angela, for inviting us here and for being so good to us in the past." As he looked at Angela, his smile faded. "You were a lovely girl but now you're a beautiful woman. Angela, you look wonderful."

His voice was sincere and his eyes had a look of tenderness. Joe knew that look spoke volumes.

"Thank you, Raymond," she whispered, blushing.

Joe glanced at Sheila, who was gazing at her husband lovingly and seemed indifferent to his last remark. As far as she was concerned there was no doubt Raymond felt deeply for Angela – as a sister-in-law. And why not? They had been through a lot together. But Joe couldn't help but think that maybe Robert Kenny had been right when he told Agnes he thought Shelia was second choice.

Dinner that evening was a real family affair with everyone sitting at the dining room table, including Aisling who was propped up by two cushions. After a few glasses of Joe's expensive wine, Raymond was in a jovial mood.

Angela smiled at Joe, then placing a finger to her lips she shook her head slightly at him and spoke.

"Raymond, in all the excitement today I forgot to ask, how is Mrs Murray?"

He put his knife and fork down.

"I was wondering when we were going to get around to her"

"She sent you a present, Angela," said Sheila.

"It's a pity she didn't send herself instead," Raymond butted in. "It would have been a lot easier living with the present next door to me!"

Angela smiled,

"I take it you two haven't gotten any closer."

He lifted his glass.

"Angela, living next to her is as close as I want to get. She's still as nosey as ever."

"Don't you like her?" enquired Joe.

"Oh, I like her," he shrugged. "I'd like her even better if she was like normal people."

Joe was curious.

"What do you mean?"

"Well, you wouldn't believe it, Joe. She can tell you what time you go out, what time you come in. She can even tell you when you flush the toilet and how often, especially during the night. The woman never sleeps. Now, that's not normal."

Joe shook his head and laughed as Raymond went on,

"She has this habit of going down the yard at night to the washing line. When the moon shines on the white hair, white dressing gown and white fur slippers, she'd give you the creeps. She looks like the ghost of Christmas past!"

Everyone laughed as he continued. "She comes in, 'any news?' Before you can open your mouth – she tells you it all! Joe, you don't know how lucky you are, living in a house on it's own. Sometimes, I think I'm living beside a private detective in drag!"

"Oh, Raymond, it's not that bad," said Sheila.

"Isn't it?" he retorted. "Well, maybe that's because you don't have to use the toilet as often as me. Especially when I've been out with Jamie."

Joe was really enjoying listening to Raymond. This guy had a sense of humour all his own.

"I must buy her a present and send it back with you," said Angela. "I'll have to think of something."

"How about a new dressing gown? Preferably in a different colour," Raymond replied.

"You'd be doing me a big favour. I suggested buying her a muzzle last Christmas but Sheila wouldn't hear tell of it!"

Sheila smiled at Angela.

"She keeps all your cards and letters in a biscuit tin," she told her.

Raymond piped up,

"I wouldn't be surprised if she kept her sleeping pills in there as well. That box only comes out of it's hiding place once in a blue moon. Maybe that's why she doesn't sleep. Now, do any of you mind if we change the subject? I came all the way out here in the hope that I could forget about her." He shook his head and smiled, "I pity poor Jamie. He couldn't wait to move in, but I'd lay odds by the time I see him again he can't wait to move out."

"Are you into sport? You know, boxing, things like that? asked Joe.

Raymond nodded.

"I bet on the horses. I get a real thrill when mine comes first past the post."

Joe smiled.

"If you like racing, we'll take a trip to Belmont Park. Who knows, if we're lucky, we might make it two or three trips."

Raymond beamed and held out his hand.

"Put it there, Joe, he said. "You're a man after my own heart!"

Joe took his hand and smiled broadly, shrugging his shoulders, "Well, I like a bet myself," he explained. "And after all, we betting men have to stick together!"

Angela gazed around the table at everyone looking so happy. She was overjoyed to have her family there and was delighted that Joe had taken to Raymond. He really seemed to like him, not to mention the rest of the family. It meant a lot to her that Joe had accepted them all as his own.

When dinner was over, Sheila excused herself and left the room. A few minutes later she returned, carrying a large plastic bag. She put it down and lifting out a brightly wrapped package she placed it in front of Robert, kissing his cheek and hugging him.

"This is for you," she smiled.

Everyone watched as he undid the paper excitedly and removing the lid from a box, he lifted out a large toy and put it down on the table staring at it with wide eyes. It was a little man with a beard, wearing a green cap and jacket. He was sitting on a wooden seat with a hammer in one hand and a shoe on his knee. As Sheila sat down beside Angela, Raymond got up and going over to Robert's chair, he leaned over.

"Do you know what it is?" He asked the boy smiling. Robert shook his head. "Well, it's one of the little people who only live in Ireland. It's called a Leprechaun." Raymond pressed a button under the seat and the Leprechaun started to tap the shoe with the hammer. "They're very hard to find," he explained as Robert watched spellbound, "And if people do see one, they make a wish and it comes true. A leprechaun can give you anything you want. Even a big pot of gold coins."

"Gee, they must have a lot of money," Robert replied, still staring.

"Yes, they have," nodded Raymond.

"Did they give you any, Uncle Raymond?"

"Well, no. But I'm working on it."

"What is he doing?" Robert pointed to the hammer.

"He's mending shoes."

"Why does he do that if he has so much money?"

Raymond looked baffled.

"I suppose he doesn't want everyone to know."

"Oh," replied Robert, satisfied with the explanation. Raymond turned to Angela.

"Now there is one smart boy. He asks more intelligent questions than our politicians do back home!"

As he went to walk away, Robert tugged his arm gently and looked up at him.

"Uncle Raymond, where does he get the gold coins?"

There was silence as Raymond stood staring at the ceiling, searching for an answer.

Sheila grinned,

"Well, Raymond, where DOES he get the coins?"

He leaned over the table and met her gaze.

"I haven't a clue," he said in a low voice. "Maybe he shites them!"

No-one knew for sure if Robert had overheard, but after turning the toy upside down and looking under the seat, he covered his mouth with his hand and started to giggle.

"Raymond Burns!" snapped Sheila, giving Joe and Angela an embarrassed look.

Robert's giggling got louder and he was soon joined by the girls. He had an infectious laugh and as Angela looked at him, she started to smile. The louder he giggled the more she smiled, until finally she broke into tearful laughter. Joe looked over at his son's bright red face, his small hand still covering his mouth as he looked from the Leprechaun to the girls, who were giggling uncontrollably. Joe leaned his elbow on the table and putting his hand on his forehead, he laughed silently.

Raymond and Sheila looked at everyone in bewilderment.

When Angela finally found her voice, she took Joe's hand away, saying,

"You know, back home there's a popular saying, 'some people never change'. Raymond is one of those people."

Joe shook his head as his shoulders heaved.

"Yeah well," he said, "He might be a big man in Belfast but he ain't so big on story telling. And that's for sure!"

After serving the coffee, Evie waited while the children said 'Goodnight'. Then she brought them upstairs to get ready for bed, leaving the adults to talk. Sheila went back to the plastic bag and taking out a package, she gave it to Angela.

"This is from Mrs Murray," she explained. "She said to tell you it's a little gift to remember her by."

Angela opened it and took out a twelve inch crystal Celtic Cross. As she placed it on the table it shone brightly. A sad look came over her face.

"It's so beautiful. But it must have been very expensive. She's only living on a widow's pension. It's far too much," she said, shaking her head.

"She still talks about you, Angela," said Sheila. "I think that's the reason she fonded so much on Aisling. She says she reminds her of you, when you were a little girl. Because she's getting on now, she talks a lot of the past. How you used to go and get her shopping, about Johnny and Mum and Dad. It nearly broke her heart, the morning we buried Mum. I don't think she ever got over that."

Joe sat quietly listening as Sheila continued,

"Anyway, we didn't really know what to get, but….." she took out two large presents and handed one to Joe, who looked surprised.

"You didn't have to do this," he said.

"Yes we did," came the reply. "Go on, open it."

He undid the wrapping paper as the others looked on. The paper came off to reveal a framed photograph of Robert and Agnes Kenny's grave. Joe studied the black marble headstone with their inscriptions written in large, gold lettering. A bunch of red roses was arranged in a black, marble flower holder in the centre. He got up from the table and embraced Sheila.

"Thank you so much," he said in a low, emotional voice. "I'm deeply touched and very grateful."

Sheila returned his embrace.

"We're the ones who are grateful, Joe. It was you who sent Mother home to rest with my Father, and you who bought the headstone for them. It wasn't cheap."

"Well, she was a very special lady and only the best is good enough for my in-laws." Raymond explained, "We wanted you to have it. After all, you've never seen the grave and it's only right you should."

Joe put his hand on Raymond's shoulder and nodded,

"That photograph means a lot to me. Agnes was a part of my life, a part I'll never forget. I appreciate it more than you know."

Shelia then handed the other present to Angela. It also contained a photograph in a similar frame.

"Where on earth did you get this?" asked Angela in surprise.

"Do you remember it?" smiled Sheila.

"Of course I remember it! But we never had it."

She held it up for Joe to see. It was a family group, Sheila, Agnes, Robert and Angela. They were standing with their arms around each other and Angela had her head on her father's shoulder. They were all smiling happily as they posed in front of a large rose bush, with a small dog at Robert's feet.

"I had it," said Raymond, smiling. "I was the one who took it, one afternoon not long before...." He stopped for a moment and looked at the floor. "Not long before he was murdered. Do you like it?"

"I love it!" she replied, brushing the tears away. She got up and hugged them both. "I'll treasure it for the rest of my life."

Joe gazed at it, taking in every detail. Agnes looked so happy and young, standing with the husband and children she'd loved so much. He could hardly believe it was the same woman. They seemed a perfect family. It was almost impossible to comprehend the horror and tragedy someone had brought into their lives. Unknown to them, this family group was to be the last time they'd be photographed together. As he looked at their smiling faces, he felt a great sadness. And as Robert Kenny's face looked at him, he felt a deep hatred for the person or persons who had given him such a cruel and untimely death. A death that had such a devastating effect on his family and had left no-one connected to him untouched, not even his dog. Raymond broke into his thoughts.

"This is for you, Joe. A little something from me!"

He handed over two bottles of Irish whiskey.

Joe held them up to Angela and smiled,

"I think I'll save one of these for Gene O'Brien."

"If you tell him it came all the away from Ireland, he won't drink it," she replied. "He'll probably get down on his knees and pay homage to it!"

"Who's Gene O'Brien?" Raymond asked Joe.

"Oh, just some guy I know. Now, let's go into the lounge and have a night-cap."

As they left the dining room, Raymond looked at him.

"You know, Joe, I don't think I've ever drank so much in one day. We don't have wine with our meals except for special occasions, like Christmas."

Joe put an arm around his shoulder.

"Well, you'd better get used to it. You've got a brother-in-law who's Italian."

Raymond turned to Angela.

"He wouldn't happen to own a chip shop?!" he whispered.

The evening ended on a much lighter note, but Joe noticed that Raymond and Sheila looked tired.

"Why don't we call it a day?" he suggested. "You both look as though you could do with some sleep. After all, it's a long journey from Belfast to New York."

Sheila nodded.

"I'm worn out, Joe. But I've been so excited; the tiredness is just catching up with me now."

Raymond got to his feet.

"You're right, Joe. I think a good night's sleep is called for."

"We can all go up together," smiled Angela. "And don't get up early tomorrow, have a lie-in. Evie and I will see to the children."

They left the lounge and went upstairs.

After saying 'goodnight' Raymond and Sheila went to their room looking exhausted but happy. Joe and Angela went along to Robert's room and entered quietly. Aisling and Robert were fast asleep. She lay clutching a small, cloth doll and Robert's leprechaun sat on the bottom of his bed.

"It's nice to see two children in here," Angela's low voice had a hint of sadness.

"Yeah, it is," agreed Joe. "And I'm happy that one of them is mine. After all, one is better then none. If I hadn't met you I might never have had any." He looked from her to Robert. "I have a fine son and that makes me a lucky man. Besides, who knows if the trouble in Ireland isn't resolved, Aisling might want to leave when she's older. It's possible. And if it ever happens she'll be welcome in this house. They all will."

"You like Sheila and Raymond, Don't you?"

"Yeah, I do. Your sister is a really nice girl. And Raymond.... Well, he's quite a character!"

Joe put his hand into his trouser pocket and taking out a few coins, he placed them under the leprechaun.

"What are you doing?" asked Angela, in a surprised voice.

"Oh, I just thought I'd give him a head start!" he smiled.

"Joe Morrelli, you're going to have Robert believing all that stuff Raymond told him."

"Well, Angel, we all need something to believe in. Life would be pretty dull otherwise."

He nodded towards Aisling. "Some day she will go from dolls to babies. And Robert ....well, I don't know. But I have a feeling he'll do o.k."

Angela gazed at him.

"I always knew you'd make a good father. If only…"

Joe put his finger to her lips.

"Don't," he whispered. "Don't punish yourself anymore. It's time to let go. It's time for something new. A new dream, Angel, everyone should have that. We all need something to hope for, something to hold onto."

"Have you got one?" she asked in a half whisper

"Yeah, I do."

"What is it?"

"To see my son grow up and make his mark in life, and to always have your love. Now, what about you?"

"I want to do what my mother never got the chance to do. I want this room to be a nursery again, some day. And I want to sit in it with my grandchildren." She took his hand, pressing it gently. "But I'll still need to feel wanted and loved, Joe. That's just the way I am. I suppose you think I'm being silly!"

He shook his head,

"No, you're not being silly. It's a good dream." He looked down at the leprechaun and smiled. "You know, I have a feeling that little man might just make your wish come true!"

Angela smiled and put her arms around his waist, hugging him tightly.

"What if I'd like some proof of that?" she teased.

He took her in his arms and kissed her.

"I'd be happy to oblige," he whispered. "You're the kind of woman who'll always be wanted and loved."

They left the room still wrapped in each others arms. As Angela closed the door gently, she looked up at him and smiled.

"You look happy," he commented.

"I am, Joe. I have my son, my husband, my family – and a new dream to hope for!"

Joe and Angela went out of their way to make sure that their guests enjoyed themselves. Most of the days were spent on family outings for the kids. The nights belonged to the adults thanks to Evie, who was in her element at having to babysit so many children. She fussed over them and enjoyed their company, organising special suppers and games around the kitchen table. Mr Smith would call to lend a hand, keeping the children enthralled with his animal stories.

Raymond and Sheila dined at 'The Safe Haven', 'The Imperial Palace', and went night clubbing with Joe and Angela. It was after one such event that Joe stopped Angela in the entrance hall.

"I'd like a word with you," he said, ushering her into the lounge and closing the door.

"What about?"

"Raymond!" Joe held out his hands. "Does he have to keep bursting into song everywhere we go?"

"Oh, he's just happy," smiled Angela.

"Maybe. But it's embarrassing, Angel. After all, I have my reputation to think about."

"What do you mean?"

"What I mean is, I feel like I've got a walking radio for company. That guy has a tune for every occasion."

"What has that got to do with your reputation?"

Joe looked at the floor, shuffling his feet. "Well," he explained. "I don't want people to think I have a brother-in-law who's…"

"Who's what?"

"Who's a bit weird!" he said loudly.

"Keep your voice down!" snapped Angela. "I don't want him or Sheila to hear you! For Heaven's sake, Joe, he likes to sing. It's just a habit. He used to sing with a group back home in Belfast."

"Well, I've got news for him, he ain't in Belfast now and I don't own a group." Then Joe got curious. "What happened anyway?"

"How should I know," she shrugged, "I wasn't there. But from what Sheila told me they weren't paying him enough for singing."

"Well, I'd gladly write him a cheque not to!" came the sarcastic reply. "And there's another thing. What's with the impersonations bit?"

"Now what are you talking about?" asked a baffled Angela.

Joe pointed to the door.

"I'm, talking about this morning when he was coming downstairs. All I did was ask him how he was."

"And?"

"He started waving his hands around and I got an impersonation of James Cagney. 'Top of the world ma. Top of the world'. What is it with him?"

Angela tried very hard not to laugh.

"Well, he watches a lot of movies and likes to make people laugh. Jokes and impersonations are his way of making an impression. Raymond's always been like that."

"Please," winced Joe, "Spare me the details. I'm just glad we're not living in Hollywood. He'd be handing out resumes like menus!"

She turned her head away and smiled broadly. Joe went over and opening the door slightly, he turned around.

"Where are we going tomorrow?" he asked.

"We're going into the city to do some shopping."

He turned his eyes upwards and sighed,

"I sure hope it doesn't rain."

"Why?"

"Because he'll probably borrow someone's umbrella and do that Gene Kelly routine on the side walk – that's why!"

As he was leaving the room, Angela burst into laughter and then began to hum, loudly.

It was the theme from 'Singing in the Rain'.

Joe put his head around the door.

"Yeah, that's the one!" he nodded, a look of dread on his face!

The time passed quickly for everyone. Sheila, Raymond and the children had only one week left. As the four adults had lunch in the dining-room, the kids had theirs by the pool watched protectively by Evie.

As Raymond gazed around he smiled,

"You know I could get used to this lifestyle. It's a pity all good things come to an end." On a more serious note he looked across at Joe and Angela. "I will miss both of you."

"It's been wonderful for us all to be together," said Sheila. "I've enjoyed it so much."

She was silent for a moment, then looked at Angela. "Why don't you come home for a holiday and bring Joe and Robert with you?"

Angela shook her head, Sheila persisted.

"But I'd like you to come home, Angela. It's been a long time. I know there's a lot of trouble going on but in some ways things have changed,"

"What do you mean?" asked Angela.

"Well, a lot of the people you knew are different now. There have been so many murders that they have forgotten about Daddy."

"How very considerate of them!" replied Angela, with an icy stare.

"You don't understand," Shelia continued. "What I mean is they are friendly. There's no hostility. They talk to me and act as though nothing happened. We're not outcasts anymore. That's all over. It's in the past."

Angela dropped her knife and fork.

"You sound almost grateful to them! They put us through Hell but that's alright now because they have forgotten. Well, I haven't! I can't believe I'm hearing this from you – my own sister." She raised her voice. "You above all people should remember what they did to us, to our family." Standing up, she pushed her chair back. "You might want to forgive and forget, Sheila but I don't."

"But Angela, I'll always remember what happened to Daddy."

"And so will I," snapped Angela.

Joe got up and put out his hand.

"Come on, Angel, she's only trying to explain."

She glared at Sheila. "You didn't see him that morning, Raymond wouldn't let you. But I did. I held my father's brains in my hands! She yelled. "And those same people who are your friends now, didn't care. They thought he got what he deserved. He was an informer – remember?"

Joe stared at Angela in amazement. He had never seen her like this and he had never suspected she still felt so deeply about her father's death.

"They might be your friends, Sheila, but they're not mine," she continued. "I hate them and with all my heart I hate and despise those who murdered him because they murdered our Mother too. I pray they die the way our Father died. 'An eye for an eye'." As Sheila burst in to tears, Angela raised her eyes. "But God has given me a son. He won't always be a child and when he's old enough I'll tell him everything that happened. He has a right to know. Someday he'll be a man and he might be a better one than the rest of the men in this family!" she clenched her teeth and her fists as she stared at her husband and brother-in-law. "He might do something about it!"

Joe watched her as she stormed out of the room. Then he stared at the table. He realised his wife carried a deep rooted hatred in her heart that he never knew existed until today. And he knew she had meant every word she'd said.

Raymond tried to comfort a sobbing Sheila.

"Oh, Sheila. Don't cry love. I told you not to bring the subject of back home up." He shook his head. "Angela can never be like you. Too much happened to her. What she saw will be with her for the rest of her life."

She got up and ran out of the room, still sobbing. Joe felt sorry for her and upset at Angela for her outburst.

He looked at Raymond.

"I'm going to sort this out!" he said in an annoyed voice. Then he, too, stormed out of the room.

On entering the bedroom, Joe found Angela standing at the window gazing out. After closing the door quietly he went over and stood in front of her.

"Don't you think you went a bit far down there?" he asked in a stern voice.

She looked directly at him.

"It's the truth. It had to be said."

"O.k. I won't argue with that. But she's your sister for Christ's sake, and you've hurt her feelings."

"And what about my feelings?" Angela replied, pointing to herself.

"I think you've made those clear to everyone!" came Joe's raised voice.

"You think I'm making too much of this, don't you?"

"Yeah, I do."

"Well, maybe that's because you don't know as much as you think you do."

"I know enough, "he retorted. "Agnes told me everything."

Angela studied him for a few moments then said,

"There were things even my mother didn't know. Things I kept to myself."

She walked over to the wall unit and pushed back the sliding door. Kneeling down, she reached in and took out a small, brown, cardboard box. Joe watched as she got up and placed it on the bed. She looked at him.

"We were a happy family with a nice home. My parents worked hard for most of their lives just to build it up. But it was all taken away from us. My mother and I were the ones who had to leave it, not Sheila. All my mother took out of that house were her photograph albums."

She pointed to the box. "And that's all I have. In there is my past, my memories and my inheritance." There were tears in her eyes as she removed the lid and revealed the contents. She took out a pair of broken spectacles, an old watch, and a dog's bowl. Holding them out to him she cried, "Take a good look, Joe. It isn't much to show for eighteen years. The glasses and watch belong to my father. They were on his body when he was found. And the bowl belongs to Prince.... Poor Prince. I had to keep them. They were all I had to remember them by. My mother never knew."

She put them down on the bed then covering her face with her hands, she sobbed loudly.

Joe went over and took her in his arms.

"I'm sorry, Angel, I had no idea," he said in a low, caring voice.

She clung to him tightly.

"I can't forgive them, Joe, and I never will. The past is always with me, lurking in the back of my mind. Someone murdered my father and they have never been brought to justice. They took an innocent man's life and got away with it. His name will never be cleared as long as they are free. That's why I can't go back there."

"Somebody must know something," said Joe thoughtfully, tightening his hold on her.

"If they do they're never going to tell. Not now, it's been too long."

He put his hand under her chin and raising her face, he looked into her eyes.

"Never is a long time, Angel. Sometimes all you need is to be patient. Things like this have a habit of coming to light, eventually. Sooner or later someone will talk – and someone will listen! Believe me, I should know. It has happened here, and if it can happen in a city the size of New York, it can happen in Belfast and it will."

"Oh, Joe, do you really think so?"

"Sure I do," he assured her, wiping the tears from her cheeks with his finger. "Now listen to me, Why don't you go and see your sister, she's all the family you have. Don't let these people split you up. If you do then they'll have taken everything from you and you will never be able to forgive yourself. Don't let them ruin the rest of your life."

"You're right," she nodded. "They've done enough to the Kenny's."

Joe kissed her cheek and whispered.

"Now, that's the kind of talk I like to hear. You're a woman of spirit Angel. You've got to fight these people every inch of the way to hold onto what's yours. If you do that then they can't win, not in the long run."

Angela put her arms around his neck and hugged him.

"I'm so glad you understand how I feel, Joe."

He stared over her shoulder, a thoughtful look on his face.

"Oh, I understand," he murmured. "I understand more than you know...."

Angela dried her eyes.

"I'm going to see Sheila," she said.

Joe nodded and walked her to the bedroom door. He watched as she went along to Sheila's room and knocked on the door. It opened and both sisters embraced each other amid tears and apologies. On seeing this, Joe retreated and sat on the edge of the bed looking at the cardboard box. He lifted Robert Kenny's spectacles and examined them. With their broken frame and shattered lense he could almost sense the brutality and force of the beating he received. He then lifted the dog's bowl and looked at the name 'Prince' written in large letters. Holding both items, Joe stared long and hard. Only now did he realise just what his wife had come through. She had kept that box hidden from everyone, including him. And only for what had taken place it would have remained hidden forever, along with her heartache. The awful tragedy of what happened to Robert Kenny and his family would never go away. It would always be there in Angela's mind and heart, and in their life together. It was something he'd have to live with until some kind of information came to light, if it ever did. But Joe Morrelli had always been an optimist. Sure, New York was a long way from Belfast he must admit, but he also had to admit something else – nothing in life is impossible and where there's a will, there's a way!

The next day Angela decided to bring Sheila and the children on a shopping spree, determined that they should go home dressed in the best. When lunch was over Joe and Raymond stood at the front door watching, as they all trouped out to the waiting limousine. Shelia was flushed with excitement as she held Senga and Deborah by the hand. Angela held onto Robert and Aisling and as Al drove down the driveway, everyone waved.

As Joe closed the door he looked at Raymond.

"It's nice to have family. It's even better to see them so close."

Raymond nodded.

"The Kenny's always were a close family."

"You must have known them pretty well," replied Joe, putting a friendly hand on his shoulder. "I'd like to have known them myself. It must have been hard for you, being around when they had all their trouble."

"It wasn't easy for any of us, Joe."

"Well, what do you say we open a bottle and you can fill me in? It's about time the men in this house had some peace and quiet!"

"I'd say you're talking my language!" Raymond grinned, as they made their way to the lounge.

Joe opened the bottle of Irish Whiskey and pouring two large measures, he gave one to Raymond.

"Just help yourself," he said, as he sat the bottle down on the coffee table in front of them. He lit one of his favourite cigars and settled down in the comfortable armchair. Raymond lit up a cigarette and relaxed on the couch. He raised his glass.

"It's been a marvellous holiday, Joe, one I will never forget. And if I know Angela, she'll probably spoil my wife and children with the latest fashions. You won't forget today either!" he smiled.

Joe shrugged dismissively.

"Oh, anything for a quiet life. Besides, it will keep them happy." He looked at the floor for a moment, rolling the glass between the palms of his hands. Then he looked back at Raymond. "You know, Angel thinks the world of you. She always talks about how good you were to her."

"Angela always was a nice girl. Different, you know?" as he took another drink of whiskey, he shook his head and smiled. "She could have had a lot of boyfriends back home but she never bothered much with men. They weren't her priority. She loved books and she loved college. Some of the boys used to say she was stuck up but in reality they were just peeved because she never paid them any attention. Angela wasn't like that. She was quiet and wanted an education. She wanted more out of life than most girls over there. Oh, don't get me wrong, Joe. She enjoyed herself by going out with her friends. If we ever met up I used to walk her home to make sure she was safe. Mr Kenny was always very grateful."

Joe watched as Raymond poured himself another drink.

"You liked her, didn't you?" he said, telling rather than asking.

Raymond looked embarrassed and said,

"Well, have you noticed you always seem to like the woman you can't have?"

"That's very true," nodded Joe.

"Anyway, I wasn't Angela's type. I was more like a brother to her and she used to confide in me. I was sorry she didn't get to go on her holiday. She worked damn hard for that money."

"What holiday?" Joe was surprised.

So was Raymond.

"I thought she'd have told you."

"She never mentioned anything about it to me,"

"She planned to go to England," explained Raymond, "with two girls she knew. They were going to tour around and visit all the places where the famous writers and poets lived. Angela was really looking forward to it. She talked about nothing else. It was a dream she's had for a long time but a few weeks before she was due to go, well... her father was killed." He shook his head. "Poor Angela, instead of getting a happy holiday she got a ship load of trouble and sorrow."

Joe poured himself a small whiskey, but Raymond a large one.

"What exactly happened?" he asked.

The alcohol had loosened Raymond's tongue and after lighting another cigarette, he related everything in graphic detail from start to finish. Joe listened intently, seeing it all in his mind's eye. When Raymond had finished, Joe couldn't help but feel a certain amount of admiration and gratitude for this guy who'd done so much for Angela and her family. Now he knew why she felt the way she did about him. Raymond was the only support they'd had in their time of need.

"I'd like to ask you one thing, Raymond, and I'd like an honest answer," Joe said in a serious voice. "Do you think Robert Kenny was an informer?"

Raymond shook his head.

"No way, Joe. He was a good, hardworking man who didn't bother with politics. He never took anything to do with the trouble over there and he never took sides. He was one of those men who thought there was something good in everyone, no matter what their religion or beliefs were. All he wanted was a quiet life, like a whole lot more. Agnes and the girls were the same." He stared in front of him for a few moments, a sad expression on his face. Then he looked at Joe. "You know, sometimes I think I've failed them all and I've disappointed Angela."

"Why?"

"Because in all this time I still haven't been able to find out anything. But believe me, I did try. You see, Joe, I'm a family man myself and I'm not in any organisation so no one will tell the likes of me what they know. It's the big men at the top who have all the information. If anyone knows, they do."

"So you think it was someone in an organisation?"

Raymond shrugged his shoulders.

"It must have been because no one's talking. Not about who killed Robert Kenny, why or who 'The Nightingale' really was. Because in all honesty, it wasn't him. Everything has been hushed up and everyone is too closed mouthed. That's what makes me feel the answers are all higher up the tree and if that's true, we will never know because I'm not in with the big boys."

Joe nodded.

"Well, don't worry about it," he said. "You did your best. You have nothing to feel guilty about and Angela will never blame you. She's too grateful for the way you stayed around and helped her." he got up and put an affectionate arm around Raymond's shoulder. "I'm grateful to you as well. And I appreciate everything you did."

Raymond smiled.

"Thanks Joe. Thanks for all you've done, including the money you and Angela send. It's a great help. You don't have to do it."

"Forget about it! That's what families are for. And speaking of families, we'd better go and get ready for dinner."

Getting up and stretching, Raymond said.

"I think I'll have a nap first. When he reached the lounge door he looked back and grinned. "If Sheila comes back in a good mood I'll be on a promise, so I'll need my strength!"

Joe smiled and shook his head. Then once alone, he went over to the window and stood gazing out. His smile faded. In his mind he was going over everything Raymond had told him. She had been through a lot of heartache in her young years and it was only now the full impact of what she had suffered, hit him. It made him love her ever more and he had a greater understanding of why she felt the way she did. He was genuinely fond of and grateful to Raymond. If it hadn't been for him, Agnes and her daughters might have suffered even more. He was also grateful for the fact that Angela had never fallen in love with some man back home, the way Sheila had, instead, she have saved her love for him and had given it completely. Just thinking about it filled him with emotion. He would never tell her about his conversation with Raymond but he was going to make tonight a special one, and give her all the love and attention she deserved. From now on he wanted her to feel loved at all times. God knows after everything he'd heard, she deserved that.

His mind then turned to what Raymond had said. Maybe the answers Angela wanted were a lot higher up than he could reach.

But Joe Morrelli had powerful friends in influential places and he knew that with their help, maybe he could reach 'Higher up the tree' to coin the phrase used by Raymond.

The vacation was coming to an end with only days to go. Joe had gotten used to having the kids around and he was going to miss them. Especially Aisling who had really taken to him and had a habit of following him around, forever holding his hand. Because she slept in the same room as Robert she had become used to Joe, who would spend some time with them at night reading bedtime stories. It was on one such occasion that Raymond came along the landing and heard Joe's voice coming from the bedroom. He pushed open the door and went in. Joe was seated on the chair reading aloud, as Aisling and Robert sat on the edge of their beds listening.

"Mind if I join the company?" he asked.

Joe felt embarrassed but tried not to show it.

"Grab a pew," he smiled. "But be careful where you sit." He pointed to the beds.

"We've got Lucky the Leprechaun and Peggy the doll!" then he winked.

"Looks like a full house," Raymond grinned, handing Aisling the cloth doll and sitting on the bottom of her bed.

As Joe continued with the story, Raymond looked around. His eyes came to rest on the bedside table and he kept staring until the story had concluded.

"Where on earth did you get that?" he asked, getting up and going over.

Joe looked.

"Oh, it's a long story," he replied.

"That's my Angel," Robert explained. "My Mom got it for me."

"Why?"

"Well, Mom says he'll look after me and be my friend. Look, Uncle Raymond." He pointed to it. "The Angel doesn't like bad men. He chases them away. He'll even kill them if he has to. Mom says he'll punish anyone who tried to harm me."

Raymond studied the statue carefully then sat down and put a protective arm around Robert. "He's an Avenging Angel. Do you know what that means?"

"No."

"Well then, I'll try and explain it to you." The boy looked up at him innocently as he continued. "You see, if the good Angel knows the bad man did something really wicked, it will follow him. No matter where he goes, no matter where he tries to hide, the good Angel will find him."

Raymond put his hand gently on his nephew's head.

"Then the good Angel will do to him what he did to others. He'll get what he deserves, the good Angel will see to that. That's why it's called an Avenging Angel. No bad man is ever really safe. Sooner or later he has to answer for his sins. You'll understand this story more when you get older."

"Is it a true story Uncle Raymond?"

"Yes, son, it is," he nodded.

"Then I'm really glad he's my friend."

"So am I. he's a good friend to have – the best."

Joe got up and put the storybook down. "Well, that's enough for tonight," he said. "It's time to go to sleep."

Raymond kissed the kids goodnight, leaving Joe to tuck them in. as he turned around he saw Angela leaning against the door frame with her arms folded. She smiled as he came towards her.

"That was quite a story Raymond! Do you believe it?"

"You know me, Angela," he shrugged, "religion was never my strong point. I don't know much about angels but Robert believes it and at the end of the day if it makes him happy that's all that really matters." He grinned. "The only angel I'll ever see is the marble one in the chapel back home. And now that I come to think of it, I don't see much of that one either!"

Angela slapped him playfully.

"Your stories about angels are about as convincing as your stories about Leprechauns!"

"Well, maybe I haven't found that big pot of gold coins under my bed yet!" came the reply.

Joe opened the back door.

"Al, bring the car around!" he shouted.

He then made his way to the pool where the rest of the houschold were relaxing. Smiling and slapping his hands playfully he said, "O.k. we are going for a drive."

The three adults got to their feet. "Sorry," he said putting up his hands, "This trip is for kids only." The children gathered around him. "Come on kids, we're going somewhere special and it will be a surprise."

"Where are we going, Uncle Joe?" asked Deborah.

He leaned forward.

"Well, if I told you that it wouldn't be a surprise, now would it?" the kids jumped up and down with excitement. "O.k. let's go!" he grinned, turning and walking away as they followed.

Deborah took his hand and Senga went to take the other one, but Aisling pushed her out of the way and grabbed hold of his fingers tightly.

Raymond looked at the two women.

"You know, for Aisling to be so small it doesn't stop her from muscling in on other people's territory!"

"Just like her Uncle Joe!" smiled Angela.

As the kids scrambled into the back of the car, Al looked at Joe.

"Where to Boss?"

"The biggest toy store we can find," he replied in a low voice.

Al smiled,

"It's a bit early in the year to be applying for the job of Santa Clause."

Joe gave him a sarcastic look and said,

"Well, it isn't too early for you. Come December you could be in a different uniform, ringing a big bell on the sidewalk!"

Al shrugged as he got in.

"You know me Boss, I always did like red."

"Yeah, I know. Every woman I ever saw you with was dressed init."

"Well. There's something about a woman in red that turns me on."

Joe leaned over and whispered,

"Would you please keep your voice down, we've got kids in the back! Besides, it isn't healthy to fantasise about things like that."

"Like what?"

"You know, sex and colours," muttered Joe.

"Well, it didn't do you any harm, Boss."

"And what's that supposed to mean?"

"I mean your apartment. You had white satin sheets and black satin sheets. And you always said they made having sex even better."

Joe glared at him.

"Maybe, but that was then. I've grown up and you should do the same!"

Al gave a sly smile.

"I'd be tempted to bet you've still got them. Boss."

"And I'll bet if you don't start this car right now, I'll wrap one of them around your neck!" snapped Joe.

"See! I knew you still had them!"

Joe opened his mouth to speak but Al beat him to it.

"I think the kids would like some music," he said in a loud voice, turning on the radio.

The kids cheered as he started the car and drove off, a huge grin on his face!

The limousine came to a halt outside a large toy store in the city. Joe and his young companions got out and made their way through the entrance, to the ground floor. The children's eyes opened in amazement.

"I've never seen so many toys!" exclaimed Senga.

"This isn't all of them," smiled Joe. "They have more upstairs." He nodded towards the escalator, then lined the kids up in front of him. "O.k., here's what we're going to do. We are going to have a look around and I want you all to choose something."

"Anything?" asked Deborah.

"Anything you like." he nodded.

They smiled and clapped their hands in glee as they followed him around the store, looking at everything and comparing toys and games. As they pointed to them and asked questions, Joe watched their faces light up with excitement. Their happiness made him happy. Finally, after they had been around the whole store and seen everything, they made their minds up. Robert chose a base-ball bat complete with glove. A pair of brightly coloured roller boots caught Senga's eye. Deborah decided on a doll that talked. As the assistant wrapped up the large packages in fancy paper, they all stood watching.

Joe looked at Aisling, who had been silent all this time. He crouched down and put his arms around her.

"Now what would you like honey?" he asked in a gentle voice.

She gazed into his face with her dark blue eyes.

"A teddy bear," she whispered.

"O.k., he nodded. "We'll go back to the next floor and get you one you really like."

When they came out onto the sidewalk, Al opened the door and Joe handed him the packages.

"I'm bringing the kids for some ice cream. I'll meet you back here in half an hour. Then we're going to the park."

Al nodded and watched as Joe made his way along the street with the four kids. He smiled. It was nice to see his boss having such a good time.

They spent the rest of the afternoon in Central Park. Joe sat and watched Robert and the girls playing. He remembered the days he and Angela had spent there before they were married. Now he was there with his son , knowing exactly what it was like to be a family man and enjoy all the little things in life that were so important. Things he could so easily have missed out on if he hadn't met Angela Kenny. He realised that all those years of women, parties and night clubs were really very lonely years. He had convinced himself it was a great life and one he enjoyed because he didn't want to admit that even with Antonia, something was missing. Like a ship without a harbour, he just drifted. However, he found that harbour in 'The Safe Haven' when he met the woman who was to change his entire future. He smiled to himself. Every man should have a woman like her but very few did. He was one of the lucky ones and he knew it. As well as being his lover, she was his friend, his confidant. They shared a deep trust and understanding. Sex only lasts for a short while but these things last a whole lifetime. Being the shrewd businessman he was, Joe knew that marriage wise – he'd gotten a good deal! As he looked at Robert running around he could only hope that if his son did half as well in his choice of a wife as Joe had done, then he would have no worries. He would do o.k.!

The front door opened and the kids ran through the entrance hall with their presents. Evie came out of the kitchen to see what all the commotion was about. Robert stopped and looked at her.

"Where's Mom, Evie? he asked excitedly.

She pointed towards the lounge. Angela, Shelia and Raymond were in conversation when Robert rushed in, followed by Senga and Deborah. They were all talking at once, telling where they'd been and what they'd seen. Then they knelt down on the floor to open the packages and show the adults what they had. After admiring their presents and watching the kids faces filled with delight, Angela turned to Robert.

"Where's your father?" she asked.

At that moment Joe appeared in the doorway with Aisling, who was holding a teddy bear so big all anyone could see were her feet! Everyone stared.

"Joe, this is far too much," said Sheila. "And the bear must have cost a fortune."

"It's going to cost even more if we have to buy a seat for it on the plane!" muttered Raymond, under his breath.

Angela laughed,

"Joe, that bear is bigger than Aisling!"

"Well, that's no big deal," he shrugged. "The good news is, it won't grow any bigger but she will. Won't you honey? He smiled down at her.

She came across the lounge with her little arms around it and put it on Sheila's knee. After making a fuss of it her mother asked,

"What are you going to call it?"

Aisling leaned over and whispered. Sheila looked at Joe and smiled.

"She says she likes that name you call her."

"What name is that? he asked, puzzled.

"Honey."

"No kidding!" grinned Joe. "Well then, honey it is!" he winked.

Raymond looked at his daughters.

"Did you thank your Uncle Joe for the presents?"

They all nodded.

"Well, thank him again," said Sheila.

They went over and one by one reached up, hugged him and kissed his cheek.

"I though you'd got lost," said Angela.

"Me, get lost in New York? Not a chance, Angel. I decided to give the kids a day out and we are going to have a night out."

"Where are we going?" she asked.

"I stopped off and made reservations at 'The Portland Club'. We are going out to dinner with champagne and dancing. This will be a special night for special people!"

Raymond got up.

"It sounds like a high-class place, Joe."

Joe just smiled.

"It is," Angela informed him. "It's very exclusive. Reservations only."

Raymond looked over at Sheila and grinned,

"Better get the old top hat and tails out, Mrs Burns. Tonight you'll make everyone jealous – you'll be dancing with Fred Astaire!"

Joe looked up at a smiling Angela, then turned his eyes upwards.

"Please God," he whispered, "don't let him sing."

Joe and Angela sat at the table watching as Raymond and Sheila danced close together.

"You know my Father had his doubts about them ever getting married," Angela nodded towards them. "He didn't say so. Well, not in so many words, but he always doubted it would last. I suppose that was because Sheila was so young. He worried that Raymond didn't really love her, but anyone can see that he does. They make a nice couple."

Joe nodded in agreement.

"Yeah, she did o.k."

Angela slipped her hand over his.

"We both did," she smiled.. "There's something to be said for marrying a man older than yourself."

"How old is he?"

"Twenty eight. Sheila's twenty three."

The music stopped and the loving couple returned to their seats, in a happy mood with all the expensive champagne they'd had to drink. Raymond refilled his glass.

"This is some place, Joe."

"I thought you'd like it."

"Come to that, it's been some holiday. I'll never forget it and I'll never forget you and Angela for making it possible."

Joe patted his shoulder.

"Well, this time tomorrow we'll be on our way home," said Sheila sadly.

"Don't remind me!" her husband winced. "Just think, in a day or two everything will be back to normal. I'll be standing in a queue waiting for a bus, half expecting Joe's limo to drive by and stop. You know, Sheila, Jamie Doyle is never going to believe all this when I tell him. All the fancy restaurants and clubs we've been to, not to mention Broadway and Belmont Park. It's just as well we took photographs of everything."

Joe looked at him and smiled,

"Yeah, you sure took a lot of those alright. I reckon you've used up more rolls of film than they did making 'Gone With The Wind'!"

Raymond pointed his finger at him as they all laughed.

"I like that, Joe," he said. "That's a good one."

Then he leaned over the table and motioned for Joe to come closer. "What do you call a cowboy with no money?"

"I don't know."

"Skint Eastwood! What's an example of Irish graffiti?"

"I don't know"

"Thank God I'm an atheist! Hey Joe, I backed a horse called 'Banana' – it never left the bunch!"

The sound of happy laughter echoed around the table as Raymond kept the jokes coming thick and fast. Everyone was enjoying themselves. It was the perfect end to a perfect vacation.

As Evie cooked breakfast for the others, Al sat at the table finishing his. The door opened and the three girls came in wearing their nightclothes. They went over to Evie and presented her with a neatly wrapped package.

"This is for you, Evie," Senga smiled.

Evie looked surprised.

"For me? Well, let's see what it is."

She took the package from the child's hand and turned down the cooker. She unwrapped the paper and discovered a black leather-bound Bible with gold lettering. Inside were brightly illustrated pictures.

"Oh, it's beautiful!" she gasped, putting a hand up to her face. Then she wrapped her arms around them and hugged them tightly, brushing the tears from her eyes.

They turned their attention to Al, who was watching the scene with great interest.

Aisling stepped forward and put a package on the table in front of him.

"We got you a present too," she smiled shyly.

Al was even more surprised than Evie!

He opened the package and produced a blue silk tie in a gift box.

"Do you like it?" asked Deborah.

He held it up for all to see.

"I sure do!" he said. "That's the nicest tie I've ever seen. I'm real pleased." He smiled broadly and patted them gently on the head. "That was real sweet of you," he concluded.

The girls looked at each other and smiled with satisfaction. Then they heard their mother calling.

"We have to go upstairs now," said Senga and they dutifully left.

Evie and Al looked at each other.

"I'm going to miss them," she said. "The house was so alive and they were great company. Wasn't it kind of them to think of us like this?"

"Yeah, they're good kids," nodded Al. "I think the boss is going to miss the youngest one. She's taken a real shine to him."

"I think she reminds Mr Joe of Miss Angela. She must have been just like her at that age. It's a shame they can't have a daughter of their own, they are such good parents. Still, the Lord works in mysterious ways. It just wasn't meant to be. I thank the Lord every night that we have Robert. He's going to miss them. And I'm sure they'll miss him."

Just then, the door opened and Robert came in on his own. He stood for a moment, one hand behind his back and the other in front of him, closed tightly. Then he came towards Evie.

"This is for you, Evie, he said, holding out a red rose he'd taken from the vase in the entrance hall.

She looked into his face, knowing right away that he'd felt left out when the others gave their presents. Taking the rose, she opened the bible to one of her favourite stories and placed it there.

"Come on, honey," she said, taking him in her arms. "A rose is a flower of love. A Bible is a book of love. I will keep both of them together. Thank you, Robert."

He put his arms around her neck and kissed her cheek. Then he walked over to the table.

"Al, I want to give you this," he said, opening his hand and putting down one of his toy soldiers. Al picked it up and looked at it.

"You know something, Robert? I've never had one of these."

"Never?"

"No, never. And I always wanted one!"

The boy smiled as he hugged Al, then went in search of his cousins.

Evie dabbed her eyes.

"Fancy a child that age having so much thought and giving me a rose."

"Yeah," smiled Al, "he's a chip off the old block alright."

"What do you mean?"

"Well, the boss was always one for giving flowers to women. I'd say Robert is going to be a real Morrelli in every way, if you know what I mean!"

She glared at him.

"Now, don't you start talking about things I don't want to hear." She warned.

"Like what?"

"Like women and such things."

"Oh, you mean sex. Well, the boss was always one for giving them that as well!" he grinned.

Evie stood rigid.

"I really think there's something wrong with you," she said, her eyes narrowing.

Al got to his feet.

"Nothing a good lay wouldn't fix!"

She grabbed a large pan.

"A good lay in the hospital for a few days would fix you even better!"

He bolted through the back door as she lunged at him.

"Now get!! She ordered.

"I'm going, I'm going!" came the reply.

Al chuckled to himself as he walked quickly towards the garage still clutching Roberts's toy soldier. He stopped and looked at it. Then shaking his head, he put it in his pocket. No matter what age he'd live to, he'd always keep it. Why? Because the boss's son thought enough of him to give it as a present. Yeah, he was his father's son aright. Joe Morrelli had given to his friends all his life and never counted the cost. Not even with personal things. – like his apartment. And Robert was going to be just like his Old Man!

The two families stood in a small group saying their goodbyes as the departure of the flight was announced. Sheila and Angela tried to console one another, tears filling their eyes. Raymond put his hand out and shook Joe's firmly.

"Thank's for everything, Joe" he said. "You're a brother – in –law in a million. It was a lucky day for Angela when she met you…."

Joe nodded in appreciation.

"Take care of yourself, Raymond… and take care of Sheila and those lovely kids."

"I will, and that's a promise," he replied.

Sheila embraced Joe.

"Mum was right," she whispered, "You're a good man."

He slipped his hand into his inside pocket and taking out an envelope, gave it to her.

"What's this? She asked, surprised.

"Just a little something for the kids."

"Joe, you've been more than good to us. I can't take this."

"Sure you can," he insisted. "You'll need it when you get home."

Raymond ushered his family towards the departure exit, carrying Aisling's teddy bear while Sheila took her by the hand. They stopped to wave, the girls shouting their goodbyes to Robert, who stood waving back sadly. Just then Aisling broke away from her mother.

"I want my Uncle Joe!" she cried running towards him, her arms outstretched.

Joe bent down and picked her up, holding her tightly as she clung to him sobbing. He closed his eyes for a few seconds, so choked up as he was unable to speak. He carried her towards Sheila.

"Now listen, honey," he whispered, finally finding his voice. "You go back home and show everyone that big teddy bear, and I'll talk to you tonight on the telephone."

"But I want to stay with you," she persisted, tears streaming down her little face.

"And you will, honey. You can come and stay any time you want to."

She looked at him pleadingly.

"You promise?"

"Yes I promise," he nodded, kissing her cheek. "But you have to go home with your mom now. she loves you and she'd miss you."

"Will you miss me?" she asked innocently. Rubbing her hand over her eyes.

"Sure I will! But I want you to do me a big favour. Look after that teddy bear for me. He doesn't know anyone in Ireland, but you. He'd be real lonely if you weren't there."

Aisling was thoughtful for a few moments.

"I'd better go home with him then, Uncle Joe, hadn't I?"

Joe smiled,

"He'd be real unhappy if you didn't."

She hugged and kissed him.

"Goodbye Uncle Joe," she whispered.

"Goodbye Aisling," he murmured.

Raymond looked at Angela, then without any warning he came running back to her and took her in his arms.

"Nothing was ever the same when you left, Angela. But you did the right thing, so don't ever regret it." He turned to Joe. "Look after her. If Hell is on earth then believe me, she's been there!" he fought back the tears as he returned to his waiting family.

As they boarded the plane, Joe and Angela stood with Robert by the hand watching. The plane taxied down the runway and took off. Joe glanced at his wife, remembering that the last time she stood like this watching a flight bound for Ireland, her mother's body was on board. He knew she must be feeling sad, so he put his arm around her lovingly.

"You know, maybe someday you should go back, Angel. After all, it is your home."

She looked at him and shook her head.

"No, my home is here with you, Joe. Where I'm happy. Where I belong."

He smiled.

"Do you really mean that?"

"Yes I do," she nodded. "New York is my home."

"Could I go to Ireland?" asked Robert.

Angela was silent but Joe looked down at him and smiled,

"Sure you can, son," he said.

"When?" he met his father's gaze.

"Oh, some day," he nodded thoughtfully. "When the time is right......."

Chapter 14

Joe was never a man who listened to idle gossip but as things got back to normal in his home and business life, rumours began to circulate concerning Dan Casey. If they were to be believed, Dan's health was failing and because of this he had decided not to run as the candidate for re-election.

Joe decided it was time to find out the truth and to make his first move. A couple of days later he turned up at Gene O'Brien's office, unannounced. As he stood in front of the secretary, she apologised as she looked at the Congressman's list for the day. "I'm sorry, Mr Morrelli but Mr O'Brien has a very busy schedule. I really don't think he can see you without an appointment."

At that, a loud voice came from across the room.

"Mr Morrelli doesn't need an appointment!"

Joe turned and saw Gene standing in the doorway of his office, smiling.

"Good to see, Joe. Come on in," he beckoned. As Joe entered the office, his friend leaned his head out.

"Janet, hold all my calls."

"Yes, Mr O'Brien."

After closing the door he went over and sat down behind his desk, motioning to Joe to take the seat opposite. He waited as Joe looked around and smiled.

"So this is where it's all happening?" he said.

"Yeah," nodded Gene, "this is it - for now anyway. But between you and me, Joe, there are bigger things to come."

"I always said you had itchy feet! What's the matter, Gene, isn't this office big enough for you?"

"There are better places," he shrugged giving a sly smile. "Where there's real power. Power you wouldn't believe." He clenched his fist. "And I've got a taste for it, Joe."

"You mean the Senate."

"I sure do," he nodded.

"Well, that's what I want to talk to you about."

Gene looked at Joe with interest.

"I was wondering what brought you to my corner of the world, old buddy. I didn't know you were so interested in the affairs of state!"

"Oh, I'm more interested than you think," came the reply. "That's the reason I dropped by. There's a couple of things I'd like to ask you."

Gene leaned back in his chair.

"Sure, Joe, I'm listening. How can I help you?"

Joe studied his hands for a moment, then looked up.

"Is it true Dan Casey won't be running for re-election?"

"Well, he hasn't given a statement confirming it, but it's true," nodded Gene. "His health isn't so good but he has plans. So for the time being he isn't confirming or denying it."

"Would those plans have anything to do with you?"

"I've had Dan's confidence for a long time, Joe. He's taught me just about everything he knows, so don't be surprised if you open your morning paper one of these days and read about me taking his place. In the not too distant future, I'll be running for the Senate. It's only a matter of time."

"I'm really pleased for you, Gene. But in the meantime, as you and Dan are so close, I'd like you to have a word with him. I need a favour."

"Sure Joe, I'll do anything I can to help. What is it?"

"Well, my son is almost five years old now but time passes so quickly it won't be long until he's a young man, and someday he'll want to travel - especially to places that will mean something to him. I guess what I'm really trying to say is, when he's old enough he will want to go to Ireland. The only family ties he has are there. I have no family on my side. It's only natural he'll want to go and see his relatives, you know, see where his mother came from and see his grandparent's grave. After all, being half Irish he has roots there. You, more than anyone, should understand that, Gene."

"You bet! So what's the problem?"

Joe put his hands out.

"The problem is, I want him to be safe. He's my son, he's all that's left of the Morrelli name and I want that name to be carried on." His tone and expression were serious. "I don't want anything to happen to him and I'll do whatever it takes to ensure that nothing ever does."

"Yeah, things are pretty bad over there."

"Bad? For Christ's sake, Gene, there's a fuckin' war going on! And if it lasts, I don't want my son caught up in it. I want him to be able to come and go in the knowledge that someone's watching out for him. I want his safety guaranteed and I'll do anything to make sure it is - and I mean anything!"

Gene stared at him, then said,

"It's a wise man who plans so far ahead. But in your position I'd do exactly the same thing." He lowered his gaze, looking at the desk for a few moments, then looked back at Joe. "I'll tell you what, why don't you leave it with me? I'll have a word with Dan Casey. If anyone knows the score about Ireland he does, and he's the man who just might be able to work something out for you."

Joe nodded,

"Thanks Gene. I knew you'd understand. I'd better not take up anymore of your time."

"I always have time for you, Joe!"

"I know, but you're a busy man now," he replied as he rose to his feet.

"Never too busy for Joe Morrelli or his lovely wife. Those speeches she's been writing for me lately are bringing the house down. Since she took up the pen, I'm getting all the right punch lines in all the right places and my point of view is coming over loud and clear at the right time. I'm hitting home hard, Joe and the applause is getting longer and louder with every speech!" he grinned.

"Well, she was always good at English and she did graduate with honours," said Joe proudly. "We even have a certificate of excellence hanging on the wall to prove it!"

Then he became more serious. "I'd appreciate it, Gene, if you kept this visit just between the two of us. I don't want Angel to know. I wouldn't want her worrying unnecessarily."

Gene came around the desk and put a caring hand on his shoulder.

"Say no more, Joe. This visit won't go any further than you, me and Dan Casey. I'll be in touch in a week or so. Your problem shouldn't take any longer than that to sort out." The two men walked to the office door and Gene opened it. Joe put his hand out "Thanks again, Gene."

"Hey, what are friends for!" he replied, grasping his hand and shaking it. "We've come a long way from the old neighbourhood and there's still a long way to go. And it wouldn't be the same if there wasn't a Morrelli around! Don't worry, Joe, that name is going to be in New York for ever! You just leave everything to old Gene, here. I'll be in touch."

Joe smiled broadly.

"I suppose when you get to the Senate I will have to make an appointment to see you."

"Not in the Senate - but maybe in the White House."

Joe walked across the room then stopped and turned.

"I hope it's the Oval office. I've never seen it in real life."

"Neither have I but where there's life, there's hope. Nothing's impossible," he beamed. "I can promise you one thing, you'll be first on my list for the President's Ball!"

"Yeah, well, you've got to aim high," Joe smiled. "And you can't get much higher than that, Gene."

As Joe left, Gene shook his head. He remembered the note and the champagne he had received from his friend, announcing he was getting married to Angela. He smiled and murmured to himself, "Well, you did it and it sure didn't do you any harm."

He went back into his office and closing the door, stood in a pensive mood for a few moments. There was a lesson to be learned from Joe Morrelli. When he wanted something, he went after it - and got it. That's why men like himself admired and respected him so much. There endth the lesson.

Just over a week later, Joe received a phone call from Gene O'Brien asking to meet him in O'Tooles Bar. They arranged to meet in the early afternoon when the place would be quiet. As Joe opened the door and stepped inside, he was greeted by a friendly smile from the other side of the bar.

"Mr Morrelli, how are you? It's been a long time."

"I'm fine Pat. How's business?"

"Oh, can't complain. Mr O'Brien is waiting for you," he nodded towards the back of the premises. "I'll see you won't be disturbed."

Joe put up his hand.

"Thanks, Pat," he smiled, walking up past the empty bar to the last booth. He sat down facing Gene, still smiling. "Well, you sure know how to pick a meeting place."

"I wanted somewhere quiet," said Gene in a low voice.

Joe looked around,

"Well, you won't get anywhere more quiet than this! What did you do, rent if for the afternoon?"

Gene laughed.

"Oh, Pat is well used to meetings. You'd be surprised at how many plans were made in here."

"What kind of plans?" enquired Joe.

"To free Ireland!" came the defiant reply.

"Really, what happened? No, let me guess. When Pat called time all the volunteers had to go home, to get up early for work the next morning!"

Gene shook his head and smiled.

"Yeah, something like that. Plans take time."

"Does that include me?"

"Maybe, maybe not," said Gene, leaning forward. "You might just be one of the lucky ones, Joe." He raised his hand. "Hey Pat, two large whiskeys." When the drinks had been brought and they were alone again, Gene continued. "O.k., lets get down to business. I had a talk with Dan Casey and there could be a way around your problem. And that way is to contribute financially to an organisation in Belfast called, 'The Celtic Awareness Society'. Their function is to get people interested in their heritage, learning to speak their native language, restoring old customs that have almost died away. In short, they want the people to be proud of their background and learn about it. It's a good way of taking their minds off the troubles and what's going on around them."

Joe's eyes narrowed.

"But who exactly would I be contributing to?" he asked.

"Joe, believe me, in Belfast there are wheels within wheels - if you know what I mean."

Joe nodded,

"O.k., I'm listening. Tell me more."

"Well, Dan can lay the ground work, but you have to appreciate he can't be seen to be directly involved. There's a lot more to it, you see."

"I understand."

411

After taking a drink from his glass, Gene went on. "Dan can provide the contacts for you, if you can provide the go-between."

"You mean, someone to go over there on my behalf to make everything legit?"

He nodded. Joe was silent for a moment as he lifted his glass and stared in front of him. Then he took a swallow, put the glass down and gave Gene a serious look.

"That won't be a problem," he assured him. "O.k., I'm in!"

Putting his hand in his pocket, Gene took out a folded piece of paper and put it on the table.

"Everything you need to know is in there," he said, sliding it towards him.

Joe lifted it and immediately put it into the inside pocket of his jacket.

"Thank's Gene."

"You're welcome, old buddy."

With business out of the way both men relaxed.

"You know, O'Tooles isn't such a bad place to hold meetings," smiled Joe.

"Or make plans."

"Yeah, but I have a hunch mine might come through a little quicker than the rest that were made in here." He leaned across the table. "What do you say we give this guy some trade, while his regulars are at work plotting the revolution?"

Gene grinned and shook his head.

"Jesus, Joe, I'm sorry I told you about that!"

"No, I'm glad you did. If I wake up some morning to hear on the news that Ireland has been invaded, I'll know who by - Pat O'Tooles secret army!" Both men started to laugh as Joe stood up. "Hey Pat, two more large whiskeys up here and one for yourself!"

Joe waited until he had thought everything through before asking Rooney to his study. He sat in the black leather armchair as Rooney took a seat facing him at the other side of the desk.

"What's up Joe, do we have a problem?"

Joe was silent for a moment as he rubbed his face with his hand.

"How would you feel about taking another trip?"

Rooney smiled.

"Sure. Where to?"

Leaning forward with his elbows on the desk, Joe looked at him.

"Belfast," he said.

Rooney's smile faded as he gasped,

"Belfast!" in disbelief. "What the hell would bring me there?"

"Business, Rooney. Business so important I need someone I can trust."

"What's going on, Joe?" he asked, staring at him.

"I've decided to donate some money to an organisation there."

"Are you crazy! What if Angela finds out?"

Joe gave a deep sigh and stood up.

"It's because of her and my son, I'm doing it. Let me explain…."

"I think you'd better!" Rooney was still shocked.

Joe scratched his head thoughtfully.

"Angel has never come to terms with her father's death and she never will. I thought by now the memory of what happened would have faded into the past, but I know now that's not going to happen. She still wakes up in the middle of the night in a cold sweat. She's still reliving it. It won't go away, Rooney, and it won't die. Not for her and not for me because I have to live with it too. Angel won't ever go back home because her father's killer or killers are still walking around free. Now, someone there knows who they are and I want to find out and get them brought to justice. It's the only way. If I can do that and prove Robert Kenny was innocent, then I can lay old ghosts to rest. I owe her that, Rooney I owe it to myself. She's never going to be totally happy until it's out of the way and neither am I." Joe went over and stood staring out of the window. "Then there's my son," he said in a concerned voice. "When he gets older, he's going to have to be told." He turned his head and met Rooney's gaze. "He may want to go there someday and my donations will ensure that if he does, he'll be safe. Someone will be watching his tail and that's what I want. It's sort of like paying life insurance and I'm willing to do that to make sure he's going to be o.k."

"How do you know you will ever find out anything?"

Joe shook his head.

"I don't. But money is a big temptation and it speaks all languages. Of course as far as everyone's concerned, I'm only doing this for my son and they won't know any different. But in time maybe, if I'm lucky, it will work both ways. But I can't do it alone. I really need your help on this one. I'm not telling you to go, I'd rather you'd make you own decision."

Rooney was silent for a few moments then said,

"Well, if you put it like that, Joe, how can I refuse? There's just something I'd like to ask you."

"Sure."

"What really made your mind up?"

Joe came towards him slowly.

"Something my brother-in-law said. He's a family man. He's not in any organisation, that's why he could never find out anything. But he reckons the 'big guys' over there know what's going on and they have all the information. So I intend to deal with the 'big guys'".

"O.k.," nodded Rooney, "I'm going to Belfast. You'd better fill me in."

He put a grateful hand on Rooney's arm.

"I knew I could depend on you. Now, lets get down to business," he said, returning to his chair. "You will be met at the airport by two guys. One of them will pass you off as a cousin he hasn't seen in years. You will stay at his home."

"How are they going to know me?" asked Rooney.

Joe smiled,

"You'll be the only person getting off the flight wearing a grey sweatshirt with 'Stacey's Gym' printed on it. A couple of days after you arrive, you'll be taken to see one of the top men. You'll open an account with him on my behalf for a specified amount to be paid on a regular basis. Reuben will have the necessary documents drawn up and ready. For every year my son gets older, the amount will go up. Call it inflation! When the business end has been taken care of, I want you to stay on for a little while. You know, blend in with these guys, get friendly with them, gain their confidence, listen to anything they have to say. You never know, you could hear something to our advantage."

Rooney looked at him knowingly.

"In other words, keep my mouth shut and my ears open!"

Joe nodded,

"It's the best way. Only tell them what they need to know. I'm told these guys can be trusted but you never can tell. I'll let you be the judge of that."

"Well, if I'm going on a trip to Belfast, where will everyone around here think I'm going?"

"That's the best part," Joe replied. "When you went to Vegas you visited a Casino that was losing money because of mismanagement. You thought if it were owned by the right people, it would be a good investment. You told me, I agreed and me and some of my friends bought into it. You've gone back to close the deal. It's perfect."

Rooney shook his head.

"You've really looked into all this."

"Every aspect."

"When do I leave, Joe?"

"The end of the week."

Rooney stood up.

"You know what will happen if Angela ever finds out about this," he warned.

Joe nodded,

"Yeah, I've given that a lot of thought, but if we keep it to ourselves she won't know. That's why I'm glad you're going, Rooney. You've never betrayed a confidence." He got up and came around the desk, putting his hands on his best friends shoulders. "Listen to me, Rooney, and believe me when I tell you that I didn't make this decision lightly. But I love Angel very much and our happiness will only be complete when the horror goes away, when she stops reliving the day she saw her father. And that will only happen when whoever did it is caught and punished. It's only then she'll be able to let go of the past. Robert has roots there. He's already asking when he can go to Ireland. What's going to happen when he gets older and learns the truth? He'll want to go and see his grandparents grave and if he's Joe Morrelli's son, he won't leave it there! You know what

I'm talking about, Rooney!"

"Yes, I do."

"Well, that's why I'm going to try and find out the truth, first. He's my son, the only kid I've got and I'm going to make damn sure nothing ever happens to him. No-one can blame me for that."

Rooney was agreeable but concerned.

"You've never been wrong about anything, Joe. I just hope you're not wrong about this."

"So do I," he replied in a serious voice. "But you'll be safe, Rooney, I've made sure of that."

"I'm not worried about me, I can take care of myself. I'm worried about you, Joe. I hope you're not getting in too deep."

He shook his head and replied,

"Joe Morrelli's too smart for that! I never take on anything I can't handle."

"Are you sure you want to go through with this?"

He nodded.

"Yeah, I'm sure."

"O.k., I'll leave at the end of the week as planned."

"Thank's Rooney, I appreciate what you're doing. I also know it's not just for me, it's for Angel and Robert."

"The three of you are the only family I've got," Rooney reminded him, his voice and expression became serious and determined. "I guess that makes it personal. I'll see you tomorrow." As he left the study he stopped and turned. "Just remember one thing Joe. There are powerful men in Ireland."

Joe smiled, "Rooney, a man is only as powerful as the city he lives in, and if you compare the size of Belfast with the size of New York - I'd say we've got the edge!"

Rooney nodded in agreement and closed the door after him.

Rooney stepped off the plane casually dressed in blue denim jeans and the sweatshirt provided by Joe. As he made his way through arrivals, two men in their mid-twenties approached him. One had black hair and a short beard. The other had short cropped, red hair and a small gold ring in one ear. The man with the beard put his arms around Rooney and grinned broadly.

"Long time no see, cousin!" he said. "It's good to have you home!"

"Its good to be here," came the reply as Rooney embraced him in return.

"Lets go and get your luggage. How was your trip?" the man asked in a deliberately loud voice, leading him away.

When Rooney had collected his large hold-all, the three men left the main building chatting happily as they passed through security. Once outside, they headed for the car-park. After they had climbed inside the car and closed the doors, the bearded man put out his hand, smiling.

"My name's Dermot Mc Cabe. Welcome to Belfast."

Rooney gripped his hand firmly.

"I'm Rooney. Thanks for coming for me."

The man with the red hair turned around in the drivers seat and shook Rooney's hand.

"Seamus Quinn," he said with a friendly smile.

The introductions over, they drove off.

As they headed for the city centre, they laughed and joked. Rooney started to feel at ease. They were ordinary, down to earth guys. The kind you feel you've known all your life. Suddenly, the car slowed down

"What's wrong?" asked Dermot.

"There's a bloody check-point up ahead," replied Seamus.

"Is it Brits or U.D.R?"

"I don't know, I can't make them out from here. There are too many cars in front."

"Alright, Seamus, swap places. If you give them any back-chat we'll be here all day, and we don't want any slip-ups." As he climbed into the drivers seat, Dermot turned to Rooney and explained, "He's a bit hot-headed with uniforms!"

As they got nearer the check-point, voices with and English accent could be heard.

Dermot gave a warning look to Seamus.

"Now, I'll handle this. Let me do all the talking and don't say anything."

Just then, a soldier's face appeared at the window. Dermot wound it down and handed out his driver's license. The soldier studied it closely, then surveyed the three men. "Please step out and open the boot," he requested.

"Certainly," Dermot nodded, getting out and going to the back of the car.

"Where are you coming from?"

"The airport. I was collecting my cousin."

"Where are you going?"

"Home!"

After searching the back of the car thoroughly, the solider informed him,

"Alright, you can go."

Dermot nodded and got back into the car. The soldier handed him his licence but seemed more interested in Seamus, giving him a long hard stare. Seamus returned it until the soldier finally stepped back and waved them on.

"What was all that about?" asked Rooney. "Why did he search the car?"

"Just in case we had guns or explosives," replied Dermot. "Don't worry, Rooney, you'll see a lot of that here. They can stop us anytime, even going into a shop or just walking along the street." He looked at Seamus and grinned. "The way he kept looking at you I thought he'd taken a fancy to you and was going to ask for a date!"

Seamus smiled,

"Maybe he knows me from somewhere."

"That wouldn't surprise me!"

"I can tell you now, they're the Green jackets, Dermot."

"How do you know that?" asked Rooney, surprised. Seamus turned and looked at him.

"It's easy. They all have a badge on their caps. Different emblems for different regiments."

"And our Seamus knows them all!" smiled Dermot.

"So would you, if you'd been stopped as many times as I have!" came the reply.

"Maybe you've just got one of those faces."

Seamus smiled again and took out a packet of cigarettes. "I like to think it's the earring." he said. "It must really stand out in all those big blown-up photographs but no information. Poor bastards," he sighed. "It must be tough for them, looking at my face and knowing that's all they can do!"

He winked, then laughed. Rooney and Dermot joined in.

As the car made it's way from one street to the other, Rooney sat in the back seat watching the different scenes. He had never seen so much graffiti in his life. Every end house and wall was covered with pictures and writing. There were huge paintings of masked men in uniforms holding guns, and tricolours were everywhere.

"Brits Go Home" and "Remember 1916" was written numerous times.

The car eventually turned into a long, narrow street with terraced houses on both sides. It stopped.

"Well, this is it. Home sweet home!" smiled Dermot, getting out and opening the rear door.

Rooney got out with his hold-all and stood looking around. Seamus moved over into the driver's seat and leaned out.

"I'll see you later," he said, closing the car door and driving off.

Dermot took a key out of his pocket and opening the front door of his home, ushered Rooney inside. The sound of the door closing brought a woman's voice from the kitchen.

"Dermot is that you?"

"I hope so!" he replied, smiling. "Unless you've given a key to the milkman!" As she appeared in the doorway, Dermot introduced her. "Rooney, this is my wife, Marion."

"Hello," she said, taking his hand and looking a little embarrassed. "Nice to have you with us."

Rooney greeted her warmly.

"Hello Marion, it's nice to meet you. I'm your new milkman!"

They all started to laugh and Rooney knew he had broken the ice with these strangers and put them at ease. Marion was a plain girl with brown hair tied back in a ponytail, but she struck him as having a friendly, kind personality. The back door opened and four kids came running in, shouting loudly.

Dermot looked at them proudly.

"These are my trusty foot soldiers," he said pointing to the three boys. "And this," picking up the youngest, "is the apple of her Daddy's eye. Aren't you, Eilish?" After a cuddle, he put her down. "Marion, put the pan on. This man must be starving." He turned to Rooney. "Come on, I'll show you where you'll be sleeping."

They climbed the narrow stairs, entering a room with bunk beds. Dermot looked around "You'll have to share with one of the boys. I know it's not what you're used to but I was told you wanted to keep a low profile. And let's face it, you can't get much lower than this!" he joked, picking up some toys from the floor.

Rooney sat on the bottom bunk.

"Don't worry about it, Dermot. This will do fine."

Dermot nodded,

"Well, I'll leave you to unpack. There's plenty of space in the wardrobe. You can come downstairs when you're ready."

Just then, loud whistles blew and a thumping noise was heard from outside. Voices shouted and swore. Rooney got up.

"What's that?" he asked, startled.

Dermot went over to the window and Rooney followed. Both men looked out. Beyond the back yard was a large open space.

"It's the army," Dermot informed him, "and that is a Saracen."

Rooney saw him point towards something resembling a tank. A large crowd was gathered, mostly youths, and they were pelting the vehicle with bricks and stones. Verbal abuse and taunts were also hurled.

"Jesus, don't those soldiers inside ever get nervous?" asked Rooney.

"I suppose some of them do. But it's their job to patrol and it's our job to make it as difficult as possible for them. Besides, a lot of those young ones only do it for fun. It helps pass the time. There isn't much else for them to do, not in this country. I'll see you downstairs."

Dermot left the room, closing the door behind him. Rooney stood watching the scene with mixed feelings. He realised that if he'd never been in the thick of trouble before, he sure was now. He would have to tread carefully. He also realised something else. For a man who had been born and brought up in Belfast, he was already homesick for New York!

The McCabes treated Rooney like one of the family. He may as well have been a cousin, and after a few days he had settled in. There was a growing friendship between him and Dermot, who shared his views with Rooney and talked openly about the situation in Belfast. As far as Rooney was concerned, Dermot Mc Cabe and Seamus Quinn's politics were their own business. They were all becoming good friends and he liked them. He felt he could trust them and at the end of the day, that was all that mattered. Although Dermot and Seamus were very close, he couldn't help but notice that

McCabe was the more subtle of the two. Quinn was inclined to be short on patience and a little hot-headed, whereas his friend, was a deep thinker. Dermot tended to mull everything over and weigh his words carefully. He was the kind of man who knew more than he would ever admit and kept well away from any involvements with the British soldiers who patrolled the streets. He went about his business quietly. Seamus on the other hand, got a lot of hassle from them. But as Dermot had told Rooney, Quinn could handle it. The Brits and police had nothing on him and he was a man who could keep his mouth shut. There was a closeness between these two men that reminded Rooney of Joe Morrelli and himself. As he gained confidence and started to go out and about, he observed everything closely. The situation in the city was bad, of that he had no doubt. Armed police and military patrolled the streets continually and Saracens and jeeps were always in full view. As he studied the faces of the soldiers, some of them only young men in their teens, they had a nervous expression. They were frightened to speak to anyone, constantly looking over their shoulders. What saddened Rooney was the fact that if you looked closely enough, they had this "I don't want to be here - I wish I was somewhere else!" look. But that was one side of the coin.

The other one was that some soldiers actually enjoyed it. They would stop people in the street and give them a hard time, making women empty out their shopping. Young men were put against walls, searched and questioned. Handbags and even babies prams were targeted. These soldiers loved the authority and it showed. With them it was a case of "You will do as I say". Rooney didn't like that. As far as he could see they were making it tough on their comrades, who just wanted to do their stint and go home. As he watched the ones who wanted to be important and get a stripe, he couldn't help but feel sympathetic towards the ordinary people. Most of them just wanted a quiet life and to go about their daily routine without causing any trouble. He was becoming emotionally involved and he couldn't control it. After all, Belfast had been his home for seventeen years. He had been born there and no matter where he lived now, when it came right down to it - he was Irish!

As he lay on the bunk bed that evening going over everything he had seen, he thought of Angela. She was lucky to be away from all this. She would never have fitted it. He had noticed that in some areas the women were very politically minded, in fact they could be downright vicious in their speech and attitude. Now he was beginning to realise just what it must have been like for her when her father was murdered and accused of being an informer. It must have been hell.

"Informer" was a dirty world to the Irish people, always had been and always would be. No-one had any sympathy for them or anyone connected to them. There was a great hatred towards any person who gave information, and their family. He knew this by listening to the every day conversations that took place. He thought of her reaction if she ever found out he was here and why. But deep inside he already knew the answer to that. She would never look at or speak to him again because she wouldn't be in Roseberry

Avenue Joe Morrelli would most certainly lose his wife forever and Rooney would lose her friendship and trust. He sure hoped all of this would be worthwhile! His thoughts then turned to why he was here. So far there had been no word of his meeting taking place and he felt uneasy. Joe had said a couple of days but he had been here for four days now and as yet he hadn't heard anything. He hoped for all their sakes nothing had gone wrong. Inwardly, he was getting worried but outwardly he had remained calm and made a point of not asking any questions about it. He had given no one the impression he was over anxious. Rooney reckoned that the man he was destined to meet was playing for time and having him watched, to see how he would behave and if he was genuine. Naturally he would go along with it, knowing that when the time was right and everyone was happy with him, he would get word.

His concentration was broken by the sound of feet coming up the stairs. The bedroom door opened and Dermot came in, followed by Seamus.

"We've got an invitation for you," smiled Dermot. "A certain man wants to meet you - tonight!"

Rooney nodded,

"That's fine by me," he replied.

"Dermot and me will take you, Rooney," said Seamus. "We know it's not much notice but we've only just got the word ourselves. I'll see you later on."

Rooney sat up and smiled.

"I'll be ready."

Dermot put his hand on Rooney's shoulder and looked at him.

"You've made quite an impression," he said. "Not just with us - but with him as well! It's a pity you live in New York. If you lived here, you'd be one of us."

"Thank's, Dermot."

"You're welcome, Rooney. If we had more men like you here, our job would be a lot easier. We'll leave at 7o'clock while there's still plenty of people and traffic on the go. Driving late at night is too risky."

Both men left the room and as Rooney heard them going downstairs, he breathed a huge sigh of relief. He got up and went over to the wardrobe, taking out clean clothes and laying them on the bed. Then he turned his attention to the hold-all, unzipping it. From a secret compartment at the bottom he lifted out a folder containing the documents Joe and Reuben had given him. He clutched it tightly and whispered, "This is it, Joe, this is it!"

The car left the terraced houses and side streets behind as it headed away from the city. Within an hour it came to a stop in a quiet suburb, so peaceful it might as well have been a million miles away for the constant explosions and gunfire Rooney was getting used to.

As the three men got out, Rooney found himself in front of a large, modern bungalow complete with garage and well kept garden. They walked up the path and Dermot rang the bell. The door was opened by a man in his forties with blue eyes and dark hair, greying at the sides. He looked rather distinguished, not at all like the men Rooney had met up till now.

He greeted the trio with a broad smile.

"Come on in," he insisted.

As they stepped into the hall, Seamus closed the door behind them.

"Harry, this is Rooney," smiled Dermot. "Rooney, this is Mr Harry Collington."

The two men shook hands.

"Pleased to meet you, Mr Collington."

"Same here, Rooney." He looked at Dermot and Seamus. "Why don't you two boys go into the lounge and make yourselves comfortable, while Rooney and I discuss some business." They did so, then Harry put a hand on Rooney's shoulder. "Follow me," he said.

Harry led him past the spacious lounge into a small hallway. Rooney noticed the expensive carpet and furnishings. He was impressed and surprised. They stopped in front of a door and taking a key from his pocket, Harry opened it.

"This used to be a spare bedroom," he smiled. "But with having just one daughter we didn't need it so I use it as an office."

They went inside, his host closing the door securely. There was a desk, some chairs, a telephone, even a filing cabinet along the wall. Harry sat down behind the desk and motioned to Rooney, who sat down facing him.

"I've been told you have something that might be of interest to me," said Harry in a serious tone.

Rooney nodded and produced the folder from inside his jacket. He gave it to Harry, who leaned back in his chair and taking out the documents, read them carefully. When he had finished, he looked over.

"I must say, Mr Morrelli is being very generous. Perhaps you could fill me in."

"When it comes to his family, Mr Morrelli can afford to be generous. His wife is Irish, his son is half Irish. That makes him sympathetic to the plight of the Irish people." Harry nodded but said nothing as Rooney continued, "Mr Morrelli is willing to give his financial support and all he asks in return is the guaranteed safety of his son, should he ever wish to come here on a visit. I'm sure, Mr Collington, being a family man yourself you can appreciate this. His son is as precious to him, as your daughter is to you. All he wants to do is safeguard the boy's future."

"I understand that perfectly. He must be a wealthy man if he is going to increase his donation every year."

What he really meant was, he thought Joe Morrelli had Mafia links.

"Let's just say Mr Morrelli is a very influential, self-made, business man," replied Rooney, emphasising the word self. Harry looked at him and smiled.

"My sources in America have told me the very same thing. I just wanted to hear it from you and be sure they were right. You must understand, I have to be very careful who I do business with."

"I understand," nodded Rooney.

"Well then, I don't see any problem with this. If Mr Morrelli is willing to pay such a generous donation on a regular basis, that will entitle his son to V.I.P. treatment. I can promise him my full co-operation and the same from my men. If his wife or son ever wishes to come here, I will personally guarantee their safety. He need have no worries about that.""

Rooney smiled, "That's all he wants, Mr Collington. I'm sure he'll be pleased by this arrangement."

"Good, I know I am. After all, we're both getting what we want. You can tell Mr Morrelli it was a pleasure doing business with him."

"He'll be happy to hear that. He's a man who likes good news!"

Harry reached over, shook Rooney's hand, then stood up.

"Now that we've taken care of business," he said, "I think we could do with a drink. We can go into the lounge and join Dermot and Seamus."

Rooney got up to follow him commenting, "Those are good men you have working for you Mr Collington."

"Yes, they are," he agreed. "We need men like that. They are dependable and expendable."

Rooney stopped and looked at him but said nothing. He didn't like that last remark and he would never have expected it from a man like Harry Collington. But he was there to do business with him, not to judge him. As they left the office, Rooney couldn't help but think this guy could never have the trust and high regard for his men that Joe had for his. This gave him an uneasy feeling.

When they entered the lounge, Dermot stood up.

"Is everything alright?" he asked.

Harry put an arm around his shoulder.

"Everything is fine, Dermot! Doing business with Rooney and his boss was a pleasure. I think tonight's little transaction calls for a drink."

Dermot smiled over at Rooney, pleased and relieved that the meeting had gone so well. Harry poured the whiskeys and handed them around. Seamus got to his feet and the four men stood together. Harry raised his glass and smiled broadly at the others.

"To the cause!" he said proudly.

"To the cause!" they echoed.

After sitting down on the elegant suite, they relaxed and discussed the main events that were taking place in Belfast. As Rooney sipped his drink and joined in the conversation, he found himself studying Harry Collington closely. He watched as Harry was all smiles to Dermot and Seamus, laughing at how the army and police were running around baffled by such well timed explosions and sniper fire, most of which had been organised by himself. Yes, he was a big man in Belfast alright, with a lot of friends. And Joe was a big man in New York with a lot of powerful friends.

They both had a lot in common, except for one very important thing. When it came to worrying about the men who worked for them and trusted them, Joe Morrelli was genuine!

After stopping outside Dermot's house, Seamus turned to Rooney.

"I suppose now that you've taken care of things with Harry, you'll be heading back?"

Rooney nodded,

"There's no big rush, is there?" asked Dermot, "I mean, you could stay on for a few days, surely."

Rooney smiled,

"Is that an invitation?"

"Call it Irish hospitality."

"Well, if you put it like that, how can I refuse. O.K., I'll stay for a little longer."

"Good," smiled Dermot, "that's settled. Besides, Seamus and me would like to show you our local landmarks."

"What local landmarks?" asked Seamus, puzzled.

"All the buildings that are still standing!" came the reply.

They all laughed.

"Hey, speaking of things that are local, why don't the three of us have a good night out at the weekend?" Seamus suggested. "We could show Rooney the night-life."

"All of which will take up only one evening of your time!" Dermot muttered.

Rooney smiled at his two friends.

"Why not? I'm game!"

"That's the ticket. What's the point in living if your going to sit in the corner and watch everything pass you by?" Seamus winked. "You've got to go out there and face danger, Rooeny, and boldly go where no man has gone before!"

Dermot turned his eyes up.

"Jesus Christ, no wonder you're not married. No woman in her right mind wants to share her life with a man who thinks he's Captain Kirk? Are you coming in or have you another planet to visit?"

There was a loud laughter as Dermot and Rooney got out and stood on the pavement. As Dermot opened his front door, Seamus started up the car and leaned out of the window.

"Hi, Dermot?"

"What?"

"Beam me up, Scotty!" he grinned, before driving off.

Dermot shook his head as they went inside.

"I tell you, Rooney, no wonder the police and military have nothing on him. He's never in the one place long enough. He zooms around Belfast in that car like it was the

Star Ship Enterprize!"

Rooney chuckled as they made their way to the kitchen and Dermot filled the kettle.

"Is he always like that?"

"No, a lot of it is just fun. He was stopped a few times and give his name as James Kirk. They got on the radio to every barracks in Belfast but no-one knew anyone by that name so they had to let him go. He's smart, Rooney, and he doesn't scare easily. He's one of the best men that Harry Collington has and Harry knows it."

Rooney sat down at the table as Dermot poured the tea and joined him. He was quiet and subdued as he smoked his cigarette and moved his cup around. This didn't go unnoticed by Dermot.

"Is anything wrong?" he asked. "I would have thought that after doing business with Harry you'd be pretty pleased. I know he was."

Rooney leaned back in the chair.

"No there's nothing wrong, everything went fine. I was just a little surprised, that's all!"

"At what?"

"Well, at his home. Haven't you ever wondered why or how he owns a place like that? I mean, it must have cost him a lot of money."

Dermot nodded, "What you mean, Rooney, is what am I doing living in a small terraced house while he lives in a fancy bungalow?"

"Yeah, I guess that's what I mean."

"We're not stupid, we've looked into all that. Harry Collington had an old uncle, a farmer who never married. When he died he left a lot of money and land to his favourite nephew - Harry. He didn't want to be a farmer, he wanted to be a republican so he sold the land at a huge profit and built that house. The reason I know is, I've seen the documents. Everything's legal and above board, Rooney. Harry has used a lot of his own money to help further the cause. He's a well respected man."

"Yeah, he really has this situation in Ireland at heart, I'll give him that," replied Rooney.

"Well, with men like that we have no worries," Dermot assured him.

"You must be very close to him."

"I am. I have his confidence."

"Then you know why I'm here?" asked Rooney.

"Yes, I do. And I'll tell you something, the contributions your boss is going to make will be a great help. Guns and ammunition don't come cheap, Rooney, especially if they have to be bought in another country."

"Did Mr Collington tell you exactly how much the contribution was?"

"Yes, he did. But maybe you should tell me," Dermot replied in a serious voice.

Rooney shook his head,

"I think we both know that talk is dangerous. It can be taken the wrong way. If he has confided in you, that's good enough for me. I like you, Dermot. You've been good to me, so I'm going to confide in you and it's only because I know you can be trusted. Did Mr

Collington tell you why my boss is making such large contributions?"

"It's because of his son."

"That's right," nodded Rooney, "so now I'm going to let you in on the rest." He took pen and paper from his inside pocket and wrote something down, then looked at this friend. "For every year his son gets older, the amount will go up by this figure." He left it on the table and got to his feet. "It's no-ones fault if I'm careless enough to leave something lying around and someone else reads it, now is it?" he asked, going over to the cooker with his cup in hand and pouring himself some more tea. He glanced around and saw Dermot holding the piece of paper, then laying it down on the table again. Both men watched as it burned in the ashtray.

"Well, Dermot, that's something else that you've seen that's legal and above board!"

"Thanks for trusting me, Rooney."

"I just wanted you to know. I think you'd do the same for me."

Dermot put out his hand and Rooney gripped it.

"I'll be sorry to see you go and I'll miss you. But, we'll stay in touch, I'll arrange something."

Rooney smiled at him,

"Thanks for everything, including your friendship and trust."

"Your boss is a lucky man to have you, Rooney. I hope he knows is."

"Oh, I think he does, Dermot, just the way your boss knows he's lucky to have you."

Both men smiled and Dermot made a suggestion,

"Why don't we get rid of this tea and have a real drink? I've a half bottle of whiskey hid in here." he went over to a high wall cupboard.

"And come to think of it, there are a couple of beers in the fridge."

"Jesus, now you tell me," said Rooney, glancing at his watch.

"Rooney you're on holiday now and the night's still young. And the best part is, we don't have to get up for work in the morning because there's no work to go to!" grinned Dermot.

"Yeah," smiled Rooney. "I guess at times like this, there's a lot to be said for unemployment!"

After a tour of pubs and clubs the three men headed for Dermot and Seamus's local. They were in a jolly mood as they opened the door and walked into "The Punters Bar". Dermot called to the barman,

"Hi Mickey, three pints of beer and three whiskeys when you've got a minute."

The barman obliged.

"You're late tonight, Dermot," he smiled.

"Well, I don't suppose I've missed much."

"Oh just the usual Saturday night crowd."

The usual crowd were many in number causing loud laughter and noisy talk in the background.

"Are we going to sit or stand?" asked Seamus.

Dermot looked at the other two thoughtfully.

"I once knew a bloke who couldn't drink sitting down," he recalled. "He'd bring his wife out at the weekend and he would stand at the bar all night while she sat looking at him. I got curious one night and asked him about it."

"And?" Seamus inquired.

"And he said he couldn't enjoy drinking unless he was standing up. I could never understand that. I guess it must have been psychological." He stroked his beard.

"Pardon me, but is there a point to this story?" asked Seamus.

"Yes. The point is, she didn't mind him standing, he didn't mind standing and I don't mind standing!" he smiled and lifted his pint glass.

Seamus looked at Rooney and shook his head.

"I hope he hasn't any more stories like that!" he muttered.

As the friends launched into conversation, their voices were almost drowned by a burst of song.

"Who the hell's that?" snapped Dermot glancing around. He then turned back and looked at Mickey. "I might have known not to ask. How long have they been there?"

"All day," came the reply.

Rooney looked at Dermot.

"Do you know them?"

He nodded,

"Yes Raymond Burns and Jamie Doyle. Ireland's answer to the Everly Brothers!"

Rooney froze. He knew Raymond Burns was the name of Angela's brother-in-law. After waiting a few moments, he turned around to get a better look. Yes, it was him alright. Rooney recognised him from some photos she'd shown him. Raymond sat in a booth with another man and some women, singing and laughing.

At that, the other door opened and a woman came in.

"Oh, oh," muttered Dermot, "here comes the wife."

Rooney looked at her as she passed by and his heart almost stopped. He was looking at a young Agnes Kenny and he could hardly believe the likeness. As he and his companions stood looking through the large mirror in front of them, they had a full view of everything. She went up to her husband and began talking to him, pointing at the door. An angry expression came over his face as he got up, gripped her arm and led her over to the bar right next to Rooney.

"I'm warning you, Sheila, don't ever do that again. Not when I'm in company," he was heard to say.

"Raymond, you haven't been home all day and you're in here spending money we can't afford on God knows who." She glanced towards the booth.

"Well, that's my business!"

"It's mine too. I wan't you to come home."

His tone grew nasty and his grip tightened.

"I'll come home when I'm good and ready. Jesus, I'm only having a drink with my friends. You know what your trouble is, Sheila? You hate to see me enjoying myself."

"That's not true," she protested. "I just don't want you squandering money."

"If your so worried about money, why don't you phone your sister?"

Rooney listened intently as Sheila replied,

"Oh, you'd like that, wouldn't you? I know how you feel about Angela. I've always known!"

Raymond looked around, hoping no-one had heard her raised voice. He released her and slipped an arm around her shoulder.

"Oh, come on, Sheila. I married you, didn't I?" he said in a low voice. "Besides, it's my money. I won it on the horses and I have plenty left. Look…." he showed her. "Now you go on home and I'll finish my drink and follow you. I promise I won't be long." he was very persuasive.

"Alright," she nodded. "But you come straight home!" She glanced towards the booth again.

"Oh, don't mind them, they're with Jamie," he lied. "Look, Sheila, this is all very embarrassing for me."

"Alright, I'm going. But I'll be waiting, Raymond, so you'd better keep your word."

Rooney kept watching in the mirror as she walked by once again and then left. Raymond went back to his friends and sat down. He rubbed his hands together and smiled broadly. "Now, where were we?" Hi, Jamie, get another round in." He slipped an arm around one of the women, the way he had just done with his wife.

Rooney leaned over towards Dermot.

"What's that guy's game?" he asked. "Is he in an organisation?"

"No way! He couldn't get into a pantomime at Christmas, never mind an organisation. He just has an eye for other women and his wife knows it. Mind you, he's a foolish man because he has a good wife. I don't know her except to see., but my Marion use to work with her in the factory. Her father was shot and killed for being an informer."

"Really?" said Rooney, casually. "Did they ever find who murdered him?"

After taking a sip of beer, Dermot shook his head.

"No, and I don't think they ever will." He stared straight in front of him, his face almost expressionless. "I'd say after all this time, who ever did it is home free, Rooney. Home free!"

Rooney got another round of drinks and as Mickey sat them on the bar, a young man came up and ordered. He was Southern Irish and he'd had quite a lot to drink. As he left the bar carrying a tray, he smiled at Dermot.

"I'm on the run!" he said in a low voice.

"Who from - the wife?" Dermot retorted.

427

The young man walked away and Dermot shook his head. "He couldn't run up an alley!" he murmured.

"I'd say he could run off at the mouth, though," said Seamus.

Rooney was puzzled.

"I don't get it. What's he doing here where there's so much trouble, when there isn't any where he comes from?"

"Well, that's simple." As they huddled together, Dermot explained. "Some Free Staters not all but some, come down here and start going out with the local talent. Before you know it, they've moved in. So that means not only have they got a woman to sleep with, they also have free board and lodging. She draws her social security down here, he draws his social security from up there. They end up being better off that the rest of us and most of them are not politically involved in anything - except making a fuckin' nuisance of themselves!"

Seamus leaned his elbows on the bar.

"You must admit," he commented, "it's not a bad set up, considering most of them can hold a pint but not a gun."

"I take it you wouldn't tell them anything." smiled Rooney.

"I wouldn't tell them when I shit last! Now take him for instance," Seamus nodded towards the young man. "He tells everyone he's on the run. What would happen if he knew something really important and he was stopped by the police or military? I'll tell you. In a state like that he'd either talk like a parrot or sing like a canary!"

"You don't like them, do you Seamus?"

"Rooney I don't like some of the Belfast one's either. No wonder it's taken so long to free Ireland, we've got too many big mouths in it and I'm talking both North and South. Why do you think the jails are so full?"

"Oh, that reminds me," said Dermot, looking at his watch. "Hi, Mickey, why didn't you tell me it was after eleven? Give us three more whiskeys and hand me that tin from behind the bar."

As asked, Mickey handed him a long, round tin with an opening in the lid.

"What the hells that?" asked Rooney.

"The Prisoners' Families Support", smiled Dermot walking away and shaking it.

"Where is he going?" Rooney was still curious.

Mickey leaned over the bar and smiled.

Seamus gripped Rooney's arm.

"Watch this!" he grinned as both men turned and stood with their backs to the bar. Dermot moved along the crowd.

"A bit of order there, till I say something!"

The noise and laughter died down and the singing stopped immediately. Dermot continued,

"Well, now that you've all had a good night and enjoyed yourselves, don't forget there are people living here who can't because their loved ones are 'inside'. So I want you all to dig deep into your pockets and give generously."

Everyone started to put money into the tin as Dermot walked around, shaking it loudly. Rooney and Seamus watched as he approached an elderly man, who was sitting in the corner smoking a pipe.

"What about you Hughie?" he asked, holding out the tin.

The man was silent for a moment, then he removed the pipe and used it to point towards Dermot's outstretched hand.

"Well now, just when you're here, Dermot, I'd like a word with you about these collections. I have a son 'inside'. Your son's inside for stealing lead off a roof. That doesn't make him a political prisoner."

"But it was a U.D.R. man's roof."

"Then he's lucky he wasn't shot, never mind put in prison! Look, are you giving or are you not?" He shook the tin impatiently.

Hughie put the pipe back into his mouth and thought for a moment, then removed it once again.

"I've no change," he replied, sarcastically.

"Ah, bugger off!" snapped Dermot, walking away.

His two friends at the bar burst out laughing as they continued to watch his progress.

Two tables down, near the bar, he stopped in front of a middle aged woman with blonde dyed hair, thick make-up and bright red, cupid lips. Once again, Dermot held out the tin.

"Jesus" she said, "you can't go out for a drink that somebody isn't rattling a tin under your nose. If it isn't you, it's the Salvation Army."

He leaned over and rested a hand on the table.

"Well, think of it like this," he said. "If anything ever happens to your Davey, we'll feed you and they can pray for you!"

Unable to answer, she reluctantly opened her purse and took out a single coin, dropping it into the tin as Dermot watched. He straightened himself and looked at her.

"Now, that was a most generous donation, Mary. Let's see...." He started counting into himself. "I reckon, at today's prices, that should just about cover the cost of one tea-bag! I just hope whoever the lucky person is, they don't have a big tea-pot!"

"Well, Dermot, I can't afford much. My Davey's not keeping well. He never leaves the Royal Victoria Hospital."

"I know that," he nodded sympathetically, walking away from her and back towards Rooney and Seamus. "And Davey is the only man I know, who gets into an ambulance in the middle of winter wearing a pair of sunglasses," he muttered under his breath.

"Is he her husband?" grinned Rooney.

"No, her husband's the lucky one - he's dead! Davey's her son and he's a total mystery to medical science. He has every doctor at the Royal baffled. To be honest with you, I think he goes there just so he can wave to the neighbours as he gets in and out of the ambulance."

Then Seamus took over as he asked,

"Do you remember the day when he was up in Court?"

Dermot nodded.

"What happened," asked Rooney.

Seamus leaned over and continued in a low voice.

"He appeared in front of the magistrate wearing the sunglasses and was ordered to take them off. He refused. And when he was asked who'd be defending him, he replied Perry Mason."

"What happened?"

"He got two months for contempt of court. You know, there's nothing wrong with him physically but mentally he's got delusions of grandeur. He watches nothing only Mafia films. But then lets face it, no harm to Mary but if she was my mother, I'd want to go to Sicily too!"

"Jesus, and I thought there was some weird people in New York!" laughed Rooney, shaking his head.

"Well, if there is they probably emigrated from here!" Dermot slapped him on the back with one hand as he gave the barman the tin with the other. "Here Mickey, put that behind the bar. Someone will be along for it in a day or two."

"You did well tonight. It's full," came the reply. "You surely know how to talk them into giving."

Seamus put his arm around Dermot's shoulder.

"Mickey, our Dermot here could sell sand to the Arabs and they'd come back for more!"

Mickey grinned and then shouted in a loud voice, "Time to go home now everyone!"

"I'm hungry. I'm going to the chip-shop," Seamus informed them.

"We all are. I promised my Marion that I'd bring home fish suppers."

As they stood and finished their drinks, the place started to clear. Raymond and Jamie passed with their arms around their female companions, talking loudly. Rooney watched as Raymond disappeared through the door. He surely didn't seem like a man who was going straight home. And as Rooney glanced at his watch, he reckoned he didn't have much of the money left he had shown to his wife earlier.

The three men said 'goodnight' to Mickey and going outside, they crossed the road to make their way to the chip-shop. Rooney stopped for a moment and looked back at the sign over the door. He'd had a really good night and he knew he would always remember "The Punters Bar", not just for that reason but another much closer to his heart. Angela. And how she would feel if she knew about Raymond and his 'lady friends'.

After leaving the chip-shop they continued down the street and on turning the corner, came face to face with an army patrol. They kept silent and tried to walk on but one of the soldiers stepped out in front of them, blocking their way.

"Look who we've got here," he said in a polite accent. "If it isn't Mr Quinn."

Seamus stared at him and gave a slight smile,

"Well, well, Corporal Melvin Sinclair from Leeds. You're a long way from home, aren't you?"

The soldier raised his gun.

"That's what I don't like about you, Quinn. You know too fucking much!"

"More than you think I do," came the reply.

"What's in those bags?" the Corporal probed.

"Fish suppers," Dermot answered, trying to take the attention away from his friend.

"Private, take those bags and search them!" came the order.

The young man looked surprised but did as he was told. He emptied the contents out onto the pavement.

"Nothing here, Corporal."

On being disappointed, Sinclair pushed the gun into Seamus's chest.

"Alright Quinn," he said nastily, "you know the drill. Up against the wall."

Before he could move of his own freewill, Seamus found himself being roughly pushed against the red bricks, his face almost hitting them with full force.

Rooney was angry and was about to step forward and intervene, when Dermot gripped his arm tightly and whispered,

"Leave it. Seamus can handle it. He's well used to this."

The two men watched as the Corporal continued,

"Put your arms up and spread your legs! The rest of you watch those two men."

Two soldiers stepped forward with guns at the ready, while the others kept watch. The Corporal began to search Seamus, kicking his legs apart further. After searching his upper body and finding nothing, Sinclair bent down to search his lower body. As he did so, Seamus glanced down.

"It wont' be long now till your going home, Corporal. Maybe it's just as well. I hear your wife is getting very lonely," he whispered.

Stopping instantly, the Corporal raised himself up and stared at Seamus.

"What do you mean?" he stammered.

There was an uneasy silence as Seamus stared back at him, long and hard.

"Why don't you ask her!"

A look of shock and fear crept over Sinclair's face as he stepped back. Then he turned to the others.

"Alright lads, lets go!"

The rest of the patrol were surprised as he motioned for them to follow him. After they'd disappeared into the darkness, Seamus brushed his jacket and straightened it. "What the hell did you say to him?" asked Dermot, as he and Rooney came towards him.

He just smiled and shrugged his shoulders.

"Oh, I just gave him something to think about. He won't be stopping anyone else tonight. He'll be too preoccupied with his thoughts!"

Dermot looked to the ground and pointed.

"Jesus, to think I stood in a queue for half and hour and spent five pounds on fish suppers for the dogs to eat. My Marion's going to kill me!"

Seamus turned to Rooney and shook his head.

"Now, that's what I call a typical Irishman. Not scared of the Brits but shit scared of his wife!"

Rooney laughed as he put an arm around Dermot's shoulder.

"Never mind. I'll bring the kids to the shop tomorrow and buy them whatever they want."

His friend looked at him forlornly and said,

"Only it's Sunday I'd ask you to buy a pound of steak."

"What for?"

"For the black eye that I'm likely to have by the time that Marion's finished with me!"

"Well, come Monday I'll go out and buy steaks for everyone. And that's a promise," said Rooney.

"I think I'll come round for my tea," Seamus grinned. "I've never known the McCabes to have steak on a Monday. Now, I've known them to have a few mistakes on a Monday but never steaks!"

"Don't talk about food anymore, for God's sake. I have to go in and face this woman and tell her the supper is lying on the street. Wait till you see this. They'll all be sitting with their mouths watering. Oh well, I suppose the wee ones will have to have cornflakes."

"I thought you only had those in the morning," commented Seamus.

Dermot looked at his watch.

"Well, it is fuckin' morning now!"

"Och, tell her it was an accident!"

"Oh, I will. But you're coming in to tell her you were the accident!"

Seamus stopped and took out a packet of cigarettes.

"In that case, I think I'll have a smoke first."

"Oh, aye?" Dermot, smiled over at Rooney. "Now who's shit scared?" His voice changed. "Private, take those bags and search them!" he said, mimicking the Corporal. "Imagine the mentality of grown men searching chip-bags. And the English thing we're bad!"

Rooney smiled and shook his head.

"I must admit, you wouldn't get an Irish man doing that."

"No, and I'll tell you why," replied Dermot, as the three men stood together smoking.

"No matter what they say about the Paddy's, our brains are in our heads." He turned and pointed along the now deserted street. "Their's is in their ass!"

They laughed as they walked along, their arms around each other's shoulders in friendship. Rooney had not only been accepted by these two men, he had become as they say in Ireland, 'One of the Boys!'

That Monday morning at around eleven o'clock, Dermot left to go and sign on the dole. Rooney had remembered him saying that Marion used to work with Sheila Kenny, so he decided this was a good time to try and bring the subject around and see what he could find out about the family, especially Robert.

He put his head around the kitchen door.

"I wouldn't say 'no' to a cup of coffee, Marion."

She turned from the cooker and smiled,

"You must have read my mind." She switched on the electric kettle. "Now, black with two sugars. Right?"

"Right," he replied pulling out a chair and sitting down.

She sat a mug of coffee down in front of him at the table.

"You've had an eventful weekend, Rooney. I mean, being stopped by the military and all."

"Yeah, you could say that," he nodded. "It was unusual and I've met some unusual people."

"I'll bet most of them were in "The Punters Bar", she smiled.

"How did you guess?"

"Oh, they get all sorts in there."

Rooney lit a cigarette, then ventured on.

"You know, at one point I thought there was going to be an argument between some guy and his wife. He was sitting with his friend and some women, singing. Then his wife came in looking for him. I can't quite remember his name, something like Brown or Burn." He scratched his head.

"That was probably Raymond Burns," Marion replied.

He pointed at her.

"Yeah, that's it. Now I remember."

"Dermot told me about that, but it isn't the first time."

Rooney lifted his coffee mug.

"Does he make a habit of it?"

"Well, sometimes. He's not a bad bloke and he's well liked but he can't resist a pretty face and he's foolish with money. He buys drinks for everyone." She shook her head. "Sometimes I wonder where he gets it from."

Rooney already knew the answer to that. He got it courtesy of Joe and Angela Morrelli.

"Dermot said you used to work with his wife," he commented casually.

"That's right, I worked with Sheila years ago in a factory. She was Sheila Kenny to her maiden name. Did Dermot tell you about her father?"

"Yeah, he told me. Did you know him?"

"Just to see, I didn't live in that area. But he worked for the council so I used to see him around. He was a quiet man but always had a smile for everyone. Sheila had an older sister, a very good looking girl. She used to work in Nolan's chip shop at night. I think she was the brainy one. She went to College and kept herself pretty much to herself, but she was a pleasant girl to speak to and very well mannered. Gerry Nolan thought the world of her. Poor Gerry! He took her back to work for him after her father was killed and they were attacked one night. They were lucky they weren't killed. Tempers were running high!"

Rooney looked at Marion and said,

"Dermot said her father was killed because he was an informer."

"That's right," she nodded, "but there were a lot of people who believed he was innocent. They were just too scared to say so."

"What do you think?" he asked.

She was silent for a moment. Then, "I don't really know, Rooney. The only thing I do know is that if he was innocent, it was never proved. I remember when Sheila was getting married, there was talk that her father's money paid for the wedding. You know, the money he got for giving information. But Sheila told me it was the money left over from the insurance policies. Then the talk started again when her mother and sister went off to America. She said her mother's old aunt had sent them their fares. Sheila's children never went without. Apparently, her mother and sister sent money home, but I can't see how they could do that and support themselves out there as well. They must have gotten money from somewhere. Either that or Sheila's sister must have been working all the hours God could send. A bit hard to believe, don't you think?"

Rooney nodded in silence. It wasn't hard for him to believe, because he knew it to be true.

Marion leaned back in the chair and folded her arms.

"Oh well," she sighed, "after all this time I don't suppose anyone will ever know if the man was innocent or guilty. But one thing's for sure, his family were given a hard time and treated very badly. Nothing was too much for the Kennys. They were a target for everyone with a grievance. But you need money for weddings and fares to America to start a new life, and that didn't help matters. To be honest Rooney, I don't believe there ever was an old aunt. Very few people do. But then, who really knows the truth? Only the Kenny's themselves."

Marion Mc Cabe could never have realised she was talking to someone who did know the truth. Someone who had been in the old aunt's apartment and seen photographs of her.

He lit another cigarette.

"What about the chip-shop?" he asked. "Is it still open?"

She shook her head.

"No. After that night, Gerry did open again but he was help up at gunpoint by two masked men and robbed twice! Dermot and Seamus tried to find out who the culprits were but they just seemed to disappear. Anyway, Gerry got frightened and gave up the shop. He left here with his family and went to Scotland. He opened a chip-shop over there and is doing very well, from what I last heard. He loves it there because there's no trouble. It's funny too, the way people's lives turn out. Angela Kenny is somewhere in America and Gerry Nolan is in Scotland, and the two of them worked together. When you think about it, no-one knows what's in front of them or where they will end up because of what's happening here."

"Yeah, call it fate or destiny but I'll bet the troubles here have a large part to play in a lot of ways, for people finding themselves in another county. And you know, Marion, maybe it's no bad thing - if they make good." He got up. "I've enjoyed our talk," he smiled. "If Dermot wants to know where I am, tell him I've gone to buy those steaks I promised him!"

"Oh, Rooney, you don't have to do that."

"Sure I do," he insisted. "And there's something else." He reached into his inside pocket and produced a thick envelope. "Here, I want you to take this for the kids."

She opened it, almost shocked at it's contents.

"Rooney, I can't take all this money, it's too much!"

He made his way to the kitchen door as she insisted, "Dermot would never let me keep it!"

He turned around and grinned broadly.

"Sure he will. Just tell him it's for his trusty foot soldiers and the apple of his eye. That ought to do it!" he winked.

Marion followed him out into the hall.

"You're going home, aren't you?" she asked in a sad voice.

He turned once again, this time with a serious expression on his face. First he nodded, then explained.

"It isn't easy for me, Marion. I've got two homes because I've got two countries and I've been pulled between them both. I'll always be Irish but I'll always love New York. The closet thing I have to family are there and I miss them. Everyone I love is there and you have to follow your heart. I guess when all is said and done, 'Home is Where the Heart is."

Marion nodded as he opened the front door and went out.

After finding a butcher's shop, Rooney went inside and bought the steaks. On coming outside, he decided to walk the same route he had taken on Saturday night, back towards "The Punter's Bar". He reckoned that if Raymond Burns was a regular there, then he didn't live far away and Nolan's chip-shop should be in the same area. Hadn't Agnes said that Angela walked home from work with Sheila the night her father disappeared? When he reached 'The Punters Bar', which was on the main road, he walked the full stretch but couldn't find Nolans. He even ventured down some side-streets but after getting some cold and curious looks from the residents, he decided to give up. Going back to the main road, he stopped an elderly lady who was coming along and asked her for directions to the familiar area he had come to know.

"Well, son, you've a fair bit to go," she said. "You'd be better taking the bus." She pointed towards a bus stop. "Stand there, you'll see one coming along in a few minutes. The name of the district you want will be displayed on the front of the bus. You can't miss it."

Relieved, Rooney thanked her and followed her voice. He was taking no chances. Dermot had warned him about taxi's. Apparently, there were members of organisations posing as taxi drivers, who lured unsuspecting victims into the vehicles, discovered their religion, drove them to secluded places and disposed of them. Usually with a bullet in the brain, or in some cases a sharp knife.

He hadn't been standing for long when his bus pulled up and he got on board. As it passed the busy streets, Rooney sat gazing idly out of the window. Then it came to a halt at another stop to pick up some more passengers. That's when he saw the sign, 'Nolan's Chip Shop'. He got up quickly and jumped off before the bus could drive away.

Rooney stared. The place was boarded up but a lot of the wood had been ripped off, revealing a large window and door with no glass. The building was covered in graffiti both inside and out. On peering more intently he saw what was left of a large, high counter. The same counter Angela had hidden behind on the night of the attack, scared out of her wits. A lump came to his throat as he realised just how close he felt to her. Not only was he in Belfast but he was standing at the shop she used to work in. He lit a cigarette and stood looking around, noticing how badly situated it was. It was on a corner where different streets met. The perfect set up for a quick get-away. He knew now how lucky she'd been that night. After all, she could have been badly injured - even killed. He also knew she hadn't lived far away but he couldn't take the chance of going anywhere near her home, as it would look too suspicious. He'd have given a lot just to see it, and Agnes's grave. She lay in the cemetery with her beloved husband, yet he couldn't even go and pay his respects to the woman he had known so well and looked upon as a mother he never knew. Although he didn't think he was being followed, he couldn't be sure so he had to be very careful. Sad and confused, he lit another cigarette and stood staring at the ground. He was Irish but he felt he didn't belong, he didn't fit in. It never dawned on him that Angela had felt the same, both there and in New York. Only Joe knew that.

As he quietly contemplated his thoughts, he realised that Agnes had done the right thing for Angela by leaving all this trouble behind. Her daughter had met a good man, the best, and she had a good life. It was all a far cry from what might have happened if they had stayed. But the one thing that saddened Rooney most of all was, how could his own people treat each other in such a way? How could they do such terrible things to each other and yet preach about human rights? They were tearing each other apart in the name of freedom and wealding a sword of justice that sometimes fell on the innocent. No wonder people were becoming frightened and disillusioned. He knew Agnes and Angela had been guilty of nothing yet they were made to suffer. As for Robert Kenny, Rooney wondered if his murder would always remain a mystery and if so, why? It wasn't the Belfast he had known and that was for sure. It seemed to him that sometimes justice was done, just to be seen to be done. And often with disastrous consequences.

It was time, too, for Rooney to be honest with himself. Why had he wanted to find this place where Angela had worked? Was it just curiosity? No. He wanted to retrace some of her steps in a bid to get closer to her. He knew, that although Joe Morrelli loved her dearly, deep in his own heart so did he. From the first moment he ever saw her in 'The Safe Haven' he had loved her. And, although it was hard for him to admit it after all this time, he still did. He had never met anyone like her and he doubted he ever would. But no-one would ever know his true feelings. He would have to hide them from the world. His only consolation was knowing how Joe felt about her and how good he was to her. He treated her like a lady. He was proud of her and showed her respect. All this was enough to make Rooney bow out gracefully, contented that Angela was in such good hands.

At that moment, he missed Joe. He missed Roseberry Avenue and everyone there. After stubbing out his cigarette he went over to the bus stop and waited, until a bus with 'City Centre' displayed on it came into view. He boarded and sat down, looking over at 'Nolan's chip-shop' one last time before moving off. Rooney had made his mind up. He was going into the city to buy a ticket for New York. He was going home.

Rooney, Dermot and Seamus stood in the airport chatting, each one doing their best to look happy. But underneath the smiles, Mc Cabe and Quinn were sad that Rooney was leaving. Even though he had only been there for a short time, a deep friendship had developed between them through a mutual respect and admiration.

Dermot asked,

"Have you got that telephone number I gave you?"

"Right here," replied Rooney, tapping his inside pocket of his jacket.

"Well, don't lose it. It's the only way you will be able to contact me. My phone is probably tapped, but that number is what we call a 'safe house', a house where the police and military would never dream of going."

Rooney nodded.

"We need houses like that," explained Seamus. "When you're on a job or need a place to hide they're a Godsend."

Rooney looked at the two men.

"Listen," he said in a serious voice. "I don't approve of everything that's going on here but I understand most of it, so I want you to do me a favour - watch your backs!"

Seamus smiled,

"Now, why do you think Dermot and I work together? We trust each other and always watch out for each other."

"That's right," Dermot agreed. "We're like Abbott and Costello! Don't worry about us, Rooney, we can take care of ourselves." He tried to sound cheerful.

"O.k., so you can trust each other but who else can you really trust, with things the way they are?" asked Rooney, putting a hand on Dermot's shoulder and continuing on, "Let me give you a bit of advice I once got from my boss. Never take anyone at face value because 'very few people are what they seem to be'. One of the best things a man has going for him is instinct. That gut feeling you get about something or someone that just won't go away. If you ever get it, don't be scared to investigate it because doing so just might save your life. You're my friends, I don't want anything to happen to you."

They could see he was deadly serious.

"That's good advice," nodded Dermot. "We'll keep it in mind."

"Good. Now you've got my number so keep in touch. If there's anything I can ever do for you guys, just let me know."

"Same here," Dermot replied.

Rooney's flight was announced over the intercom.

"Well, this is it," he smiled, putting out his hand.

Seamus gripped it firmly.

"It's been good knowing you, Rooney. I hope we meet again," he said. "If you ever need a 'safe house' you know where I am!"

"Indeed I do."

Then it was Dermot's turn. He shook Rooney's hand.

"I'll miss you, Rooney," he admitted. "But maybe you'll be back some day. Your boss might send you again and you know my door is always open."

"I know, Dermot. Thanks for everything."

"Even if you don't come back on business you could always come for a visit. You know, help us fight the Brits!" Seamus suggested.

"Who knows, I might take you up on that!" smiled Rooney. "Well, I'd better go."

Dermot put his hand on Rooney's arm.

"Thanks for the money," he said in a low voice. "It was much appreciated."

"No problem. Just make sure Marion buys herself something nice."

"I will." Dermot assured him.

Rooney leaned towards him and whispered,

"The money's not important, Dermot, but the advice is. Promise me you'll always remember it."

"I promise Rooney."

"Well so long fellas and thanks again. We'll keep in touch." He walked towards the departure lounge, then stopped and looked back. "Hey, Dermot," he called, "do yourself a favour - don't send Seamus for any fish suppers. Marion and the kids mouths weren't the only ones that were watering that night!"

They all laughed together.

"You got steak, didn't you?" Seamus reminded him.

"Yeah, on Monday. But I'll always regret not getting the fish supper on the Saturday!"

"Maybe next time, Rooney," smiled Dermot, feeling the tears coming in his eyes.

"Yeah, maybe," he replied smiling sadly, as he waved and walked away.

Dermot breathed a heavy sigh.

"You know, Seamus, for the short time I knew that man he became like a brother to me. I'll never forget him."

"Maybe that's because he is a man, in the truest sense of the word. He's honest, reliable and genuine. The kind you know your life is safe with, not like some of the scum-bags out there."

"Speaking of scum-bags, we have a job to do tonight. We'd better get a move on." Dermot insisted.

As they walked across the airport car-park Seamus turned to Dermot.

"You know there's a lot of truth in what Rooney said. Take this bloke we have to see tonight, for instance."

"I know, he couldn't have known just how near the mark he came when he said 'very few people are what they seem to be'. I can tell you one thing, his boss is one very shrewd man, who-ever he is. He knows the score and he's smart. I'll give him that!"

The next afternoon, Rooney arrived at Roseberry Avenue and let himself in. He had spoken to Joe on the telephone, so he went straight to the study and opened the door. Joe looked up from his desk and putting down the gold pen, he smiled broadly.

"Glad to have you back."

"I'm glad to be back," Rooney smiled, closing the door and taking a seat.

Joe leaned his arms on the desk and clasped his hands.

"Well, how was the trip?" he asked.

"Fine."

"What about the business end, did everything go o.k.?"

"Mr Collington was most impressed by your generous donation," Rooney replied, lighting a cigarette. "He has personally guaranteed the full protection of your son. If ever he goes to Ireland he will get V.I.P. treatment, not only from himself but also his men."

"Now that's what I've been waiting to hear," nodded Joe. He studied Rooney for a moment then said, "So tell me, were you impressed by Mr Collington?"

"I guess so."

"You don't sound too sure. What's the matter, don't you like the guy?"

"Joe it's not important whether I like him or not," shrugged Rooney.

"It is to me!"

"What difference does it make? We got what we wanted."

"Come on, I want to know what you think."

Rooney looked at him and said,

"O.k. I like him. I just don't know if I would trust him."

"Why?"

"Oh, just some remark he made about his men. Nothing to do with us."

Joe nodded. "I see. Well, you don't have to like people you do business with, but you always need a certain amount of trust."

"Maybe it's me Joe. I just had this gut feeling he might not be as loyal to his men as they are to him, if his back were to the wall."

Joe's eyes narrowed as he considered Rooney's comments.

"Well, that's not our problem," he said thoughtfully. "As long as he's loyal to me, that's what really counts. But I'll bear in mind what you've just said. I take it you like the other guys?"

"Yeah, I do."

"Do you trust them?"

"Joe, I'd trust them with my life – I just did!" Joe nodded satisfied.

"Well, one day my son might have to trust them with his. For now, I pay my annual donation and do nothing. Later on it might not be a bad idea to investigate Harry Collington, just to be on the safe side. After all, it's always best to keep one step ahead of guys like that. The main thing is, I've got my foot in the door and once you've got your foot there, there's always a chance that one day you can kick it wide open!"

"That might not be so easy."

Joe leaned back in the leather chair.

"What do you mean?" he asked.

Rooney sighed,

"I mean, trying to get information about Robert Kenny. You've got no idea what its like over there, Joe. They are finding bodies every day. It has become part of life. People are being murdered all the time. You can't turn on the T.V. set that you don't see some victim lying on a road or in a street. I'll tell you now, it's worse then the Mafia!"

"As bad as that?" Joe was surprised.

"Yeah, as bad as that!" Rooney nodded. "And the worst part is, no one is getting caught. Let's be realistic, Joe, Robert Kenny was murdered nearly eight years ago. If you want my opinion, getting information about it is going to be almost impossible, especially the way things are."

Joe's face became serious.

"Nothing's impossible, Rooney. Besides, it's early days yet and I'm in no hurry. When the time's right and I've paid enough money, then I'll start asking questions and believe me, I better get some answers! And I think it will be men like Harry Collington who'll be able to tell me what I want to know!"

"Well, if he can't, no one can. When I asked about it nobody seemed to know anything, and if they did they sure weren't talking."

"Did you find out anything?"

"Just bits and pieces. It was never proved if Robert Kenny was really an informer, but everything Agnes told us was true. They were given a really hard time. I fear to think what might have happened if they'd stayed. And I heard about what happened Angela at her work. Believe me, she was lucky it was stones that came through the window – and not bullets!"

Anger swept over Joe's face.

"That's why someday I'm going to make damn certain the people responsible pay the price. Even it that price is their life. Because of what they did to her mother, they took away my wife's right to give life. It's only fair to want the same from them and I want it, Rooney, I want it real bad!" His tone changed and he tried to be light-hearted, holding out his hands. "Anyway, they did me a favour. If Angel hadn't come to New York I never would have met her and I'd never have known what true happiness is. It's just sad that my happiness had to come through such a tragedy and heartbreak." He smiled at Rooney. "I'm glad you're home. I thought maybe you'd meet some nice Irish girl and want to stay."

"Not a chance!" replied Rooney, shaking his head. "If I want to meet a nice girl, I'll meet her here in New York – where I belong."

Joe nodded in agreement and picked up the pen.

"Well, now that you've told me everything, why don't you take the rest of the day off?" After a few seconds he glanced over at Rooney, aware that he had remained sitting and had lit another cigarette. "What's the matter, is something bothering you?" he asked.

"No, not really."

"You have told me everything?"

"Sure… but…"

"But what?"

"Oh, its nothing."

Joe put the pen down again.

"Look, if you've got something to say to me, Rooney spit it out."

Rooney looked uncomfortable as his gaze met Joe's.

"There's something I think you should know. It's your brother-in-law, he's not the happy family man you thought he was."

"What do you mean?"

"I mean, he goes out with other women, Joe."

"How the hell would you know something like that?" Joe was stunned.

"I know because I saw him."

441

"Wait a minute, Rooney, are you telling me you saw Raymond Burns?"

"That's right. I saw him in a bar. I also saw his wife, Sheila. She came in looking for him and they had an argument right beside me."

"Go on," said Joe, in a voice of almost disbelief.

"He was with his friend. A man called Jamie Doyle. They were with some women. His wife came in and asked him to go home."

"And did he?"

"No. He promised he would and she left. He spent a lot of money and at the end of the night, he left with his arm around another woman. I asked around and it seems he does it quite often. He likes a pretty face. He also likes to spend money, unfortunately he's not spending it on his wife. Some people are wondering just where he's getting it."

Joe closed his eyes for a few seconds, trying to take in what he's just heard.

"Yeah, well, we know the answer to that!" he said. Then he looked at Rooney. "He's not slapping her around, is he?"

"No," replied Rooney, shaking his head. "And he's not in any organisation, either. He just likes a good time."

"What night was it?"

"Saturday."

Joe banged the desk with his hand.

"Damn it!" he snapped. "He could bring his wife out on Saturday nights and have a good time with her. What the hell's the matter with guys like that?" He got up angrily and stood looking out of the window. Then he turned and pointed a finger. "I don't ever want Angel to find out about this, Rooney. It would hurt her deeply and she'd worry about Sheila and the kids so much, she'd make herself ill. Besides, if Sheila is pretending everything is o.k. and won't tell her, why should we?"

"She wont' hear it from me," Rooney assured him. "I was supposed to be in Vegas not Belfast, remember?"

"Yeah, that's true," nodded Joe. "Belfast is strictly between you and me and it will have to remain that way. We can't divulge anything we know to anyone else."

"I know, but I'll bet you never dreamed when I went over there, I'd end up seeing your in-laws!"

Joe shook his head and stared at the floor.

"It's a small world, Rooney, and you can take it from me, Raymond's spending sprees are going to get smaller."

"What do you have in mind?" Rooney was puzzled.

Looking at him with a stern expression, Joe replied, "I'm going to have Rueben draw up a trust fund for the kids. The parents will only be allowed to draw out a certain amount of money twice a year, for vacations and Christmas. That will end the regular cheques Angel and I send. And that means Raymond can't spend my money on other women – not if he doesn't have it!"

"Good thinking. But how are you going to explain all this to Angela?"

"Oh, I'll get around it. I'll explain it's for the kids own good. They will have money when they need it most, when they're older and maybe want to further their education, or travel and settle in some other country. Angel will go along with that. After all, she came to this country with no money. She'll understand how important it is to have it."

Rooney got up.

"Well, I think you're making a wise decision and I'm sure she will too."

Joe came over and put an affectionate hand on Rooney's shoulder.

"Thanks for going to Belfast, Rooney," he said, sincerely. "I couldn't have pulled this donation business off without you."

"Anything to oblige."

"How did it feel being back there? Did anything exciting happen?" asked Joe, as Rooney went over to the door and opened it.

"Don't ask!" came the reply. Then after a few thoughtful moments, "You know, I really missed this house and everyone here," he admitted.

Joe smiled,

"Yeah well, we missed you too. And although I wouldn't want it to get around, I missed you the most!"

Rooney stood still and put his hand up to his ear. Joe stared, puzzled.

"What's the matter?" he asked.

"I thought I heard violins playing. Next thing I know you'll be sending me a bouquet of red roses!"

Joe pointed a warning finger and tried hard not to smile.

"Hey, I said I missed you, I didn't say I was in love with you!"

Rooney grinned,

"You know something Joe? Deep down inside I think you really care, you just don't want to admit it."

"What is it with you Irish? You're all so full of wit."

"We like to call it charm, Joe and you're a sucker for it. After all, you married Angela."

Joe lifted the pen and aimed it at Rooney, who ducked just in time.

"You always were a smart ass!" he said.

"That makes me the perfect man for the job then, doesn't it?" smiled Rooney, closing the door behind him. He turned and saw a smiling Angela coming downstairs.

"Welcome home, Rooney. How was your trip?"

"Fine," he nodded.

She crossed the entrance hall.

"Why don't you come to dinner this evening and tell me all about it?"

"Well, I'd like to, Angela, but I can't," he replied, feeling guilty at having to lie.

"Don't tell me, Joe has more business for you to take care of."

"No, it's nothing like that. I promised a couple of guys I'd meet up with them, that's all."

She put her hand lightly on his face.

"You look tired, Rooney. It must have been all those late nights in Vegas!"

"Yeah, I am a little. I was just on my way home to get some sleep."

"Well, in that case I'll walk you to the door."

Angela slipped her arm through his as they both walked slowly up the entrance hall, in silence. On reaching the door, she turned and looked at him.

"You know, Rooney, I think you need the love of a good woman," she smiled.

"Maybe, but good women are hard to find," he insisted.

"Why don't you let me help? I'm sure I could introduce you to a few I know."

"Well, I just hope your choice of women is better than Joe's!"

Angela bit her lip and tried not to laugh.

"That bad, was it?"

"Worse than you can imagine! When it came to picking women for me, lets just say he was no expert. And the best part about it was, he thought he was doing me a favour!"

"I think I know the type," she nodded. "Big breasts and no brains!" Rooney gave her a surprised look. "Oh, don't look so shocked, Rooney. Joe told me about his trips to Vegas! With so much glamour on offer, I often wonder why he chose me."

He thought for a few moments, then said, "Angela, a woman can be like a bottle of wine. It's not the shape that matters, but the contents. And lets face it, there's nothing worse than an empty bottle! Joe realised that. Besides, in you he got a Dom Perignom!"

"But he'd known a lot of beautiful women in his time."

"True, but none of them were like you. Their beauty was only skin deep, yours isn't. Do you ever feel jealous about those other women?"

She smiled and shook her head,

"No, I don't. If Joe forgets to tell me he loves me during the day, he remembers to tell me at night."

"Now that doesn't surprise me! Joe always was the hearts and flowers type. But he'll never love anyone the way he loves you."

"I don't know why!" she joked.

"I do. You're the only woman who ever made it difficult for him. You were your own person, he admired that. You had a temper, he always liked a woman with spirit. You had a good mind, he was proud of that. But most important of all, you didn't throw yourself at him. He had to do all the running and deep down he respected that. So, put all those together and then you'll know why!"

Angela blushed and looked away but Rooney put his hand on her arm.

"Listen, Angela, don't ever think those women meant anything to Joe. He's no fool. When he met you he didn't think he was in love, he knew he was!"

She looked at him almost innocently.

"Rooney, a lot of the committee women I have lunches with are having affairs, mostly with younger men. They brag about it! It's so embarrassing when they launch into all the details of what they get up to. But somehow, it doesn't seem to bother them. I suppose that's because most of their husbands are having affairs too. They always seem so shocked that Joe and I haven't done it. But I could never do that to Joe, and I would never forgive him if he did it to me."

"Well, it only goes to prove that one very important thing is missing from those women's lives. A strong, loving relationship like the one you and Joe have. They're only trying to shock and embarrass you because deep down they envy you and what you have. There's more than enough love in your marriage, Angela. Neither of you have the need for any affair, and you never will," he winked.

She smiled, grateful and relived.

"I guess out of all those committee women, I'm the lucky one."

"You bet."

"Thanks for listening, Rooney. I don't know what I'd do without you. You go home and get some sleep now. All those late nights in casinos have taken their toll!"

Angela stood at the door and waved as Rooney got into his car. After she went inside he lit a cigarette, his thoughts going back to Belfast. Back in Nolan's chip shop, 'The Punters Bar' and Raymond and Sheila. If Angela; knew Raymond was cheating on his wife, she'd never get over it. She always talked so lovingly about him, always praised him for his strength and loyalty. She must never know of his weakness for other women and his disregard for Sheila. That's why he'd made and excuse about dinner. He couldn't talk about a trip to Vegas when he'd really been to Belfast for reasons she'd never approve of. Joe was right. It should remain strictly between the two of them, each shouldering a certain amount of guilt. But if Robert Kenny's killer or killers were ever to be found and brought to justice, it would be a small price to pay.

Rooney was sad that so much had been done without her knowledge, but he and Joe were laying the groundwork for some serious results concerning her father. The trip to Belfast had been important to both men, for Joe it proved just how far Rooney was willing to go for him and how much he could be trusted. For Rooney, it proved just how close he felt to Angela and how much he still loved her. He sighed as he started the car engine, determined to keep all secrets to himself.

At this point in time, honesty would not be the best policy!

Chapter 15

The next two years passed quickly. Joe still took his family to Miami for their summer vacation but he had kept his word to Angela and had taken her to Italy. Even though he was getting older, he was still a romantic at heart and liked to be completely alone with her. Angela had wondered why he didn't bring Robert along too but as Joe pointed out, Robert had his whole life in front of him to travel, he didn't. That's why he made any trip with her extra special. He still needed the closeness and love his wife gave him and the shared moments of these trips brought him a lot of happy memories.

Joe was also a devoted father and loved his son dearly, spending every spare moment with him. They had season tickets to football and baseball games and whenever they visited Stacey's Gym, Robert was treated like one of the guys. It was after one such outing that the boy came home to dinner with his father and Rooney, looking happy and excited. As they sat around the table Joe glanced down at him, then smiled at Angela.

"Guess who we met today? Go on, son, tell your mom."

Robert smiled at her broadly,

"Wild Man Wilson!"

"Is that the same Billy Wilson I used to hear you talking about, Joe? The small time boxer?"

"The very same," he replied. "Only he's not small time any more, no sir, Billy has climbed the ladder to success. He's big time now and one hell of a boxer." Robert put his glass of milk down on the table.

"Yeah," he agreed, his eyes narrowing. "He's real mean!"

"That's right, son," said Joe, proudly gazing at him with that 'chip of the old block look!' Then he leaned back in the chair and continued, "You know, if I hadn't become a businessman I'd like to have been a boxer."

"I think you'd have been a great boxer, Dad."

"Yeah, so do I son."

"What would you have called yourself?"

"Oh, I don't know. Something that would look good with my picture. Something to interest the fans," Joe looked at the ceiling, thinking hard. "Something like ... Mean Man Morrelli!" He announced, smiling with satisfaction.

Rooney and Angela looked at each other while Robert beamed,

"Gee dad, that sounds great!"

Joe stared straight ahead, wrapped up in his thoughts and totally unaware of the others staring at him.

"You know, I think I'd have liked it - all that excitement," he smiled. "Yeah, I can see it all now. The glare of the lights. The roar of the crowd. The ding of the bell."

"The sound of the ambulance!" Angela interrupted.

He threw her a sarcastic look and sneered,

"Do you have to spoil everything? Your problem is you have no confidence in me, Angel. You don't think I could have made it, do you?"

"Not back to your corner without help, Joe!"

Rooney bent his head low and tried hard to keep from laughing.

Joe rose from the table.

"Well, I can see this conversation's going nowhere," he said in a peeved voice. "Come on, son, we'll finish it somewhere else."

Robert slid off the chair and taking his father's hand, they both left the room. Angela lifted her glass and looking at Rooney, shook her head.

"Mean Man Morrelli. Honestly, Rooney, the older he gets the worse he gets. Sometimes I think I'm married to Peter Pan!"

"Yeah, he was really living the part. For a few moments he could see it all happening to himself."

"Really? He didn't happen to see himself lying stretched out on the canvas and being carried out by the paramedics! Or the headlines over his picture in the early editions, 'Mean Man Morrelli Hospitalised!' I wonder how much interest his fans would have had then!"

Rooney laughed,

"I take it Joe's right, you don't think he would have made it?"

"Believe me, Rooney, he's better off the way he is now. At least he's gotten to forty eight and never had his nose broken."

"Did you see the look on his face when you butted in?"

She nodded,

"If looks could win a fight instead of fists, I'd be out cold! But never mind. Tonight I'll tell him how attractive I think he still is, then he'll be glad he isn't a boxer. You leave Joe to me," she winked.

In the meantime Joe had taken Robert outside. He sat by the pool and watched as his son played. The boy was seven years old now and growing up fast. He was intelligent and good looking with an outgoing personality and showed great affection to those he knew and loved. Joe was proud of him and recalled the first time he had ever seen him, a tiny, helpless, premature baby. Now he was strong and healthy and a big part of his life. No matter what might change in the future, one thing was for sure - Joe's plans for Robert would not. Here was the only one who'd be left to carry on the Morrelli name. His father knew it and wanted it more than anything. It was Joe's dream and he hoped to see that dream come true.

But his good friend, Gene O'Brien, also had a dream. One which was about to become a reality. Dan Casey had decided not to run for re-election and wanted Gene to take his place. Yes, Gene O'Brien was going to run for the United States Senate! He had waited a long time but now the time was right and he was ready. Dan Casey had taught him everything he knew and had been a good friend. But Gene wanted and needed more good friends behind him. So, as he waited patiently for Joe to answer the telephone in his study, Gene couldn't help but feel a certain amount of satisfaction and excitement. He was on his way and he wanted Joe to be the first one to know before the headlines hit the morning papers.

The last couple of years had been quiet and laid back for Joe and Angela, but as the phone rang they weren't to know that all that was about to change - in more ways than one. Helping Gene O'Brien to realise his dream would open up new territory for both of them. Once again, fate was waiting for Joe and Angela. They would take their paths towards it unaware of what it had planned for them and unsuspecting as to the outcome of their journey and what lay in store.

On Angela's advice, Gene O'Brien opened his campaign headquarters in a large office block in downtown New York. As Angela had put it,

"What better place is there to be than among the people."

He had become a very busy man and never missed an event that would bring him publicity, rarely appearing without his loyal and supportive wife by his side. Kate and he had a happy marriage and had always been a devoted couple. Gene used this to his advantage and became a crusader for the importance of family values. Because of his time consuming schedule, Angela was given a free hand in running his office and helping to organise his campaign.

Joe campaigned too, but in his own way. 'The Safe Haven' was made available and used by Gene and his staff whenever necessary. Although Joe stayed very much in the background, he was not without influence. Being well known and trusted within his own business circles, he could reach those people with wealth and status. And if he couldn't he always knew someone who could. That's why he decided to pay Antonia a visit. When she opened the door to him a look of surprise swept over her face.

"Joe! Come in!"

He closed the door and followed her into the lounge. After fixing some drinks she sat facing him, across the large glass coffee table. Joe took a couple of sips, then put his drink down.

"How are you, Antonia?"

"I'm fine. And you?"

"Couldn't be better," he smiled, leaning forward and clasping his hands. "I'd like you to do me a favour. Well, not me personally. More a favour for Gene O'Brien."

"I read in the papers he's running for the Senate."

"That's right and you could help him. After all, he's an old friend."

Antonia smiled.

"What would you like me to do, Joe?"

"Well, I've been thinking. You're a big Broadway star and you're in with the high society, the jet set. You could do him a lot of good. People admire you. They listen to what you have to say and value your opinion. Why don't you give a few interviews to the press and magazines? Tell them you're voting for Gene O'Brien because he's the best man for the job. Stuff like that always goes down well and brings a lot of publicity. It can't hurt either him or you."

She listened intently as he continued,

"Then there's always the parties. You could bring his name up, praise him a little, tell people how much good he'll be able to do. If you say it they'll believe it, why shouldn't they, you're Antonia Flemming - the finest actress on Broadway." He smiled at her warmly. "If anyone can pull it off you can!"

"Is that a compliment?" she asked, almost in a whisper.

"I guess it is," he nodded.

"You always did have confidence in me, Joe, even when I was dancing in the chorus line."

"I know a good actress when I see one," he grinned. "Even in the old neighbourhood I knew you were different."

Antonia looked away, obviously embarrassed.

"Very few people know where I come from," she reminded him.

"Yeah and Gene O'Brien's one of them! But I've never heard him say it." She gazed at him, almost grateful.

"Neither have you. I guess I owe you both something for that. I'll do anything I can to help and to be honest, I'm delighted you want me to be involved. By the time I'm finished singing Gene O'Brien's praises, everyone will want to vote for him." She thought for a moment, then a tone of excitement entered her voice. "I'll organise a few functions at 'The Portland' and invite everyone who is anyone. I'll expect Gene to be there and mingle and of course I'll do all the introductions."

"Of course," nodded Joe, happy to have won her over.

"You know, the more I think of it the more I'm convinced it's a wonderful idea."
"Sure it is!" he replied, lifting his glass and finishing his drink.

"Would you like another?" she asked.

"No thanks, I'd better be going."

She looked into his face.

"Does your wife know you're here?"

He met her gaze.

"No." He glanced at his watch. "But she will by the time we sit down to dinner." "Then I don't suppose there's any point in me asking you to stay on - just for a little while?"

"I can't Antonia."

"Oh well, you can't blame a girl for trying!"

"What about Judge Thompson?" he enquired. "He's a nice man."

"Yes he is." She lowered her gaze, then looked back at him. "But he's not you, Joe. You were the best lover I ever had."

Joe's expression and voice was full of affection.

"You know something, Antonia? You weren't so bad yourself."

She smiled bravely as he got up to leave.

"I'll walk you to the door," she insisted.

As they crossed the lounge together, she slipped her arm around his waist and he put a protective arm around her shoulder. He looked around at the decor.

"Well, nothing's changed."

"Of course it has. You're an old married man with a wonderful son and I'm the toast of Broadway with a highly respected Judge to escort me to dinner."

"Yeah," he nodded, "I guess we did o.k."

When they reached the front door, Joe turned to her. "Why don't you marry the guy?"

"Why didn't you marry me?"

He looked into her eyes, then kissed her forehead.

"I had my reasons, Antonia."

"And I have mine, Joe."

He nodded and opened the door.

"I'm proud of you," he whispered. "Don't ever forget that."

"I know. I'm the one you're proud of Angela's the one you love!"

"Well, that's life. But I guess I did the Judge a favour because there's a man who really loves you."

Antonia's voice became hard and haughty.

"Oh, I try not to see him as often now. My new friends are a bit out of his league." Joe stepped out, then turned.

"Well if that's the case, what chance would I have had?"

For a moment she was stunned into silence.

Perhaps Joe had known her better than she'd known herself, finally, she found her voice. "Were they your reasons?"

"Maybe," he shrugged, "but whatever they were, they saved us both a lot of grief" "If I send you an invitation to 'The Portland Club' will you come?"

"You bet!" he winked.

"Goodbye, Joe, and thanks for asking for my help. It means a lot to me."

"There's no one I'd rather ask because there's no one more capable."

Her face lit up and she beamed.

He waved to her from the lift.

"I'll see you real soon," he promised.

Antonia leaned seductively against the door frame, still hoping Joe would change his mind. However, the lift doors closed and it began to move. As Joe waited for it to come to a halt he thought about Antonia. How she really lived up to her actress status, regardless of anyone. It was just further proof that he had made the right choice in marrying Angela Kenny and he could hardly wait to get home. With her there was no glitz and glamour and no pretence. Antonia, on the other hand, had been such a good actress for so long she just couldn't stop, even in her private life.

"Once an actress, always an actress!" he muttered.

At least his love with Angela was real. With Antonia he could never be sure, especially now. In a way he felt sorry for her and all those like her. They became lost in the characters they played until their lives became as empty as the theatres they left behind. Sure, they had money and all the trappings it brought along but even money is a poor substitute when you don't know who you really are!

Angela worked long and hard for Gene O'Brien. She was out of the house most of the time and there were evenings when she came home looking and feeling exhausted. Joe wasn't seeing her as often as he would have liked and he was beginning to worry about her health. One evening, she arrived home to find him busy in the kitchen.

"What are you doing?" she asked. "And where's Evie?"

He turned and smiled at her.

"I'm cooking us a 'Joe Morrelli Special'. Robert's asleep and I have everything under control, so I gave Evie the night off. Actually, she was all set to babysit. I was going to bring you to Mario's for a change of scenery so I phoned to tell him we'd be there. It's just as well I did because they're closed."

Angela was surprised.

"Closed? Why? Has he given up the restaurant?"

Joe shook his head.

"No. Mario's ill, Angel."

"Is he in hospital?"

"Not yet. He doesn't want to go to hospital, he wants to stay with his family. So Gino and his wife are looking after him. That's why the restaurant's closed. He needs rest and quiet. Let's face it, he wouldn't get either living over a room full of people and a juke box playing."

"Poor Mario. I'm sorry to hear about him. I always liked him." She became thoughtful. "I think I'll take tomorrow afternoon off and go and see him."

Joe nodded.

"He'd appreciate that and a break wouldn't do you any harm either. I think you're doing too much Angel. Why don't you get someone else involved? That way you could shorten your hours. You're working too hard. Besides, I hardly ever see you."

Angela went over and kissed him lightly on the lips.

"Is that your way of telling me you miss me?" she smiled.

Joe turned down the pans, then took her in his arms. He kissed her.

"You're damn right I do! I miss you and I worry about you."

She noticed the tenderness in his voice as he held her close.

"I'm fine Joe," she assured him. "The parties and functions will be starting soon and we'll be able to spend more time together."

"Yeah well, I guess expensive champagne and a beautiful woman to share it with is worth the wait!" he joked.

Angela smiled and teased,

"You always did like a night out and believe me, you're going to get plenty!" She lifted the lids off the pans. "That looks good."

"And it tastes delicious - trust me! Now, why don't you go upstairs, have a hot shower and slip into something more comfortable."

"Any suggestions?" she asked, walking towards the door.

"Well, off the top of my head I'd say just a bathrobe would do! By the time you're ready, dinner will be ready." He turned back to the stove and stirred the contents of the pans. "And so will I!" he whispered to himself

Angela put her head round the door.

"By the way, what's for dessert?"

"With a 'Joe Morrelli Special' you never really know," came the reply.

"Oh, I think I can guess!"

As she disappeared Joe continued with the cooking, singing happily to himself in a low voice.

Angela woke to see Joe holding a breakfast tray.

"Good morning," he smiled.

She rubbed her eyes.

"What time is it?"

"Ten thirty," he replied.

"What?" She sat up quickly. "Joe, why didn't you wake me? I have to be down town by eleven!"

"Angel, don't panic." He put the tray down in front of her. "I phoned and told them you were taking the day off. Besides, you need the rest and you're going to see Mario this afternoon anyway."

Joe grinned as he sat down on the side of the bed.

"You're looking very cheerful," Angela observed.

"Yeah well, that's because I am."

"I can't believe I slept until now."

"Maybe it was that Italian meal I cooked."

"I think it was the dessert, Joe. I've never had one that lasted so long!"

He leaned towards her.

"Well, you always save the best till the end. Now you know what a 'Joe Morrelli Special is!"

"You're a very talented man."

He kissed her cheek.

"We aim to please! And may I say I enjoyed myself immensely." On standing up he continued, "I'll be out most of the day, Angel. I'm meeting Reuben for lunch but I want you to do something for me." Reaching into the inside pocket of his jacket he took out a large, brown envelope and placed it on the bedside cabinet. "Give this to Gino. The restaurant's been closed for over a week now and he has a wife and two kids to support. It will help pay some bills and keep him afloat. After all, we have to take care of our own." He kissed her tenderly. "I'll see you this evening."

She reached over and took his hand gently.

"I enjoyed last night too, Joe," she whispered. "You really know how to make a woman feel wanted."

He pressed her fingers lightly with his own and replied,

"It's not hard to do, Angel, when you love that woman and she loves you."

Angela smiled, "Was it that obvious?"

Joe nodded, "It was to me, and it's good to know you still feel the same way about me."

"Why shouldn't I?"

"Well let's face it, I'm forty eight years old."

She looked at him sheepishly and smiled, "With all the stamina you had last night, I'd never have guessed it."

"Yeah well," he shrugged, "it just goes to show that after all this time the 'Joe Morrelli Special' still works! I'd better go. Tell Mario I'll call and see him." He walked over and opened the bedroom door, then looked back at her. "Come to think of it, I guess I did o.k."

"You did more than o.k., Joe. I suppose it's because you've still got that 'Joe Morrelli Charm'."

"Angel honey, every man has charm. The trouble is, most of them don't know how to use it. I do. I've always been lucky that way and I've never had any complaints!" he winked.

Angela shook her head.

"I might have known you'd end up singing your own praises - but don't forget it takes two!"

"Now, how could I forget? I've only had a couple of hours sleep. I've got to admit, you're all woman Angel." He pointed his finger. "And I've got to admit something else. When it comes to dessert, not a restaurant in town could serve up anything to compare with what I had!" he grinned, closing the door behind him.

As she left Mario's and stepped out into the bright sunlight, Angela stood for a few moments and looked around. A few small boys around Robert's age were playing with a ball in the street and from an empty space left by some demolished buildings, she could hear loud laughter. Out of sheer curiosity she followed it and found children playing happily on make-shift swings, large car tyres suspended from rusted scaffolding by thick ropes. Others were playing netball, with nets attached to long, wooden poles that wobbled each time the ball went in. At first Al sat in the car watching. Then he got out and went to join her.

"Anything wrong, Mrs. Morrelli?" he asked.

She looked at him.

"Don't these children have a proper playground?"

Al shook his head.

"I guess not. But then, neither had we when we were their age. Some things never change."

They began to walk along the street. Older boys stood outside pool halls and bars.

"Why are they standing there?" she asked.

"They're waiting to run errands for the big guys," he explained. "It's the best way to earn a few dollars. Besides, they have nothing else to do and nowhere to go." "Don't they go to school?"

"Some of the time. But if there's no food on the table, their parents are grateful for the few bucks they make on the street."

Angela stopped and turned to him.

"Tell me something, Al, is this what it was like for Joe?"

He nodded.

"Yeah, the boss did the same thing. He had to. It's called 'survival'! He was smart, though. He went from running errands to full time employment. Then when he'd made enough money, he got out. A lot of guys never get out. They don't plan ahead. The next thing you know they're trapped by booze, drugs or crime. They end up with no education and no jobs."

Angela became concerned.

"Couldn't someone do something for these youngsters to try and help them?"

"Who cares? Everybody's too busy looking out for themselves. If you're lucky and make it big, you move out. That's the way it works in the old neighbourhoods, Mrs. Morrelli, and nobody expects anything different."

"I see," she nodded. "But don't you think it's selfish to get out and just forget?" Al shrugged his shoulders.

"I never really thought about it like that. Anyway what can you do for these kids?"

As they walked back towards the car, she studied the busy street and crowded play area. A hint of sadness came into her voice as she shook her head and said,

"I don't know, Al, but there must be something..."

That evening Joe watched t.v. with Robert upstairs, then made his way down to the lounge and poured himself a drink. Sitting down, he glanced at Angela who was curled up on the couch reading a book.

"Is anything the matter?" he asked. "You've been quiet all evening."

"No, everything's fine," she replied and put the book down. "It's just that there's something I want to talk to you about."

"What is it?"

She got up and coming around the back of his chair, draped her arms over his shoulders. She didn't do that often but when she did, Joe knew there was something bothering her. He took a swallow from his glass, then put it down.

"O.k. I'm listening."

"Well, it's about today." Angela was hesitant.

"Are you worried about Mario?"

"It's more than that Joe."

"Angel, did something happen today that I should know about? Because if it did you'd better sit down and tell me."

She returned to the couch and remained silent as she clasped her hands. Then she looked at him earnestly.

"Joe do you remember this morning when you said we have to take care of our own?"

"Yeah."

"Did you mean it?"

"Sure I did."

Angela seemed relieved and said, "Well, when I left Mario's today I took a short walk. I couldn't help but notice the children in the neighbourhood have nothing, Joe. No proper playground, no facilities, nowhere to go. I felt really sorry for the younger ones but I also felt sorry for the older ones. They were just standing around on street corners waiting to run errands."

He stared at her and replied.

"What's so wrong with that? I did exactly the same thing. If they're smart they won't be running errands all their lives."

"I know," she nodded, "but they won't all be as smart as you. You invested your money and became a successful businessman. Most of them won't get that chance. There's too much crime now and too many drugs and drug dealers. Once those boys get involved they'll never be able to break free. Their lives are over before they've really begun."

Joe shrugged.

"Yeah well, that's life and there's nothing you can do about it."

"There's something you could do."

"Me?" He pointed to himself in a surprised voice.

Angela leaned over.

"Yes. You Joe. You see I've been thinking. What if you were to buy some run-down property and fix it up. You could build a proper play ground for the children and renovate a couple of derelict buildings, make them into youth centres for the older ones and keep them off the streets."

Joe looked amazed as he held out his hands.

"Listen to me, Angel. I know you like kids and your intentions are good but let's be honest here, you can't save the world."

"I'm not asking you to save the world," she replied, "just your own neighbourhood! It's all very well making good and moving out, but don't you remember what it was like for you? I mean, too many people want to forget and that's wrong. I think when you hit the big time and the money starts rolling in, you should give something back."

Joe lowered his gaze and was thoughtful for a moment. He shook his head. "They wouldn't go to youth centres."

"They would if it appealed to them."

"What had you in mind?"

She knew she had him interested so she asked,

"How many good boxers have you known who came from poor neighbourhoods?" "I must admit, quite a few."

"And there are a lot more, Joe. All they need is a chance and you can give it to them. Open a gym. You might get a surprise and end up with a world champion!"

He smiled broadly.

"Yeah, now wouldn't that be something! Well, that's one building. What about the other one?"

"I was thinking along the lines of youth training, teaching them skills. Perhaps giving some general education. I could help in that department. Books are an education in themselves and I think some of the kids would be interested in reading. You'd be opening up a whole new world for them, Joe, and giving most of them a start. You'd be helping them to believe in themselves and giving them a chance to prove their worth." She took his hand. "Listen to me Joe. We have a good life. Our son goes to a good school. We have a lovely home and we don't want for anything. Why don't we try and help those less fortunate than ourselves? You made your mark in life but it's getting tougher in all the old neighbourhoods now. Drugs are getting a hold in this city. No one knows that better than you."

"Yeah. I guess they go from making deliveries to taking the stuff. After that it's down hill all the way. Believe me Angel, there's a lot of money to be made in that quarter but it's the one thing I'd never get involved in. It's a dirty business and if anyone ever tried to hook my son, I'd kill them and have no remorse." There was silence between them as he finished his drink. Then he nodded, "O.k. I'll think about it." As she smiled he insisted, "I'm not making any promises Angel. But when I go to see Mario I'll have a look around for myself. If I decide to do it, I'll see Reuben. If anyone can get a rock bottom price on disused property, he can!"

Angela went over and sat on his lap.

"That's all I want you to do. Just think about it."

Joe put his arms around her.

"You know, I always thought that in this life you looked after number one. Why do you care so much about other people, even people you don't know?"

"We all need a lucky break and there's always someone out there who can give it to us. Finding them is the difficult part."

He drew her close.

"You talk a lot of sense. No wonder Gene O'Brien wanted you to work for him! I'm a fortunate man. I'm married to a very caring and generous woman and I wouldn't have it any other way."

She stroked his cheek lightly with her finger.

"Do you mean that, Joe?" she whispered.

"You can't begin to know how much," came his reply.

He kissed her passionately, lifted her in his arms and carrying her over to the couch, he laid her down gently.

"The longer I live with you, the more I seem to love you. And I do love you," he assured her.

"I know. And I love you, so I guess we're both fortunate," she smiled.

As he joined her and they lay holding each other tightly, no more words were needed and none were said.

A few days later, Joe paid Angela a visit. Pushing open the large, glass doors of Gene O'Brien's headquarters, he looked around. He saw her at the back of the room talking on the telephone and waved as he walked towards her, passing rows of desks and equipment. As he was making his way along, a very attractive young woman stepped in front of him and smiled,

"Can I help you?"

"No, I don't think so," he replied.

"There must be something I can do for you," she insisted. "Perhaps you would like some information. You don't need to be shy with me, I'm here to help you."

She gave him one of those 'I'm available for the asking' smiles. A smile Joe knew only too well. Then moving closer to him, she pushed out her breasts provocatively. For once, Joe was lost for words as he stood staring at them.

"Let me guess," she said, "I bet you're here to offer your services."

"No, actually I'm here to take my wife out to lunch," he smiled as Angela tapped her on the shoulder.

"Sorry Susan, not this one. He belongs to me."

Then she smiled at Joe. "What are you doing here?"

"I've got a surprise for you and figured it would be your lunch break, so shall we go?" He slipped his arm around her waist and guided her towards the door.

As they walked away, Susan put her hands on her hips and glared after them. "How come all the best men are married!" she snapped aloud.

Angela looked at him, smiling "You've made quite an impression there."

Joe shook his head.

"She's not my type. She's too pushy."

"I bet there was a time when she'd have been exactly your type!"

"Not any more," he replied, opening the doors for her. "Besides, I'm getting too old for that. The last thing I need is to wake up in the morning to find Miss Whiplash standing over me, expecting me to perform like some circus trained animal!"

"Joe, that's a terrible thing to say. Susan isn't like that."

"Oh no? Well, I wouldn't bet on it Angel. There are a lot of Susan's out there who are nice and respectable during the day - and real weirdos at night!"

Angela shook her head as they crossed the sidewalk to the car.

"'Where are we going?" she asked, getting in.

"You'll see!" he teased.

The car came to a halt outside Mario's.

"Are we having lunch here?" Angela asked.

"Not exactly. There's something I want to show you."

They both got out of the car and Angela looked around at the crowded street, surprised. "Joe what are all these people doing here?"

He took her arm as they crossed over.

"Sight seeing. Just like us." He smiled nodding over the heads of the crowd.

She followed his gaze and found herself looking at a large earth remover and a team of construction workers. Some were clearing the old playground area and others were busy renovating two large buildings nearby. Most of the neighbourhood looked on, talking excitedly. She turned to Joe in disbelief.

"You did it!" she exclaimed. "You actually did it!"

He nodded and smiled,

"Yeah, I did but no one knows it's me, Angel, and I'd prefer to keep it that way." Just then the upstairs window of the restaurant opened and a voice called, "Hey Joe!"

On turning around he saw Mario leaning out and waved up to him.

"What's going on?" he asked the old man, pretending not to know.

"A miracle," came the reply.

Joe smiled at Angela.

"He's an even bigger miracle!" he joked. "The last time I saw him he was on his deathbed!"

Mario pointed to the workmen.

"Plenty business, Joe. They all come to Mario's. My Gino, he busy all the time now."

"That's great," Joe nodded. Then he smiled again at Angela. "There's nothing like the colour of money and the sound of a busy cash register to bring you back from death's door!"

"You look pleased," she observed.

He lowered his gaze for a moment.

"I am. You know, I'd have really missed that old man."

She put her arm through his.

"I know," she whispered. "We both would."

"Joe!" came Mario's voice again. "You come inside and have some lunch. Gino! Where is that boy?"

Gino came out onto the street.

"I'm here, papa. What do you want?"

"What do I want? I tell you what I want!" yelled Mario, waving his hands around and looking flustered. "Where's your manners? Bring Joe and his beautiful wife inside and give them some lunch. On the house, Joe. Anything you want!"

"Thanks Mario, but we can't stay," he replied. "We'll call again some other time."

"Any time Joe. You always welcome, workmen or no workmen. I always see to you first. Mario never forget his friends, Joe. And Joe Morrelli, he a good friend to Mario. I not forget."

Gino smiled at Joe.

"I better get Papa inside before he takes a stroke. He's all excited. The whole neighbourhood is, especially the kids. It's good to see someone doing something for them at last."

"What exactly are they doing?" Joe enquired.

"They're making a new playground for the kids, a big one. It's going to have swings, slides and a basket ball pitch." He pointed towards the buildings and continued, "I hear there's going to be a gym and training centre for the young people. We need it Joe. Too many of them are getting into trouble. May be now the old neighbourhood won't be as bad or look as bad. No one seems to know who's footing the bill for it all, but someone is. Those construction workers are employed by a private company."

"Well, at least that someone is doing something," replied Joe, trying to sound impressed.

Gino nodded,

"Whoever they are they'll always have the gratitude of the people living here. Are you sure you won't stay and have something to eat?"

Joe patted his shoulder.

"Thanks, Gino, but we really have to go."

"O.k. but remember what papa said. You're always welcome Joe."

"I know. I'll see you later."

Joe and Angela said their goodbyes but as they turned to leave Gino put his hand on Joe's arm and in a low voice said, "When papa was ill and I had to close the restaurant, only for your help I might not be open today and doing so well. We owe you a lot."

"You don't owe me anything. That's what friends are for," said Joe, glancing up towards the window. "Take care of your father, we go back a long way."

"I will."

Gino disappeared as Joe and Angela walked back to the car. Before getting in they waved to Mario, who was still surveying the scene. Once settled inside she put her arm around her husband's shoulder and kissed his cheek.

"I'm very proud of you, Joe Morrelli," she said, as he gave an embarrassed smile. "Now, are we going to lunch?"

"Soon," came the reply. "We have one more stop to make."

As Joe turned into Westmere Avenue, Angela looked surprised.

"What are we doing here?" she asked.

"You'll see!"

He drove down towards the local Church and stopped.

She looked at him, puzzled.

"Don't tell me you've turned religious Joe."

"Angel, there have been a lot of things in my life I couldn't get enough of - but religion wasn't one of them!" he grinned, glancing at his watch.

A few minutes later, Father Ryker appeared through the vestry door and walked over to them, leaning in through the open window.

"Hello, Angela," he smiled.

"Hello, Father." She looked from one to the other.

"O.k. Father, hop in," said Joe. "I may not be able to save your soul but I can save your feet!"

Father Ryker shook his head as he climbed into the back of the car.

"What's going on?" she asked him.

"I think you should see for yourself."

Joe remained silent until the car finally came to a halt some streets away. The two men got out and encouraged Angela to do the same. When she did they ushered her around the corner, where she stopped in her tracks. A construction team was also at work here, assisted by a large number of young people. They were all helping to clear out an old warehouse.

"What are they doing?" she asked.

Father Ryker put a hand on her arm and informed her, "They're converting it into a youth centre for training and a hostel for the homeless." She could hardly believe it and turned to Joe.

"You bought property here?"

Before anyone could say another word she threw herself into his arms.

"Oh, Joe! I'm so happy! Thank you!"

"We're all happy, Angela," smiled the old priest, nodding appreciatively. "When the word got around the kids were queuing up to offer their help. It's going to make big changes in their lives, not to mention the neighbourhood itself. And I believe we have you to thank for coming up with the idea."

Angela shook her head.

"I can't believe it!" she kept saying.

"Well, you'd better," smiled Joe, "because it's all happening just the way you wanted it to."

"Sometimes I can't believe it myself," Father Ryker admitted. "It's the answer to all my prayers. I can't thank Joe enough. He's turned out to be God's messenger."

With raised eyebrows, Joe looked at him.

"Yeah well, I bet that surprised you, Father. Considering that God and me were never exactly bosom buddies!"

"If God isn't going to hold that against you, Joe, neither am I. That should make you sleep better," joked the priest.

Joe leaned over.

"Father, I've never had any trouble sleeping at night. Just like I've never had any trouble in other ways," he winked.

An embarrassed Angela gasped.

"Joe Morrelli, you're talking to a priest!"

"I know but Father Ryker here doesn't marry people just so they can play poker! Now do you, Father?"

"That's perfectly true Joe," he laughed, nodding in agreement.

Angela glared at her husband, who avoided her attention!

As they watched all the activity, the priest put a hand on both their shoulders.

"You know, Angela," he said, "God does work in mysterious ways. If you hadn't left Ireland and come here to live you'd never had met Joe and none of this would have happened. Your father's death was so tragic, yet out of all the bad a lot of good has come. Robert Kenny's death has brought hope to the living and that should make you both very proud."

"I am proud, Father," she replied. "I'm proud of his name and his memory. But I'll never forget what happened to him and I'll never forgive those who did it." She took Joe's hand and smiled at him lovingly. "I'm also proud of your name."

"And I'm proud you took it," he said in a soft voice. "That was the happiest day of my life."

Father Ryker looked on approvingly.

Joe then checked his watch.

"We'd better be going, Father. Can I give you a lift back?"

"No thanks, Joe. I think I'll stay a while." He took Joe's hand in a firm grip. "Thanks for everything. I wish there was more I could say!"

"There's no need," Joe assured him. "As my wife says, we should give something back."

"And you have. You both have. You've given hope were there wasn't any and you've made an old priest and the people he cares for very happy. God bless you both - and I know he will!"

On saying their goodbyes, Angela took Father Ryker's hand gently.

"I'll be back to help out when everything's finished," she promised. "There are a lot of smart kids in these neighbourhoods and we're going to make sure they get the chance to prove it."

"You really believe in them, don't you?"

She nodded,

"Yes I do. After all, God's own son was born in a stable and look what he achieved."

"That's so true, Angela," he agreed. "But unlike you, too many people forget about that."

She looked at him with sincerity and said,

"What they really forget is - just because you're born poor, doesn't mean you're born stupid!"

When they had both gotten into the car, Angela turned to Joe and put her arms around his neck in a loving embrace.

"It was a wonderful surprise Joe," she whispered. "Thank you. I really love you." Joe smiled,

"Well, if you love me so much, why don't you take the rest of the day off? We could still have lunch."

"What did you have in mind?"

"Well, what about sharing some coffee and sandwiches with me in the park?"

"I'd like that," she said, kissing him.

A broad grin spread over Joe's face as he started the car.

"O.k. the park it is!"

Joe and Angela spent the afternoon relaxed and happy. As they sat on the grass she studied him for a moment then said,

"Joe, I feel a little bit guilty."

"Why?"

"Well, buying the property and hiring those construction workers must have cost you a lot of money. I'm beginning to wonder if perhaps I asked too much of you." He took her hand.

"Listen Angel, Reuben got me a really good deal on that property and the construction firm was about to go under because of bad management. I stepped in and straightened things out. I saved those guys their jobs, now they work for me."

"Are you telling me you bought the company?" she asked in surprise.

"That's right," he nodded. "It's only a small one but it can make money. Of course, now it's changed hands I've given it a new name. We now own 'K and M Enterprises'." Angela looked puzzled.

"Is that short for something?"

"It sure is! Those guys now work for 'Kenny and Morrelli Enterprises'."

She could hardly believe her ears.

"Why did you use my name?"

"Why not? It was your idea so it's only right that you share in this venture. What do you think?" he smiled.

Her hand tightened in his.

"I think you're a wonderful man who's just full of surprises!"

"Well, I always knew we'd make a great team. With your brains and my know how, we're the perfect combination!"

"You've made me very happy, Joe." she whispered.

Pulling her down gently onto the grass beside him, he smiled,

"We aim to please. Besides, you've made me very happy, Angel. Every time I make love to you is like the first time. There can't be many men who can say that." As he gazed lovingly into her eyes, he smiled and stroked her face lightly with his fingertips. "You know," he went on, "I feel pretty good with myself. All those kids in the neighbourhoods will get a chance to go straight, make something of themselves. And those guys in the construction company will have steady employment now. Most of them have got wives and kids so they need the work. By listening to you I've been able to do something positive for the future and the best part is, everyone's got a good deal - including me!"

"I think you and Reuben make a good team as well!" she joked.

Joe nodded in agreement,

"Yeah, Reuben's one smart guy when it comes to business deals. He always knows when the time is right to buy and invest, never a day early or a day late. He gets it from his father. Isaac had great judgement. Between the two of them they've made me a wealthy man. But all the money in the world wouldn't matter to me if didn't have you and Robert."

Angela knew Joe meant what he said. She looked at him and commented,

"You know, I've heard people say that money can buy you anything."

"Believe me it can," he agreed, "but the night you gave me back my tip in 'The Safe Haven', I knew it couldn't buy you. You were different and I guess I fell in love with you that very night only I didn't realise it. You're a woman who's impressed by the man - not his bank balance. When you married me I knew it was because you loved me and not my money!"

She smiled and kissed him tenderly "I'm so glad I've made you happy, Joe. I'll always love you."

Joe leaned over and gazed into her deep, blue eyes.

"And I'll always love you," he whispered, taking her in his arms and kissing her long and wantonly.

His hands caressed her body as she drew him closer, responding sensually to his touch. As their embrace became all the more passionate Joe was getting so carried away, he almost forgot he was in the park.

Joe sat at the table in the spacious kitchen enjoying a cup of coffee and reading the morning paper. He always read the Stocks and Shares page first, keeping a shrewd eye on the money market when the back door opened slightly and Rooney popped his head round, a huge grin on his face.

"Where's Robert?" he asked Angela.

"Oh, he's playing somewhere around here. Why?"

"You'll see. Go get him, Angela. I have a surprise out here!"

Joe put the paper down as Angela went out into the hallway and called Robert, who came running out of the lounge. Angela took his hand and led him into the kitchen. "Hi Uncle Rooney," greeted Robert as he made a dart for the back door. Rooney stopped him with a wave of his hand.

"Wait there!" he ordered.

Angela sat down and drew Robert close to her. All three were staring at the door when, suddenly, it was flung open and in strode Rooney with a long lead attached to an adorable golden Labrador puppy. Robert shrieked with delight.

"Uncle Rooney! Is it for me? Is it mine?"

"All yours," replied Rooney.

Robert dived onto the floor and started hugging the pup. Rooney joined the others at the table. Wagging it's tail, the little animal made it's way over to Angela who lifted it into her lap and started to pat it.

"He's beautiful, Rooney, and so cute!"

She handed the pup to an excited Robert who had just finished hugging Rooney. Both boy and dog ran out of the kitchen and into the hallway. There was more room to play in there.

"It will be great fun for him to have a pet he can play with, Rooney."

"I bought him a pony!" Joe reminded her, more than a little bit perturbed.

"I know you did, Joe," replied Angela, "and he adores it. But you can't bring a pony into the house and run about with it."

"Look," said Rooney reaching into his pocket, "he has papers and everything."

"That's all we need!" muttered Joe under his breath.

"What was that, Joe?" enquired Angela.

"That's nice - we can breed." Joe was trying to get back to his paper.

Angela smiled.

"I love dogs. We always had a dog at home. It was one thing my father insisted on.

When I was young I used to watch all the films on T.V. with dogs in them."

"Mmm," agreed Rooney, "and they were always sad."

Joe sat staring from one to the other, totally out of the conversation. He decided to pipe in.

"Well excuse me if I don't weep for joy when Lassie finds her way home through the door of my back porch!"

He waved his hand towards the back door, as if to make a point. He was ignored. "Rooney, did you ever read the story of 'Greyfriars Bobby'?" asked Angela.

"No, but I saw the film when I was a boy. It was really good."

"Yes it was. I saw it twice and cried both times. Being a true story made it all the more sad."

Joe sat in disbelief, but he was curious. He looked at Angela and asked,

"Who was that guy?"

"What guy?"

"That guy!" maintained Joe, "that friar! Aren't they some kind of priests who wear robes? And who was this Bobby character?"

Angela's gaze was fixed on her husband as she explained,

"Greyfrairs is a graveyard in a city called Edinburgh in Scotland and Bobby was the name of a dog."

"Well who owned him then?"

"A man, Joe," replied Angela raising her voice like a school teacher. "An ordinary man who lived in a boarding house. He died and the dog lay on his grave until it finally died. They erected a statue of the dog as a reminder to everyone of it's loyalty."

"Well, pardon me for asking!" snapped Joe sullenly.

He got up from the table, folded his paper and put it under his arm. As far as he was concerned, this conversation was leading nowhere! As he reached the kitchen door Rooney commented,

"What's the matter, Joe? You look kind of sulky?"

"Oh, don't mind him, Rooney," said Angela. "He'll be alright. It's just that time of the month!"

Joe refused to retaliate and walked out of the kitchen instead. Angela gripped Rooney's arm and they both started to giggle like teenagers. Angela covered her mouth with her hand, leaned back on the chair and watched Joe make his way to the study. Robert ran to his father, accompanied by his new pet.

"Dad, aren't you and Uncle Rooney best pals?"

"Yes, son, we are."

"Then that's what I'll call my dog - Pal."

"That's real nice son," commented Joe, as he bent down to pet the new addition to the family.

Robert started running around squealing with delight as the puppy started chasing him. Joe stopped at the study door and called out,

"Robert, could you keep the noise down - please!"

He retreated into his study, grateful for the peace and quiet it held. As Angela and Rooney heard the door close securely, Rooney threw back his head and roared with laughter. Angela giggled uncontrollably now.

"I have to hand it to you, Angela," he said. "You're the only one who could talk to Joe Morrelli like that and get away with it!"

There was admiration in his eyes.

Over the next three months things were really hotting up in the election campaign. However, Angela couldn't help but notice that there were times when Gene O'Brien seemed a little pre-occupied, even dismayed. She knew something was bothering him so she decided to find out what it was. After discussing the matter with Joe, she invited Gene and Kate to dinner.

As they all sat at the table enjoying one another's company, Joe brought up the subject of the election. Lifting his wine glass, he looked over at Gene.

"So, how's the campaign going?" he enquired.

His friend's smile faded as he replied,

"It's going pretty well but ..."

"But what?"

Gene shook his head,

"I won't lie to you, Joe. It's getting tougher all the time, Matt Hayden is making damn sure of that. He's going all out to win."

Joe put the glass down.

"Sure he is. And so are you. I've never known the opposition to bother you before and I've never known you to walk away from a fight, especially one that involves politics."

"Oh, I'm not going to walk away from this one, Joe. I'll be there until the very end, you can count on it. But running for the Senate is a whole new ball game compared to Congress."

Joe shrugged,

"Well, at the end of the day it's the people who decide who the best is for the job."

"I know that," Gene nodded, "but Matt Hayden is a very shrewd man. What he says and what he thinks are two totally different things and believe me, I know. He's like so many before him. He's promising the people the moon but he won't deliver, and I'll tell you why. Matt Hayden is a very rich man and he has surrounded himself with even richer friends. He doesn't give a damn about people, poverty, creating jobs or the interests of our country abroad!" He tapped the table angrily.

"Maybe, but you've got Dan Casey on you side," Joe reminded him . "He's rich and he's well respected. That should count for something."

"Yeah, Dan's been great but even he admits that Hayden and his friends are dangerous. And they'd be even more dangerous if he was elected." He rested his elbows on the table. "Matt Hayden is a highly educated Yale man and he comes from a moneied family. He's never had a poor day in his life and he's never mixed with anyone who had. His friends are all business executives and industrialists. The more money they have, the more they want. They're spending a bundle on this campaign in the hope that they'll get it back twice over, through favours Hayden can give them if he gets into the Senate."

Joe leaned back in the chair and gazed at his old friend.

"Aren't you forgetting something, Gene?" he said. "You're a Harvard man and highly educated yourself. O.k. Matt Hayden paid for his, but you won your scholarship. You've got more brains than he'll ever have. You were one of the finest lawyers in the City and do you want to know why? You had to prove yourself, he didn't. And you did it by going into Courts of Law and fighting for the man in the street - and winning! You didn't care if your client lived on Park Avenue or Seventh Avenue, you fought for them, Gene, and you got them the best deal you could. I know I was always satisfied with anything you ever handled for me. You were a damn good lawyer and you'll make one damn good Senator!!"

"That's what I keep telling him," said Kate, somewhat concerned, "but he won't listen. Maybe he'll listen to you."

Gene smiled over at Joe,

"Thank's, old buddy."

"What for? I'm only telling the truth."

The door opened and Evie came in with a tray to clear the table.

"Evie, we'll have our coffee and brandy in the lounge," Joe informed her.

"Yes, Mr. Joe."

Gene watched as she left the room, then turned to Joe.

"And there's another thing," he nodded towards the door. "If Matt Hayden had his way we'd be living in an all white America."

Joe pondered for a moment, then leaned over.

"Is that so? Well, we'll just have to make sure he doesn't get his way then - won't we!!" They all left the dining room and went into the lounge.

After the coffee and brandy was served, they sat relaxed in the comfortable chairs and couch. As both men enjoyed Joe's favourite cigars, he said, "Tell me something Gene. How do you know so much about Matt Hayden's friends?"

"My best source of information is Kevin Mitchell," smiled Gene. "Don't forget, being a high flying executive he knows them all."

Joe shot a quick glance at Angela, who lowered her eyes.

"I didn't know he was still around," he said, trying not to sound too interested.

"Oh, he's around alright," Gene replied, "and I must admit that he's proving very valuable with information about what's going on in the other camp. He keeps Dan and me up to date with everything." He turned to Angela. "You know, when I told him you were working in my headquarters down town, he was very pleased but not surprised. He said if anyone could help me get votes, you could. Dan agrees with him. You made quite an impression with those guys."

Kate smiled broadly,

"Even though Dan isn't running in the election, Kevin knows he wants Gene to take his place. So he's working very closely with them. Ever since Gene told him you were campaigning for him, Kevin always asks about you, Angela."

"That's nice of him," she replied, trying to force a smile and finally succeeding.

"Yeah, I wouldn't be a bit surprised if he paid you a visit one of these days," said Gene. "He's never been in my headquarters."

Kate looked at her husband.

"You'll have to bring him along and show him where it's all happening," she suggested. They both sat smiling, completely unaware of what had happened in the Morrelli household concerning Kevin Mitchell.

"Is he married yet?" Joe asked casually.

Gene nodded,

"Yeah, he is. But I wouldn't say it was a marriage made in heaven."

"What do you mean?"

"Well, he married some rich debutante but Kevin still has an eye for other women, although his wife is very attractive. From what I can gather they both go their separate ways. She's having an affair with her tennis coach and he has a string of models coming and going from his penthouse suite. The only time they're really together is when they need to be. You know, functions and parties. That's the only time they act like the ideal couple. But then, they have to do it for Dan's sake."

Joe was finding this conversation very interesting, and neither Gene or Kate had noticed how quiet Angela was.

"Any kids?" Joe asked.

"Not on your life!" came the reply. "She works out six days a week in a gym to keep in shape. Then there are the beauty parlours, the hair salons and of course the tennis!"

Joe smiled at him,

"How come you know so much about them?"

"Dan told me. He knows what's going on, Joe, he's not stupid. Mind you, he did try to warn Kevin that glamour wasn't everything. Dan still maintains if his nephew had married someone with a little less glamour and a bit more brains, he'd be a lot happier today. And you want to know something? So do I. All these models are just a pass time," shrugged Gene. He thought for a moment then continued, "I think deep inside Kevin Mitchell's unhappy. If you want my opinion I'd say he's searching for something he can't find." He looked over at Joe. "Who knows, maybe he did find it but couldn't have it!"

Joe tapped the arm of his chair with his fingers, feeling uncomfortable as he avoided looking in Angela's direction.

There was silence for a moment, then she spoke.

"Why don't we change the subject? I'm sure some people would find Kevin

Mitchell's love life very interesting," she remarked looking at Joe, "but personally I think there are far more important things to talk about. Kevin Mitchell's problem may be women but our problem is Matt Hayden and I think we should discuss what can be done about it."

"I agree, Angela," said Kate. "Men talk about the way we women gossip but believe me, they like a bit of scandal themselves!"

"I guess I did go on a bit," Gene confessed, "but you're right, Angela, I do have a problem and I'm open to any suggestions on how to deal with it."

Angela got up and poured some drinks, serving her guests first. When she came to Joe he looked into her face only to be met by an icy stare. She held it defiantly for a few moments, then returned to her seat.

"Now," she said, turning to Gene. "Why are you so worried about Matt Hayden?"

He took a sip from his glass then, putting it down on the coffee table, he leaned over and clasped his hands.

"We're neck and neck in the polls," he explained, "and he's gaining ground fast. Everything I come up with, he comes up with something that sounds better. Every promise I make, he makes one the same." He clenched his fist and sounded deadly serious. "I need to come up with something he hasn't thought of I need to get the edge!"

Angela looked at the floor for a few moments, then at Gene.

"I have an idea," she said, "but it's really up to Joe whether or not I can discuss it." "What is it?" asked Joe.

"The property."

He shrugged.

"I guess it's alright to tell Gene, he's an old friend."

Angela put her glass down and explained,

"Well, Joe bought some run-down property in his old neighbourhood and mine. It's being turned into a playground for the children and the buildings are being renovated into youth training centres. No one knows Joe is the benefactor. He wanted it that way. Now Gene, if you were to become involved, pay a few visits, talk to the young people, take an interest in what's going on, the t.v. and press would be onto it right away. They'd want to interview you to get your thoughts and comments about it. Just think of the media coverage you'd get, not to mention the personal appearances. You'd be reaching people in their own homes. If they see you doing something positive and worthwhile for the old neighbourhoods, then they'll know you care about them and they'll vote for you."

Gene slapped the palms of his hands on his knees.

"Jesus, Angela, that's it! That's the one thing nobody thought about, not even me. And as for Matt Hayden, he wouldn't even dream of it."

"Well, there's your edge," smiled Joe, as Gene got up and embraced Angela.

"I always knew you were smart," he said, "but this is one plan that could push the doors of the Senate right open for me." He looked at Joe. "And what about you?" he asked. "Don't you mind me taking the credit, Joe?" There was an earnest look on his face.

"Why should I mind?" Joe replied. "I'm more than willing to take a back seat, so long as it gets you what you want."

"I can hardly believe it," Gene smiled, shaking his head. "But I'll have to tell Dan Casey. Is that a problem?"

"No, I guess Dan isn't going to tell anyone what your plans are."

"You bet he won't. He'll be thrilled and listen ..." he pointed his finger, "if I get in I'm going to get government funding to do the same in other neighbourhoods. This is only the beginning."

Joe grinned,

"Don't tell me - tell the public!"

"Oh I will, Joe, believe me. I'll tell it to every t.v. and press interviewer I meet. That's my promise to everyone who votes for me and it's one promise I'm going to keep." As he went back to his seat, Kate put her arms around him and said,

"It's going to work, Gene, I just know it is! Young people are important, not just to their parents but to the future of our country. You'll have to show them you care. You're a parent yourself, after all."

"I know Kate, and I will. This is the chance I've been waiting for." He was silent for a few moments, then turned to Angela. "I'm going to need a slogan to make this work."

"I thought you already had one," Joe reminded him. "You know the one, 'If you forget where you've come from, you'll never know where you're going'."

"I'm using that one as it is, Joe. But need something else. Something that fits in with Angela's plan to make the public sit up and take notice of me."

They all stared at Joe, who immediately put his hands up.

"Hey, don't look at me! You're the ones with the college education," he reminded them. True! So they each lapsed into deep thought. Suddenly Angela stood up.

"I think I've got it," she said. "What about this - 'All kids are my kids'?"

Gene O'Brien repeated it to himself several times. Each time the smile on his face got bigger.

"Yeah, I like it Angela. It's a simple phrase that Matt Hayden can't use. He's not involved with the kids on the street, just the kids of the wealthy and the privileged.

"But all kids are the same to you, Gene. You don't make distinctions. You never have and you never will. You were once one of those kids yourself and look at you now. You're an example to the ordinary people, Matt Hayden isn't."

Gene threw his hands in the air and clenched his fists.

"We've got him, Angela," he yelled. "We've got Matt Hayden by the balls!!"

Joe couldn't help but laugh as Kate slapped her husband on the shoulder.

"Really, Gene, do you have to talk like that in front of Angela?" she snapped.

"I'm sorry, honey, I just got excited," he explained, reaching for his drink and glancing at Joe. "But after all," he murmured, "if she's married to you she'll understand. You were one guy who always liked to use yours!" he winked.

"Yeah and I still do. Believe me, that hasn't changed!"

Gene stood up and raised his glass.

"Here's to you, Little Lady. I knew from the first time I ever met you that somehow our paths would cross. But I never dreamed it would be for the Senate. I'm very grateful to you, to both of you. I can't thank you enough but if there's anything I can ever do for either of you, don't hesitate to ask." He took a sip then went over and shook Joe's hand firmly and embraced Angela warmly. "I'm going to keep every promise I make in this election," he assured her.

"I know," she nodded.

Kate got up and took Angela's arm.

"We're going to order a taxi and have a little chat. Excuse us," she smiled. As the two women were leaving the room Gene called out,

"Hey Irish!" Angela turned. "You're okay!" he nodded.

She smiled, then closed the door.

"Now, that's some woman," he sighed.

Joe smiled,

"I'm glad to see she didn't waste any of her education."

"You know, old buddy, I have a good feeling about her idea. It can really work. If this country ever decides it wants a lady President, she'll walk it!"

"Yeah, I'll say one thing about my wife, she has a good head on her shoulders. I'm proud of her."

"And so you should be," said Gene, returning to his seat. "Not many people thought it would last between you two, but they've all been proved wrong."

"Were you one of them?" enquired Joe.

"Not me! I know you too well. I knew back then that if Joe Morrelli was finally getting married it was because he'd found someone very special - and you did. You really love her, don't you?"

"Yeah I do," Joe admitted. "And I'll tell you something else. The worst thing that could ever happen to me is some young guy coming along and taking her away."

"Someone like Kevin Mitchell?"

Joe was surprised but Gene smiled.

"Oh come on Joe. I knew the first time you ever laid eyes on him you felt threatened. But believe me, as far as the Kevin Mitchell's of this world go, you have nothing to worry about. Angela is way ahead of them. She's too smart to fall for the smooth talk and the compliments guys like that dish out. If you think she's so clever in other ways, then why don't you give her some credit for being clever concerning other men? She loves you, Joe, and I think she's proved that. Take a tip from me, if you love her - trust her. Trust her completely because if you don't you're going to end up loosing her, and you'll only have yourself to blame."

Joe nodded,

"Yeah, you're right."

"Sure I am! And besides, Angela's got all the things she wants in a man right here. There are a lot of Kevin Mitchell's in this world but there's only one Joe Morrelli and she knows it!" He leaned over and patted Joe's arm, a roguish glint in his eye. "Mind you, Dan Casey would have loved someone like Angela for a niece-in-law! He's mighty disappointed with his nephew's choice in women."

"Oh really? Well I'm more than pleased with mine. I guess when it comes to getting what you want, Gene, we've both got the edge!"

Angela and Kate returned and the four friends talked and joked until the taxi arrived. As they all stood at the front door, Gene put a hand on Joe's shoulder.

"Thanks for everything, old buddy. I really enjoyed myself tonight."

"Then you'll have to come again real soon," Joe smiled.

Gene nodded and looked at Angela.

"I really do appreciate what you've both done for me. It's going to be one hell of a fight but I can win, and I want you right there along side me if I do."

She returned his smile.

"It's the perfect plan, Gene, and you're the right man to carry it through. The people like and respect you, and when the time comes they'll show it - by their votes."

"You're right, Angela," he agreed. "I came here tonight low on hope but I'm leaving with plenty, thanks to you. We'll give the opposition a run for their money!" He then turned to Joe. "You don't know how glad I am you married someone Irish. I've been telling you for years we're just as smart as the Italians and now I've finally proved it!" Joe smiled and asked,

"How come all you Irish want to be Senators and Presidents?"

"Because all you Italians get the job as Popes! Let's face it, Joe, have you ever heard of a Pope called 'Kennedy'?"

Joe shook his head.

"Jesus Gene, you have an answer for everything!"

"You're damn right I do," came the reply. "Why do you think I'm running for the Senate? At least we Irish have a chance of getting into 'The Whitehouse'. We sure don't have a hope in hell of getting into 'The Vatican!!"

The taxi driver sounded the horn.

"Come on, Gene, we'd better go," Kate smiled, taking his arm.

After all the goodbyes were said the O'Brien's headed for the taxi.

"Hey Gene!" called Joe.

Gene looked back.

"What?"

"I guess when you're elected you'll tell the Senate all about the famine in Ireland."

"I sure will and don't you forget to tell all your Italian friends to vote for me. Just remind them that when we were out hunting for a potato, they were probably sitting down to spaghetti and meatballs!"

The Morrellis stood waving until the taxi disappeared from the driveway, then they closed the door and walked across the entrance hall. Joe put an arm around Angela's shoulder.

"Now there goes one happy guy," he said, "and it's all thanks to you. That was one smart plan you came up with tonight."

"Well, he's a good man. Sincere and caring. He'll make a great Senator." As they approached the stairs, she stopped.

"You go on up, Joe."

"Aren't you coming too?"

"I'm going to have a word with Evie," she replied.

Joe had a puzzled look on his face as he watched her enter the kitchen. Climbing the stairs he thought she seemed rather quiet and subdued, not at all like someone who had successfully sorted out Gene O'Brien's campaign tactics. She didn't seem to be very happy.

Evie was putting away the last of the dishes as Angela laid an affectionate hand on her shoulder.

"I want to thank you for tonight, Evie," she smiled. "It was a wonderful meal and every one enjoyed it."

"Oh I'm so glad, Miss Angela. Is there anything else I can do for you?"

"No Evie. You've done quite enough for one night. Now why don't you go to bed and get some rest?"

"Well if you're sure."

"I'm sure," Angela insisted.

Evie smiled and nodded.

"Okay Miss Angela. Goodnight."

"Goodnight, Evie. And thank you again."

Once she had the kitchen to herself, she poured out some coffee and sat down at the table. A while later the door opened and Joe appeared in his dressing gown. Finding her deep in thought he joined her and asked

"Is anything the matter, Angel?"

She shook her head,

"No, I've just been thinking."

"About what?"

Angela sighed and leaned her elbow on the table. "You know, I think Gene O'Brien is really on his way now, Joe. I think he's going to win this election and take his seat in the Senate."

"Sure he is! Why wouldn't he, when he's got friends like you behind him?"

She gave a faint smile and said,

"Gene's got a lot of fiends, more influential than I am and they're all behind him. I think the time has come for me to bow out gracefully."

Joe stared at her, clearly surprised.

"Angel, you can't do that. Not now. Not after coming so far. Gene needs you and he wants you with him right to the end. You heard him say so yourself, tonight. You've done a great job for him and don't forget, everything he plans to do was your idea. It's only right that you should stick with the guy until it's all over. You can't throw the towel in now."

Angela was silent as she lowered her gaze. Joe studied her for a moment, then put out his hands and said.

"I just don't understand why you want to do this. There must be a reason." She looked straight at him.

"You know the reason Joe," she replied. "I didn't know Kevin Mitchell was back in the city and helping Gene O'Brien until tonight. When the fund raising dinners and functions start, he'll be there. I just can't ignore him, it wouldn't be right. After all, I worked with him on Dan Casey's committee and he was my friend." She paused, then continued, "If we're not there then we won't see him. I don't want any unpleasantness, Joe. I couldn't come through all that again and to be honest I won't!"

It was time to reassure her, so he stood up and cupped her face in his hands.

"You won't have to," he said softly, gazing into her eyes. "Listen to me, Angel. I made a big mistake that time and it almost cost me my marriage, but I'm not going to make that same mistake twice and that's a promise. Just give me the chance to prove it."

"But you don't like him, Joe, and when you see us together you imagine all sorts of things."

He shook his head,

"Not any more. I trust you. I trust you completely, with Kevin Mitchell or any other man. I want you to believe that."

"Do you really mean what you're saying?" she asked, almost innocently.

"Yeah I do because I'm the lucky one. They might talk to you and dance with you, but at the end of the night I'm the one you leave with. I realise that guys like Kevin Mitchell would want to go to bed with you and I don't blame them. But why should I be jealous of them? They're probably jealous of me because I'm the only man who's ever had that privilege." He kissed her. "Now, I'm not going to let you give everything up just because of how you think I might feel. You've worked too hard. I'm proud of you, Angel, and I'll be even prouder when you're standing at Gene O'Brien's side celebrating his win. And believe me, after what you advised him to do tonight I'd say it's in the bag! So I don't want to hear anymore talk of you leaving him."

Angela stood up, smiling.

"Why don't you give yourself some praise?" she asked. "It may have been my idea but it's your money that bought the property. You deserve the credit, you're the one who's paying for everything."

He held her close.

"Oh, let Gene have the praise and the credit. After all, I've got you!"

After leaving the kitchen and going upstairs, they went to Robert's room. As he looked down at the sleeping child, Joe couldn't help but think that this was one thing Kevin Mitchell didn't have and might never have - a son! He watched Angela kiss Robert and smooth his tousled hair. He was a proud and happy man, who loved his family above all else.

In their own bedroom, Joe lay on top of the bed with his hands clasped behind his head. He gazed admiringly, as Angela got undressed.

"Why are you staring at me like that?" she asked.

"Because I get a lot of pleasure out of it" he smiled. "You know, Angel, you've got the same figure now you had when I married you. That's saying a lot for a woman who never works out at a gym."

"I don't have to. I get enough work outs with you!"

"Yeah and you're getting a good deal. You get to stay in shape and you also get to enjoy yourself?" he grinned.

Angela shook her head in despair.

"Joe Morrelli, I always said you were a big head."

"Right now, that's not all that's big!"

She lifted a scatter cushion and threw it in his direction.

"I just don't know what I'm going to do with you!" she exclaimed.

He patted the bed with his hand.

"Well, if you come over I'll show you."

Joe's grin faded as he watched the thin, silk nightdress fall over her slender curves and cling to them. This was something else Kevin Mitchell didn't have. A loving wife, devoted and loyal. A marriage that was based not just on physical desire and passion, but on a union of souls. Kevin Mitchell would never know Angela the way Joe Morrelli did - and Joe would make damn sure of that!

Gene O'Brien didn't waste any time putting his plans into action. A few days later he turned up in the old neighbourhood to the surprise and delight of its residents, and he was followed by newspaper reporters and t.v. cameras. He showed great interest in what was going on, paying particular attention to the kids. He talked to them about the projects and listened to their views, picking up some of the smaller ones and holding them in his arms. He chatted and joked to the construction workers, who showed him around and pointed out all the many changes that were taking place. Gene shook hands with them and congratulated them on the work they were doing. He also shook hands with the large crowd of people who surrounded him, while the newspaper photographers flashed their cameras and the t.v. crews scrambled to get a few words from him for the '6o'clock News'.

When asked for his comments he was only too pleased to give them, springing into action by saying that he came from a part of that neighbourhood and how good it was to see something being done for the kids. How he was going to do the same in other areas and of course he rounded off his interviews with his catchy slogans, which brought cheers from the crowd and smiles from Gene. When his visit was over and after promising to be back, he got into his car and was driven away still smiling and waving. He turned around and saw the camera crews and reporters following him. His face lit up as he leaned back in his seat, the car now heading for Westmere Avenue. Gene O'Brien never dreamed his first visit would be so successful and he knew now that the best place to campaign was on the streets!

Father Ryker was waiting for him when he arrived and proudly gave him a guided tour. They were photographed shaking hands and Gene deliberately took a great interest in the youth hostel for the homeless, letting it be known that too many young people had no homes and were living on the streets. That's why they were getting into trouble and turning to prostitution and crime. But he was going to ensure that more hostels and training centres would be built in all areas (black and white) because - all kids, were his kids!

Gene went home a very happy man that day. He had achieved the trust of the people. They believed in him and he had received more media coverage in one day, than he had done throughout his campaign. For the first time in quite a while, he made the t.v. news and the front page of every newspaper had photos of him with his slogans written in large print above them.

After all the publicity, Gene knew he was on course for the Senate but he wasn't a man who made empty promises. He had genuinely been touched by the way the old neighbourhoods had been forgotten and the plight of some of the kids he had met. He wanted to get involved, not just because of the votes but because he was concerned for the people. So he made up his mind there was no time like the present. After a meeting with Dan Casey and getting his backing, Gene got his committee together to set up a fund raising dinner for donations to go towards more property developments. Joe gave him the use of 'The Safe Haven' and its staff for the occasion and Angela worked alongside Freddie Barrett, organising everything.

The dinner was by invitation only and on the night it proved to be a gathering of glitz and glamour. Everyone who was anyone turned out and as Gene and Kate greeted them, Angela noticed that most of their guests were wealthy, influential people. Gene O'Brien and Dan Casey were shrewd. They wanted "big bucks" to get their project started and it looked like they were going to get their wish. The who's who" of society were there. As the evening wore on, everyone was enjoying themselves - including Joe, Rooney and Angela, who looked stunning in a long, black evening gown, her hair swept up making her look all the more elegant. The champagne flowed as Gene O'Brien took the podium to deliver his speech.

He looked around at the large gathering, a hush falling on the entire room.

"I'd like to thank you all for coming. I never realised I had so many friends and I never realised you all wanted me to get into the Senate so badly!" he joked as they laughed. Then his face became serious. "I'm a family man. I love my kids and I want to do the best I can for them, just the way so many of you want to do the same for yours. But not all kids are as lucky as ours because a lot of their parents don't have the money to do it. A lot of them are in low paid jobs or on welfare. Some kids don't even have any parents to care." He paused. The silence had returned. "But we are going to try and change that tonight by showing that we care. I came from a poor neighbourhood and I know how hard it can be and unlike some other candidates, I won my scholarship. That's why I'm here today running for the Senate. I'm not ashamed of my background because a wise man once said, "If you forget where you've come from, you'll never know where you're going". He looked at Angela and smiled. "I never heard truer words." He looked around at all the nodding heads. Antonia dabbed her eyes with her handkerchief as Gene looked straight at Joe. "You know, a great friend of mine has always maintained, "you can take the man out of the Bronx but you can't take the Bronx out of the man!" When I went back to my old neighbourhood, I knew he was right." Gene nodded knowingly as Joe smiled and lowered his head, taking

Angela's hand and pressing it gently as tears stood in her eyes. Gene continued, "There are a lot of kids out there who need our help and I think we should give it to them. We can provide them with hope for the future by taking them off the streets and giving them the chance they never had. The chance to learn a trade, to excel in sports, to be educated. If we can help them do that, not only are we giving them the chance to succeed, we're helping them to become responsible citizens of this great country of ours. And it shouldn't matter what colour their skin is or what their religious beliefs are, because this country is big enough for all of us. This is America and it's the land of the free. Every kid has the God given right to live the American Dream." He put his hands out towards his spellbound audience. "I'm asking you tonight to please help them to do it. Don't take that away from them, just because they live in a poor neighbourhood or the wrong neighbourhood." He then pointed his hands towards himself and concluded in a loud voice, "All kids, are my kids!"

There was a thunderous applause as everyone rose to their feet and gave Gene O'Brien a standing ovation. He nodded and thanked them as Kate joined her husband, wiping the tears from her eyes and putting her arms around him proudly. As they left the podium together, Joe shook his head and smiled. He had to admit, that was one hell of a speech and it had brought the house down. Judging by the ongoing applause, Joe was left in no doubt that that speech would be a landmark in Gene O'Brien's career and get him the help he needed for the old neighbourhoods. It would also get him something else - his seat in the United States Senate!

When the podium was taken away, the band struck up the music. It was time for the guests to take to the temporary dance floor and enjoy the evening. It was also time to mingle. The first to make his way to Joe's table was Gene. As he sat down, Joe greeted him with a smile. "That was some speech. I don't think there was a dry eye amongst the ladies. To tell you the truth, you almost reduced me to tears!"

"Then it sure must have been a lot better than I thought it was!" joked Gene. Then he looked around and leaned over. "Believe me Joe, these people can afford it and what they give can be written off as expenses."

"You were a great success tonight Gene," Angela assured him.

"Well I couldn't have done it without you. I have a lot to thank both of you for. I won't ever forget what you did for me and that's a promise." he replied in a sincere tone. Rooney patted his arm.

"Maybe one day you'll run for President, Gene."

"Who knows. Nothing's impossible. Not when you've got the friends I have." At that moment, Antonia came through the crowd followed by Judge Thompson. "Gene darling!" she gushed, embracing him and kissing his cheek. "What a wonderful speech and so very true. Why, of course those kids need our help. Now listen, I've just had a marvellous idea."

Rooney was staring at her.

"That's a first!" he muttered.

Angela suppressed a smile. Joe shot him a sarcastic look.

"I think the centre should have a small drama school," Antonia continued. "I'll employ the teacher and in my spare time, I'll give lessons. Why, there must be dozens of budding young actors and actresses just waiting for a chance. And of course with me working on Broadway, I can give them the benefit of my experience. I would be like a role model for them."

Gene looked clearly surprised, as did everyone else! He put his hand up to his mouth and coughed, not knowing what to say and hoping Joe and Angela would comment. Joe did.

"I think that's a great idea, Gene. What do you think, Angel?"

"I agree."

Gene then looked at Antonia and smiled.

"I'm always open to suggestions and that's a good one. Who knows, we may even find another Marlon Brando."

"Or a Katherine Hepburn!" she quipped. "Well, what do you think?"

"Antonia, I think it will work."

"Darling, I just knew you would! When the centre opens I'll start it all up and get everything running. You just leave it to me." Gene took her hand and kissed it graciously. "Thank's Antonia."

"Oh, there's no need to thank me. After all, we mustn't forget where we came from. I'll see you all later," she waved, walking away. Judge Thompson had a look of bewilderment on his face, as he leaned over the table.

"I never knew she came from that old neighbourhood. Did you?"

There was silence as the company of four looked at each other.

Finally Joe admitted,

"Yeah, we did."

The Judge shook his head.

"I'd never have guessed it. Now there's one woman who can really keep a secret!"

"Well, it only goes to show just how good an actress she really is!" smiled Joe.

The Judge nodded and turned to go but before leaving, he congratulated Gene.

"Oh by the way, that was a great speech."

"Thanks Judge. I appreciate it."

As he watched Judge Thompson walk away, Gene shook his head.

"Jesus it must have been - to jog Antonia's memory! After just one speech I've made her come clean about where she came from and given her an idea for a drama school. You know something old buddy, I don't think I'll try for the White House after all. God knows what surprises she'd have in store."

Joe shrugged.

"Well, look on the bright side. If you ever get into the Oval Office, she can come and perform for you."

"Thank's Joe, but as much as I like Antonia I have to admit I'm a Frank Sinatra man myself "

"Aren't we all!" chuckled Joe. "Aren't we all!"

Rooney was thinking aloud.

"Could you picture Antonia in the White House?" he asked.

Joe looked at him.

"Believe me, Rooney, when you've known her as well as I have, you could picture her anywhere."

He then looked at Gene and both men began to laugh.

"Well, I'd better go." Gene got up and took Angela's hand. "Don't forget to save me a dance, little lady," he smiled.

"I will."

After Gene O'Brien had made his way through the crowd, a waitress came with another bottle of champagne. Joe poured three glasses.

"What do you say we all really enjoy ourselves tonight? Especially you, Angel. You've earned it, helping Gene and getting this place ready."

"I'll drink to that," agreed Rooney, holding up his glass.

Joe lifted his.

"To my wife," he proposed proudly, smiling and taking a few sips.

As he casually looked around the tables he caught sight of Antonia, surrounded by her jet-set friends and loving every minute of their attention. She posed happily for them, while poor Judge Thompson sat waiting in the wings looking uncomfortable if not unhappy.

Joe studied the scene, then said,

"You know something, Rooney? I'm sure glad I didn't marry an actress."

Rooney followed his gaze and watched with him.

"Amen!" he smiled, raising his glass once more.

Rooney sat tapping his feet to the music, then looked across at Angela.

"What do you say we have a twirl on the dance floor?" he smiled.

"I'd love to," she replied, without hesitation.

As they both got up from the table, Joe looked around.

"I'm going to ask Antonia," he informed them.

When the music had ended, Angela took Rooney's hand.

"Follow me. There's someone I'd like to introduce you to." She led him towards one of the tables and stopped. "Rooney, I'd like you to meet Rachel Levine. Rachel, this is Rooney. He's one of the family!" she smiled. The instant attraction was obvious. They both liked what they saw.

"I'm pleased to meet you," he said, putting out his hand.

"Same here," she nodded returning his gesture. As Angela turned to walk away she whispered, "It's up to you now, Rooney."

He wasted no time!

"Would you like to dance, Rachel?" he asked

"Yes I would."

They held hands as they walked onto the dance floor. As he took her in his arms he thought of how attractive she was, with her blue eyes and shoulder length brown hair. She wore an expensive evening gown of pale blue satin, which complimented her eyes and figure.

By now, Angela had made her way back to her husband and sat down.

"Where's Rooney?" asked Joe.

She nodded towards the crowded dance floor and he turned around to see Rooney holding Rachel closely and gazing into her face, captivated.

Joe watched them for a little while then said,

"You know, Angel, I've only ever seen him look that way at one other woman."

"You mean there was someone before?"

"Yeah, there was someone."

"Who was she?"

"Oh, just a girl he met."

"What happened?"

Joe shrugged, determined not to give anything away. "It didn't work out. She met some other guy."

Angela looked back towards the dance floor.

"Well, he must have been very special if she let someone like Rooney go."

"I guess he was," he replied, lifting his glass. "Who is that girl anyway?"

"Rachel Levine. Her father's a wealthy business man. Maybe you've heard of him, Samuel Levine?"

Joe thought for a moment, then shook his head.

"No, I can't say I have."

Angela continued,

"Well, he's Jewish and owns a large clothing firm. Her mother is American. They're really nice people, Joe. There's Rachel and an older brother, Aaron. He's married and lives in Los Angeles. They have a business out there too."

Joe had become quite interested.

"How come you know so much about them?" he asked.

"Because Rachel's mother, Joan, was on Dan Casey's committee."

He smiled broadly.

"You know Angel, I never thought I'd see the day when you'd know people in this city that I didn't!"

"Neither did I," she admitted.

It was quite a while before Rooney returned to his seat. Joe winked playfully at Angela.

"What took you so long?" he enquired.

"Oh, Rachel was just introducing me to her parents," Rooney informed him smugly.

"Oh really? I guess her old man was giving you the once over before he invites you to dinner."

"It's not like that Joe."

"I'll bet you'll get your feet under the table before the week's out. And who knows, if you're lucky you might even score before the night's out!"

"She's not that kind of girl!" snapped Rooney.

"How do you know?" asked Joe, trying hard not to smile.

"I just do - that's all!"

As the night wore on, Rooney kept disappearing and surfacing on the dance floor with Rachel.

Eventually he would come back and join Joe and Angela, but every few minutes he'd gaze over towards the Levine's table.

Joe leaned towards Rooney.

"Why don't you go over and sit beside her. It would save all that walking backwards and forwards every five minutes!"

Rooney shook his head,

"I don't like to and besides, I came with you and Angela."

"Well, don't let that stop you. Every time I turn around to talk to you, you aren't here anyway. You're up and down off that chair so often, you're making me dizzy."

"Oh, very funny!" smirked Rooney.

Joe smiled slyly,

"I'm beginning to think you're in love. Either that or the chef made a mistake with your meal and gave you a helping of jumping beans. You haven't sat still all night."

Rooney glared at him.

"You're the one who said we should all enjoy ourselves - remember?"

"Yeah," Joe nodded, "but I didn't think you were going to give me indigestion doing it."

"Now listen Joe ..."

Before Rooney could finish, Rachel stood before him smiling.

"My father wants to know if you would like to come to our table and join us?"

"Why sure he would!" smiled Joe. "Isn't that right, Rooney?"

Rooney's mouth was still lying open as he nodded in agreement. Peeved, he turned to Joe and whispered,

"I can speak for myself, you know!"

"Oh yeah? Well, up until now you're not doing such a great job," came the whispered reply.

Rachel turned her attention to Joe.

"You must be Angela's husband. My father says you're an important business man, Mr. Morrelli."

They shook hands.

"That's right. And this is my business partner," he smiled, nodding at Rooney.

"Really? He never said." Rachel was impressed.

"He's very modest," Joe explained.

Without further ado, Rooney rose to his feet rather hastily.

"I'd love to join you!" Then he looked at Joe and Angela. "Excuse me."

"Delighted to." Joe really meant it.

Rooney threw him a sarcastic glance as he and Rachel walked away. But Joe wasn't finished.

"See you later, Rooney." he called. Rooney turned and grinned,

"Joe, somehow I don't think you will!"

As they disappeared through the crowd, Joe and Angela couldn't help but laugh.

"I think I can safely say we will have the rest of the evening to ourselves," he said. "And it looks like we will be going home without Rooney."

"He looks very happy," smiled Angela. "And so do you."

"That's because I am! It's good to see him with someone he really likes, and all this very fine champagne is putting me in a romantic mood. Would you like to dance, Mrs. Morrelli?" he smiled, gazing into her eyes.

She leaned over, her lips almost touching his.

"Well, you've danced with just about everyone else, you know. I thought you'd never ask."

"Angel," he whispered, "I like to keep the best till the end."

He got up and pulled out her chair. Then taking her hand, he led her towards the dance floor.

As they manoeuvred their way past the crowded tables, a voice called out,

"Angela!"

She and Joe looked around to see a smiling Kevin Mitchell. Angela's fingers tightened in her husband's hand, as she stood rooted to the spot forcing a smile. She didn't know what to do, so Joe acted quickly by placing his other hand on her back and steering her gently towards Kevin Mitchell's table.

"It's been a long time, Angela. How are you?" asked Kevin getting to his feet.

"Oh, I'm fine," she informed him.

His eyes swept over her in an admiring glance.

"You haven't changed a bit," he insisted. "You look terrific."

"Thank you," she replied, looking a little embarrassed.

Joe stood surveying the scene, as Kevin extended his hand in greeting.

"Nice to meet you again, Mr. Morrelli."

"Same here," he lied, turning to shake hands with Dan Casey and Alma.

"Good to see you again, Senator."

"And it's a pleasure to see you, Joe. It's been a while but Gene here keeps me up to date on everything," he winked. "What did you think of his speech?"

Joe leaned his hands on the table and smiled,

"I think after tonight, Matt Hayden has a lot of running to do to catch up with him."

Dan nodded, "That's just the way we want it, Joe."

"Let's just say I've got the edge!" beamed Gene.

Out of the corner of his eye, Joe saw Dan Casey give his nephew a sharp look. Kevin responded immediately.

"Angela, Mr. Morrelli, I'd like to introduce you to my wife, Vivienne."

After exchanging a few pleasantries, Joe tried to reclaim Angela for the next dance. But Kevin beat him to it.

"Angela, would you like to dance?" he asked. "That's if you don't mind, Mr. Morrelli." Joe did mind. He minded a great deal but he couldn't say it, not in front of the rest of the company. So he shrugged his shoulders.

"No, why should I mind?"

Kevin escorted Angela onto the dance floor, just the way Joe had hoped to.

As the music played they held each other and swayed slowly. Joe could only watch helplessly. After a few moments, he turned his gaze back to the table to find Gene O'Brien staring at him. Gene shook his head slightly at Joe, nodded in Vivienne's direction, then at the dance floor.

Joe finally got the message!

"Would you like to dance, Mrs. Mitchell?" he asked/

"Why I'd love to," came the reply.

They danced and made small talk while Joe kept a watchful eye on Kevin who was engaged in deep conversation with Angela.

He had to admit the fact that Kevin Mitchell was still a very handsome guy and his smile had a boyish quality. That was the one thing that had always needled Joe. Kevin Mitchell had a smile that could melt any woman's heart - and he knew it! He used it to his advantage all the time. Any woman would find it irresistible.

As the music ended, Joe walked Vivienne back to the table and waited for a few moments. However, it seemed that Kevin was determined to keep Angela on the dance floor, so he returned to his own seat feeling a bit rattled. He'd almost reached it when he felt a hand on his shoulder. It was Gene O'Brien.

"Joe, listen to me, old buddy. Don't let him get to you. If it wasn't Angela he was trying to smooth talk, it would be someone else."

"I don't think so Gene," he replied, shaking his head. "And neither do you."

"O.k. so he happens to like your wife. So what?"

"So I don't like the way he looks at her! And he knew damn well I was taking her up to dance."

"I know." nodded Gene. "But does Angela like him enough to do the dirty on you? I don't think so and neither do you! She's only being polite. You've got to trust her Joe. And more importantly, show her you trust her."

"I guess you're right. But you said yourself he had a string of models."

"Yeah, that's right. It just goes to show you how gullible they are. But Angela isn't a model and she sure as hell isn't gullible! She wants to be number one in a man's life, not number three or four. If anyone should know that, you should."

Joe looked towards the dance floor and saw Kevin having yet another dance with his wife. Nodding towards them he said,

"I think if he had his way, he'd make her number one."

"Maybe, but Angela loves you - not him! So why don't you show him?"

"What do you mean?"

Gene smiled and replied,

"Play him at his own game. After all, you own this place. Send up a special request for some of your favourite music and take your wife up to dance. Show him you're both still in love and happily married. You know what I mean," he winked.

"Yeah, I know what you mean," Joe nodded as Gene patted his shoulder and walked away.

After finding Freddie Barrett and having a few quiet words in his ear, Joe returned to his seat. The band took a five minute break, so Angela came back to join him. She looked at him hesitantly and in a low voice said,

"I'm sorry about our dance, Joe."

"No problem honey. Here have some more champagne."

He poured two glasses but instead of drinking, Angela lowered her gaze. Clasping her hands, she studied them silently for a few moments. Then she looked up at him.

"Perhaps we'd better go," she said.

"Why?" asked Joe. "I'm enjoying myself, aren't you?"

She didn't reply, only forced a smile. He leaned towards her.

"Listen Angel, I'm not going to cause a scene, if that's what's bothering you."

"But what about when we get home?"

"I'm not going to cause a scene there either. I'm a much wiser man than I used to be, so stop worrying. Please."

He gently put his hand over hers and gave her a reassuring smile. Deep inside he felt bad that the scars of what had happened that night had never really healed, not for her anyway. She had a look of dread on her face and what made him feel even worse, was that she seemed almost frightened. He couldn't blame her. He had acted so badly back then and his temper had been uncontrollable, especially the last time he'd encountered Kevin Mitchell. But Joe was determined that history should not repeat itself. As the band prepared to play again, the lead singer came to the microphone.

"Ladies and gentlemen, we would like to play a special request for Mr. and Mrs. Morrelli."

Angela couldn't hide her obvious surprise.

Joe laughed a little, then said,

"Do you honestly think I would let that guy steal my dance? Come on, they're playing our song."

There was loud applause as they made their way onto the dance floor. Joe wrapped her in his arms, while she placed hers around his neck. They danced slowly to "Strangers In The Night".

"Did you ask them to play that?" she asked.

"You bet! Are you surprised?"

"Yes, I am. I never expected it in front of all these people."

He gazed into her eyes.

"The people don't matter, Angel. As far as I'm concerned there's only you and me, just like that first night in Mario's."

"I love you, Joe Morrelli," she smiled.

"And I love you."

Instinctively they embraced to kiss, regardless of the onlookers. Just as he was closing his eyes, Joe threw a quick glance towards Gene O'Brien's table. Kevin Mitchell was watching them together, a stunned look on his face.

"That ought do it!" thought Joe, closing his eyes completely and enjoying the warm and passionate response that only Angela could provide.

As the weeks went by, Gene O'Brien was rapidly gaining ground in the opinion polls. He had kept his promise to the people of the old neighbourhoods, by returning to visit them and keep a watchful eye on the development projects. He had also raised enough funds to further this scheme in other areas and all of this was making him a very popular man. So popular in fact, that wherever he went crowds of people were waiting to see him and shake his hand. He was becoming quite a celebrity and a lot of people felt sure they were looking at a future president. That's why he always drew such great crowds. When the time came for the opening of the new playground and centres in Joe's old neighbourhood and Westmere Avenue, he and Angela stayed out of the limelight and let Gene do the honours. Joe arranged for Billy "Wild Man" Wilson to show up at the gym, which brought a huge response from newspapers and t.v. stations. Billy had become a big name in sporting circles and he assured all concerned that he would visit the gym regularly to give the kids support and advice. He and Gene posed for photographs, shaking hands and smiling happily.

In the playground the t.v. cameras followed Gene around as he pushed the smaller children on the swings and lifted others off the slides. He even shot some basketball with a newly formed team calling themselves "O'Brien's Boys."

At Westmere Avenue, he and Father Ryker opened the youth hostel and training centre. Everyone listened as Father Ryker sang Gene's praises, telling the crowds that if more politician's were like him the country would have fewer problems and more stability. Photographs depicting all these events were in the front pages of all the newspapers and even appeared in the glossy magazines. Everyone wanted to interview Gene O'Brien and write about him.

His was a regular face on t.v. and he was fast becoming a household name, with his slogans being well known by everyone.

As the weeks passed into months he took a clear lead over his opponent and it was obvious to all around him that he had won the respect, trust and admiration of the people. At this stage in the campaign it would be true to say that he was proving to be, in Angela's own words, the right man for the job and the people's choice. Gene O'Brien was on route to the Senate and it looked like nothing and no one was going to stop him.

Angela and Evie stood chatting in the kitchen while Joe sat at the table with a cup of coffee and a newspaper. Robert arrived home from school. He was eight years old now. Evie's face lit up when she saw him and smiling broadly she held her arms out to him.

"How did my beautiful baby get on today?" she asked. "Have you got a hug for Evie?"

Robert always hugged her, but not today. He backed away and stood silently looking at her. Evie grew worried.

"Why, what's the matter with you honey? Don't you feel well?"

Robert still didn't speak, so Angela knelt down and put her hands on his waist.

"Robert, are you alright? Tell me, did something happen at school?"

Joe put the paper down.

"What's the matter, son?" he asked in a concerned voice. "Answer your mother."

Robert's bottom lip began to quiver and his eyes filled with tears.

"David Baker said I'm a nigger lover!" he blurted out and then began to cry. "David says his dad says niggers shouldn't live with white people like us. His dad said they should know their place and white boys shouldn't let niggers touch them."

Joe got up from the table.

"David's dad seems to have an awful lot to say!"

Evie put her hands up to her face and burst into tears.

"Oh, Miss. Angela!" she sobbed, "I wouldn't have anyone hurt that baby for the world. If I leave, no one will ever be able to say that to him again."

Angela's face was white with temper.

"Evie, you are not leaving this house! You are a member of this family and I can promise you that after today no one will ever remark on it again. Come on, Robert." She took Robert's hand and headed for the kitchen door.

"Where are you going?" asked Joe.

"We're going to David Baker's house!" replied Angela angrily.

They both marched down the driveway as Joe watched from the patio. Angela wanted to walk. It would give her time to prepare herself for the confrontation with David's father. They made their way along the very select avenue and up the path to the Baker's house.

Tom Baker answered the door.

"I want a word with you!" Angela said in a polite but angry voice and told Tom Baker what his son had said.

"Yes, it's true," he admitted. "I said it and I'll say it again. We don't need niggers around here."

"And we don't need people like you!" Angela retorted.

Tom's wife, Barbara, came to the door. Her platinum blond hair was piled high on top of her head and her make up looked like it had been applied by a trowel!

"My husband only employs young, white staff," she said, looking adoringly at Tom.

"And we all know why!" said Angela. "So he can screw them when you're not around! That's why none of them will stay." Angela became even more polite. "My husband may employ a negress but even before he did, he never screwed his own staff"

Barbara Baker's mouth fell open. Angela continued,

"Your husband might not want negro's living around here, but that doesn't mean he's not partial to them in other ways! From what I've heard his car is pretty well known for curb crawling on the other side of town. And there's one more thing, Tom Baker. My husband is Joe Morrelli. He's Italian. And if he has to pay you a visit you'll be looking for somewhere else to live. So if you want to stay here, I suggest you keep your big mouth shut and tell your son to do the same. If not, it won't be me you'll be talking to next time!"

Angela turned and still clutching Robert's hand, came back down the path leaving Tom and Barbara Baker speechless.

On the way home she looked down at Robert.

"Listen son. If you really care for someone the colour of their skin or their religion doesn't matter. You'll understand all that as you get older."

She stopped and took his face in her hands.

"Evie loves you more than anything. She's helped me to look after you since you were a little baby and she's been loyal to us all. I know you're getting to be a big boy now, so if you don't want to hug and kiss anymore it's o.k. But even age shouldn't stop you from showing people you care. Evie's black, Robert, but I'm Irish and your father's Italian. There are some people who aren't exactly crazy about us!"

Even though Robert was just a child, he understood what his mother was trying to say.

"Is David Baker still my friend?" he asked.

"Well, we'll talk about that later," came the reply.

When they arrived back into the kitchen, Joe and Evie were sitting at the table. Without a word of encouragement, Robert rushed over and flung his arms around Evie's neck, hugging her tightly.

"Well, that's that!" said Angela. "I don't think we'll be hearing any more from Mr. Baker or his son."

"Come on son," said Joe. "You and me will take a walk in the garden with the dog." Robert released his grip on Evie and went outside with his father, leaving the women to talk. He clutched Joe's hand tightly as they both strolled along the little winding path, watching Pal chase his shadow.

After a few moments Robert asked,

"Dad, what does the word 'screw' mean?"

Joe looked down at him.

"Where did you hear that word?"

"Mom said it when she was at the Baker's house."

"Oh, what exactly did she say?" asked Joe, a little amused as well as surprised.

"Well, she told Mrs. Baker that the only reason Mr. Baker had white staff was because he could screw them when she wasn't around."

Joe grinned from ear to ear.

"Did she now! And what did they say?"

"Nothing. But what did mom mean?"

"Well son, it's kind of hard to explain," said Joe, searching for the appropriate words. "It's like making someone do something that might not be the right thing to do - at the time."

It was at times like this when Joe was glad he was a business man and not a diplomat!

"Oh," said Robert, "now I know why mom told them none of their staff would stay. Mr. Baker must have made them do things that weren't right."

"Yeah well, your mom's one smart lady!"

Robert sighed,

"I don't think David Baker will be my friend anymore. But I don't care!"

"What makes you say that?"

"Well, mom says I'd be better off without him. She says if he grows up like his father, he'll be able to use his balls but not his brains!"

Joe turned his head away and laughed quietly. Some of Joe Morrelli had certainly rubbed off on his wife, he thought. And he was proud that with her Irish temper and Italian lingo, she was coming into her own. Nobody was going to get the better of Angela Morrelli!

It was just after 2 a.m. when the phone rang in Joe's bedroom. He rubbed the sleep from his eyes and stretching out his hand, he lifted the receiver.

"Hello," he said in a low voice. As he listened to the caller, a worried look came over his face. "Just stay calm!" he answered loudly.

Angela gave a startled jump and switching on the light, turned around.

"Joe, what's wrong? Who is it?" she asked anxiously.

He put his hand up and looked at her. She was silent. Then he covered the receiver with the same hand.

"It's Antonia," he whispered. "Of course I'm still here!" he snapped, returning to the caller. "Where do you think I'd be at two o'clock in the morning?" He sounded annoyed and glanced at the phone sarcastically. "No I'm not shouting at you, Antonia. No I'm not angry with you either." He looked at Angela and cast his eyes up towards the ceiling. "O.k, now calm down and listen to me. Don't say anything to anyone until I get there. I'm on my way."

He put the receiver down and pulling back the bedclothes, he jumped out of bed. A pair of trousers and a shirt were hastily snatched from the unit and Joe struggled to put them on.

"Joe what's going on?" demanded Angela. "Is she in some kind of trouble?"

"That would be an understatement. She's in big trouble! She was at a party tonight and the joint was raided. They were all busted for drugs. Right now she's down town in the narcotics division and she's hysterical!"

"Did she have any drugs?"

Joe shook his head,

"No, Antonia has never done drugs but some of her high flying friends have. The cops were watching the place." He hit the unit with his hand in dismay more than temper. "Jesus Angel, she's a friend of Gene O'Brien's, she campaigns for him. She opened the drama school, for Christ's sake! If this gets out, Matt Hayden will have a field day. It will ruin Gene's chances and everything we've worked for, not to mention Antonia. It will almost certainly destroy her career. I tried to warn her but she wouldn't listen. Now she's sitting in a police precinct like a criminal with the same rights as everyone else there - one phone call!"

"But why didn't she phone her lawyer?"

"Because it's going to take more than a lawyer to get her out of this mess and she knows it. If she involves a lawyer she'll have to go to court. By involving me she won't have to!"

"What do you mean?" Angela was puzzled.

By now Joe was putting on his jacket.

"I mean, this calls for people a lot higher up than a lawyer. Like a District Attorney and a Judge. Both of who just happen to be friends of mine. If I can pull a few strings, I can get her out of there and make sure nobody knows about it."

"Do you think you can do it, Joe? It's a serious offence."

"I know but I'm sure going to try. There's a lot at stake here, Angel . If I don't pull this off and she's charged, she'll have to go to court and it's going to mean big headlines. That would give Matt Hayden the chance to implicate Gene and dish the dirt he could never find before. I'd better go honey. I'll see you later." He went over to the bed and kissed her cheek, then turning to leave the room he shook his head. "Damn it!" he muttered. "I've said it before and I'll say it again - for an actress, her timing's lousy!"

The lift carried them from floor to floor and as it did so, Antonia became more restless. "I don't like this Joe. I don't like it at all. I think we're making a big mistake."

"Listen," he explained. "I got you out on bail but he's the only one who can get you off the hook!"

"Well, what do I say to him?"

"You don't say anything. You let me do the talking."

"And what am I supposed to do?"

"You're an actress - so act!"

The lift doors finally opened and after ringing the bell to one of the apartments, they were greeted by Judge Thompson.

"Antonia dear....and Joe. Please come in."

Although he'd been expecting them he really didn't know the full story about the night's events concerning Antonia's arrest, so Joe filled him in on all the details. He sat with them, listening intently and sympathetically, patting Antonia's hand every time she held a handkerchief to her eyes.

"Well Judge, that's about it," Joe concluded. "What do you think?"

"Why I think it's all been a terrible mistake!" came the reply.

"Judge," sniffed Antonia, "you've known me long enough to know that I don't do drugs. I never did and never will."

"Of course my dear. Now don't you worry. I'm sure we can get this mess sorted out before morning. Just you leave everything to me."

He rose to his feet and looked at Joe. "I'll just go and make some phone calls," he said. On reaching the lounge door, he paused and turned. "There's just one thing ..."

"What?" asked Joe.

"Well in order to make things more convincing in all of this, I will have to say that Antonia and I are more than just good friends."

Antonia opened her mouth but before she could utter a word, Joe said,

"Whatever you say, Judge. We're behind you one hundred percent. Isn't that right Antonia?"

When she saw the warning look in his eyes, she gave a faint smile and nodded.

"Excellent!" exclaimed the Judge, then left the room.

Antonia's expression changed.

"I knew it! I knew it! 'More than just good friends'," she mimicked. "I said it was a mistake coming here! God knows what he'll tell people!"

As she ranted on, Joe got up and started searching the room. He looked behind chairs, scatter cushions, curtains. In the end she could contain herself no longer.

"Joe, what are you doing?" she snapped.

He spun round, an angry look on his face.

"I'm looking for your arty farty friends! Funny how they're never around when you need them, isn't it?" He came across the room and stood before her. "So what if he tells a few people you're his girlfriend? Being the girlfriend of a judge is no mean feat." Joe pointed towards the door. "He happens to be a very important man in this city, Antonia, and right now he's got your reputation in one hand and your career in the other. So you watch what you say and how you say it!"

Antonia bowed her head. She knew Joe was right. He returned to his seat and the room remained silent until Judge Thompson appeared again.

"Well, I think we can say that tonight was a clear case of wrongful arrest," he smiled. "Even the authorities make mistakes!"

Antonia breathed a deep sigh of relief as Joe stood up and shook the Judge's hand.

"What can I say?" he asked.

"What you always say Joe. What are friends for?"

"Thanks Judge. We won't forget this, will we Antonia?"

"No. No we won't," she replied, her smile sincere.

"Well, we won't take up any more of your time, Judge. We'll be going now," said Joe looking down at her.

But Antonia didn't move. Both men waited, then she said,

"Actually Joe, I was going to stay with Judge Thompson for a while. That is, if it's o.k. with him."

The Judge couldn't believe his luck!

"I think I have a bottle of wine in the cooler," he said, excitedly. "I'll go and get it!" As he did so, Joe bent down.

"Are you sure about this Antonia?" he asked.

"Yes," she insisted. "You'll be going home to a wife and child, Joe. I'll be going home to an empty apartment."

He kissed her affectionately on the forehead.

"I guess we all need somebody," he said softly.

Judge Thompson returned with the wine and two glasses, so Joe took his leave of them. He walked out of the building and over to his car. As he put the key in the lock, he looked up at the Judge's apartment and smiled. He was glad Antonia had decided to stay behind. Like he'd said, "We all need somebody".

Joe opened the kitchen door.

"Evie, have you seen Angel?"

"She's gone to do some shopping, Mr. Joe."

"Well, when she gets back would you tell her I'd like a word with her? I'll be in my study."

"Surely," Evie nodded, as she returned to her baking.

About an hour later a gentle tapping could be heard on the study door and as it opened slowly, Angela's face peered around it.

"Evie said you wanted to see me."

Joe put the pen down and motioned to her. "Come on in and sit down," he invited.

She looked surprised as she closed the door.

"You must have something very important to tell me if I'm being invited into your sanctuary!" she smiled, taking a seat facing him and looking around.

"Well," he explained, "it's the one place in this house that's totally private. And it's the best place for what I'm about to say."

He leaned back in the leather chair.

"You look every inch the business man Joe." she observed.

"Well right now I have other things on my mind besides business. There's something I'd like to discuss with you." He studied her thoughtfully for a few moments then said,

"You know Angel, the night I had to go down town to sort things out for

Antonia, I got talking to a couple of guys. Jeff Lang was one of them. Actually, we were talking about Gene O'Brien."

Angela looked at him, puzzled.

"I don't understand," she said.

"Well, Gene's way ahead in the polls, mainly because of what we did in the old neighbourhood. But it hasn't gone down too well with some of the big guys. There aren't as many kids hanging around the streets to deal for them or run errands." He looked at her earnestly. "Did you know Gene O'Brien was getting hate mail?"

"No, no I didn't!" she replied obviously shocked.

"Yeah well, he is and the police are taking it seriously. Everywhere he goes now, he has a bodyguard - but you don't!"

"What do you mean?"

"Angel, what I mean is, this city is full of nuts and weirdos. What's to prevent one of them from walking into those campaign headquarters and opening up with a gun? Or stalking you because you're working for Gene. What if some crazy lunatic showed up here when me and the guys aren't around. I worry about you, Angel, and I worry about my son. Both of you are unprotected when you're alone."

Angela cried,

"Joe stop it! You're frightening me!"

"Honey I don't want to frighten you but I want to make you aware of the dangers out there," he replied in a calming voice.

"Well, what do you suggest we do?" she asked. "Hire a bodyguard?"

Joe shook his head and opened the desk drawer.

"No, I suggest you learn to use this."

He put a gun down on the desk in front of her. Angela stared at it in horror.

"You can't be serious."

"I'm perfectly serious."

"Joe Morrelli, my father was murdered in cold blood by one of those. Now you want me to learn how to shoot so I can do the same to someone else. How could you. I won't do it!"

Tears came to her eyes. Joe leaned over and rested his arms on the desk.

"Angel, I'm not asking you to murder anyone. Listen to me, please."

"I don't believe this!" she interrupted, shocked and upset.

He took both her hands in his and held them tightly.

"Listen to me," he repeated in a serious, determined tone. "I'm a wealthy man and I've only got one son. You don't know how ruthless these people are. They could kidnap him and believe me, no matter how much money I'd pay I'd never get him back alive. I know the way these nuts operate, you don't. If anyone comes onto my property or into my home to endanger you or Robert, all you have to do is shoot them in the legs. If you do that they can't run so they won't be going anywhere. Then all you do is call the cops." There was silence in the room as she lowered her eyes.

"Believe me Angel," he continued, "It's for your own protection, that's all. I have some business trips coming up and I'd feel a lot happier if you could defend yourself and Robert, when I'm not here. What do you say?"

She looked up at him.

"Do you really think something like that could happen?"

Joe nodded,

"There's always that chance and I don't like to take chances, not where my wife and son are concerned. You're well known in this city for helping Gene O'Brien, so you've got to be one step ahead of anyone who doesn't like him or want him to get into the Senate." He let go of her hands gently and watched. Angela stared at the gun, slowly she moved one of her hands towards it, then quickly drew it back.

"It's o.k. honey. There's nothing to be scared of. It's like a lot of other things in life, you only use it when you have to."

Without taking her eyes off it she asked,

"Who's going to teach me?"

Joe was relieved.

"That won't be a problem! I know a guy who gives lessons, mostly to women. He shows them how to protect themselves, where to aim, how to wound someone without doing much damage, just enough to save your life. Believe me, Angel, you'd be doing yourself a favour and an even bigger favour for Robert."

He waited for her reaction. After a long pause, she reached over and lifted the gun. She gazed at him, a look of sadness in her moist eyes. She nodded,

"Alright Joe, I'll learn how to use it."

"I'm glad. And I'm relieved you see things from my point of view. I don't ever want you to feel threatened by anyone, when I'm not around. A gun can be a good friend in the right hands, always remember that."

Angela stood up, clutching it tightly with a mixture of dread and acceptance. Joe came around the desk and took her in his strong arms.

"It's just a precaution, Angel. You probably won't ever need to use it."

"I hope you're right."

"I just want you to feel safe at all times. I love you too much to let anything happen to you. You must believe that."

"I do Joe."

They kissed tenderly, then she left the room in silence.

Joe stood, staring thoughtfully towards the door. He knew how she must be feeling. She would always remember what had happened to her father and now he was asking her to keep the one thing that was responsible for his tragic death. The one thing that would serve as a constant reminder for something he'd always hoped she'd forget. But it was for the best. He was being cruel to be kind. There was a lot of slime out there, roaming the streets of New York. There was a lot of slime everywhere. He wanted Angela to be able to take care of herself in any situation. What he told her was true but there was something he didn't mention.

Joe knew he wasn't getting any younger and he wouldn't always be there for Angela. She depended on him but the day would come when she'd have to depend on herself. He wanted to prepare her for the future as well as the present and when the time came he would do the same for his son, and if he wasn't spared to do it for him Angela would. She would protect their son at all costs and their son was always uppermost in his thoughts. Nothing must ever happen to Robert - Joe Morrelli had his reasons!

From the night of Gene O'Brien's charity dinner, Rooney had been seeing a lot of Rachel Levine. Joe and Angela had been out with them on several occasions as a foursome and both of them had been to dinner at Roseberry Avenue. Rooney was always smiling and acting very much like a man in love.

Everyone was happy for him.

That morning at eleven, Joe arrived into the kitchen dressed up and ready to go out for a day of business meetings. He looked around.

"Where's Rooney?" he asked.

"He hasn't shown yet, Boss." replied Frankie, leaning his back against the sink.

"Well, I can't go without him I need him today."

Joe went over and poured himself a cup of coffee. He took a seat at the table.

Al came in.

"I'm ready when you are, Boss."

"I'm waiting for Rooney," Joe informed him "Why don't you both grab a cup of coffee?"

"It's not like him to be late," remarked Al.

"Well, maybe he got held up."

A few minutes later, the door opened and Rooney came in.

"Sorry I'm late Joe. I overslept."

Al raised his eyebrows as Rooney passed Frankie and muttered,

"Yeah, and he probably did it while he was over some woman!"

"Did you say something?" Rooney snapped. Joe intervened by putting up his hand.

"It's no big deal Rooney, we've got all day. Come on and sit down. Hey, Al, get him a cup of coffee too."

Al poured one cup and re-filled his own. Bringing them both to the kitchen table, he sat down facing Rooney.

"You must have had a late night," he beamed. "Was it a night on the town or a quiet night at home?"

Rooney stared at him.

"Al, why are you so interested in my love life?"

"Because he doesn't have one of his own!" grinned Frankie. Al turned, looking at him sarcastically.

"Well, maybe that's because I don't get the chance to go to important parties."

"What's that supposed to mean?" asked Joe.

"Nothing," he shrugged. "Except ..."

"Except what?"

"Well boss, I don't get the chance to meet the right women."

Frankie put his hand on Al's shoulder and smiled,

"Al, no woman you meet is the right woman. What makes you think a party would make any difference?"

"Well, it sure would make a change from the room service I'm getting used to!" he replied in a huffed tone.

Frankie pulled out a chair and sat down beside him.

"I'm always telling you, you're going to all the wrong places."

"I don't have much choice!" came Al's curt reply. Joe sat with a bemused smile on his face/

"Al, I remember in the old days you always did like a good party and you could always pull a broad."

Al smiled as he reminisced.

"Yeah, those were the days, Boss. Wine, women and sex. I miss all that and you're right, I always managed to get somebody."

"I guess that was your problem," smirked Rooney. "They were always 'some body'!" Al looked at Frankie, then at Joe.

"Well, would you listen to Mr. High and Mighty, here. Ever since he met a woman who's father makes clothes for a living ..."

"Now you listen to me a minute," warned Rooney, pointing a finger. "Her father doesn't make clothes, as you put it. He happens to own the factories."

"Well, whoopee for him!"

"O.k. you guys, knock it off," said Joe, trying to hide a smile. He looked at Al. "I'll tell you what, if Gene O'Brien wins this election he's going to throw a big party and you're invited."

"Really?" asked Al, sitting up in surprise. "Who's inviting me?'

"I am," replied Joe.

"I have a feeling you're going to regret all this when the time comes," muttered Rooney.

Al had just put his coffee cup to his mouth when the back door opened and Evie came in, smartly dressed and carrying a large hat box. Everyone was silent and all eyes were upon her as she walked passed them and out of the kitchen.

Al, still holding the cup, looked at Rooney.

"Does she know something I don't?" he asked.

"Like what?" Rooney was puzzled.

"Like when's the big day? She wouldn't happen to have a new hat in that box, would she?"

"Don't be stupid!"

Joe leaned forward and gazed thoughtfully.

"You know, I think Al's right," he commented. "That sure looks like a new hat box to me. When is the big day?" he smiled.

"I don't know!" muttered Rooney, looking uncomfortable. Joe ignored that last remark.

"Rachel Rooney. I like that. It's got a nice ring to it," he continued. "Angel's getting pretty excited at the thought of it. To tell the truth, I guess we're all excited," he joked. Rooney lifted his cup casually and began to drink his coffee.

"Yeah it looks like we're all excited - only him!" Al observed.

"Oh, Rooney's just playing it cool," Joe explained. "Maybe he wants to wait until he's the same age as I was, before he says 'I do'."

Rooney put his cup down and shrugged.

"I'm in no big hurry," he said.

Joe looked at him and was inclined to agree. For a man who seemed to be in love, Rooney surely didn't seem to be in any hurry at all. As the three men looked at him, Rooney gave an embarrassed smile.

"Maybe I'm waiting until Gene O'Brien's election party!" he teased/

"Maybe," thought Joe, "and maybe not."

"Hey, that would be really something, Rooney!" grinned Frankie. "Wouldn't it Boss?"

"It sure would," nodded Joe giving a side glance to Rooney. "It sure would ..."

After all the months of hard work and campaigning, the day finally came for the election results. Joe and the guys sat in the lounge waiting for news of it on t.v. Angela was down town in the headquarters with Gene O'Brien, his wife and the rest of the workers, nervously awaiting the outcome. There were t.v. cameras and pressmen waiting patiently on the sidewalk. As word of the results started to filter through, Gene was pleased but not over-confident. After a long wait, the number of votes was confirmed. The majority of the people had given him their vote and he had won by a landslide victory! When it was announced, Gene clenched his fists tightly and punched the air, smiling broadly. Kate threw her arms around him and they held each other. It was a very emotional moment for him. He was overwhelmed at the amount of votes he had received. Turning to Angela with tears in his eyes, he embraced her.

"We did it, Irish!" he exclaimed. "We really did it!"

"Congratulations, Senator," she replied. "I always knew you would."

"Your ideas and Joe's money, that's what has made all this possible. I'll always be grateful to you both."

The rest of his staff clambered around him excitedly as he shook hands and thanked each one of them individually. Then he looked towards the large, glass doors and nodded,

"Well, I think it's time to thank the public. Better let the press and cameras in." As two members of his staff went and opened the doors, Gene wiped his eyes with the back of his hand.

Angela turned to walk away.

"Hey, where are you going?" he asked.

"Oh, you don't need me," she smiled.

"Now that's where you're wrong! I told you I wanted you by my side and that's where you're going to be."

He put an arm around Kate's shoulder and the other around Angela's, and stood looking proud and happy as the place was suddenly besieged.

Over at Roseberry Avenue, loud cheers filled the lounge as the results of the voting were announced on t.v. Joe leapt to his feet.

"I knew he could do it," he grinned. "My boyhood friend is now Senator Eugene O'Brien. Not bad for a poor kid from the Bronx!"

He looked across at a smiling Rooney.

"Jesus Joe, he got in by some majority. I'd love to know what Saint he prays to!"

"Believe me Rooney, saints had nothing to do with it. If he has anyone to thank - it's the people. When it comes right down to it, if you want something bad enough you'll get it. He wanted to be a Senator and the people wanted him!"

Frankie shook his head and remarked,

"I guess the old neighbourhood hasn't done so badly Boss. After all, the Andrettis came from it, you came from it too and so did Gene O'Brien.

Joe smiled,

"Yeah, from little acorns, big trees do grow. And they don't come much bigger than those guys. The Andrettis got Gene a lot of votes and I'm really proud of him. I think this calls for a drink. Who knows, maybe the Senator of today will be the President of tomorrow!"

Al hovered around with excitement and anticipation.

"Does this mean he'll be having that big party, Boss," he asked.

"It sure does," Joe nodded.

Rooney stared at Al and snapped,

"Is that all you can think about? The man has just been elected Senator!"

"Yeah, and Senators know some very high class women. So whoever he'll be inviting, I'll be there - ready, willing and able!"

Rooney looked over at Joe and shook his head.

"You know, I think all those visits he makes to brothels are affecting his brain."

"How come?" Al piped in.

Rooney turned to him to explain.

"Well, you don't go to a high society party to proposition women."

"And why not? I'll bet most of the women go in the hope that someone will!" Joe chuckled.

"I don't think there's an answer to that."

Frankie got up to pour the drinks and Joe was talking to Rooney, when Al pointed to the t.v.

"Hey Boss, look at this. There's your wife."

All eyes looked to the screen and sure enough, Gene O'Brien was being interviewed with Kate on his right side and Angela on his left. He was thanking the people for their votes and commenting on the election. He thanked his staff and much to Joe's delight, paid a special thank you to "Mrs. Angela Morrelli" for all her help and support throughout the long months of campaigning. Angela was asked for her views as to why she thought Gene O'Brien had won.

She smiled,

"He won because of his honesty and integrity. The people love him, he's their choice. In him they see the qualities all politicians should have. When he fights, he fights fair and square. He doesn't try to bring his opponents down by ridicule or mud slinging. Gene O'Brien is a decent man and that's why he is now our Senator."

Joe nodded in agreement and smiled proudly.

"You know, she's right. Gene always said politics could be a dirty game, but it's a smart man who doesn't have to stoop that low or kiss the asses of the rich and famous." As Frankie handed round the drinks, Joe raised his glass.

"To Gene O'Brien. I think he'll make one hell of a Senator. And to my wife. Behind every great man there is a good woman and believe me, I should know!" he beamed, his face full of admiration.

It was late that afternoon when Joe saw the taxi stop and Angela get out. She let herself in and was making her way past the study when Joe appeared at the door.

"Well, he did it!" he smiled.

She threw her arms around him.

"Oh Joe, I'm so happy!" she replied, her face flushed with excitement. But that wasn't all.

"Have you been drinking?" asked Joe, as he studied her. She nodded,

"Yes I have. The finest champagne money could buy. We were all celebrating Gene's victory." She walked across the entrance hall followed by Joe and continued, "Gene had left in a few bottles for us but Dan Casey turned up with Kevin and they had a lot more." Joe stared after her as she climbed the stairs.

"You didn't tell me that when I phoned," he said.

Angela stopped and turning around, looked at him for a few moments.

"I didn't think I had to, Joe."

"No you didn't have to," he shrugged. "I just thought you would, that's all."

"Anyway, it didn't happen until after you phoned."

"How convenient!" he muttered.

"I thought you would have come down town. It isn't to say you weren't invited. Gene asked you and so did I."

"Yeah, I know but I thought I'd just phone and congratulate him. And you, you did really well on t.v. honey. I was proud of you."

Angela smiled and they both continued onto the landing.

"Where's Robert?" she asked.

"He's in the garage playing. Al's with him."

"Well, I'm going to shower and change and then I'll have dinner with my son. Maybe now I'll be able to spend more time with him."

On entering the bedroom, Joe closed the door behind them. He sat on the bed, while Angela took off her jacket and unbuttoned her blouse.

"Was he alone?" Joe prodded, trying to sound casual.

"Who?"

"Kevin Mitchell."

"No, He was with Dan Casey."

"I know that!" he turned his eyes upward as Angela hid a broad smile. "What I mean is, was his wife with him?"

Joe was so obvious for information that it was all she could do to keep from laughing. Biting her lip, she decided to give him more than he was asking for. She kept undressing.

"No, his wife wasn't with him."

"I had a feeling she wouldn't be!"

"You know, when he walked in you should have seen the look on Susan's face."

"Why?"

"She looked like she'd just seen some big Hollywood heart throb."

"Oh yeah!"

Angela held the blouse in her hand and looked towards the window, thoughtfully.

"Now, what was the way she described him!" she teased. "Oh yes, I remember. She said he was drop dead gorgeous!"

"Really!" replied Joe, in a sarcastic tone.

She turned and looked at him.

"Come to think of it, he does have a very attractive smile."

"Yeah and come to think of it, he knows it!"

"His eyes sort of light up his face and it makes him look very sexy. Have you noticed it?"

Joe was becoming really annoyed.

"I can't say I have but then he's not my type!"

"I was quite surprised to see him," she commented.

"I don't know why, a bad penny always has a habit of turning up!"

"He made quite an impression, I can tell you."

"With who?" he demanded.

"With everyone really. Susan says it's his boyish smile."

"Yeah well, someone like her would!"

"Maybe he should be a movie star."

Joe looked at her sarcastically.

"He'd like that. He'd have a big camera all to himself to smile into. If you ask me he's all ego and no character. What a pity his money can't buy him a personality! That smile of his just says it all - I love me, who do you love?"

Angela dropped the blouse onto the floor and scrambling onto the bed, she pushed him down.

"You!"

Kissing a surprised Joe, she undid his shirt and ran her smooth hands over his chest. Then taking her lips from his, she used them to explore the rest of his body, pressing her fingertips gently into his flesh.

Engulfing her in his arms, he rolled her onto her back and looked into her eyes.

"How much have you had to drink?" he asked.

"Not much," she answered smiling. "You know I don't need alcohol to want you." Joe shook his head as he realised the truth.

"You've been winding me up, haven't you? All that stuff about Kevin Mitchell!"

"You asked for it."

"Yeah I guess I did," he admitted. "And now you're asking for it!"

He smiled mischievously.

"Joe Monrelli," she said softly, "you've got the nicest smile I've ever seen."

"Angel, are you trying to tell me my smile pleases you?"

"Yes, I am."

"Good, let's see what the rest of me can do!"

What began as fun became more passionate and intense with every kiss and caress. Joe knew exactly how to please his wife and she knew exactly how to respond . He had missed her during the months of campaigning but that was over now and he was glad. Angela was where she belonged. In his arms.

Senator Gene O'Brien decided to have his celebration party at "The Imperial Palace", with no expense spared. He and Angela drew up a guest list which was to include not only the rich and privileged, but all those who had helped him in his election campaign and those he knew well . Freddie Barrett and all the staff from "The Safe Haven" were invited as well as old Mario and his family, Father Ryker and of course, everyone from Roseberry Avenue. Angela made sure not to leave anyone out.

As the day of the party arrived, the house was a bee-hive of activity. Joe assembled everyone in the kitchen.

"O.k., here's what we're going to do," he informed them. "Frankie, you and Elena will go by taxi. Evie, a taxi will also collect you and Mr. Smith. I've hired a limousine for Angel and me." He turned to Rooney. "Now, do you want to come with us or have you made other plans?"

"I'm going over to Rachel's house. I'll be sharing a limousine with her and her parents."

"O.k." Joe nodded. "I think that just about takes care of everything. You can all have the rest of the day off"

Al stood with a glum look on his face/

"What about me Boss?" he asked. "Everyone else seems to have transport." Frankie nudged him and said, "New York is full of taxis. All you have to do is phone one!"

"That won't be necessary. Al's coming with us," replied Joe looking over at Angela who smiled in approval.

Al's face lit up in surprise.

"You mean I'm going in the limo with you and Mrs. Morrelli?"

"That's right. You spend most of your time driving one but tonight someone else is going to drive and you'll be the passenger."

Al gave a broad grin.

"Gee Boss, that's great!"

"Yeah, I thought you'd be pleased," smiled Joe. "We're leaving at 7:30 so be here." "You bet!"

As the three friends turned to leave, a beaming Al looked at Rooney.

"Hey, I've got ten dollars here says the Boss's limo is bigger than the one you're going in."

Rooney glared at him. "Don't start," he warned, "or you'll be arriving at "The Imperial Palace" in a hearse!"

Al pointed to Joe and said smugly,

"It takes a big limo for a big man."

"And a big mouth!" retorted Rooney, pushing past.

"Yeah well, we're all expecting you to open yours tonight Rooney. Isn't that right Boss?" he winked, closing the door.

"What was all that about?" asked Angela.

Joe shrugged,

"Oh nothing. I might get a surprise tonight. Someone in our company may be making a speech." He nodded towards the door and smiled.

Angela was still puzzled but Evie claimed her attention.

"Miss Angela, are you sure Robert will be alright with the baby sitter?" There was anxiety in her voice.

"Of course he will. Now don't you worry Evie. Robert will be just fine, you'll see. I want you and Mr. Smith to go to that party tonight and enjoy yourselves."

Evie put her hands up to her face in a fluster.

"Oh Miss Angela, I'm so excited! And Mr. Smith is so pleased he was asked."

"You're family," smiled Angela, putting her arm around her. "You have every right to be there. And if Mr., Smith is your friend, that gives him the right to be there too." After giving her an affectionate hug, Angela left the kitchen.

Evie turned to Joe.

"You know, Mr. Joe, I remember saying a long time ago, that Miss Angela had her feet firmly on the ground. In all this time she's never once rose above herself and she never will."

"I know," he agreed. "That's why I love her!"

Just after seven that evening, Al arrived immaculately dressed in an expensive suit. A few minutes later the taxi came with Mr. Smith inside, to collect Evie. Shortly after they'd gone, Joe came downstairs.

"Gee Boss, you look terrific!" Al commented, giving him the once over.

They stood together in the entrance hall. As time wore on Joe kept glancing at his watch. It was now 7:30. He was growing impatient.

"What's keeping her? You know Al, I can never understand that about women. When they're going somewhere, they're always the first to get ready but end up being the last!"

"Well, I don't have that problem."

A knock came to the door.

"Jesus, that's our car," muttered Joe, walking up the hall to answer it.

The driver touched his cap.

"Mr. Morrelli?"

"Yeah, that's right. We'll be with you in a minute."

He returned but there was still no sign of Angela.

"I'd better go and see what's keeping her."

Joe had just made it to the bottom of the stairs when Angela appeared at the top and started to walk down gracefully. The two men stared at her, then at each other. Al's mouth fell open.

"Jesus Boss, she looks like a princess!"

Angela came towards them in a dark blue velvet evening gown. It was strapless, with a band of dark blue satin across the neatly fitted top. The tailored bodice showed off her slender waistline and the full skirt reached to her ankles. The outfit was completed by an evening bag and high heels in the same rich material.

Joe looked stunned as he watched her, her deep blue eyes fixed on him. As she reached him her light makeup gave her a natural glow and her hair was swept up at the sides, allowing it to fall softly behind her smooth shoulders. On seeing the reaction of both men, she put a hand under Al's chin.

"Better close your mouth Al," she advised, "or you'll catch flies in it!"

Joe gazed at her.

"You look beautiful honey." As Angela took his arm, he smiled. "You know, Angel, this reminds me of the day we got married."

"That's almost nine years ago. Would you do the same thing again?"

"You bet! Would you?"

"Yes I would. I did alright," she smiled. "After all, there's only one Joe Morrelli." "Yeah and I only ever met one Angela Kenny," he nodded.

"Looks like they broke the mould when they made you two," Al chimed in. "The only other couple I've seen to go so well together was Rhett Butler and Scarlett O'Hara."

Angela put her other arm through Al's and looked from him to Joe.

"Well who knows, after tonight we could rename this place 'Tara'!" she said in a very convincing southern accent.

They laughed as they made their way to the front door. Maybe Al wasn't wrong in his comparisons. The Morrellis did make a handsome couple and one thing was for sure, both men were feeling very proud to have "Miss Angela" on their arm.

On entering the almost palatial dining room, Joe stopped and looked around.

"Well, I've got to hand it to Gene. Apart from our friends, everyone who is anyone is here tonight." He spotted Rooney waving to them through the crowd. "I've just seen our table honey. Let's go." He put his hand on her back to help guide her.

"What do I do now Boss?" asked Al.

Joe leaned over.

"If you see something in red - go for it!" he winked. Al smiled and nodded then disappeared into the crowd, as Joe and Angela joined Rooney and Rachel.

An orchestra was playing and Ralph Lennox had laid on his most expensive champagne in silver ice buckets and a buffet of exotic and mouth watering foods that looked delicious. Everyone was relaxed, happy and talkative. After a few glasses of champagne, Joe made his way to Gene's table. He tapped his friend on the back.

"Congratulations Senator!"

Gene smiled and gripped his hand firmly.

"Thanks Joe. I can hardly believe it."

"Tell me something, how does it feel to have all that power?"

"It sure beats the hell out of being Pope!"

They both laughed.

"I'll see you later," promised Joe.

"You bet!"

After speaking to several of his friends, he made his way back and sat down.

"I see Gene didn't leave out any of his old pals, anyway. He must have had some guest list!"

"He had," Angela confirmed, "but he wanted them all here and he's happy to see them." As another ice bucket and bottle were brought to the table, Gene crossed the floor and stepped onto the podium. The orchestra stopped playing and a hush fell on the crowd. He looked around at all the faces.

"I'm not going to give any long winded speeches. I just want to thank each of you for coming. I want to thank you also for your hard work, your support and your votes. I will do everything in my power to keep my promises to you and every man and woman in New York who voted for me. Enjoy yourselves. There's plenty to eat and drink and if you're wondering who is picking up the tab for all this, believe me - so am I!!" There was laughter and loud applause as he waved and went back to his seat.

Angela stood up.

"Where are you going?" asked Joe.

"I have to make a speech."

"You didn't tell me you were making a speech," he said, surprised and looking at her empty hands.

"Where is it?"

Angela pointed to her head and smiled,

"It's up here Joe."

He watched as she turned and walked away.

She took Gene O'Brien's place on the podium, lowering her gaze for a moment. Then she raised her head confidently and began to speak in a strong, clear voice.

"'How do I love thee? Let me count the ways'. These words are the first sentence of a poem written by Elizabeth Barrett-Browning, for her husband Robert, and I think they are appropriate for the man we have all come here tonight to honour, Senator Gene O'Brien." She paused thoughtfully for a few seconds. "There are many ways to love someone and I am sure every one of us have our own. We can love the honesty and truthfulness. The work and convictions. The belief, the loyalty, the trust. Many of us will love his friendship and," she smiled at Kate, "the man! But there is someone else for whom those words are appropriate. Someone who also had the conviction to do something. Who gave his time and money to help others, in an effort to try and make things better for the community because just like Senator O'Brien, he cares and more importantly, he never forgot where he came from. He never sought the lime light and refused to take credit but I think the time has come for all of you to know who this man is. I would like to dedicate the last three lines of this poem to him." She looked directly at Joe. "'I love thee with the breath, smiles, tears of all my life. And if God chooses, I shall but love thee better after death'." She held out her hand and pointed towards him. "Ladies and gentlemen, the man I speak of is my husband, Mr. Joe Morrelli." There was silence throughout the dining room. Then Gene O'Brien rose to his feet, pushing his chair back. He looked up at Angela and began to applaud loudly. Soon everyone else followed his example. He turned his smiling face towards Joe and winked, as the applause grew louder. Evie wept openly into her handkerchief, comforted by Mr. Smith. Frankie was so chocked up he couldn't speak. Al sniffed as he wiped his eyes with the back of his hand. A proud Freddie Barrett stood gazing at Angela, nodding his approval. Overcome with emotion, Mario sobbed unashamedly, while Reuben pretended he had something in his eye and removed his gold rimmed spectacles. Father Ryker's applause grew softer as his thoughts carried him back over the years to when he first saw Angela Kenny, kneeling beside her mother in the dimly lit Church of Our Lady of Lourdes. No one but God could have known her destiny and no one but God could have guided her along. Yes she had known a lot of sorrow but had brought so much happiness.

It took all of Rooney's strength to fight back the tears. He was full of admiration for Angela and both pleased and happy for Joe.

Although there was a sea of people, Joe Morrelli could see only one - his wife. After hearing what she had to say and the way she said it, he was at a total loss for words. She stood before him, beautiful and elegant. He was very proud of her. All the guests turned and looked at him, still applauding. Joe smiled and nodded his appreciation but his eyes were filling up with tears. He had always been respected by those who knew him but he had always craved respect from the elite. Now thanks to Angela, he had it. All these people who would never have given him a second glance because of his background and the way he had achieved his success, were giving him a standing ovation. He had wanted this kind of recognition for years, now it was his. His wife had made it all possible.

Many times she had told him she loved him but tonight she had told everyone. As he blinked back the tears he was filled with happiness and emotion because Angela had just paid Joe Morrelli the ultimate compliment.

Rooney had never known any woman to show her husband so much love and respect by reciting such beautiful words, and in front of so many people. Joe had a love most men only ever dream of and Rooney knew in his heart he wanted the same. If he couldn't have love like that, he didn't want any. But love like that had to come from a very special person. Someone you would only meet once in your life and only then if you were lucky! That someone was Angela. But she was married to his best friend, in many ways his brother. He did not feel jealous of Joe Morrelli but he did feel sad for himself. When Angela returned to her seat, Joe took her hand and held it gently but firmly under the table. He gazed at her, his eyes still moist.

"Thank you," he whispered.

"I was only telling the truth. I love you."

"Yeah I know. And now, so does the world!"

"Good," Angela smiled. "That's the way I want it."

Rooney poured more champagne and Joe made a toast.

"To us," he proposed.

In the midst of laughter and clinking glasses, Antonia appeared at the table.

"Joe darling, I'm so happy for you," she smiled then turned to Angela. "What a pretty speech my dear. You were very convincing."

Joe detected a note of sarcasm in her voice. He and Rooney shot a quick glance at each other.

"Would you like to dance, Antonia?" Joe asked, getting to his feet.

"Well actually, I came to have a little chat."

"Oh I think you'd rather dance," he insisted with a glare. Then taking her arm he led her away from the table and onto the dance floor.

"I had no idea your wife was educated enough for Gene O'Brien to let her make speeches," she commented.

He looked at her and said,

"What's the matter, Antonia, are you jealous it wasn't you up there? Or maybe you think no one can remember their lines only you!"

"Really Joe, don't tell me a man of your age was taken in by all that sentimental nonsense written by some woman no one has every heard of"

He was determined to stay calm. No one was going to ruin this special evening for him, especially Antonia.

"I thought the words were very beautiful," he replied casually.

"That's all they are, Joe, just words. And I should know."

He stopped.

"You never thought it would last between Angel and me, did you? You always thought I'd come back to you."

She smiled.

"Who knows, maybe you will. Things change and people change."

"What do you mean?"

"Well, the election's over and Gene's in the Senate now. He doesn't need Angela's help anymore. Do you honestly think a woman so young can go back to being a good little housewife after getting a taste of high living?" She shook her head. "She'll get bored Joe, and we all know what happens to young bored women. They get their excitement in other ways, with other people their own age. I'm only thinking of you, Joe. Angela has gained a lot of admirers. I don't want to see you get hurt." She nodded over his shoulder. He turned to find Kevin Mitchell, sitting at one of the tables and staring intently at an unsuspecting Angela.

Joe turned back.

"I trust my wife completely!"

"I hope so. But let's be honest, you never would have had that problem with me. You were always number one in my life and you knew it."

"You still don't understand, do you? I love her."

"You told me you loved me too. Remember?"

As the music came to an end she put her hand under his chin and continued,

"I'll always be here for you. We had good times and great sex. It can be like that again." She glanced towards Kevin Mitchell and smiled. "You'll be back Joe," she whispered.

"I wouldn't count on it Antonia."

"Oh, but I am," she nodded. "It won't last. You'll be back and I'll be waiting."

He stared after her as she walked away, then felt a hand on his shoulder.

"Anything wrong, old buddy?" It was Gene.

Joe shook his head and replied,

"After all this time she still thinks my marriage won't last and I'll go back to her."

"Well, you were with her for quite a while. If you ask me she just won't accept the fact that you fell in love and married someone else . She loved you Joe. Oh, not as much as her career, but Antonia always thought she was the one who was going to be Mrs. Joe Morrelli. She's still bitter Joe, and she's jealous because you married a much younger woman. You know the old saying, 'Hell hath no fury like a woman scorned'."

"Yeah, I guess you're right," Joe nodded. "She wasn't pleased at Angela giving a speech."

"What did you think of it?" Gene smiled.

"I'll never forget it. She made me feel like a million bucks. Did you know about it?" "Yeah. We decided it was time you got a little credit. One good turn deserves another. After all, you took a back seat to give me my chance in the election and it paid off"

"Oh, it was no big deal," he shrugged.

"Maybe not to you, old buddy, but it helped put me in the Senate and before I start to make comments and give advice in corridors of power, here's a little advice for you. Don't worry about your marriage, Joe. Angela loves you and she proved it tonight. I've never heard words spoken more sincerely in my life. Believe me, after all the women you went with you sure ended up with a prize catch!"

"Yeah I did," Joe agreed. "I just hope she feels the same way about me when I'm in my fifties!"

Gene patted his shoulder in assurance.

"You can count on it. Angela will be faithful to you no matter what age you are. She's that kind of woman."

They parted company and Joe made his way through the crowd.

"Mr. Morrelli!" came an unexpected voice.

Joe turned smiling to come face to face with Kevin Mitchell. His smile faded as Kevin held out his hand.

"Mr. Morrelli, I'd like to congratulate you on having a wife like Angela. She did you proud tonight. You're a very lucky man."

Both men's eyes were fixed on each other as they shook hands.

"I am a lucky man. I always knew she loved me but now everybody knows. And if they don't, they'd better realise it fast because if not it could prove to be very unhealthy for them. I never was a man who liked to share my women and I don't intend to share my wife with anyone - ever!"

Kevin nodded and gave a bemused smile.

"I understand but I'm a man who was never easily frightened of anyone."

"Well, I guess maybe that's because you never had to be. But there's always a first time!"

"Does that mean I can't dance with your wife?"

"No, that means you can dance with her but that's all I want you to do."

Kevin Mitchell's face broke into that charming, boyish grin that Joe disliked so much!

"I think you're making too much out of this situation, Mr. Morrelli. After all, Angela and I are just good friends."

Joe nodded.

"I know, she told me. And as long as you stay just a good friend, you don't have a thing to worry about. Do I make myself clear?"

"Perfectly".

Joe turned to go, then hesitated.

"There's just one more thing," he said. "I trust my wife. It's you I don't trust, Mr. Mitchell. Let's just say your track record doesn't impress me. If you're planning on staying in New York, take some good advice and stay well away from her. If you don't you may well live to regret it!"

Joe walked away and returned to his table.

"Where have you been?" asked Angela.

"Oh, I was just talking to a few people. You know how it is," he shrugged, sitting down beside her. He lifted his glass and gazed into her eyes. "You have my full attention for the rest of the night and the next dance - that's a promise!" he smiled.

Rooney and Rachel went onto the dance floor, leaving Joe and Angela alone. As she sat quietly, sipping her drink, she gazed around wistfully.

"What's the matter, honey," asked Joe.

She shook her head.

"Oh, nothing. I was just thinking of something my father said to me the day he was murdered."

"What was it?"

She looked at him and recalled,

"Well, we were talking about my exam results and he said, 'Who knows, maybe one day you'll be standing in front of important people giving a speech and I'll be there among them all applauding and feeling very proud. My Angela, mixing with the cream of society'." She shook her head again. "I can remember his words as though it was yesterday."

Joe saw the sadness creep into her eyes. He placed his hand over hers.

"The memory of that day won't ever fade for you, will it?" he said softly.

"I won't ever let it Joe. I loved him too much. He wasn't here tonight to hear me but you were. He didn't live to see me achieve it but you did. I could never have done it without your help Joe. You always believed in me, just the way he did and I love you for that."

He pressed her hand.

"You know," he said sincerely, "I'd have liked Agnes to have been here to see you. She would have been so proud."

"You were very fond of her, weren't you?"

Joe nodded.

"Yes I was. She was a special lady and a good friend. But I've got to tell you Angel, no-one could be more proud of you, than me. Your words will always live in my heart, just the way your father's words will always live in yours. The best thing you can do for them now is to be happy. That's what they'd want. That's what I want."

"I know and I am happy. I've got you and Robert and believe me Joe, I wouldn't swop that for anything - or anyone!"

He was both delighted and relieved.

"Listen, why don't we go and mingle for a while. Say hello to all our old friends. I'm sure they'd like to dance with you. After that, we can grab a bite to eat."

Angela smiled and nodded her approval. As they got up from the table he took her hand.

"It might be Gene's party but it's our night so let's enjoy it. Besides I'm with the most beautiful woman in the place!"

Although he was smiling, he couldn't help but think about Robert Kenny and the dream he had for his daughter. He never lived to see that dream come true. However, Joe did and was grateful. Grateful to Robert Kenny for having such a wonderful daughter, who had proved to be an equally wonderful wife and mother. He owed a lot to him and Agnes and if ever he could repay them, he would. He knew there was only one way to do this - find out who murdered him and why.

When they finally got back to their table, they rejoined Rooney and Rachel. The four of them were in happy conversation when Rooney nudged Joe's elbow and nodded towards the dance floor. There was Al, his arms draped around a woman. He steered her in their direction and looking over her shoulder, he smiled and put his thumb up as he danced by. Joe smiled,

"Well, it looks like he's on a promise judging by the look on his face."

"I might have known it," said Rooney, shaking his head.

"What?"

"That if Al scored, she'd be blonde and wearing red!"

"We all have our weaknesses," Joe shrugged.

Rooney stared after them.

"I wonder who she is."

"Her name's Gloria Randel." replied Rachel.

"Do you know her?" Rooney was surprised.

"Yes. She's divorced now. Her husband is an executive with a real estate firm. She receives a large alimony cheque from him every month. She lives alone in a fancy apartment with her poodle."

Joe looked at Rooney.

"Well, this is one night Al will get to keep his money in his wallet."

"She really loves that dog," Rachel commented. "It sleeps on her bed."

Now Rooney looked at Joe.

"Maybe not! He might end up paying the poodle to sleep outside the door!" Joe shook his head.

"It would be just his luck to get a dog that won't budge. And somehow I don't think three in a bed is his bag."

Rooney started to chuckle.

"Can't you just picture his face, talking real nice to it in front of her and ready to strangle it when she turns her back. I'd love to know it's name."

"She calls it 'Toots'," Rachel informed him.

"Really," said Joe, raising his eyebrow. "Well, if it won't get off the bed, I know one guy who sure won't be tooting his horn tonight!"

Angela smacked his arm as both men laughed loudly.

"Honestly Joe! Is that all you can think about?"

He glanced at his watch.

"Well, starting from now - yeah, it is!" he grinned.

The party was in full swing and the dance floor was crowded. Joe and Angela sat at the table alone. He reached over and took her hand.

"So tell me, what are you going to do with yourself now?" he asked.

"What do you mean?"

"Now that Gene's been elected, all the hard work is over. Won't you miss it? After all those parties and functions and organising, I guess you'll be a little bored."

She smiled.

"I must admit it was fun. But Gene will still need a committee and there'll be fund raising events in the future. I'll be a part of that but for now I'll be happy to be at home with you and Robert. I missed not being able to spend as much time with you both. He's growing up now Joe, and although he has his friends, he still needs us to share his life. I'm going to bring him to movies and shows the way I always did. To parks and museums. I want our son to see the beauty in the world and to read about it. That's the best way to broaden his interest. I've also promised Father Ryker I'd do a couple of days a week at the centres, teaching basic English and a little poetry. I'm looking forward to all of that and I'm looking forward to being at home every evening with you!"

He kissed her hand.

"I've missed you Angel. We can go back to doing all the things we used to do. Like going out together in the afternoons, or going to Mario's or "The Safe Haven" in the evenings - just the two of us. I've really missed all that."

"Well, after tonight I'm all yours," she promised.

"Why wait until after tonight? Do you know what I'd really like to do?"

"No what?" she asked.

"I'd like to go home, open a bottle of champagne, bring it upstairs with two glasses and drink it in bed with you. Then I'd like to lie and hold you in my arms. I'm proud, I'm happy and I'm in love."

"I've never known you to want to leave a party early."

"Why stay when I have everything I need and want at home?" he whispered.

"Joe Morrelli, you're a romantic," she smiled.

He gazed into her eyes.

"Yeah, well I guess I am."

"Well in that case we'd better go. I'm feeling rather romantic myself." As they stood up, Joe leaned towards her ear.

"Thank God we don't have a poodle!" he said in a low voice.

Chapter 16

Angela lifted her eyes from the book and looked at Joe. She found herself studying him as he sat reading the evening paper. He was wearing dark framed glasses and his hair was greying at the sides. As he turned the page, he saw her.

"What's the matter?" he asked.

"Oh, nothing. I was just thinking, in another week you'll be fifty."

Joe winced, "Please don't remind me! That's one birthday I'd rather forget."

"Oh come on, Joe. Surely you want to celebrate this one. After all, you haven't had a big party in years and it's not every day you reach the Big Five O!" she joked.

He put the paper down. "That's the problem with being fifty. You realise you've been around for half a century and it makes you feel old."

Angela smiled, "You're not old, you're just mature."

Joe nodded, "Yeah, so mature I can't read the small print anymore!"

She went over and sat on his lap.

"I think you look quite handsome," she said in a low voice, removing his glasses and stroking his hair gently.

He looked embarrassed. "To be honest Angel, this is what I've always dreaded. Me starting to look my age while you're still an attractive, young woman."

"But Joe, I love you just as much now as I've always done and that won't change, no matter what age you are."

"I'll remind you you said that when Al's helping me in and out of the car with my walking stick!" he smiled.

"It's going to be a long time before you need one of those – Mr. Seducer!"

He slipped his hands around her waist. "Are you telling me I'm still o.k. in that department?" She nodded. "Well, I always did aim to please!" he smiled broadly.

Angela put her arms around his neck. "Now, there must be some way you want to celebrate your birthday."

"Well, maybe a small dinner party. You know, just close friends. Rooney and Rachel, Reuben and Miriam. A sort of family affair." He looked thoughtful for a few moments and then continued, "There is one thing I'd really like to do but I guess you would think I was being silly."

"What is it?" she encouraged.

Joe explained, "Well, a few weeks ago while I was waiting for my dental appointment, I picked up a magazine and I saw some pictures of Venice. You know, the most romantic city in the world, the City of Lovers and all. It looked really nice and I've had this idea that I'd like to go there." He noticed the look of surprise on Angela's face and shook his head. "I knew it was a silly idea. It's only for young people."

She leaned close. "Joe, the City of Lovers means exactly what it says. You don't have to be a certain age to be in love or want to go there. I don't think it's a silly idea at all. I think it's a wonderful idea."

"You mean, you don't think I'm too old?"

"Of course not!"

Relieved, he smiled, "I'd really like to ride in one of those boats."

"They're called gondolas, Joe."

"Yeah well whatever, they're still boats."

"True," she nodded, curbing a smile.

He was becoming excited at the thought. "You know Angel, I think I'll call into the travel agents and book a trip for us. We could go in a couple of weeks. It would be sort of a belated birthday present to myself. What do you say?"

"I'd say for a man who wanted to forget his fiftieth birthday, you're really pushing the boat out!"

"Oh, very funny," came the reply.

Angela got to her feet and smiled down at him with a mixture of affection and amusement.

"I never thought I'd see the day you'd be like Charlie." she commented.

"Well, you have to take some of the blame for that," he insisted. "Every time we went to Miami we went on boat trips. I got to like it, that's all."

"Joe, you can walk around Charlie's boat," she reminded him, "but you can't walk around a gondola. If you do we will all end up in the canal!"

He quickly stood up. "I know that, I'm not stupid! But I haven't told you the best part. Some of those guys play music and sing to you while you're taking in the sights."

"Really? Well, I'll put up a request for you. Maybe they'll sing Happy Birthday."

He nodded sarcastically. "Now, that's like something Rooney would say."

"Oh, I'm sure Rooney will have a lot to say when he hears about it."

Joe raised his finger like a stern school teacher. "If you ask me, that guy says every thing but the right thing. Like when's the engagement or the wedding? I'm still waiting on that speech he was supposed to deliver. I think if he followed my example and brought Rachel somewhere romantic, he'd end all the suspense for everyone."

Angela's smile faded. "Joe, maybe Rooney isn't finding it as easy to fall in love as you did "

He took her in his arms. "Yeah, I guess you're right. And looking back on it, I'm sure glad I didn't waste all that time. Now, about Venice. Would you like to share one of those boats with me?"

"I'd love to," she whispered, reaching up and kissing him. "But seeing as we have to wait a couple of weeks, why don't we go upstairs and I'll sing to you."

"Would that be before or after?" he grinned.

"Which ever you prefer," she teased. Then she gazed into his eyes. "You know something Joe, to me you don't look a day older than when I first met you."

"Well, I'm sure glad about that!" he joked, returning her kiss. "Now, what about that singing you promised me?"

As they left the lounge and climbed the stairs, Angela put her arm around Joe's waist and said, "Maybe you're right about Rooney, Joe. Maybe it would help if he did bring Rachel somewhere romantic. We could ask them to come to Venice with us."

Joe stopped. "No way, Angel! If Rooney wants to propose on water, I'll build him a raft and he can do it on his way down the Hudson River. Venice was my idea - for us."

She laughed and shook her head. "That's what I like about you, Joe. You're all heart!"

Angela decided to recruit Rooney's help on the matter of Joe's birthday. She phoned his apartment the following afternoon, when Joe and Robert had left for a baseball game, and asked him to call. As she sat in the kitchen going over a shopping list for Evie, Rooney arrived through the back door with an anxious look on his face.

"What's wrong?" he asked.

"Nothing's wrong," she replied, "I'd just like a word with you."

He joined her. "O.K. I'm listening."

"Well, it's Joe's birthday next week."

"Yeah, I know."

"And I'm thinking of giving him a party."

Rooney sighed, "Jesus Angela, I thought something bad had happened. Why all the secrecy?"

"He won't know anything about it. He thinks he's getting old, Rooney, and I suspect that deep down he feels insecure. You know Joe, he always loved to celebrate his birthday. But not this one. I think the thought of being fifty scares him a little. We are both a lot younger than him, and Robert's only nine."

Rooney nodded, "Yeah, you're probably right . What did you have in mind?"

"Well, he said he wanted a small dinner party," she explained, looking thoughtfully around the kitchen. "But I think this is one occasion when this house should be filled with people, laughter and conversation."

"You mean, have it here?" he asked, surprised.

"Why not? Evie told me he used to have some really fancy parties here, when he went with Antonia."

"That's true, but it was a long time ago."

"Maybe too long. I'd like to bring those days back for him," she smiled. "Make it an open house. Invite all his old friends, the ones he's known for years and really likes. I think he'd enjoy that. What do you say?"

When Rooney smiled, Angela knew she'd won him round.

"Sure, I think it's a great idea. Now, what do you want me to do?"

"Well, there are some of Joe's friends I don't know as well as you do, so that's where you come in. If you could get in touch with them and explain what's being planned. There'll be no formal invitations, just a lot of phone calls. Between the two of us we should get around everyone in time. I'll bring some caterers in and the guests can help themselves to whatever they want."

"Great," said Rooney, "but there's only one problem. How do we keep Joe from finding out?"

"Why ask me?" she smiled. "That's your department. Keep him occupied on the day. The less time he spends in the house, the better. That way, he won't know what's going on."

"O.K. What about presents?"

"Oh, I think the best present we can all give him is to be here. Besides, Joe has already given himself one."

She'd sparked off his curiosity. "What is it?"

"A trip to Venice."

"Venice?"

"That's right," she nodded. "He wants to ride in a gondola."

Rooney leaned back in his chair and grinned,

"You're joking!"

Angela assured him, "No, I'm not. In fact, not only does he want to ride in one, he wants some poor man to play music and serenade him while he's taking in the sights."

He threw back his head and laughed, "Well, I'll be damned! No wonder he never mentioned it. Joe Morrelli in a gondola. Jesus, how did he think of that one?"

"He didn't. He saw some pictures in a magazine while he was waiting at the dentist's. He says it would be really romantic."

Still laughing, Rooney shook his head. "Then I hope he's a good swimmer. You know Joe, if he gets romantic, he's bound to rock the boat!"

She giggled, "I never thought of that. I've already warned him not to stand up. Looks like either way, I can't win. He's an accident just waiting to happen! He's really got his heart set on this trip but on our return it wouldn't surprise me one bit if someone asks him, "How was Venice?" and he says, "Very wet!"

Rooney popped his head around the study door.

"Happy Birthday!" he smiled.

Joe nodded and smiled back, as he sat in his leather chair with Robert by his side. "Thanks for the card, Rooney. I'm just admiring my present from my son. What do you think?" he asked pointing to the desk.

Rooney went over for a closer look. There on top of the polished wood, stood a bright glass paperweight of a boxer.

"I'd say that was one of the nicest presents I've ever seen."

"And the best!" piped Joe, winking. "It's the one thing I've always wanted and it sure will be useful to have."

Robert smiled with satisfaction as he and Joe looked at each other.

"What are you doing after lunch?" Rooney asked, sitting down.

Joe shrugged, "Oh, nothing special. Why?"

"I was thinking maybe we could go to the race track. It's a beautiful day. We could bring Robert. He'd be with the two favourite men in his life."

Joe looked surprised. "Since when did you develop a love for horse racing?" He thought for a few seconds, then screwed up his face. "I don't think it's such a good idea. Robert's too young and Angel would never approve."

"Oh come on Joe. He's not going to bet on them, he's only going to watch them. It would be fun. Afterwards we could grab some burgers and sodas. He'd enjoy it and so would we."

Robert clutched Joe's arm in excitement.

"Please dad, can we go? It would be great. Please."

His father shook his head. "I don't know son. Maybe we should go to a ball game instead."

"That's O.K. by me," replied Rooney.

Joe looked at him sarcastically. "Oh, so you've suddenly developed a love for baseball too? Or maybe it's because I just happen to be fifty years old today and you figure it's dangerous for me to be let out on my own. Maybe I'll need help to cross the street!"

"Don't start!" snapped Rooney.

"Oh come on, dad. We went to a ball game last week. Can't we go and see the horses?" Robert pleaded.

Joe nodded. "O.K. But only if your mom agrees."

The boy clapped his hands with excitement and ran towards the door. "I'll go and ask her."

As he turned the handle, Joe added, "Robert, don't forget to tell your mom this was all Uncle Rooney's idea."

He nodded and disappeared.

Joe smiled at Rooney. "I can assure you if Angel blows a fuse, this is the one time I won't be taking the rap!"

A few minutes later Robert returned with a big grin on his face. "Mom says I can go." Joe stood up.

"O.K. The race track it is." He put an arm around his son's shoulder and guided him out of the room. "Come on then. Let's go upstairs and get ready." Rooney followed and watched as the two climbed the stairs together in deep conversation. Angela came to the door of the lounge and as he held up his thumb, they both nodded and smiled to one another.

It was 6:30 when Angela heard Rooney's car stop in the driveway and when she looked out of the window, she saw Joe and Robert making their way to the front door. When they arrived into the entrance hall, she was waiting. Both father and son were all smiles.

"Well, I take it you had a good day," she remarked.

"We sure did," replied Joe.

"Yeah mom, it was great. I saw the horses walking around and I watched them racing. It was terrific!" said a grinning Robert.

His mother smiled lovingly. "Well, I think we should all go upstairs now and get ready for dinner. After all, we have guests coming and we don't want to keep them waiting."

Joe waved his hand. "Oh, there's plenty of time. What I need right now is a cup of coffee."

He headed for the kitchen but Angela quickly stepped in front of him and blocked his way.

"Why don't you have a drink instead?" she suggested.

"Coffee will do just fine."

As he reached for the handle, she put her hands on his chest/

"Joe, you can't go in there."

"Why not?" he asked puzzled.

"Because Evie has baked you a birthday cake as a surprise and she doesn't want you to see it until tonight."

"Well, I won't look," he shrugged.

But Angela was adamant. "Joe you know what Evie's like. Besides, she's gone to a lot of trouble and she'd rather you wouldn't go in."

He threw his hands up in the air. "This is great. I can't even go into my own kitchen. I don't know why I bothered to buy this house. Evie seems to have more of a say than I do!"

Angela put her hands on her hips. "Really, Joe, I don't know why you're being so childish."

"Maybe it's because I'm being treated like one. I think I'll have that drink after all." He went into the lounge and reappeared with a scotch in his hand.

"I think it's a bit much when a grown man of fifty isn't allowed to see his birthday cake," he muttered.

"Well, I think it was very good of Evie to bake it for you."

Joe nodded in agreement. "Yeah, I guess you're right. Maybe I could take just a peek

"Joe Morrelli!"

"O.K., O.K., lets go," he beckoned, walking towards the stairs.

As they all went up together, Robert hurried on in front. Joe turned to Angela and in a low voice said,

"You know something Angel? That is one smart kid."

"What do you mean?"

"Well, while Rooney and I were studying the form book, he was looking at the names and he picked the winner in nearly every race. We had a pretty good day, I can tell you. Yeah, he's a Morrelli alright. He's just like his dad."

She smiled and put her arm around his waist. "Then some woman is going to be very lucky."

"Now that compliment is a very nice birthday present."

"Really? Well I have something else for you later!" she whispered.

As Joe fixed his tie in the mirror, he glanced at Angela.

"Is it my imagination or do I keep hearing the door bell?"

"I haven't heard anything," she replied casually, zipping up her dress.

He leaned over and stared at himself. "Jesus, I'm beginning to think my age is affecting my ears."

"Honestly Joe, you're acting like there was something really wrong with you."

"Yeah well, if I keep hearing bells that aren't ringing, something must be wrong. How come it never happened to me before?"

"Because you've never let any other birthday get to you like this one," she answered, straightening his tie. "Now let's go downstairs."

Joe put his jacket on as he followed her out of the bedroom. Robert came running along the landing to meet them. Each parent took his hand and led him downstairs. As they reached the bottom, the doorbell rang.

"Don't worry, I heard that bell too," Angela smiled. Joe nodded sarcastically, then looked towards the kitchen waiting for Evie to answer it, but she didn't come. He shook his head, "I'll get it!

Angela and Robert went into the dining room and Joe opened the front door to find Rooney and Rachel.

"What's the matter, did you forget your key Rooney?"

"No, I just thought you'd like to welcome your friends."

"What friends?" he asked, looking out at the empty driveway.

Suddenly familiar faces appeared from both sides of the door.

"Happy birthday Joe!" they smiled.

He viewed them all with surprise, then grinned.

The guys from the gym, Jeff Lang and his wife, Carlo and Sandra Capaldi.

"Come on in," he insisted, opening the door wide.

As they filed passed he punched Carlo's arm playfully. "You son of a gun. What are you doing here?" he joked.

"You know me Joe. I always did like a good party - especially if the booze was free! Besides, you can fill me in on what it's like to be fifty!" he winked.

"Watch it!!" warned Joe.

He escorted them all to the dining room and flung open the door to surprise Angela with his unexpected guests, but it was Joe who got the surprise.

Bunches of balloons hung everywhere, the table was laid with an expensive buffet, waiters and waitresses stood with trays of champagne and even more familiar faces greeted him with, "Happy birthday Joe!"

He put his hand up to his forehead and took a deep breath.

"What can I say?" he smiled, in disbelief

"It's not like you to be lost for words," said Rooney, patting his shoulder affectionately. Frankie and Elena, Reuben and Miriam, Evie and Mr. Smith, Antonia and Judge Thompson and Freddie Barrett were all there, as well as some of Joe's old business partners from his various ventures.

Angela stood smiling with her arm around Robert. He walked over to her.

"So I did hear bells after all," he whispered. She nodded. "Well, thank God for that!" he sighed.

Antonia threw her arms around him

"Joe darling. Happy birthday," she beamed, kissing his cheek.

He put his arms around her. "Thanks for coming, Antonia."

"Oh I wouldn't miss your birthday party Joe, especially this one."

"Yeah well, I'm not as young as I used to be," he smiled.

She looked into his face. "Maybe not, but you're still as handsome."

It was an open-house. The guests mingled, moving around. Some even sat on the stairs, talking and laughing. The happy and relaxed atmosphere only added to the occasion. The hired staff followed each other continuously with food and drink, and Angela made sure to show her appreciation by having food and refreshments for them in the kitchen.

"You sure know how to surprise a guy," said Joe as he handed her a glass of champagne.

She smiled, "Happy birthday to my darling husband," as she raised it.

He kissed her, then looked around at all the smiling faces. However, one was missing.

"Where's Al?" he asked. "It's not like him to miss a party."

Angela shook her head. "I was wondering the same thing myself. He was invited and I told him he could bring a friend, but so far he hasn't shown.

Just at that moment, Al made a grand entrance with a woman on his arm. Joe recognised her

"Well, it looks like he took you at your word Angel," he said in a low voice, as Al ushered her towards them.

"Gloria, I'd like you to meet my boss and his wife, Mr. and Mrs. Morrelli," said Al as he presented her proudly. "This is Gloria Randal."

Joe shook her hand. "Nice to meet you."

"It's nice to meet you too. It was so kind of you both to invite me," she smiled.

"Not at all. Thanks for coming."

"You know Mr. Morrelli, Al has told me so much about you."

"Really? I hope it was all good," replied Joe, glancing at Al who looked a little uncomfortable.

Angela put her arm around Gloria's shoulder. "Why don't you have a drink and we can get better acquainted, Gloria," she smiled, leading her away.

Joe watched them, then turned to Al.

"I didn't know you were still seeing her."

"Oh, it's nothing steady," Al shrugged. "But I couldn't bring just any woman to your party, boss. If you know what I mean."

"Yeah, I know what you mean."

"I'm sorry I'm late boss. I guess you were wondering where I was."

"The thought had crossed my mind," Joe nodded.

Al explained, "Gloria had a problem with her dog."

"What dog?" Joe pretended not to know.

"She's got this poodle and I swear boss, I've never seen anything that walks on four legs so fuckin.' jealous of anyone who walks on two!"

Curiosity got the better of Joe as he leaned over and asked, "Then how do you two ..."

"What?"

"You know ..."

"What?"

Joe tutted and turned his head up towards the ceiling. "Get it together! Make out!" he explained.

"Oh that," Al nodded. "Believe me boss, it isn't easy. I have the bite marks on my ankle to prove it."

"Just be thankful it's your ankle! But tell me, where does she put the dog when you're there?"

"Outside the bedroom door and it barks all night. Now you know why our relationship isn't permanent. She loves that poodle boss. She's always going on about it's cute little face. If I had my way, I'd put it outside the window instead of the door. I'd like to see how cute it's face would look then, after dropping six stories onto the sidewalk."

Joe chuckled, "I never thought I'd see the day you'd get a woman with her own apartment."

"And I never thought I'd see the day I'd be in competition with a poodle!" Al retorted.

"Yeah Al, life's a bitch."

"Hey boss, how did you know what sex it was?"

Both men laughed loudly at their private joke.

As Joe stood in deep conversation with Rooney and Reuben, this was the one time he didn't hear the door bell.

"Hey Joe," said Rooney, nodding towards the open dining room door.

Joe turned and saw Evie ushering in some guests. Frankie smiled, "Well, well. It looks like the mountain has come to Mohammad."

Joe hurried over. "Nick, good to see you."

Both men shook hands, then Nick Andretti placed an affectionate hand on Joe's shoulder. "Happy Birthday Joe. I hope I'm in time to see you cut your cake!"

"I'm honoured to have you as a guest in my home - all of you," he replied in an emotional voice, shaking Anthony's hand and kissing Maria's.

"I'm both proud and pleased you could all come."

A waiter came over directly with a tray of champagne and as they each took a glass, Nick held his up and said, "I always make time for my friends, Joe. Congratulations!"

Angela appeared with Robert by her side. "Mr. Andretti, I'm so glad you could come."

"Not at all, it was good of you to invite me. Joe and me go back a long way."

"Yeah, maybe too long," smiled Joe. "When I was running errands for you I never thought I'd end up like this, a business man with my own home."

Nick nodded, "Well, we all have to start somewhere. Besides, you were always a bright kid. I knew you'd go a lot further and I was right."

"Speaking of kids, I'd like you to meet my son. Joe put an arm around Robert's shoulder and proudly stood him in front of the old man.

Nick Andretti smiled. "He's a fine boy, Joe, and he resembles you very much. He must be your pride and joy."

As Angela chatted to Anthony and Maria, Joe moved closer to his guest.

"Believe me, Nick, he is. But he's also my future. He's the only child I have and I don't ever want anything to happen to him"

Robert smiled warmly and innocently, then turned his head. In a low voice his father continued, "If anyone ever tried to harm him I'd kill them and have no regrets."

Joe was serious, but then so was Nick when he replied, "Now you know how I felt all those years ago. Dominic didn't have a long life, but neither did the men who killed him and let's just say, I sleep better at night knowing it."

Angela led Maria away to introduce her to the other female guests and Robert followed. Joe watched him walk away.

"Yeah," he nodded thoughtfully, "I know what you mean."

Changing the conversation to a lighter not, Nick put a hand on Joe's arm.

"So tell me, how does it feel to be fifty?"

"O.K." he laughed, "but I'm married to a much younger woman, don't forget."

"So what?"

"Well, I'm worried in case my stamina won't hold out! I just hope I can get to your age and look as good as you do Nick."

The old man smiled broadly and held his hands out. "Joe, you're an Italian. We don't grow old, we're like a good wine - we mature with age!"

"I'll remember you said that," came the reply.

Then Joe turned to Anthony. "Your grandfather sure knows how to boost an ego!"

Nick laughed, "Well, if I can remember rightly, you always had plenty of that."

"Yeah, I did," he agreed. "And it helped me do a lot of bed-hopping. No-one ever knew exactly where to find me - including you," he winked.

"And what about now Joe? Most men I know have a mistress somewhere."

Joe shook his head, "Not me. I got who I wanted most." He looked across the room at Angela. "Why play away from home when the one you really love is in it?" Nick Andretti put an arm around Joe, drew him closer and looked at Anthony. "Now you know why I respect this man. He has many qualities."

His grandson nodded in agreement. "He's also very good on business trips. I learned a lot from him."

Robert came over and took Joe's hand.

"Dad, mom says it's time for your birthday cake."

"O.K. son. Let's go. I'll see you in a little while," he explained to his two friends. They nodded.

After everyone was supplied with fresh drinks to toast Joe, the lights dimmed and a man appeared in the doorway carrying a large cake with coloured candles and sparklers. He made his way to the table and carefully sat it down. Joe thought he was a waiter until the lights went up and he saw his face.

"Charlie!! Jesus. Where did you come from?"

Charlie beamed, "Well now, I wouldn't leave my boats for just anybody. But for you Mr. Morrelli, I was happy to."

They embraced like the old friends they were.

Angela took Joe's hand. "Hurry up and blow out those candles, before they go out by themselves!"

"O.K. honey. How many candles are there?" he whispered.

"Fifty," she whispered back.

He shook his head. "You never did do things by half, Angel."

"Oh hurry up, Joe. We'll help you. And don't forget to make a wish."

"I wish there wasn't fifty candles on this cake!" he muttered.

Everyone counted, "One, two ..." and on the count of "three", Joe took a deep breath and assisted by Angela and Robert, blew out all the candles. Everyone concluded by applauding and singing, "Happy Birthday".

He wiped his brow with his hand. "Thank God for that," he sighed. "I thought I wasn't going to make it!"

As he smiled and nodded to them all, Angela leaned over and whispered, "I had every confidence in you, Joe Morrelli. One thing you can always do is 'make it'!" He gave her a surprised look as she kissed him on the cheek.

Robert threw his arms around Charlie, excited and happy to see him. Then he returned to his father's side for the cutting of the cake. As it was being distributed to the waiting guests, Joe looked at Charlie, then Angela.

"Now I know why I wasn't allowed into the kitchen for that cup of coffee," he smiled, looking very pleased.

"Are you happy?" she asked.

"You bet!" He looked around. "I couldn't have wished for a better birthday. You've given me a great present and a great life, Angel. Yeah I'm happy."

He gazed into her face, took her hand and squeezed it gently. There was no need for him to say anymore.

After a few moments, Angela lifted an envelope off the table.

"Gene couldn't be here, he's in Washington," she explained, "but this arrived for you."

"O.K. but I guess I'd better say a few words first." When they'd gotten everyone's attention, Joe began. "Now, I'm not big on speeches, as most of you will already know!" Laughter broke out. "So before we get down to some serious drinking ...," a loud cheer went up, "I'd like to thank you all for coming. It's great to see so many friends together in the same place at the same time. I'd like to say a big thank you to my wife and Rooney for this wonderful surprise party. And a big 'thank you' to my housekeeper, Evie, for baking such a fantastic cake."

Evie smiled with pride and a little embarrassment as she was applauded.

Joe continued, "Enjoy yourselves and have a good time - I know I will." He waved the envelope in the air. "One last thing. I have a telegram here from Senator Gene O'Brien, an old friend who couldn't be here tonight. Let's see what it says." He opened it and read it aloud. "Congratulations, old buddy. Now you know how I feel! P.S. Here's a crate of Irish whiskey - give everyone a real drink!"

As everyone cheered and applauded, Joe shook his head, grinning. "That guy's a ...!"

Then he turned to the waiters. "O.K. fellas, better do as he says. Bring it on in." He looked around his guests. "What do you say we drink the hell out of it?" he asked. The roar of approval was his answer.

Joe eventually made his way over to Charlie. "I can't believe it's really you," he smiled. "When did you get here?"

"I arrived today, about the same time as the caterers. When Angela phoned me and told me about your party, I just had to come." He looked at Joe in amusement. "It was either me or some stripper jumping out of a cake, dressed in black leather. I hope you're not disappointed!"

Playing along with the joke, Joe shrugged. "To be honest Charlie, I'm glad it was you. Have you ever tried blowing out fifty candles? Believe me, there isn't a lot of air left for heavy breathing at such a sight. Angel would have seen to that!" He screwed up his face. "Besides, leather never did turn me on. I prefer a nice, sexy nightdress." Charlie agreed. "Yeah, you're right. I guess that's more what we were used to. There's something about satin or lace that can make a woman look good."

Joe leaned over and in a low voice said, "Charlie, when a guy's walking around with a permanent 'hard-on', even a bag lady looks good!" When both men had finished laughing, he continued, "Well. I hope after coming all this way, you'll be staying with us."

"I wanted to book into a hotel but Angela wouldn't here of it, so I'll be staying in the guest room for a couple of days."

"Good," Joe nodded. "I'm glad. I always told you if you came to New York you were welcome to stay here."

"Thanks, Mr. Morrelli," Charlie smiled, shaking Joe's hand warmly. "And happy birthday!"

"Thank you Charlie. It was good of you to come and it's great to see you. Enjoy the party."

As Joe moved on, Robert came over and held Charlie's hand tightly. It wouldn't be long before their conversation would turn to stories of tall sailing ships and the voyages of sailors on the high seas!

Angela was the perfect hostess, mingling with the guests, joining in their conversations and making sure they were enjoying themselves. Eventually, she made her way to Charlie, who was in a light-hearted conversation with Robert. She held out her hand to him.

"Come with me, Charlie. I want to introduce you to the others."

"Oh, that's O.K. Angela, I'm happy just to be here. Besides, I think some of them might be a bit out of my league."

She gripped his hand firmly. "Now that's where you're wrong. You're an intelligent businessman."

He smiled, "I hardly think renting beach-houses and cars is worth mentioning and don't forget, I'm paid to do it. It's my job. I don't own the business, I only manage it."

"Well, what about the diner you opened at the Marina a couple of years ago, you own that don't you?"

He nodded, "Yeah, that's true."

"And you own sailing boats, don't you?"

"I sure do."

"Then you're a businessman in your own right, Charlie. And Joe says you make the best hamburgers in Miami."

He stood up and sighed. "O.K. but I warn you, they might not want to know me."

Angela took his arm. "They might not have wanted to know John Masefield - but we would!" she smiled. "You're a fine, decent man, Charlie. Most of the people you see around you started at the bottom. Joe was one of them. You're going to get along with everyone just fine." She pressed his arm in re-assurance. "It has taken all these years to get you here, I'm determined to show you off!" She proudly led him into the crowd.

Charlie was soon feeling right at home. Everyone he met was friendly and down to earth. Angela, in her own subtle way, was steering plenty of business in his direction, by telling about his wonderful boat trips and how much she and Joe enjoyed the food at his diner, not to mention the friendly atmosphere and excellent service.

Not to be outdone, Antonia asked for Charlie's phone number so she could book a vacation. Judge Thompson was delighted and enquired if he did moonlight cruises. Gloria Randal decided that she'd like to go and do some sunbathing on board one of his boats. Al stood with a huge grin on his face. He'd never been to Miami, but maybe now he'd get his big chance to live it up like his boss!

When Angela caught up with Charlie again, he looked very happy.

"I have enough business here to last all year. I've got to hand it to you, Angela, you've got a good head on your shoulders."

"I hope so," she replied, smiling. "I'd hate to think all that College education was wasted!"

"Not on you. They say behind every great man there is a good woman. But behind Joe Morrelli there's a great one!"

She hugged him affectionately. Then she glanced around the room until she saw Joe leaning against the wall, talking.

"Speaking of Joe," she said, "there's someone else I'd like you to meet."

She steered him over. "Mr. Andretti, I'd like to introduce you to a very dear friend of both Joe and myself. This is Charlie Gordino. Charlie, this is Mr. Nicholas Andretti."

Joe looked surprised, but said nothing as he watched the reaction of each man. Charlie smiled as he held out his hand.

"I'm pleased to meet you."

He looked at Nick Andretti as though he'd never seen him before. In return, Nick shook his hand.

"And I'm pleased to meet you, Mr. Gordino."

As Joe took in the scene he noticed that nothing passed between these two men. Not even a knowing glance.

Angela continued, "Charlie lives in Miami. He runs a business there."

"Really?" asked Nick. "And what business are you in?"

"Oh, mostly hiring . Beach houses, cars, boats. Whatever's needed."

"Is business good?"

"It's pretty steady."

"Do you work for yourself?"

"No, I have a boss. We've known each other for years."

Joe kept studying them as Nick nodded, "It's a wise man who has a back-up. Especially in places like Miami. I hear things can get pretty rough down there. You know, people trying to muscle in on your territory."

Joe looked directly at Charlie, who never flinched even in his expression.

"Somehow I don't think that's likely to happen, Mr. Andretti. You see, my boss would never allow it."

Nick smiled, "Good, I'm glad to hear that."

Angela touched Charlie's arm. "Charlie this is Anthony Andretti, Mr. Andretti's grandson, and his wife, Maria."

After shaking hands with them, he and Angela turned to go.

"It has been really nice meeting you all," he smiled.

Nick nodded in approval. "And it has been really nice meeting you, Mr. Gordino."

As the night wore on, everyone was in high spirits. Rooney joked with the guys from the gym. Judge Thompson was relating a story to Jeff Lang and Reuben and most of the ladies were talking about the latest fashion - or scandal. Angela gazed at them all as she sat with her arm around a sleeping Robert. The people there in her home were treating it just like their own and that's exactly the way she wanted it. Her eyes moved towards the loud laughter in the corner. Joe, Nick and Anthony had been joined by Carlo, Frankie and Al. This company of men were talking, laughing and waving their hands around. Nick Andretti was laughing so hard, he was drying his eyes with his handkerchief. She knew they were swopping stories about the old neighbourhood. Joe was really enjoying himself. He'd never looked happier. This party had been a good idea and had worked the way Angela had hoped. She had surrounded Joe with all his old friends. The people who had shared good times and bad with him. The people he cared about and whose friendship he valued . He stood grinning, looking like a man half his age. Angela pushed two chairs together and laid her son down carefully. Then she got up and fetched two drinks from a tray. Charlie stood gazing around. She handed him a glass and slipped her arm through his.

"Why don't we have a chat?" she said, in a low voice. "I know the perfect place."

She guided him out of the dining room, unaware that Antonia was watching from a safe distance!

A few minutes later, Rooney tapped Joe on the shoulder. "Robert's fast asleep. Do you want me to see to him?"

Joe looked around. "Where's Angel?"

"I don't know, she's probably talking to someone."

He nodded. "That's O.K. Rooney, I'll see to him." He crossed the room to the small boy and looked down at him. "Poor little guy!" he murmured.

Antonia's eyes studied Joe's face. She noticed the loving look he gave his son and how gently he lifted him in his arms. At that moment all the old passion she had ever felt for Joe Morrelli came surging back. She yearned for that look and those strong, yet gentle arms. As Joe carried Robert out of the room, she followed and watched him climb the stairs. She loved her god-son dearly but she had to admit to herself she wished it was her in Joe's arms and not Robert.

Angela and Charlie sat by the pool enjoying the cool breeze.

"You're not much of a drinker, are you Charlie?" she remarked.

"No, I'm not. I never felt the need, not even when my wife left. I felt sad, depressed, I even worried about her. After the pain and hurt had gone, I actually hoped she'd find the happiness she couldn't find with me. But not once did I reach for a bottle. That's the one thing I didn't do."

"That shows a great strength of character."

He gave a faint smile, "To me I was just being sensible. I had a business to run and people depended on me."

She gazed at him "What's bothering you, Charlie? I know something is."

Charlie stared across the swimming pool. "Well, to be honest Angela, I'm chomping at the bit."

"What do you mean?"

"For a while now I've been thinking of leaving my secluded life and heading back

531

to the city. I'm not getting any younger." He looked into her face. "You know, when you phoned me I was feeling pretty low and mixed up. That's why I made the trip. When I looked around tonight I couldn't help but think that if I'd moved back to the city, things might have been different. I might have had a wife, a home, a family and friends - real friends. I guess I have missed out on all that. But then, there's a part of me doesn't want to leave Miami. When I get up early and go down to the beach I see a beautiful ocean rolling in onto white sand. I look up and see bright sunshine coming from a clear, blue sky. That's when something here, deep inside," he put his fist on his chest, "tells me I can't leave, I just can't!"

Angela put her hand on his arm. "You belong there, Charlie. All you need is a good woman to share it with. Sometimes, I think if anything happened to Joe and Robert was old enough to lead his own life, I'd go back to Miami, to the beach house. I don't think I could stay here if Joe wasn't with me."

He shook his head. "You'd be making the biggest mistake of your life, Angela."

She looked surprised. "But why?"

"Because some people are meant to go through life alone but you're not one of them. You give a lot of love but you also need to get it. You're the kind of woman who needs to feel loved and wanted, don't ever think of closing yourself away. Besides, I don't think your husband would want you to do that, or expect you to. O.K. you would never find another Joe Morrelli, but whoever the guy would be, he'd be close enough. You're too smart to settle for anything less. Trust me on that."

She sighed. "I suppose in my heart I know you're right Charlie. We all need to love and be loved, it's only human nature. If only you could meet the right woman, you'd be truly happy."

"Life is full of 'if only s'," he shrugged. "But I'm glad I came. Talking to you has helped me more than you know. At least now I realise my true feelings and I feel a lot better. The city's fine Angela, and at times I'll want to be back here. But back in Miami I have a lot to be thankful for, believe me. I guess I was just feeling sorry for myself but I should have remembered that old saying I once heard in my neighbourhood."

"What was that?"

Charlie looked into the pool for a moment, then at her. "I cried because I had no shoes, until I met a man who had no feet."

Angela didn't reply, she just nodded.

Meanwhile upstairs, Joe had just put Robert to bed. As he left the room, closing the door quietly behind him, he turned to find Antonia standing there.

"Don't tell me, let me guess. The bathroom's occupied," he smiled glancing over to it. She moved towards him "No, I just wanted to give you my congratulations in private." Putting her arms around his neck, she pulled his face close to hers. "Happy Birthday Joe," she whispered, closing her eyes and kissing him passionately.

He quickly put his hands on her arms and pushed her away. "Are you crazy? Anyone might have seen us!" he said in a loud whisper, looking cautiously around.

"Well, if we went into the bedroom, no one would."

"I happen to share that room with my wife."

"Your morals are very commendable, Joe, but there was a time when you shared it with me. Or have you forgotten?"

Joe didn't like her sarcastic tone. "That was a long time ago, Antonia. I have been married for ten years, for Christ's sake."

"I know," she nodded, "and I've counted every one of them. I should have been giving this party tonight, and I should be sleeping in that room because I should have been Mrs. Joe Morrelli!" Her sarcasm had turned to anger.

Joe stared at her with just as much anger. "Yeah well, you blew your chance so don't lay any guilt trips on me. You wanted to be the best actress on Broadway and everything came second - including me! How many afternoons did I spend on my own because you had rehearsals? How many nights did I sit in your apartment listening to you going over your lines? How many evenings did I spend in the theatre watching the same play over and over again, just so I could bring you out to dinner?" His eyes were flashing as he pushed his face close to hers.

"How many, Antonia? Tell me! Everything has a price and fame can be the most expensive of all. But I guess you know that now."

Tears came to her eyes. "I loved you Joe."

"I know," he nodded, his voice becoming calmer, "and I loved you too. But it wasn't the kind of love to build a marriage on. It would never have worked. We wanted different things, that's all."

"Why her Joe? She can't be any better in bed than I am. Give me a chance to prove it," she pleaded, gripping his hand firmly.

He pointed a warning finger at her. "I'm going to overlook all of this, Antonia, because I think you've had too much to drink."

"You never used to complain about that. You used to like it when I drank a lot. You said it made me more sexy."

Joe shook his head. "Like I said before, all that was a long time ago." He rubbed his forehead. "Look Antonia, I don't want to hurt your feelings. That's the last thing I want to do, believe me, but I love my wife. I never thought I could love any woman the way I love her. She married me, Joe Morrelli the man. Not the image. Not the tough businessman. She wanted me for who I am, not what I am. And she's made me very happy."

Antonia stared at him. "And what about later?"

"What do you mean?"

"Well, let's face it Joe, you aren't getting any younger. What happens when you can't keep up with her? Shall I tell you? She'll start looking for someone her own age. She won't want you anymore and you're a fool to think she will. She's still young and sooner or later she'll want an attractive young guy."

Joe was silent for a few moments. "You never liked her much, did you? You always doubted her. The truth is, you never thought this marriage would last so long and you're jealous."

"Why should I be jealous of a waitress?" she replied haughtily.

"Because she's everything you're not."

Antonia immediately raised her hand. "How dare you!" she cried.

He pointed his finger once again. "No, how dare you come into my home and think you could end up in my bed!"

"She wouldn't care. She's too busy strolling arm in arm with that man from Miami, or hadn't you noticed?"

Joe smiled. "Charlie? Why, he's an old friend and has been since Angel and I were married."

For a moment she was lost for words, due mostly to his cool reply.

"What is it with that woman and older men? Didn't she ever have a father?"

His expression changed as he gripped her arm firmly. "That's enough, you leave her parents out of this and don't you ever refer to her father again, not in my presence and most certainly not in hers. That's final. Do you understand me? Do I make myself clear?"

She saw a determined yet sad look sweep over his face. "I'm sorry Joe, I never meant to go so far. I've really hurt you, haven't I?"

He shrugged, "We've hurt each other. Now do you see why it would never have worked between us? We would have said and done things to hurt each other for the rest of our lives, and we would have made each other miserable. You and I together, Antonia, would have been so destructive. You've got a good man downstairs. Why don't you forget the past and find some happiness with him? He really loves you."

She nodded. "I know, but I guess I'll always want what I can't have. And I want you, Joe, and I'm not going to give up. Not yet, anyway. Somewhere deep inside I have this feeling that what you've got won't last. Angela will find herself another man and you'll come back to me, I just know it!"

He looked at the floor thoughtfully for a few moments, then at her. "Maybe. Nothing is certain in this life, but I know one thing that is. If Angel finds us together like this it will ruin my marriage. And if that happens, Antonia, then I won't ever be back to you."

"You're still a very shrewd and careful man, Joe. What you're really trying to say is, if your marriage ever goes wrong then she will have made the first move."

"Well, let's just say, it will be her choice."

"I can live with that," she smiled.

"So can I. Now why don't you rejoin Judge Thompson? I'm sure he's wondering where you are."

Antonia touched his hand sensuously. "You'll always know where to find me," she whispered.

Joe watched her walk away, shaking his head in both disbelief and despair. After waiting for a few minutes he straightened his tie, smoothed his jacket and made his way to the stairs. As he descended, he looked around the entrance hall. He thanked God he had persuaded Antonia to come down on her own. If Angela had seen them both together he could never have convinced her that nothing had happened. No woman, not even Angela, would have believed him. Antonia Flemming would have been the cause of the break up of his marriage, which was probably what she wanted anyway.

The rest of the evening went off without a hitch. As Joe and Angela waved goodbye to the last of their guests, he put his arm around he shoulder and dutifully escorted her down the entrance hall. Charlie was standing at the bottom of the stairs smiling

"It's been a long day and I could sure use some sleep!"

"Did you enjoy yourself?" Joe asked.

"You bet! It was a great party and well worth the trip."

"Well, I'll tell you what Charlie. While you're here with us Angel and me will bring you out to dinner at my restaurant, 'The Safe Haven'. After all, that's where I met her," he smiled proudly.

"Now I'd say that was one lucky place, Mr. Morrelli."

"It was also my lucky night."

"I can't argue with that," Charlie replied, holding out his hand. "Goodnight to you, Mr. Morrelli."

Joe took it gladly.

"Goodnight Charlie and thanks for being here."

"I wouldn't have missed it for anything." Turning to Angela he rested his hands on her shoulders. "Goodnight Angela, and thanks for inviting me. Thanks for everything - I mean that." He gave her a knowing look.

She in return embraced him, kissing him on the cheek. "What are friends for if not to be here for each other, and you are a very dear friend, Charlie. Goodnight."

As he climbed the stairs he felt both proud and honoured to be a guest in Joe and Angela's home. He also knew that being invited to the party as Joe Morrelli's friend would stand him in high regard with his boss, Nick Andretti. And that would lead to better things in the future. It was only a matter of time before he would become his own man in Miami, of this he was sure. Maybe this was his lucky night. He had a feeling that the tide of fortune was about to change for him at last, and he owed it all to the kindness and friendship of Angela Morrelli.

Joe dismissed the caterers and hired staff with a hefty tip and sent a tired but happy Evie off to bed.

As they left the kitchen, Angela went over to switch off the lights in the dining room.

"Hold it," said Joe, taking her hand and leading her inside.

He stood her by the table and reaching up, loosened one of the balloons and handed it to her.

Holding it by the long, silver string she smiled,

"What made you think of that?"

He shrugged his shoulders, "Oh, I saw someone do it once and I thought it looked romantic."

After pouring two final glasses of champagne, he placed one of them in her hand.

To the sound of the clinking crystal he smiled broadly and winked, "Here's looking at you, kid."

On hearing those words, Angela's thoughts went back in time to the night of Gene O'Brien's Congress party, when she remarked about Joe being like Humphrey Bogart! In her wildest dreams she never thought she would one day be his wife.

When they had finished, they put the empty glasses down on the table. She put her arm through his.

"Well now that you've said your words for this occasion, there a few I'd like you to hear."

On arriving in the lounge, she closed the door securely. Joe sat down on the couch with a happy grin on his face.

"I know, you've written a poem for me."

"Not quite," she replied, unwrapping a record and holding it up for him to see, "but I want you to listen to this very carefully."

"Why?"

"Because it's everything I ever felt about you."

She placed it on the turn-table and joined him. As it began to play he was silent, and remained so until it had finished. Then he looked at her with moist eyes.

"Those are some of the most beautiful words I've ever heard."

"And every one of them is for you, Joe."

He took her hand. "What's the title?"

"'The Power of Love'. I chose it because it says everything about how I feel about you, about us. It's our song, Joe."

He took a deep breath. "You know, Angel, the party was really something, but I never expected anything like this. What can I say?"

She squeezed his hand. "It's just my way of telling you how much I love you. You taught me to love and I'll always be grateful for that, and for meeting you."

Joe blinked hard, then got up and crossed the room. He put the record on again, this time fixing it so it would keep replaying. Turning around to her, he held out his hands. "Would you like to dance, Mrs. Morrelli?"

They wrapped their arms around each other and swayed to the music. He held her so close he could feel her heart beating. He listened once again to the words of the song. From that night on Jennifer Rush would be in Joe's special collection - right next to 'Ol Blue Eyes'!

He took her lovely face in his hands and gazed into it. "Thank you," he whispered. "Not just for the song, but for being my wife."

He kissed her passionately, then led her over to the couch. Laying her down gently, he stretched himself out on top of her.

"Joe, don't you think we should go up to the bedroom?" she asked, as he covered her face with small kisses.

"Angel, right now I don't think I could reach the stairs!" he replied resuming his kisses, only this time making them longer and more passionate.

The more he caressed her body, the more she responded and pretty soon Joe and Angela were making love to 'their song'.

When Joe arrived back from Venice his happiness and contentment was plain to see. It had far exceeded his expectations in everything from sightseeing to art and sculpture. Over the years he had lived with Angela, he had come to appreciate beauty from whatever source. In Venice she had shared her knowledge with him and was able to comment on things of interest. All those books she'd read had certainly been of great benefit - to both of them! To Angela it was all a dream come true and Joe had derived a great deal of pleasure in seeing his wife so happy. After all, if Angela was happy then he was happy.

Waiting for them were three pieces of news. Rooney and Rachel had gotten engaged. Angela was thrilled and Joe was delighted that Rooney was finally going to follow in his footsteps and get married. So much so, that he threw an elaborate dinner party for them at 'The Safe Haven'.

The next piece of news was of a more sombre nature. Dan Casey had died of heart failure. Naturally, they paid a visit to his home to offer their condolences to Alma. Although they stayed for just a short time, it was long enough for Joe to discover that Kevin Mitchell was moving in with Alma to keep her company and manage things. There was no mention of his wife, Vivienne, and this gave Joe an uneasy feeling. Dan had always made Kevin tow the line, but Alma had always loved him as the son she never had. She would go along with anything he wanted to do and this left Joe wondering just what his plans would be for the future, especially concerning his marriage to Vivienne. He also wondered about his own marriage. He'd never trusted Kevin Mitchell when it came to Angela, and he never would!

The third piece of news came by way of two theatre tickets and a note from Antonia. She was appearing in a new Broadway play that had attracted the attention of a

Hollywood film director, who was interested enough in the story line to turn it into a movie for the big screen with Antonia as the possible leading lady. She wanted Joe and Angela to attend the performance and a special party she was giving afterwards at "The Portland Club". Joe was very pleased for her, but not so pleased when Angela came up with an idea.

At dinner that evening the day's events were being discussed as usual, when Angela said, "I suppose Judge Thompson will be escorting Antonia to the party."

Joe shrugged, "Yeah, I suppose he will."

"Why don't you escort her?"

"Me?" This was something he didn't expect.

"Why not? I think it would be a nice gesture, Joe. She's really going to the top now and you helped her on her way. Besides ..." she became silent.

"Besides what?" he asked.

"Well, you two were an item long before I came on the scene. You were lovers for a long time and to be honest Joe, I don't think she ever really stopped loving you - in her own way. It would be a nice surprise if you showed up. I think that would make her very happy."

Joe tapped his fingers lightly on the table.

"I don't think that's such a good idea, Angel."

"Why ever not?"

"Well, I don't think it would be fair on Judge Thompson. He really cares about Antonia and he might be offended if I stepped in."

"Oh, I'm sure he wouldn't mind, not if you explained it to him," she replied. "You'd only be escorting her to a party Joe. I can't understand why you're being so hesitant. It's only one night!"

Joe thought hard for a few moments. After what had taken place at his birthday party, how could he begin to explain that one night with Antonia back on his arm was all it would take for her to think that their relationship was back on track. Trying his best to come up with an excuse he said, "What about you, what are you going to do?"

"I can partner Judge Thompson and be at "The Portland Club" with everyone else when she makes her grand entrance with you," Angela smiled.

He shook his head. "Don't you mind? I mean, wouldn't you rather go to the party with me?"

"I think Antonia would rather go to the party with you. Anyway, why should I mind? You're my husband Joe, and I trust you. Now why don't you telephone the Judge and set it all up?"

Joe wasn't happy about the situation but there was nothing he could do. Reluctantly, he agreed. "O.K. I'll phone him later."

Angela lifted her wine glass to take a sip.

"While we're on the subject of Judge Thompson, what was his first wife like?"

He looked across the table. "To tell the truth, Angel, I don't know how he ever came to marry her."

"Why?" She was obviously surprised.

"Well, I only ever saw her once and once was enough!" He screwed up his face. "She was the hardest looking woman I ever saw, and he must have thought so too. He sure paid a lot for his divorce."

"Oh come on Joe, you're exaggerating."

"No I'm not, honest. He told me once that it was worth the alimony just so he didn't have to wake up in the morning and look at her."

Angela gave him a sarcastic glance. "What is it with you men? You all think you're so handsome."

Joe smiled, "Well, compared to her Quasimodo was in with a chance!"

"Well he must have liked something about her," she insisted.

"Yeah, I guess you're right. But it must have been below her waistline."

"Joe Morrelli!"

He put his hands up. "Well, you did ask!" he grinned.

As the curtain came down at the end of the play, Joe and Angela stood applauding loudly with everyone else. Antonia got three standing ovations and he was really proud of her. The theatre began to clear so he made his way back stage and knocked on her dressing room door.

"Come in Judge," came the reply.

Antonia was putting the finishing touches to her already perfect make-up, when Joe walked in. When she caught sight of him in the mirror, a look of complete surprise appeared on her face. She got up from the chair and turned quickly around.

"Joe, honey! I wasn't expecting you."

"I know but I had to come and congratulate you on a great performance," he smiled.

"Oh thank you darling, and thank you for the flowers. They're beautiful." She kissed his cheek. "Have you seen Judge Thompson anywhere? I don't want to be late for my own party and he's my escort."

"Not tonight he isn't. There's been a change of plan. I'm escorting you."

She clasped her hands and smiled. "Really? Oh Joe, that's wonderful! It's just like old times." She gave him a sly look. "There wouldn't happen to be something wrong in your marriage?"

"No, Angel has already gone onto the party with the Judge. Everything's fine."

"Well, it's early days yet," she replied.

Joe shook his head. "You never give up, do you Antonia?"

"If I did, I wouldn't be where I am today," she smiled.

"Now that's very true, and Broadway would have lost it's brightest star."

"You always did know how to compliment a woman, Joe."

"Yeah, well it's true. Are you ready?" he smiled, holding out his arm.

Antonia stepped back and twirled around, showing off her expensive sequined dress. "What do you think?" she asked.

"I think you look terrific!"

Satisfied, she put her arm through his and looked into his face. "Now I'm ready for anything. After all, I've got my favourite man at my side."

On leaving the theatre they were quickly surrounded by a large gathering of fans who had been patiently waiting.

"Miss Flemming, could I have your autograph?" one of them asked.

"Not now, I'm in a hurry," Antonia replied with a wave of her hand as she pushed her way through the crowd, towards the waiting limousine.

Joe gripped her arm firmly and leaned over.

"These people have been here a long time. It wouldn't hurt to be nice to them."

She tutted. "Really Joe, I have a party to go to."

"I know, but it won't start without you. Surely you can give them a few minutes of your time."

"Oh, alright then!" she snapped, hurriedly signing a few autographs.

When they had climbed into the limousine, Al closed the door and got into the driver's seat.

Antonia sighed, "You'd think seeing me on stage would be enough for them, without waiting outside for my autograph. It can be very annoying!"

Joe looked at them through the window, then turned to her. "It would be more annoying if they weren't there Antonia, because that would be the time to start worrying."

"I don't know what you mean."

"Oh, it's very simple to explain. You see, when someone wants to become an actor they want fans. But when they become an actor they don't want fans. They don't see the need for them anymore. It's too much hassle. But fans can make you and fans can break you, Antonia. If you ever get to Hollywood ask the has-beens, I'm sure they wish they still had theirs. After all, an empty theatre doesn't earn any one any money or bring rewards but it can bring an end to a career. When the fans stop coming, the phone stops ringing and then you're in big trouble. You'd do well to remember that."

"And what makes you such an expert?"

Joe shrugged his shoulders. "I'm not, it's only common sense. Very few stay at the top forever. There's always someone just as good coming behind and they want to be where you are. The way I see it, stardom is like climbing a ladder. When you reach the top you can't stay there indefinitely, sooner or later you have to climb down."

There was a heavy silence as Antonia turned her head away. Joe looked towards the driver's seat and saw Al watching him in the mirror. Both men exchanged knowing glances and Al nodded to his boss in agreement. Then he started up the car and drove away from the kerb.

When Joe and Antonia entered "The Portland Club" there was loud applause. She stood holding onto his arm firmly, beaming with delight and nodding in appreciation. Looking around him, Joe realised it was a real high society gathering with people he either didn't know or knew only slightly. Just when he was about to despair he saw two faces he recognised. He was happy and relieved to see one, but not so happy to see the other. He leaned towards Antonia and in a low voice said, "Why don't you go and mingle with your guests? I'll see you later." Removing her arm gently he directed her towards the crowd.

"Don't forget to give me the first dance," she smiled, leaving him.

Joe made his way over to Angela and the familiar face of his old friend.

"Hey Gene, good to see you," he grinned.

They grasped each other's hand.

"It's good to see you old buddy."

As Angela and Kate entered into deep conversation, Gene put his hand on Joe's shoulder. "That was some entrance. Are you thinking of auditioning for this movie I'm hearing so much about?"

Joe stared at him. "Before you say another word, it wasn't my idea, it was my wife's!"

"Well, you've sure made Antonia happy."

"Yeah? Well, I just hope I haven't made her too happy," replied Joe as they each lifted a drink from a passing waiter's tray.

"What do you mean?" asked Gene.

Joe turned towards him so Angela and Kate would not hear. "The night of my birthday party she made a pass at me."

"I don't believe it!" came the surprised reply.

"To be honest Gene, I could hardly believe it myself"

"What kind of pass?"

"Jesus Gene, use your imagination!" snapped Joe, as his friend tried very hard to keep a straight face.

"How did it happen?"

He glanced around and leaned over. "She followed me upstairs and gave me the come-on."

"What did you do?"

"I talked my way out of it."

Gene shook his head and patted Joe's shoulder.

"You're getting old Joe," he smiled. "I remember the time when you'd have talked your way into it!"

"Oh thanks a lot, you're a great help!"

"I take it Angela doesn't know."

"Do you honestly think I would have been her escort tonight if she did? Besides Antonia is convinced I'll go back to her. You'd think after ten years she'd get the message."

Gene smiled again. "Yeah well, she always did have a soft spot for you." Then he whispered, "Maybe you should have given her a wam-bam-thank-you-mam!"

"She's not the wam-bam type," Joe muttered. "Antonia is an all night affair - and I should know!"

"Oh, I believe you alright," Gene grinned, "and it looks like your night's only beginning." Joe followed his gaze to find Antonia coming towards them, smiling. She took his hand then turned to Angela.

"I'm sure, Angela dear, you wouldn't mind if I borrowed you husband for a dance?" she said, light-heartedly. Then, without even waiting for a reply, she led him away.

Joe reached back and handed his drink to his wife saying, "Why don't you and Kate get a table honey. I won't be long."

Just as he and Antonia stepped onto the dance floor, Kevin Mitchell appeared before Angela. His mouth broke into a charming smile as he fixed his eyes on hers.

"Would you like to dance Angela." he asked.

She was hesitant. Kate took the glass from her hand and urged,

"Go on. Gene and I will find a table."

On hearing this, Kevin took Angela's hand and guided her onto the dance floor. Gene O'Brien stood surveying the scene. Kevin's timing had been perfect. Too much so for his liking. He had been amused at Joe's account of what had happened at his birthday party, and his reaction had been of harmless fun. But as he looked at Antonia with Joe and Kevin with Angela, it gave him an uneasy feeling.

Gene O'Brien was nobody's fool and it seemed to him that someone wanted to keep Joe and Angela apart. And he was pretty sure that someone was Antonia. She had always wanted Joe Morelli and the best way to get him would be to cause a split in his marriage. If Angela had a liking for Kevin and was swayed by him, then Joe would go back to her. There had always been a spark between them and a handsome young guy like Kevin Mitchell could be the one to re-kindle it.

He was deep in thought as he and Kate sat down at a table. Time would tell. But for now this was Antonia's night and she was going to see that everything went her way. Of that, he was sure!

As the evening wore on, a self-assured Kevin Mitchell danced Angela at every opportunity, which did not go un-noticed by Joe. He also noticed that his presence did nothing to deter this young man. In fact, Joe was beginning to think he was deliberately trying to provoke him. Kevin's whole attitude was so obvious and the way he smiled and gazed at Angela was blatant. He didn't seem to care who saw him, especially Joe. Then there was Antonia. She seemed to be paying him a lot more attention than was needed, insisting he met her many friends and holding onto his arm tightly as he did so. Joe knew that to many of these strangers they looked like a couple and he was beginning to feel annoyed.

When Kate and Angela went to the ladies room, he turned to Gene.

"Is it my imagination or am I being deliberately kept away from my wife?"

"I don't know Joe, but it's sure starting to look that way," Gene admitted.

"Let me ask you something. Where is Kevin Mitchell's wife?"

"Oh, they parted company after Dan Casey died. There wasn't any reason to keep up the pretence any longer. I hear they're getting divorced."

"Well, with all the women he has hanging around, you'd think he'd have brought one tonight."

"Maybe he didn't want to," replied Gene, lifting his glass.

Joe looked at him. "Maybe that's because he knew Angel would be here. Come on Gene, don't tell me you haven't noticed the way he looks at her. That guy fancies my wife!"

"Yeah, I know. It's sticking out like a sore thumb. To be honest with you Joe, I think your gut instinct about him was right all along. I think he liked her from the first time he ever laid eyes on her."

Joe rested his elbows on the table. "I can understand that, Gene, but he's been dating some of New York's topmodels for Christ's sake! What does he want?"

His old friend stared at him. "Probably the same as you Joe - intelligence and breeding. You see, you might think Kevin Mitchell has it all but he hasn't. He wants what you have, a woman like Angela. Those other women may look beautiful on a cat-walk or smiling at you from the cover of glossy magazines, but it's all show. Nine times out of ten they don't have much up here." He tapped his head. "Angela's different. She's got brains and she knows how to conduct herself. She's not the kind you take to dinner and then to bed. You should know that better than anyone. My guess is, that's what he likes and admires about her."

Joe shook his head. "I warned him once before to stay away from her."

"Yeah well, maybe he's trying his luck again since he became twice as rich, thanks to his uncle. He can match anybody now Joe, and I hear our Kevin is setting his sights pretty high."

"What do you mean?"

"I mean he's thinking of going into politics and believe me, he has the backing of some powerful and influential friends."

"What about you?" Joe enquired.

"Oh he wouldn't do me any harm. After all, we'd be on the same side."

"But wouldn't a divorce stand in his way?"

"Not necessarily. I know quite a few politicians who are divorced. Come to think of it, half the country is divorced - and they would be the voters!" He looked into his glass for a moment. "You see Joe, Kevin isn't without brains either. He knows if he got the right woman, someone the public would like, down to earth and caring, that's what would matter most to the ordinary man and woman in the street. The fact that he'd be divorced wouldn't enter into it. Know what I mean?"

Joe nodded. "Yeah, I know what you mean. Someone like Angel."

"That's right, old buddy."

His eyes narrowed. "Well, I don't know what his dreams and schemes are but I can tell you one thing, they won't have anything to do with my wife!"

Gene put a hand on his shoulder. "Then you'd better make sure of that Joe," he advised, "because if anything happens you can't put all the blame on Angela. Not when you're spending so much time with Antonia."

Joe stared intently in her direction. "Well, there's no time like the present„" he said in a serious tone, getting to his feet.

Gene nodded and watched as he walked towards Antonia. The band was playing slow, soft music as Joe asked her to dance.

He waited until they were on the dance floor before he spoke again.

"I didn't know you knew Kevin Mitchell," he said casually.

"Joe, in my profession you get to know a lot of people. Besides, we have something in common."

"And what's that?"

"We both know you and your wife. He's very fond of Angela. He thinks she's the perfect woman and he should know, he's had the best ."

"Well, I don't see any of them here tonight," he commented.

"He must have decided to come alone. Anyway, he and Angela seem to be getting along very well. But then, he's an attractive and charming man, don't you think? And he's so cute!"

"Oh yeah, real cute!" he replied, sarcastically.

Antonia looked at him and smiled. "Why Joe, anyone would think you were jealous. Well, he is paying Angela a lot of attention and let's face it, not many women can resist him."

Joe studied her for a moment then said, "Maybe that's why he's here alone."

"I don't know what you mean," she insisted.

"Oh, I think you do, Antonia! You planned this, didn't you?" He gripped her arms tightly.

Her smile faded as he glared at her.

"I wasn't born yesterday," he continued, "and you of all people should know that. Let me guess ... You knew if you invited him he'd spend the evening trying to attract my wife's attention and that would leave the door open for you to get mine. You'd like nothing better than to see them together because you know if they had an affair, I'd leave her."

"And would that be so bad?" she asked. "You can't play happy ever after forever Joe. Sooner or later someone's going to come along. If it isn't Kevin Mitchell it will be someone else and then I'll be able to say, 'I told you so'!"

Joe shook his head, feeling both hurt and angry. "You'd stoop to anything to get what you want."

"I'm sick of waiting for something to happen between you two!" she snapped.

"So you thought you'd hurry things along? Well, let me tell you something. I'm sick! Sick of the way you've treated my wife tonight by taking over my evening and trying to keep me away from her. What is it with you? Can't you let go?"

"You loved me before she ever came along . Is it so terrible to want that love back?"

He was losing patience. "O'.K, if you want the truth then you're going to get it. I never loved you the way I love Angel, and I never could."

Her eyes flashed. "I don't believe that!"

"Then that's your problem - not mine."

"I love you Joe."

He stared at her. "Do you? Or do you just want something you can't have - like your friend, Mr. Mitchell? You're trying to wreck my marriage but it won't work. Angel has never been unfaithful to me and I'm not leaving her. Do you understand?"

"But you don't have to leave her," she explained, "just visit me from time to time at the apartment. No-one will know."

Joe could hardly believe what he was hearing. "I feel sorry for you, Antonia. You've got everything you ever wanted, fame, fortune and the jet set lifestyle. But you're still not happy and now you want to ruin my happiness. Can you really call that love?"

"I'll settle for what I can get," she replied determinedly. "Just as long as we can be together. One or two evenings a week isn't much to ask for and you owe me that, Joe Morrelli."

He tightened his grip. "And what about my son, does he owe you too?"

Antonia lowered her gaze for a moment, then looked back at Joe. "Robert's only a boy," she said in a low voice.

"But he's growing up Antonia. He won't always be a boy and what is he going to think of his father, when he's a man? When he finds out about us. When he finds out I've been unfaithful to his mother because his aunt and godmother wanted it that way. I don't owe you anything except the name of a good psychiatrist! You're hell bent on destroying my life and everything I love because of the past." He looked and spoke sternly. "I'm warning you, don't ever pull another stunt like you did tonight. I've never cheated on my wife and I don't intend to start now. Not with you or any other woman. If you won't let go for me, then do it for Robert. If you had an ounce of decency left, you would."

She was silent as he took her by the arm and pushed his way through the crowd. On reaching her table he gave a wry smile. As he sat her down somewhat roughly, he looked across the table and said,

"There you go Judge. She's all yours!"

Antonia scowled at him as he turned and walked away.

Joe went back to his table and rejoined his wife and friends. As he sat down both men exchanged glances but when Joe nodded his head slightly, Gene knew he had taken care of things. After that, the four friends enjoyed their evening and each other's company. However, there was some unfinished business for Joe.

Standing before the large mirror in the men's room, he saw Kevin Mitchell come in. As he turned, Kevin smiled at him.

"Are you enjoying the party, Mr. Morrelli?"

Joe nodded. "Yeah, but I'd enjoy it even more if you would find a woman of your own and stop chasing after someone else's."

"I'm afraid I don't know what you mean," replied Kevin, still smiling.

"Then let me make it clear to you. You see, Mr. Mitchell, I know you fancy my wife." The charming smile soon disappeared.

"Now that's where you're wrong Mr. Morrelli. I don't fancy your wife - I want her!" Joe stared at him through narrowed eyes. "Only I admire your taste in women, I'd bust you in the mouth so hard you wouldn't be able to smile for a month."

"I don't think that would be wise, do you? How would you explain that to Angela?"

"Oh, I'd think of something."

Kevin looked at him. "Why don't you tell her the truth? You're getting old and you're scared of losing her. You can't bear the thought of her finding happiness with another man, a younger man, who can give her everything she wants."

"And I suppose you fit the bill?" asked Joe, with a look and tone of sarcasm.

"As a matter of fact, I think I do."

Joe stepped closer. "I warned you before, stay away from her."

"And I told you I didn't scare easily."

If Kevin Mitchell was trying to get him riled, he succeeded. Pushing him against the wall hard Joe snapped,

"Now you listen to me, Mr. High-flying Executive, you might want my wife but you won't ever get her!"

"Why don't you let Angela be the judge of that?"

Kevin leaned his face towards him as if to prove his courage. But Joe had come across other Kevin Mitchell's.

"Not with the likes of you," he said. "You see, I know how guys like you operate. You're only in love until a new face and figure comes on the scene. Men like you want a woman, sure, but you never love them. I think the fact that you have a broken marriage and a string of broken affairs proves my point."

"Maybe that's because none of them was Angela," came the angry reply.

"Yeah," Joe nodded, "I guess she has even more brains than I gave her credit for. She never was easily swayed, especially by a smooth talker."

"Well Mr. Morrelli, maybe that's because with you being so jealous and possessive, she never had the chance."

Joe stood back and studied him. "She had plenty of chances, especially when she worked with you on your uncle's committee. You see, you might want her - but does she want you?" He looked him up and down. "I don't think so! After all, I'm the one she always came home to. But you're right, I am jealous and possessive of anything I love. And I love my wife!" He poked a warning finger into Kevin's chest. "If you ever come between me and Angel I swear you'll regret it - and I don't make empty threats!"

"And I don't give up easily. If she ever wants me I'll be waiting and there's not much you can do about that, now is there?" he smirked, pushing Joe's finger aside.

Joe's eyes narrowed once again. "I wouldn't count on it, because nobody fucks with Joe Morrelli. And I mean nobody! You'd do well to remember that."

Without another word, he turned on his heel and left the men's room.

Antonia had kept her distance but she had watched Joe and Angela's every move. The attention Joe was paying to his young wife was really beginning to get to her. As they talked, laughed and danced together, Antonia was consumed with jealousy. So much so, she couldn't contain herself any longer.

Joe saw her coming towards the table and looked hurriedly at Gene.

"Why don't we all have a dance?" he suggested, then stared directly in front of him.

Gene followed his gaze. "Yeah, why don't we?" he replied.

As both couples left the table, Antonia stopped in their path.

"I hope you are all enjoying my big night," she said.

"We sure are," Gene assured her.

"You must be feeling very relieved and lucky Angela," she smiled sweetly.

"I beg your pardon ..."

"Well my dear, my big break is a movie. Your's was getting a job in 'The Safe Haven'. If Joe hadn't seen you waiting on tables in his restaurant, you wouldn't be here with him tonight. He probably would have married me and we would be on our way to Hollywood soon. But then, Joe never could resist helping someone down on their luck. And he always was a sucker for a woman telling him she loved him, just like most men."

She put her hand on Joe's arm. "I'll bet you never thought I'd come this far darling. I hope you have no hidden regrets." Her smile remained.

There was total silence and Antonia was feeling very pleased with herself

Angela remained composed, then spoke in a soft, polite voice. "I hear Hollywood can be a very bitchy town to live in. I also hear the women there are forever chasing after someone else's husband. I think you'll fit in very nicely, Antonia." She glanced over the actress' shoulder casually. "Do excuse me. I've just seen someone I'd really like to talk to."

As she brushed by, Antonia stood stunned.

"I don't believe the nerve of that woman! How dare she insult me here!" she seethed.

Angela turned back and leaned close to Antonia's ear. "Why, where would you prefer to go?" she asked innocently, before walking away.

Gene O'Brien smiled broadly. However, Antonia was not amused.

"Aren't you going to do something?" she snapped at Joe.

He removed her hand. "Yes I am. I'm going to congratulate my wife. That was a great performance, even better than the one you gave. You can tell she studied Shakespeare. What a pity you never learned any Antonia - you really lost out!"

She clenched both fists and stamped her foot in anger before storming off. Kate O'Brien smiled as her husband burst out laughing.

"Jesus, this is one night when I'm really proud of the Irish!"

"Yeah, and this is one night I'm really proud to be married to someone who is Irish!" came Joe's reply.

Gene shook his head. "I've never seen anyone brought down with such style."

"Angel always did have a way with words," Joe smiled. "Besides, Antonia did ask for it."

"Somehow Joe, I don't think you'll be hearing from her for a while."

Joe grinned. "Neither do I Gene, Neither do I."

Gene and Kate took to the dance floor while Joe went in search of Angela. He found her standing alone, leaning her back against the wall and watching the crowd.

He stood in front of her. "Hey lady, would you like to dance?"

She gave a faint smile. "I thought you'd be angry with me."

"Why should I be angry?"

"Because of what I said to Antonia. After all, you were her escort."

"Believe me Angel, she had it coming. But that's Antonia for you, give her your hand and she wants your whole arm. Maybe now you'll understand why I wasn't too keen on the idea. Anyway, I'm proud of the way you handled the situation."

"Really?"

"Really," he nodded. "You hit where it hurt and still managed to do it with grace and charm. I'll tell you one thing, you made my night - and Gene's!"

Angela smiled. "I don't care if this movie gets an Academy Award, this is the last time you will escort her anywhere."

"Is that a promise?" he asked.

"Yes it is. I know what she was trying to do tonight, Joe. She wanted you all to herself but I wasn't prepared to let that happen. You're my husband and I love you."

He leaned over and kissed her cheek . "And I love you," he whispered.

She gazed into his face. "But she's right about one thing, I was a waitress."

"Yeah, I know. But I'm sure glad it was in my restaurant and not someone else's. Otherwise I might never have met you. Besides, if Antonia ever makes it to Hollywood she's in for a big surprise."

"Why?"

"Well, she's going to discover that most of the actors and actresses there were waiters and waitresses themselves while they were waiting for their big break."

Angela looked surprised. "How do you know?"

He tapped the side of his nose with his finger. "When I was younger I used to spend a lot of time at the movies and I used to read a lot of magazines too," he smiled.

"Joe Morrelli, I never thought you were interested in movie stars."

"Oh, we all have our favourites," he grinned, holding out his hands. "How do you think I got this macho, tough guy image?"

She shook her head. "I suppose you'll be telling me next you learned how to make love by watching your favourites do it on the big screen."

"Not me! That part is strictly Joe Morrelli. I never had to copy anyone."

"Now I can believe that!" she smiled.

He smiled back and took her hand. "Why don't we finish this dance?" As he led her towards the dance floor, he looked around. "It's getting pretty noisy in here. What do you say we find Gene and Kate, then we can all leave together?"

Angela agreed.

As the four friends reached the door, Joe stopped. "Why don't you say goodnight to Kevin Mitchell?" he urged.

Angela nodded and went across to his table, as Joe watched. Kevin got up and he and Angela talked for a few moments, then he bent over and kissed her cheek. When she returned, Joe put his arm around her and both men stood staring directly and coldly at each other. Then Joe smiled as he ushered Angela out of the door, leaving Kevin Mitchell in deep thought.

Things hadn't gone the way he'd hoped they would, tonight. But he consoled himself with the fact that there would be other nights. He knew in his heart the chances of him breaking into politics were slim because of his impending divorce and past womanising, but Gene O'Brien was doing a good job as Senator and at a later date would probably want to further his career. Kevin had given him 100% of his backing and always would, not just because of his uncle but because he genuinely liked him. He knew there would be other fund raising events in the future and charity evenings. He also knew that Angela would be on the committee- and so would he. If he wanted to unlock the door that would lead him to Angela, only one man held the key and that man was Gene O'Brien. His committee work would bring him into contact with Angela again, of that he was certain. Only the next time he would try harder to get the woman he admired so much. He didn't mind waiting because one day he was going to wipe that smug smile off Joe Morrelli's face!

Over the next few months things were back to normal at Roseberry Avenue. Joe had had enough of the parties for the time being, so when he and Angela did go out it was usually just an intimate dinner for two. Sometimes Rooney and Rachel joined them for a foursome making it one big happy family, full of fun and conversation. But Joe couldn't fail to notice that there were times when Rooney seemed pre-occupied with his own thoughts, especially when they were alone together dealing with business. He had a gut feeling something wasn't quite right but he never asked any questions. He knew Rooney well enough to know that if something was troubling him, he would hear about it sooner or later. He didn't have long to wait.

Joe sat in his study going over some business propositions, when Rooney came in. "What are you doing here?" smiled Joe . "It's your day off."

"I know, I just thought I'd call. Are you busy?"

Joe put the papers down and shook his head. "No."

Rooney closed the door and came towards the desk. Then he gazed at the floor, shuffling his feet in an uncomfortable manner.

"What's the matter? You're acting kind of weird," said Joe, as he studied an anxious Rooney.

"Joe, I need to talk to you, I've got a problem."

"Sit down."

Joe leaned back in his chair while Rooney took a seat. Both men looked at each other. "O.K. Let's hear it," he encouraged.

"Well, it's Rachel."

Joe leaned forward quickly. "Jesus Rooney, you haven't got her in the family way, have you?"

"No!!"

"O.K., O.K., don't bite my head off" replied Joe, holding up his hands.

Rooney was silent for a moment, then explained,

"She wants us to get married."

"Like when?"

"Like in three months. Just long enough for her parents to arrange a really big wedding."

"Hey that's great news! Well, isn't it?" he asked hesitantly, looking at Rooney's sombre face.

"To tell you the truth Joe, I don't think I can go through with it. Don't get me wrong, Rachel's a really nice woman and I love her but ..."

"Hey hold it a minute!" Joe put his hands up again. "You've lost me. She's a really nice woman, you love her but you don't want to marry her. Am I right?"

Rooney nodded

Joe shook his head. "For Christ's sake, Rooney, that doesn't make any sense. If you love her you'll want to marry her. That's the way it's supposed to work, anyway. What makes you so different from the rest of us?"

Rooney lowered his gaze. "Maybe I don't love her ... enough."

"What do you mean?"

"I mean, I don't think it would be fair to marry her. You see, I don't love her as much as I should."

"Have you spoken to her about it?"

Rooney nodded. "She says if we get married, I'd learn to love her as much as she loves me."

"Well there you are! Maybe she's right," said Joe, trying his best to find some thread of hope.

Rooney stared at him. "Oh come on Joe, you know that isn't true. Could you have learned to love Antonia the way she wanted you to? Be honest."

There was silence while Joe soul searched.

"No ... I guess not," he admitted.

"Well, there you are. I guess I'm not so different after all."

Joe studied him carefully, "Rooney, how much is enough? What I mean is, why do you feel you can't build a marriage on what you've got?"

"Because it would never work, Joe. I could never have the happiness you and

Angela have. I could never love Rachel the way you love Angela and I want that, Joe. I don't want to settle for anything less."

"O.K then end it. End it before it's too late," Joe sighed.

"I guess you think I'm pretty stupid about the whole thing."

"No I don't Rooney. I think you're making a wise decision. It's better to pull out now and hurt her feelings for a while, than marry her and make her unhappy for the rest of her life. If you can't love her completely, don't love her at all. You'd both end up hating each other." Joe was earnest and sincere in his advice. "I know if I'd married Antonia, I'd have been very unhappy. At the time I thought I was in love - I wanted to be in love, but I was only kidding myself. When Angel came along I really knew I was in love. But I guess I don't have to tell you that because you loved her too."

Rooney became flustered. "I swear to God, Joe, I've never envied you your happiness, you've got to believe that. But the night Angela gave her speech for you, I knew then that the love you both had was special and that she was special. I guess it was on that night I realised I wanted the same. I thought maybe I could find it with Rachel but I can't . I've tried Joe, I've really tried."

Joe reached over and patted his arm. "I understand, Rooney. I do, honest. I'm just sorry it didn't work out for you. Nothing would give me more pleasure than to see you as happy as I am. Now is there anything I can do to help?"

"Well, there is one thing."

"Just name it."

Rooney looked embarrassed. "I don't want to tell Angela and I don't want to tell the guys."

"That won't be a problem," Joe promised. "You leave that to me. I'll just tell Angel things didn't work out - and before you say another word, I won't go into details!"

Rooney gripped his hand firmly. "Thanks Joe. I'd hoped you'd understand and I know I can count on you to straighten things out with everyone. I don't want any of them asking me questions."

Joe nodded. "I'll have a word with Frankie and Al."

"Especially Al!" Rooney insisted. "If he makes any smart comments about this, I'll wring his neck!"

"No-one will mention it. You've got my word on that."

"Well I guess I'd better go and see Rachel. There's no point in putting it off any longer."

"Yeah, there's no time like the present. That's what I always say. I'll see you tomorrow."

Rooney got up and left the study.

Joe shook his head and lowered his gaze to the desk. He felt gutted that things hadn't worked out for his best friend. But he knew why. Both of them had fallen in love with the same woman and Rooney was waiting for another Angela Kenny to come along. But there was little chance of that. There was only one Angela and he had been the lucky one to get her. But he felt guilty.

If his house rules in 'The Safe Haven' had been different, Rooney would have been the lucky one. However, Joe consoled himself with one thought. Rooney had let Angela go too easily. He should have persuaded her to leave by finding her another job. It was a mistake not to and a mistake he would always have to live with.

Joe on the other hand, never gave up easily. If he wanted something badly enough, he'd do anything to get it - and did. It was just a pity that Rooney hadn't learned that from him all those years ago.

Chapter 17

Over the next few years, things went well for Joe. Thanks to his shrewd business deals with the Andrettis and his sound investments with Reuben, he was making a lot of money. The profits were huge, pleasing him and delighting his trusted accountant, who kept a watchful eye on every transaction and could trace every dollar!

Joe was an extremely wealthy man now and could afford to be generous to all those in his employ. He was, but nothing pleased him more than lavishing his money on his family. He could have bought a mansion away from the city but Angela wouldn't hear of it. He was glad. Roseberry Avenue was home to both of them and as she had often pointed out, "Home is where the heart is". Besides, it was a happy house with a lot of happy memories and Joe's heart was certainly there.

During this time Antonia had gone to Hollywood but found herself disillusioned with everything there. So she had returned to the two places she loved, New York and Broadway.

Sheila had two miscarriages, both boys, and was told she would never carry a baby boy full term. This distressed her greatly, as Raymond had always wanted a son. She suffered from bouts of depression and anxiety attacks, which worried Angela. Joe persuaded them into sending Aisling back to the States for school vacations, which they did. Her visits made him very happy. He and Angela treated her like their own and Joe loved her dearly. To him, she was the daughter he never had and Aisling returned that love, idolising her Uncle Joe and looking up to Robert as her big brother. Her time spent with them was filled with fun and laughter. The older she got the more she resembled Angela, especially when she got into a temper! Yes, Joe really enjoyed having her around.

He still brought his family to Miami, but he travelled with them too. His wealth made sure that he, Angela and Robert could have first class tickets to anywhere in Europe, staying at the finest hotels. Robert loved Italy, which pleased Joe, so they went often. But every now and again he would make sure to book a long weekend or a few days away for just him and his wife. There were times when he wanted to be alone with her and places like Paris were perfect. Joe was still a romantic at heart. He still liked the candle-lit dinners and the evening when they could stroll hand in hand. He still needed her company, conversation and undivided attention. After all these years he still loved Angela as much as he did when they first married. For Joe Morrelli, that had never changed.

The years had been good to him. His life was like a river running smoothly on it's way. But unknown to Joe, he was about to hit a current. One he would have to fight ruthlessly, in order to save those closest to him.

The phone rang in Joe's study. Lifting the receiver to his ear, he immediately recognised the familiar voice on the other end.

"Hey Nick, how are you?"

"Fine Joe," came the reply.

"I'm glad to hear it," Joe smiled. "Is this a social call or is it business?"

"A little of both." Nick Andretti's voice sounded serious and Joe's smile faded.

"Is there something I can do for you, Nick?"

"I hope so. I'd like you to come to my home this evening. It's important and I'd appreciate it."

"Sure, that's no problem. What time?"

"Oh, sometime after dinner. Say nine o'clock?" Nick suggested.

Joe agreed. "o.k. I'll be there."

"Thanks Joe."

After thinking for a few moments, Joe asked, "Hey, Nick would you mind if I brought Rooney along? It's just that he's managing a lot of my affairs right now and the more he learns, the more I'll benefit later on."

"Not at all Joe. Bring him along by all means. I think he might find it very interesting."

Joe was relieved. "Thank's Nick. I'll see you tonight. Goodbye."

"Goodbye Joe."

He put the receiver down and stared in front of him, puzzled. It wasn't like Nick Andretti to discuss business at his home. That was the one place he had always kept private. Nick always used his office for meetings and discussions. Joe knew instinctively that something was wrong, he just didn't know what. However, come tonight, he would surely find out.

At nine o'clock that evening, Joe rang the door bell. He was accompanied by Rooney, while Al waited in the parked car. The door was opened by a maid and before he could speak she said,

"Please come in Mr. Morrelli, Mr. Andretti is expecting you. This way ... " she smiled. Joe and Rooney glanced at each other as they followed her across a spacious entrance hall. Stopping outside a thick oak door, she knocked and waited.

"Come in," came the reply.

She ushered the two men into the room, closing the door after them. They found themselves in a lounge, tastefully and expensively furnished . Nick Andretti got up from behind a large desk smiling.

"Good of you to come Joe." He gripped his hand firmly.

"Yeah well, I was curious to see how the other half lives!"

Nick nodded. "I remember the time I had to conduct my business from the back of a small restaurant in the old neighbourhood."

"So do I and it had red and white check table-cloths. But come to think of it, all the restaurants in the old neighbourhood had them. It must have been the fashion. Either that or all the Italians bought their table-cloths at the same place!" joked Joe.

Nick laughed, "It wouldn't surprise me to learn that you and Dominic sold them at a discount."

Joe gave a sly smile. "Now that would be telling!"

The old man shook Rooney's hand, then looked at them both. "You are welcome in my home. Please sit down," he motioned.

"It's an honour to be here," Joe replied.

Rooney agreed. At that moment, the door opened and Anthony appeared.

He greeted Joe warmly. "It's good to see you again, Mr. Morrelli." He then shook Rooney's hand and went to pour some drinks, while the two guests sat down on the couch.

When everyone was settled, Nick Andretti began to fill Joe and Rooney in on why they were there.

"There's something I'd like you to see," he said nodding to Anthony, who unlocked a desk drawer and took out a video.

Going over to the television set, he put it into the recorder and switched it on. Returning to his seat, he waited. There was silence as the four men sipped their drinks and watched the blank screen. A few moments later, the video started to play. It became clear to Joe right away that this was a home made video, containing lurid sexual acts between an adult male and under-aged teenagers of both sexes. These kids were so high on drugs they stumbled around barely knowing what was happening to them and too helpless to resist.

Joe leaned forward and watched closely. He had never been interested in pornography of any kind, but something was bothering him. He couldn't see much of the man's face but thought he recognised the loud laugh. He didn't want to watch such filth but felt compelled to. Following a series of sickening and depraved acts, the man finally got up off the bed and reached for a small package on the bedside table. Turning around, he placed some white powder on the back of his hand and snorted it up his nose. Then walking forward, he leered into the camera for a close-up shot.

A wave of shock and revulsion swept over Joe as he stared at the face confronting him on the screen. "Jesus, that's Benny Bangles!" he said out loud.

Rooney shook his head. "I can hardly believe what I've just seen. But I said a long time ago if he wasn't stopped there wouldn't be a decent kid left in this city, he'd ruin them all. It looks like I was right."

Anthony switched off the tape, as Joe looked across at Nick.

"How did you get hold of that?" he asked.

"I have my connections Joe. One of his men stole it from his collection." "You mean he's got more?"

"Believe me, he's got a lot more - and a lot worse!"

Joe and Rooney looked at each other in almost disbelief as Nick Andretti continued. "Fortunately, not all of Benny's men are loyal to him now. Some of them don't like what he's into. They're scared it could lead to something more serious and they want out."

"I'm not surprised," said Joe. "That guy's a fuckin' psycho! He's trash, and trash like that ought to be taken off the streets for good."

"Then maybe you could help us to do just that."

"Me?" asked a surprised Joe.

While Anthony refilled the glasses, his grandfather remained silent, examining his own thoughts. Then he lifted his eyes and looked at Joe. "I heard about the run-in you had with him some years ago in a nightclub."

This was news to Rooney!

Joe shrugged, "Yeah well, that was a long time ago. Besides, I haven't seen him since."

"Maybe that was because you warned him to keep out of your way. Listen Joe," Nick explained, "we all want to do business without stepping on anyone's toes but this guy is becoming an embarrassment - and a threat! He's stepping on quite a few toes, including mine and it won't be long before he steps on yours. Benny Bangles has made a name for himself but it has made him arrogant. He's muscling in on territory that doesn't belong to him. He's selling drugs and picking kids up off the streets, and you've just seen what he's doing to them. Benny's a problem, and one I'd like to be without."

Joe thought for a moment then suggested, "Why don't you get that video delivered to the cops and let someone down town deal with him?"

"Because it wouldn't do any good. He's got cops on his payroll. That tape probably wouldn't get any further than the enquiry desk and even if it did, some hot shot lawyer would make sure Benny walked away. That's what he's paying them for." He stared intently at Joe. "No, this is one time when I want him put away for good. And to do that, we'll have to deal with him ourselves. That's where you come in."

It was obvious now to Joe that Nick Andretti wanted a favour from him, a favour he just couldn't and wouldn't refuse. After all these years, it was payback time!

He nodded. "O.k. Nick, what did you have in mind?"

"He doesn't like you Joe, but he fears you. You once told him he'd made an enemy for life. I think he has enjoyed himself enough since then, don't you? I want that life ended. Believe me, we would be doing this city a great service."

"Well, after what I've just seen I'm inclined to agree with you. But I'll need time to figure out what to do and how to do it. I'll also need some information, like times, places and who he hangs out with."

Nick smiled, "That won't be a problem, Joe. Some of Benny's men are already in my pocket. They'll tell us everything we need to know." He raised his glass to Joe and then spoke in Italian saying, "On your wedding day you told me if there was ever anything you could do for me, just to ask. I am touched by your loyalty after all these years."

And in Italian Joe replied, "I owe you a great debt of gratitude and I will repay it. I am honoured to be of service to you."

Nick turned his attention to Rooney. "I would be very interested to know what you would do?" he asked.

Rooney met his gaze and held it. "I'd blow his brains out. Better one dead pervert than a dozen dead kids."

"Now that's very true. That's what I admire about the Irish, they're truthful. They say what they mean and mean what they say - a bit like the Italians!"

"We have to be, Mr. Andretti. Where I come from your life can depend on it."

After finishing their drinks, Joe and Rooney were ready to leave. Nick and Anthony walked them to the door, where the old man put his hands on Joe's shoulders.

"Let me explain something to you Joe," he said. "If this guy ever does anything to a kid who's father is connected, all hell is going to break loose. There will be dead bodies all over this city and once a feud starts it can take years to settle. Believe me, I know, I've lived through a few. Everyone has to choose sides and business goes down the tubes. No one has anything to gain but they have a lot to loose. I don't want that to happen." He sighed deeply. "I may be an old man but I'm trying to prevent a war here and I need people I can trust. People like you, Joe."

"Yeah, I know. Leave it with me, Nick. I'll get back to you," Joe promised.

The four men took their leave of each other and as the front door closed, Joe and Rooney stood in the cool night air.

"What are you going to do?" Rooney asked.

"What do you think? You saw that video, I have no choice. I'll have to take Benny Bangles down, just the way I did with his friend, Lenny Shultz."

"You don't look too happy about it."

Joe shrugged, "Well personally I have no beef with the guy but Nick Andretti has been good to me over the years and I owe him a lot. More than you'll ever know, Rooney. If I do him this one favour, he won't ever ask for another one."

"How can you be so sure?"

"Because I know him. The slate will be wiped clean and that's the way I want it. Besides, that fuckin' Benny has gone too far. Old Nick's right, he's an embarrassment and a threat to every Italian who wants to be respected."

"But why you Joe? Why couldn't he take care of it himself?"

"Because no one would ever suspect me. No one ever suspected me with Lenny Shultz - and he knows that . I'm a businessman. Maybe that's why Benny has never shown his face on my patch. I don't deal in drugs and don't run brothels. I'm no threat to him. How I make a living is a lot higher up the ladder and he knows he can't compete." Joe turned the collar of his jacket up and shook his head. "No I have nothing Benny wants. Nothing he can get his hands on. Maybe I'm just lucky."

As they reached the waiting car, Rooney was still hesitant. "I don't know Joe. I still think Nick Andretti could have handled this himself. He's a big man with a big say."

Joe looked at him. "So is Harry Collington but he stays in the background, remember? That doesn't mean to say he's not involved, though. I might be the one who's going after Benny but Nick will set it all up. It's the same difference except for one very important thing."

"What's that?"

"Nick Andretti has as much loyalty for his men as they have for him."

"Point taken," Rooney nodded, as he opened the car door. "How long are you going to let this guy enjoy what he's doing?"

Joe's eyes narrowed as he looked around thoughtfully. "Oh, I don't know. As long as it takes, I guess. I'll have to think everything through very carefully. There's no great hurry."

He and Rooney got into the back. Al turned around.

"Do you want to go somewhere Boss?"

"No. Why?"

Al smiled. "I was thinking, maybe we could drive though the city and see the night-life." Joe scratched his forehead. "No thanks Al, I've seen enough for one night! Let's go home."

Joe, Angela and Rooney were sitting at the kitchen table in jovial conversation when Robert arrived home from school. He was thirteen now and besides being a very bright boy, he was also very good looking with his black hair and large, dark eyes. Although he had just entered his teens, Evie still fussed over him. She always had a glass of milk and some cookies waiting for him, a habit she could never break   since he first started school. As he came through the door with his books, Rooney put his arm out and punched him playfully.

"Well, how goes it champ?" he smiled.

Usually, Robert would have responded with a broad grin and some playful sparring. But not today. Instead he nodded. "O.k. Uncle Rooney."

Evie turned away from the vegetables she was preparing. "Robert honey why don't you sit down at the table and have your milk and cookies?"

"No thanks, Evie. I'm not hungry," he replied, leaving the kitchen.

She stared after him and shook her head. "I've a notion there's something troubling that boy. And I know what I know!"

Angela looked at Joe, then got up. "Evie's right Joe, it's not like him to be so quiet and withdrawn. There's something wrong with him. Maybe he's ill and doesn't want to tell us." She was worried.

Joe put his hand on her arm. "Don't panic, Angel, it could be anything. Maybe he's just had a bad day at school or an argument with one of his friends."

"Well, whatever it is I'm going to find out."

"No, you stay here and I'll go. He's not a child anymore and if that's what it is he'll probably tell me. After all, I was his age once. He might feel a man would understand more than a woman."

As Joe got up, Angela nodded. "I suppose you're right."

"Sure I am. Just leave it to me, I'll go and have a word with him."

Leaving the kitchen, he went straight to Robert's bedroom and opened the door quietly. Robert sat on the side of the bed, staring at the floor.

"What's the matter son?" he asked, sitting down beside him.

"Nothing dad," came the reply.

"Well now, I don't think that's true. Listen son, if something happened at school today, don't you think I should know about it? I am your father."

The boy kept his eyes on the floor. "I don't want to talk about it."

Joe put a caring hand on his shoulder. "Oh come on, son, you can tell me," he coaxed.

Robert looked up at him "O.k. I was hanging around with one of my friends at lunch time, outside the school. We where just passing a basket ball to each other, when a car stopped and a man called us over. We thought he was looking for directions."

"And was he?"

"No, he started to ask us stuff"

"What kind of stuff?" Joe was becoming concerned.

"What we were studying in school and if we liked it. Who we hang out with and what we do. Then he asked us our ages."

"Go on," Joe urged.

"He took out some pills and asked us if we wanted any. I said no. My friend said he couldn't because he didn't have any money. But the man just laughed and said we could have them for free."

"Was he driving a big car?"

"No, just a small one, like the car Al picks me up from school in."

"Was he alone?"

"No, he was sitting in the back and another man was driving. But he didn't say anything."

"O.k.," nodded Joe, "did anything else happen?"

Robert was silent for a moment as he clasped his hands nervously. "He was staring at us and asked us to come closer. He wanted us to get into the car and go for a drive with him. He said it would be fun."

"What did you do, son?"

"I told him we had to get back to class. But he said, 'Some other time'. Then he reached out of the window and stroked my face. He started to smile and said I was a pretty boy and he liked me." Tears came to his eyes. "It was really creepy dad. The way he looked at me and touched me was wrong. I hope he doesn't come back!"

Joe stared into Robert's face, earnestly. "Listen son, there are different kinds of love in this world and what people choose to do in the privacy of their own home is their own business. Do you understand what I'm saying?"

He nodded, so his father continued,

"O.k. But when people bring it out onto the streets and around schools, then it becomes everyone's business - especially mine because I'm your father. Can you describe this man?"

Robert thought carefully. "Well, he looked Italian. He was dressed in flashy clothes. And he had this loud laugh."

"Anything else?"

"Yeah dad. He wore a lot of jewellery around his neck and wrists. Real gold."

Joe turned away so the boy couldn't see his expression change. Benny Bangles !!! He filled with such anger and disgust, he was finding it very difficult to suppress it.

"Do you know him?" the boy asked.

Joe turned back and shook his head. "No, I can't say I do."

"Dad, I'm scared. What if he does come back? I don't like him"

His father embraced him protectively and they met each other's gaze. "He won't be back, Robert. I can promise you that."

Robert nodded. He loved Joe and knew he'd never lie to him about something so serious. He could always believe his father and felt sure that this would be no exception.

"Did he ask you your name?"

"Yeah, but I wouldn't tell him."

"Good boy," Joe nodded. "What about the other boy."

"He wouldn't tell either. We both ran back to school."

"Well, I'm proud of you. You did the right thing son." He got up off the bed and stood staring down at Robert for a few moments. "Are you o.k. now?"

561

he asked.

"Yeah, I'm o.k. I'm glad you came, dad. I didn't want to tell mom." He looked uncomfortable and embarrassed so Joe said,

"Speaking of your mom Robert. I think we should keep this conversation just between the two of us. You know, men's stuff. Besides, we don't want to worry her."

"What will we tell her, then?"

"Oh, we could say you had an argument with your best friend. What do you think?"

"That's fine by me, Dad." The boy was obviously relieved.

Joe forced a smile but inside the thought of what might have happened to his son was tearing him apart. "O.k. that's what we'll tell her. Agreed?"

"Agreed," Robert nodded.

Embracing him once more, Joe said, "Never hide anything from me son. I'm your father and I'm here to listen and help you. I won't ever let anything or anyone harm you." He ran his fingers through Robert's hair, lovingly. "No one will ever harm a hair on your head - not while I'm around. That's my promise to you son. And Joe Monrelli never breaks a promise! Now, I better go downstairs and see your mother. She thinks you're ill. I'll see you later," he smiled.

He left the bedroom, closing the door after him. As he reached the top of the stairs, he stopped and grabbed hold of the wooden rail, digging his fingers into it viciously. Benny Bangles would regret this day with all his heart. Joe Morrelli would see to that personally!

All eyes were upon him as he entered the kitchen.

"Did you find out what's wrong with him'?" asked Angela.

He nodded. "Yeah, it was just what I thought. He had a disagreement with his friend and it led to an argument. He's pretty cut up about it. You know what kids are like at that age."

"Did you talk it through with him, Joe? You were up there quite a while."

"Sure I did. I told him it happens to everyone at some time and in a day or two it will all be forgotten. It takes more than one argument to break up a friendship. He knows that now. It's all part of growing up Angel."

She was relieved. "Thank God he isn't ill. I'm going upstairs to see him " Joe didn't try to stop her but advised, "O.k. but don't question him about it."

"Why not?"

"Because he's feeling stupid and embarrassed about the whole thing. Anyway, I wouldn't be surprised if they were best friends again tomorrow!"

"You're right Joe. Best not to mention it," she agreed.

"I've got some business to take care of honey . I'll be in the study."

He motioned for Rooney to follow and when both men were sure of their privacy he said, "Sit down Rooney, I've got something to tell you."

When Joe had finished, Rooney leapt to his feet. His face was white with rage. "That slime, that fuckin' pervert slime! I'll kill him for this, I'll fuckin' kill him!"

"No you won't," came the determined reply. "That pleasure is going to be all mine." Banging his fist hard on the desk, he raised his voice. "That bastard touched my son! That son-of-a-bitch put his hands on Joe Morrelli's son!"

Rooney tried to calm things a little. "Joe, are you sure Robert told you everything? Would you like me to have a talk with him, just to make sure?"

"No it's o.k. He told me everything that happened. If there was something else, I'd know about it. Robert wouldn't hold anything back from me, not about this. Besides, I told him it was just between him and me. He doesn't know I've told you."

Rooney was visibly upset. "Joe, as far as I'm concerned Robert is my own flesh and blood, you know that. What happened between you and Benny Bangles in the past is your business. But what happened today to that boy, is my business too."

"Yeah, I know," Joe nodded.

"Well, what I want to know is, what are we going to do about it? Jesus Christ, if he'd been dumb enough to get into that car ... Well, you know what might have happened. You saw that video!"

"Thank God he's a smart kid. I always laid down two rules to him. Never take anything from strangers, and never go anywhere with them. No matter what they promise or offer. He learned those rules and he learned them good. That's what saved him today. Him and that other kid."

Rooney stared. "Joe, Benny Bangles will be back - and we both know it. We have to stop him. Next time Robert might not be able to get away."

"There's not going to be a next time," he was assured.

"What are you going to do?"

"What the law can't do," Joe replied. "I'm going to take him off the streets - for good. And I'll be doing every kid a favour, not just my own." He walked around the desk and sat down in the leather chair. Lifting the receiver, he dialled. "Hey Nick, it's me. We need to talk." After a short conversation, he replaced the receiver and looked across at his friend. "We have a meeting this evening at Nick Andretti's office but don't say anything about today. I promised him I'd do him a favour and I will. I just don't want him to know I have my own personal reasons. That way, my debt is paid in full and no one knows I'm doing it for my son. I trust Nick but there are other guys I don't trust. In these situations, it's always best to be one step ahead. As far as everyone's concerned, I have no beef with Benny Bangles and that's the way I want it to stay."

"What time do we meet?"

"Seven thirty. Tell Frankie and Al I want to see them here at nine thirty."

"Are you going to tell them about Robert?"

"Yeah I am. They have a right to know."

Rooney nodded and walked towards the door. On reaching it, he turned around. "We all love him, Joe."

"I know, believe me, I know. But he's my son, Rooney and I love him more. That fuckin' junkie pervert is going to pay with his life for what he did today."

"Yeah, and we will all make sure of that. You want to be the one who kills him, Joe, but we would all like to be there."

Joe stood up and rested his clenched fists on the desk. "Don't worry, you guys won't miss a thing."

"I'm glad to hear it. I'll see you later."

Left on his own, Joe unlocked the desk drawer and took out a gun. Holding it in his right hand, he examined it closely then stared into space.

"And Benny won't miss a bullet!" he murmured.

Frankie and Al knew if their boss was calling a meeting it must be something important, so at nine thirty on the dot the four men were assembled in the study. When they were all seated, Joe leaned back in his chair and looked at his two friends.

"There's something I think you guys should know." He glanced towards Rooney and nodded. "I've already told him and the rest he's known for a few weeks." Joe proceeded to tell them about the video he had seen at Nick Andretti's home, followed by what had happened to Robert that day. When he concluded there was silence as a look of shock came to their faces.

"Jesus, I can hardly believe it!" said Frankie, shaking his head.

Al leaned forward in his seat and looked at Joe. "He stroked his face? That fuckin' low life stroked his face?" His anger was boiling over. "Jesus boss, that piece of shit was making a pass at your son. At a kid who had his thirteenth birthday just a few weeks ago. I say we kill him!" He looked around at the rest of the company. "I say we shoot his fuckin' hands off, then blow his brains out - that's what I say!"

Frankie agreed. "Al's right, Boss. We've got to get rid of him before it's too late. If he's offering drugs to kids in school then we have to stop it."

Joe nodded. "I intend to. Rooney and me just came from a meeting with Nick Andretti. Benny won't be around after the weekend."

Al was puzzled. "What do you mean?"

"I mean, Saturday night is party night."

"So Nick Andretti is going to deal with him?" asked Frankie.

"No, I am - with his help!" Joe leaned his elbows on the desk and explained. "Some of Benny's friends will throw a party for him on Saturday night, with the best booze and cocaine money can buy. Afterwards, two of his most trusted friends will drive him home. Only he won't be going home, he'll be coming to us."

Al looked at Frankie with a raised eyebrow. "With friends like that, who needs enemies!"

Frankie was wary. "Boss, can these men be trusted?"

"Yeah . They want out, Frankie. They've already sworn allegiance to Nick and they know if they back out now, they're dead."

"Do they know about us?"

"No Al, and they won't. They'll only be told where to take him. The only other person who knows I'm involved is Nick Andretti and since it's been all his idea, he'll hardly have it broadcast, now will he? If he's setting it up he can't afford to take unnecessary risks or drop names."

Rooney looked at them. "We've been over it all tonight and it's perfect. Some might suspect old Nick but they won't have the proof. Joe isn't connected to anyone or on anyone's payroll, so that's him off the hook. As for Benny's friends, they'll be taken care of when the time comes, Nick Andretti will see to that. He doesn't trust anyone who can change loyalties so easily, but right now they're useful to him. At the end of the day it's going to look like Benny was killed in revenge by these two friends, then they were killed in revenge by the others. An internal feud. Everyone else will just walk away."

Joe looked at the two men, waiting for their reaction. "Well, what do you think?" he asked.

"I think Rooney's right," said Frankie. "It's a perfect set up."

Al nodded, "Me too. I have just one question. Where will they be taking him, Boss?"

"To an abattoir on the south side. It closes for the weekend and the last shift is Saturday. It doesn't open again until Monday morning."

"And how are we going to get in?" asked Frankie.

Joe smiled, "I'll have a set of duplicate keys."

Al looked at him. "Well, you sure picked the right place. He's more of an animal than the ones they've got in a joint like that!"

"That's the idea. It's the best place for him." Joe got to his feet. "Well, that's it for now. We will go over everything in detail come Saturday. In the meantime, Al I want you to hang around the school after you've dropped Robert off. Keep your eyes open in case that bastard comes back."

"No sweat Boss. I'll even go in and take lessons if you want me to."

"You should have done that years ago," smiled Rooney.

"I never had the time!"

"He was too busy taking lessons of a different kind," Frankie joked.

"Yeah well, as I always say - stick with what you know!"

Joe shook his head and smiled. "You never were the academic type, Al. But you sure would have gotten good grades on a woman's anatomy."

"Yeah boss. From their necks down, I know about. But I never could understand their minds!"

"Maybe that's because you never got that far up," teased Frankie.

Al nudged him. "Now why would I want to go all the way to the top when all the excitement's at the bottom?" He looked over at Rooney. "You see, I'm not as dumb as you think I am. Al Colleano did his homework a long time ago! Isn't that right boss?"

"Yeah, that's right Al," Joe nodded. "After all, why bother with an empty head when you've got a full penis?" he shrugged.

The study rang with the laughter of the four men . Still laughing, Frankie and Al got up. "See you tomorrow boss," they said.

"Yeah. Goodnight." Joe watched the door close behind them, then turned to Rooney. "They didn't need any persuading."

"That's because they're your friends Joe."

He nodded and stared towards the door. "Yeah, they're good guys, Rooney. The best!"

The four men stood huddled together in the darkness. Rooney lit a cigarette and checked his watch. "It's well past midnight Joe. Maybe they're not coming."

"Yeah," agreed Frankie. "Maybe they've changed their minds about the whole thing, Boss."

But Joe was confident. "Relax. You know what parties are like, they never finish early."

"What about Angela, Joe?"

"What about her?"

"Where does she think you are?"

"Don't worry, Rooney. I told her I had some business meetings at the nightclubs. She knows I'll be home late."

The place was dimly lit and silent.

Al looked around nervously. "This place gives me the creeps. It's so quiet it's like a fuckin' graveyard!"

"Well it is full of dead animals inside," Frankie reminded him.

"Yeah well, as long as their ghosts aren't walking around out here!"

Frankie nudged Joe and Rooney, then placing a pointed finger at each side of his head he crept up behind Al . "Moo," he said in a low voice.

Al's eyes widened and he gave a startled jump.

"Hey, that's not fuckin' funny!" he snapped, as his three friends laughed quietly.

A few minutes later, a car screeched to a halt. Stamping out his cigarette, Rooney peered around the comer of the building. He then turned to Joe.

"Looks like we've got company."

They all watched as the car door opened and Benny was pushed out

"Hey come on you guys, a joke's a joke," he laughed loudly, stumbling as he got to his feet. As the car sped off he stood waving his hands. "Hey come back!" he yelled, as it disappeared into the night. Realising his companions had deserted him, he began to mutter to himself "Oh, fuck you! Fuck all of you! This is fuckin' party night!"

Suddenly, an arm closed tightly around his neck. "And the fuckin' party's over!" came a voice from behind as Rooney dragged him round the side of the building, out of sight. When he was finally freed, Benny found himself face to face with Joe Morrelli. He was both surprised and afraid.

"What the hell's going on, Joe?" he asked.

Joe put his hand over Benny's face and squeezing hard, pushed him against the wall. "What's going on? I'll tell you what's going on. You offered my kid drugs outside a school playground. And not only that. You put your hands on him!"

He pushed Benny's head hard off the wall. "You put your filthy hands on my son!" Slapping his face from side to side forcefully, Joe continued. "You fuckin' scumbag you touched my son - Joe Morrelli's son, and I'm going to kill you for it!"

His victim began to plead. "Joe, please listen. I'm sorry. I didn't know he was your kid. I swear to God, I'd never have done it if I'd known. Honestly!"

"And you think that makes everything O.k. Right? Well, you're wrong!" Rooney kneed Benny in the groin and as he doubled over, Al glared into his face.

"How would you like to have no hands? Then you couldn't touch another kid - ever."

After breathing deeply for a few moments, Benny then straightened up and looked at Joe. "You're a fuckin' tough guy with your back-up, Morrelli. But you wouldn't be so tough if my men were here!"

In a split second, Joe had gripped him by the throat and pulled him forward. As his eyes flashed he said, "My men are only here to observe. Tonight it's just you and me. Come on, you piece of shit, stroke my face!" he demanded. "Come on, you bastard, touch me the way you touched my son. Or maybe I'm too old for you. Maybe you only like to do it to kids who can't defend themselves." He let go and put his hands on his hips, staring menacingly. "Come on, what are you waiting for?" he urged.

Benny stepped back and held his hands up.

"Wait a minute Joe, we can sort this out."

"That's where you're wrong. I'm going to sort you out!"

Moving forward, Joe took a swing and landed a heavy fist on Benny's jaw, knocking him over. As he lay on the ground, Joe grabbed him by the shoulders and pulled him up, for more. Another punch got Benny on the nose, causing blood to pour from it. Both men lunged at each other as Rooney, Frankie and Al watched. Benny's punches missed so Joe grabbed him by the hair, punched him in the stomach and booted him between the legs. As Benny fell on his back, Joe booted him again. He lay on the ground moaning loudly, clearly no match for Joe Morrelli.

"No more, no more!" he gasped. "I swear on my mother's life it won't ever happen again."

Joe stood over him, consumed with rage. "I don't think you ever had a mother, you fuckin' freak! I warned you once to stay out of my way."

"I will Joe. Just let me go, please."

But Benny's pleas meant nothing as his attacker bent down and pulled one of his arms out straight. He could feel the pain as Joe deliberately stamped on his hand, pushing it down onto the rough ground and squeezing the fingers until it was too much to bear. Benny squealed. Al smiled with satisfaction. After his other arm had received the same treatment, Benny Bangles lay helpless. He saw Joe lean over him.

"You'll never touch my son again - never! That's a promise and Joe Morrelli never breaks a promise."

A forceful kick to the side made Benny squeal again. But Joe continued,

"You're not a man, you can't even fight like one. You're a pervert like your friend, Lenny Shultz!"

A look of fear spread over Benny's face, at the mere mention of his dead friend. "What are you going to do to me?" he asked in a terrified voice.

"Exactly what I did to Lenny!"

"It ... it was you, wasn't it? You killed him."

Rooney stepped forward. "It was us."

Looking from one to the other Benny pleaded, "Jesus, don't kill me. Please, don't kill me. Please don't kill me." He began to sob, "I'll never touch your kid again. Please Joe."

"Maybe not," came the cold reply, "but you'll touch someone else's. I saw one of your videos and I can't allow that to happen. You are a menace to every kid in this city but it stops here and now."

"Joe, I'm begging you. Don't hurt me, please."

As Joe stared into Benny's terror stricken face he could see all those poor kids with that same look.

"Is that what they said to you? All those kids you've used and abused. "Don't hurt me, please", because if they did you didn't listen. So why should I?" He pulled out a gun and nodded to his three friends. "Lift this piece of slime and stand him up. I want to look him in the eyes."

Benny struggled as they got him to his feet.

Joe went over to him and put the gun to his head.

As Rooney, Frankie and Al encircled him, Benny knew there was no escape and shook uncontrollably.

"Joe I swear to you, I won't ever touch another kid as long as I live."

"Now, that's very true!"

Without the slightest guilt or emotion, Joe Morrelli pulled the trigger and watched as Benny Bangles collapsed in a heap. He reached into his pocket and exchanged his gun for a set of keys.

"O.k., let's get him inside."

He unlocked the door and held it open, so that the others could carry the body into the building. Ten minutes later the four emerged, their assignment completed. Joe locked the door and wiped it clean of prints. Then, putting the keys back into his pocket, he followed the others to the works car park where Rooney's car was waiting.

After letting himself in, Joe went straight to the lounge and poured himself a Scotch. He drank it slowly, staring thoughtfully into space. When finished, he put the empty glass down and left the lounge, making sure to switch off the lights on his way to the study. Once there, he opened the desk drawer and carefully placed the gun and keys inside it. Locking the drawer securely, he walked out and up the stairs to Robert's bedroom. He opened the door silently and walked over to the bed where he stopped and looked down at his son, sleeping soundly. Bending down, he touched the boy's hair lightly with his fingers and whispered, "Everything's o.k. now son. You're safe."

Joe left as he had entered, unnoticed. Going to his own room he checked to make sure Angela was asleep, then went into the bathroom. Switching on the lights, he stood before the mirror. There was blood on his shirt and jacket - but it wasn't his. He undressed quickly and washed his face and hands. Then taking the bloodstained clothing, he rolled them up and quietly carried them into the room. In the darkness he managed to push them under the bed. He would dispose of them later.

Angela stirred. "Joe is that you?"

He climbed in beside her. "Yeah honey."

"What time is it?"

"It's late. You go back to sleep," he whispered, slipping an arm around her waist and kissing her cheek. She nodded drowsily and was soon sleeping.

Joe breathed a sigh of relief and rolled over onto his back. Staring into the darkness he went over the night's events in his mind. He had killed Lenny Shultz to protect Angela and tonight he had killed Benny Bangles to protect Robert. On both occasions he felt no pity or remorse because both men had deserved it.

This was the one side of his character Angela had never seen. The one side she didn't know about - and he hoped she never would. Although Angela knew he was capable of many things, she would never believe him capable of murder. But he was. His only hope was that she'd never find out. After what had happened to her own father, she wouldn't be able to deal with it and he would lose her for sure. Yes, he had done it for all the right reasons but how could he ever convince her that murder was a right reason for anything?

He sighed again and closing his eyes he said a silent prayer. Not for forgiveness, but for his sins to remain hidden.

That Monday morning, Carlo Capaldi's car came to a halt outside the abattoir. Going inside, he joined the rest of his colleagues who were already on the crime scene.

"Well, where's the body?" he asked looking around.

Sergeant Delaney pointed upwards and Carlo's eyes followed.

"Jesus, what have we here?" He took a stick of gum from his pocket and popped it into his mouth. Both stared at the body of a man, hanging on a meat hook. In the corner, two other cops were swopping jokes unperturbed by the scene they beheld. Carlo turned around. "Hey, Romano, Bronski, are you guys on vacation? Get over here!" As Romano approached he covered his nose with his hand. "Christ Lieutenant, I can't bear the stench."

"Well, my nose isn't exactly overjoyed at the smell either," came the casual reply. "O.k. let's go to work. Bronski, get me something to stand on."

"Like what, Lieutenant?"

"Like steps or something!"

"What are you going to do?" asked a puzzled Bronski.

"I'm going to go up there."

"Why?"

"Because I promised him the last waltz!"

As Bronski walked away Carlo looked at Sergeant Delaney and shook his head. "No wonder that guy's still in uniform!"

At that moment a young policeman came in. He took one look at the body, covered his mouth and ran outside.

Carlo stared after him. "Who's that?"

"Oh, that's Palmer. He's a rookie and this is his first homicide."

"Really? Guess who won't be eating hamburgers for a while!"

Delaney nodded and smiled. "Yeah, we were all like that to begin with. When he's on the force for a while he'll be fine."

Bronski returned with some steel steps.

"Wait till he goes on his first treasure hunt," Romano grinned. "I'll never forget mine. We found a leg on the south side, an arm on the east side. There were bits everywhere. We were running around all over the place. We eventually found the torso in the trunk of a car outside the city."

Bronski stared at him. "What about the head, did you ever find it?"

"Yeah, it was right here in the middle of town in a garbage can. Someone had played football with it."

"Jesus, imagine someone playing ball with your head."

Romano put a hand on Bronski's shoulder. "Don't worry about it, the guy didn't feel a thing. It wasn't attached to his neck at the time!"

As Delaney turned his head to hide a smile, Carlo slipped on a pair of surgical gloves and climbed the steps.

"What's he like close up, Lieutenant?" Romano asked.

"Well, he ain't no Al Pacino!!" came the reply, as he studied the broad features of the now discoloured and distorted face of the deceased. Observing the gold jewellery around the neck and wrists, he flicked open the jacket to discover the victim's wallet and cash still intact. "Well, he sure wasn't robbed," he informed the others.

The only thing that was missing was the man's identification. There was nothing on him that could give a hint as to who he was. However, Carlo had an eerie feeling that he knew him - or knew of him. Anyway, he would keep it to himself until he was sure.

"Well, lookee here!" he said, removing two packets of white powder from the jacket pocket and holding them up for the others to see. "Looks like this guy was either an addict or a dealer. Maybe even both."

He replaced the packets and climbed down. As he reached the ground he heard a loud voice coming towards him. It was Jeff Lang, and he was in a foul mood. He stood for a moment surveying the body, then rubbing his worried brow with an unsteady hand, he looked at Carlo.

"Jesus Christ, this is all I need! It's a gangland killing, isn't it Capaldi? I'll bet a fuckin' war has broken out in this city and we'll be finding dead bodies everywhere!"

Carlo had other ideas. "I don't think so, sir. If you ask me it's just a one-off killing. The guy has drugs on him. It could have been a deal that went wrong, or more likely he was muscling in on someone else's territory."

"How did he die?"

"One clean bullet wound to the head, probably done with a silencer. But he has bruising on the face. I reckon he was punched a few times before he was shot. There could also be bruising on the body. We'll know after the coroner's finished with him."

"Any idea who he is?"

Carlo shook his head. "Not at the moment, sir."

Jeff Lang motioned him to one side, away from the others. "I hope you're right. I hope it is a one off, or I'm in for a lot of pressure from the Mayor's office. If a feud has started, the shit's really going to hit the fan - especially when the press gets hold of it!"

He leaned closer. "Carlo, you're an Italian, what's going on?"

Carlo studied the facts in his head. "Well sir, judging by where he was found and the way he was found, I'd say this guy did something really bad."

Jeff nodded. "O.k. Carlo, investigate it."

"Wait a minute," he advised. "If I were you, I wouldn't dig too deep."

"What do you mean?" Lang was puzzled.

"If it's not a feud among the 'families' it could turn out to be something more sinister. You could open up a can of worms that might crawl all over this city. My instinct tells me that there's more to this than meets the eye. Who knows the guy might have had it coming. So do yourself a favour, if no more dead bodies show up don't push this. Investigate it, sure, but take my advice and leave well enough alone. Don't make a big issue out of it."

Jeff Lang agreed and walked away. Half way to the door, he turned and pointed. I want that guy taken down off that meat hook now, and I want a handle on him. He must have a name. And I want evidence, statements, anything! There are elections coming off in this city and the Mayor will be breathing down my neck," he yelled. "Lieutenant Capaldi, I want you in my office just as soon as you come up with something." He then stormed out.

Romano stared after him. "That's what I like about this city, there are always elections. But I never notice a raise in my pay cheque."

"Wait till you're married with kids," Carlo told him, "then you definitely won't notice it! O.k., let's get him down. Bronski, get that kid Palmer back in here, we need him."

Palmer ventured in looking pale and nervous. As the others removed the body and laid it on the ground, he stared at it. Once again he covered his mouth.

Carlo looked at him. "Listen son, why don't you go and get a stretcher?"

Romano agreed. "Yeah and just remember, Palmer, it's for the stiff- not you! I ain't carrying you out of here."

Bronski winked, so Palmer couldn't see. "Hey Lieutenant, isn't it beef stew in the canteen today?" Palmer's walk broke into a run. "That ought to hurry him up!" he smiled with satisfaction.

As the camera flashed over the dead body, Romano and Bronski were in deep conversation about the base ball game shown on T.V. the night before. Carlo and Sergeant Delaney stood in silence.

Eventually, Delaney shook his head. "Jesus, who could do such a thing? What kind of mind would hang a man on a meat hook in this place?"

"A very smart one!"

"What do you mean by that?"

"Well, you've asked who would do it but the big question is, why? I've got a hunch this place was specially chosen for him. You see, where do you put a dead animal?" He stared at his colleague. "You put it with other dead animals. Maybe this guy wasn't as human as he looked and somebody wanted us to know."

"You could be right, Lieutenant/"

The body was covered over. Just then, a man was ushered towards them, clasping his hands and visibly shaken.

"I swear to God, I don't know nothin' about this!" he maintained.

"Who are you?" Carlo asked.

"I work here. It was me who discovered the body, but I don't know nothin' about no murder."

"O.k. I believe you, but we need some details. Romano, I want you to take down this man's statement. Now, just tell this officer what you saw, in your own words."

Taking out his notepad and pen, Romano approached.

"O.k.," he said to the man.

"Where do you want me to start?"

"I think it's best to start at the beginning. Don't you?"

He nodded. "Well I came in early to get everything ready for the rest of the guys. I always do that."

"Yeah? Good for you."

"I switched on the machinery to get things moving and then I see's it. I see's this shape on a meat hook coming towards me and I says to myself, 'Archie, that ain't no cow up there!!"

"That was real clever of you," Romano praised.

"Come to think of it, it was - wasn't it?" The man was obviously pleased with himself. "Anyway, when it got closer I says to myself, 'Gee Archie, that's a man!"

Tapping the back of his pen hard against the notepad, Romano turned to Carlo. "Thanks a bunch, Lieutenant! I'm going to be here all day taking down what this guy kept saying to himself."

"It's all part of the job," Carlo reminded him, smiling and walking past.

"By the way, my name is Lowe," the man interrupted. "Archie Lowe - with an E. Don't you wanna hear what I says to myself next?"

"Sure, I'm all ears," Romano replied staring after Carlo, who left the building with a broad grin on his face!

When he got back to the precinct, Carlo pulled the files on all known narcotic dealers. He sat in his office pouring over them all afternoon, and getting nowhere

. Rubbing his tired eyes, he leaned back in the chair and stared out of the window, trying hard to piece everything together.

The victim, in some way, looked familiar. He knew he had seen this guy before. Nobody could forget a guy who wore all that jewellery! Carlo wrecked his brain. Maybe he was going in the wrong direction. After all, if this guy was smart he wouldn't be in the up-to-date files. But if he hadn't been so clever in the past, there was a chance he had a file way back. He decided he would just have to dig deeper. It was also very likely that the dead man had others working for him. He looked every bit the "King Pin". If tracked down, they could provide the answers. He picked up the phone to the Narcotics Division.

"Jamison? I want you to dig up the files on known drug dealers but you'll have to go back ten, maybe fifteen years. And listen, when Willis gets in, tell him I want to see him."

Some of the files were delivered with more to follow so Carlo asked for some coffee, then made a start. Working his way through the stack of paper work, he shook his head. Finding this guy was like looking for a needle in a haystack and he was proving to be a real headache. Opening the next file, something clicked. He was looking at another guy who had given him a headache some years ago - Lenny Shultz!

Carlo remembered that Lenny had worked for someone called Benny Bangles, who got his nickname because of his love for gold jewellery. Suddenly, the pieces of the puzzle were starting to fit together. He sat Lenny's file to one side and flicked through the rest, hurriedly. As he reached the end of the pile - Bingo! There he was! Comparing the two files carefully, he found so many similarities it was more than coincidence. On more than one occasion these men were arrested and charged together. They both had the same team of high class lawyers who always seemed to get them off on technicalities. Later on, when Lenny Shultz had been arrested on his own for violent attacks against women and drug possession, those same lawyers stepped in once again and saved his ass! Carlo knew Lenny could never have paid them - but Benny could.

As he was studying all the information, the door knocked and opened.

"You want to see me, Lieutenant?"

"Yeah. Come on in Willis and take a seat. I need to talk to you."

Willis worked in Narcotics, an undercover cop who was street wise and knew everything that was going down. No one would ever suspect he was on the police force. He wore faded denim jeans, an old check shirt and the bandana around his head kept his long hair off his face. In his late twenties, some might have considered him a bit young for such a dangerous and vital role, but Willis was as tough as old boots when he had to be. As he sat down Carlo held up the photograph.

"Do you know this guy by any chance?"

Willis studied it. "Well, it's a bit out of date," he smiled, "but yeah, I recognise him. I recognise the jewellery even more. His name's Benny Bangles and he's one shrewd dude."

"Well, he's one dead dude now," Carlo informed him.

"You mean someone killed him?"

"They sure did. We found him this morning, hanging on a meat hook over at the abattoir."

Willis shook his head. "Jesus, somebody really had it in for him."

"So, what can you tell me about him?"

"He owns 'The Blue Paradise Club' on Albany Street. He deals in drugs and street prostitution . He's the supplier mostly, with other low-lifes to do the dirty work for him. Last I heard, he was into kids. I've been trying to get that son-of-a-bitch for a long time but he's been so well protected I could never get past his fuckin' goons. But it looks like somebody did!"

"Yeah," Carlo agreed. "Somebody with a grudge or a score to settle."

"That could be anybody, Lieutenant. This guy was an evil bastard who didn't care how he made a buck. His friends were the same, they didn't care either."

"Then why don't we pay some of these friends a visit?"

"Sure, why not."

Willis got up and waited as Carlo put on his jacket. They were just about to leave the office when Carlo stopped and said, "Why wasn't something done about this guy? How the hell did he get away with it all these years?"

Willis stared at him. "I'll put it this way. When you find yourself in trouble, who are you supposed to go to?"

"The cops!"

"Well, there's your answer, Lieutenant. Now you know why I prefer to work alone." Carlo Capaldi shook his head in disgust and realised that although Willis was a loner - he was a damn good cop!

Joe and Angela were relaxing in the lounge when the six o'clock news came on. As the reporter at the crime scene gave the details of the abattoir murder, Joe looked over the top of the newspaper, at the T.V. screen. He listened with interest and paid great attention to the live report from outside the building. It looked a lot different in broad daylight.

When it was over he went back to his reading muttering, "Serves him right. If anyone had it coming, Benny had."

Angela looked at him, surprised. "How did you know his name?"

Firstly he glanced at her, then putting the paper down he pointed towards the television. "The guy just said it a few minutes ago."

"No he didn't. He said as yet the body was unidentified. But you called him Benny."

He shrugged. "Well, I thought he gave a name. I must have misunderstood, that's all."

She stared at him, as her hands gripped the arms of the chair tightly and a look of horror swept over her face. "My God!" she cried. "You know about this, don't you?"

"Oh come on Angel, don't be silly. How could I know about something like that?" He tried to dismiss her fears but it didn't work.

She jumped off the chair. "Because maybe you were there! You weren't the least bit surprised or sorry to hear about him or the way he was found. And you called him by his name! What do you know about this murder, Joe?"

Joe quickly got up, turned off the television and put his hands on her shoulders. "Angel, honey, calm down."

She pushed him away in disgust. "Don't touch me, don't you dare put your hands on me! What are you anyway?"

"I'm your husband."

"You're an animal! That poor man was left hanging on a meat hook. You stay away from me!" she warned.

Joe gripped her wrist tightly. She tried to break free but he forced her to turn and look at him. "You don't want me to touch you because you think I was involved in a murder. But let me ask you something Angel. If I'd helped to kill your father's murderers, would you still feel the same?"

"That's an unfair question, Joe Morrelli, and you know it."

"Maybe, but I'd still like an answer. You're the one who's always talking about justice for the innocent victims. What if the men who killed your father were found hanging on meat hooks somewhere in Belfast? Would you feel sorry for them or would you say they got what they deserved? Be honest with yourself, then be honest with me!"

Tears filled her eyes. "I'd say they got what they deserved."

He nodded. "Then how do you know that that guy didn't get what he deserved? The truth is, you don't Angel. You don't know what that guy did to end up like that and you don't know if I had anything to do with it. You're accusing me, sure, but you don't know. Do you?"

She stared at the floor as he let go of her wrist. There was an awkward silence between them. After a few moments she looked into his eyes earnestly.

"Did you kill him?" she asked, in a half whisper.

He held her gaze and shook his head. "No, I didn't,"

"Were you there?"

"No."

"Then how do you know his name?"

Joe took a deep breath and hoped he would sound convincing. "You know I don't discuss my business but tonight I'll make an exception because I think it's important that your mind is put at rest. A while back I heard some rumours that this guy called Benny was doing some bad things - I mean really bad! He made a lot of enemies, Angel, and it was just a matter of time before someone caught up with him. When I heard the news I had an idea it was Benny. I just put two and two together and got four! And that's all I know, Angel. Honest."

She took his hand. "I'm sorry, Joe, I should never have accused you of something like that. Not murder. I know you could never be capable of it. You're such a good man. I feel so ashamed."

He gently wiped her tears away. "It's o.k. honey, we all make mistakes. The main thing is, you know the truth now."

Angela walked towards the door but on reaching it she looked back at him. "You should never have brought my father into this. It was hard for me to deal with his murder when it happened but it's even hard now after all these years, knowing that whoever did it will never pay. Maybe if there were men in Belfast like those men who killed Benny, there would have been some justice for my father and for us."

"Yeah I know. New York's a big city but sometimes it isn't big enough, as Benny found out. If your father had lived here, things might have been different. Who knows?" As the door closed, Joe breathed a deep sigh of relief. He wasn't proud of the way he'd lied to her but in this case lies were better than the truth, for her sake as much as his. Some things were best left hidden if he wanted to remain happily married. His thoughts were interrupted as Robert came in.

"Dad, mom was crying as she went upstairs. Did you two have an argument?"

"No son," he assured him. "We were talking about your grandfather and you know how upset she gets when she talks about him. It brings back a lot of painful memories for her."

Robert went over and stood looking out of the window. His eyes roamed around the garden but it was obvious he had something on his mind. Finally he said, "Dad, why would anyone want to kill my grandpa? What reason could they have? And how come they were never caught?"

Joe put a comforting arm around his son's shoulder. "I don't know, son" he said.

"Well, someday I want to go there and find out. I want to go there and let them see we don't forgive or forget."

Father and son embraced.

"You sound like your mother," Joe smiled.

"Yeah, but I think like you!" the boy replied.

The next day at noon, Carlo Capaldi arrived in Jeff Lang's office. He carried a file and notepad under his arm, and knew by the look on the D.A.'s face he was still anxious about the recent events.

"Well I got the information on that guy at the abattoir," he informed him.

Jeff nodded, "O.k. Lets hear it."

Opening the file Carlo began. "His name is Benedict Lusari, better known as Benny Bangles. He started off small time but over the years he made a name for himself, mostly through drug dealing. He was arrested a couple of times but we couldn't make the charges stick – thanks to his fancy lawyers! Years ago he opened 'The Blue Paradise Club' on Albany Street, a haunt for junkies, dealers and weirdos." He then referred to his notes. "At first he made his money from drugs, then moved onto other things."

"What other things?" Jeff enquired.

"He owns a couple of brothels. Real low class, where the customer is always right and the girls have the marks to prove it! They were scared of Benny and just as scared of his pimps. Most of the time they're doped up. He liked it that way, they didn't make trouble. The only way out for some of them was suicide. Shall I continue?"

"You mean, there's more?"

"Oh, there's more alright. Lately he's been taking an interest in kids, mostly under aged runaways. He'd feed them a line about taking care of them, make big promises, give them dope, then put them to work on the street. He told them if they didn't earn, they wouldn't live! Yeah, our Benny was a real nice guy, wouldn't you say?"

Jeff Lang stared at him. "How did you get all this information so fast?"

Carlo explained, "Willis and me made a few calls yesterday evening. He pointed out the places and the people, I asked the questions."

"Well, if you could find all that out in just a few hours, why the hell didn't someone find it out sooner and fix this guy? How did he get away with it for so long? That's what I want to know," he said, angrily.

It was time for both men to forget their positions and be straight with each other.

"Oh come on, Jeff, you already know the answer to that. Not every cop is a good cop. There were some on Benny's payroll who always looked the other way."

"But we're talking about kids, damn it!"

Carlo nodded. "I know and I have a gut feeling that's why he ended up on that meat hook. Somebody didn't like what he was doing, Jeff. And who knows, maybe he picked the wrong kid!"

"I think you're right, Carlo. What do you suggest we do?"

"I suggest we end this investigation now. Whoever killed Benny Bangles had their reasons. They sure did us a favour because we would never have nailed him."

Jeff thought for a moment as he rubbed his forehead. "Any ideas who it might be?"

"No, but I wish I had, I'd send them a medal. They deserve it." He sat the file and notepad on the desk. "Listen Jeff, nobody is going to shed any tears over Benny Bangles. He was the lowest form of life this city could produce. If you'll take my advice you'll wrap this case up in a neat little package and tell the Mayor he doesn't have a thing to worry about."

Leaning back in his chair, Jeff Lang opened a desk drawer and took out a package. He held it up for Carlo to see.

"Everything you've told me fits in with this," he said.

"What is it?"

"It's a homemade video of our friend Benny with some young teenagers. The guy was a real pervert."

"Where did you get it?"

"It was delivered here to my office this morning by a mail man and addressed to me personally. Sergeant Delaney said you told him yesterday that someone wanted us to know about this guy, and you were right, Carlo. That bastard was an animal! I could hardly believe my eyes when I watched that tape. At least now this jungle has one less beast to feed." He stood up. "The investigation into this scumbag's death is over and when the Mayor sees this video he won't want it any other way, believe me." They shook hands. "You did a good job Carlo. Thanks for all your help."

"I was only doing my job," Carlo smiled.

Jeff studied him. "You knew this investigation wasn't going to lead anywhere, didn't you?"

"Let's just say, being an Italian I had a hunch."

"You're a good cop, Carlo Capaldi. I wish there were more like you."

"Yeah well, money can be a big temptation to a lot of guys. But out there, someone's walking around who doesn't care about dollars and cents. He saw a piece of filth on the street and got rid of it. He did our job for us. Maybe you should wish for more guys like him "

"Maybe!" he joked in reply. "What the hell, at least now the file on Benny Bangles can be closed for good."

"And a lot of kids will be grateful. It looks like Santa has come early for them this year."

"Yeah," Jeff agreed smiling. "See you Carlo."

"See you Jeff- Sir!!"

Chapter 18

If Joe Morrelli thought his problems were over he couldn't have been more wrong, there was another one waiting just around the corner.

The study door opened and Rooney came in with an anxious look on his face. "Joe I need to talk to you," he said.

Removing his glasses and putting them down on the desk, Joe clasped his hands and leaned forward.

"Sure. What's up?"

Rooney sat down. "I think we've got a problem."

"What kind of problem?"

"A serious one. Since the time I was in Belfast I've always remained friends with Dermot McCabe and Seamus Quinn, you know that."

"Yeah," Joe nodded.

"Well, Dermot has kept in touch over the years and I got a phone call from him about an hour ago. He told me that funds over there have been getting low. It's been happening over a period of time and he wanted to know if my boss had second thoughts about increasing his donations. Apparently, the amount you send has remained the same for the last couple of years."

"I see," came the thoughtful reply. "And how does this guy know I was to increase my donations?"

There was silence for a moment before an uncomfortable Rooney admitted, "I told him."

"You trusted him that much?"

"I did Joe, and I still do. He's honest and decent and I think he's proved himself by telling me about the fund situation. At least now we know that something's wrong because a lot of your money is unaccounted for."

"Yeah, and the only one who can account for it is Harry Collington."

Rooney leaned over. "Look Joe, you've been paying him for a long time but none of your family have ever been to Belfast. Maybe he thinks none of them ever will and he's skimming off the top. If he's doing it to you, he's probably doing it to other people."

Joe slammed the palms of his hands down on the desk. "Yeah? Well I don't care about other people and their money. I'm only interested in mine and finding out where it's gone."

"I'm ready to go back to Belfast any time you say," came the offer.

But Joe shook his head. "That won't be necessary. I think it's high time Mr. Collington earned his money. I think I'll give him a surprise."

"What do you mean?"

"I mean, I'm the one who's going to Belfast."

"You?!"

"Why not? After all, it's my money and besides, I think I've paid enough to entitle me to ask some questions and demand the answers."

Rooney became anxious once again. "But Joe, you don't understand. Belfast is a whole different ball game to New York. You don't know these men, they're dangerous. I'll come with you."

"Not this trip, Rooney," he insisted. "I can play ball with the best of them and I think Mr. Collington and me will have a pretty interesting game when we meet face to face."

"But you don't know anything about him."

"Not now," he admitted, "but I will. Before I confront him I intend to do a little investigating of my own. By the time we meet I'm going to know everything there is to know about him."

"And just how the hell are you going to do that, when you're here in New York and he's over in Belfast?"

Rooney was becoming annoyed but Joe just smiled.

"Watch and see," he advised, winking.

Reaching over to the telephone, he picked up the receiver and dialled. He didn't have to wait long before he heard a friendly voice on the other end. Replying with equal friendliness, he leaned back in the chair. "Yeah Gene, it's me.... Oh I'm fine .... Listen, I was wondering if you had any time to spare? .... Sure, your office tomorrow afternoon sounds great .... Thanks, Gene, I'll see you then."

As Joe put the receiver back down, Rooney shook his head.

"Jesus I'd forgotten Gene helped you to get your connections in Belfast."

"Yeah, Dan Casey told him everything and if he knows about the fund there's a good chance he knows about the man. And whatever he doesn't know, he can always find out. Who knows what we might uncover?" He smiled broadly, "Now, what was that you were saying about ball games, Rooney?"

On entering Gene O'Brien's office, Joe was greeted with a smile from his old friend.

"Come on in, Joe," came the invitation. "It's good to see you. Have a seat." He waited until his guest was settled, then leaned across the desk. "Now old buddy, what's so important that I had to cancel all my calls and appointments for the next hour?" he joked.

Joe looked at him. "I want to tell you a story."

"Now that's one thing you were always good at! I hope it's as interesting as the rest," Gene grinned.

"Oh it is," Joe assured him, in a serious voice. "And it's also very true."

He proceeded to tell everything that had happened to Angela, both before and after he met her. Joe went into every detail of her life in Belfast and that of her family. He then went on to explain why they never had any more children. After he'd finished, Gene looked shocked and sad.

"Jesus Joe, I'm sorry. I had no idea."

"I know you must have wondered at us having only one kid. Angel was a young woman after all, and you know what the Irish and Italians are like for families!"

Gene nodded. "To be honest with you Joe, there were times when I did. But Angela's such a lovely woman, I thought maybe you wanted to keep her that way and not have her tied down with kids all the time. I should have known I was wrong!"

He looked across at Joe, his face ridden with guilt. "Christ, I feel so bad about all this. When Angela joined my committee I used to joke with her about you two holding out for twins. She would just nod and smile. She must have felt terrible but she never showed it."

"She never ever told me that, Gene," he replied sadly.

After a few moments silence, Gene O'Brien continued, "Well, at least now I know why you joined that fund. You weren't really worried about your family, were you? Your real reason was Robert Kenny. You hoped in time to find out who murdered him. Why didn't you tell me?"

"I had my reasons. Besides, no-one else knew except Rooney." Joe leaned forward.

"Listen Gene, Rooney's connections in Belfast have informed him that my payments aren't what they should be. There's a lot of my money unaccounted for - and I mean a lot! I'd like to find out where it's gone but I need your help."

His friend took a deep breath and shook his head. "I don't know Joe. It's a sticky situation and I'm a United States Senator. I can't get involved. I'd be laying my political life and career on the line. Surely you understand that."

Joe stared coldly. "I think you're missing the point here Gene. Maybe you're the one who should understand. Understand that you might not be a Senator if it hadn't been for the help and support Angel and me gave you. We did everything we could to get you elected and my wife worked long and hard to see that you were. Now, I don't know about you, but in my book one good turn deserves another. You owe me, Gene, and you owe Angel. I'm not asking that you get directly involved, just that you get me some information. I'm asking for your help. What I want to know is, will I get it?"

Joe soon realised that pricking Gene's conscience had worked. After a thoughtful pause, O'Brien admitted,

"You're right! If it weren't for you and Angela I probably wouldn't be in the Senate. I know I'll be taking a risk here, but you've been good friends to me.

What exactly is it you want me to do?"

"Get me everything you can on Harry Collington. Dan Casey must have known something about him. Go back on his records and ask around . If I'm going to go to Belfast and confront this guy, I want to be prepared and I want to be one step ahead. It's the only way and we both know it."

Gene nodded in agreement. "O.k. I'm going to Washington tomorrow, leave it with me and I'll see what I can do. I'll have to be very discreet so give me a few days. I'll call you when I get back."

Relieved, Joe smiled. "Thank's Gene, this means a lot to me."

"Tell me, when you go to Belfast, are you taking Rooney with you?"

"I can't. He'd be a dead give away. You see, Harry Collington's men know him but they don't know me. They don't even know my name and that's the way I want it. Besides, my business is with Mr. Collington and no one else. He's the one who's been handling my money. He sure knows my name and exactly how much I've donated over the years. He's the only one who can explain where my money is." He paused. "To be honest with you, he might be able to explain a lot of things."

Gene looked at him. "I'll do my best for you Joe, but guys like that are their own masters. Aren't you scared of rubbing him up the wrong way?"

Joe stood up and shrugged. "Gene, I worked for Nick Andretti in the Bronx. That's enough to scare a lot of people."

"Yeah, but Collington doesn't know that."

"Not yet he doesn't, but from what I've been told about the situation over there, they are just like the Mafia only on a smaller scale. If Mr. Collington thinks he's the Godfather of Belfast, he sure hasn't met any Godfathers from New York. I have. And let me tell you, what Nick Andretti teaches you, you never forget. Believe me, Gene, I've been taught by the best!"

Gene got up to see him to the door. "I'll be in touch," he promised, putting a caring arm around Joe's shoulder.

"Look, Gene, I know how much your career means to you," he said sincerely. "I know there could come a day when you'll be running for the White House, but I'd appreciate anything you can do for me."

"At the minute I can't make any promises. Getting information like that won't be easy, but I'll see what I can do."

Both men parted on this understanding and in the knowledge that each one had a difficult task ahead.

It was over a week later when Joe returned to Gene O'Brien's office. The serious expression on his friend's face prepared him for what was to follow.

"Listen Joe, about this business in Belfast, are you sure you want to go through with it?"

"You know I do," he insisted.

Giving a deep sigh, Gene nodded. "O.k. then, I think I have uncovered some information to help you."

"Did you look through Dan Casey's files?"

"Yeah, but that was only the tip of the iceberg. I had to dig a lot deeper than that and it wasn't easy. I had to use all my influence and pull a few strings in the right places."

Joe smiled. "Thanks Gene."

"Don't thank me just yet. Not until you know what you're letting yourself in for. Mr. Collington is a very smart and dangerous man, Joe. I sure hope you know what you're doing. Maybe you should withdraw your payments and just leave things as they are."

"This isn't just about money," he reminded him, "it's about murder. I have some questions and maybe this guy has the answers. Let me ask you something. If what I told you had happened to your wife and her family, what would you do?"

"Probably the same thing as you."

"Yeah, I think so," he nodded. "I've got to meet this guy Gene, he's overstepped the line. He's playing me for a fool but Joe Morrelli is nobody's fool and I want him to know that." He was obviously determined.

"O.k.," his friend agreed reluctantly, "but on one condition. You don't go on your own."

"But I've already explained why I can't bring Rooney."

"Who said anything about Rooney?" Gene leaned over. "You're going into unknown territory Joe, and I'm not letting you go on your own. When you board that plane you'll be accompanied by two men with links to the organisation. They go backwards and forwards to Ireland all the time and they know all the top men. These guys have been instructed to keep an eye on you at all times. They'll even be staying in the same hotel. You can't bring a weapon with you, so they will get them at a pick-up point in Belfast. I hope to God you won't need them but it's better to be sure than sorry. We have to cover every aspect."

Joe rubbed his forehead. "You've thought of everything. Who are these guys?"

"The best!" Gene replied. "And that's all you need to know. " Opening the desk drawer, he took out a folder and handed it to him. "It's going to be a long trip so I got you something to read. I think you'll find the contents very interesting."

Taking the folder from him, Joe said, "I really appreciate all this Gene."

"What are friends for?" came the reply.

Joe watched as Gene got up and walked over to the large window, gazing down at the streets below. He joined him and they both stood in silence for a while. Then O'Brien turned and rested a hand on his shoulder.

"You know, old buddy," he smiled. "there are around eight million people in this city and less than half a million in Belfast."

"Yeah well, I guess that gives me the edge!" Joe grinned.

"Yeah, I guess it does! And you know it wouldn't do any harm to mention that to Mr. Collington."

Joe nodded. "Believe me Gene, I intend to." He put the folder inside his jacket and made his way to the door.

"You take care and watch your step," Gene advised.

"I will. I'll see you when I get back."

Before he could leave, his anxious friend reminded him, "Hey Joe, Belfast isn't the Bronx and Harry Collington isn't Nick Andretti. You remember that!"

"But they all have things in common."

"What things?"

"Money, murder and corruption. If I can survive here Gene, I can survive there. You worry too much!" He gave a wry smile before closing the door.

Gene O'Brien returned his gaze to the sprawling city below. The city Joe Morrelli loved. Even with it's high crime rate and it's fast and furious pace, it had been both mother and father to him. Where else could a young, penniless Italian orphan rise to become a wealthy, admired and respected man? Yes, Gene understood his old friend and knew he'd come so far because of one golden rule - always be one step ahead. He hoped with all his heart that Joe would hold fast to that rule, while in Belfast. But more than anything he hoped he'd done the right thing in helping him.

"This business trip has come up so suddenly, Joe, are you sure nothing's wrong?" Angela asked, as she helped him pack his suitcase.

He put his arm around her. "Everything's fine honey. I've already explained about Reuben's phone call." Sitting down on the bed he took her hand, so she joined him "It's just business, Angel, that's all. One of the investors in Chicago wants to sell his shares and Reuben got to hear about it. If the price is right I'm going to buy him out. It's a good deal and one I don't intend to miss, but this guy isn't going to hang around. There are other interested parties so that's why I have to make my move now. I could be there and have the deal clinched while the rest are still thinking about it."

She smiled. "You know, for someone who never went to college you're a smart man."

"Well if you want something badly enough you've got to go after if."

"How long will you be gone?"

He shook his head. "Now, that I don't know. It could be a few days, there again, it might take longer. It depends. But I'll phone, just like I always do."

Pressing his hand gently she said, "I'll miss you."

"And I'll miss you," he assured her. "But Chicago isn't that far away." He got up and kissed her forehead. "I'd better go downstairs and have a word with Rooney. I won't be long. Then we can spend some time together before my flight."

As he opened the bedroom door he looked back to see Angela resume his packing. He felt badly about all the lies and deceit but he couldn't tell her where he was really going and why. He had carried the secret of his payments to the Irish fund for years. Now he would have to add to that with the secret of his trip and what he might find out. Standing silently looking at her, Joe hoped and prayed that what he had done and intended to do, would be worth it. If not, he had everything to lose and nothing to gain. Closing the door quietly behind him he knew that if anything went wrong with his plan he could be closing the door on his marriage!

Joe found Rooney waiting in the study. Sitting on the edge of the desk, he glanced at his watch.

"O.k. I don't have much time," he explained, "so let's go over everything again. You've got the time of my arrival in London'?"

"Right here," said Rooney, patting the inside pocket of his jacket.

"Good. I'll be on the next connecting flight from there to Belfast, but I don't want Harry Collington to know that. There's another flight three hours later and that's the one I want him to think I'm on."

"I've got that written down as well."

"O.k. When that second flight goes out I want you to telephone him from your apartment and say exactly what I told you. Your boss was in London on business, decided to pay a visit to Belfast and would like to meet up with him. That way, if he enquires about flight times he'll get the right information. The journey is only going to take about an hour, so he won't have any time for cover-ups. I want to take him totally by surprise. Meanwhile, I'll have arrived and checked into my hotel. If he sends someone snooping around the airport or decides to come himself, he'll draw a blank because I won't even be there! I don't want our friend Mr. Collington to see me and I don't want to see him, until we come face to face."

"Why?" Rooney asked.

"I have my reasons," Joe replied.

Rooney studied him thoughtfully for a few moments.

"Joe, is there something you're not telling me? Did you find out something about him?"

He nodded. "Yeah, but I'll have to go over it in more detail when I'm onboard the plane. But I'll fill you in on what I know on the way to the airport. Don't forget to tell Mr. Collington where I'll be staying and that I expect to hear from him as soon as possible."

"Don't worry, everything will be done exactly the way you want it," Rooney assured him.

Going over and putting a hand on his shoulder Joe said, "A lot depends on you, Rooney."

"I know and everything will go according to plan. Trust me."

"I do and there's one more thing. Look after Angel and my son while I'm gone. My family and my business are in your hands."

Rooney looked at him anxiously. "They will be quite safe, Joe. I just wish I could say the same about you!"

"Oh, I'll be o.k. You'll understand when I explain a few things to you." He breathed deeply. "Well, now that business has been taken care of, I want to spend the next couple of hours with my wife and son. We can talk some more when you pick me up."

"Right, I'll see you later then," Rooney nodded, as he got up and made his way to the door. Resting his hand on the handle, he turned. "Joe, I know you've got a lot on your mind and there may be certain things you don't want to tell me, but I want to tell you something. I hope you have thought out every word and every move real carefully before you confront this guy. Because if you haven't, you could be in big trouble. Harry Collington is an important man in his part of the world and he's highly respected and trusted - which makes him dangerous!"

That was the second time Joe had heard that word to describe Harry Collington. He nodded, "Yeah, you're probably right. But no man is invincible, they all have their weaknesses and we know that his is money. At least that's a start."

Rooney agreed, then left. Joe stared thoughtfully at the closed door. He was convinced that at the end of his journey he would be dealing with a man who was just as careful and shrewd as himself. He would have to play his hand with great skill if he wanted to win the game.

The flight was called. Rooney stamped out his cigarette and both men looked at each other.

"Well, this is it," said Joe.

They shook hands firmly.

"Good luck Joe."

"Thanks. You know what to do?"

"Sure. By the time I contact Harry Collington, the flight you're supposed to be on will be halfway to Belfast. He won't have time to think straight, never mind be prepared."

"That's the way I want it," Joe replied in a serious voice.

As he went through the departure area, he turned and held his hand up in a farewell gesture. Rooney returned it then watched him disappear. He waited until the air craft had taken off and was finally out of sight, before making his way to the car park. He felt relieved that Joe wasn't making the trip alone. On the way to the airport, he had been told about the two companions Gene O'Brien was sending to Belfast with Joe, and Joe had also confided in him about a piece of information regarding Harry Collington, that was causing him great concern.

As he got into his car, Rooney had a sombre look on his face. He was deeply worried about Joe and even more worried about the outcome of his meeting with such an unsavoury character.

Meanwhile, on board the large aeroplane, Joe Morrelli sat quietly confident armed with the relative information he needed. Opening his brief case, he took out the folder. After making himself comfortable for the long journey ahead, he opened it and began to read, absorbing every word.

After checking into the hotel, Joe went straight to his room and unpacked. As he put the last of his clothes away, a knock came to the door and on opening it he found two well dressed men standing before him.

"Mr. Morrelli, we have a mutual friend in New York," the first one informed him. "He wants to ensure your stay is a safe one," said the other.

Both had American accents and Joe quickly realised who they were.

"Come in," he invited.

They entered the room, closing the door securely.

The first man held out his hand. "My name is Eddie Kovak." Seeing Joe raise an eyebrow in surprise he quickly added, "I'm Irish on my mother's side!"

"Oh I see."

They exchanged friendly smiles. Then the second man stepped forward and shook Joe's hand.

"Patrick Molloy," he said in a strong, positive tone.

"Let me guess," Joe grinned. "You're Irish on your father's side!"

"Actually, on both sides! Both my parents are Irish."

"Well, that sure explains your name."

Patrick smiled, "Yeah, I guess it does. We saw you get a taxi from the airport but we couldn't follow you. We were being picked up by a friend who had something for us. He had to make a stop on the way here." Reaching into his coat he produced a gun and gave it to Joe. "It's already loaded. We figured you'd feel better if you had your own. Eddie and me have ours." He opened his coat fully to reveal a hand gun tucked into a shoulder holster that fitted snugly under his arm.

Eddie Kovak lifted his trouser leg showing a weapon down inside his leather boot. You'll be quite safe, Mr. Morrelli," he promised. "If necessary we won't think twice about using them. I've had a word with the manager of the hotel. As far as he's concerned, we are three American industrialists over here for some business meetings."

"That's fine by me," Joe replied.

"I suggest that if you are going to any business meeting of your own, you decline any offers of transport," Patrick advised him. "We know this city well and we can get someone to drive us any where you want to go."

Joe looked at him intently. "I take it trust isn't high on the agenda over here!"

"Let's just say there's always room for doubt."

"I understand. I guess not everyone is what they appear to be."

Eddie nodded. "That's right. With things the way they are you have to be one hundred percent certain - and then some. Why do you think we need weapons?"

Patrick agreed. "You see Mr. Morrelli, the years of trouble here have resulted in conflicting ideas and many disputes. It's getting to the point where there are too many chiefs and not enough Indians. The sad part is, some people will do anything to become a chief. Some of those who claim to love Ireland are usually among the first to betray her. But thank God there is still a majority who won't."

"Well, we'd better go and get settled in," said Eddie, turning towards the door. "We're just along the corridor, the third door from here. So if you need us, you know where we are."

"Thank's guys," replied Joe sincerely. "It was nice meeting you."

"Same here, Mr. Morrelli," Patrick smiled as they left the room.

After they had gone, Joe locked the gun in his briefcase. He checked his watch. Soon, Rooney would be telephoning Harry Collington. In the meantime, Joe would shower, change and lie down on top of the bed. He'd rest and wait for that all important call that would at last bring him face to face with one of the chiefs!

He drifted off to sleep but was awakened by the telephone ringing. Sitting up, he paused for a moment then lifted the receiver.

"Hello," he said.

"Mr. Morrelli

"Yeah, speaking."

"Harry Collington here. Reception put me through to you. I hope I'm not disturbing you at all."

"No, not at all, Mr. Collington," Joe insisted.

"I know I haven't given you much time to get settled, but Rooney did say you wanted to hear from me as soon as possible on your arrival."

Harry Collington sounded polite, almost charming.

"Yeah, that's right," said Joe.

"You can imagine how surprised I was when he telephoned to say you were on your way to Belfast. I wish I'd known sooner."

"Well, it was a sudden decision. I just thought that while I was in London and so near, it would be a shame not to pay a visit."

"Is there anything I can do for you, Mr. Morrelli?" Collington enquired.

"As a matter of fact, there is." This was the chance he had been hoping for. "I'd like to meet you."

"That can be arranged. Why don't you come to my home? I'll send someone for you at two o'clock tomorrow afternoon."

Joe immediately remembered what Patrick and Eddie had told him. "That won't be necessary, Mr. Collington, I'll get a taxi. You just give me the address and I'll be there," he promised.

"Well, if you're sure."

"Yeah, I'm sure." Joe's friendly voice put Harry Collington at ease.

"Alright," he agreed. "The address is number four, Mount View, Birchwood."

Joe lifted a pen from the bedside cabinet and wrote it down on the notepad provided. "That's fine," he said. "See you tomorrow."

"I'm looking forward to it, Mr. Morrelli. Goodbye."

"Goodbye, Mr. Collington."

He put the receiver down and stared at the notepad. So far, things were going according to plan.

It was just after two o'clock when Joe stepped out of the car, immaculately dressed and carrying his briefcase. He walked up the path and rang the doorbell, which was answered almost immediately by Harry Collington himself.

"Mr. Morrelli, it's nice to meet you. Come in."

Both men shook hands and Joe followed him inside through to the lounge. Looking around him, Joe couldn't help but admire the tasteful decor and expensive furnishings. Harry turned. "Can I offer you a drink, Mr. Morrelli?"

"Not for me, thanks."

"Is this trip business or pleasure?"

"A little of both, actually."

"I see," Harry nodded. "Well then, perhaps we should go through to my office. We won't be disturbed there."

He led Joe to his office, just as he had done with Rooney, and took him inside.

"Please sit down." He waited until Joe was comfortable, then sat down behind his desk. "Now, how can I help you?" he asked, unprepared for the reply.

"As I'm sure you know, Mr. Collington, it's almost time for me to make my annual donation to the fund." Joe reminded him.

"And may I say how grateful we are for such a generous one, Mr. Morrelli. It is much appreciated and I can assure you the money goes a long way in helping the cause."

"Now, that's what I'd like to talk to you about. You see, it has come to my attention that not all of my money is going to the fund, or cause, or whatever you want to call it."

Harry looked surprised.

"I don't understand."

"Oh, but I think you do," Joe insisted. "There's a lot of my money unaccounted for and I want you to tell me where it is."

"Mr. Morrelli, every penny goes to the fund."

"Yeah, but who's fund? We are both men of the world, Mr. Collington, so let's not play games." He placed his briefcase on the desk and opened it, taking out the folder Gene O'Brien had given him. He held it up. "Have you any idea what this is?"

Harry looked at it and shook his head. "No, I haven't."

"It's information - about you!"

"Information? What kind of information?"

"I'd say just about everything. It confirms who and what you really are, and just how far my money has gone. You see, I know for a fact that my missing money is in a Guernsey bank account, number 57200693. It's in the name of one John Cunningham, along with a lot more money you receive for services rendered."

Harry became angry. "This is all lies, nothing but lies! When you are in a position like mine, there's always someone who wants to discredit you."

Joe shook his head. "No Mr. Collington, you did that all by yourself. Besides, why would British Intelligence lie about one of their most trusted informers? You are on their records as one of the most reliable sources of information they have in Belfast and they have paid you a lot of money, which is deposited in your account regularly. No wonder you go to Guernsey so often for vacations! Of course, you're much too smart to use your own name and they are too smart to let you. It's a good set-up considering it has worked to your advantage and theirs, all these years." He gave him an icy stare and continued. "You have a codename, Mr. Collington. You're known as 'The Nightingale'."

He leaned over and waved the folder in front of Harry's face. "It's all here in black and white, if you care to read it."

He watched as Harry Collington's eyes widened and his look of surprise was replaced by one of fear.

"How the hell did you find out?" he asked.

"That's not important," dismissed Joe. "What is important is that you tried to make a fool out of me by taking my money for your own personal use. But no body makes a fool out of Joe Morrelli!"

"Look, we can come to an arrangement. I'll give you back your money. Jesus

Christ, if anyone finds out about this - I'm a dead man!"

"I know," Joe nodded. "But I don't want the money."

Harry stared at him "Then what do you want?"

"I want some information and I'm willing to make you a proposition."

"I'm listening," Harry replied anxiously.

Joe sat back in the chair and looked at him long and hard. "A man was murdered here in 1973, his name was Robert Kenny. No one seems to know just why he was murdered, except that he was accused of being the informer known as 'The Nightingale'. But you and I both know that isn't true. Whoever killed him was never brought to justice. Not by the police or any organisation. This man was an innocent victim, not politically involved in anything. I want to know who murdered him and I want you to find out."

"Why are you so interested- in him?"

Keeping his eyes fixed firmly on Harry, Joe replied,

"Because Robert Kenny was my father-in-law."

There was an uneasy silence as Harry lowered his gaze. "I can tell you now Mr. Morrelli, no order to shoot that man came from me."

"Maybe not, but you played along with it. Only you could have spread the rumour that he was 'The Nightingale, to take any suspicion from yourself."

Lifting his eyes, he met Joe's gaze. "The man was already dead. What harm could it do?"

Shaking his head in disgust, Joe explained, "That man left a family and you did more harm to them than you'll ever know. They were treated so badly they had to leave their home and their country. He was shot, then blamed for something he wasn't/ I could have you shot for something you are but I don't want you, Mr. Collington, I want whoever did it. The price of my silence is the name or names of whoever killed him - and why!"

"It was a long time ago."

"Yeah, but you remembered, didn't you? Now I want you to remember that your own life is at stake here. Not by me, but by your own men."

"It may take time. How long were you planning on staying?"

"For as long as it takes."

Harry nodded. "Alright, I'll see what I can find out."

"Good. I'll be expecting a call from you," said Joe replacing the folder in his briefcase. Both men stared at each other. Finally Joe gave a confident smile. "I wouldn't try anything foolish like having me bumped off," he advised. "Because if anything happens to me my lawyers have been instructed to send copies of this information to your men and we both know that if that happens, you won't live long!"

There was almost a look of hatred in Harry's eyes. "You've got it all sown up, haven't you?"

Joe shrugged. "That's the only way to do business."

"Don't underestimate me, Mr. Morrelli. I'm a big man in Belfast."

"A man is only as big as the city he lives in," Joe informed him. "There are eight million people in New York but less than half a million in Belfast! Need I say more?" They both got up and Harry escorted him to the front door.

Stepping outside, Joe turned. "I'll be waiting to hear from you. Oh' and there's one more thing. Don't go to the trouble of having me followed. I've got my own men to do that." Harry looked towards the waiting car and saw two men standing beside it. On seeing him, they opened their jackets to reveal their weapons. The driver of the car got out and joined them, producing a gun of his own. Beads of sweat formed on Harry Collington's forehead and he used a trembling hand to wipe them away. As the car and it's passengers drove off, a frightened and worried man was left behind!

While waiting for Harry Collington to contact him, Joe was finding his surrounding increasingly disturbing. Armoured trucks and Saracens cruised along the streets, soldiers and police were on constant patrol and gunfire and explosions were a part of every day life in Northern Ireland. Back in New York he was used to seeing armed police but here they carried large rifles, just like other members of the security forces. The sound of low flying helicopters was beginning to get on his nerves.

"It's just like Vietnam!" he thought.

He watched the local news every day in his hotel room. Dead bodies were being found at an alarming rate. Pictures of murdered victims, funerals and women and children crying, were being flashed onto the T.V. screen. Joe found it all very depressing. After one six o'clock news round up, he switched off the set and lay on top of the bed. His thoughts turned to Angela, just as Rooney's had done on his visit.

For the first time in his life he realised what she and her family had been through. All the heartache and pain she and Agnes had come to terms with. He was left in no doubt that Angela carried horrific memories all these years. Ones she could never forget and how could he expect her to? She had knelt beside the body of her murdered father. Joe would never forget the sadness he felt at seeing the pictures of victims he didn't even know, so he knew what it must have been like for her. At last he could understand her feelings and share the tragic memories that had overshadowed her life and left such deep scars. His visit to Belfast had made him more aware of Angela's circumstances and it would leave a lasting impression on him. He would love her even more now, if that were possible, and do everything in his power to make sure she was happy. At that moment he missed her with all his heart and longed to be back in New York and Roseberry Avenue, with his wife and son.

It was four days later when Harry Collington called him to arrange another meeting at his home. On the advice of Eddie Kovak and Patrick Molloy he again followed the same procedure as he'd done with his first meeting, using a car and it's driver especially on loan for the visit.

On his arrival, Harry opened the door and after glancing quickly down the path at Joe's minders, he took him inside and brought him straight to the office. When they were seated Harry leaned his elbows on the desk and looked directly at Joe, with an air of self- confidence.

"First of all, Mr. Morrelli, there is something I should explain to you. We have a problem here in this city. There are some people who cannot be controlled, even by an organisation. Disagreements turn into feuds and some men decide to go their own way. We call them 'splinter groups'. They do things that are not sanctioned by us but we get the blame anyway. Then you have others who will threaten, rob and terrorise people - even murder them, and they make it look like an organisation is responsible. The fact is, they are only out for what they can get. They are known as 'free-lancers'. Last but not least, we have those who are in an organisation but don't obey the rules. They too are out for what they can get but they cover their tracks so well, no one would ever suspect them. I do what I can to try and find out about these people and warn them what the consequences will be if they keep stepping out of line. But it's a very difficult job as I'm sure you will appreciate. After all, this is a big city."

Joe nodded. "I can see you've got your hands full but where exactly does that leave me?"

"Well, in your case we were lucky but it took quite a bit of searching to get to the truth. I had to investigate your request very carefully." He sat back in his chair and from the top desk drawer, produced two plain covered files. Holding them up he gave a broad smile. "This is what you asked for. But you see Mr. Morrelli, this places me in a position to call the shots - if you'll pardon my expression! I now have something you want. That gives me something to bargain with."

Looking deadly serious, Joe nodded. "Yeah, that's right - your life! You've got a nice set-up going here Mr. Collington. The point is, do you want to live long enough to enjoy it? If you do, you'll give me those files. If you don't, you'll be taken down by your own men and if that happens, sooner or later I'm going to get hold of those files anyway."

Harry's smile faded. "You don't scare easily, do you?"

"Not when I'm holding all the aces! Don't get smart with me Mr. Collington, because believe me you'll regret it when you're looking over your shoulder at every sound you hear. Now, I made you a proposition, do you want it or not?"

Putting the files down on the desk, Harry placed his hand on top of them. "On one condition," he replied. "That my name is never mentioned in connection with what happened to Robert Kenny. You know I was responsible for having him labelled as an informer but no one else must ever know. It was a long time ago and I want no repercussions. Give me your word that no one in this city will ever find out what I'm doing or who I work for."

"That's two conditions! But I can promise you that as long as I live, no one in Belfast will ever know that you are 'The Nightingale'. And Joe Morrelli never breaks a promise."

Harry nodded and pushed the files across the desk. "All the information you want is there along with a little extra. Photographs of the men you're looking for. Let's just say, I thought you'd like them for identification purposes. It's much easier to find someone if you know what they look like. I hope you will appreciate this gesture as one of trust, Mr. Morrelli. After all, a man in my position needs to know that he has that from someone like you."

"Believe me, your double life is perfectly safe with me. But just out of curiosity, don't you think the risks you take far outweigh the benefits?"

"How do you think I bought this house?" he smiled. "There are risks in everything, even in being a top man. I won't always be one. There are too many young men coming along with big ideas. When the time is right I'll have enough money to get my family out of here. I'll be able to live abroad in comfort for the rest of my life, with no money worries."

"Yeah, I guess we all make plans," said Joe, putting the files into his briefcase and standing up.

Harry rose too and shook his hand." Well Mr. Morrelli, maybe we'll meet again and maybe not. It all depends on what you decide to do in the future. But if you ever need me, you know where I am."

He escorted Joe out of the office and to the front door.

On his way out, Joe turned to him. "By the way Mr. Collington, I won't be making any more payments to the fund. I think you have enough of my money to live abroad in style . After all, I've been donating a lot of money for a long time."

"How am I going to explain your sudden decision?"

"Oh, you'll think of something."

"You're a very shrewd man Mr. Morrelli."

"Yeah, too shrewd to keep you for as long as you live!"

Harry shook his head. "I suppose all good things must come to an end."

"I guess they do," Joe agreed. "It's nothing personal Mr. Collington, it's just good business sense."

"Well goodbye Mr. Morrelli and have a pleasant journey. I know if you decide to read, you'll have an interesting one."

Joe tapped his briefcase. "I hope what you've given me was worth the trip. If not, I'll be back. You can count on that."

As they held each other's gaze, Joe knew deep down that for all Harry Collington's failings the information he had given him was correct.

He turned and walked down the path, having in his possession what he had planned and paid for all these years - the names of Robert Kenny's murderers!

The next morning Joe booked a flight back to New York but as it wasn't due to leave until late that evening, he decided to pay a visit to two places he had always wanted to see.

After talking it over with Eddie and Patrick, who were reluctant to let him out of their sight, Joe explained that he wanted to do this on his own. They agreed to let him have his way but as before. By doing that he would be perfectly safe. He understood and appreciated their concern. Besides, they were only carrying out Gene O'Brien's instructions. His first stop was Glensdale Park. Sitting in the back of the parked car, he looked out of the window at the red bricked houses. Staring over at number 23 he did so with mixed emotions. This had been Angela's home. The house where she had been born and raised. The place she had shared for seventeen years with a loving, happy family. This in turn gave a feeling of happiness. But it was also the house that had held it's share of grief for her. Her murdered father's body had lay in there, his funeral had left from there and not long afterwards she and Agues had left too. Driven out by hostility, abuse and hatred, even towards a small dog. A faithful friend to a kind master who had also paid the price with his life and lay buried in the back garden. Sadness replaced the feelings of happiness, but he was still glad to be there. He felt close to Angela because now he was sharing a part of her life he had only ever heard about.

At that moment the door of number 23 opened and a young girl came out. His heart stopped for a moment. With her long red hair, blue eyes and slim build, it was as if he was looking at a younger version of Angela Kenny. He couldn't help but recognise her immediately. It was Aisling!

She came down the path, opened the gate and went up the next path. He noticed she was carrying a shopping basket and he smiled to himself. She must be running errands for old Mrs. Murray, just the way Angela had done.

"I guess old habits die hard." He thought. "Yeah, Aisling's just like her auntie Angela, in so many ways."

When Aisling disappeared into Mrs. Murray's house, he nodded to the driver. A few moments later they were on their way to Joe's next destination, leaving Glendale Park and all it's memories far behind.

As the car came to a stop for the second time, Joe got out. He made his way though the cemetery carrying a large bouquet of red roses. Walking from one pathway to the other, his eyes kept searching until he finally found the name he was looking for. Going over, he stood at the foot of the grave and read the large gold lettering on the black marble headstone.

In loving memory of
Robert Kenny
And his beloved wife Agnes
Gone but not forgotten
Rest in peace

He paid particular attention to the years in which they had died. Robert in 1973 and Agnes not long after him in 1975. How could he or Angela ever forget it? Agnes died and their son had been born on the same day. She never saw the grandchild she longed so much to hold. With a heavy heart he bowed his head, a solitary figure.

"Agnes, what can I say?" he murmured in a low voice. "There's so much I want to tell you. About my life with Angel and how happy she's made me. And about my son. He's a fine boy, Agnes, you would have been very proud of him. But the most important thing is, I know who killed your husband and my son's grandfather. I just don't know what I'm going to do about it. Not yet anyway. That's why I can't tell Angel. She mustn't know until the time is right. I've carried a lot of secrets in my time Agnes, but this is going to be one of the hardest. But I promise you, one day justice will be done. I've waited this long to find out, I can wait a little longer. Someday they'll probably be lying in this very cemetery, then you and your husband can really rest in peace." Bending down, he carefully placed the bouquet on the grave. "I never thought that after all these years I'd be delivering this in person." He closed his moistened eyes in silent prayer, then crossed himself and took one last look. "Goodbye Agnes," he whispered as he turned and walked away.

Eddie Kovak and Patrick Molloy were having a drink in the hotel lounge, so he joined them and called for another round. As the waiter sat it down on the table Patrick asked, "Have you anything else planned, Mr. Morrelli?"

Joe shook his head. "No, only to enjoy my drink."

Eddie looked at his wrist. "My watch has stopped. What's the time?" he asked.

"It's time to go home guys," smiled Joe.

The two men grinned as they lifted their glasses.

"We'll drink to that!" they said together.

"I had a feeling you would!" he replied.

On the long flight back to New York, Joe had plenty of time to think about the

597

past and present. It was only now he realised just how much he had asked of Gene O'Brien. He could never have succeeded in getting a man like Harry Collington to help him without the important information Gene had supplied. He knew that now. It was Gene's help that had given him everything he needed to force Harry Collington's back to the wall, leaving him no way out but one - to give him the names of Robert Kenny's killers. Angela had always believed her father to be an innocent victim but Joe knew he was, thanks to his old friend who had put his career on the line for him because of two things, friendship and loyalty. They had shared them since childhood and would continue to do so for as long as they'd live, of that Joe was certain.

He rubbed his face with his hands and looked out of the window, before settling back and closing his eyes. He was leaving Ireland a much wiser man with a lot to think about. But for now he only had one thought in his mind - he was going home.

As Joe came through the arrivals area, Rooney was waiting.

"Am I glad to see you!" he grinned.

"Same here!" smiled Joe.

"How was the trip?"

Looking back towards the large aircraft on the tarmac Joe nodded, "Pretty good." After picking up the luggage they left the airport and went to Rooney's car.

"It's great to be back," said Joe looking out of the window at all the hustle and bustle going on around him. "I really missed this city."

"I know the feeling!" smiled Rooney as he drove along.

"Oh, by the way, did you get the presents for Angel and Robert like I asked? I was supposed to be in Chicago not Belfast, remember? I don't want to give the game away."

"Don't worry, that's all been taken care of and added to your account. I managed to get Robert one of those sweatshirts of the Chicago Cyclones."

Joe was surprised. "How did you get your hands on one of those? They're pretty hard to come by."

"Not if you know where to go. One of the guys at the gym has a brother-in-law who can get you anything you want, if the price is right. I got Angela some expensive french lingerie."

"What kind of lingerie?"

"A black nightdress and negligee."

Joe leaned sideways and stared at him. "Why didn't you get her some perfume?"

"Oh I got her that as well. The very best I could find. I also got a bottle for Evie. You know how excited she gets when you go on business trips."

"I don't believe this!"

"Stop griping Joe," Rooney smiled. "After all, if you count the time difference from one country to the other, you've been away about eight days."

"Yeah well, anyone would think I'd been away eight weeks, the way you've been splashing my money around. Just remind me never to send you to do my Christmas shopping!" He reached into his pocket. "Speaking of countries, I picked this up for you on my way through Belfast airport. It's for good luck." He pulled out a key ring with a plastic leprechaun dangling on the end.

Rooney looked at it, then looked at Joe. "Are you sure you could afford it? I mean, I wouldn't want you to go spending all your money on me!"

"Well, you're the ones who believe in little men dressed in green that run around granting favours! Besides, I've got some Irish whiskey in my suitcase for you and Gene."

"How did you get on with Harry Collington?" asked Rooney, keeping his eyes on the road.

"I'll tell you all about that this evening. I want you to come to the house after dinner. I'll fill you in then."

"O.k. I'll be there between nine and nine thirty."

"Fine," replied Joe.

The car entered the driveway and stopped at the front door. It opened and Robert came running out, followed by Angela and Evie.

"Where are the presents?" Joe whispered.

"On the back seat, all wrapped up in expensive paper and ribbons."

"You're one expensive guy!" he muttered, climbing out.

"Just like my boss! I'll hand the presents out to you."

As he did so, Joe leaned towards him and in a low voice said, "I sure hope this stuff doesn't give Angel the wrong idea and make her suspicious."

"What about?"

"Me! She might think I've been with another woman and I'm feeling guilty."

"Oh come on Joe! Angela would never think that of you. She knows you too well - we all do. I can promise you, she'll be thrilled with these presents."

"Yeah well, if she decides to wear them tonight that will make two of us!" he winked.

Rooney shook his head as he went to get the suitcase from the boot, leaving Joe to be welcomed home by his loving family.

That evening, Joe and Rooney closed the study door behind them and prepared for some serious business.

Joe leaned back in the black leather chair. "There's something I want to show you," he said turning the key in the securely locked drawer and producing the two files Harry Collington had given him. "Here." He handed them to Rooney. "Those are the men who murdered Robert Kenny."

Rooney noticed the sombre look on Joe's face but he remained silent as he opened the files and stared at the photographs. Joe watched for his reaction. Almost immediately the blood drained from Rooney's face, leaving it pale and death-like. He put his elbow on Joe's desk to steady a shaking hand that was trying to rub his cold and clammy forehead.

Joe held a stony expression as Rooney finally met his gaze, shaking his head in disbelief.

"No Joe," he said almost pleadingly, then returned his gaze to the photographs. "Oh Jesus. Jesus no!"

Chapter 19

Joe had been out that afternoon on his usual round of business calls. As he headed home, he glanced at his watch.

"Hey Al, drop by the College and we can give Robert a ride home."

"Sure Boss," Al nodded, turning off the busy street and making his way to the large buildings that were so familiar to him.

When the car stopped, Joe sat for a few moments looking around at the many students coming out. Then he opened the door. "I think I'll surprise him, he smiled, getting out and going through the entrance gates. Never having been to College himself, he was curious to see what he had missed. Walking up the path towards the large campus, he could hear loud roars and cheers coming from the side of one of the smaller buildings. Deciding to investigate, he put his head around the corner and saw a large circle of boys shouting and swearing at the two in the centre, who were having a fight.

Joe was surprised to see such a spectacle, but even more surprised to discover that one of them was Robert! He stood silently for a few moments, watching. It was a vicious fight as both boys lunged at each other with their bare fists. However, Joe decided not to intervene. After what he termed were a couple of even rounds, the other boy kicked Robert on the legs and head-butted him in the stomach, sending him crashing to the ground. Joe winced as his son lay on his back while his opponent threw himself on top of him, putting a hand on his throat and pressing hard. After a lot of scuffling and struggling, Robert managed to put his hand under the other boy's chin pushing it upward and forcing his head back, throwing him off. He quickly got to his feet and waited for the other boy to do the same. As they squared up to each other once again, Robert's eyes flashed with temper he had a look of sheer determination on his face. He raised his fists and started throwing punches in quick succession to the face and body.

They were fast and furious, coming too quickly for his rival. As Joe watched, he was going through all the motions himself with his own fists and looking rather pleased. All those sessions in Stacey's Gym had paid off! By now the other boy was taking a real beating and could hardly stand. A few moments later, Robert threw a right punch to his face and a left to his body. That was enough! Down the other boy went, flat on his back and stayed there. Joe nodded to himself in approval. Yes, there was no getting away from it, Robert was a chip off the old block alright. Joe Morrelli had just witnessed a younger version of himself. As cheers rang out from the crowd and a lot of swear words were hurled at the boy still on the ground, Robert stood over him and glaring down pointed a warning finger into his face.

"If you ever call my father a guinea again or my mother a mick, there's plenty more where that came from!"

Now Joe knew what the fight was about and he was full of pride and admiration for his son. Robert had stood up for his own kin and no matter what he might ever do in the future, Joe could never feel any prouder of him than he felt today.

As the crowd dispersed, Robert turned around and saw him. He looked embarrassed. "Dad, what are you doing here?"

"I came to give you a ride home," he smiled. "After what I've just seen, maybe I should carry you there on my shoulders!"

Robert tucked his torn shirt inside his trousers. "He had it coming "

"Now, I can believe that," Joe nodded, going over and putting an arm around him. "It was a good fight, one of the best I've ever seen. I'm real proud of you, son."

"Really?" The boy wiped the blood from his mouth.

"You bet!" winked Joe. "I think this calls for a celebration. Why don't you let your old man buy you a drink?"

"Dad, I'm not old enough to drink. No one will serve me."

"They will where we're going. What do you say? You've earned it."

Robert smiled. "O.K."

His father nodded. "You know, watching you brought me back to when I was your age, living in the old neighbourhood. I've got to tell you, some things never change - except the surroundings." He looked around at the buildings and grounds.

"You never talk much about those times and what you did," Robert commented.

"Well, I have my reasons." Taking out a handkerchief, he wiped the remaining blood from his son's mouth. They looked at each other. "You beat him fair and square son. Wild Man Wilson couldn't have done it any better."

"Coming from you that's one hell of a compliment, Dad."

"Yeah well, it was one hell of a fight!"

They both smiled broadly and began to walk down the path with their arms around each other's shoulders.

They had always been father and son but at that moment they became more than that. Now they were buddies!

After hearing what had happened, it was a delighted Al who brought the car to a halt outside Mario's. Stepping onto the sidewalk, Joe paused and looked up at the sign. He turned to Robert.

"You know, I brought your mother here on our first date. Now I'm bringing you here for your first drink. I'm just sad Mario isn't around today to see you."

"Mom often talks about him. She really liked him."

"Yeah, so did I. We knew each other a long time. I really missed that old man after he died." He went forward and pushed open the door.

As they walked to the bar, he glanced around. Nothing had changed. It was as though time had stood still and he was glad. It brought back a lot of happy memories. A smiling Gino greeted him.

"Joe Morrelli! It's so good to see you again. How are you?"

He nodded and returned the smile. "It's good to see you too. I'm fine." He placed a hand on Robert's shoulder. "Gino, this is Robert, my son."

Gino looked surprised. "Robert? You mean, little Robert?"

"That's right. He's at College now and he's had a busy day. I think he could use a drink!"

Joe gave a knowing wink and Gino responded by shaking Robert's hand warmly and saying,

"Sure, no problem! What will it be?"

"Oh, I think two beers will do just fine," said Joe.

"Dad, I've never seen you drink beer," Robert remarked, lifting the two glasses and following him to a table.

"I only drink it on special occasions."

They sat down and he took the glass from the boy and smiled, "Here's looking at you, kid."

Robert nodded but as Joe began sipping his beer, he was amazed to see his son gulp his own down like water. Anxious, he leaned over and put a caring hand on his arm. "Hey now, slow down. That's your first drink and I don't want it going to your head. Your mother would have a fit if she knew I'd bought you alcohol. And besides, the last thing I want is to get the blame for bringing my own son home drunk."

"Dad, it's not my first drink," confessed Robert in a low voice.

Joe raised his eyebrows. "What do you mean? Are you telling me you've done this before?"

"I like beer."

"Really? And when did you acquire a taste for it? No, let me guess that one. I suppose it happened with your friends on that fancy campus. Am I right?"

"No, it happened at home. Mom shares a beer with me when you're not there, but she told me not to tell you."

"I'll bet she did!" Joe replied, stunned. "You mean to tell me she's been giving you beer at home and I've come halfway across town to buy you one, so that she wouldn't know?! He shook his head. "Now that is one sneaky lady."

Robert smiled. "Well it wasn't a wasted journey. I'm enjoying it." He put the empty glass down on the table.

"I've noticed! I suppose you'd like another one. Can you handle it?"

"Yeah, I think so."

"O.k, but if your mother asks, you only had one."

"Now who's being sneaky?"

Joe shook his head. "You know, that woman is just full of surprises."

"Maybe that's why you love her so much," said Robert.

Joe gave an amused smile as he looked around, "Well I can tell you this, I really fell in love with her right here. That was some night for me."

"I'll bet you didn't need any help getting her to feel the same way, dad."

"Oh, I wouldn't say that." He glanced towards the juke-box. "As a matter of fact, Frank Sinatra helped me a great deal!" They both smiled broadly at each other, then Joe turned. "Hey Gino another beer and two large Scotches."

"Coming right up!" came the reply.

Robert looked at his father in surprise. "Two Scotches?"

Joe got up. "Yeah well, Al was so pleased about today, I'm sure he'd like to join us."

"Won't mom be wondering where we are?"

"Maybe, but I've got the perfect excuse. We were in the old neighbourhood. Besides, seeing as this isn't your first drink, I don't think there's much she can say. Do you?" he winked.

Robert grinned and shook his head as Joe went to get Al. There was one thing he had to admit about his father - Joe Morrelli always came out on top.

After Evie had served dinner, Joe, Angela and Robert sat at the table in happy conversation. The boy was in his sixteenth year now and quite mature for his age except when it came to Pal, who sat dutifully beside his chair. For every mouthful of food Robert ate, he smuggled a helping to his four legged Friend. Joe watched as the food disappeared from the plate.

"That must be the only mutt in New York to be fed on prime steak."

"He's not a mutt," Robert replied, rather hurt at his father's comment. Putting his hand down, he stroked the dog affectionately.

"Uncle Rooney got papers with him."

"Well, I got papers with your pony!" Joe reminded him, still smarting after all this time. Angela pointed a warning finger in his direction.

"Now don't start that again, Joe." He lowered his eyes and returned to his meal with the look of a scolded schoolboy. Angela decided to change the subject.

Looking at Robert she enquired, "What about that new boy you're always talking about? Has he settled in yet?"

"John? Yeah, he's fine. Actually, we've become really good friends. He wants to be a lawyer too, so we have a lot in common."

She nodded. "What about the exams, won't he find it difficult with being in a new school?"

"It won't be any trouble for him, mom, he'll sail through them. The guy's got a computer for a brain. No matter what he's told or reads, he never seems to forget it."

Joe listened, finding it all very interesting. Then putting down his knife and fork, he looked at his son. "I read about people like that somewhere. Maybe he's got one of those photographer's memories!"

Robert smiled. He was well used to his father's misrepresentation of certain words and phrases, so as usual he didn't contradict. "You're probably right, dad." he agreed. "I've been thinking the same thing myself. He's trying to talk me into taking a speech and drama course with him."

Joe raised his eyebrows. "What for? You're going to be an attorney, not an actor!"

"But that's the whole point dad. John says that all great attorneys have to be great actors as well. The way he figures it, a courtroom is like a stage and when it's our turn to say our lines, we have to give an award winning performance every time. You see, he reckons it's not just what you say - but the way you say it." He held up his hands, his voice full of enthusiasm. "If you can captivate an entire courtroom, have them hanging on your every word and win a jury over to your way of thinking, then that's how you become popular and in demand."

There was silence for a few moments as Joe thought carefully, then nodded. "Mmmm, I see your point. That's not a bad idea. The kid's smart, I'll give him that. Why don't you ask him over some time?"

"Well, I was kind of hoping you and mom would let me invite him for the weekend. What do you think?"

"Sure son, why not? Your friends are always welcome, you know that. Right Angel? By the way, what's the kid's name again?"

"John. John Sullivan."

"And what business is his father in?"

"Well, his father isn't really in a business, as such ...

Joe looked puzzled. "What do you mean - 'as such'?"

"He's a delivery man for a bakery."

After staring at him for a few moments Joe then glanced over at Angela. "Well, at least we won't starve to death!" he said, in a sarcastic tone.

Robert looked from one to the other, hesitating. Finally he asked, "Well ... can I still invite him?"

Before Joe could say another word, Angela put a hand on her son's arm. "Of course you can. You know your father isn't one to be impressed by a person's background. Right Joe?"

Dare he disagree? Better not!

"That's right," he nodded. "Now, why don't you go and call the kid? Tell him we'd like to meet him After all, you've had plenty of friends here, what's one more?"

Robert got to his feet. "Thank's dad. Thank's mom," he smiled, leaving the table to make his phone call accompanied by the ever faithful Pal.

After they'd both gone, Joe rested his elbows on the table and looked across at Angela.

"Tell me something. How come that with all the different nationalities in this city, the Irish always seem to home-in on their own kind?"

"What do you mean, 'home-in?'"

"Well, take this John Sullivan kid, for instance. Now why couldn't he be called ... Johnny Corrolla or Vinnie Santino. Or is that too much to ask?"

Angela's voice became quite curt. "Oh I see. You'd like it better if his friend was an Italian. Now who's homing in on their own kind? Besides, the Irish in this family have done very well by you, haven't they?" Her curtness took on a sarcastic note. "Anyway, I don't see why you're making such a fuss. What's in a name?"

"Try telling that to Willie Dick on 45th Street," came the quick reply.

"Joe Morrelli!!" she exclaimed. "What am I going to do with you?"

His face broke into a mischievous grin as he lowered his gaze and played around with the food on his plate. "Well, now that you've brought it up, Mrs. Morrelli, I have a few suggestions. That is, if you've got a couple of hours to spare!"

That Friday afternoon Joe and Angela were in the lounge when the door opened and Robert popped his head around.

"Mom, Dad, I'd like you to meet John Sullivan."

He looked back over his shoulder, beckoning his friend. "Come on," he coaxed.

The door opened wider and in they both came. As Angela got up to greet their guest, Joe sat staring in amazement. John Sullivan was black! Hastily putting the newspaper down, Joe got to his feet and held out his hand as the boy approached.

"It's nice to meet you, Mr. Morrelli. Thanks for inviting me."

"My pleasure," he replied barely able to hide his surprise. "Robert tells me you want to be a lawyer."

John smiled, "That's right, I do."

Stepping forward, Robert put a hand on his friend's shoulder. "Maybe we'll end up in the same practice one day. 'Morrelli and Sullivan, Attorneys at Law'. Come on, I'll show you to your room."

"Why not?" thought Joe. They were both dressed the same in casual jeans and sweatshirts.

As they reached the door, Robert turned around.

"Mom, can we have dinner early? Frankie Junior's coming over with a few friends and we're all going to the movies." He looked at John. "You're going to love this guy. He's a movie fanatic and pretty good at acting all the tough guys."

"Really, like who?"

Robert opened the door, then spun around and pointed his finger,

"You talkin' to me?"

John's face beamed. "Hey, you're not so bad yourself?"

They left the room laughing, with Joe staring after them.

"You know Angel," he said glancing over at her, "I'm getting a little worried about this drama course. I just hope he never says that to a Judge, because if he does it will be the last thing he'll ever get to say in a courtroom!"

As she heard the boys heading for the kitchen, she stood with a smug smile on her face. "Well, so much for the Irish homing in on their own kind!"

He looked embarrassed, if not a little guilty.

"O.k. so I made a mistake," he admitted with outstretched hands. "Besides, this house is like the subway. When the doors open, you just never know who you're going to see!"

"It just goes to prove you can't go by names," she called after him as he left the lounge. Joe met up with Robert and John in the entrance hall where they passed Al, who stared long and hard at the new house-guest. As the boys climbed the stairs he made his way over to Joe.

"Hey boss, who's that?"

"Don't ask, it's a long story. His name is John Sullivan."

"John Sullivan?"

Joe nodded. "I know what you're thinking, believe me." He glanced up towards the loud laughter at the top of the stairs, then leaned over. "I thought I was going to be introduced to an Irish kid. How wrong can a guy be?"

Just then Evie appeared from the kitchen.

"Mr. Joe, I've decided to do something special for that nice, young Mr. Sullivan."

Al winked at Joe. "What about spaghetti and meatballs, Evie?" he teased.

She turned and gave him a stony glance. "In case you haven't noticed, young Mr. Sullivan is not an Italian."

"No kiddin'? And here was me thinking he came all the way from Little Italy!"

Joe was trying hard not to smile at all this, so he decided to butt in. "What did you have In mind?" he asked.

"Oh, roast chicken with all the trimmings and a nice big chocolate cake for dessert."

He nodded in approval. "Sounds good to me. Maybe we should all change our name to John Sullivan."

"Yeah," Al agreed. "It would sure give the meat loaf a rest!!"

Evie tossed her head haughtily and went to find Angela.

Al looked at Joe. "She couldn't be more pleased about 'young Mr. Sullivan'," he mimicked, "if she were carrying a banner!"

"I think she's more pleased with Robert," Joe replied, staring after her as she entered the lounge. He shrugged his shoulders then turned back to Al and pointed his finger. "It just goes to prove you can't go by names," he smiled, echoing his wife's words and pretending they were his own!

Robert and John remained firm friends and studied hard together. When Gene O'Brien heard what their plans for the future were, he offered them a place in his law firm whenever they'd graduate. This pleased Joe and made the two young men very happy. Gene knew it wouldn't do him any harm either, to have a white man and a black man working side by side in his offices.

Antonia was very proud of Robert. He was ambitious and she admired that. When he told her about Gene O'Brien's offer, she decided it was time to introduce her godson into the select circles she moved in. That way he would become well known and with the right acquaintances it would be a lot easier for him to make a name for himself. With his parent's permission, she set about her task. Robert escorted her to parties and functions where he rubbed shoulders with the rich and famous. Although he was a down to earth young man with his feet firmly on the ground, he enjoyed it. There had always been a special bond between himself and Antonia. From his childhood they shared a love for the theatre and on many occasions he sat in the front row applauding loudly as he watched his godmother perform. It was on the opening night of her new play that he was to be her escort to a party afterwards.

Joe and Angela were in the kitchen when the door opened and Robert came in. "How do I look?" he smiled.

"Very handsome," his mother replied, proudly.

Joe gave him the once over. "Yeah, you look great."

"I'm not over-dressed in this monkey suit, am I?"

"Now, that all depends on where you're going."

"The Portland Club for a champagne bash. Aunt Antonia wants to wait for the early reviews."

"Well in that case," Joe smiled, "I'd say you were dressed just right." He lifted his coffee cup and looked rather thoughtful.

"Yeah, she never could sleep until the early editions hit the streets. She's a great believer in the critics - just as long as they don't criticise!"

Robert looked from one to the other. "I wish you two were coming "

Joe shook his head. "Son, I was Antonia's escort for years. I've done the 'theatre and parties' bit, now it's your turn. You go and enjoy yourself, besides, I'm getting too old for all of that. Me and your mom's going to have a nice quiet evening at home with Frank Sinatra." He smiled over at Angela.

She nodded, "That's right, your father and I are going to have our own champagne party."

"You see," he winked, "things are looking up for your old man already!"

"Well, I think I'll go now and let you get an early start," Robert joked, making his way to the door.

"Hey," called his father, pointing a finger. "Don't you let any of those young actresses sweet talk you. You hear?"

"Don't worry, Dad. If they didn't get Joe Morrelli they don't stand a chance of getting his son!"

"Enjoy yourself," smiled Angela.

"I will mom. See you later."

After a few moments the front door closed and he was gone.

Joe put his cup down. "You know Angel, I've got to admit he's grown into a handsome guy."

"Why wouldn't he? He's very much like his father."

"Yeah, he's a Morrelli, alright!"

She looked at him and leaned her elbows on the table. "I think that's part of the attraction for Antonia."

"What do you mean?"

"I think when she looks at Robert she sees you, all those years ago. She always loved you, Joe, we both know that. And although she loves Robert dearly as his aunt and godmother, he's so much like you he's bound to be a reminder of how things used to be."

He nodded. "Well, if having him around makes her happy then why not? I guess I owe her that much. I really thought she'd have married Judge Thompson by now. After all, they're practically living together. But then so were we at one time, but like I always used to say, Antonia is married to the theatre and she always was."

"I think maybe now she regrets it. I think she realised a long time ago she wanted to be married to Joe Morrelli. That's why having his son so close to her, makes her happy."

"Don't you mind?" he asked.

"No, why should I mind? I'm the one who married Joe Morrelli and Robert is my son. That makes me the lucky one. I don't need reminders of the past, Antonia does. After all, she isn't getting any younger."

He smiled. "Well I'll give her one thing, you'd never know it. She sure doesn't look her age, she's still a very attractive woman. I can see why the Judge stayed around, he really loves her."

"And what about you?" she asked in a low voice.

Joe reached over and placing his hand in hers, he pressed it gently. "I've always cared for her in my own way, but I've always loved you. From the day I proposed to you in 'The Safe Haven', I've never been with any other woman. You must believe that, Angel."

Angela looked deeply into his eyes. Like his voice, they were honest and sincere. "I do," she nodded, holding his hand firmly. "Do you know what I'd like to do now?"

"No, what?"

"I'd like to open a bottle of champagne, bring it upstairs with two glasses and drink it in bed with you ..."

He smiled. "Then I'd like to lie and hold you in my arms," he finished for her. "I didn't think you would remember that."

"How could I forget? It was better than the party!" she teased.

They got up, still holding hands.

"Yeah, who needs parties and crowds, when all we really need is each other?"

"My sentiments exactly, Mr. Morrelli."

Joe's smile became a broad grin. "I hope my son enjoys himself as much tonight as his father intends to!"

She waited in the entrance hall while he fetched the champagne and glasses from the drinks cabinet in the lounge. As he turned, he glanced at the stereo.

"Sorry Frank, but I have other things on my mind!" he murmured, rejoining Angela and climbing the stairs.

As Robert sat in the theatre watching Antonia portraying the heroine brilliantly, she wasn't the only one he was watching. A young actress in a small supporting role caught his eye. He studied her with great interest every time she came on stage. She was very talented but also very attractive and by the end of the show, he knew he wanted to meet her. When he went back stage to Antonia's dressing room, he mentioned it to her and she happily agreed to do the introductions.

After making her grand entrance in 'The Portland Club' on Robert's arm and greeting her many friends with smiles and kisses, she led him across the room to a table where two young women were in light conversation.

She gave one of them a cold stare. "Excuse me, my dear." Whereupon the young woman immediately got up and left. Turning her attention to the other one, she smiled sweetly.

"Camilla, dear, I'd like to introduce you to my godson, Robert Morrelli."

"It's nice to meet you."

"Same here," he replied as they shook hands. "Mind if I join you?"

"No, not at all. Please, sit down," she motioned. He pulled out a chair and sat down facing her.

Antonia looked over his head and beckoned to a waiter, who came at once. "Yes Miss Flemming?"

"I'd like you to bring a bottle of your best champagne to this table."

"Right away, Miss Flemming."

As he hurried off she looked down at Robert and his companion. "Well, I'll leave you both to get acquainted . I'm sure you'll find lots to talk about."

"But won't you join us?" he asked.

She put her hands on his shoulders and brushed her cheek lovingly against his. "Not now darling. I really must go and mingle with my guests. I'll join you both later," she smiled, then returned to the crowd.

A bottle of champagne in an ice bucket was soon sat before them, with two glasses.

After filling them both, he lifted his.

"O.k. let's have a toast."

"What will we drink to?" she asked.

"Well, what about the play? I though you were great."

She looked embarrassed. "It was my first real part and a rather small one, I'm afraid."

"All the more reason to drink to it, then. Sooner or later a small role can lead to a big one, just ask my Aunt Antonia!" he smiled. "Besides, the part may have been small but it was important to the play, so don't put yourself down."

Camilla smiled and raised her glass. "Maybe you're right."

"I know I am. Trust me."

As they sipped from the glasses they studied each other carefully, yet warmly. "Is Camilla your stage name?" Robert enquired.

She shook her head, still smiling at him. "No, that's my real name."

"Well I guess like the rest of us you've got another one. What is it?"

"Bruce."

"That doesn't sound very New Yorkish."

"My mother is half Jewish and my father is Scottish descent."

"Really? My father is Italian and my mother is Irish, so I guess you could say we're neighbours."

"Neighbours? How?"

"Well, my mother always said the Irish and Scots were very much alike - the same clan! So you'd be right at home in our house," he grinned.

Her smile began to fade. "I doubt it. If Miss Flemming is your godmother then your parents must move in the same circles. Mine can't afford to. My dad is a salesman and he's out of town quite often. That's why he couldn't be at the theatre tonight. Mom works nights in a hospital because the extra money helps to pay for my drama lessons. I was a part-time waitress in a diner until I got my audition."

Robert smiled. "All good actresses were waitresses at one time or another."

He shrugged his shoulders, a habit inherited from his father. "Besides, my mother was a waitress before she met my dad."

"Maybe, but I guess what I'm really trying to say is that perhaps I'm not the one you should be with." She glanced around at all the many beautiful and wealthy young women. "Perhaps there's someone more ... suitable," she suggested.

"Why don't you let me be the judge of that?" he replied, holding her gaze.

Her large, dark eyes and long eyelashes were the dominant features in her finely shaped face. Her flawless skin had a natural glow and her long fair hair was in a casual yet feminine style. But for all her loveliness and obvious honesty, it was clear that when it came to young men of Robert's status, she lacked confidence in herself. If he'd met her some where else, he'd never have guessed she was an actress. She didn't go on about her ambitions or how great she wanted to be. And she certainly wasn't forward or pushy. This young woman was down to earth, just like himself, and gifted with good manners. Her personality was friendly but not overly familiar and he was sure she had many qualities.

They continued to talk openly to each other and Camilla soon became attracted to Robert's charm and sense of humour. She was smitten by his warm and generous nature. But unlike his student girlfriends, she had worked for what she wanted. There were no wealthy parents to indulge her with expensive cars and shopping trips, the things those other girls took for granted. Coming from a middle class background she understood the difficulties and hardships some families have to face, and greatly sympathised. Just being with her awakened emotions in him, Emotions he had never felt for any other young woman. He knew deep down inside that she was different from all the other actresses he had met, far removed from the glitz and glamour they all loved so much - especially his Aunt Antonia! He enjoyed her company and didn't want it to end there. Camilla Bruce was the sort of girl he could bring home to his mother and father, and he was convinced they would like her just as much as he did.

Joe and Angela couldn't fail to notice a change in their son. He had always been a happy boy but now he went around the house beaming and he was going out a lot more often than he used to. Joe suspected he had a girlfriend but what puzzled him was, why was he being so closed mouthed about it? One evening after dinner, he decided to find out. When Angela had left for the bowling alley, Robert came down the stairs and crossed the entrance hall to the front door.

"Robert, I'd like to talk to you," called Joe from the door of the lounge.

"Dad, I'm in a hurry."

"It won't take long."

He turned back and followed his father, closing the lounge door after him.

They stood facing each other.

"Son, are you dating someone on a permanent basis?"

Robert didn't speak, just nodded.

"Well, I'm pleased for you," Joe continued. "But I don't understand why you're being so secretive about it. Who is she?" he smiled.

He looked at him and took a deep breath. "She's an actress."

In a split second Joe's smile had gone. "You're dating an actress? No wonder you've been keeping it so quiet! Where did you meet her?"

"At a party. She's appearing on Broadway in Aunt Antonia's play."

"And I suppose your Aunt Antonia knows all about this?"

"She introduced us."

"I might have guessed!"

"Dad, it's not like that, honestly."

"Then why don't you tell me what it is like?" Joe invited.

"I wanted to meet her," he admitted. "And before you say anything more, she's a very nice girl and very talented. This is her first theatre role and she's good, even if it is only a small part."

His father nodded sarcastically. "Yeah, for now! With your name and my money she knows she'll get a bigger part next time!"

"She isn't like that," he insisted.

Joe stared at him "How do you know what she's really like, she's an actress isn't she?"

Robert stared back. "What have you got against them?"

"I don't have anything against the acting profession but you've got to understand that they can be very temperamental, especially the women. And, believe me, I should know," he replied, taking a step back and putting his hands on his hips in a stern fashion.

"Now, I want you to listen to me. Some of them are o.k. but others will do anything to further their careers. They'll tell you anything - including 'I love you', and I sure hope you're not in love because if you are, you could be heading for a lot of grief."

Robert became defiant, much to Joe's surprise and annoyance. "Dad, I'm old enough to know what I'm doing and how I feel."

Joe became angry now. "Oh yeah? Well, I sure hope so for your sake because if you persist with this relationship, it's going to cost you and me! If she's using you to get ahead and you're foolish enough to marry her, it will only end in tears. Then she'll walk away with a big fat alimony cheque every month. Either way, she wins."

"You haven't even met her," he replied with clenched fists.

"And I don't want to!" Joe's voice was loud and forceful. "I'm your father and

I'm not going to stand by and watch you throw away your future. You're going to be an attorney. Maybe some day a District Attorney and no two bit actress is coming along for the ride!!"

Robert's temper rose to the surface as his eyes flashed and his tone became strong and determined. "Dad, I've always listened to your advice and I've never gone against your wishes, but you're wrong and I don't want to hear anymore!"

"Well, you're going to. You could have your pick of young women. Women who are educated enough to be an attorney's wife and you're attending a College that's full of them. What's the matter with you, son? You're not thinking this through."

But he was adamant. "I'm not going to stop seeing her."

"Oh yes you are," Joe nodded. "I've never asked you to do anything for me but I'm asking you now. Break it off. This is the first argument we have ever had and it's over an actress. Need I say more?"

He walked over to the door, opened it, then turned and pointed a warning finger at Robert. "I want it ended and I want it ended now!" he ordered, storming out and slamming the door loudly.

Rooney got out of his car and came towards the front door but before he had a chance to reach it, it opened swiftly.

"Am I glad to see you!" Frankie exclaimed, turning his eyes upward. "Maybe you can calm him down."

Rooney became anxious. "What is it, what's wrong?"

As both men reached the entrance hall, Joe's voice could be heard as it boomed from the lounge.

"Robert's only gone and gotten married," Frankie explained.

"What?!"

They hurried across to the open door and joined the others. Joe Morrelli was pacing up and down looking as if his entire empire had just crumbled. Angela sat on the couch, clearly distressed. Looking at Rooney she shook her head, then lowered her gaze to the floor. Between sobs, Evie was blowing her nose with a crisp white handkerchief and Al and Frankie looked like they were pall-bearers at a funeral.

"Rooney!" Joe yelled. "Come on in, join the party. No doubt you've heard the glad tidings."

"Is it true?" he asked.

"Oh, it's true alright," he was assured.

He shook his head, still unable to believe it.

"Well, who is she?"

Joe stopped and put his hand up. "No Rooney, not who is she? What is she.

What is she? And you know what she is? An actress, that's what!"

Angela finally broke her silence. "All we know is that he met her at a party, Rooney. She's a young Broadway actress and her name is Camilla."

Rooney screwed up his face. "Camilla?"

"Yeah," Joe nodded sarcastically. "Can it get any worse? They were married yesterday by a Justice of the Peace and guess who was chief witness at the ceremony? None other than his beloved aunt and godmother, Antonia Flemming!" He started to pace again, then turned.

"You know what this is? Revenge! Joe Morrelli didn't marry an actress but she's made damn sure his son did. Well, this time she's gone too far!"

"Please Joe, would you calm down," Angela pleaded. "We all know how much Antonia loves Robert. I can't believe she would deliberately stand by and watch him do something he'd live to regret."

Joe stared at her in disbelief; then walking over to her he bent down and glared into her face. "Oh yeah? Well, you don't know her like I do. This is her way of getting even. And besides, since when did you two become such bosom buddies?"

Angela was deeply upset by the whole situation and Joe's sarcasm was making it almost unbearable.

Rooney decided it was time to interrupt. "Oh come on Joe, things might not be as bad as you think Robert is a sensible boy. He knows the score and he's not the type to be taken for a ride."

Throwing him a quick glance Joe replied, "Yeah, I thought so too. But now I'm not so sure."

"But the girl might be o.k. Maybe if you met her ..."

"I don't want to meet her!"

"Why?"

"I have my reasons and just how the hell can she be o.k. Rooney? She doesn't come from an important family. She doesn't have any money. She's nothing! My son has married a nobody."

Angela rose to her feet, her eyes filled with tears. "Why shouldn't he?" she asked her husband. "You did!"

Joe stood speechless as she left the lounge, closing the door behind her. For a few seconds there was total silence. He turned to Rooney and put his hands out. "You see, you see the position he has put me in, my own son! How could he do this to me? Well I can tell you this now. Nobody, and I mean nobody, makes a fool out of Joe Morrelli!"

"Have I got news for him!" Al muttered, under his breath.

"What was that you just said?" Joe demanded.

Al glanced at him quickly, then lowered his head. "I said, I sure wouldn't like to be him" he lied.

"You better believe it!" his boss replied, as he stormed out of the lounge, leaving the others glancing sheepishly from one to the other. Al began to laugh quietly, Frankie followed and they were soon joined by Rooney and Evie.

Angela was sitting at the window in Robert's room wiping the tears from her cheeks, when Joe entered and closed the door quietly.

"Angel honey... "

"Don't! Don't say any more!" she ordered him. She felt so hurt. This time he had gone too far.

"He's my son too, Joe. How do you think I feel?"

"But Angel I didn't mean ..."

"You were the one who insisted she be his godmother."

Joe bowed his head. "Well, yeah, I know ..."

"You were the one who insisted he spent so much time with her."

"Yeah, well, I know that, too ..."

"And you were the one who insisted they have a close loving relationship."

He surrendered. "O.k., o.k., it's my fault! It's all my fault!"

There was a stony silence as Angela gazed out of the window. He studied her for a moment before continuing, "I only ever wanted the best for him, Angel. Is that so wrong?"

She looked at him. "No, my mother felt exactly the same way about me, Joe. That's why she never wanted me to be a waitress. But if I hadn't taken the job in 'The Safe Haven' we never would have met, we never would have gotten married and we never would have had Robert. So you see, sometimes you just have to stand back and let fate take a hand."

Joe nodded. He knew she was right. Sighing deeply he made his way over and sat down beside her, putting his arms around her protectively and pressing her gently against him. He kissed her forehead and stroked her hair lovingly.

"What are we going to do?" she whispered.

"Well I guess it wouldn't do any harm just to meet her. Maybe Rooney's right. Maybe she is o.k."

Angela tightened her hold on him in agreement and appreciation. "She's Robert's wife, Joe, and our daughter-in-law. However we might feel about it."

"Yeah, I know. I just think he's too young for marriage. It's a big responsibility, Angel, and I just don't want to see him get hurt." As he stared out of the window his eyes narrowed and his voice changed tone. "But she hasn't heard the last of this. I'm holding her responsible," he snarled. "By the time I'm finished with Antonia Flemming, they'll be picking her up with a vacuum cleaner!"

Things changed in the Morrelli household after the news of Robert's wedding. Joe was still angry and hurt. So much so, he had changed his mind and dug his heels in, refusing to even see his son and new daughter-in-law. He never spoke

Robert's name to those in his employ and they in turn did the same. He still blamed Antonia for the marriage and had sent a strong message of disapproval, which had given her a few sleepless nights. She relayed it to Robert upon his return from the honeymoon. This meant there had been no contact between father and son for a long time, or anyone else for that matter, and it showed. Angela always had a sad lost look. She was deeply unhappy and Rooney came and went with a face like a wet weekend.

Joe was in the study alone going over some business files, when the phone rang. He lifted the receiver to hear Antonia's voice at the other end.

"Joe, it's me."

"I know who it is. What do you want?" he asked coldly.

"I must see you. Can you come over?"

"I'm busy."

"Joe, we need to talk," she insisted.

"I have nothing to say to you," he ended, putting the phone down.

Antonia sat in her apartment still holding the receiver. Robert was staring at her as he stood with his arm around Camilla.

"Well, what did he say?" he asked anxiously.

"He won't come," came the reply, as she finally replaced the receiver.

He looked annoyed. "I knew it. Dad can be really stubborn when he wants to be."

She threw him a quick glance. "Tell me about it!" Sighing, she continued, "Oh well, if that's his attitude I'll go to him. This whole situation has gone on long enough."

"Maybe that's not such a good idea."

"Have you a better one?" she asked, standing up and putting a loving hand on his shoulder.

"Robert we have to try. The longer we leave it the harder it's going to be for everyone."

His eyes were moist and clouded. "I miss him, Aunt Antonia. He gave me his love and I don't want him to think I'm not grateful, I feel so bad about it."

"I know," she nodded. "He gave me his friendship from we were kids. How do you think I feel?"

An hour later the flashy red car zoomed up the driveway to Joe's house and stopped. Angela hurried down the stairs just as Evie was opening the front door. The beautiful actress swept in without as much as a glance in Evie's direction.

"Angela, I must talk to you and Joe." She sounded serious and determined as she made her way to the lounge, unaware of Evie glaring at her in a vengeful way!

Angela went to the study at once. "Joe, I think you'd better come with me. Antonia's in the lounge and she wants to talk to us."

Without hesitation, he followed her.

When all three were seated there was an awkward silence as Antonia prepared herself "Joe, I've come to talk to you about Robert."

He leapt to his feet, shaking his head, "I knew it, I knew it! I knew it wouldn't work out. He's regretting it already, isn't he? Well I hate to be the one to say it but I told him so. I warned him."

She shook her head. "It's not like that Joe. Robert and Camilla are not the problem - you are!"

Shocked, he pointed a finger towards himself

"Me?!"

"Yes. He's very upset."

"He's upset? What about us?"

She gave a polite cough and tried again. "He wants to see you."

"Oh really, he wants to see me," he replied in a loud voice. "Well, that makes a nice change, considering he didn't want to see me at his wedding!" Turning to an anxious Angela he continued sarcastically, "My son wants to see me. I must have forgotten to write the cheque for his monthly allowance. It must be overdue!"

"Oh for God's sake Joe, sit down!" Angela snapped, then she looked at Antonia. "I want to know the real reason you're here. Is Robert alright?"

"Well, to be honest, he's distraught. He loves you both very much and it's tearing him apart not being able to see you." She lowered her gaze. "Alright, I admit, he should have told you he wanted to get married." She raised her eyes again innocently. "But everyone makes at least one mistake in their life. The main thing is, he's sorry."

Joe stared long and hard. Antonia was every inch the actress and with her soft voice and sad face, she was giving an Academy Award performance. She might be fooling Angela but she sure wasn't fooling him. If his instinct was right, and it usually was, Antonia was feeling more guilty than Robert. She's the one who was sorry!

"Then why didn't he tell us?" he asked. "After all, he told you and you're only his godmother. We are his parents." He threw his hands in the air. "I don't understand it, he could have had the biggest wedding day money could buy."

"No, that's where you're wrong Joe," Angela contradicted. "There never would have been a wedding. You would have found some way to stop it. Robert knew that. Don't you see, he was frightened to tell you."

Sitting down, Joe put his head in his hands despairingly. "I had such big plans for him. Such big plans. With his brains and my know how he could have gone all the way. Robert Morrelli, District Attorney."

Angela studied him. "My God! That's what this is all about, isn't it? It's not just the fact that he has hurt you, the real reason is because he went his own way. You think he'll never make it without you but he still can. You'll have to show him that you believe in him. Can't you see that?" She leaned forwards and grabbed his arm. "He's Joe Morrelli's son!"

He finally nodded. "Yeah, I guess that gives him the edge."

"Angela's right Joe," Antonia agreed. "None of your plans have to change just because Robert has a wife. If anything, it might make him more ambitious. He can still be District Attorney. Please talk to him Joe. Let him put things right between you two. If you don't, you could live to regret it one day."

Her words made him think, then relent. "This is his home. It always will be. If he wants to come and see us, it's o.k. by me."

"Good!" she smiled, getting up and walking over to the french windows. "You can tell him yourself."

She waved towards the car and a few moments later, Robert walked in holding his wife's hand. Both were unsure of their reception. Joe stood up and beckoned his son towards him Robert rushed over and put his arms around his father.

"Oh dad, it's so good to see you! I love you."

"I love you too, son" he replied, holding him tightly.

Angela cried as she kissed her son and Robert tried hard to conceal his own tears. "I've missed you mom."

"And I've missed you Robert. You'll never know how much," she said in a soft whisper, stroking his cheek with her finger.

He turned and went back to Camilla, taking her hand once again and leading her towards his waiting parents. He introduced her, "Mom, Dad, this is my wife," he smiled. To his delight she was welcomed with open arms. Antonia watched with tears in her eyes. Robert looked at her with deep affection and gratitude. "Thank's Aunt Antonia."

She nodded, then looked over at Joe. "Does that mean I'm forgiven too?"

Stepping forward, he put his arm around her and kissed her on the lips.

Gazing into his eyes she smiled, "Now that was worth waiting for. Maybe I should do things to be forgiven for more often!"

"Why not quit while you're ahead. Your next performance may not be as good as this one!" he winked.

Antonia smiled even more. "You're still the same Joe Morrelli. You always could see straight through me."

"Right from way back in the old neighbourhood," he reminded her. Turning to his son and daughter-in-law, he grinned. "Hey this calls for a celebration! I'm going to open a bottle of my best champagne. On second thoughts - I'd better make it two!"

Robert held up his hand. "Hold on a minute dad. Where's Uncle Rooney?"

"Oh, he's out there somewhere," Joe gestured. "If he's not in the garage, try the pool. He's been spending a lot of time out there lately." As Robert hurried through the door, Joe was almost shouting now in order to be heard. "Seeing you will bring a smile to his face. And believe me, it will be the first in a long time!"

Rooney peered around the study door. "Angela has just told me the good news. Congratulations!" he smiled.

Joe was as pleased as punch. "Yeah, it sure is something, me a grandfather. I can hardly believe it!" He tossed the pen onto his desk and leaned back in the leather chair. "Well, my kid sure didn't take after his old man. When it came to women I always liked to play the field, but not Robert. He falls in love and gets married at eighteen."

Rooney sat down. "I guess the reason it took you so long was the fact that you were looking for something you couldn't find. Robert found it and being a Morrelli, he went for it."

"Yeah," Joe agreed. "You know, I've been thinking. Maybe it's not a bad idea to marry young and start a family. At least time is on your side. Did Angel tell you about my wedding present?"

"No."

"Well, I had this nice little apartment lined up for him near the law school but when he told me about the baby, I changed my mind I paid Reuben a visit and he started searching for something more suitable. He found a nice house just a couple of blocks from here." He shrugged, "Why go all the way across town to visit your grandchild, when you can have it close by? That way, I can see it whenever I want to. You know something Rooney? I'm going to spend a lot of time with this kid. I can hardly wait for it to be born. It won't want for anything. Angel's over the moon at the thought of a baby in the family and she and Camilla get on really well." He paused for a few moments, looking thoughtful. "I have to say, that girl has really surprised me by putting her career on hold to have a baby. I thought she was one of those young actresses who wanted to get to the top in a hurry. I guess I was wrong. She's intelligent and she comes from a good background." Joe leaned forward and rested his arms on the desk. "I was talking to her at dinner the other night and guess what?"

"What?" Rooney was intrigued.

"She can trace her family way back. You're not going to believe this, but one of her ancestors was a King of Scotland and his name was Robert too! We've got royalty in the family!" he smiled proudly. "What do you think of that?"

"I think Robert's done very well, considering he married a nobody - remember?" Joe winced with embarrassment.

"So I made a mistake. It happens."

"Well, with Camilla it looks like you made a big one!"

"Now how was I supposed to know she had a King called Robert Bruce in her family?"

He grinned, "Just think, Rooney, my grandchild will have royal blood in it's veins."

"Before you get too carried away and rush out to the nearest jewellery store for a crown and sceptre, may I remind you that it was all a very long time ago." With a studious look, Rooney continued. "If I remember correctly, Robert the Bruce was King of Scotland in the thirteenth century."

Joe was curious. "How do you know?"

"I learned about him in school," he was informed.

"Wait a minute! Are you telling me you went to school in Ireland and learned about a King in Scotland?"

"That's right," Rooney nodded.

Joe threw his hands up in the air. "Jesus, and people think the New Yorkers are weird!"

"Well, it looks like Camilla got one over on you."

"What do you mean?"

"Let's face it Joe, I've never heard of a King in Sicily called Morrelli," Rooney smiled broadly.

Throwing him a sarcastic glance, he explained, "We didn't need Kings! We had some pretty good men who ruled instead. And believe me, they did o.k. They made life good for the people."

"Sure they did. Why, life was so good for the people that's why it's deserted and they're all over here!" Trying hard to keep a straight face, Rooney waited for Joe's reaction. He watched as he screwed his face up.

"You know, Rooney, you can be a real smart ass - like a whole lot more where you come from!"

"Well for a big man like Joe Morrelli, you made a big mistake about Camilla Bruce," chuckled Rooney, as they both stood up.

"Yeah, and it looks like you're not going to let me forget it. Go on, get out of here!" he grinned, waving his hand.

Turning to go, Rooney noticed the medicine bottle on the desk. "Joe, why don't you pay the doctor a visit?"

"What do I need to see a doctor for? There's nothing wrong with me," he insisted,

"Well, if that's true, why do you need that?"

Nodding towards the bottle, Rooney was obviously concerned.

"Oh, I've just got indigestion, that's all. What do you expect when you get to my age?" He smiled and patted his shoulder. "You worry too much. I'm fine, believe me. And with a grandchild on the way, I expect to be around for a long time to come - you can count on it!"

Chapter 20

The back door opened and Angela came in laden with packages.

Joe turned and smiled. "Well, it looks like you've had a busy day. I guess I don't have to ask how the shopping trip went!"

"I had a wonderful time," she beamed, "and I bought some beautiful things for the baby. I'll show them to you later."

"I'll bet you could use some coffee."

"You read my mind," she replied, putting the packages on the table and pulling out a chair.

Joe went to fetch a cup, which suddenly smashed to the floor as he doubled up in pain clutching his stomach.

Angela rushed to him. "Joe, what is it? What's the matter?" She was both startled and anxious.

He shook his head. "I don't know. But this pain is so bad I can hardly move." Gritting his teeth, he stood rooted to the spot.

"Joe, don't try to walk, just stay where you are," she advised. "I'm going to get Frankie and Al."

Disappearing quickly from the kitchen, Angela soon returned with the two men who hurried to their boss's side.

Close to tears she told them. "Help him upstairs. I'm going to phone young Doctor Walker."

They both looked upset and worried as they encouraged Joe to lean on them. Helping him to walk slowly out of the kitchen, they glanced at each other.

"Just take it easy, Boss. You'll be fine," said Al, determined to hide his true feelings of dread.

Frankie nodded. "Sure you will Boss. Al's right."

After speaking to the doctor, Angela then phoned Rooney and told him what had happened. She tried to calm herself down as she fumbled through the leather bound book of telephone numbers that lay on the hall table, but her hands continued to shake as she searched for the number of the Law School. On finding it she left an urgent message for Robert, then ran upstairs and into the bedroom where Frankie and Al were putting Joe on the bed.

"Evie should be home from the market soon and Rooney's on his way," she explained. "But in case the doctor arrives first, would you let him in and show him up?"

They nodded and left the room silently. Going over to her husband, Angela knelt by the side of the bed and held his hand. "Joe, everything's going to be alright. The doctor's due any minute." By now she was in tears. "What ever it is, whatever's wrong with you, we'll make it better. You'll see, Joe. You're going to be fine, I promise."

"Sure I am," he agreed. "Don't cry honey, it's probably nothing more than indigestion or an ulcer."

She stroked his hand lovingly and waited for the doctor to arrive, which didn't take long. On completing his examination of Joe, the doctor turned to Angela. "Mrs. Morrelli, I'd like to admit your husband to hospital for some tests, just to be on the safe side. I'll phone for an ambulance."

"Oh come on Doc," tutted Joe. "Do I really need an ambulance? Why can't I go in my own car? I'm feeling better already, I don't see what all the fuss is about."

The doctor smiled, "I'd rather you'd go by ambulance, Mr. Morrelli. Besides, you're one patient I never see. I think that entitles you to some V.I.P. treatment, don't you?"

"O.k. if you say so - but just this once!"

Using the phone on the bedside cabinet, the doctor ordered the ambulance with a request for urgency. Then he and Angela left the room, closing the door quietly behind them. "What's wrong with him?" she asked.

"I'm not sure, that's why I want some tests done. We can find out rather than speculate. I'll ring the hospital and ask them to keep me informed. Don't let him fool you, he's in a lot of pain. More than he cares to admit but he's going to the right place. Don't worry, I'll be in touch."

Angela nodded. "Thank you Doctor."

As the doctor was making his way down the stairs, Rooney was making his way up. "Is he alright?" he asked, breathlessly.

"I don't know Rooney. He has to go to hospital." She broke down. He comforted her.

"Come on Angela, Joe's a tough guy. He's going to be o.k. You wait and see." As the paramedics carried Joe down the stairs and across the entrance hall, Frankie and Al stood with sombre faces. Evie, still carrying her shopping basket, wept openly. "Oh Mr. Joe, Mr. Joe," was all she could say.

Although he was in excruciating pain, he looked at her and forced a smile. "I always knew that one day all that meat loaf would catch up with me!"

Angela accompanied Joe into the waiting ambulance and as it sped off Rooney followed in his own car. Frankie, Al and Evie watched. By now all three of them were in tears. Al wiped his away with his sleeve while Frankie stared up at the sky, swallowing hard. When Evie finally retreated to her room to pray and they were left alone, they gazed at each other. It was only now, after all these years, that the look they shared had that one dreadful thought behind it. What would they do without the Boss? And only now did they realise just how much they had depended and leaned on him.

Until today, Joe Morrelli had never needed anyone to lean on. That's what had made him "The Boss"!

On arrival at the hospital. Joe was taken to an examination room, while Rooney and Angela waited outside. It was an anxious Robert who came rushing along the corridor towards them.

"I got your message mom, but by the time I got to the house I'd just missed you. How's dad?"

"I don't know son, they haven't finished examining him. yet."

He embraced her. "Don't worry mom, he's going to be alright."

Angela held onto her son tightly. "I hope so Robert, I really hope so."

Just then, the door opened and the doctor came out to join them. All eyes were upon him.

"How is he?" she asked earnestly.

"I've given him something for the pain."

Robert stepped forward. "What's the matter with him, Doctor?"

"It's too early to say. With your permission, I'd like to bring him to the theatre and do a biopsy. That way we'll find out a lot sooner."

"You do whatever you have to," Angela agreed. "Will it take long?"

"Well, the biopsy won't take long but it could be a few hours before we get the results back from the lab. Mrs. Morrelli, why don't you go home and get some rest? When your husband is given the anaesthetic he'll be out for some time. I'll call you when I know for sure what the problem is."

She shook her head. "No, I'm not going to leave him. I'd rather stay, if that's alright with you."

"We're all very worried about him, Doctor," Rooney explained. "We'd all like to stay."

"I understand. I'll have a nurse show you to a private waiting room where you won't be disturbed. But remember these things take time."

"I know but his wife and son would like to be here when he comes round."

"Well, in that case I'd better get on with my job!" he replied, turning to re-enter the examination room.

Angela quickly put her hand on his arm and in a tearful voice she pleaded, "Please help my husband. Do anything you can, no matter what it costs. Just make him well, please."

He looked into her worried face, sympathetically. "I'll do everything I can," he promised in a low voice, then went back to Joe.

Almost immediately, a nurse appeared from the room and brought them down to the end of the corridor, where the cosy waiting quarters where situated.

As they sat there waiting none of them was in a talkative mood. Robert left the hospital briefly to fetch Camilla, leaving a tearful Angela in Rooney's care.

"Do you think he'll be alright?" she asked.

"Sure he will. Joe's a healthy man, he always has been."

"But what if it's serious Rooney? What if he's really ill? What's going to happen then? I can't go on without him - I just can't!"

He could see how her panic was beginning to show. Leaning over, he took her hand.

"Angela, look at me." She did. "Joe did everything he could to make you independent. The committees for Dan Casey and Gene O'Brien. The parties, the functions. Helping Gene to run for the Senate. Getting involved with all the right people. None of those things were coincidence, you know. Joe wanted it that way. He wanted you to be your own person and you are. He always knew you could do it and he also knew that being so much older there'd come a day when he wouldn't be around anymore, and you'd have to stand alone. In his own way he's been preparing you for that. You're a strong woman, Angela, and if he's really ill he's going to need all the strength and courage you can give him. Don't give in now. Let him see that all those years haven't been wasted." As the door opened and Robert and Camilla entered, she nodded at Rooney. "I will. I owe him that much."

They drank endless cups of coffee, checked the time constantly and spoke rarely, until the doctor finally came to see them. Standing up together they closed ranks, waiting for the news.

The doctor looked directly at Angela. "Mrs. Morrelli, I've just received the test results from the lab. Unfortunately it's not good news."

"What's wrong with my husband?" she asked, dreading the reply.

"I'm afraid he's got cancer."

As the blood drained from her face, she steadied herself.

"But you can operate," she insisted. "You can remove it, can't you? You can save him. You've got to save him"

He shook his head. "The biopsy tests not only proved malignancy, they also confirmed my worst fears. The cancer has spread rapidly and an operation is out of the question. There's nothing we can do."

"I won't accept that. You must try, you have to try," she cried out. "My God, you can't just let him die!"

"Believe me, if there was the slightest chance I wouldn't hesitate but an operation wouldn't help. Mrs. Morrelli, your husband is dying."

For a few seconds there was silence, then mother and son threw their arms around each other, sobbing loudly.

"Oh no! Oh, God no," she kept saying over and over.

Robert took a deep breath and wiped the tears from his eyes. "How long does he have?" he asked.

The doctor thought for a moment. "Four months, six if he's lucky. With the proper drugs he won't be in much pain until the final stages. After that, his own doctor will need to increase the medication."

Angela put a shaking hand to her forehead. "Does he know?"

"Not yet, but he's out of the anaesthetic and wants to know what's wrong with him. I haven't said anything. I thought it best to speak to you first. I wasn't sure if you wanted him to know."

"I'm not going to hide something like that from him," she replied, determined to continue with the openness and honesty she'd had all through her married life. "My husband has the right to know."

Nodding, the doctor offered, "Do you want me to tell him?"

"I think it would be best coming from you."

"I'll speak to him now. Then you can see him."

"When can I bring him home?"

"Any time you want. Today, if you like."

"Thank you," she replied in a half whisper.

He studied all four of them, before placing a consoling hand on Angela's shoulder. "I'm sorry," he said with sincerity and understanding, "I truly am. He's had it for quite some time. I just wish I had gotten to him sooner."

As the doctor left the room, Rooney stood in stunned silence. He watched Joe's family as they wept in each other's arms. Not only did he feel sorrow, but anger too. He lit a cigarette and went over to the window, gazing out but not seeing anything because of the tears welling up in his eyes. He couldn't believe that Joe Morrelli was dying! He was going to lose his best friend and a brother. How could he ever come to terms with that?

About fifteen minutes later, the doctor came back to tell Angela she could see Joe and escort her to his room. She stood up and wiped her face with a handkerchief. Then looking over at Rooney, she straightened up, clenched her fists tightly and nodded.

On opening the door to Joe's private room she found him sitting up in bed, sombre and thoughtful. After closing the door quietly, she sat down on the bed. He looked at her sadly and shook his head.

"Well, this is it, Angel. It looks like I've come to the end of the road."

She took his hand and held it firmly. "Joe, I'm taking you home."

"That might not be such a good idea. I don't have much time left."

"Doctors can be wrong."

"Not this guy, and from what he's told me I'm going to get a lot worse." He lowered his gaze. "I've been thinking, maybe I should go into one of those hospices, it would be a lot easier all round."

Her heart breaking, she took his face in her hands and gazed into it. "Joe we can fight this. And even if we can't. I want you with me every minute of every day we have left." Putting her arms around him she drew him close to her. "I love you, I always have. Do you honestly think I'm going to love you less now that you're ill?"

He pressed his face against her breast as she cradled him, rocking back and forth gently. "I'm dying, Angel!" he sobbed, clinging to her tightly.

"I know," she whispered, holding back the tears. "And you're going to die at home with me, where you belong. We're all going to die, Joe, it's just a question of 'when'. But please listen to what I have to say. We have been married for twenty years and we have been happy because we loved each other. But there are thousands of people in this city who will grow very old and very lonely before they die. Unloved, uncared for and so unhappy. What kind of life is that? I'm sure most of them would gladly change places with you. We've had such a good life Joe, and we're lucky. We found a love that those poor people only ever, dream about, and we can still have that love right up to the end. That's why I'm taking you home."

"I want to go home Angel," he admitted. "I want to be with you and Rooney. And Evie and the guys. I want to see Robert's baby when it's born, I want to see my grandchild."

"You will Joe," she promised.

"I love you. I've always loved you."

"I know," she nodded, "and it doesn't have to end before it's time. That's why I want you to come home. I don't want to hear anymore talk about hospices. When you die you'll die in Roseberry Avenue, with your family around you."

Eventually he released his hold on her allowing her to wipe the tears from his eyes. They kissed, just as passionately as they had always done. "Now, I'm going to help you get dressed," she told him. "And then, we're going home!"

Having been prescribed the proper medication, Joe was ready to leave. A nurse brought a wheel-chair but Angela insisted on pushing him herself Reaching the end of the long corridor, she allowed Robert to take over. He put his arms around his father hugging him tightly, while Camilla bent down and kissed Joe's cheek lovingly. As Robert wheeled the chair along slowly, Angela held her husband's hand and Rooney patted his shoulder and walked alongside him.

Leaving the hospital, they made their way to the crowded car park. As Joe sat sampling a taste of what was to come, he looked up at Rooney and put out his hands. "You see what has to happen a guy before he can get a fee ride in this city!!" Rooney's mouth broke into a broad grin. Joe Morrelli might be losing his fight for life, but he wasn't losing his sense of humour. That was one of the things Rooney was really going to miss. He wasn't going to have it for much longer and although he had a smile on his face, he had tears in his eyes.

Thanks to the drugs he received on a daily basis, Joe had more good days than bad. However, every one knew that it wasn't going to last, none more so than himself. All his old friends came to visit, even Charlie from Miami. And although they were shocked and saddened by the news, no one spoke of death but were cheerful and humorous in his company.

Angela went out of her way to make sure that everything continued normally and Joe decided to put all his business affairs in order. Reuben became a constant visitor to the house. Some days he and Joe spent their time in the study, on others they conducted their business from the bedroom. It was after one such meeting that Joe sent for Angela. "Come in and sit down honey. We need to talk," he said.

After glancing at Rooney and Reuben, who were already seated at the side of the bed, she closed the door securely and joined her husband.

Propped up by pillows, Joe was thoughtful for a few moments then began to explain. "Angel, as you know I have a lot of business deals and interests. Most of them are right here in the city and the rest are out of town. With Reuben's help I've got most of them sorted out but I want to discuss things with you. You're my wife and you have a right to know what's going on. For your sake and Robert's I've decided to keep all my legitimate businesses and sell the rest. Robert will be going to work for Gene O'Brien's office in the not too distant future. He's smart and ambitious and he's going to make one damn good lawyer. If he goes all the way, and I think he will, he's going to end up working with the District Attorney and he can't afford to be mixed up in any shady dealings. The development company I bought, K and M Enterprises; The 'Safe Haven' and my shares in the nightclubs are all legit'. Stacey's Gym is fine too." As Angela raised an eyebrow, he shrugged. "O.k. so I fixed a few fights over the years and got Billy Wilson and a few more into the big time. But they deserved a break and besides, no one got hurt or ripped off. Apart from that, the gym's a sound investment." He checked over some papers that were lying on the bed and then continued. "I'm selling my out of town interests. Most of them were with the Andretti's anyway, and old Nick and Anthony are willing to buy my shares, so that's easily taken care of. And I'm selling the numbers rackets and the Escort Agency."

"No, you're not," she replied.

"But honey, I have to. Besides, there's no one to run it."

"That's where you're wrong Joe. I know someone who can."

"You do. Who is it?" he asked, greatly puzzled.

"Me."

"You? But you've never liked the idea of an escort agency!" he reminded her.

"Yes, that's true," Angela admitted, "But I paid a visit to it a few weeks ago and had a talk with the girls. They're frightened of losing their jobs and they don't want to work for anyone else. They earn good money and are well looked after. Some of them have families to support and how they choose to support them is their own business. We provide escorts for important and influential clients who just happen to need an attractive partner. Whether it's for business or pleasure isn't really our concern, that's up to the girls. What is our concern is that they are treated with courtesy and respect, which they seem to be. No, the Escort Agency stays Joe. Reuben and I can run it between us, just the way you did. Isn't that right, Reuben?" She asked, looking over at him.

He peered through his gold rimmed spectacles as Joe sat upright, surprised at what he had just heard.

"Of course Angela ," Reuben stammered "If that's the way you want it."

"That's exactly the way I want it," she nodded, before turning to Joe. "Robert will have nothing to do with the agency, I'll be the boss. That way he won't be involved. The same applies to the numbers you run. Rooney knows all about that. My guess is he handles most of it anyway, so that can stay too. Right Rooney?"

"Sure. Me and Frankie can see to that, no problem."

She took Joe's hand. "I'll have a talk with Mr. Andretti and his son. If your investments are sound and Anthony can conduct your business along with his own, then I don't see why we should sell them either. And if at any time we should run into difficulties or someone gets too smart for their own good, Rooney and the guys can handle it by paying them a visit."

The three men were stunned into silence. Joe stared at her in amazement. She held his hand and his gaze.

"Joe I didn't watch you build up an empire over all these years, only to see it crumble. You might be dying but that doesn't mean the Joe Morrelli business has to die with you. Living with you has taught me a lot. But the most important thing of all was - if you want something badly enough, go out there and get it. What you have you hold, Joe. You don't give it away and you certainly don't sell it if you don't have to! I had a good college education and I think it's time I put it to use concerning business."

"Angel are you sure about this? It's a big responsibility," he reminded her.

"I've never been more sure about anything in my life. The business stays the same and that's my last word on the subject." Letting go of his hand and standing up, she looked at Reuben once again. "All the legitimate business can go into Robert's name. He will have full control and it will make him a rich man. That should give him the backing he needs to be independent, and a good future for our grandchild. The rest we can deal with between ourselves. No one has to know except those involved, just like it's always been."

Reuben nodded in approval. "I agree."

She then looked at Rooney and waited for his comment. He smiled at her with a mixture of pride and admiration.

"That's fine by me," he said.

"Good. Well, now that business is concluded I'll go and get us something to eat."

Joe could hardly believe what had taken place. As he looked from one to the other he had to admit, "Angel, I think it just might work!"

Reaching the bedroom door, she turned and smiled.

"Trust me Joe," she said, leaving the room to the three friends once more.

It was a cheerful Reuben who removed his spectacles and cleaned them with a handkerchief

"Well, it looks like the Joe Morrelli business is still intact," he grinned.

Joe shook his head. "Yeah. I always knew she was smart but not that smart. She's sure surprised me."

"I never thought I'd see the day when I'd listen to a woman who made so much sense" said Rooney.

"Yeah, you've got to hand it to her," smiled Joe proudly. "You really got to hand it to her!"

The weeks went by and Joe's health started to deteriorate. The doctor had increased his medication which meant he was confined to bed. Angela knew his time was limited and decided it would be best if those closest to him said their final goodbyes, before he became too weak for long conversations. So she telephoned Gene O'Brien and Antonia to explain the situation.

That evening, Joe's bedroom door opened and Gene O'Brien came in quietly. Going over to the bed he stood looking down at his old friend. Joe opened his eyes and smiled. "Hey Gene, nice to see you again."

"How's it going old buddy?" he asked, pulling up a chair and sitting down.

"Not so good but I can't complain. I've had a good run for my money. I've been thinking about Dominic Andretti a lot. That poor guy never got this far, he was wiped out in his late twenties."

"Yeah, life sucks."

Joe looked thoughtful for a moment. "Gene, I want you to do something for me."

"Sure, anything. Just name it."

"Don't leave Angel on her own after I've gone. Get her involved in something, get her back on a committee. I don't want her sitting here alone, grieving. Robert and Camilla are going to be parents any day now, they have their own life to lead and I want Angel to have one too. She's young and still has a lot of years left in front of her." "You're running for the Senate again, aren't you?"

Leaning over, he clasped his hands and smiled. "No, this time I'm going all the way, old buddy. I've decided to run for the Whitehouse!"

Joe was both surprised and pleased. "No kidding, you're going to run for President? Well, it's about time. When did you decide all this?"

"Just before I heard about your illness," he replied, looking sad. "I wanted you in my corner Joe. When I realised you weren't going to be around, I had second thoughts. Then I remembered."

"Remembered what?"

"You've got to aim high - Joe Morrelli always did! Besides, I'm not getting any younger and I've always had my eyes on the prize. I guess now's as good a time as any."

Joe smiled. "President Eugene O'Brien. Not bad for a kid from the old neighbourhood and Joe Morrelli's life-long friend! We did o.k. Gene."

"We sure did," he agreed. "And Angela's going to be fine. I want her with me every step of the way. She's going to be a very busy lady. I just wish you were coming along too."

Sighing heavily Joe replied, "Well, if I can't be there in body, you can bet your life I'll be there in spirit. I'm really proud of you Gene."

"Not as proud as I am to have known you, Joe. If I get into the Whitehouse I'll have you to thank. Your friendship and loyalty will have helped put me there, not to mention that wonderful Irish lady you married."

"You don't owe me anything. What are friends for?"

Joe's voice had become weaker and he looked tired as he closed his eyes. Gene got up and leaning over, he covered Joe's hand protectively with his own. Opening his eyes again slowly, his old friend looked at him. Both men knew they would never see each other again but neither of them wanted to say "goodbye".

Gene forced a smile. "Well, I'll be seeing you, old buddy."

Joe nodded, smiling faintly. "Yeah, but not on this side of the track."

Turning and walking away, it took every ounce of strength Gene O'Brien had not to look back. Leaving the room as quietly as he had entered, he stood on the landing wiping away his tears. For a few moments his thoughts went back to the old neighbourhood. To two young boys playing happily in the street, with no money and old clothes on their backs. Yes, Joe Morrelli was right. They'd both done o.k.!

The following afternoon, Antonia and Angela came out of the lounge and crossed the entrance hall in silence. But on reaching the bottom stair, Antonia burst into tears.

"I can't believe it," she cried. "I can't believe I'm never going to see him again. Never speak to him again. How can I face him knowing that? What am I going to do?"

Angela took her by the shoulders firmly. "Look at me, Antonia. Look at me!" she demanded. "I'll tell you what you're going to do. You're going to go up there and give the best performance of your life."

Calming herself, Antonia nodded. Then making her way up the stairs, she dried her eyes and cheeks with an initialled lace handkerchief. Arriving at the bedroom door she took a deep breath, held her head up high and entered.

"Joe darling," she smiled, embracing him and kissing his cheek. After fixing his pillows, she sat down beside him.

He studied her closely. "Have you been crying?" he asked.

She put a hand to her face. "Oh so you've noticed it too. You'll never believe it Joe, but I have an allergy. Imagine, at my age! It's such a nuisance, especially in my profession."

Joe nodded, but she was right. He didn't believe a word of it, not for a second! "You look wonderful," she smiled.

"Well, that's nice to know - considering my condition."

"You'll be fine, Joe."

"Antonia, I'm dying!"

"Don't talk like that," she replied sharply. "I won't listen."

"Now, that's where you're wrong because I want you to listen," he insisted. "I worry about you. You're not getting any younger, you know. What if some day you take ill? You have no family and no husband to look after you. You're going to be all alone and I don't want that to happen. I'm lucky. I have my wife and son and believe me, I'm very glad I have! We all need someone, Antonia, and I don't want you to wait until it's too late before you find that out. Friends are o.k. but it's times like this you need real love. Take my advice and find someone," he almost pleaded. "I only want what's best for you."

She turned her head away and fought back the tears that were stinging her eyes.

"Look at me Antonia," he said softly.

She did, then with trembling lips asked, "Joe, did you love me? I've got to know the truth."

He stretched out his hand. "Of course I loved you."

Sliding onto the bed beside him, she rested her head on his shoulder.

Putting his arms around her he continued, "You didn't need to ask me that. I've always loved you in my own special way."

"And I've always loved you," she whispered.

"I know honey. But it's time to move on. You've wasted a lot of years, don't waste any more. I'm not going to be around for you when you need me but I'd like to think you'll have someone who will. I just want you to be happy."

She sighed, "The only time I was really happy was with you. I never realised it until you married someone else. I always thought you'd come back to me."

"Well, that's life. We don't always get what we want."

"You did."

"Yeah," he nodded, "I guess I was lucky. But so were you. I remember a young girl who dreamed of becoming an actress, and she did. She became the toast of Broadway! But everything has a price Antonia, especially fame and we all have to pay."

"I know that now Joe," she admitted. "My price was you."

"Well, it doesn't matter now honey, because I'm very proud of you. I just wish you and Angel could have been more friendly."

Antonia raised her head and looked into his eyes. "Joe, I was wrong about Angela. I thought she married you for all the wrong reasons but I know now she really loved you. I don't know what I could ever do to make it up to her for the way I behaved and the things I said."

He looked at her. "Well. There is one way, Antonia."

"What is it?"

"Be there for her in the future, if she ever needs you."

"I will Joe, I promise."

He gripped his stomach and winced in pain.

She kissed his lips gently. "I'm going to miss you Joe. But you won't ever die, not to me. I will keep you alive in my mind and in my heart for as long as I live. We did have some good times together, didn't we?"

Joe nodded and gave her the answer he knew would make her happy. "The very best!" he smiled.

Antonia Flemming stood up and nodded back, a look of deep satisfaction on her face. She walked to the door but on opening it, turned around.

"You know, maybe you're right. Maybe we do need love. I think I'll marry Judge Thompson."

He smiled in approval. "Now there's a guy who'll never leave you on your own. Do you love him?"

"I guess deep down I do. But there will always be a corner of my heart that's strictly for Joe Morrelli."

She put her fingers to her lips and blew him one last kiss before closing the door behind her.

Joe lay back on the pillows and stared at the ceiling. "You know God, I always used to say her timing was lousy but yours is even worse! Gene O'Brien is running for President, Antonia has finally decided to get married and I won't be around for any of it. So here's the deal. If you keep me alive long enough to see my grandchild and hold it, then after that I'm all yours. And believe me, you won't get better odds than that anywhere!"

Rooney had moved back into his room permanently to be close to Joe and Angela. The two men spent a lot of time together as there was still some old ground to cover and unfinished business to discuss, some of it relating to Joe's employees.

Evie, Frankie and Al stood at the bottom of Joe's bed, wondering why they had been summoned.

"O.k.," he said, "this won't take long. I just want you to know what I've decided." He turned his attention to Evie. "You've been a great housekeeper over the years, Evie. I don't know how we would have managed without you. But like the rest of us, you're not getting any younger. However, I don't want you to worry about the future. I've left you well provided for."

Evie nodded in appreciation. "Thank you Mr. Joe. I suppose with that and the money I've saved over the years, I could find a nice apartment." There was silence for a few moments before she blurted out, "But Mr. Joe, it's going to break my heart to leave this house!"

"Who said anything about leaving?" he asked. "You've been here so long you're like part of the furniture. This is your home, Evie, and we're your family. That room downstairs is yours for as long as you want it."

"You mean I can stay, I don't have to leave?"

"That's right."

She clasped her hands, surprised and relieved. "Praise the Lord!" she smiled. Going over and taking Joe's hand she cried, "Oh thank you, Mr. Joe, thank you! I thought you and Miss Angela had decided to get a younger housekeeper. I thought you wanted me to go."

"What would be the point? You'd probably end up coming back to my front door in a taxi!" he joked.

By now she was sobbing. "You know, coming here in a taxi all those years ago was the best thing I ever did, Mr. Joe."

He patted her arm affectionately. "Sure it was, Evie. For both of us."

"I've never regretted it."

"Neither have I. Now don't cry anymore, you're going to stay here."

Evie's large dark eyes gazed into Joe's face. In them he saw the great devotion and respect she had for him and he was deeply touched.

"You've been so good to me, Mr. Joe. All these years you made me feel wanted and the Lord will reward you. Why, you're the one person he's going to take to heaven, you'll see. And I know what I know!" she nodded.

He smiled, "Yeah well, that I can handle. Just so long as he doesn't give me wings and expect me to sit on a cloud playing a harp. That would be a bit up-market even for Joe Morrelli - and very boring!"

"Now Mr. Joe, don't you go blaspheming the Lord," she warned.

"Evie from where I'm sitting I wouldn't dream of it. After all, with any luck I might get to meet him pretty soon!"

"I'll pray for you, Mr. Joe," she promised, then leaning over she whispered, "Just like I've always done."

"Sure you will," he nodded

"God bless you, Mr Joe."

He put his arms around her. "And you too, Evie."

She left his room and went straight to her own, where she kept the promise she had just made.

"Why do women cry so much?" Joe asked in a puzzled voice.

Al looked at Frankie. "I think you'd better answer that, you're the one who's married."

Frankie shrugged, "I don't know. Maybe they've got more emotions than us and that's how they show them. Or it could be their hormones. Who knows?"

"Not you!" replied Al. "After all these years of being married you don't know much, do you? Not if that's the best answer you can come up with!"

"Well, if you can come up with something better I'd sure like to hear it!"

Joe decided to intervene by putting his hands up. "O.k. you guys, knock it off." There was a silence so he continued. "I've left each of you well provided for too. Let's just say you won't have any lean days in the future. You both deserve it. You've been good and loyal friends to me over the years. Rooney and Angel are going to run the business end of things when I'm not here. Everything is going to stay the same, except that you'll be working for them. They'll be giving the orders, so if you don't want to stay around I'll understand. At least you won't have any money problems, if you do decide to leave." He waited for their response.

Frankie looked at the floor, then at Joe. "I'm not going to pretend I won't miss you, Boss, you know I will. But you can count me in. I'm staying."

"That goes for me too," Al nodded in total agreement.

"We've come a long way together and that counts for something in my book," said Frankie, sadly. "If I could go back, I'd do it all again. You gave me a chance, Boss, and it paid off. Because of that me and my family have a good life, and I have you to thank. Not only have you been a good boss, you've been a good friend. The best any man could hope for so I'm not going to desert you now. It doesn't matter to me who's running things because deep down in my heart I'll know it's still your business and believe me, when you've worked for a boss like Joe Morrelli you don't ever want to work for anyone else."

Joe nodded as they shook hands. "Thanks Frankie, I appreciate everything you've said and I'm glad you'll be around for Angel."

"You bet! She's a Morrelli, isn't she? Anything she wants me to do she only has to ask and you have my word on that. I owe you, Boss."

Joe beckoned him close and spoke in a low voice. "Frankie, don't leave Al on his own. Invite him over to dinner now and then and always make sure he's o.k. He's family and I want you to be there for him. That's what family is all about, looking out for each other."

"Don't worry Boss, I will," came the whispered reply.

They could see he was getting tired so as Frankie walked towards the door, Al came forward and shook Joe's hand, forcing a smile.

"You know me Boss, I don't mind working for a woman - I always liked them!" His smiled was soon replaced by the sadness he really felt. "Jesus, I'm going to miss you," he admitted in a choked voice. As he turned to walk away, Joe watched him. "Al, come here a minute," he said, as Frankie left the room. "Can I ask you something?"

Al shrugged. "Sure Boss, what is it?"

Joe sunk back into the pillows. "I've been married for twenty years and in all that time I've never heard you refer to my wife as Angela, you always called her Mrs. Morrelli. Why is that?"

He looked thoughtful and a little embarrassed as he began to explain. "Well you see Boss, when all us guys hung out together in the old neighbourhood, I know some of them laughed at me behind my back. You know, my parents being so strict and all. But not you. You treated me the same as the rest. You were my friend and that made me feel good. Then when you got enough money together and decided to leave and go it alone you asked me, Al Colleano to come with you."

Joe listened intently as Al shook his head. "That was the proudest moment of my life. I went back to my apartment and packed so fast I passed my mother on the way out, still standing where I'd passed her on the way in! I was so worried you'd change your mind. From that moment on you were the Boss - and you always will be, no matter what. I've always admired you. I guess deep down inside I wanted to be just like you."

Joe shook his head. "I never knew that."

"Well, I always knew I didn't have what it takes to be a Joe Morrelli, but working for you was the next best thing. No matter where I went, I only had to mention your name and I was treated like a VIP. The best seats for a show, the best table in a restaurant, the best room in a hotel. That really used to impress the women and it made me feel like a big shot. I got respect. That's why I've always called your wife Mrs. Morrelli, out of respect. That name means something in this city and I'm proud to have been connected with it all these years. Proud to have had you as my boss." Tears trickled down his face. He hastily wiped them away with his hand and said, "Well, now you know."

Joe stared at him. "How come you never told me any of this before?"

"You know me Boss, I always did love the movies and we all know that the tough guys always hide their true feelings."

"Yeah, it's harder being a man than most women think. And speaking of women, I want you to do me a favour."

"Sure Boss, anything you want."

"Make sure Angel's o.k. when I've gone. Sit at the table with her and have a cup of coffee. Make her smile the way you always did."

Suddenly, Al looked and felt important. "You leave that to me Boss, I'll always find some thing to say - I'm a natural!"

"Yeah I know. But I'm warning you Al, if you make any smart-assed remarks at my funeral believe me, wherever I am I'll hear you."

Both men smiled at each other in mutual understanding.

"Go on, get out of here!" Joe waved.

Frankie was waiting as Al closed the door . No words were spoken, there was no need. They just embraced one another as the family they had come to be, thanks to Joe.

Angela sat the tray down in front of him but it was obvious his thoughts were elsewhere. "What's the matter?" she asked.

"Camilla. That's what's the matter."

"Has something happened?" she became anxious.

Joe held out his hands. "That's the whole point. Every day she waddles in here and waddles out as big as a house but nothing's happening. Are you sure she knows when this baby is due? I mean, maybe she's got her dates mixed up."

Angela smiled. "The baby's due any day now."

"So everyone keeps telling me but I've come to the conclusion that that baby doesn't want to see the light of day. I think I'll have a word with the doctor when he comes."

"Oh for heaven's sake Joe, don't fuss."

"Well, I'm worried about her, Angel. If I didn't know better I'd swear she's been pregnant for more than nine months."

"Well, she is over her time," she admitted.

On hearing this he threw his hands up in the air.

"I knew it, I just knew it! If you ask me she's making life too comfortable for that kid. It's probably lying thinking how great things are. Why doesn't she do some exercises and waken it up? Let it know it's supposed to be outside, not inside."

"Now Joe, don't get yourself all worked up. The baby will know when it's time to come."

"Well, I sure hope so! I don't know how much longer I can hold on, waiting for it. I still say she needs more exercise. Why doesn't Robert take her for a walk through Central Park or something?"

Looking shocked she reminded him, "There are a lot of unsavoury people who frequent that park."

"That's right," he nodded, "and coming face to face with one of them just might do the trick."

"Joe Morrelli! Are you saying you want your own daughter-in-law to be frightened into giving birth?"

He shrugged his shoulders. "Well, if it helps, why not?"

"I'm surprised at you."

"Yeah well, it's Camilla who needs the surprise! And coming face to face with some weirdo would end all this waiting. That baby would be born faster than I could eat this lunch!"

Spreading out his napkin, Angela tutted. "I don't see how being a week overdue is going to make such a big difference."

Sarcastically he replied, "Oh really? Well maybe that's because you're not sitting where I am. And I'm still going to have a word with that doctor!"

After dinner that evening Joe and Rooney were discussing the day's highs and lows, when Angela came rushing into the bedroom.

"Joe, I've got good news. Robert just phoned to say Camilla's water has broken!"

"I'm surprised she didn't flood the joint it's been that long!" he muttered to Rooney. Then looking at Angela he gave a broad smile. "That's great news, honey."

She clasped her hands excitedly. "I'll let you know when it's born."

Disappearing as quickly as she had arrived, Angela left them together again. Joe sighed deeply, leaned his head back on the pillows and turned his eyes upward.

"At last! I'm finally going to see my grandchild." He looked at a smiling Rooney. "You know, I was beginning to think it would never happen."

Joe sat up in bed full of anticipation with Angela and Rooney standing by. The door opened slowly and Robert appeared with his arm around Camilla, who was carrying the baby.

As they reached the bed he grinned, "Dad, I'd like you to meet your grandson."

Smiling, Camilla placed the tiny bundle into Joe's waiting arms.

"Well, he sure is a fine little fella. Aren't you?" he said proudly.

Everyone watched as he gazed into the baby's face adoringly, placing a finger into it's tiny hand. He looked up at the happy parents. "I'm real proud of you son. And you, Camilla, you did a great job. He's real handsome."

"Why wouldn't he be?" she replied. "He's a Morrelli!"

Noticing the baby's black hair and large dark eyes, Joe had to agree. "Yeah, he is isn't he? I was thinking the same thing myself but I didn't like to say."

"Well, I'd say he's the image of his dad and grand dad," she smiled.

He nodded. "What are you going to call him?"

Robert placed a loving hand on his father's shoulder.

"Joseph Rooney Morrelli - after my two favourite men!"

Still looking at the baby, Joe smiled broadly.

"Yeah, I like that. It's got a nice ring to it." He then looked at his best friend. "I tell you Rooney, with a name like that this kid's going to be a winner. He'll go a long way."

Clearly pleased at Robert and Camilla's choice of names, Rooney smiled and nodded. "Who are the god parents going to be?" Joe asked/

"Camilla's sister, Heather, is going to be god mother," Robert replied. "She's an actress."

"Now that sounds familiar!" muttered Rooney.

If Joe had heard that remark, he chose to ignore it. "And who's the god father?"

"John Sullivan," he was informed, without hesitation.

"Really?" He looked at Robert. "Well, I must admit we've sure got variety in this family. Your father's Italian, your mother's Irish, your god father's Irish and your god mother's part Jewish. Camilla can trace her ancestors in Scotland and I suppose John Sullivan can trace his roots all the way back to Africa!"

His son smiled, "No - Alabama, actually!"

"Same difference!!" Joe looked down at the baby again. "Yeah, we Morrellis are a real mixed bag!" He gave the baby to Angela and watched as she cradled it lovingly.

"He's so perfect Joe, and it looks like the Morrelli name is going to live on," she smiled.

"Yeah, that was always my dream Angel, and after all these years I've got it. It was well worth the wait. I'm a happy man."

Placing the child into Rooney's arms she said, "Here, it's just like old times."

"It sure is. And it's nice to know the name Rooney will live on too, considering I'm not even married!"

After holding it gently for a few moments, he gave it back to Joe with the words, "Yeah, he's a Morrelli alright."

"You bet. Third generation and that's not counting the ones before me . You know something, Rooney, this city hasn't seen the end of us. There'll always be a Morrelli in New York. Now, ain't that something?" His pride and satisfaction were obvious.

"It sure is Joe."

The room seemed to be filled with an air of hope and happiness, brought by this new arrival. All those present savoured it gratefully.

"Now, when is he getting baptized?" Joe asked.

Robert shot a quick glance at his mother. "Well, we thought maybe next week, Dad."

"That soon?"

Angela nodded and putting his arm around his father he went on, "Yeah. If he's baptized next week we could all get together here at the house and have a small party. You know, to wet the baby's head."

"Now that's a good idea," Joe nodded. "I always did like a party. But why wait till next week to wet my grand son's head? We can do that right now. Let's all have a drink. After all, we've got something to celebrate ...Haven't we, little man?" he said softly.

"Rooney go downstairs and get a bottle of my best champagne. Only the best is good enough for this little guy. Come to think of it, you better make that two. Crack open a bottle for Evie and the guys. This is a special occasion. Joe Morrelli is a grand father!"

As Rooney left the room, he took Angela's hand. "You know honey, if little Joseph grows up like his dad they won't have any worries."

She smiled as he gazed into her eyes, his own becoming moist. "If I hadn't married you, Angela Kenny, I wouldn't be holding this precious gift. You've given me everything in my life that has made me happy." He kissed her hand. "Because of you I have a fine son and a beautiful grand son. If that's not proof of how much we've loved each other, then I don't know what is. I love you so much.

She leaned over and stroked his face before kissing him tenderly. "And I love you," she whispered, fighting back the tears.

But Robert and Camilla couldn't. As they witnessed such a heart rendering scene, their tears flowed. Watching this deep display of the warmth and affection his parents still had for each other after all this time, made Robert realise what true love really was.

Two days after the christening, Joe took a turn for the worse. At first Angela thought it was all the excitement of the new baby and the party but as the day wore on she could see his pain increasing steadily and although she had given him the required medication, his condition was giving her great cause for concern.

He groaned loudly, then opened his eyes to find her sitting at the side of his bed. Holding out his hand to her he said, "I think you better get the doctor honey." Taking it gently, she nodded. "I will Joe. I'll get him to give you an injection for the pain. You'll be alright after that, you'll see."

He pressed her hand firmly and shook his head. "It's time Angel."

"No, not yet. I want you to stay with me."

"It's time to let go. I can't fight this any more. I'm tired," he sighed deeply, looking drained and sounding weak.

Leaving the room, she made her way downstairs in tears. After phoning the doctor, then Robert and Camilla, she went to the kitchen knowing Rooney and Evie would be there.

"What's the matter," Rooney asked getting up and giving her his seat.

Through her sobs she was able to tell him, "Joe's ill, very ill. The doctor's on his way. Please God, let him be able to ease my Joe's suffering."

Evie joined her and both women were comforted by a worried Rooney.

A short while later the doorbell rang. Angela got to her feet and dried her eyes.

"That will be the doctor now. I'll let him in and take him upstairs. Rooney, will you wait for Robert and Camilla"

He nodded.

Doctor Walker went over to Joe as Angela looked on, but Joe was in too much pain and discomfort to warrant an examination. His expression was that of a man in agony and distress, his breathing heavy and stifled. The doctor turned and looking at Angela, shook his head. The moment she had been dreading had finally arrived. She had to admit to herself that Joe was dying.

Opening his case the doctor explained "Now, Mr. Morrelli, I'm going to give you something that will ease the pain."

"I sure hope it's strong Doc."

"Oh believe me, it is. Almost as strong as your heart!" he replied, forcing a smile. After administering the injection he told him, "That ought to do the trick for now and let you get some proper sleep."

Joe nodded in gratitude and managed a quiet, "Thanks."

"Don't mention it. I'll call by this evening and see how you're getting along." Angela followed him onto the landing and closed the bedroom door.

"How much time does he have?" she asked anxiously.

He took a deep breath. "Very little, I'm afraid. He's on his way out, Mrs. Morrelli, but I don't want him to suffer any more than he already has. I'll come back after dinner and give him another injection. In the mean time you could send for your family's priest." Those words pierced her heart, for she knew now the end was near.

"Thank you doctor," she whispered.

He nodded and put a caring hand on her arm. "I'm sorry Mrs. Morrelli, I really am. For a man like that to die, is such a waste."

Father Murphy had given Joe the Last Rites and after the doctor's second visit, Angela, Rooney, Robert and Camilla kept a constant vigil at Joe's bedside.

Late that evening he slowly opened his eyes and gazed drowsily around at his family.

Looking directly at Robert he told him, "Son, I'd like a few minutes alone with your mother."

"Sure dad," he replied, leaning over and kissing him.

Gripping his arm Joe whispered, "I love you son."

"I know, and I love you too."

It was Camilla's turn to kiss him.

"You take real good care of my grand child."

"I will, and all the others to come!" she smiled through the tears.

He beckoned to Rooney. "You know, for a smart-assed kid from Ireland you did o.k.," he smiled faintly. "You ended up as close to me as a brother and I loved you like one. I'll be seeing you Rooney."

"Yeah, I did o.k. didn't I Joe? But then, I had the best brother any man could wish for." He took Joe's hand and held it for a moment before leaving the room.

When they were alone, Joe looked at Angela. "Angel, I don't have much time. Open my bedside drawer. Inside there's a key."

She followed his instructions, then sitting down beside him she put the key in his hand. But he immediately gave it back to her placing it in her palm and closing her fingers tightly around it.

"That belongs to you now," he insisted. "It's the key to the bottom desk drawer in my study. There are some things locked away that I want you to see - but not yet. Promise me you'll wait until after my funeral."

"I promise Joe," she replied, a little puzzled.

"And promise me something else."

"What is it?"

His speech was slow and his voice weak. "I don't want my son to see me dying. He's always looked up to me. I want him to remember me the way I was all his life - strong." She agreed and left the room.

The others were waiting at the top of the stairs.

"Robert," she said, putting a hand up to his tear stained face, "Your father and I need to be alone for a while."

"But mom, he's my dad! I should be there with him. We all should."

Angela studied him for a few seconds, searching for the resemblance between father and son. On finding it she said, "Son, I've never asked you for anything but I'm asking now. Please, give us our last chance to be alone."

He looked across at Rooney, who nodded.

"O.k. mom, if that's what you want."

"That's what I want. And it's what your father wants."

Returning to the bedroom, she sat the key on the bedside cabinet. Then slipping of her shoes she climbed under the covers and moved over to her dying husband. She lifted his arms and putting them around her shoulders, rested, her head on his chest. He opened his eyes. "Oh Angel, I'm not much good to you now."

Lifting her head, she looked into his glazed eyes. "Don't say that, Joe Morrelli, don't you ever say that. You're as much of a man to me now as you've always been." She kissed him tenderly on the lips. "I love you," she whispered.

"I love you too."

He closed his eyes.

Placing her head back onto his chest, she held him tightly and listened to his shallow breathing. As it grew fainter she knew he was slipping away from her.

"Don't leave me Joe, please don't leave me," she sobbed, her heart about to burst with grief. "I can't go on without you."

Gradually, she felt the life leave his body until there was a final sigh and his arms went limp. She lay as motionless as the man she loved, hoping against hope he would start breathing again.

"Oh, dear God, don't do this, please. I need him here with me," she pleaded.

But Joe was gone, from the suffering that had become so unbearable for him. Angela looked into his face. It was pale and still. Stroking his cheek, she kept saying his name over and over. But there was no answer. Smoothing the front of his greying hair with her fingers, she kissed his forehead and whispered, "Goodnight, sweet Prince; and flights of angels sing thee to thy rest."

She then looked at the clock. Joe Morrelli had died at ten minutes to midnight on a Friday night, four and a half months after being diagnosed and in his sixtieth year.

Angela climbed out of the bed, put on her shoes and smoothed the cover around him with shaking hands. Unable to believe he was really dead she felt his still warm wrists for a pulse. Then taking his hands in hers she gazed into his face.

"Oh Joe, what am I going to do without you?" she said softly, as more tears spilled from her eyes. Kissing him once again, she ventured out of the room. Robert was waiting. She had to confirm what he'd already guessed.

"Robert, your father has just passed away."

He hurried past her, followed by Camilla. Angela and Rooney stood in silence listening to his loud cries as he embraced his dead father with all the love that was in him. Camilla was trying desperately to console him, even though she too was overcome.' Rooney was motionless until the shocking truth that Joe Morrelli was dead, finally hit him.

"Joe!!" he cried. Then turning, he threw himself against the wall and pounded it with his fists, shaking his head in disbelief.

Angela had never seen Rooney go to pieces like this. Going over she hugged him tightly, pressing her face against his back. His shoulders heaved as he wept unashamedly.

"What am I going to do, Rooney?" She asked in a frightened voice.

"Joe was my life. I can't face the future without him."

He turned around and took her in his arms. "Sure you can . Joe would want that", he replied in a low comforting voice, stroking her hair and kissing her forehead.

She closed her eyes and clung to him for a moment, everything that had happened seemed like a bad dream. It felt as though it was Joe who was holding her, as Rooney stroked and kissed her just the way he had done. For that short time she didn't feel lost any more, until Rooney spoke. Then Angela opened her tear filled eyes and returned to reality.

"Angela, listen to me. You've got to be strong, for yourself and for Robert. You've got to find the will to carry on for Joe's sake. So much depends on you now. The family, the business. He always believed you had the ability to follow him, now's your chance to prove it. You owe it to yourself and to his memory."

She looked up at him and nodded.

"What arrangements do you want me to make?" he asked.

"I want you and Robert to get him the best casket money can buy."

"What about the funeral parlour?"

"He's not going to one. Joe will stay in his own home."

Rooney forced a smile. "Are you planning on giving him an Irish wake?"

Her tone was determined "You bet!"

Coming down the stairs, he met Evie. "I thought I heard crying," she told him. "Is Mr. Joe getting worse?"

Putting his arm around her shoulders, he broke the news. "Evie, Joe died just a little while ago." She came to the top of the stairs wringing her hands and sobbing loudly,

"Miss Angela, Miss Angela".

They put their arms around each other, then Angela escorted Evie into the bedroom. As she approached the bed she buried her face in her hands.

"Oh, Mr. Joe poor Mr. Joe," she cried, as she gazed at his lifeless body.

Robert and Camilla were standing at the bed side as Angela comforted Evie. However, it wasn't long before all four of them were embracing, sharing their concern and their grief. Mother and son held each other tightly. They wept. One for the husband she had loved with all her heart, the other for the best father any son could ever wish to have. After phoning the doctor and the undertaker, Rooney then phoned Frankie.

"Hello," came a sleepy voice.

"Frankie, it's me, Rooney. Joe's dead."

First there was silence, followed by a muffled sob. "I'll be right over."

Next it was Al. The phone rang for a few moments, then he answered.

"yeah?"

"Al, it's Rooney. I've got some bad news. The boss is gone. He died a little while ago, Al are you still there?"

"Awe, Jesus!" came the cry. "Not the boss, Rooney!"

Once again, Rooney's eyes filled with tears as he held the receiver and listened to Al weeping on the other end.

Roseberry Avenue became an open house both day and night to many people from all walks of life who came to offer their sympathy and condolences to the bereaved. Angela made sure everyone was greeted warmly and there was an abundance of food and drink on hand at all times. Gene O'Brien had often heard about an Irish wake but had never actually been to one, until now. As he, Reuben and Joe's many friends from way back sat around telling yarns and stories about certain events in his life they each remembered, it's brought happy smiles to many faces especially Gene's!

He looked into the casket, then around at the company.

"You know, my old buddy would have loved this! Yeah, Joe could sure tell a good story, himself."

On the morning of the funeral, Joe's family and closest friends spent a few moments alone with him as they said their last farewells. Angela waited until they had all left the room, before going over and fastening the gold claddagh tie pin onto Joe's silk tie. Rooney watched, deeply vexed by the memories it held.

Leaning over, she kissed her husband and covered his cold hands with the warmth of her own. Then stroking his cheek gently with her finger she whispered, "Goodbye, Joe. I will always love you".

The undertakers offered to provide pall-bearers for Joe's Casket but his friends insisted that the privilege be theirs. There was no shortage of men willing and proud to carry him, even for a few steps. And Angela watched full of emotion, as some of New York's finest citizens paid tribute to her husband.

The funeral mass was held in the church of Our Lady of Lourdes, where she and Joe had married. Father Ryker was now a very old man and living quietly in a parochial home but on hearing the news of Joe's death, he came out of retirement to conduct the service as a mark of respect and gratitude for all Joe and Angela had done for his parish and neighbourhood over the years.

Once again the "Ave Maria" was sung by a single choir boy. As his voice filled the church with it's melodic beauty, there wasn't a dry eye anywhere.

In the cemetery, Father Ryker gave a small but meaningful sermon. As he did so, Rooney studied Angela. Her face was pale but there were no tears, as others around her wept openly. She was trying her best to be strong but he knew she was grieving inwardly, which was the worst kind. Her simple but elegant outfit made her look striking, the long red hair Joe loved so much swept back and covered by a black lace mantilla.

He glanced across the open grave at Antonia, who was inconsolable.

Angela gazed around at the packed cemetery and mountain of wreaths. It seemed as though everyone had come to pay their last respects to Joe Morrelli and those who couldn't come had sent Floral Tributes of one kind or another.

As the casket was lowered into the ground she stepped forward and dropped a single red rose on top of it as a symbol of her undying love. Antonia stood hesitant, clutching a rose of her own. She looked pleadingly at Angela, who nodded and motioned her to do the same. Antonia did so and through her tears acknowledged Angela's kindness and understanding with a look of sincere appreciation.

The girls from the Escort Agency stood together crying. Al leaned over and nudged Frankie's arm. "I haven't seen so many tears since that batch of faulty condoms hit the street!" he whispered, nodding towards them. Frankie smiled, then Al suddenly remembered what Joe had said. He looked up to the sky. "Sorry, Boss!"

It was time to shake hands and thank everyone for coming, which Angela did gracefully. As she and Antonia held hands they looked at each other knowingly. At last they had something in common, the loss of Joe.

"Angela, thank-you, "Antonia sobbed.

"You loved him too. I understand."

"You always did. I'm grateful for that."

The only sign Angela showed of breaking down was when Gene O'Brien put his arms around her. She gripped his shoulders tightly, her eyes stinging.

"Oh, Gene, what am I going to do?"

"What Joe would want you to do, pick up the pieces. Get on with your life and be happy, Angela. I'm always here for you and I'm going to need you. Just remember, I can't get into the White House without help." He looked into her face. "I need you, little lady. Will you help me? That way, we can help each other."

She nodded. He gently lifted her chin. "You know, Irish, you're o.k. Joe would be real proud of the way you've handled everything, I know I am!.

Anthony Andretti helped his grandfather towards her. The old man put his hands on her shoulders and kissed her cheek, his face still wet from the tears he had shed. "Thank you for coming. Both of you," she said.

Nick shook his head. "Nothing could have kept me away today. I buried one son along time ago, now I feel as if I've buried another. I've known Joe since he was a kid. My Dominic and him, well they were like brothers, "he sighed.

"I know how hard it must be for you."

"I'm an old man, it's sad to live to my age and bury those you love, when they are so much younger. Your husband was a much respected man by everyone and much loved by me. I'm going to miss him". He glanced towards the grave. "Joe

Morrelli had his reasons for everything, I know, and never let anyone tell you different. He was a good man. If there's ever anything I can do for you or if you ever need me, Mrs, Morrelli, I'm here for you. It would please this old man greatly to have your friendship, just the way I had Joe's. It was an honour to have known him."

She smiled faintly. "Thank-you for your kind words, Mr. Andretti".

He took her hand. "The business will continue between the names Morrelli and Andretti. I promise you that,"

Nodding in appreciation, she watched as Anthony led his grandfather away. The next one to approach her was Kevin Mitchell.

"Angela, I'm so sorry about Joe. I know this is a sad loss for you."

Rooney was taking everything in! "Perhaps I could call some time in the near future," Kevin continued, "Just to see how you're getting along. After all, that's what friends are for. Maybe we could get together and talk."

Angela nodded. Rooney threw him a sarcastic glance as he passed by, then looked over at Joe's grave. He couldn't help but think that wherever Joe Morrelli was, he would turn summersaults if ever Kevin Mitchell showed up at his home! When everyone had left the cemetery, only the family remained. Frankie and Al stood side by side, while Robert comforted Camilla, Evie, still in tears, was becoming concerned for Angela.

"Robert, I think it's time your mother went home she must be worn out."

He went over to the graveside. "Mom, I think it's best if we leave now."

Angela shook her head. No, I can't go yet Robert."

As he turned away he shrugged his shoulders helplessly at Rooney. They all waited for another few minutes, then Rooney went over and took her arm. "Angela, there's nothing more you can do here. Come on let's go home", he said in a low voice.

"Not yet. I want to stay with him just a little longer. I want to be on my own with him please."

He nodded and walking back to the others, he led them away.

She stood alone looking down at Joe's casket. Suddenly, she burst into tears.

"What am I going to do without you?" she cried. "You were my life and without you, what good is it to me now?" Her eyes closed tightly. "Please, Joe you've got to help me through this because my heart is breaking and I don't think I will ever be happy again, not without you." She reached into her pocket and produced the key he had given her. "I don't know what secrets I'm holding," She whispered, "and I don't know what the future will bring, or even if I can face it. But I know one thing, Joe Morrelli, I always loved you."

Chapter 21

Everyone grieves in their own way and Angela was no exception. By day she was quiet and subdued, wandering around the house aimlessly and lost. At night she cried herself to sleep, clutching Joe's pillow tightly for comfort.

Meanwhile, the key lay undisturbed in the bedside drawer where she had left it after the funeral. She couldn't bear the thought of going into the study. It was the one place that had always been Joe's domain and it held too many memories of him, but she knew deep down sooner or later she would have to. In order to run the business she would need to use the study.

Several days went by and they were worrying days for Robert and everyone at Roseberry Avenue. Rooney had moved back to his own apartment but took care of things as best he could, with the help of Reuben, Frankie and Al. He knew Angela needed time, but was secretly beginning to doubt if she had the willpower and determination to keep her promise to Joe.

Then one morning out of the blue, she put her head around the kitchen door.

"Rooney, I'd like you to come to the study."

"Sure," he replied, surprised.

Getting up from the table he looked across at Frankie and Al and nodded before following her.

As Angela sat down in the black leather chair, he closed the door and took a seat facing her. She held up the key.

"I think it's time to get down to business," she said, unlocking the drawer and taking out the contents. She laid two large folders down on the desk, but opened the white envelope with her name on it in Joe's handwriting. It contained a letter and she read it in silence.

"My Dearest Angel,

By the time you read this I'll be gone and I will have brought a lot of secrets with me, but not this one. This secret I must share with you . It is one I have had to live with for a very long time and believe me, it wasn't easy. You see, I found out a long time ago who murdered your father, and I could have done something about it - but I had my reasons. You will understand when you open the folder. I thought it best to keep it from you. All my married life I've tried to make you happy and I hope I've succeeded. But now, what you are about to discover will make you unhappy, that's why I've kept it hidden away all these years. No-one can tell you what you should do about it Angel. Even I can't offer any advice. It's up to you now, you do what you think is best. Rooney's there to help if you need any, he knows all about it. Maybe I should have left well enough alone.

Sometimes I wish I had but you always wanted to know the truth and now it's right in front of you. I figured I owed you that for the happiness you brought into my life. No man ever had a better wife. I love you Angel. I always have and I always will, even death can't change that. I want you to be happy because wherever you are, I won't be far away - you can count on it! That's a promise and Joe Morrelli never breaks a promise. We had a good life together and I want the rest of yours to be just as good. So let there be no tears, Angel, just a lot of happy memories.

Be happy honey.

Joe"

With tear stained cheeks, she folded the letter neatly and put it back into the envelope. Then she opened the folders. Rooney watched as the colour drained from her face and a look of horror spread over it. She studied the photographs enclosed, before breaking down.

"My God, I don't believe it! Tell me it's not true," she pleaded, "tell me Joe has made a mistake!"

He shook his head. "I can't do that Angela. It's all true."

She covered her face with her hands. "Raymond, Raymond Burns killed my father! My own brother-in-law and his best friend, Jamie Doyle, killed my father! But why, why?" she sobbed.

Rooney leaned over and gently took her hands away. "The answer's in the files, Angela, every detail is there. I'd advise you to read them, then you'll know why."

After a little while she composed herself and did as he said. As Rooney gazed at her silently, he couldn't help but wonder just how much more Angela could take. He was filled with a feeling of self-doubt and dread, and was beginning to wish he and Joe had never gone to Belfast.

As she went over the documents in front of her, Angela read aloud,

"Raymond Burns. Also known as Raymond 'The Rat' because of his night-time activities which include assaults, muggings, robbery. Jamie Doyle. Also known as 'Dodger Doyle' because he always had an alibi which placed him well away from the scene of a crime - and his partner.

Through a lack of definite evidence no disciplinary action was ever taken against either. These two men do not hold membership nor are they part of any organisation." She looked at Rooney. "I don't understand. What does that mean?"

"Exactly what it says. Those two have been doing that off their own backs for money. Over there they're called 'free-lancers'."

"But why would they kill my father?"

"Well, my guess is they jumped your father with the intention to beat him up and rob him. But Raymond didn't realise who it was until it was too late. Your father recognised him and then knew these two guys were responsible for what was going on."

Within seconds Angela thought back to the day her father was killed. Hadn't Raymond told him about old Pete Flanagan and the way he had been attacked and robbed coming from the pub? No wonder Raymond had known so much about it!

Rooney continued. "Think about it for a minute, Angela. Your father was a decent man. There's no way he would have kept quiet and let them carry on, and there's something even more important. He'd never have let Raymond Burns into his home again or let him near your sister. His good times with your family and his easy way of making money would have come to an end. I reckon he knew his secret life was on the line and the only way to keep it secret was to take your father's life. That way no-one would ever know about him, especially you and Sheila. Raymond had to silence the only witness who could ever point a finger at him - and he did!"

Angela fought back the tears. "How did Joe get all this information?"

"At a very high price. He made a contact in Belfast and I went there to set things up. He paid a lot of money over the years, then when the time was right he went there himself"

She was shocked. "You and Joe were in Belfast? But that's impossible! When?"

He leaned back in the chair. "When I was supposed to be in Vegas. And when Joe took that business trip to Chicago and had to stay longer than planned. Remember?"

Staring at him intently she asked, "Rooney, why didn't Joe take things into his own hands? Why didn't he deal with them? I would never have known."

"He couldn't. Raymond was your brother-in-law and you loved him, Joe knew that. Then there was Aisling. Angela, you know how close she and Joe were. For him to leave her without a father the way Raymond had left you without one, wouldn't have been right. You see, he couldn't do that to Aisling. It would have made him no better than Raymond Burns."

Angela nodded with understanding. "Who was the contact?" she asked.

"A guy called Harry Collington. But he has nothing to do with those two scumbags, he just provided the information. He's a big man in Belfast but he was never involved in the murder of your father." He shook his head. "No, Harry's not guilty of that, but he is guilty of something else."

"What is it?"

"He's the one who spread the rumour about your father being an informer, to cover his own tracks," he replied. "Harry Collington is the real 'Nightingale' and Joe found out. But to get those files Joe promised him he would never tell anyone as long as he lived."

There was an icy silence before she nodded, "Well, he kept his promise. But Joe's dead now."

Rooney looked uncomfortable, but decided to tell her the rest. "I think there's something else you should know about, Angela. Raymond's a bit of a lady's man and spends most of his money on other women. Sheila knows it."

"How can you be so sure?"

"I saw him myself when I was in Belfast and I made some enquires about him to some friends of mine. They only confirmed what I already suspected." He shrugged. "If you want my opinion, that's why Sheila's health isn't so good. She knows what's going on but she can't do anything about it. That's why Joe stopped sending them money on a regular basis and set up a trust fund for the kids. At least that way Raymond couldn't spend it on good times with other women."

"Rooney, there's so much I didn't know. So much he never told me." She sounded hurt.

He leaned over and touched her hand. "I know it's a lot to take in. The big question is, what do you want to do about it?"

Raising her eyes, she looked into his face. It was the first time he had ever seen those lovely deep blue eyes look so cold and calculating.

"I want justice," she said determinedly. "Raymond Burns and Jamie Doyle killed my father and the only way they can pay is with their own lives. I also want Harry Collington to pay. After all, it was Joe who made the promise to him - not me!"

Rooney was thoughtful. "I don't see how that's going to be possible, not now with Joe gone." He thought even more. "O.k., let's look at the whole situation. Firstly, you've got some straight up-front guys who work for Harry Collington. They are loyal to him. They do whatever he asks and they never question his motives because he's their boss and they believe him to be as genuine as themselves. They don't know that Harry is giving information and getting well paid for it. They don't know about his deal with Joe to get those files, and they certainly don't know about Raymond Burns and Jamie Doyle, believe me. Secondly, when Harry Collington finds out Joe's dead he's going to feel real safe and very relieved. As far as he's concerned, it's all over. There's no more deal and nothing to connect him to the 'Nightingale' or any money that's been going astray and into his own bank account. Thirdly, because Joe kept his mouth shut all these years, would Harry's men ever believe it?"

"They might if they had the evidence. Did Joe have a file on him?"

"In the same drawer, at the very back."

Reaching in, she found it. Laying it on the desk with the others, she got up and went to the window. She gazed out, just as Joe used to whenever there was something on his mind.

Rooney waited, reluctant to interrupt her thoughts. Eventually, she turned around. "What if Mr. Collington was to get a visit from Joe Morrelli's wife, telling him she knew everything but wanted the deal brought to an end once and for all? If what you say is true, Joe paid an awful lot of money but only got half the goods. I think it's time Mr. Collington delivered the rest. Let's suppose Joe's widow wants her father's murderers brought to justice and she gives him an ultimatum. All he has to do is set them up and collect $50,000 for doing so. A gesture of my appreciation! Or I tell his own men about the real Harry Collington and his activities. What do you think he would do?"

"What could he do? If he didn't go along and word got out about him - he's dead meat!"

"That's exactly what I'm going to do," she told him.

Rooney became concerned and protective.

"Now, hold on a minute Angela! There's no way you can go to Belfast and carry that through, it's too risky. What if someone should see you, someone you know? You've got family over there."

"Who said anything about me? Harry Collington has never seen Joe Morrelli's wife and I know the perfect woman to take my place."

"Who?" he was baffled.

"Antonia!"

"Antonia?" he repeated.

Angela nodded. "Why not? She's the best actress on Broadway. If anyone can carry it off, she can. All I have to do is convince her."

"And just how are you going to do that?"

"Leave it with me," she smiled faintly. "Which brings me now to your friends. Can they be trusted?"

"You bet!"

"Do you still keep in touch with them?"

"I've always remained friends with them. Why do you ask?"

"Because we're going to need them and it's important that they know what's going on. If Antonia goes to meet Harry Collington, she's going to ask for his most trusted men to deal with the set-up."

"Then she'll get McCabe and Quinn," he assured her.

"Good. In the meantime, I want you to get in touch with them and tell them everything you know about Harry and the deal he made with Joe. When Raymond Burns and Jamie Doyle are dealt with, then they can deal with Mr. Collington. That way, we will be bringing everyone to justice."

Rooney had listened intently to Angela's plans. "And just where do I fit into all this?" he asked . "Joe made me promise that if you ever decided to bring things further, I'd be the one to go to Belfast."

"And so you will." She returned to the chair and sat down. "But knowing you will have your two friends on your side will make it a lot easier."

He stared at her and in a low voice said, "Angela, if you set up your own brother-in-law you know I'm going to have to kill him and leave your sister a widow. How do you feel about that?"

She returned his stare. "Well, from what you've told me she'd be better off without him. I'm going to finish what Joe started, Rooney, and I don't feel any remorse. Raymond Burns took my father's younger daughter, his home, his furniture, his money. But not before he took his life!! How would you feel?"

"Exactly the same," he had to admit. "And if all this goes according to plan and Collington takes the bait, then I know he'll send McCabe and Quinn on the job. I'll make sure of that when I contact them. But I have one request, Angela."

"What is it?"

"That I'm the one who pulls the trigger on that bastard and his side-kick! It's important to me. I promised Joe and I owe him that."

She nodded her approval. "After dinner tonight we can go over what's in these files in detail. If we're going to carry this out, everything must be perfect with no slip-ups."

Rooney got to his feet. "That's fine by me. After you've spoken to Antonia and if she agrees, I'll contact Dermot McCabe and explain everything. When he hears what I have to say, we won't have any problems."

As he turned to leave Angela reminded him, "This is just between us, Rooney. Robert mustn't find out about any of this. I don't want him involved, it would ruin his future."

"Yeah," he agreed. "If he knew what had really happened, there's no telling what he'd do. He's got a brilliant career in front of him. There's no way we can let him jeopardise it, no matter what. I'll see you later."

When Rooney had left the room, Angela returned her gaze to the two photographs on the desk, then burst into tears.

"Oh Joe, you were so right," she whispered, recalling his face and his voice. "Very few people are what they seem to be!"

The next afternoon, Evie knocked on the study door and opened it.

"Miss Angela, Miss Flemming is here to see you."

Before Angela could reply Antonia swept into the room, her arms outstretched. "Angela, dear! How are you? I know I'm a little early but as the great actors and actresses always used to say, 'Be early, know your lines and don't bump into the furniture,'" she smiled.

After embracing, Angela nodded to Evie.

"Thank you Evie. That will be all."

"Yes Miss Angela," came the reply as she threw a sarcastic glance in Antonia's direction and left the room.

They were now alone.

"I was surprised to get your call. Is anything wrong?" Antonia asked, taking a seat.

Angela made herself comfortable in Joe's chair. "I need to talk to you."

She proceeded to tell her everything in great detail watching closely as her expression changed.

"It's all too awful to imagine!" said a shocked Antonia. "I can understand why you would want to get your own back. Especially after everything Joe did to uncover the truth. But I can't see how I can be of any help to you."

"You can," Angela insisted.

"How?"

"I need someone to go to Belfast in my place. I can't take the risk of going myself, someone might recognise me. Harry Collington has never met me so if Joe Morrelli's wife turns up to persuade him to keep his part of the bargain, why should he suspect?"

"You want me to be Joe's wife?"

"I can't think of anyone more suited. Can you? After all, if anyone could convince Harry Collington you could. Joe always said you were the best actress on Broadway."

Antonia raised her eyebrows. "Well, I must admit the role does appeal to me. It's a very challenging one." She gave a slight smile. "I would be Mrs. Joe Morrelli to everyone over there. It's an interesting proposition."

"Before you make up your mind, I think there's something you should see." Angela opened one of the drawers and took out Joe's leather bound personal file. Turning to the back cover she showed it to Antonia.

Two photographs were securely fixed to it. One of Joe and Angela taken on their wedding day outside the Church, and the other of Joe and Antonia taken on the same day in the same place!

As she studied it, Antonia's eyes filled with tears. "I never thought he'd keep that so close to him all these years, but he did."

She gazed longingly at the photo of Joe and her smiling happily. "I guess Joe was telling me the truth all along. He did love me - in his own special way. I know that now for sure."

"Yes, he did," Angela assured her.

"Alright, I'll do it! I'll meet with Harry Collington and give the performance of my life. I'll be the best Mrs. Joe Morrelli you could wish for," she said adamantly.

"I know you will Antonia, you're perfect for the part. Thank you."

"Don't thank me Angela. This is one part it will be a pleasure to play.

Besides, I owe Joe a lot, I'm only repaying a debt in the best way I know how. Now, you'd better fill me in on everything . How much time do we have before I go to Ireland?"

"Not a lot. A few weeks."

Antonia smiled. "Oh, that's long enough for any good actress to learn her lines. We'll just have to spend a lot of time together. I need to know everything I have to say to be convincing. I want to be word perfect for our Mr. Collington!"

Angela returned her smile. "That won't be a problem. I have your script right here!" She produced the three folders and gave Harry's to Antonia. As she began to read it, Angela leaned back in the chair with a feeling of deep satisfaction. Perhaps she should have been surprised by Antonia's sudden change of heart towards her but she wasn't. Because she knew she was offering her something she just couldn't resist. She was giving her the chance to play the one role she has always wanted. At long last Antonia Flemming was about to become Mrs. Joe Morrelli!

When Rooney heard Antonia was going to Ireland, he set the wheels in motion by contacting Dermot McCabe and confiding everything to him. McCabe was gutted when he heard about Raymond Burns and Jamie Doyle, but even more so when he heard about Harry Collington. Dermot was making a name for himself in Belfast and gaining respect. He had come a long way from when Rooney last saw him and Collington had given him and Seamus a high position of trust. Because of this he doubted the accusations made against his boss, not really wanting to believe them. After a lengthy conversation Rooney promised him proof, and told him a copy of Collington's file would be sent on by special delivery. Only then would Dermot be totally convinced and make up his own mind what to do. Rooney agreed to this and after discussing it with Angela, it was in the post the very next day.

As they waited for word Angela and Antonia worked closely together, mostly at Antonia's apartment so that Robert and everyone at Roseberry Avenue would not have cause to wonder why they had become such good friends after all these years.

Nearly two weeks later, Rooney arrived into the lounge with an anxious look on his face.

"What's the matter?" asked Angela, putting down her magazine.

"We've got a problem."

She stood up. "You've heard from McCabe. He doesn't believe us about Harry Collington, does he?"

"He believes it alright. I never doubted it for a minute - not once he saw the file."

"Then what's the problem?"

Rooney gave a deep sigh. "The problem is, there's going to be a cease-fire pretty soon and no-one knows about it only those directly involved. Dermot says its only weeks away. All organisations are going to call a truce." He stared at her. "Don't you see what this means, Angela? No more bullets and no more dead bodies. We don't have as much time as we thought. When the deadline comes McCabe and Quinn can't help us and Harry Collington certainly can't help!" He shook his head. "Raymond Burns and Jamie Doyle will have a free hand just like always and Collington can't be touched. He need never keep his end of the bargain now. Joe kept those secrets for so long and now that they're out in the open, it looks like it's too late." He looked towards the ceiling. "I don't believe it! After all these years they are actually going to stop killing. Jesus, it looks like it's either bad timing on our part, or those three guys have got charmed lives. I don't know what we're going to do."

She walked towards him. "Well, I do. We will just have to bring our plan forward. I'm not having Joe's secrets blown apart for nothing. Rooney, not until those men get what's coming to them. Are your friends willing to help?"

"Sure, I've explained everything. They want Collington just as badly as we want Burns and Doyle."

"Alright," she nodded, "then this is what we're going to do. I want you to contact Dermot McCabe and tell him we are going through with everything just the way we planned. Tell him Antonia will be arriving in Belfast early next week."

"Will she be ready?" asked Rooney. "I mean, will she know exactly what to do and say?"

Angela smiled. "Well, she's never missed a cue yet! She'll be ready." She bit her lip and looked thoughtful. "She'll only be there for three or four days. Just long enough to put some pressure on Mr. Collington and convince him to help her, for his own sake. After that, it shouldn't take long to set up Raymond and Jamie. Not if he knows there's a cease-fire coming and he's going to make £50,000 with no hassle. That's where you and your friends come in. One evening will get the job done, then you get the next flight back leaving them to deal with Collington. He doesn't need to know Mrs. Morrelli's coming until she's on her way. If we act now our timing won't be bad at all Rooney. We can have the whole thing over and done before the cease-fire."

They stared at each other.

Then Rooney shook his head. "You know Angela, you're running Joe's affairs like a real professional. You're a shrewd lady with a hard head for business. But I must admit, I never thought you could plan something like this in such detail."

"Why, because I'm a woman?" she smiled.

"Yeah, I guess so," he admitted.

"You're forgetting something Rooney. I learned from the best - Joe Morrelli was my husband!"

He nodded. "Yeah, and right now I wouldn't doubt it for a second!"

Antonia answered the door of her hotel suite and came face to face with a smartly dressed man in his early sixties.

He smiled courteously as he held out his hand.

"Mrs. Morrelli? I'm Harry Collington."

Taking his hand she greeted him warmly. "Mr. Collington, it's so nice to meet you. Please, come in."

As he stepped inside she closed the door and motioned to a chair. "Why don't you make yourself comfortable and I'll get us both a drink." She smiled, "Now let me guess. I'll bet your drink is a whiskey. Am I right?"

"That was a good guess!" Harry replied.

She went over to the brightly lit mini bar and opening two miniature bottles, poured them into crystal glasses. Harry looked around the expensively furnished room. After giving him his drink, she settled in the chair opposite.

"Well, I must admit Mrs. Morrelli, I've never been in a hotel room quite like this one. I can see you're a woman of taste," Harry commented admiringly.

Antonia smiled coyly. "It's really kept reserved for V.I.P.'s but I like the best, if the best is available. And it was, for the right price. Money can buy you anything, Mr. Collington."

"It's the patron saint of luxury!" he joked. "You can't get far without it. I suppose that's why most of us have prayed for it at one time or another."

She nodded in agreement. They sipped their drinks.

"I was very surprised when Rooney telephoned me to say you were coming," he continued. "He said you had some business you wanted to discuss with me. That surprised me even more, I thought your husband would be making the trip. How is Mr. Morrelli?"

Putting her glass down on the long polished coffee table, Antonia lowered her gaze. When she raised her eyes again they were full of sadness. "My husband passed away."

Harry was shocked. "I'm sorry to hear that. It must be a great loss to you."

"Yes, it is. But I learned a lot from him. He left me in charge of everything and I'm pleased to say the Joe Morrelli empire is still going strong and making money." She paused for a few moments, looking at him intently. "Joe and I had no secrets, Mr. Collington. He told me everything about his trip here. I know all about Raymond Burns and Jamie Doyle. And I know about you! That's the reason I'm here. You see, I don't think my husband got his money's worth, not when you consider the large amounts he paid all those years."

"Well, he did get the files," he was quick to point out.

"That's true. But for such large sums of money he should have gotten the men as well. As far as I'm concerned, you still owe him and I'm here to collect."

"I don't think you understand Mrs. Morrelli. Let me explain. I told your husband if he ever needed me, he knew where I was. But he never contacted me again. Naturally, I assumed he didn't want those men."

"Oh, he wanted them alright, but he didn't want to leave my sister a widow and her children without a father. To Joe, that would only have meant history repeating itself. But now let me explain something to you. Joe is dead and I'm here to take care of unfinished business and tie up all loose ends." Leaning forward she stared at him. "I want those men, Mr. Collington. I've waited a long time and now I want justice for my father."

He shifted uncomfortably in his chair. "Am I included in that?" he asked.

She shook her head. "No. I want the men who murdered my father and you can help me get them." She leaned back. "Of course, if you refuse, that places you in a dangerous situation. I mean, if your men were to receive copies of your file detailing your activities, we both know you wouldn't live long." She sighed, "It would be such a shame, all that money you've got hidden away in Guernsey. You'd never get to spend it. Why, it would be such a waste! Speaking of money ... if you were to help me, of course there would be an added bonus. We Morrelli's like to show our appreciation for services rendered."

"How much appreciation are we talking about?"

Without replying, Antonia got up and went to the telephone. She dialled reception and asked for the manager.

"This is Mrs. Morrelli," she said. Suite 139. I have a briefcase in your safe and I'd like it brought to my room right away, please. Thank you so much."

A few minutes later the briefcase was delivered as she asked. The manager agreed to wait at the door.

"I only need it to check something," she explained. Returning, she placed the case on the coffee table in front of Harry, then fetched a key from her bedside drawer. On opening the case she saw his eyes widen in disbelief as he looked at the neatly stacked bundles of crisp notes.

"How much is there?" he asked.

"$50,000."

"That can buy any favour!"

Antonia smiled. "Does that mean you're going to accept my proposition?"

Still gazing at the money he replied, "I'd be a damn fool not to!"

She closed the briefcase and locked it, them brought it back to the waiting manager. "Thank you. I'm so very grateful," she smiled.

"Not at all, Mrs. Morrelli. I'll put it back in the safe right away."

As she rejoined her guest she put the key on the table. "Now why don't we get down to business," she said.

He nodded and they lifted their drinks. "If you have a plan, I'd be more than happy to hear it."

Running her finger around the rim of her glass, Antonia crossed her long slim legs. Harry watched with admiration.

"Oh, I have a plan alright and believe me, it will be the easiest $50,000 you will ever make."

"I'm listening."

"Well, for years now these two men have taken the law into their own hands. By their actions they have become a threat to the community you promised to protect. I'm sure a lot of people wonder why men like this are not punished. Indeed, some may even think you have something to gain by allowing this conduct. It doesn't exactly boost a lot of confidence in you, Mr. Collington. I think I would be right in saying that in some quarters people are so frightened that you are involved in, or sanction what these men do, it actually puts you in a bad light. In all honesty these men are nothing more than an embarrassment to you, and one I'm sure you could well do without. If justice was seen to be done, it would prove to the community that you are a man of your word and put you in even higher standing with the people. That's where I come in. All I want you to do is set these two men up. That shouldn't be difficult for a man in your position. If you can have them in a secluded place, preferably out of the city, on a certain day at a certain time - Rooney will do the rest."

"Rooney?!" Harry was greatly surprised.

"Yes, Rooney. He will do in Belfast what Joe would have done in New York - take care of business! But he will need a couple of men to drive him there and back and provide a weapon for him. And an alibi, in case he gets stopped by the police or military. I want to ensure he gets the best and most trustworthy men you have. Men who are totally loyal to you and can keep their mouths shut. All they have to do is accompany him, they won't even have to use a weapon. So you see, Mr. Collington, I'm not asking you or your men to kill anyone. Rooney will do that job for you. I get what I want and so do you. You will get respect from the people, I will get justice for my father. I'm sure you will admit, yours is a small part to play for my silence, the debt you owe my husband and $50,000!"

Harry was silent as he considered all she had said. Then he leaned over and put his drink down. "Count me in!" he said, determinedly. "As a matter of fact I know just the men for the job and the best part is, Rooney knows them too. They became good friends when he was here the first time. He trusts them and I can guarantee he will be quite safe. You have my word on that."

Antonia smiled. "I'm very glad to hear it."

He looked thoughtful. "I think the best way around this is to take the men in question, Burns and Doyle, into my confidence. Nothing of great importance, mind you. I'll just give them a few jobs to do. Nothing heavy, but they'll be well paid. If I do that, their suspicions won't be aroused when they're asked to go out of the city on another job. When they get there, I'll have my men drive Rooney to the same place. Then everything can be taken care of." He looked across at her. "Of course there is no reason why my own men should know about the money. I'd prefer we kept that strictly between us."

She shrugged slightly. "It's your money, Mr. Collington. I don't see why anyone else should know about our little arrangement." Holding up the key in front of him, she continued. "There's just one thing I'd like to get straight. Tomorrow morning I'm putting the briefcase in a safety deposit box at the bank. When the job's done and Rooney is leaving, he will bring the key and number of the box to you personally, in a brown padded envelope. I'm sure you will agree, it's not good business to pay until the goods are delivered. It's nothing to do with you personally, let's just say it's my insurance that nothing goes wrong and Rooney is safe. Do we have a deal?" she asked offering her hand.

He gladly took it and shook it firmly. "We have a deal! You know, Mrs. Morrelli, you're very much like your husband when it comes to doing business. He was thorough and covered every aspect. You are the same, nothing is left to chance."

"Joe was a good teacher," she replied.

Harry nodded. "He would have been proud of you. When you started to talk to me, I was left in no doubt that you were his wife."

She beamed with satisfaction. "Did it really show that much?"

"Yes it did," he smiled, then became quite serious. "Tell me something, Mrs. Morrelli. If your husband didn't take action all these years because of your sister and her children, why are you? Don't you feel guilty about it? After all, Raymond Burns is your brother- in-law."

Antonia looked at him and raised an eyebrow. "We can choose our friends, Mr. Collington, but we can't choose our relations."

"Now that's very true," he agreed.

She stood up. "Well, now that we've had our little chat and we understand each other, I think that concludes our business for this evening."

He got to his feet and they shook hands once again. "And may I say it was a pleasure doing business with you Mrs. Morrelli."

She glanced at her Rolex watch. "Would you care to dine with me, Mr. Collington? Or perhaps you have another appointment?"

"Not at all," he replied hastily, seizing the opportunity to spend some more time with her. "I'd be delighted to," he smiled.

"Good. I'll just get my purse."

Antonia walked towards the bedroom, the key still grasped tightly in her hand. Harry gazed after her. She was a very attractive woman, not just in appearance but in her intelligence and gutsy attitude. He could tell she was a woman who was used to getting what she wanted and would go to any lengths to ensure she did. She was just the sort of woman Joe Morrelli would marry and the ideal choice to carry on his business. In the hands of a woman like that, it could only prosper!

As they sat in the dining room talking and laughing in friendly conversation, Harry found himself quite taken with her. She was polite, charming and had impeccable table manners. Not at all like the women he was used to.

Sipping the last of his large brandy, he leaned forward "You know Mrs. Morrelli, what we discussed earlier on this evening will take time. It will take some days, maybe longer, for me to sort it all out. By then I will have more details for you. When I have spoken to my men and explained a few things, especially about Raymond Burns and Jamie Doyle, then we can put our plan into action. They won't shed any tears about seeing hoodlums like that taken off the street, not when I tell them what they did. And I know they'll be pleased to hear Rooney will be paying a visit. But these things can't be rushed, I will have to discuss everything with them."

"I understand," Antonia smiled and nodded. "I don't mind waiting. It will be worth it, to get what I want."

"In that case, Mrs. Morrelli, you will have some time to spare. Tell me, do you like the theatre?"

"Oh, I just love it!"

"Well, we have some very fine plays on here and I would like to return the hospitality you have shown me tonight. How would you feel about going to a show tomorrow evening and having some supper with me afterwards in a nice hotel or restaurant?" Harry waited anxiously for her reply.

Antonia smiled sweetly at his invitation. "How very kind of you. I would be delighted."

"The delight will be all mine," replied a happy and relieved Harry Collington.

Putting her hand to her mouth, she yawned discreetly. "You must excuse me, Mr. Collington, I think I will retire now. A woman needs her beauty sleep."

"Certainly not a woman as attractive as you! But you must be feeling very tired from your long journey." He excused himself, trying his best to make a good impression. "Thank you for a lovely evening, Mrs. Morrelli. I'll telephone you tomorrow and let you know what time I shall be calling. Good night."

"I'll look forward to it. Goodnight, Mr. Collington."

As she watched him leave, Antonia knew she had Harry Collington exactly where she wanted him. After waiting for a few moments, she returned to her suite and dialled direct to Roseberry Avenue. On hearing everything from her, Angela expressed how pleased she was at the way Antonia had handled things, and the way the plan was working out.

After their conversation had ended, Antonia decided to take a shower. After undressing, she slipped on a robe and went into the bathroom. Feeling pretty pleased with herself she stood in front of the mirror and smiled. Removing her make-up with the cold cream and tissues, she began talking in a low voice.

"I have just given the best performance of my life, Joe, because this was the one part I always wanted to play." She leaned forward and stared at her reflection for a few moments. "You see, all that money you paid for acting lessons wasn't wasted darling," she whispered.

While Antonia enjoyed the attention of Harry Collington, back in New York someone was turning their attention to Angela.

As Rooney came along the entrance hall, she was replacing the receiver.

"Was that Antonia?" He enquired.

"No, Kevin Mitchell. He has invited me out to dinner tonight."

"Are you going?"

"Yes I am," she smiled.

He looked at her with disapproval. "Well, I sure hope he isn't calling for you. Joe would turn in his grave if Kevin Mitchell ever set foot in this house. He never liked the guy, and neither do I!"

Angela's smile faded. "Joe had a reason - I was his wife! What's yours?"

Her sarcastic tone made him look at the floor. Then lifting his eyes, he met her gaze. "I just don't think he's your type."

"I'm not going to marry him, I'm only having dinner with him."

He nodded. "O.k. Where's he taking you?"

"The Imperial Palace."

"Where else!" Rooney shrugged. "Only the most expensive place in town. No lowly restaurant with common people would be good enough for him. After all, they probably wouldn't know who he was. But 'The Imperial Palace' - well! Everyone knows him there that would suit him just fine. That guy has an ego as big as the Empire State Building. I doubt if he's ever eaten in a diner like the rest of us mortals!" He was obviously peeved.

Angela, being Angela, was taking no nonsense. "Now you listen to me Rooney. Kevin Mitchell is my friend and has been for a long time. Gene O'Brien will be running for President any day now and Kevin and I will be seeing a lot of each other when the campaigning starts. I don't know why you're taking this attitude but I know one thing, he has asked me to dine with him tonight and I'm going. And just to put your mind at rest he isn't calling for me, I'm meeting him there!" she snapped, walking away.

He stared after her. "A guy like that doesn't stop at asking a woman out to dinner, so don't say I didn't warn you!" he called.

She stopped and turned defiantly. "What happens after dinner is my business." Then casting her eyes, she continued towards the kitchen.

"That's fine by me!" he said in a raised voice as he opened the study door, slamming it loudly after him.

He stood looking at Joe's empty chair. In the past he could never understand Joe's bitter feelings towards Kevin Mitchell, but now he did. For the first time in his life he understood perfectly. The very thought of the woman you love being with another man was hard to take, even if it was an innocent relationship like committees, lunches and dinners. He knew Joe had always been threatened by Mitchell. He was young, handsome and could give a woman anything she wanted.

Rooney loved Angela, but out of respect for his best friend he had never asked her out for an evening. He kept telling himself it was too soon, and she'd probably refuse. But Kevin Mitchell picks up the telephone, turns on the charm and gets himself a dinner date! Rooney felt annoyed with himself at passing up the chance of asking Angela out, and giving the opportunity to someone else. And he was surprised and upset at her going. But his feelings went a lot deeper than that. Rooney was jealous of Kevin Mitchell!! After all these years he had ended up in the same situation as his friend and brother. He knew now how it felt. He wasn't just standing in Joe Morrelli's study - he was standing in his shoes as well!

The following day, Rooney arrived through the back door and into the kitchen. "Hi Evie," he smiled, half-heartedly.

"Oh Rooney, I've got something to tell you," she beamed. "Miss Angela went out to dinner last night with the late Senator Casey's nephew!"

"Yeah I know. She told me yesterday she was going."

Evie glanced towards the door leading into the entrance hall and lowered her voice. "Well, I think it's time she had a proper evening out. From Mr. Joe died she's only been to the bowling alley and the movies. The rest of her nights are spent reading or watching videos alone. That's no life for a young woman, and she spends too many hours in that study working. I was worried about her."

Rooney felt a pang of guilt. "Yeah, we all need a break Evie."

She nodded in agreement. "Miss Angela has grieved enough. I think it's time she went out and enjoyed herself, and a man like that may be just what she needs."

"Did she have a good time?" he was curious.

"Why, she had a wonderful time!" she replied excitedly. "I'm sure she really likes him, and I know what I know." She smiled slyly.

"Was she late home?" he asked casually.

"I don't know. I never heard her come in but she over-slept this morning and that isn't like Miss Angela. I'm really happy for her."

"So am I." He forced a smile, then made his way to the study.

He felt embarrassed about what had happened the day before but was determined not to show it as he went inside.

Angela looked surprised to see him. Putting the pen down, she greeted him with a warm smile. "I thought this was your day off?"

"It is but I just dropped by to have a word with you." Taking a seat, he proceeded to explain. "I had a telephone call from Dermot McCabe. Harry Collington sent for him and Seamus Quinn and had a long talk with them. Harry is going to set up Raymond and Jamie with their help and they are going to accompany me when the time comes. We got the two men we wanted for the job, so it looks like our plan has been put into action."

"I had a call from Antonia telling me much the same thing. She's done everything she had to and has gotten all the details and information she could, so she's coming home."

"Well, all we can do now is wait," he shrugged. "I hope Harry Collington doesn't take too long. Time isn't on our side."

Angela nodded, "I know. But according to Antonia he wants that $50,000 badly and the only way he'll get it is to see that everything is taken care of before the cease-fire. I don't think we have anything to worry about. Mr. Collington knows a good thing when he sees it, and this is one deal he won't want to miss out on."

Rooney stood up. "Yeah, I guess you're right. It looks like everything is going to go our way. Burns and Doyle don't know Harry is going to get them dealt with, and Harry doesn't know McCabe and Quinn are going to deal with him. Its the perfect set-up. We get rid of three scumbags instead of two. Well, I'd better be going."

"Why don't you come over tonight for dinner, Rooney?" she asked.

"I can't Angela, I have other arrangements. I'm going to a nightclub with an old girlfriend," he lied, convincingly.

She lowered her gaze for a moment, then looked at him again. "Anyone I know?"

He shook his head. "No, I don't think so."

Angela gave a faint smile. "Well, I hope you enjoy yourself."

"Believe me, I intend to!" he winked, with a broad smile. "We all need the right company to have a good time and this woman fits the bill perfectly!" He walked towards the door, then turned. "I'll see you tomorrow."

She nodded in silence as he left the room.

Once outside he took a deep breath. He knew Angela was taken aback by his refusal to spend the evening with her, but although he felt bad about offending her, he wanted her to realise that he wasn't there to be used as a convenience. If Evie was right and she really did like Kevin Mitchell, then she would be going out with him again. Rooney was letting Angela know in his own subtle way, that if she was going her own way in the company of someone else, then he could do the same.

It was with deep regret that Harry Collington said goodbye to Antonia. It had been a short but pleasant friendship and he had grown quite fond of her, but she had promised to return in the near future. As he watched the large aircraft take off, he hoped her next visit would be a longer one. He wanted to see her again but knew this was only possible if he kept his end of the bargain. Harry was determined that "Mr.s, Morrelli" should see him in a good light, a man of integrity, a man who kept his word and someone to be trusted to take care of things. And of course there was also the matter of the $50,000! He would never get an offer like that again for doing so little. The fact that there was going to be a ceasefire had never been mentioned by him - he didn't see the need. Being a shrewd and careful man he knew if he handled things right, the job would be done and the money would be his before the cease-fire would be announced in Northern Ireland and the rest of the world. As he left the airport he decided to waste no time in dealing with the situation.

Burns and Doyle were recruited into the organisation by McCabe and Quinn. They were lured by the prospect of working for such highly important men and the promise of big money. It would also give them something they never had, respect from the community they lived in and the power and authority over other individuals, they had always craved. At last these two men would rub shoulders with the "big boys" at the top of the tree and earn a reputation even greater than the one they already had! Working for Harry Collington had it's compensations. It brought an element of fear to the ordinary people, enabling Burns and Doyle to have a free hand and take control. And with McCabe and Quinn at their backs, no one would dare approach them or ask any questions. Power and money are the two best weapons any man can have in any country and it was for this very reason that Raymond Burns and Jamie Doyle became such willing recruits.

In the few weeks that followed they had done various jobs and everyone involved was satisfied with them. The money flowed in and the good times had come. Life was good. Their dealings were strictly with McCabe and Quinn. Although their boss was Harry Collington, they had not as yet met him, but they were kept informed of how pleased he was with their progress. However, Harry was biding his time. After lulling the two men into a false sense of security, he decided the time was right for the set-up. They received word through McCabe that he wanted to see them. Finally Burns and Doyle were going to meet " The Main Man"!

On the day in question they were picked up outside "The Punters Bar" by Seamus Quinn, and driven to the end house at the corner of Belmore Street next to the patch of waste ground known locally as "The Alamo." It was aptly named because of the many shootings that had taken place there and the many dead bodies that had been found. As the two men got out of the car and looked around, they also glanced at each other. Whatever Harry Collington had in mind, they both knew there was no turning back now. As Seamus led them up the stairs, they noticed it was a two storey house made into offices. On climbing the second flight they saw McCabe standing outside the second door on the square landing. He smiled, then knocked on the door and opened it.

"Burns and Doyle are here, Mr. Collington," he announced.

"Send them in," came the strong reply.

On stepping inside the door was closed promptly behind them, leaving them alone with the man they had been so eager to please.

He looked up from behind his desk and smiled. "Take a seat." Motioning to the two empty chairs in front of him, he waited until they were seated. "So, we meet at last," he said. "I've been hearing good reports about you, so there's no point in beating around the bush. How would you both like to be involved in a major job and earn some big money?"

Raymond nodded. "It sounds good to me, Mr. Collington. Right Jamie?" He looked across at his friend, who readily agreed.

"That's right Mr. Collington. You've just got to name it and we'll do it."

"Good." This was just what Harry wanted to hear. "I take it you're happy with our arrangement. You know, the jobs and the money I've been putting your way."

"More than happy," Raymond assured him. "And we'd like it to continue."

Harry could sense they were nervous at meeting him, so he took a packet of cigarettes from his jacket pocket and passed them around. Then he leaned forward and lit their cigarettes for them.

"Relax boys! You work for me now and I look after my own. You're as safe as houses while I'm around, you have my word on that."

Jamie sat back in the chair. "We never thought we'd meet someone in your position."

Harry placed his hands on the desk. "The reason you have is because I'm always on the look out for good men. Men who aren't afraid to take chances. And your reputations have preceded you."

At this comment they both looked embarrassed.

Harry waved a dismissing hand. "Oh, forget all about that stuff you did in the past. It's what you're doing now that's important."

This put them at their ease.

Stubbing out his barely used cigarette in the ashtray, he stared at them for a few moments. "Now, I think it's time we got down to the business of why you're here. I have a job coming up soon and I need two very reliable men who can keep their mouths shut and I think you two might just be what I'm looking for."

"That won't be a problem Mr. Collington," said Raymond. "Me and Jamie never tell anyone what we're doing."

Nodding, Harry began to explain. "Well, the truth is we have an informer in our midst and as if that isn't bad enough, he's been skimming off the top, taking money that doesn't belong to him . Money that was meant for other things. The bastard has been lining his own pockets while the rest of us are risking life and limb!"

Raymond looked totally disgusted. "What kind of man could do something like that?"

"Believe me, you'd be surprised at who could do it and who is doing it. But I fully intend to put a stop to it."

"And quite right too - that bastard should be shot!" Raymond's answer was obvious.

"You read my mind. I can see you're the right man for the job. You - and your friend," Leaning his arms on the desk, Harry continued. "Here's what we're going to do. The tout will be sent on a job out of the city, accompanied by McCabe and Quinn. That way he won't suspect anything. When they get to their destination both of you will be waiting. He will be fully interrogated and made to confess on tape. After that, my orders are that he be shot. And I want one of you to do it. One bullet at close range should do the trick. End of problem for me, end of job for you."

Without hesitation, Raymond said "You leave it to us Mr. Collington, it's as good as done!"

Harry was pleased with this response. "Of course, you will be paid for your time. Say, £.500 each up-front and another £500 when the job's done."

Their eyes lit up and Jamie drew a deep breath. That's a lot of money Mr. Collington," he commented.

"Maybe, but it's money well spent. Just think how much we'll save when he's out of the way."

Raymond Burns couldn't help but show his admiration for Harry Collington's way of thinking. "You've picked the right men," he assured him. "Hasn't he, Jamie? I'd shoot the bastard and be happy to pull the trigger!"

"That's what I like to hear. And needless to say if all goes well with this job and you prove yourselves, there'll be other jobs and bigger money. Can you handle that'?"

"We can handle anything you put our way Mr. Collington."

"That's all I need to hear." Harry got up and came round the side of the desk. Raymond and Jamie got to their feet as he came towards them. " I want this business taken care of at the end of the week. Dermot will give you the money and the details of where you're going on the day. He will also provide a car to get you there, the gun will be in the car. Any questions?"

The two friends shook their heads in silence.

"Good," Harry smiled. "I think this plan is going to work out perfectly for everyone. Just remember, I'm putting a lot of trust in you both. I wouldn't want to regret it."

"Don't worry, you can count on us."

After shaking hands with them, he placed a fatherly hand on each shoulder. "I know I can count on you to do the job right. I wish I had more men of your substance. Believe me boys, Ireland needs them."

Raymond and Jamie felt proud and important as Harry walked them to the door and opened it. McCabe and Quinn stood talking. Leaving the office, the two unsuspecting friends were led back down the stairs by Seamus, while Dermot followed Harry inside and closed the door.

"Well, did they fall for it?" he asked.

Harry nodded and smiled. "Like apples of a tree Dermot." Watching McCabe's face break into a broad grin, he could appreciate his feelings of joy and relief "I wish everything in life was as easy as setting those two up." Walking over to the window, Harry looked onto the waste ground below.

"What made them go for it?" Dermot asked. "Was it the money?"

After a short silence the thoughtful reply came.

"I suppose so. Money is a big temptation. Even Jesus was betrayed for thirty pieces of silver." Then he turned and looked at McCabe. "What a pity those bastards will never get to spend it!"

Rooney was looking pleased with himself. He leaned over the study desk and looked at Angela.

"I've just had a telephone call from Harry Collington. Raymond and Jamie took the bait and everything is set for the weekend."

She was surprised. "This weekend?"

"Yeah, I must admit he planned it well. He's sending them right out of the city and with it being a Saturday night the pubs and clubs will be full to all hours, which makes it most unlikely anyone will be around to see or hear anything. It's a busy night for the police and military so we might be able to avoid them. They'll be more interested in street crowds and trouble makers."

Angela got up and walked around the desk. "When are you leaving?"

"I can get a flight out on Thursday and get the next available flight back. I don't want to spend any more time there than I have to."

She nodded. "That's perfect. We can be in and out before anyone realises what has happened."

Rooney stared at her. "WE? What do you mean, WE?"

"I'm coming with you," she informed him.

"Oh no you're not!"

"Give me one good reason why I shouldn't go?"

"I could give you a dozen, but here's a few off the top of my head. McCabe and Quinn are expecting me on my own. I have somewhere to stay, you don't. And there's no place on a job like this for a woman."

"Why not? It was a woman who planned it!" she interrupted sarcastically.

Rooney was beginning to lose patience. "For Christ's sake Angela, it's too dangerous for you to go! We are talking about murder here and I don't want you to have any part in it. I don't want you involved and neither would Joe."

She clenched her fists and glared at him. "Well you're NOT Joe!" she yelled angrily.

"Maybe not!" he yelled back. "But I'm the nearest thing you've got to him." His eyes flashing with temper, he stormed out slamming the door behind him.

Angela went over to the window and gazing out into the garden, she fought hard to keep back the tears. She hadn't meant to hurt Rooney but she knew she had. It was only then she realised just how dependent she had become on him since Joe died. He was kind and thoughtful and since she'd taken over the business, they had become close. Very close.

A lot closer than she wanted to admit.

She heard the door open and close quietly. Rooney walked across the room with his head bowed. There was silence. Then he looked at her. "You had planned to go to Ireland all along, hadn't you? I'd like to know why."

Turning around and meeting his gaze, she explained, "Raymond Burns was the brother I never had and I loved him like one. We were family, even back then. Yet he and his best friend killed my father. I just want to hear from his own lips, WHY. All I want is to hear them confess and give their reasons. That's all Rooney. I promise I won't get in the way. They don't even have to know I'm there."

Rooney sighed. "I don't suppose I can persuade you not to go?"

"No. Nothing you can say will make me change my mind. I've waited too long to find out the truth."

He shook his head. "I'm not happy about any of this Angela. And God knows what McCabe and Quinn are going to say when they find out. Different travelling arrangements will have to be made, we can't be seen together. I just hope these guys will understand. They are taking a big risk as it is, I'd sure hate for anything to go wrong for them."

Seeing his great concern, Angela walked over and looked into his face with equal understanding.

"Nothing will go wrong," she insisted. "You're flying into Belfast, I'll go by Dublin and stay in a hotel under a different name. All I have to do is meet up with you on Saturday night. Phone Dermot and tell him. I'm sure he'll think of some way of getting me there, once you explain everything."

Rooney closed his eyes for a few seconds, as if to help him think straight.

"O.k." he agreed. "But you'd better make all the arrangements now. I need the flight times, the name of the hotel and the name you'll be using, before I contact him. We don't have much time."

"I'll see to all of that today. What made you change your mind?"

"Well, the job Burns and Doyle are supposed to be going on, Harry Collington asked them to shoot someone and they agreed. They don't even know the guy or if they've been told the truth about him, but they're willing to do it anyway - for money! That makes them even more ruthless than the man they're working for. Wouldn't you say?"

He didn't have to tell her this but she was glad he did. It showed he understood how she felt. She took his hand. "This is important to me Rooney, I have to be there. I have to hear for myself what Raymond and Jamie say."

He looked at her, forlorn. "I'm sorry about my outburst earlier Angela. I should have know you had your reasons for wanting to go. But I'm worried about you."

"I'm the one who's sorry Rooney. I keep comparing everyone to Joe and that's wrong. But you were right about one thing, you can be very like him at times."

He smiled. "I guess all those years with him are starting to show."

"Yes they are," she nodded. "And in more ways than you know!"

The car came to the end of the narrow country road and stopped in front of a lonely derelict farmhouse a few miles from the border. Already waiting inside, Raymond looked out and saw McCabe dragging a strange man from the car with one hand, while he held a gun to his back with the other. He pushed the victim roughly, as he was reluctant to walk. The dimmed headlights were immediately switched off and the driver's door closed. Quinn's voice could be heard ordering the man to enter the farmhouse. Raymond flicked his cigarette through the broken window as the voices and footsteps drew nearer in the now dark surroundings. He glanced over at Jamie.

"It looks like we've got company. You can light that lamp now. It's a good job Dermot told us to bring it."

Jamie lit the oil lamp and smiled as he watched the glow brighten up the damp room littered with rubbish and straw. "I don't know about you," he said gleefully, "but with £500 quid in my pocket, I intend to enjoy myself tomorrow!"

Nodding in agreement Raymond replied, "This is our chance to show McCabe and Quinn we're just as good as they are when it comes to doing jobs for Harry Collington. After tonight we'll be made Jamie. It's going to be 'hello big time' from now on!" The door was pushed open and the stranger was thrown forward by McCabe while Quinn closed it securely behind them.

Raymond stood in front of the man and stared into his frightened face. "So, you're the bastard who's been passing information and stealing money," he smirked, pointing a warning finger. "I'm going to enjoy rattling your cage before I shoot you off your perch!"

But as quick as a flash, the man grabbed Raymond's wrist and spun him round, twisting his arm up his back. "Not as much as I'm going to enjoy doing exactly the same thing to you!" he snarled.

Raymond struggled to free himself but the grip was so tight he yelped in pain, as Jamie stood wide-eyed in surprise. "You're breaking my fuckin' arm!" he cried. "What the fuck's going on here?"

"I'll break your fuckin' neck!" replied the stranger, over Raymond's shoulder. Jamie looked at McCabe and Quinn. "Don't just stand there - do something. Shoot the fucker!"

Pointing a gun straight at his face McCabe ordered, "Move away now, or I'll shoot you!" As Doyle stepped back in shock, McCabe went over and put his hand on the man's shoulder.

"He's all yours Rooney," he said.

Rooney nodded and loosening his grip, pushed Burns away. Turning around Raymond pulled the gun out of the waistband of his trousers. His eyes had a look of fear and disbelief

"I don't know what's going on, but I know one thing. I'm going to shoot you, you bastard!"

"The same way you shot Robert Kenny?"

A deafening silence filled the room!

"I ... I don't know what you're talking about," Raymond stammered.

"Oh come on . Don't tell me you've forgotten how you and your friend murdered your future father-in-law. You know, the man who provided you with his home, his money ... his daughter. Surely you remember him!"

"I didn't kill Robert Kenny," Burns insisted, "and I'm not taking the blame for someone who did. Move out of the way, I'm walking out of here."

Rooney never flinched. "You'll have to get by me first."

"That's going to be the easy part." Raymond smiled with a ruthless look on his face, pointing the gun at Rooney as he pulled the trigger.

The only noise to be heard in the room was a clicking sound. He kept pulling the trigger, but nothing happened. He stared at McCabe and Quinn.

"This fuckin' gun isn't working!" he squealed.

McCabe nodded. "Maybe that's because it isn't loaded."

Quinn went over and pulled it out of his hand. "You see Raymond, if you want to play with the big boys you should follow the rules. Always check your weapon. If you had, you'd have found out it was empty."

"You bastards!" he cried. "I trusted you. I trusted Harry Collington."

"Well, that just goes to show you can't trust anyone, doesn't it?"

As Quinn stepped back, Rooney produced his own gun. "O.k. Burns, down on your knees."

Raymond was unable to move.

"Didn't you hear me?" Rooney asked, coming closer and holding the gun to his head. "DOWN ON YOUR KNEES!"

As his captive sank to the floor, he turned his attention to Doyle. "You, move over here and do the same," he ordered.

Jamie started to cry. "Jesus Christ, somebody do something!"

Grabbing his shoulder, McCabe advised him, "Why don't you do like the man says." He pushed him towards Rooney.

Without another word, Doyle knelt down a few yards from his friend.

Standing in front of them pointing the gun, Rooney looked from one to the other. "O.k. the interrogation starts now and I want the truth about why Robert Kenny was murdered."

"Who the hell are you?" asked Raymond, receiving a hard slap across the face.

"I'll ask the questions Burns," he was told, "and I want answers. I'm not a patient man so I'd advise you to start now."

"Why should I tell you anything?"

At this, Rooney grabbed him viciously by the hair and pushing his head back, placed the barrel of the gun between Raymond's eyes and cocked the trigger. "Because this is all that stands between you and eternity. Now, start talking!" he demanded, his voice filled with rage.

"Alright, alright!" Raymond whimpered.

As Rooney released him and stepped back, McCabe and Quinn looked at each other. "If that's how they do it in the States, I wish they'd send a boat-load of them over here!" Seamus whispered, as he handed Dermot a cigarette. Then both men stood in silence and watched.

Doyle broke down sobbing, "I didn't want to do it, it was all his idea."

"Shut up - keep your fuckin' mouth shut!" shouted Raymond, as he glared at him. Then he looked at Rooney. He knew nothing but the truth would satisfy this man. Besides, the cat was out of the bag so he'd have to come clean. "It was an accident," he insisted. "It wasn't meant to happen but he was just in the wrong place at the wrong time. I really liked Robert Kenny, I didn't want to hurt him. I was going with his daughter for Christ's sake!"

"Then why did you murder him?"

"Jamie and me had a scam going and it was a nice little earner, mostly robbery and muggings. We knew no-one would suspect us. If anything, people would blame splinter groups, that sort of thing."

McCabe looked at Quinn. "No prizes for guessing who robbed Gerry Nolan's chip shop!"

Rooney waved the gun in Raymond's face. "Keep talking!"

"It was just starting to get dark. We were standing in the doorway of a derelict house when we saw a man coming down the street. As he passed we jumped him and dragged him inside. He put up a struggle and tried to fight back as we beat him up. It was only when I got him to the floor I realised who it was. I just wanted to rob him and get out of there, but as I was taking his wage packet he pulled off my hood and recognised me. I'll never forget the look on his face. He knew there'd been a lot of mugging going on, we'd even talked about it, but now he knew it was me! Robert Kenny was one decent man and there was no way he was going to keep quiet. I was scared word would get out. I knew if it did someone would come after us, we'd be beaten up or knee-capped. But worst of all I knew he would never let me near his home again and he'd stop his daughter from seeing me. By that time I'd got her pregnant. Then there was Angela. I was very fond of her. She would never forgive me or speak to me ever again and I just couldn't take that chance. Although I was going with Sheila, it was Angela I admired most. I wanted to be close to her and I knew if I let him go, all that would change and I couldn't let it happen. I just couldn't."

"You bastard!" Jamie cried. "You never told me that was the reason."

"That's because it was none of your fuckin' business! Raymond snapped. Looking at Rooney once again he explained, "Anyway, I panicked and shot him. There was nothing else I could do, I couldn't let him go. If he opened his mouth about me, I knew I could be shot . It was either him or me."

Rooney glared at him in disgust. "Did he ask you to let him go?"

Before he could receive the answer, Jamie butted in.

"He pleaded for his life. The man begged us to let him go, but he wasn't having any of it. He said we'd be in too much danger and we wouldn't be able to make any more money, unless we killed him. He talked me into it. But I didn't shoot him - he did!"

Shaking his head Rooney replied, "Maybe you didn't pull the trigger Doyle, but you went along with it. You both beat up and murdered an innocent man, for money. For a wage packet he was bringing home to support his family." He held the gun directly in front of them. "You both deserve each other and you both deserve to die."

With tears streaming down his face, Doyle shook uncontrollably. "Oh Jesus, I don't want to die!"

"Neither did Robert Kenny," came the cool reply. As Rooney aimed the gun at Raymond's head, the door opened and Angela walked in.

A petrified Raymond's eyes widened in surprise.

"Angela! What are you doing here?" he stammered.

"I came to find out the truth and I heard every word." She nodded towards the broken window.

He joined his hands as if in prayer. "I swear to God Angela, it was all an accident. I didn't want to kill him, you have to believe me. I'd no choice. Now this guy wants to kill me!"

"I know. I told him to and he's very good at his job." She gave him a wry smile. On hearing this Raymond's fear increased.

"Listen Angela, you're all the one who can stop this. Just think for a minute. I know what I did was wrong and I'm sorry, so very sorry. But it would be just as wrong to kill me. What good would it do now, after all these years? You'd only be leaving your sister in the same position that I left Agnes. You can't do that to Sheila. Think of her Angela. Think of my children, my three girls. It would only bring the same heartache to them, that I brought to you."

Angela thought deeply. "You're right Raymond. Being a widow brings its own grief and losing someone you love causes a lot of sorrow. I should know." She put her hand out to Rooney.

"Give me the gun."

He was bewildered by her reaction, as was McCabe and Quinn.

"You're not going to fall for that surely," he said, surprised. "This slime only wants to save his own skin."

Raymond watched anxiously as Rooney kept hold of the gun, then reluctantly placed it in her hand.

Slumping forward, Raymond gave a heavy and deep sigh of relief "Jesus, thank God. I knew I could depend on you to see sense Angela, and not let him kill me."

She looked at him coldly and deliberately saying, "It's alright Raymond, he's not going to shoot you. After all, you're MY brother-in-law, so I AM ! Just the way you shot my father...." She pointed the gun.

McCabe and Quinn stared at her in surprise, as Rooney tried to intervene. "For Christ's sake Angela, give me the gun."

"You stay out of this Rooney!" she snapped, without flinching or taking her eyes off her brother-in-law.

"Do you remember the story you told my son about the Angel in the nursery all those years ago?"

As Raymond recalled the incident to mind, his face went white with fear and realisation. Angela continued, "You told him if a bad man does something really wicked, the good Angel knows and will follow him. No matter where the man goes and no matter where he tries to hide, it will find him. Then, the Angel will do to him what he did to others. He will get what he deserves. You said that's why it was called an 'Avenging Angel'. Well, after all these years Raymond, I've finally caught up with you. I'm YOUR 'Avenging Angel' and I've come to see you get what you deserve."

"No Angela, no!!" he pleaded.

As Rooney looked on there was a split second when Angela actually reminded him of Joe. She showed no emotion as she pointed the gun steadily at Raymond's head and pulled the trigger. He fell back and lay motionless as Jamie Doyle's squeals pierced the night. Suddenly there was confusion.

"Shut the fuck up!" Rooney yelled at him, pulling the gun from Angela's hand. Then he turned on her. "I hope you realise what you've just done!"

"It was MY father he murdered."

"Yeah, and now you've committed murder. I can't believe what I've just seen and Joe Morrelli would never have thought it possible, not of you Angela."

She stared into his face. "How can you be so sure of that? It was Joe who forced me to take shooting lessons and gave me my first gun. And Joe never did anything without a reason. Looking back I never really was in any danger working for Gene O'Brien. Was I Rooney?" she was answered by his silence as he deliberately looked away. "No, Joe would have made sure of that," she insisted. "I think he knew this day would come eventually and he was trying to prepare me, in his own way."

Rooney looked back at her, still angry and upset. "And I promised Joe if this day ever DID come, I would shoot Raymond Burns and you promised me I could. You broke that promise Angela and in doing that I broke my promise to Joe!" He sounded so cold and unforgiving. "Get her out of here!" he yelled at McCabe and Quinn, who were still rooted to the spot, trying to come to terms with what they had just witnessed. As they led Angela outside, Rooney took care of Jamie Doyle with a single shot. His lifeless body lay beside Raymond's.

In the dark farm yard Dermot held his hand up and beckoned. The rear door of Seamus' car opened and two young men got out. They were Dermot's sons. As they came towards their father he both looked and sounded serious.

"Alright boys, you know what to do. Emmett, you get Mrs. Morrelli's suitcase out of the boot of the car and put it into Burns and Doyle's. Paul, sit in the back seat with her and let Emmett do the driving. If you're stopped going over the border remember, she's your auntie and she's been here on holidays. You're driving her to the airport to catch her flight."

They lost no time in doing what they were told. As the three of them drove off Angela kept looking back out of the rear window, hoping to catch a glimpse of Rooney - but he never appeared.

McCabe and Quinn went back inside.

"Right, let's get to work," said Seamus, in a matter of fact way.

The three men lifted the bodies one at a time and carried them to a dark corner. Dermot started to search their pockets.

"What are you doing?" asked Rooney.

His friend held up the two thick brown envelopes he had given Burns and Doyle that afternoon.

"Harry Collington wants his money back," he explained, putting them in his inside pocket. They then proceeded to cover the bodies with straw and rubbish.

Once done, Rooney said "Listen you guys, we're going to need at least twenty four hours to get out of the country and back to the States, before these two scum bags are discovered."

Seamus smiled, "Rooney, in an out of the way place like this, it could be twenty four weeks! Don't worry about it. They're covered up just as good here as they would be in a cemetery."

"That's right," Dermot agreed. "You'll have plenty of time. In three or four days I'll get Emmett to tip off the security forces in an anonymous phone call. That's about the only way they'll be found."

Rooney nodded. "They are good boys Dermot."

Shrugging, their father smiled. "Well it's good to have your own family as foot-soldiers - especially at a time like this. At least you know you can trust them!"

After looking around to make sure nothing had been forgotten Seamus put the lamp out and picked it up. He carried it outside and waited as Rooney and Dermot closed the door securely after them. On reaching the car, the front passenger seat was removed and all their weapons placed inside. Putting it back in position again, they climbed in and Seamus started the engine. Turning, the car sped back down the lonely road and headed for the city.

There was a long silence. McCabe and Quinn glanced at each other, while Rooney sat with a face like thunder! They both knew he wasn't pleased about what had happened earlier. Finally the silence was broken when Dermot passed around a packet of cigarettes.

As Rooney lit up, he thumped the back seat of the car with his fist. "Jesus, I'm so angry I could fuckin' explode! I'll bet she had that planned all along, that's why she insisted on coming. What the hell made her do it?"

"Who knows?" Seamus shrugged. "But I'll tell you one thing Rooney, I thought the woman I live with had guts but I've never seen a more gutsy lady that I did tonight back at that farm house. She was something else. Cool, calm and collected. Now, that's the kind of woman I would marry."

"Well, not me!" he snapped in reply. "She didn't have to murder him, that was my job and I could have handled it. Why? Why the hell did she have to get involved?"

Dermot turned and leaned over the seat. "Oh come on Rooney, from what you told me last night she had plenty of reasons. That bastard killed her father and sent her mother to an early grave. She nearly lost her baby because of it and couldn't have any more. I'd say those were reasons enough. Raymond Burns' hand reached a lot further than the trigger he pulled in Belfast. It reached all the way to America and caused a lot of heartache and pain. He didn't just ruin the Kenny's lives, he ruined your boss' life as well.

"How do you think Joe Morrelli felt, having to live with that all those years?"

"You don't understand Dermot. Joe loved her because she was good and kind - and innocent. And that's the way he would have wanted her to stay."

"Are you sure about that Rooney? Or is that the way you wanted her to stay?"

"I don't know what you're talking about!" he insisted.

"Oh, I think you do." Dermot knew him too well. "You're in love with her and tonight she shattered the image of herself you loved. But ask yourself a question. Do you think if her husband was still alive, he'd love her any less because of what she did? I don't think so! I think he'd be proud of her. Why are you so angry? Is it because you didn't get to do the job yourself, or is the real reason the fact that you can't come to terms with what you saw back there?"

Rooney stared at him. "I'm angry because she used me to get what she wanted and she doesn't care!"

"How do you know? Why don't you tell her how you feel?"

Stubbing out the cigarette, Rooney shook his head. "I can't, not after tonight and not after what she did to me. I can't tell her I love her because right now my feelings are so mixed up, I don't even know if I want to love her. But I know this Dermot, I can't forgive her!" Sighing deeply, he leaned back.

Dermot turned away and the three friends sat in silence until they saw the bright lights of the city come into view.

"Well, what's the plan now?" asked Seamus.

"We'll drop Rooney off at my house," Dermot replied checking his watch.

"Then you and me will go to 'The Punters Bar' for the last hour. I'll go around and do my collection as usual. That way, when word gets out that Raymond and Jamie are missing, we will have an alibi. Everyone at 'The Punters Bar' will have seen us and as far as they are concerned, we never left the city. After that, all we have to do is act as surprised as everyone else when we hear the news."

Seamus looked at him admiringly. "I'll say one thing for you McCabe, you've got a good head on your shoulders."

Grinning broadly he replied, "Well, living in a place like this it pays to be one step ahead."

Rooney shook his head and smiled to himself. He couldn't help but think, that's exactly what Joe Morelli would have said!

Harry Collington stood at a safe distance in the cemetery watching the mourners. As he heard the sound of approaching footsteps, he glanced around to see McCabe and Quinn coming to join him. Standing together in silence, they observed what was going on. Harry was puzzled. "I thought Mrs. Morrelli would be here. I mean Raymond Burns' wife is her sister."

"She is here," McCabe replied.

"Where?" Harry's eyes lit up as he looked through the crowd.

"Over there."

As McCabe pointed to the grave side, Harry's gaze followed and came to rest on a young, attractive woman with red hair.

"That's not Mrs. Morrelli Dermot! Mr.s Morrelli is a little older with a more rounded figure and blonde hair. I should know - I met the woman."

"Harry that is Mrs. Morrelli and Sheila Burns' sister. She was Angela Kenny to her maiden name and lived in Glensdale Park."

"Then who the hell did I meet? Who the fuck was the Mrs. Morrelli I made the deal with?"

McCabe shrugged. "I don't know. But speaking of deals, there's something we'd like to talk to you about." He held up the key to the safety deposit box.

Harry made a grab for it. "That's mine, Rooney was to give it to me before he left!"

"Well, he gave it to me and he's long gone," McCabe smiled cooly.

"That bastard set me up!"

"No Harry - she did." He nodded towards Angela. "And you fell for it hook, line and sinker. You see, Joe Morrelli may be dead and gone but his file on you isn't. He left that behind. Well, you know the old saying, 'You can't take it with you when you go'. Come to think of it, he's the one who really set you up all those years ago. But it was his wife who carried it through."

McCabe and Quinn each laid a firm hand on Harry's shoulders. Then staring into his face McCabe said, "I think you'd better come with us. We've read the file!"

Their captive struggled, a look of fear in his eyes. "I'm not going anywhere. I'm a big man in this district!"

Quinn moved closer and pressed a gun into his back. "Well, the big man has two choices. He can come quietly with us for a little chat, or be made to confess right here in front of all these people. And if you choose the last one, there'll be a line of men all queuing up to shoot you - and you won't be so big anymore!"

McCabe agreed. "He's right. How do you think the people in this area would react if they knew what you were and what you'd been doing all these years. You've put many a good man behind bars - and worse! Raymond Burns isn't the only one in this cemetery because of you and your love for money. The game's up Harry, and you have to answer for what you've done. Now, MOVE IT!" he was ordered in a stern voice, "after all, we wouldn't want to cause a scene at a funeral. Now, would we?"

"Where are we going?" asked Harry in an anxious voice.

"Oh somewhere quiet and appropriate," Quinn replied, "where we won't be disturbed." They tightened their grip on a shaking Harry Collington, the gun still pressed firmly into his back. As he was led away, he turned his head in the direction of Angela and took one last look at her. He knew now he would never find out who the woman was who'd posed as Mrs. Morrelli. But he had to admit to himself, whoever she was, she had done a really good job. She had been so convincing, she should have been an actress!

As Raymond's coffin was lowered into the ground, Sheila sobbed loudly and clung to Angela.

"Who could have done such a thing? My Raymond never hurt anyone in his life."

Angela put her arms around her. "Neither did our father Sheila," she reminded her. "But I promise, I'll take care of you. You and the girls won't want for anything." Raymond's wife and daughters stood grief-stricken and trying desperately to console one another, as the service came to an end.

Angela carried her own grief inside as she watched them, then left and made her way along the path alone. Coming to her mother and father's grave, she stopped and looked at it for a few moments. Then kneeling down, she placed a large bouquet of red roses there. The tears ran down her cheeks as she moved her fingers gently along the gold lettering that spelt out their names on the black marble stone.

"I loved you so much daddy," she whispered. "I had to do it for both of you. But it's over now. Rest in peace."

At that moment Aisling appeared. She clenched her fists tightly and cried, "If I ever find out who murdered my dad and granddad I'll kill them!"

She sounded so angry and determined that Angela saw herself as she was at seventeen. The likeness was uncanny. Standing up, she took Aisling in her arms and held her tightly.

"Maybe they are already dead Aisling. If not on the outside, then perhaps on the inside."

"Auntie Angela, I loved my dad but he wasn't perfect."

"None of us are darlin."

"He did things."

"What kind of things?"

"Well, he went with other women. Mum knew it, we all did. It used to cause such terrible rows. He could be so mean to her and hurt her so much, but she still loved him. Now, I feel guilty because there were times when I used to wish Uncle Joe was my dad. I loved him and was so happy when I was with you both and Robert. Uncle Joe didn't shout and argue with you over other women. He would never have gone with anyone else, he loved you too much. I could tell, just by the way he looked at you."

Fresh tears came to Angela's eyes as she stroked Aisling's hair. "Your Uncle Joe and I had a good marriage and a good life together. We loved each other and all that is very hard to find. I was one of the lucky ones."

"Maybe that's because you left here and went somewhere else,"

Letting go of her Angela looked into her face.

"What are you trying to say Aisling?"

"Auntie Angela, I want to leave here. Senga has a baby and she's living at home. She's happy with that. Deborah is going steady with a boy who doesn't have a job - and doesn't want one! She's happy too. But I'm not. I want to try and make something of my life, but not here. I want to go to New York and get work. Maybe I'll meet someone and be happy. Someone like my Uncle Joe!"

Wiping the tears from her neice's eyes, she smiled. "Aisling if that's what you really want, I'll help you in every way I can. Robert would be so happy to have you there and your Uncle Joe always wanted that. He loved you very much."

"I know. Will you talk to mum about it? Please Auntie Angela."

She nodded. "I'll sort something out before I go. If your mother knows you're unhappy she won't stand in your way. But you will have to stay with her for a while, until she gets over your father's death. After that, you can come."

Aisling smiled, "Is that a promise?"

Angela nodded again. "Yes, that's a promise!"

The next day Angela visited the Nursing Home to see old Mrs. Murray, who by now was very frail and almost blind. As they sat together, the reporter's voice could be heard clearly coming from the television in the corner...

"In the early hours of this morning, the body of a man was discovered on a patch of waste ground known locally as 'The Alamo'. A taped recording believed to be that of the dead man was found on the body. Police say they received an anonymous phone call and have identified the body as that of Harry Collington, a well known public figure in the area. The police have also stated that the tape contains a confession by the victim, in which he admits to being an informer and for many years sold information to the Special Branch under a secret code name, 'The Nightingale'. Sources within the police and security forces have said they would prefer not to comment as this has proved to be an embarrassing situation for them. However, if it is true (and its widely believed so) it proves the innocence of a man named Robert Kenny, who was murdered in 1973 for being 'The Nightingale' informer. When asked about this, police would only say that according to past and present records, no man by that name was ever known to be connected in any way to either the security forces or any organisation. Ironically, Harry Colligton's murder took place just hours before a cease-fire was announced by all organisations, which seems to prove that those close to him had gained knowledge of his activities and decided to make them public before the cease-fire began. A statement by the Chief Constable of the RUC issued a short time ago, said he hoped this would be the last killing and it would be under investigation."

Angela tried to fight back tears as Mrs. Murray gripped her hand tightly.

"I always said there was more to your father's death than we knew," she said.

"Yes, you did," Angela agreed.

"All these years I believed Robert was innocent and every night I prayed it would be proved. I never thought I'd live to hear it but I have, and so has everyone who doubted him. Thank God my prayers have been answered before I die."

Even though Angela shed her tears, inside she had a deep feeling of satisfaction. She held her head up and closed her eyes tightly. After all this time she had finally got what she wanted. Her father's innocence had been proved and his name vindicated. Only now could Robert Kenny truly rest in peace with his beloved wife Agnes, and Angela Morrelli could go home.

She returned to Roseberry Avenue and the family business, but things had changed. Rooney was no longer around. The last time she'd seen him was that night at the lonely farmhouse. After that they'd both gone their separate ways. She had caught the first flight back to New York to await the phone call she knew would come from Sheila, telling her of Raymond's death. Rooney had also left Ireland, of that she was certain, but he had not returned to work.

Antonia married Judge Thompson in a blaze of publicity and Angela had attended the reception in the hope she would see him but was greatly disappointed. For although an invitation had been sent to his apartment, he never showed up.

She went to Reuben's office and asked for his help in locating Rooney. He readily agreed and started his own investigations but no-one had seen Rooney or heard from him, so both he and Angela came to the conclusion that their close friend was no longer in New York.

As the weeks went by without even a phonecall, Angela consoled herself to the fact she would never see or hear from him again. She began to realise just how much she'd hurt him and she realised something else - just how much she missed him! Joe and Rooney had been a big part of her life and now they were both gone. She would have to come to terms with that, and the reality that Rooney could never feel the same towards her. She would never expect him to. Angela Morrell had committed murder. Killing her own brother-in-law and Rooney had watched her do it. Any feelings he had for her now must surely be contempt and disgust, but deep in her heart she knew she'd done the right thing. It was HER father Raymond Burns had murdered and HER family who had suffered all the grief and heartache because of it. It was family business and she had meeted out family justice. Because of this she could live with herself and justify her own actions - even if Rooney couldn't!

Robert could not understand why Rooney had left his mother's employ. His uncle hadn't even paid a visit to Roseberry Avenue and this upset the young man greatly. As he entered the lounge, Angela sat gazing out of the window. He went over and bending down, took her hand.

"Mom, why can't you tell me what happened between you and Uncle Rooney when you both went on that business trip?"

She decided to tell him exactly what she had told Frankie and Al. "We had a disagreement about how some business should be handled, that's all."

He shook his head. "It's not like Uncle Rooney to hold a grudge. He and Dad had plenty of disagreements over the years, but he never stayed away. Are you sure it was nothing more serious?"

Angela pressed his hand and forced a faint smile. "Of course I'm sure. Now don't worry Robert."

"But I am worried. I'm worried about you mom. You lost grandpa and grandma, you lost dad and Uncle Raymond and now Uncle Rooney. That's a lot to cope with. You shouldn't be on your own like this. You're still young and there's a big world out there. What are you going to do?" His voice was full of concern.

"Well, I think I'll travel," she replied. "I've had a word with Reuben and he's going to take over for a while. He will be able to manage everything just fine with the help of Frankie and Al."

"Hey, that's great news!" he smiled. "You deserve a break. Where are you going?"

"I was thinking of going to London. After all, I never did get the first holiday I planned there. But first, I think I'll go to Miami for a while and see Charlie. We can go on some boat trips together."

"Are you sure you can handle staying at the beachhouse without dad?"

She nodded. "That house holds a lot of happy memories Robert, and I will always remember the good times. Then when I come home from my trips, Gene O'Brien's Presidential Campaign will be well underway and there'll be lots of functions and dinners to organise. Your mom will have a committee to see to and she'll be one very busy lady, with the help of Kevin Mitchell."

"Oh him!" he muttered, standing up and turning his head away in disapproval.

"You sound just like your father," she said, trying hard to hide a smile.

Robert turned back and looked at her. "Well, maybe that's because I'm his son!"

"How come I'm the only one in this family who seems to like him?" she asked.

"Because the rest of us are men and we don't swoon when he smiles!"

"Robert, I have never swooned at Kevin Mitchell's smile in my life," she gasped, surprised.

"Then you're one of the very few! Have you ever watched that guy at parties? No one can smile for that long - it's not natural. He makes the muscles in my face ache just looking at him!"

"I take it you wouldn't approve of us becoming an item?" she teased.

"I don't mind," he shrugged. "Just as long as you don't seat me across the table from him at dinner. I couldn't bear to witness the expression on his face when he has to eat and smile all at the same time!"

Angela lifted a cushion and threw it at him playfully, as they both burst out laughing. "Poor Kevin! What is it with you Morrellis? Your father never liked him either."

"Maybe that's because dad was a man - not some Hollywood poster version of the real thing! Besides, we Italians are very sensitive about our women."

"And jealous!"

He pointed a finger at her. "Yeah maybe. But it works. That's why you Irish and Scots love us so much, we respect our wives and know what to do to keep them happy. Dad always said there never was a divorced Morrelli, even all the way back to Sicily!" He smiled broadly. "Dad also said Italian men were good lovers."

Angela returned his smile. "Did he really? Well your father always did like to blow his own trumpet, but I can't argue with that."

As she watched him leave the room she shook her head. When Robert was a young boy Joe always used to say he was a chip off the old block - and he was right. Robert had grown up with the same values, looks, mannerisms and wit that he had. Robert Morrelli was indeed his father's son!!

That evening Robert stopped on the stairs and turned to his mother. "Are you sure you don't mind babysitting mom?"

She put her arm around him fondly. "Of course I don't mind, I love having Joseph here. It reminds me of when you were a baby."

"Yeah," he smiled, "It's hard to believe my son is sleeping in the same nursery as his dad."

"Well, it looks like it's going to be a family tradition and he couldn't be in a safer place or in safer hands. So don't you worry. I want you both to go out and enjoy yourselves." She watched as Robert descended the rest of the stairs to a waiting Camilla, and crossed the entrance hall with his lovely young wife on his arm. But as he opened the front door Robert's smile quickly turned to surprise and delight.

"Uncle Rooney!!" he exclaimed. "Hey mom, it's Uncle Rooney!!"

As the two men embraced, Rooney stared towards Angela. She felt her hands start to tremble as she tightened the belt on the long white satin robe.

"Where have you been all this time?" Robert asked him.

"Oh I've been out of town. I took a long vacation."

"You sure did! But it's great to have you back."

Camilla agreed and kissed Rooney's cheek affectionately.

Robert checked his watch. "Well, we'd better go or we'll be late. I'll see you tomorrow Uncle Rooney," he smiled, ushering Camilla out of the door to the waiting limousine. Rooney stood in silence until it drove off, then he looked at Angela once more.

"Can I come in?" he asked.

"This is your home, Rooney," she replied. "You are always welcome here, you know that."

He closed the door and came towards the staircase, stopping as he noticed the two suitcases. "Are you going somewhere?"

"Miami. I'm leaving tomorrow morning."

He shrugged. "I just dropped by on the off chance. I thought maybe you'd be going out to dinner."

She shook her head. "No, I'm babysitting. Gene O'Brien wants Robert and John Sullivan to meet some prospective business clients."

"Well, I'm at a bit of a loose end myself. Would you mind some company?"

"Not at all," she smiled, turning and walking back up the stairs.

He followed her. On entering the nursery, he looked around. Robert's bed had been moved to the corner of the room and the baby's crib stood in the centre.

"Nothing's changed," he smiled as he went over and joined Angela.

They stood looking down at the sleeping baby.

"He's the spitting image of his father and grandfather. Aren't you Joseph Rooney?" he said in a low voice, bending over and touching the tiny hand gently.

"Yes he is." She looked at Rooney with relief and a little uncertainty. "Where have you been?"

He met her gaze and held it. "I needed to be on my own. I needed time to think. So I rented a place by the ocean. I spent hours just walking along the beach or sitting looking out to sea. I needed to get everything straight in my mind."

"And did you?"

"Yeah," he nodded. "I guess I finally did. I began to realise just how much I missed this house and everyone connected to it, especially you."

Angela lowered her gaze. "Rooney, about that night at the farmhouse, I need to explain...."

He put his finger to her lips and shook his head. "No, you don't have to explain anything to me. You did what you had to do. I know that now Angela. But it's over in the past, for both of us."

"Do you forgive me?" she whispered.

"Look at me," he said, placing his hand under her chin. She did. "I'd forgive you anything Angela Kenny. I love you."

Drawing her close, he kissed her gently. She did not resist, but put her arms around his neck and clung to him as the lingering kiss became more intense for both of them. All Rooney's longing for her erupted into passion and desire, as she responded willingly to his caresses.

Eventually he asked, "What time will Robert and Camilla be back?"

"They're not coming back," she told him. "Joseph is staying with me. I'm going to drop him off in the morning on my way to catch the flight."

"There isn't going to be any flight Angela. Not for you ..."

After so many years two people who were destined to be together, came together! As they did so Agnes Kenny's words rang true for a second time, "What starts out as friendship can end up as love."

A cool night breeze fluttered the curtains and swept across the room, catching the door. As it closed slowly a clear view of the crib could be seen, where Joe Morrelli's grandson lay in peaceful slumber guarded by the statue of the Angel that Angela had brought into her home all those years before. How could she have known then the importance of the story she had told Robert and the effect it would eventually have on her own life? It was now over twenty years since Joe Morrelli had instinctively chosen the name "Angel" for her, and Joe never did anything without a reason.

Angela had earned that title and showed herself worthy.

As the door finally closed, so does this story.

Angela Morrelli had proved beyond all doubt that nothing is impossible -

"WHEN THE ANGEL COMES"

THE END